MEDICINAL CHEMISTRY-I

FOR
T.Y. B. PHARM.
SEMESTER - V
AS PER NEW REVISED SYLLABUS W.E.F. JUNE 2015

K. G. BOTHARA
M. Pharm., Ph. D.
Principal and Professor
Sinhgad Institute of Pharmacy,
Narhe, Pune - 411 041.

NIRALI
PRAKASHAN
ADVANCEMENT OF KNOWLEDGE

N1719

MEDICINAL CHEMISTRY (SEM. V)   ISBN 978-93-5164-801-7

First Edition : June 2016

© : Dr. K.G. Bothara

Published By :   Polyplate
NIRALI PRAKASHAN
Abhyudaya Pragati, 1312, Shivaji Nagar,
Off J.M. Road, Pune – 411005
Tel - (020) 25512336/37/39, Fax - (020) 25511379
Email : niralipune@pragationline.com

☞ DISTRIBUTION CENTRES

PUNE

Nirali Prakashan : 119, Budhwar Peth, Jogeshwari Mandir Lane, Pune 411002, Maharashtra
Tel : (020) 2445 2044, 66022708, Fax : (020) 2445 1538
Email : bookorder@pragationline.com, niralilocal@pragationline.com

Nirali Prakashan : S. No. 28/27, Dhyari, Near Pari Company, Pune 411041
Tel : (020) 24690204 Fax : (020) 24690316
Email : dhyari@pragationline.com, bookorder@pragationline.com

MUMBAI

Nirali Prakashan : 385, S.V.P. Road, Rasdhara Co-op. Hsg. Society Ltd.,
Girgaum, Mumbai 400004, Maharashtra
Tel : (022) 2385 6339 / 2386 9976, Fax : (022) 2386 9976
Email : niralimumbai@pragationline.com

☞ DISTRIBUTION BRANCHES

JALGAON

Nirali Prakashan : 34, V. V. Golani Market, Navi Peth, Jalgaon 425001,
Maharashtra, Tel : (0257) 222 0395, Mob : 94234 91860

KOLHAPUR

Nirali Prakashan : New Mahadvar Road, Kedar Plaza, 1st Floor Opp. IDBI Bank
Kolhapur 416 012, Maharashtra. Mob : 9850046155

NAGPUR

Pratibha Book Distributors : Above Maratha Mandir, Shop No. 3, First Floor,
Rani Jhanshi Square, Sitabuldi, Nagpur 440012, Maharashtra
Tel : (0712) 254 7129

DELHI

Nirali Prakashan : 4593/21, Basement, Aggarwal Lane 15, Ansari Road, Daryaganj
Near Times of India Building, New Delhi 110002
Mob : 08505972553

BENGALURU

Pragati Book House : House No. 1, Sanjeevappa Lane, Avenue Road Cross,
Opp. Rice Church, Bengaluru – 560002.
Tel : (080) 64513344, 64513355,Mob : 9880582331, 9845021552
Email:bharatsavla@yahoo.com

CHENNAI

Pragati Books : 9/1, Montieth Road, Behind Taas Mahal, Egmore,
Chennai 600008 Tamil Nadu, Tel : (044) 6518 3535,
Mob : 94440 01782 / 98450 21552 / 98805 82331,
Email : bharatsavla@yahoo.com

niralipune@pragationline.com | www.pragationline.com

Also find us on [f] www.facebook.com/niralibooks

PREFACE

Paul Ehrlich's assumption that protozoal diseases could be cured by drugs which selectively react with the target tissues of the protozoa where the target tissue may be an enzyme, DNA, RNA or even a structure of unknown constitution was the foundation of chemotherapy. The emphasis in this book is given on the principles upon which chemotherapy is based. These principles are appropriately illustrated by groups of drugs in current use. The author aims to provide a framework of basic drug-design which explains the development of drugs under clinical use.

The specific aim of drug design is the maximal reduction of the trial-and-error factor in the development of new drugs via optimal rationalization. Computerised statistical methods are now routinely being used in drug-design.

Since this book is written basically for degree students, a backbone understanding in basic disciplines is assumed.

I wish to place on record my sincere thanks to the publisher Mr. D. K. Furia for his kind co-operation. The author is also greatly indebted to his colleagues for their generous help and criticism.

Suggestions from all corners of profession are welcome. The author is responsible for any deficiencies or errors that might have remained, and would be grateful, if readers would call them to his attention.

Pune

Dated : June 2016   *Author*

SYLLABUS

1. **General Considerations :** Structure of biological membrane, physicochemical properties affecting drug action; solubility, partition coefficient, ferguson principle, stereo chemical aspects of drug action, bioisosterism, Introduction to drug absorption; distribution, metabolism and elimination, protein binding, blood brain barrier.

2. **Receptors :** Types of receptors, types of forces involved in drug receptor interaction; intracellular cyclic nucleotides and other mediators of biological response, drug-receptor mechanism including signal transduction.

3. History and general aspects of the design and development of drugs including classification, nomenclature, structure activity relationship (SAR), mechanism of action, adverse effects, therapeutic uses and recent developments of following categories and scheme of synthesis of drugs mentioned in bracket.

3.1 **Adrenergic Agents :** Agonists and antagonists, biosynthesis, release and metabolism of noradrenaline, receptor subtypes and their strucutral features. (Methyldopa, atenolol, Prazocin, Guanethidine, Terbutaline.

3.2 **Cholinergic Agents :** Biosynthesis, release and metabolism of Neurotransmitters, Acetylcholine, Cholinergic receptor subtypes and their strucutral features, cholinergic agonists, cholinergic antagonists, acetylcholinesterase inhibitors, ganglionic blockers and neuromuscular blockers. (Carbachol, Dicyclomine hydrochloride).

3.3 **Cardiovascular Drugs**

   (a) Cardiotonic drugs

   (b) Anti-anginal agents

   (c) Anti-arrhythemic agents

   (d) Anti-hypertensive agents

   (e) Anti-hyperlipidemic drugs

   (f) Anti-coagulants and anti-thrombolytics

   (Losartan, Clofibrate Hydralazine, Captopril)

3.4 **Diuretic Agents (Furosemide, Chlorthiazide)**

CONTENTS

1

GENERAL CONSIDERATIONS

1.1 INTRODUCTION

The desired pharmacological response of a drug can only be achieved if it is present at the sites of action in an appropriate concentration for sufficiently long time. This appropriate concentration is generally governed by many factors. The important amongst them are :

(i) Amount and frequency of drug administered.

(ii) Route of administration.

(iii) Factors affecting drug absorption, distribution and elimination.

(A) Factors affecting accessibility of drugs to the active sites :

Once the drug is administered in the body, it undergoes a chain of complex events till it reaches to its site of action, which is represented in Figure 1.3. The process by which a drug is released in the body from its dosage form is known as 'absorption'. Since the duration and the intensity of drug action is a function of rate at which the drug is absorbed, an understanding of the factors which can affect the rate of absorption of a drug is necessary. These factors include,

(i) concentration of the drug administered or dose.

(ii) route of administration.

(iii) drug solubility.

(iv) in case of solid dosage forms, the rate of dissolution may govern the rate of absorption.

(v) in the local application, the blood circulation to the site of application and area of absorbing surface are the important factors.

(vi) physico-chemical parameters of the drug play an important role in governing the rate of absorption.

These factors are lipid solubility, dissociation constant, pH-partition theory, dissolution rate, Donnan membrane equilibrium principle, salt forms, effective surface areas, crystal form, complexation, viscosity, surface active agents and drug stability in gastrointestinal tract.

(B) Passage of drugs through natural membranes :

To yield the desired effect in optimum measure, the drug should reach the site of action quickly and remain there in adequate concentration for adequate period of time. To reach the site of action, drug molecules have to cross one or more membranous barriers. This passage is a function of physical and chemical properties and the pharmaceutical make up of the drug.

Biological Membrane :

The biological membrane, though lipoidal in nature, is intermittently interrupted by small aqueous channels or pores of different sizes. In addition to this, the absorption of the drug molecules may be accelerated by the electrical charges present on these membranes on both sides.

Main Variables :

Many weak acidic or basic drugs do not present in their ionized form. Similarly, many drugs are lipid soluble. These features characterise slow elimination of such drugs. Hence, metabolism of such drugs usually tends to produce such drug metabolites which are more polar and hence can be excreted readily from the body. If a drug is already polar in nature, it may not even require the bio-transformation and may be excreted unchanged. Though kidney is a major site for elimination of a drug or drug metabolite, other sites like milk, saliva, sweat, tears, bile, intestine, lungs and skin are also recognized as the sites for elimination.

Structure of Membrane :

A membrane surrounds all living cells. It separates components of vital metabolic processes from the external medium. Thus, the membrane provides an identity to a cell. Since a cell depends upon and communicates with the external environment, its membrane must allow the passage of certain molecules while preventing the passage of others. Thus, cell membranes are sites of a large variety of cellular processes ranging from permeability, transport and excitability to intercellular interaction, morphological differentiation and fusion.

Biological membrane is essentially a two dimensional matrix. It is a membrane of thickness equal to two lipid molecules i.e., some 50 to 60 A°. The three major components of the membrane are proteins, lipids and water. Although the different membranes have the same general pattern, they vary widely in the proportion in which proteins and lipids form their composition.

Most biological membranes consist of a lipid bilayer which contains proteins and other molecules that serves as recognition sites, signal transmitters or parts of entrance and exit. The thermodynamic properties of membranes are then described in terms of surface properties such as surface chemical potential and surface tension.

Communication between the inside and outside of a cell includes the exchange of metabolites and electrical signals, the flow of heat and changes in shape. These processes depend on the differences in temperature, pressure and electrochemical potential on both sides of the membrane. Temperature differences cause heat flow, pressure differences cause changes in shape and electrochemical potential differences cause molecular transport and electrical signals. Usually, membranes consist an assortment of lipid molecules with diverse chemical structures, together with proteins and sometimes polysaccharides. The lipids are typically fatty acid esters that differ in the length of fatty acid chain, the degree of unsaturation, the change or polarity of the esterifying group and the number of fatty acids esterified per molecule.

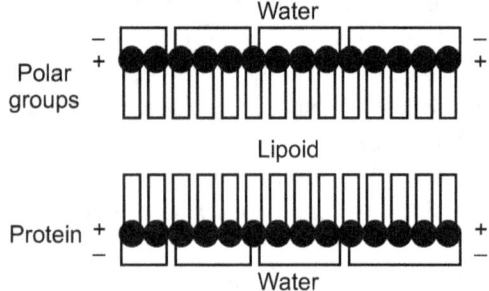

Fig. 1.1 : General pattern of a biological membrane

Proteins may constitute upto 80% of the cell membrane (e.g., red cell membrane) or as little as 18%. (e.g., nerve myelin). Variations are even wider in bacteria. The lipid contents also vary widely from membrane to membrane, constituting upto 80% of myelin, but only 15% of skeletal muscle membrane. Not only the total lipid content varies, but also the chemical nature of the lipids. The hydrocarbon chains vary widely in the nature of polar groups, length and saturation extent.

Although biological membranes are known to be complex and highly variable both in structure and in function, it seems probable that there is a common structural basis to all of them. Under the electron microscope, all the natural membranes thus far examined are in the order of 100 A° in thickness and are generally considered to consist of a lipid bilayer of the Gorter - Grendel type with adsorbed protein or non-lipid layers.

1.2 PROCESSES OF DRUG ABSORPTION

The main processes by which a drug molecule crosses the natural barriers are :

(a) Simple diffusion

(b) Diffusion of ions across the membrane

(c) Facilitated diffusion

(d) Active transport

(e) Pore transport

(f) Filtration

(g) Phagocytosis and pinocytosis.

Table 1.1

Some important functions of biological membranes

Function	Membrane
Permeability barrier of ions and molecules	Plasma
Ion accumulation or active transport	Plasma, nerve
Conduction of nervous impulse	Nerve axon
Conversion of light into chemical energy	Thylakoid
Conversion of light into electrical energy	Visual receptor
Oxidative and photosynthetic phosphorylation	Mitochondrial chloroplast
Site of immunological reactions	Plasma
Protein synthesis	Cell organelle
Phagocytosis and pinocytosis	Plasma

(a) Simple diffusion : The drugs are absorbed from gastrointestinal tract, cross the intestinal endothelium by simple diffusion. This process can be defined as, the flow of drug across a cell membrane from a solution of higher concentration (C_A) to the solution of lower concentration (C_B) without energy utilisation.

The important features of simple diffusion are :

(i) It depends and proceeds along a concentration gradient.

(ii) It does not involve energy expenditure.

(iii) Partition coefficient plays a governing role in the transport of lipophilic drugs by this process.

(iv) The transport of ionic or polar drugs by this process is influenced by the difference in pH on both the sides of the membrane.

(v) The process terminates as soon as the concentration of free drug is same on both the sides of the membrane (i.e., at equilibrium).

Simple diffusion can be expressed mathematically using Fick's law, which is as follow :

$$\frac{dm}{dt} \propto \frac{dc}{dx}$$

$$\therefore \quad \frac{dm}{dt} = -DA\frac{dc}{dx} \quad\quad ... (1.1)$$

where,

$\dfrac{dm}{dt}$ = Rate of drug diffusion

A = Surface area of the absorbing membrane

dc = Difference in solute concentration on both sides of the membrane

dx = Membrane thickness

(i.e. $\dfrac{dc}{dx}$ = concentration gradient)

D = Proportionality constant. Here it is distribution coefficient. It includes all other factors that may affect drug, nature and condition of the absorbing membrane

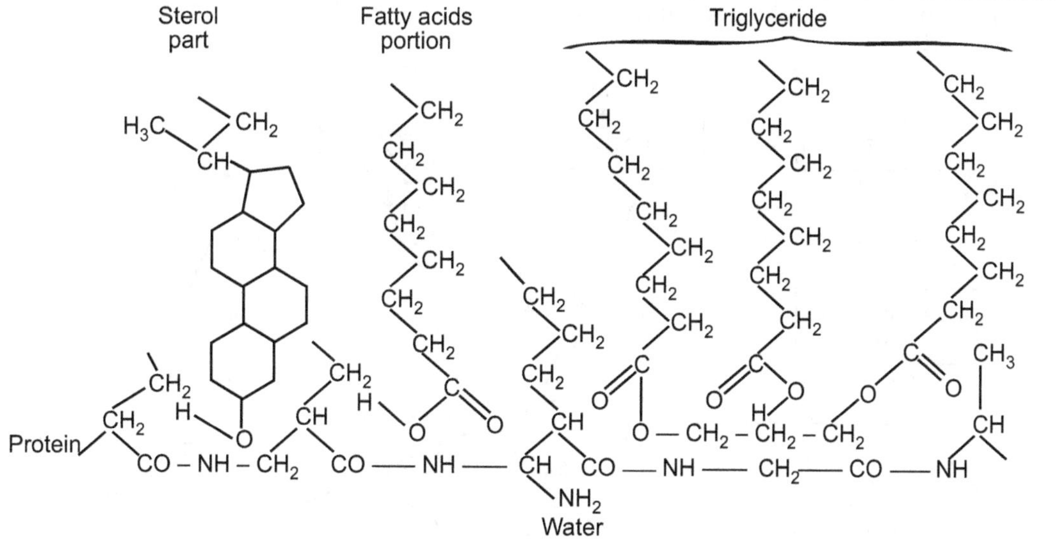

Fig 1.2 : Central features of the Davson and Danielli's model of biological membrane

Movement of GIT membrane facilitates the contact of drug molecules with the absorbing surface. This leads to an increased absorption of drug. Food in the stomach interferes in the drug absorption, hence drugs that inhibit gastric emptying (e.g. atropine, amphetamine, morphine etc.) may decrease the rate of absorption.

If we replace $\dfrac{D}{dx}$ by another term, P (i.e. diffusion constant), equation (1.1) can be rewritten as,

$$T = - PA \cdot dc \qquad ...(1.2)$$

Fick in 1885, derived this equation and now it is known as Fick's law of diffusion. The minus sign indicates the passage of a drug from the area of higher concentration to the area of lower concentration. The continuous removal of the drug molecules from the serosal side of the intestinal wall by blood circulation tends to keep the concentration on the other side always negligible. This serves as an additional driving force for the transport of drug molecules.

The rate of diffusion of a drug is a function of an area of absorbing surface. It is much greater in the small intestine due to its folding and refolding into valves of Kerckring and villi. It, thus provides an absorbing area of some 4500 m^2.

The pH difference across the cell membrane and the dissociation constant (pKa or pKb) of drug also govern the rate of drug absorption. Since most of the drugs are either weak acids or weak bases, their acidity value (ratio of ionised and unionised forms) is dependent upon pH and pKa. Hence, the dissociation constant plays a vital role in determining the ability of drug to cross cell membrane e.g. barbiturates.

(b) Diffusion of ions across the membrane : Sometimes, a potential difference develops which leads to polarisation of biological membrane. One side of the membrane becomes positively charged and other side gets a negative charge. When a positively charged ion (i.e. cation) comes in contact with the positively charged face of the membrane, it will be kicked away from the membrane. Similarly, anions will be driven away by negatively charged face of the membrane in the opposite direction. This process works on the forces of repulsion and naturally does depend upon the electrochemical concentration gradient i.e. on bioelectrical properties of the membrane generated due to polarisation of the membrane.

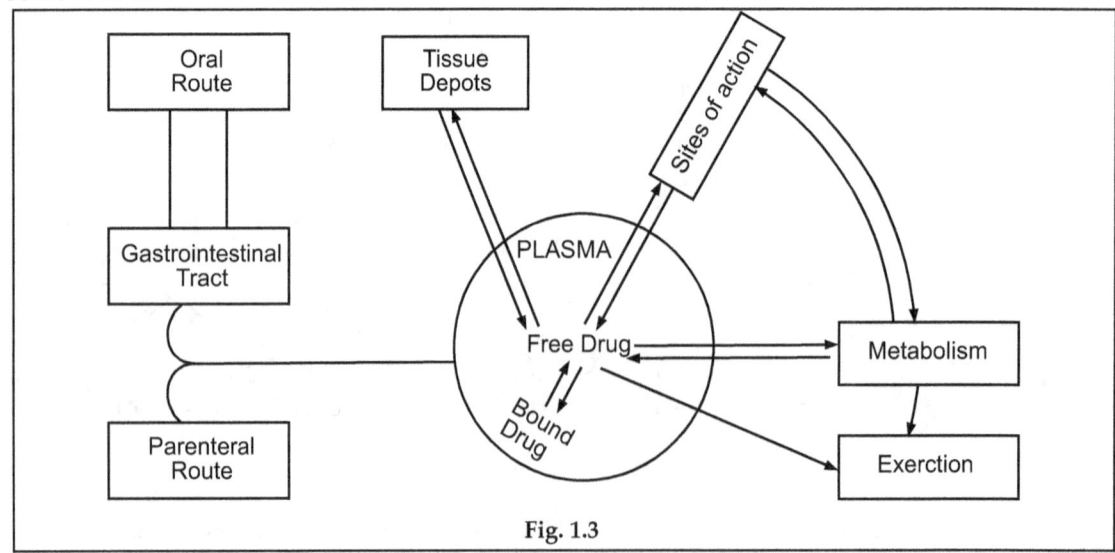

Fig. 1.3

(c) Facilitated diffusion : As the name indicates, it is an accelerated movement or diffusion of molecules that can not be justified by their lipophilicity or molecular size. This diffusion proceeds generally along the concentration gradients. Such diffusion is termed as downhill diffusion (i.e. from higher concentration to lower concentration). Downhill diffusion requires no net expenditure of energy. A series of acceptor-donor macromolecules carry out this diffusion. But sometimes, facilitated diffusion also trains away molecules against concentration gradient. This is known as uphill diffusion where energy is expended. Uphill diffusion is also termed as Active transport.

The accelerated diffusion of drug molecules is brought out by carrier macromolecules which oscillate back and forth across the cell-membrane. The loose complex is formed between carrier and drug molecule. Arriving at another side, loose complex dissociates to relieve the molecule and carrier returns back to lift again a new passenger. The process to certain degree, exhibits substrate specificity. Facilitated diffusion can be well illustrated with the example of transport of antibiotics like, valinomycin or gramicidin A. The eight carbonyl oxygens of the four valine residues in valinomycin skeleton, face inward, forming a cage within which, potassium ions can easily be held by co-ordinate bonds. Thus, potassium ions can get entry through the hydrophobic interior of the membrane when it is in "sound-sleep" within a mosaic of hydrophobic side chain of the antibiotic. Gramicidin A acts as transport antibiotic by forming channels that transverse the membrane.

Limitations of this process include -

(a) Its saturable nature due to limited number of carrier macromolecules and

(b) Competitive inhibition of transport of one drug by the presence of another drug bearing similar structural features.

(d) Active transport : Some substances diffuse across the biological membrane at much more faster rate that cannot be accounted on the basis of their lipid solubility or molecule size. This transport which proceeds against the concentration gradient and utilises a series of specialised carrier moieties is termed as 'active transport of drug'.

This carrier aided transport system is characterized by,

(i)   utilization of energy supplied by metabolic activity of membrane,

(ii)   proceeds against the concentration gradient,

(iii) absorption rate is independent of concentration.

The mechanisms that bring these and similar movements are often termed as pumps e.g., Ca^{++} ATPase pump, Na^+, K^+-ATPase pump etc. Under the conditions of non-availability of energy, the material thus transported, drifts back again until equilibrium on both sides of the barrier is reached.

Active transport is identical in most of the aspects with facilitated transport. The only difference exists between facilitated transport and active transport is, that the former does not utilize energy (i.e. proceeds along concentration gradient) i.e. downhill diffusion whereas the latter process proceeds against the concentration gradient i.e. uphill diffusion and needs energy consumption. In the case of ionic molecules, transport may occur against an electrochemical potential gradient. The exact mechanism of active transport is still not clear but it would appear that, on the mucosal surface side of GIT, carrier proteins form a loose complex with the drug molecule. This complex trains away the drug molecule to the serosal side where the complex dissociates to relieve its passenger.

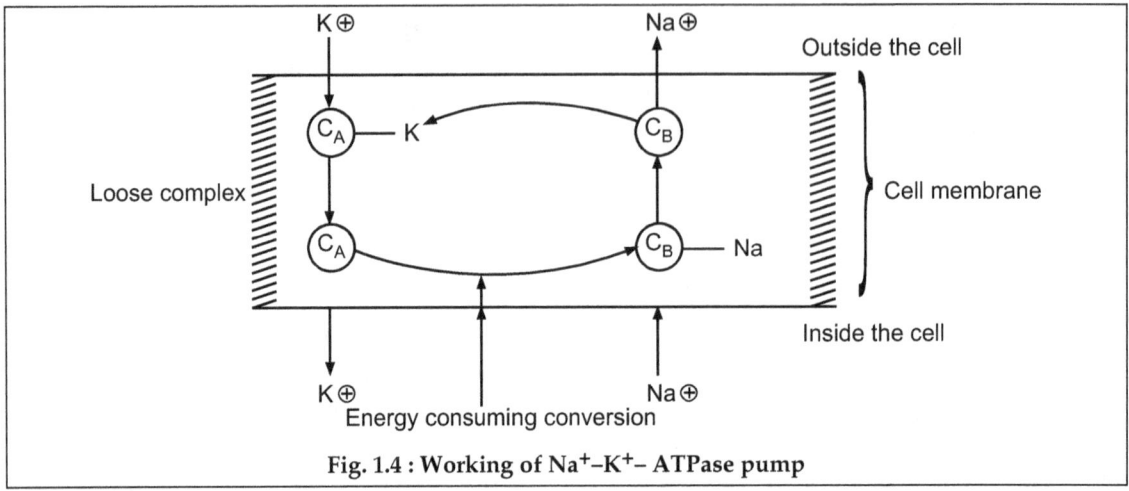

Fig. 1.4 : Working of Na$^+$–K$^+$– ATPase pump

The carrier may then return to the mucosal surface empty handed or may pick up another molecule during its journey back to mucosal side. Before picking up another molecule, it is involved in an energy consuming chemical reaction that converts the carrier protein (C_A) into a new form (C_B). The new form C_B, releases that molecule to mucosal side and undergoes a spontaneous change to its original form, C_A.

Limitations :

(a) Active transport is site specific as well as a substrate specific process. It means that special carrier channels are appointed to carry particular types of chemical structures. Similarly these substrates are usually absorbed from their corresponding specific sites located in a limited segment of the small intestine. For example, ileum is a site of diffusion for bile acids.

(b) Since carrier channels with a specific carrier molecules are allotted to transport drugs from particular chemical structural class, the carrier system becomes saturated,

(i) if the drug is present at higher concentration or/and

(ii) if another substrate of close structural similarity is simultaneously administered.

(c) Substrates that interfere with cell metabolism or in energy generation, may cause non-competitive inhibition of active transport system.

Active transport plays an important role in renal tubule reabsorption, secretion of H$^+$ into the stomach, accumulation of iodide ions in the thyroid gland, absorption of glucose, amino acids, some vitamins and metabolites in intestine, absorption processes across placenta and blood brain barrier. The process is of great importance and enables the cell to accumulate metabolites from an external environment where the concentration of the substance may be relatively very low, to excrete unwanted substance, to develop membrane potentials and probably to maintain a normal cell volume.

The active transport of glucose across biological membrane is aided by sodium ions. The glucose molecule and sodium ion both, bind to a specific carrier protein. This complex when enters the cell, the sodium ion is effluxed out through the operation of Na$^\pm$ K$^+$ ATPase pump. Such aided type of transport mechanism is termed as co-transport.

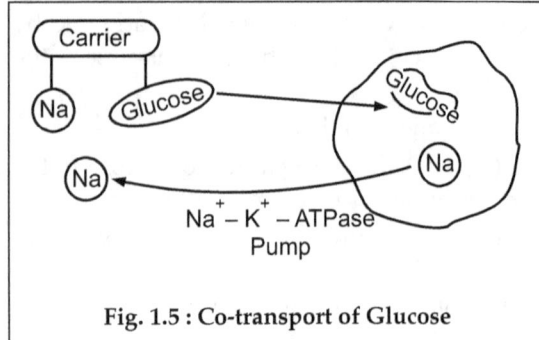

Fig. 1.5 : Co-transport of Glucose

$Na^+ - K^+ -$ ATPase pump is widely distributed in the cell-membranes and especially present in high number in different secretory cells along with excitable tissue such as nerve and muscle cell. It is mainly concerned with the transport of amino acid and glucose during nerve excitability and maintenance of cell-volume. The enzyme, $Na^+ - K^+ -$ ATPase was discovered in 1957 by Jens Skou in the cell-membrane. It hydrolyses ATP molecule to release energy necessary for functioning of this pump. The enzyme and the pump, both are tightly bound with the plasma membrane. The hydrolysis of ATP molecule needs the presence of Na^+, K^+ and Mg^{++} ions.

The phosphorylation reaction is catalysed by Na^+ and Mg^{++} ions whereas the dephosphorylation needs the presence of K^+ ions.

The $Na^+ - K^+ -$ ATPase enzyme is the pharmacological receptor for digitalis. Digitalis like drugs bind to the external surface of the enzyme. Cardiac glycosides induce conformational changes and inhibit dephosphorylation reaction of the $Na^+ - K^+ -$ ATPase enzyme.

(d) Pore transport : The aqueous filled pores or channels are present across the cell-membrane. The diffusion of small sized polar molecules is mainly governed by these channels.

The diameter of these pores was estimated to be near about $4°A$ which serves as a major limitation to the transport process. It is an example of passive diffusion where the rate of transport depends upon the concentration of drug and does not utilize energy. Various electrolytes, urea, low molecular weight sugars, etc. are transported by this mechanism.

(e) Filtration : The natural membrane consists of numerous pores of different sizes embedded in it, which generally control the diffusion of small sized molecules of water-soluble or lipid-insoluble substance. If a mechanical pressure (hydrostatic pressure) is imposed on the biological membrane, the drug molecules will ooze out to the other side. Such transport mechanism is termed as filtration. It means,

$$\text{Filtration} = \frac{\text{Simple}}{\text{diffusion}} + \frac{\text{Hydrostatic}}{\text{pressure}}$$

The hydrostatic force arises due to the pressure of a drug solution (solvent drag) at one side of the membrane which imposes its pressure at the site of absorption. These pores may have electrical charges that may influence the diffusion of charged bodies, like cations or anions.

In summary, there are three possible routes through which a polar substance can be passively transported across a membrane.

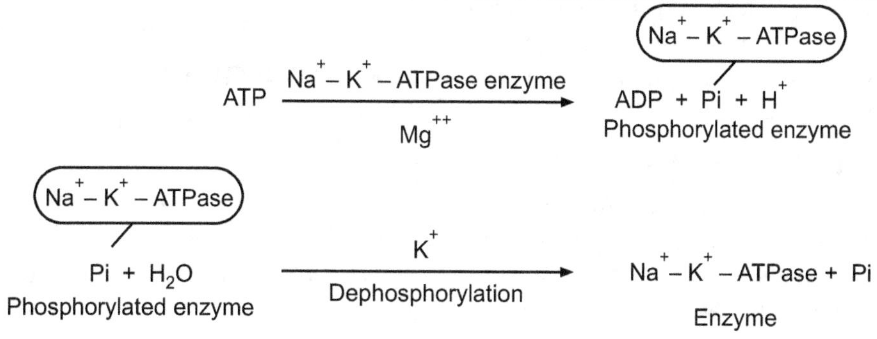

Fig. 1.6

These are :

(i) Diffusion down a concentration gradient (polar transport).

(ii) Diffusion down a gradient of electric potential (ion transport).

(iii) Filtration.

In this case of diffusion restricted by a lipid barrier, the penetrating molecule can enter the cell provided it has the appropriate solubility characteristics to dissolve first in the lipid of the membrane and then in the aqueous phase on the other side. This mechanism does not require aqueous pores in the membrane. It has been supported experimentally by the correlation of lipid-water partition coefficients with membrane penetration rates in the case of many non-electrolytes.

(g) Phagocytosis and pinocytosis : Droplets of extracellular fluid along with solute molecules are carried into the cell through the formation of vacuoles.

Phagocytosis is described as cell eating process whereas pinocytosis is referred to as cell drinking process. Both these processes are examples of engulfing of extracellular fluid and substances dissolved in it. Phagocytosis can carry macromolecules (such as proteins) into the cell, whereas pinocytosis has limitations of carrying large molecules.

Principle behind these processes has been exploited to develop new drug delivery system. Recently, techniques have been developed to envelope drug molecules by 'liposomes' which can be engulfed by the cells by pinocytosis.

1.3 DISTRIBUTION OF DRUGS

If a drug is administered into the body, blood circulation serves as a transport system for it, to reach at its site of action. The most prominent organs like heart, kidney, liver and brain share major portion of the drug, thus characterising the first or initial phase of distribution. The entry of drugs into the cells depends upon many mechanisms. Very small water-soluble molecules and ions (e.g., K^+, Cl^-) evidently diffuse through aqueous channels. Lipid-soluble molecules of any size diffuse freely through the cell-membranes. Water-soluble molecules and ions of moderate size including the ionic forms of most drugs, can not enter cells readily except by special transport mechanisms. Drug that is too large to pass through any pore and is also practically insoluble in the membrane, can form a lipid-soluble complex at the membrane surface. The complex then moves by diffusion within the membrane. In a complex biological system like human body, along its way to the site of action, a drug may meet with a number of outward instances which control the distribution of the drug. These instances, however, are dependent upon the physico-chemical properties of a drug and may be one of the following types :

(1) A considerable amount of drug administered may be retained by reversible storage depots.

(2) The drug may undergo certain metabolic alteration by biological enzyme systems before it reaches to its site of action, which may result into more or less active form.

(3) Before a drug gets a chance to act on its normal site, it may be excreted unchanged or in its metabolic form.

1.4 STORAGE DEPOTS

Plasma proteins, certain tissues, neutral fat, bone and transcellular fluids (gastrointestinal tract), are found to act as drug reservoirs or storage sites for drug.

The drug stored in these depots is in equilibrium with that in plasma and is released as the plasma concentration of the drug falls below its therapeutic concentration.

Thus, the plasma concentration of the drug is maintained which sustains and prolongs the duration of action of the drug.

Plasma Proteins : Approximately 6.5% of the blood constitute the proteins, of which 50% is albumin. Most drugs bound to plasma proteins in the albumin fraction; binding to other plasma proteins, generally occur to a much less extent. Albumin has a net negative charge but can interact with anions as well. The binding generally involves ion-ion interaction which is further strengthened by the presence of secondary binding like hydrogen bonding (non-ionic polar portions), hydrophobic and van der Waal's forces (non-polar portions) of the molecule. Ionization is thus not a major factor in the specificity and intensity of protein binding. The protein binding is found to be a reversible process.

Protein binding reduces diffusion of the drug to the sites of action, metabolism and excretion. The size of drug-protein complex is large and hence cannot pass through glomerular filtration which prolongs its duration of action. Protein binding also delays the metabolism of the drug.

Since protein binding is rather a non-selective process, other drugs with similar physicochemical characteristics, may exert an indirect biological effect by displacing active substances from protein binding which may result into (a) dangerous, adverse effects and (b) misinterpretation about the actions and dose of the drug.

Tissue Reservoirs : Depending upon its physico-chemical characteristics, a drug may be stored in various tissues, like liver (antimalarial drugs), thyroid (Iodine), lung, spleen and muscle. Tissue binding of drugs usually occurs with proteins, phospholipids or nucleoproteins and is generally a reversible process.

Neutral Fat : Since fat constitutes around 10% (starvation) to 50% of the total body weight, it serves as a main storage site for drugs having a high partition coefficient (lipid/water system) or a high lipid solubility (thiobarbiturates).

Other drugs which get readily deposited into the fat, are adrenergic blocking agents (dibenamine), neuromuscular blocking agents (hexa-fluorenium) etc.

Bone : Heavy metals (like lead or radium), divalent metal ion chelating agents and antibiotic (tetracycline group) are the examples of the compounds which, in considerable concentration, are retained by bone.

1.5 METABOLISM AND EXCRETION

The termination of drug effect is caused by biotransformation (alteration in the structure of a drug due to the action of enzymes or due to other biochemical processes) and excretion.

The effects of drugs are terminated by: redistribution between the compartments, storage, excretion of the unchanged drug and its metabolites. Compounds having a molecular weight less than about 400 are excreted in urine; larger molecules are cleared by the liver. Bile is excreted into duodenum, where a proportion of drugs (e.g., antibiotics, cardiac glycosides, vitamins) is reabsorbed by the enterohepatic cycle.

Drugs excreted unchanged in urine
- Digitalis
- Phenformin/metformin/chlorpropamide
- Bretylium
- Gonadotropin
- Methotrexate
- Thiacetazone
- Sodium stilbogluconate

- Amino glycoside
- Acyclovir
- Neomycin
- Gallamine
- Norfloxacin

1.6 FERGUSON PRINCIPLE

Pharmacologically active compounds can be divided into two major groups :

(a) the structurally specific and

(b) structurally non-specific.

The structurally specific drugs bring about their effects by combining with a specific receptor. The SAR of such groups can only be varied within relatively narrow limits.

The structurally non-specific drugs do not act on specific receptor. Instead, they penetrate into the cell or accumulate in cellular membranes, where they interfere by chemical or physical means, with some of the fundamental cellular processes e.g. general anaesthetics, hypnotics, volatile insecticides and certain bactericidal agents. The biological effect of such drugs is more closely correlated with the physical properties of the molecule than with the chemical structure e.g. cyclopropane, diethyl ether and chloroform, though having different structures, are good general anaesthetics.

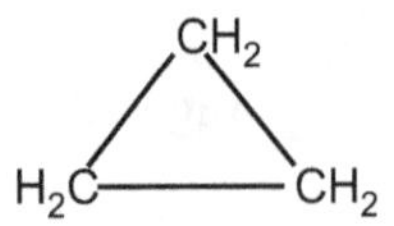

Cyclopropane
(Hydrocarbon)

$C_2H_5 — O — C_2H_5$			$CHCl_3$

Diethyl ether (Ether)			Chloroform

Fig. 1.7

Ferguson suggested in 1939, that the potency of structurally non-specific drugs was determined by their thermodynamic activity. This quantity is a measure of the proportion of the molecules which are free to react with enzyme systems, nerve membranes and similar biologically important sites. The molecules which are not free to act in this way, are reacting with one another, with the molecules of the solvent or with molecules of other solutes. It follows, therefore, that the thermodynamic activity of a drug in solution is not determined entirely by its concentration. In the case of volatile anaesthetics administered with air or oxygen, the thermodynamic activity is proportional to the relative saturation of a drug (a). The relative saturation of a drug is defined as $\dfrac{P_t}{P_o}$ for volatile drugs and gases.

$$\text{Relative saturation (a)} = \frac{P_t}{P_o} \qquad ...(1.1)$$

where,

P_t = partial pressure of the drug in solution or in the gaseous mixture and

P_o = vapour pressure of the pure drug at the same temperature.

For non-volatile drugs of limited solubility the relative saturation (a), is given by

$$\text{Relative saturation (a)} = \frac{S_t}{S_o} \qquad ... (1.2)$$

where,

S_t = molar concentration required to produce the biological effect and

S_o = molar solubility of the drug.

Ferguson's theory predicts that the anaesthetic agents will show the same degree of biological activity if their concentrations are adjusted so that their thermodynamic activities are equal (or relative saturation value (a) are equal). This theory is also applicable to substances other than anaesthetics and it was originally applied to insecticides and antibacterial substances.

Table 1.2

Concentrations of gases and vapours producing the same degree of anaesthesia in mice at 37°C

Anaesthetic agent	Saturation pressure at 37°C (P_S) (mm Hg)	Activity (P_t/P_S)
Nitrous oxide	59,300	0.01
Acetylene	51,700	0.01
Methyl ether	6,100	0.02
Ethylene oxide	5,900	0.01
Ethyl chloride	1,780	0.02
Diethyl ether	830	0.03
Methylal	630	0.03
Ethyl bromide	725	0.02
Dimethylacetal	288	0.05
Diethylformal	110	0.07
Dichlorethylene	450	0.02
Carbon disulphide	560	0.02
Chloroform	324	0.01

Table 1.3

Bactericidal concentrations of miscellaneous organic compounds toward Salmonella typhosa

Compound	Bactericidal Con-centration (S_t)	Solubility (S_0)	Relative Saturation (S_t/S_0)
Thymol	0.0022	0.0057	0.38
Propaldehyde	1.08	2.88	0.37
Methyl ethyl ketone	1.25	3.13	0.40
Acetone	3.89	9.7	0.40
Aniline	0.17	0.40	0.44
Cyclohexanol	0.18	0.38	0.47
Butyraldehyde	0.39	0.51	0.76

1.7 IONIZATION

Ionized form imparts good water solubility to the drug which is essential for good binding interactions of drug with its receptor. While non-ionized form helps the drug to cross cell membranes. Hence, a good balance of ionized : non-ionized forms is essential for better pharmacokinetic and pharmacodynamic features. Most of the effective drugs are amines having a pKa value in the range 6 - 8. Hence they are partially ionized at blood pH to create balanced ratio of ionized : non-ionized forms.

The rate of absorption of a drug which is capable of existing both in ionised and unionised forms, is dependent on the concentration of its unionised form rather than on its total concentration. The unionised form is a function of both, the dissociation constant (pKa or negative logarithm of acidic dissociation constant) and the pH of the environment which is represented by Henderson-Hasselbach equation.

For Acid, pKa- pH = log (Cu/Ci)　...(1.3)

For Base, pKa - pH = log (Ci/Cu)　...(1.4)

where, Ci and Cu are the concentrations of the ionised and unionised drugs respectively. It can be seen that a solution of weak acid, aspirin (pKa = 3.5) in the stomach, (pH = 1.0) will be more than 99% unionised and since unionised form is lipid soluble, it will get more easily absorbed in the stomach. Quinine, a weak base (pKa = 8.5) in stomach (pH = 1.0) would have only one out of 10,000,000 molecules in unionised state, hence would be most unabsorbable in stomach. Inspite of the fact that certain drugs exist in unionised state, they are poorly absorbed due to their low lipid solubility. The distribution or partition coeffi-cient of drug in unionised state between fat-like solvents (such as chloroform) and water or an aqueous buffer mixture nearly at the pH of the site of absorption gives an idea of the lipid solubility of the drug.

Table 1.4
pKa Values of acids and bases

	Acids	pKa Scale	Bases	
Strong	Sulphonic acids Benzyl Penicillin	1	Antipyrin	Weak
	Salicylic acid	3		
	Aspirin	3		
	Benzoic acid	4		
	Phenyl butazone	4		
		5	Amidopyrin	
	Sulphadiazine	7	Reserpine	
	Barbital	8	Morphine	
	Sulphapyridine	8	Quinine	
Weak	Diphenyl-hydantoin	9	Procaine Ephedrine	Strong

For weak bases or acids, the pKa value together with the pH of the medium determine which fraction of the drug molecules is undissociated and thus available for penetration through the various lipid barriers. The rate of penetration thus is strongly dependent on the lipophilicity of the drug molecule in its unionised form.

The lipophilic-hydrophilic balance plays a role not only in passive transport but also in active transport and drug metabolism.

Table 1.5
CHCl$_3$/H$_2$O partition coefficient of unionised barbiturates and % absorption from rat colon

Barbiturates	Partition Coefficient	% Absorption
Barbital	0.7	12
Amobarbital	4.9	17
Phenobarbital	4.8	20
Cyclobarbital	13.9	24
Pentobarbital	28.0	30
Secobarbital	50.7	40

Table 1.6
Anaesthesia produced by primary alcohols in tadpoles (Overton and Meyer)

Alcohol	Anaesthetic concentration in aqueous medium	Partition coefficient (cottonseed oil/water)
CH_3OH	0.57	0.00966
C_2H_5OH	0.29	0.0357
C_3H_7OH	0.11	0.156
iso-C_4H_9OH	0.045	0.588

As the length of the hydrophobic chain increases, both the partition coefficient and the anaesthetic potency increases while the aqueous concentration decreases. For weak acids and bases the ionised and non-ionised forms have completely different lipid/water partition coefficients. The ionised groups (usually COO^- or $-N^+HR_2$) interact strongly with water dipoles and consequently penetrate only poorly or not at all into the lipoidal cell-membranes. Thus, drugs that are partially ionised at body pH enter cells at rates that are strongly pH dependent.

Phenobarbital, a weak acid, caused a drop in the plasma drug level, when the plasma pH was lowered by CO_2 inhalation in dog. It is because the greater fraction of the total phenobarbital in the blood assumed the non-ionised acid form. The plasma concentration of undissociated diffusible phenobarbital was thus increased and a large amount of the drug moved across the cell-membranes and into cells where the pH remains relatively stable. Plasma alkalosis produced opposite effect. Hence to promote just such a shift of the drug out of the tissues, alkalosis is induced therapeutically in the treatment of barbiturate poisoning.

The co-ordinated effect of pKa and lipid solubility of a drug on its absorption led to the development of erythromycin propionate. The pKa value of erythromycin is 8.6 while that of ester is 6.9. Since the partition coefficient of ester form is about 180 times larger than that of erythromycin, the ester yields 2 to 4 times higher blood levels than does erythromycin. These observations are in accordance with the Handerson-Hasselbach equation.

1.8 COMPLEXATION

Since complexes of drug molecules cannot cross the natural membranous barriers, they render the drug biologically ineffective. The rate of absorption is therefore, proportional to the concentration of the free drug molecules i.e., the diffusible drug.

Due to the reversibility of the complexation, there always exists an equilibrium between the free drug and the drug complex. Such equilibrium is represented below :

$$\text{Drug} + \text{Complexing Agent} \rightleftharpoons \text{Drug Complex}$$

Complexation reduces the rate of absorption of the drug but does not affect the total availability of it, because the absorption of the free drug molecules shifts the equilibrium to the right, causing the free drug molecules to be released from the drug complex.

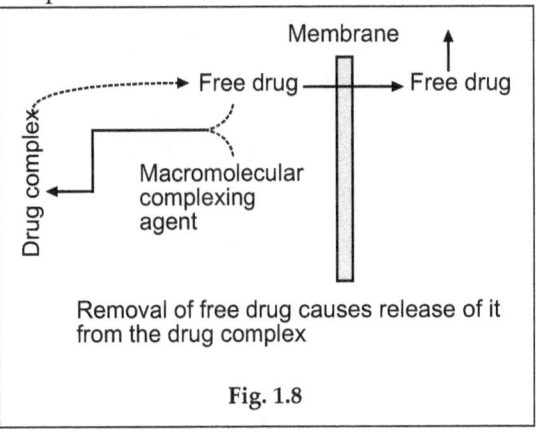

Removal of free drug causes release of it from the drug complex

Fig. 1.8

Examples of Drug-Complexes :

(1) Phenobarbital forms a non-absorbable complex with polyethylene glycol-4000. The dissolution rate of phenobarbital tablets containing PEG-4000, is only one-third of that of control tablets.

(2) Amphetamine carboxymethylcellulose is yet another example of non-absorbable complex.

(3) Tetracyclines have been known to form complexes with divalent and trivalent cations, which are much less effectively absorbed.

(4) Calcium is an important constituent of the mucous membrane of GIT. The complexation of this calcium with EDTA, increases the permeability of the membrane, probably due to the widening of space between epithelial cells due to removal of calcium. Therefore, presence of EDTA, increases the absorption of mannitol, quaternary ammonium compounds of sulphanilic acid and heparin, which are very poorly absorbed in ordinary condition.

1.9 SURFACE-ACTIVITY

As regards to the effect of surfactants or surface active agents on drug absorption through biological membrane, there have been opposing claims both in favour of enhancement and retardation of drug absorption. The main controlling factors in this regard are - the chemical nature of the surfactant, its concentration, its effect on biological membranes and the micelle formation.

It is evident that while in lower concentrations the surfactant enhanced the rate, the same in higher concentrations reduced the absorption rate. In lower concentration, the amphiphiles reduce the surface tension and bring about better absorption through better contact of the molecules with the absorbing

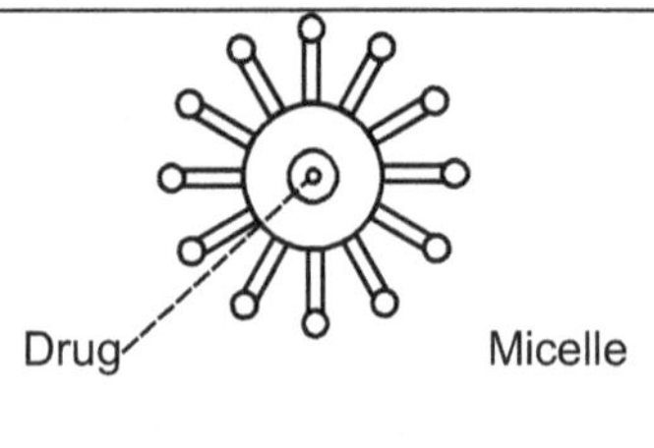

Fig. 1.9

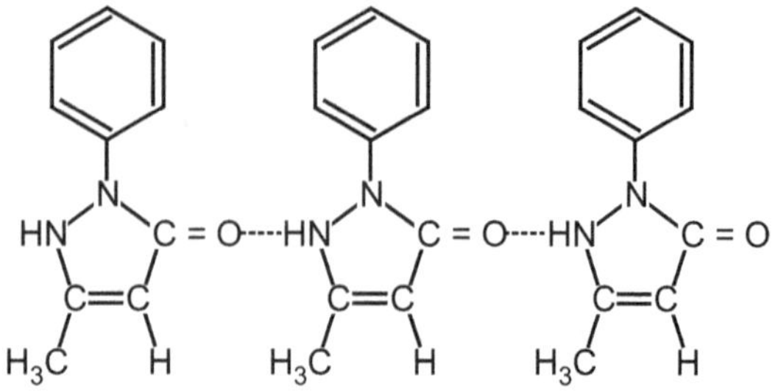

Intermolecular hydrogen bonding
1-Phenyl-3-methyl-5-pyrazolone

membrane. But when the concentration crosses the critical micelle concentration (C.M.C.), the surfactant molecules in the bulk of the solution form colloidal aggregates comprising nearly a few hundreds of themselves, and these molecular aggregates are called micelles, which entrap the drug molecules in their hydrophobic core, resulting in the retardation of the rate of absorption.

Bile salt solutions of approximately physiological concentration greatly enhance the dissolution rate of poorly water-soluble drugs like griseofulvin and hexestrol by virtue of micellar solubilization effect.

1.10 HYDROGEN BONDING

Atoms which are capable of forming H-bonds are electronegative atoms; these include F, Cl, N, O and S.

Though H-bonds are relatively weak bonds their presence may have a profound effect on the biological action of a drug.

For Example :

(1) 1-phenyl -3-methyl -5-pyrazolone shows no analgesic properties while 1-phenyl-2,3-dimethyl-5-pyrazolone (antipyrine) is a well known analgesic agent. This effect appears to be best explained by the fact that the first compound through intermolecular H-bonding forms a linear polymer.

The resulting large attractive force between molecules lowers the solubility, especially in the non-polar solvents which are not capable of breaking the H-bonds.

On the other hand, antipyrine cannot form H-bonds and has only comparatively weak attractive forces between its molecules and hence it is freely soluble in non-polar solvents and has the proper partition characteristics to penetrate the CNS.

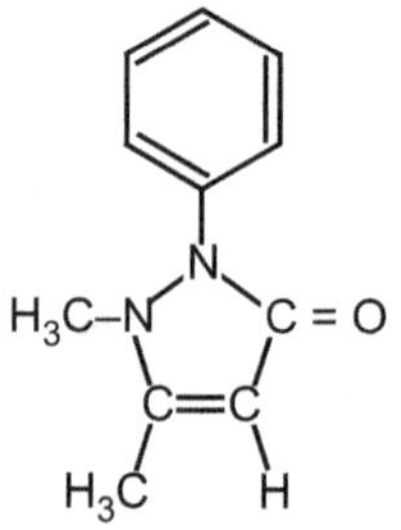

1-Phenyl-2,3-dimethyl-5
pyrazolone (Antipyrine)

(2) Salicylic acid (o-hydroxy benzoic acid) has quite an appreciable antibacterial activity, but the para isomer (p-hydroxybenzoic acid) is inactive, because salicylic acid is the ortho isomer that can form intramolecular H-bonds.

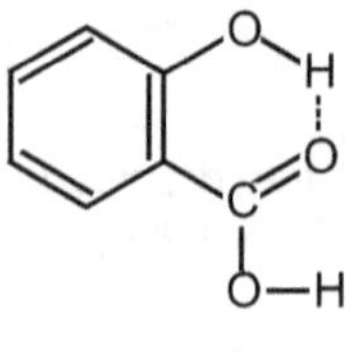

Salicylic acid

The m - and the p-isomers can form only intermolecular H-bonds.

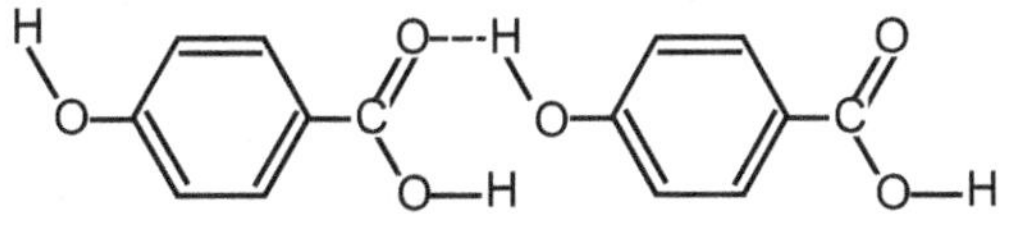

p-Hydroxybenzoic acid (dimer)

Salicylic acid is less soluble in water than the p-isomer but its partition coefficient (benzene water) is approximately 300 times greater, while p-hydroxy benzoic acid has low partition coefficient and hence low anti-bacterial action. In salicylic acid, intramolecular H-bond has the phenolic hydroxyl group masked but the carboxylic acid group is free and can function as an anti-bacterial agent similar to benzoic acid.

(3) The nucleic acids, fundamental reproductive units of cells, provide an important example of molecules held together by specific hydrogen bonds. The genetic code of the cell, which constitutes the instruction for the synthesis of the cell proteins, is present in the cell nucleus, in the form of DNA. The code consists of sequences of 4 purine and pyrimidine bases-pyrimidine pairs are held together by specific hydrogen bonds.

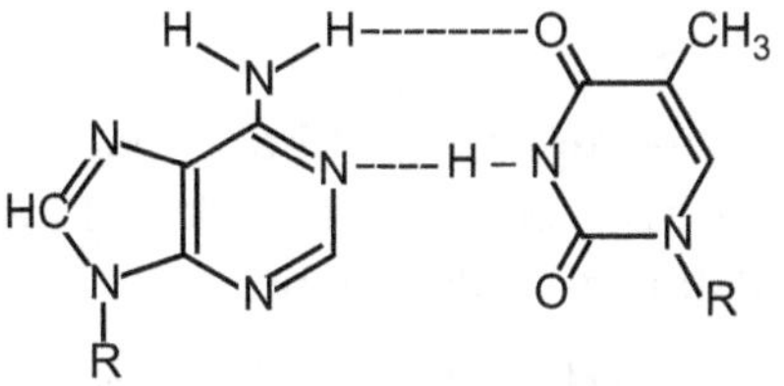

Adenine　　　　　　　Thymine

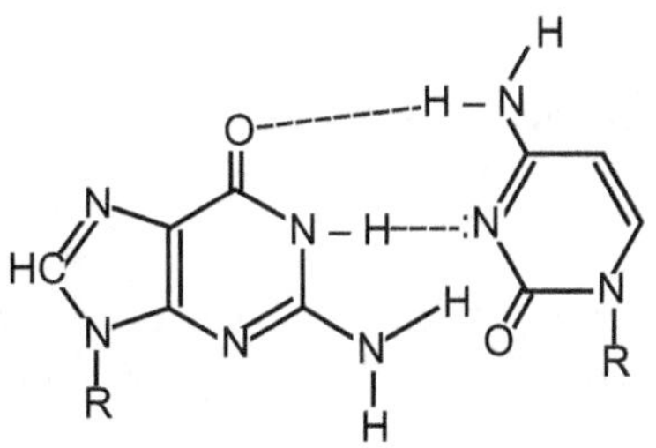

Guanine　　　　　　　Cytosine

Thus, H-bonds play a key role in maintaining the structural integrity of the base pairs of DNA.

1.11 OXIDATION-REDUCTION POTENTIALS

The tendency of a compound to give or to receive electrons, is measured quantitatively by its oxidation-reduction potential or redox potential.

Since the oxidation-reduction potential applies to a single reversible ionic equilibrium which does not exist in a living organism, the correlations between redox potential and biological activity can only be drawn for the compounds of very similar structure and physical properties. Following are the examples :

(1) The optimum bacteriostatic activity in quinones is associated with the redox potential at + 0.03 volt, when tested against Staphylococcus aureus.

(2) The biological activity of riboflavin is due to its ability to accept electrons and is reduced to the dihydro form. This reaction has a potential of $E_O = -0.185$ volt. By retaining most of the structural features and altering its redox potential, one may develop compounds antagonistic to riboflavin. Kuhn prepared the analogue, in which the two methyl groups of riboflavin were replaced by chlorines and having a potential of $E_O = -0.095$ volt. Its antagonistic properties are due to the dichloro-dihydro form being a weaker reducing agent than the dihydro form of riboflavin. It may be absorbed at specific receptor sites but not have a negative enough potential to carry out the biological reduction of riboflavin.

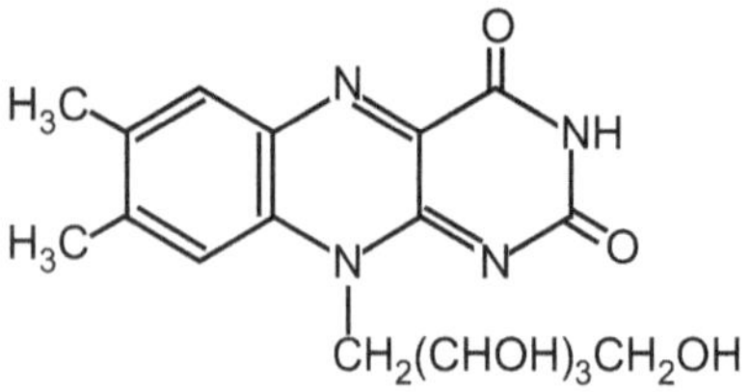

Riboflavin $E_0 = -0.185$ V

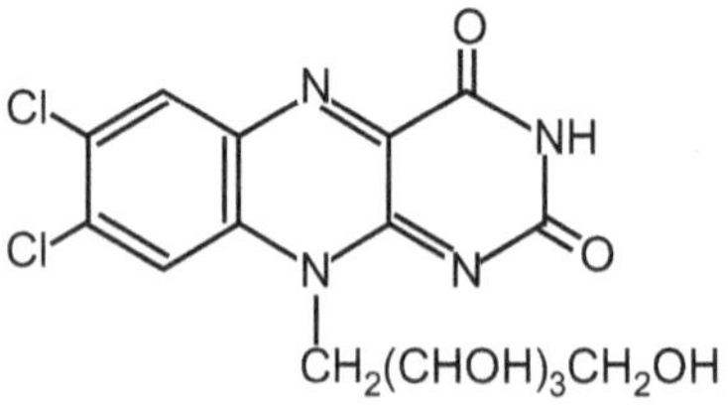

Riboflavin analogue $E_0 = -0.095$ V

(3) The optimum anthelmintic activity in a series of substituted phenothiazines is associated with the E_m potential of 0.583 volt (acetic acid - water) which could lead to maximal formation of semiquinone ion (a radical ion) at physiologic pH. (against mixed infestation of Syphacia obvelata and Aspirculurus tetraptera in mice). The semiquinone facilitates an essential biological electron transfer reaction, producing a toxic or paralysing effect.

The necessity of a free 3 or 7 position in the phenothiazine nucleus for significant anthelmintic activity and the inactivity of phenothiazine tranquillising drugs (2-substituted 10-dimethylaminopropyl phenothiazines) is only due to the difficulty of correlating redox potential and activity.

1.12 BIO-ISOSTERISM

In SAR studies and drug design, it is always necessary to compare the formal and three dimensional structure with the substituent and functional groups of compounds that show a similar spectrum of biological activities. In most instances, one may find similarities in molecular shape and overall chemical functions and will base one's explanation of biological similarities on these resemblances. This total complex of analogies that comprises steric, electronic and molecular orbital comparison is called bio-isosterism.

Bio-isosteric replacement is the principal guide followed by medicinal chemists in developing analogues of the 'lead' compound, whether as agonists or antagonists of biological effects. The parameters being changed are molecular size, steric shape, bond angles, hybridisation, electron distribution, lipid solubility, water solubility, pKa, the chemical reactivity to cell components and metabolising enzymes and the capacity to undergo H-bonding (receptor interactions).

In order to develop a new drug the structure of the drug is considered to consist of two parts,

(1) Critical or essential.

(2) Non-critical or non-essential : The non-critical part allows sufficient changes without a considerable change in the biological activity. The various molecular modifications done on this non-critical part are classified as follows.

(a) Selectophores : Those modifications which confirm selectivity in action of the drug by regulating drug distribution.

(b) Contactophores : The modifications which by increasing penetration, help the drug to reach the receptor site.

(c) Carrier moieties or conducting moieties : These moieties increase affinity of a drug.

Thus, non-critical part of a drug molecule is not involved in drug receptor interactions but is involved in passive transport of the drug.

While any change or modification of critical part of the drug molecule will result in the change of its biological activity, only those groups having similar steric, electronic and solubility characteristics can be interchanged. The study of such groups (bio-isosters) and their application in medicinal chemistry is known as Bio-isosterism.

More recently Burger classified and subdivided bio-isosters as :

(1) Classical bio-isosters :

(a) Monovalent atoms and groups,

    e.g. CH_2, NH_2, OH and SH.

(b) Divalent atoms and groups,

    e.g. R–O–R', R–NH–R', R–CH_2–R'

    and R–Si–R'

(c) Trivalent atoms and groups,

    e.g. R – N = R', and R – CH = R'

(d) Tetrasubstituted atom,

    e.g., $= C =$, $= \overset{\oplus}{N} =$, and $= \overset{\oplus}{P} =$

(e) Ring equivalents

    e.g. – CH = CH –, – S –, – O – , – NH

    and – CH_2 –

(2) Non-classical bio-isosters :

These non-classical bio-isosters do not rigidly fit the steric and electronic rules of the classic bio-isosters. These are further subdivided into,

    (a) Exchangeable groups

    (b) Rings versus non-cyclic structures.

BIO-ISOSTERIC APPLICATIONS

(1) An important compound of catecholamine series is phenylephrine.

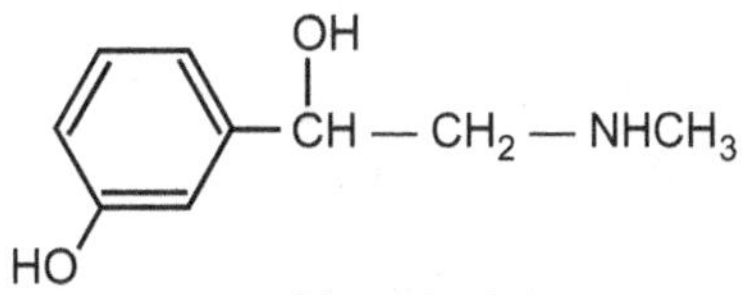

Phenylephrine

An alkylsulphonamido group may be substituted for the phenolic hydroxyl group. Some of the resulting compounds have agonist activity whereas others are antagonist.

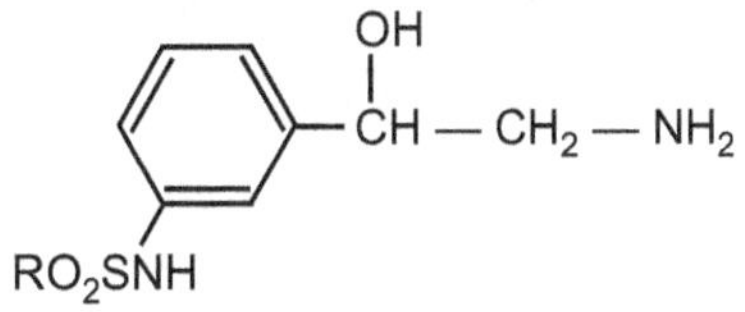

Alkylsulphonamidophenylethanolamine

While a classic example of rings versus non-cyclic structures is diethylstilbestrol and estradiol.

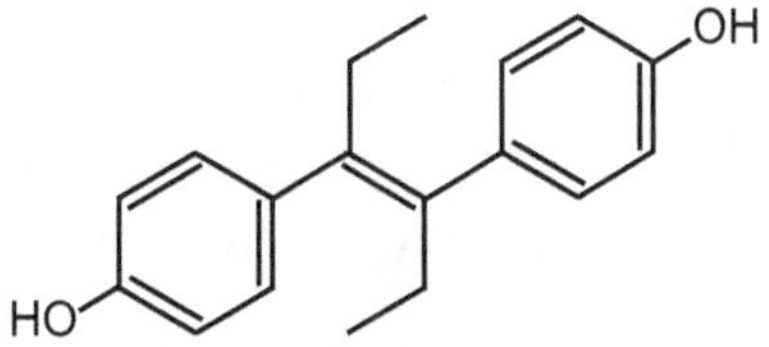

Diethyl stilbestrol

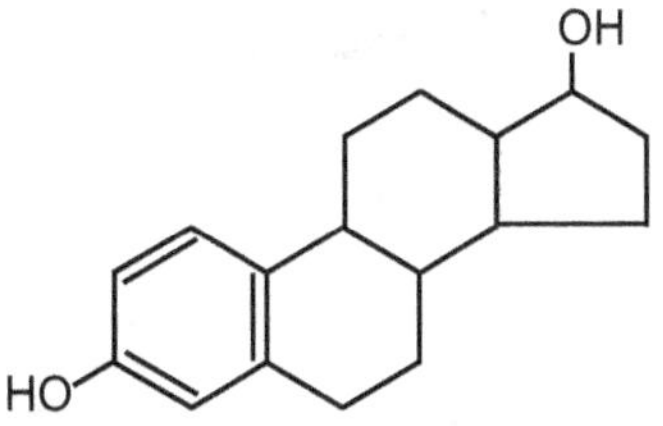

Estradiol

Diethylstilbestrol has about the same potency as the naturally occurring estradiol. The central double bond of diethyl stilbestrol is highly important for the correct orientation of the phenolic and ethyl groups (trans) at the receptor site. Table 1.6 contains a variety of bio-isosters including classical and non-classical examples, incorporating marketed drugs as well as interesting experimental compounds.

Applications of bio-isosterism were also found in the designing of histamine -1-receptor antagonists and anticholinergics (antispasmodics) by replacing benzene by thiophene,

$$\diagup \!\!\! \diagdown CH - by \diagup \!\!\! \diagdown N-, - CH_2 \text{ by O or S and so on.}$$

The first application of classical isosterism may be found in ring equivalents. Examples include pyridine and thiazole, benzene and thiophene.

The sulphur atom of the phenothiazine ring system of neuroleptic agents was replaced by – CH = CH – or – CH$_2$CH$_2$ – leading to the azepine ring analogues that opened up the field of tricyclic antidepressants. In imipramine by isosteric exchange of $\diagdown N -$ with $\diagdown C =$, amitriptyline was obtained.

The purpose of molecular modification is usually to seek subtle change in the compound that should not alter some properties but change others in order to improve potency, selectivity, duration of action and reduce toxicity. Bioisosterism makes it possible to limit some of these changes. All aspects considered, retention of overall molecular shape is the overriding condition for analogy of action.

In the design of bio-isosters an appreciation of the biochemical mode of action may play an important role e.g., aspirin acetylates prostaglandin synthetase and thereby deactivates this enzyme which ordinarily catalyses the biosynthesis of nociceptive prostaglandins. Isosters of aspirin in which the phenolic oxygen atom (X) has been replaced by 'classical' isosteric groups or atoms are inactive because they cannot release the acetyl group at all (X = CH$_2$) or at an adequate rate (when X = S, NH).

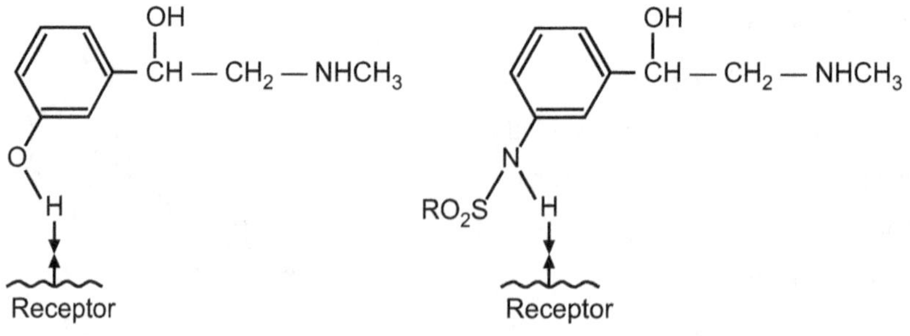

Table 1.7

Parent compound	Bio-isosters	Activity of parent compound
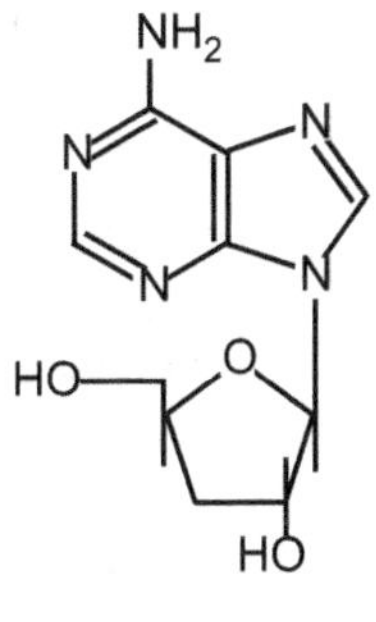	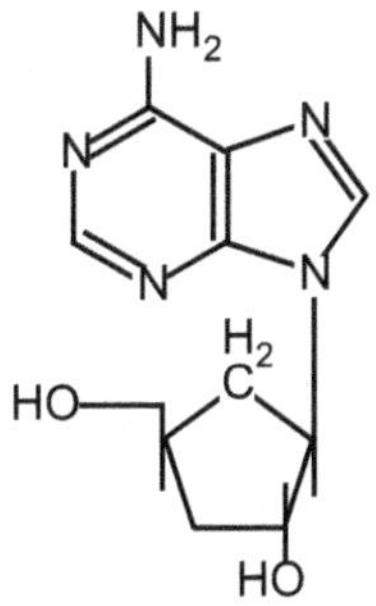	Adenosine deaminase activity (−)
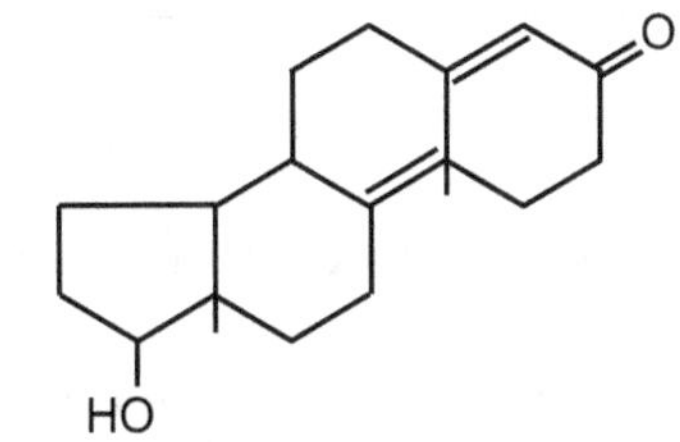	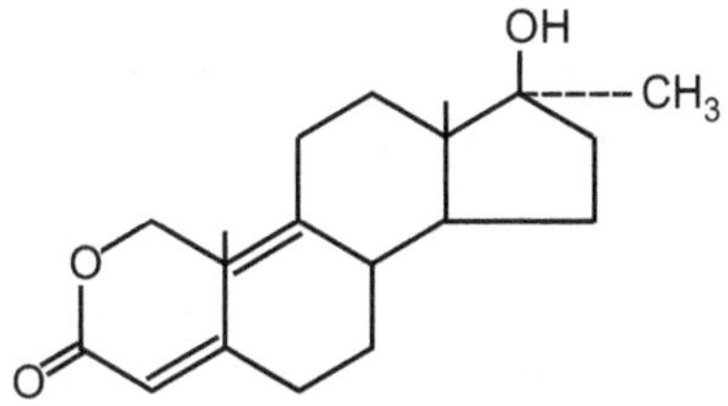	Androgenic (+)
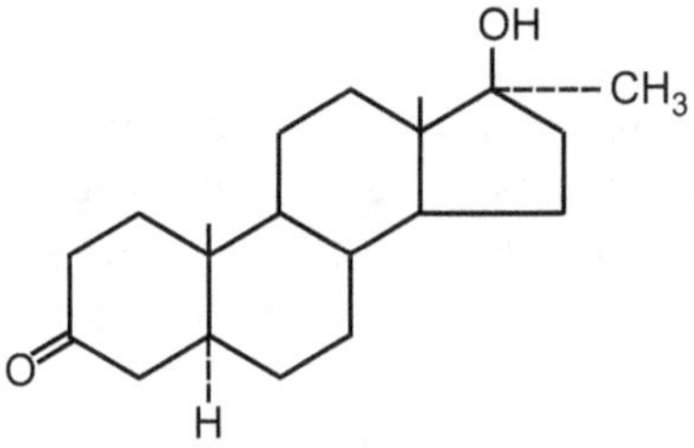	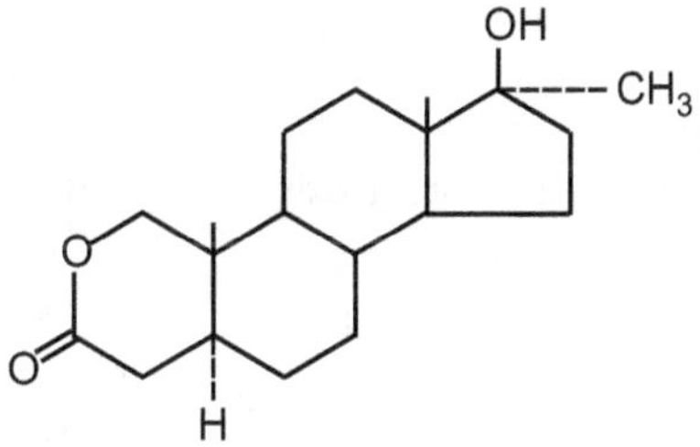	Androgenic (+)
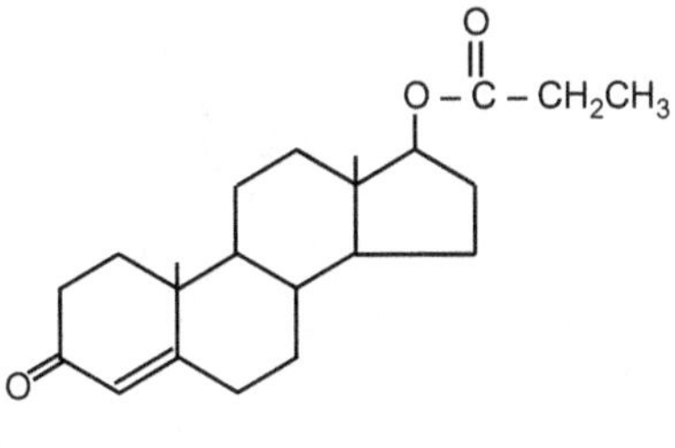	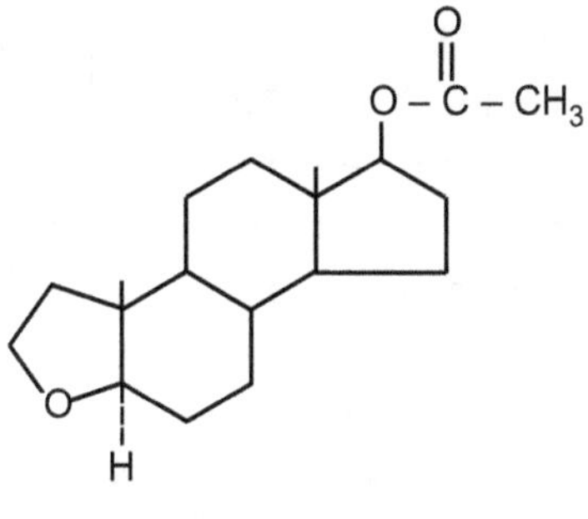	Androgenic (−)

Contd...

$CH_2 — Hg — O$ | $CHOMe$ | $CH_2 — NH — C$ (phthalimide ring)	$CH_2 — Hg — O$ | $CHOMe$ | $CH_2 — O — C$ (phthalide ring)	Diuretic (+)
HO—(benzene, HO)—$CH_2CH_2NH_2$	HO—(benzene)—CH_2ONH_2	Increases inhibition

(+) → activity of bio-isoster greater than parent compound.

(–) → activity of bio-isoster less than parent compound

1.13 BODY PROTEINS

The reversible binding of drug with non-specific and non-functional sites on the body proteins without showing any biological effect is called as *Protein Binding*.

A drug molecule, to less or more extent, has a capacity to enter into specific combination with plasma-proteins. These molecular interactions play an important role in deciding the intimate nature of drug action. For example, using paramecia as test organism, Busck, in 1906, observed the inhibitory effects of serum on the photodynamic and other toxic properties of certain dyes. This inhibition was attributed to the formation of dye-albumin complexes. Moore and Roaf reported that protein binding of volatile anaesthetics, ether and chloroform make them more soluble in plasma than in saline. Rabbit serum has excellent binding properties towards various drugs.

Drug molecules in blood are present in two forms :

(a) Free form : This form is pharmacologically active. It is diffusible and available for both, metabolism and excretion.

(b) Bound form : It is non-diffusible (being complexed with plasma-proteins) and hence inactive. It acts as reservoir of drug.

The free drug diffuses into various body compartments through biological membranes and barriers. It is consumed at sites of action for physiological effects, for metabolism and excretion.

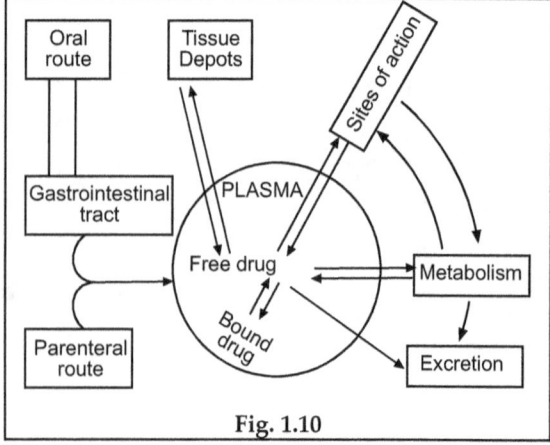

Fig. 1.10

Numerous alliances of drug molecule with different body proteins are possible. The one which is responsible for pharmacological response, is known as *'Primary interaction'* whereas all other interactions fall under the term, *'Secondary interactions'*. These secondary alliances are responsible for side-effects and storage of drug. It means the key fits many locks but there is only one door.

The body proteins which take part in binding are mainly available in blood and to small extent in tissues. They function as a specially designed transport system for the regulated distribution of drugs throughout the body.

Human plasma is a circulating fluid tissue. The protein portion occupies about 7% (or 200 gm) of total volume (3000 ml) of plasma. Albumin is the most important protein fraction which constitutes about 59% of total body proteins. On the basis of differences in size, shape, composition, physical and chemical properties, over 25 distinct proteins are categorised into different groups or fractions.

(a) Fibrinogen : It is not generally involved in binding with drugs except certain substituted naphthoquinones. It forms loose complexes and requires drug at comparatively higher concentration.

(b) γ-globulins : No specific reactivity of γ-globulins in drug binding has been witnessed. They are more involved in highly specific protein-protein interactions e.g., immune responses.

(c) α- and β-globulins : These include enzymes like choline esterase, peptidase, lipase and amylase. Due to their lipoidal nature, they can easily form conjugates with steroids, phospholipids and other non-polar molecules.

Table 1.8

Fraction	Major components
I	Fibrinogen
II	γ-globulins
III-0	β_1 – lipoprotein
III – 1, 2, 3	Isoagglutinins, plasmin, thrombin
IV – 1, IV-4	Various α- and β-globulins and several enzymes
IV – 7	Metal combining β_1-globulin
V – 1	Bilirubin-containing α_1 – globulin
V	Albumin

(d) Albumin : It is the most important protein fraction involved in binding of drugs and scatters greatest diversity in drug-protein interactions. Albumin has a molecular weight of 69,000. At blood pH 7.4, it has a net negative charge. It has about 109 cationic and 120 anionic residues. Hence, it can interact with both, anion as well as cation. It is a macromolecule, composed of hundreds of amino acids. It is the side-chain of composite amino acid structure that possesses the functional groups necessary for attracting and binding of the drug molecules. For example, epsilon amino groups of lysine residues and phenolic groups of tyrosine residues actively participate in binding of drug by albumin. Beside this, many and varied sites, capable of binding, exist in albumin.

Large molecule size (either due to inclusion of aromatic rings or due to increase in chain-length) contributes to increase an affinity of albumin towards drug molecule. This has been observed with penicillins, sulphonamides and barbiturates.

All the acidic drugs bind to plasma protein albumin

Ex. : Valproic acid, phenytoin, barbiturate Benzodiazepines, sulphonamides, Tetracycline, Polbutamide, Warfarin, NSAIDs.

All the basic drugs bind to α-1 acid glycoprotein

Ex. : Beta blocker, Prazosin, Bupivacaine Lignocaine, Verapamil, Disopyramide Imipramine, Methadone.

1.14 FORCES INVOLVED IN DRUG-PROTEIN INTERACTION

Drug binds with plasma-proteins which hinder their access to the sites of drug action, metabolism and excretion. It remains stored in an inactive form. Thus, drug molecules not only form alliances with the receptors responsible for their pharmacological action but also interact with several other secondary receptors in the body tissues. In the plasma, plasma-proteins play the role of secondary receptors.

Drug molecule binds with proteins through two different modes.

(a) Primary binding : A firm binding results through primary binding. This is an ionic interaction in which an ionised form of the drug molecule interacts with the charged molecule of the plasma-protein.

(b) Secondary binding : The primary binding alone, is not sufficient for plasma-protein to hold the drug molecule. It is to be supplemented with other secondary binding forces. These forces mainly operate between the non-ionic part of drug and non-polar portion of protein molecule.

The forces involved in secondary binding are :

(1) Hydrogen bonding
(2) Hydrophobic bonding
(3) Van der Waals forces.

(1) Hydrogen bonding : A sort of electrostatic union always exists between a hydrogen atom and an electronegative atom. This bonding can be illustrated as :

$$A - F \ \ldots\ldots\ldots\ H - B$$
$$A - O \ \ldots\ldots\ldots\ H - B$$

The hydrogen atom may be a part of drug molecule or the plasma-protein. This is an example of *intermolecular hydrogen bonding.*

(2) Hydrophobic bonding : According to the principle of 'like dissolves like', the hydrophobic portion of drug molecule always has a tendency to avoid an aqueous phase. Hydrophobic bonding results through this tendency. Actually bond formation does not take place but association of two hydrophobic portions occur to form micelle like structures in order to avoid water.

Thus, an attraction of non-polar portion of drug molecule towards non-polar portion of another molecule results through their unwelcome reception to water, is known as *hydrophobic bonding.*

(3) van der Waals forces : This force operates mainly between dipole and induced dipole portions of the molecules. This is categorised as a weak binding force. All the above mentioned secondary binding forces help a non-ionised drug molecule to bind with plasma-protein e.g. steroidal drugs, like hydrocortisone.

There are usually one or two primary binding sites available per protein molecule with several possible secondary sites. The characteristics of each such site depend not only upon the properties of its ionic residues but are also influenced by the properties of neighbouring non-ionic groups, and upon surface configuration and steric hindrances offered to approaching molecules.

1.15 FACTORS AFFECTING DRUG-PROTEIN BINDING

These factors are categorised as :

(a) Physical factors,

(b) Chemical factors, and

(c) Physiological factors.

(a) **Physical factors** : The pH of blood, ionic strength and temperature are top amongst the list of physical factors. They affect the degree of drug binding in plasma by affecting the number of binding sites available per protein molecule.

(b) **Chemical factors** : Polarity of drug molecule increases its affinity for protein. For example, salicylic acid binds more strongly with protein than benzoic acid due to increase in number of sites for primary binding.

Table 1.9

Drug	No. of binding sites per protein molecule (η)	Association constant $K \times 10^4$
Phenol	Negligible	Negligible
Benzoate	0.3	1.5
Salicylate	0.4	3.0

Similarly, an increase in non-polar portion of drug molecule through addition of non-polar substituent or by lengthening the side-chain results into more firm binding due to increase in number of sites for secondary binding.

Table 1.10

Compound	η	$K \times 10^4$
Octanol	4.5	3.0
Octyl sulphate	4.5	60.0
Dodecanol	4.5	15.0
Dodecyl sulphate	8.5	120.0

Such enhancement is due to an interaction between the lipophilic portions of drug and protein.

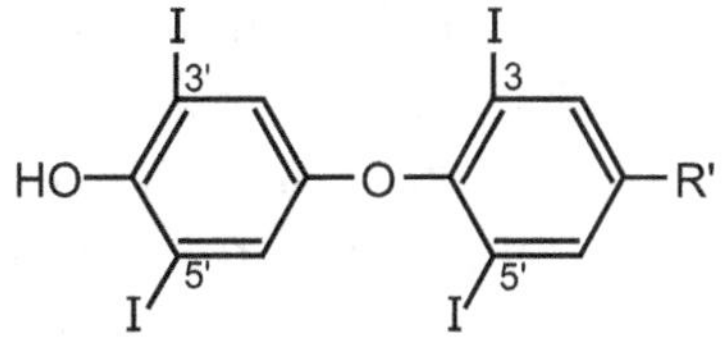

Thyroxine; R' = $- CH_2 - \overset{\overset{\displaystyle NH_2}{|}}{CH} - COOH$

Plasma-proteins, while interacting with small molecules, exhibit a high degree of structural specificity. The specific structural features of thyroxine analogues necessary for binding with thyroxine binding albumin fraction have been well characterised. The following structural features favour more efficient binding with plasma-proteins.

(1) A diphenyl ether nucleus.

(2) A free phenolic hydroxyl function.

(3) An ionised moiety separated by about three carbon atoms away from aromatic ring.

In general, the extent of binding of any substance to plasma-proteins is greatly influenced by its partition coefficient value. Other factors which determine the extent of protein binding include decrease in albumin concentration, dose of drug given, route of administration, pathological conditions and genetic factors. These factors affect the number and type of protein binding sites. For example, the protein binding of phenytoin found to increase two times in a healthy person than that in nephrotic or uremic patient.

1.16 PHARMACOLOGICAL SIGNIFICANCE OF DRUG-PROTEIN INTERACTION

Depending upon their structural features, most drugs interact at their therapeutic concentration with one or more of the plasma-proteins. This may give rise to different possibilities like :

(1) Drug bound to plasma-protein is pharmacologically active and can penetrate the sites of drug action.

(2) When only unbound or free drug is active, then protein binding may :

(a) act as a reservoir of drug and prolong the duration of action,

(b) facilitate the distribution of drug throughout the body,

(c) retard the excretion of drug,

(d) lower the therapeutic concentration of the drug by not allowing a sufficient concentration of free drug to develop at the receptor site,

(e) unbound drug is freely diffusible and the drug-protein complex is generally confined to the circulating plasma.

[A] Effect of protein binding on drug distribution :

(i) Protein bound drug is unable to penetrate membranes and is confined to the circulating plasma. It cannot diffuse to the site of action or metabolise in other compartments.

Only free drug can cross biological membranes. This transfer is mainly influenced by partition coefficient and concentration gradient of the free drug. Protein binding, therefore, by acting as reservoir of drug, can decrease the rate of drug disappearance from general circulation. When required it dissociates to release free drug and maintains a steady state concentration level of free drug. It thus compensates the loss of free drug by excretion or metabolism e.g., the affinity and extent of binding of different sulphonamides enable these drugs to be classified into long and short acting categories. Sulphamethoxydiazine strongly binds with plasma-proteins. Hence, it is a long acting drug, whereas sulphathiazole weakly binds to proteins resulting into its short duration of action.

(ii) Protein binding of drug slows the rate of distribution of drug into peripheral compartments.

(iii) Placenta is a demarcation line between the maternal and the foetal circulation. Hormones such as thyroxine, is not required in foetus before the appearance of foetal endocrine glands. Since the placenta is not permeable to the proteins, protein binding of thyroxine limits its access to the foetal circulation.

(iv) Ferrous ions are transported to the bone marrow with transferin, a β-globulin. They are utilised in the formation of haemoglobin but are toxic when they are not bound in the plasma.

(v) Protein binding of a drug may project misleading conclusions, if two drugs of the same pharmacological category, are compared on the basis of concentration of drug in the plasma.

[B] Effect of protein binding on drug metabolism :

In general, the drug present in the unbound form is available for metabolic processes. Hence, the rate of metabolism is inversely proportional to the extent of protein binding of a drug.

[C] Effect of protein binding on drug elimination :

Even though renal blood supply consists of both, bound and free drug, only the free drug is filterable through the glomerular filter. The concentration of free drug in the glomerular filtrate equals to the concentration of free drug in the plasma. Hence, the drug elimination via the kidneys is influenced by the extent of plasma-protein binding of a drug.

Glomerular filtration rate of a drug

$$\propto \frac{1}{\text{Extent of protein binding}}$$

It means that increased protein binding decreases the rate of elimination of a drug, resulting into prolonged biological half-life. But it does not hold true, if the rate of dissociation of drug-protein complex is high. For example, the rate of dissociation of penicillin-protein complex is considerably high. Hence, penicillin can be completely removed from the blood during single passage through the kidneys.

1.17 EFFECT OF DISPLACEMENT OF BOUND DRUG

There are obvious occasions where drugs bounded with plasma-proteins can be partially or completely liberated by another drug. This leads to increase in pharmacological response of the displaced drug due to an increase in the concentration of free drug in plasma and biophase. In such cases, the dissociation constant and the apparent volume of distribution determine the rate of excretion of the displaced drug.

The effect of displacement could be sudden if the binding exceeds 90-95%. For example, in the case of a drug which is 98% bound, a displacement of 2% drug will lead to a substantial 100% increase in the unbound drug concentration in plasma. In such cases, if the volume of distribution (VD) is large the effects may be minimal. Serious toxic effects may appear if VD is small. This is due to a significant rise of drug concentration in plasma and biophase.

Some drugs may exert an indirect biological effect by displacing other drugs from plasma-proteins. This can reasonably be attributed to competition between the drugs that are known to act on same physiological receptors or that share some common structural features.

(1) Sulphonyl urea anti-diabetic agents displace insulin from its complex with protein.

(2) Atropine displaces pilocarpine.

(3) Salicylates and sulphonamides displace bilirubin.

(4) Acetylcholine displaces carbonic ester inhibitors from their complex with the plasma cholinesterases.

(5) Similarly, benzoates and salicylates displace thyroid hormone.

The impairment of the binding capacity of plasma-proteins (e.g., hypoalbuminemia) may be a significant factor in justifying an unusual sensitivity or resistance to drugs. Moderate hypoalbuminemia may be caused by a number of diseases and conditions such as cancer, myocardial infarction, pregnancy, prolonged immobilisation, G.I.T. disorders, etc. Severe hypoalbuminemia is observed in severe burns, liver and renal impairments. In renal impairment, decreased binding of acidic and neutral (but not basic drugs) drugs to plasma-protein is found.

1.18 DRUG PERSISTENCE

Beside plasma-proteins, tissue proteins also exhibit an affinity for certain drugs. They thus provide drug depots outside the plasma. This process obviously is reversible. The effective intracellular protein concentration is considerably higher for certain body organs, e.g. liver, lung, spleen, muscles etc. They have much higher affinity for certain drugs which include emetine, suramin, quinacrine and organic arsenicals and antimonials. For example, quinacrine and antimalarial drug, after 4 hours of administration, shows a 2000 fold concentration in liver than in plasma. After 14 days of daily administration, the concentration of drug in liver touches to 20,000 times to that in plasma. It is not entirely clear whether albumin or a globulin is primarily involved in it.

1.19 DRUG ALLERGY

An allergy arises due to antigen-antibody interaction, which itself can be interpreted in terms of protein-protein interaction. Landsteiner has developed a method of producing an artificial drug antigen (by coupling particular drug to protein through diazo-linkage) which can be utilised to get specific antibody responses in experimental animals. Strychnine, epinephrine, aspirin, sulphonamides are among the drugs which have been tried. In many cases, only albumins qualify themselves to act as antigens but purified globulins could not give expected results.

1.20 SUBSTANCES THAT PPARENTLY DO NOT INTERACT WITH PLASMA-PROTEINS

Though most of the drugs bind with plasmaproteins, there still remain a short list of substances which are least interested in forming association with plasma-proteins.

This list includes :

(a) Sodium and potassium ions

(b) Nitrous oxide

(c) Thiamine

(d) Histamine and choline

(e) Streptomycin

These agents interact with plasma-protein weakly if at all.

1.21 BLOOD BRAIN BARRIER

Not all the categories of drugs administered in the body, can reach the CNS area and cause CNS-effects. Their entry into the region of CNS is supposed to be governed by a permeable barrier, known as the blood--brain-barrier. This barrier operates to regulate the passive diffusion of both, macromolecules as well as micromolecules from the systemic circulation into the various regions of the CNS. Certain properties like, molecular weight, charge and lipophilicity of the molecules play an important role in controlling the passage of bioactive substances in the CNS.

In human body and other complex organisms a steady state concentration of hormones, amino acids, sugars and ions (like Na^+, K^+, Ca^{++}, etc.) is maintained in circulation. Frequent small fluctuations in their concentrations are expected after meal or exercire. These fluctuations do not affect the functioning of different organs of the body, leaving brain as an exception.

Table 1.11 : Some central-neurotransmitters

Transmitter	Agonists	Antagonists
1. Acetylcholine	M_1 : Muscarine	Atropine
	M_2 : Bethanechol	Atropine
	N : Nicotine	Dihydro-β–erythroidine
2. Norepinephrine	α_1 : Phenylephrine	Prazosin
	α_2 : Clonidine	Yohimbine
	β_1 : Dobutamine	Practolol
	β_2 : Terbutaline	Butoxamine
3. Epinephrine	same as above	Same as above
4. Dopamine	D_1 : Dihydrexidine	Phenothiazine
	D_2 : Apomorphine	Butyrophenone
5. 5-Hydroxytryptamine	$5\,HT_1$: LSD	Methylsergide
	$5\,HT_2$: LSD	Spiroperidol
6. GABA	A : Muscimol	Picrotoxin
	B : Baclofen	Saclofen
7. Glycine	Taurine	Strychnine
8. Dicarboxylic amino acids	N-Me-D-aspartate	α-amino adipate

Brain is a highly specialized organ of the body. Even a slight fluctuation in the composition of blood supplied to brain, may affect nervous function. Since some hormones and amino acids serve as neurotransmitters, such fluctuation may lead to uncontrolled nervous activity. Hence, the brain must be kept rigorously isolated from such transient changes in the composition of the blood. The concept of Blood-Brain-Barrier, whose existence was first demonstrated conclusively in the 1960's has been put forward. It possesses the unique and specialized mechanisms by which, brain excludes unwanted substances presented to it by circulation. The barrier serves a critical function as stringent gatekeeper between blood and brain to create the unchanging environment, the brain needs.

Fortunately to receive the essential nutrients needed for brain functioning, there exists specialized transport systems that recognize and carry nutrients into the brain. There are several different types of transporter, each of which has a specific function. These transporters not only carry nutrients into the brain but also pump surplus substances out, in order to maintain a constant environment for neurons.

The first evidence for the existence of such barrier came out in 1913 through the observations of Edwin E. Goldmann when he showed that the central nervous system is separated from the blood by a barrier of some kind. With an introduction of Electron microscopy, it can be stated with certain surety that the endothelium of brain capillaries is the anatomic site of the blood-brain-barrier. These capillaries that supply blood to the tissues of the brain, has a unique structure. In contrast to any usual animal cell, the endothelial cells forming the tube of a brain capillary are locked by continuous tight junctions that prevent substances in the blood from diffusing freely into the brain. In addition, the brain capillaries are almost completely surrounded by processes of the brain cells, known as astrocytes. Previously it was thought that the astrocytes form the blood-brain-barrier. But now it is proved that the endothelial cells govern the transport across the blood and brain cells. Hence, they constitute the barrier site.

Lipophilicity is an important parameter which governs an ability of a molecule to reach the blood-brain-barrier. Lipid soluble substances easily cross the barrier and enter the brain. The reason lies in the lipophilic nature of cell-membrane of capillary endothelium. But certain substances which are of vital importance for brain function (e.g., glucose, certain amino acids) are not lipophilic. A special transport control system exists in capillary endothelium to recognize and to bring nutrients across the membrane. Recently S.I. Harik proved that each endothelial cell is richly supplied with such transport sites. Each transporter is undoubtedly composed of proteins that span the cell-membrane, thereby forming a channel through which nutrients and other substances needed for brain metabolism cross the barrier.

If an unwanted substance enters the endothelial cells from blood, it can be modified through enzymatic steps into a chemical form, in the endothelium and rendered unable to enter the brain.

For example, L-dopa is converted in endothelium into dopamine and DOPAC in successive steps by the enzymes AADC and MAO. Hence the enzymatic conversions can serve as a means of controlling how much L-dopa reaches the brain.

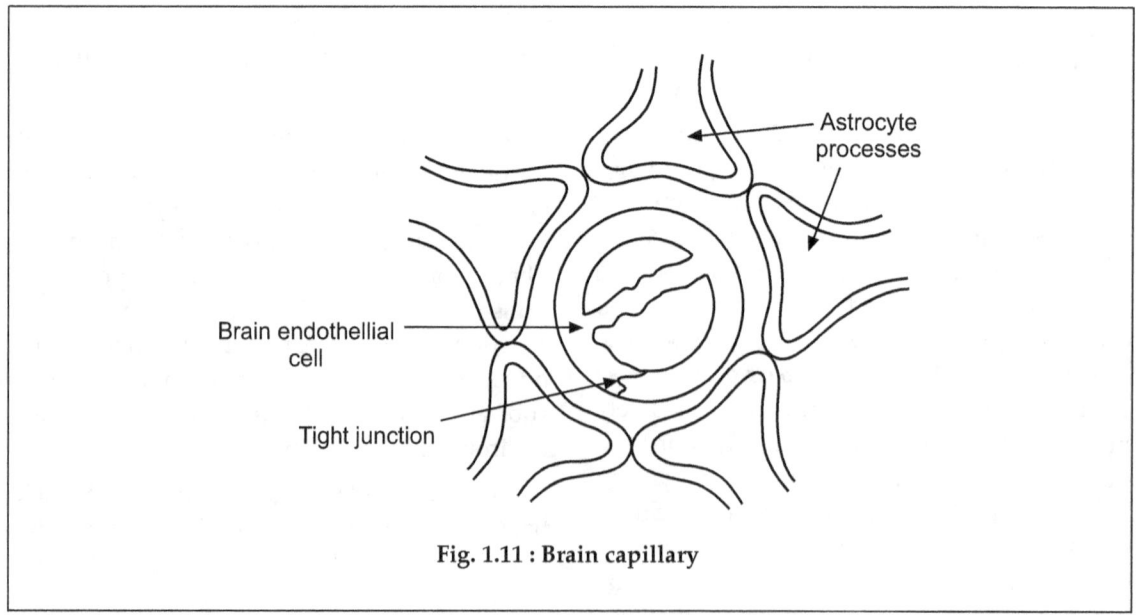

Fig. 1.11 : Brain capillary

An interesting experiment by Stanley I. Rapoport indicated that the concentrated sugar solution temporarily loosens the tight junctions between endothelial cells. When the sugar solution is removed, the barrier is re-established. This presents a more precise way of administering medicines which enter the brain slowly. e.g., penicillin. This technique is of clinical value in patients with brain tumors where the entry of drugs in brain can be facilitated using this procedure.

The operation of metabolic and physical barriers across blood and brain cells is collectively known as blood-brain-barrier. The term describes all the obstacles to the free passage of a substance from the blood stream to the brain cells.

The barrier is not equally strong in all parts of brain. It is relatively liberal in the hypothalamic region and in the area postrema.

2

RECEPTORS

2.1 INTRODUCTION

To exhibit the same pharmacological action, the two drugs must possess certain structural features in common along with the same spatial arrangement of such groups. Such requirements cannot logically be explained unless it is assumed that for a drug, in order to produce its pharmacological action, it must react or interact with the complementary chemical groupings of a biologically important integral part of the organism known as *receptor*.

The term receptive substance or, receptor was coined to denote a relatively small region of a macromolecule which may be an isolable enzyme, a structural and functional component of a cell-membrane or a specific intracellular substance like protein or a nucleic acid. Enzymes are biological catalysts.

Most enzymes are proteins but the active sites often contain groups other than amino acids. There are metalloenzymes in which zinc, iron, cobalt, manganese or other transition metals are the catalytic centers. Many enzymes require cofactors – small molecules bound to the enzyme – to become effective catalysts. For example, all the vitamins from B complex family are all cofactors. Some enzymes are complexes of protein and RNA in which the RNA also participates in catalysis e.g. ribosomes.

Ion channels mediate ion permeation with both efficiency and specificity. Ion channels may be classified by a number of criteria including electrophysiological properties (i.e., conductance, activation and inactivation), ion permeation (i.e., sensitivity to specific drugs). Ion channels thus may be regarded as pharmacological receptors and possess both activator and antagonist ligands which exhibit defined and discrete SAR.

The receptor concept goes back to 1878. It was formulated by John N. Langley, a British physiologist who worked on antagonism of atropine and pilocarpine. The term, receptor was introduced in 1907 by Paul Ehrlich, the famous pioneer of chemotherapy and immunochemistry. He said "compounds do not act unless bound. "Drug receptors consist of a cascade of cell-membrane bound lipoproteins and/or glycoproteins and/or cellular nucleic acids. The binding of drugs to receptors, in various cases, involves all known types of interactions. like, ionic, hydrogen, van der Waals, and covalent bonding. Non-covalent interactions of high affinity may appear to be essentially irreversible. It is likely that, in most cases, multiple type binding may be present.

The biological response of a drug is a result of drug-receptor interaction which alters the function of that specific cellular component and thereby initiates the series of biochemical and physiological changes that are collectively recognised at the gross level of observation as its biological response. Thus, by virtue of such interactions with receptors, drugs do not create the effects but merely modulate the rates of ongoing function. In simple pharmacological words, one can state that a drug cannot impart a new function to a cell but is potentially capable of altering the rate at which any bodily function proceeds.

The receptor diversity, their complexity in coupling to regulatory proteins, signal trans-duction pathways and subsequent cellular events reflects the root of a variety of diseases.

The ability of a drug to bind to the receptor is termed as affinity of the drug for the receptor. While the drug ability to elicit its pharmacological response is termed as its intrinsic activity or efficacy. The receptor recognises the arrangement of certain functional groups in three dimensional space and their electron densities. Intrinsic activity is the recognition of these groups rather than the structure of the entire drug molecule that results in an interaction, normally consisting of non-covalent binding. Intrinsic activity defines the drug as an agonist, an antagonist or a partial agonist. For example, when a drug molecule possesses a high affinity as well as high intrinsic activity, it is known as 'agonist'. Those having a high affinity but poor intrinsic activity, are known as 'antagonists' and drug with an affinity equal or less than that of the agonist but with less intrinsic activity is termed as 'partial agonist'.

2.2 TYPES OF RECEPTOR

The three main criteria for receptor classi-fication are operational (i.e., agonists, anta-gonists), transductional (intracellular transduction) and structural (gene and amino acid sequence of the receptor).

Certain receptors are exposed at the external surface of the cell membrane to recognize and interact with hormones, neurotransmitters or drugs. Second category includes effector enzymes such as adenylate cyclase (which generates second messenger, c-AMP) ion channels, which are exposed at the inner, cytoplasmic side of the cell. The third category of receptors is located within the nucleus domains and is called as intracellular receptors.

(a) Membrane bound receptor systems :

Certain hormone and neurotransmitter receptors are associated with structural and functional elements of the cell by relatively weak covalent bonds and may be solubilized and isolated by treatment with non-ionic detergents, without loss of their binding affinity, e.g. nicotinic cholinergic receptors. These receptors appear to result from the association of several (three or more) subunits of molecular weight 40,000 which carry binding sites for cholinergic agonists and

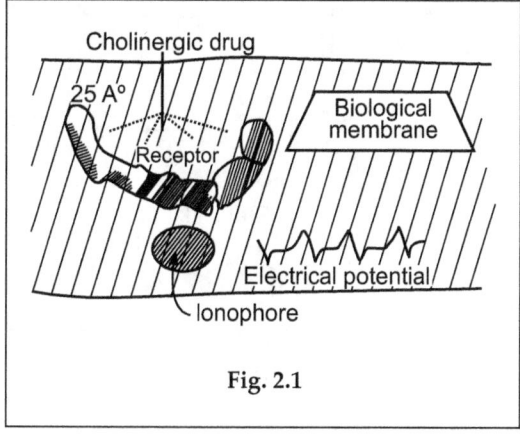

Fig. 2.1

antagonists (along with a common or overlapping site for both agonist and antagonist). The interaction of cholinergic agonist with the receptor results in changes in transmembrane electrical potential [changes in cation (Na+) flux through the membrane] as a result of change in state of specific ionophore or ion conductance modulator.

The ionophore is a protein that is distinct from the receptor, perhaps of the molecular weight 43,000, and the receptor and ionophore are strongly associated in the native membrane.

(b) Receptors acting through second messenger :

Receptors for a number of hormones and autacoids function by regulation of the concentration of the intracellular second messenger, cyclic adenosine 3', 5' monophosphate (cyclic AMP) through the activation of intracellular adenylate cyclase. In this system, the receptor - drug binding sites

and enzymes catalytic sites are clearly on separate proteins e.g. β-adrenergic receptors.

(c) Intracellular receptors :

Intracellular receptors play a dominant role in the actions of the steroid and thyroid hormones. The steroid receptor complex undergoes a conformational change and is thereby activated. This activated complex then enters into the nucleus and binds to acceptor sites on chromatin (actual or true receptors), resulting in an increase or decrease in the production of certain RNA's and m-RNA's along with the corresponding enzymes and other proteins which cause the steroid-hormone response.

2.3 RECEPTOR SITE THEORIES

(a) Occupation theory :

This theory, proposed by Gaddum and Clark, states that the intensity of the pharmacological effect is directly proportional to the number of receptors occupied by the drug.

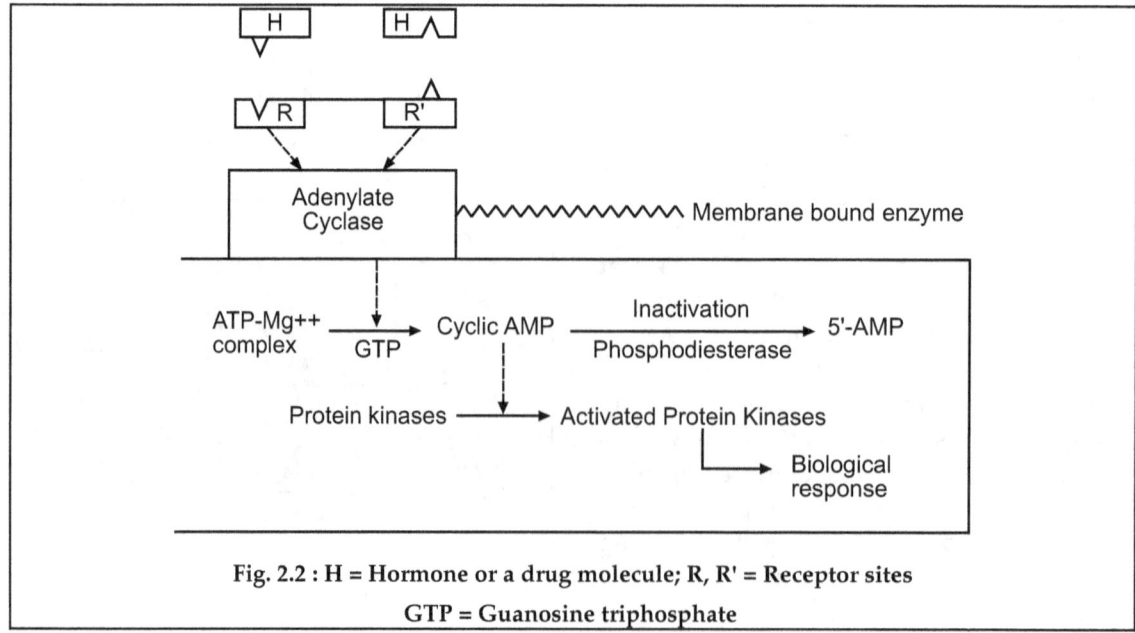

Fig. 2.2 : H = Hormone or a drug molecule; R, R' = Receptor sites
GTP = Guanosine triphosphate

The pharmacological response of a drug molecule is a function of dose, number of receptors available and its intrinsic activity. The rate of combination of drug and receptor can therefore be expressed as -

$$K_1 [R] \times [A]$$

where,

K$_1$　=　association constant

R　=　concentration of the receptors not occupied by drugs and

A　=　concentration of drug molecules or dose.

Similarly, the rate of dissociation of the drug receptor complex is given by the expression

$$K_2 [RA]$$

where,

K$_2$　=　dissociation constant

[RA]　=　concentration of receptors occupied by the drug.

At equilibrium,

$$K_1 [R] \times [A] = K_2 [RA]$$

This relationship can be more conveniently expressed by taking account of the fact that [R] + [RA] is equal to [r] = total concentration of receptors. Thus,

$$K_1 [A] [r] - [RA] = K_2 [RA] \qquad ... (2.1)$$

Or 　$$\frac{[RA]}{[r]} = \frac{K_1 [A]}{K_1 [A] + K_2}$$

$$= \frac{1}{1 + K_2 / K_1 [A]} \qquad ... (2.2)$$

$\dfrac{K_2}{K_1}$ can be replaced by, KA = equilibrium constant.

It is reciprocal of the drug's affinity for the receptors.

The term $\dfrac{[RA]}{[r]}$ represents the fraction of the total number of receptors occupied by the drug. When [RA] = [r], i.e. all the receptors are occupied and the response is thus proportional to its intrinsic activity, X$_n$.

Relative response　$= \dfrac{[RA] \, X}{[r]}$

$$= \frac{X}{1 + KA/[A]} \qquad ... (2.3)$$

This theory does not rationalise partial agonists.

(b) Rate Theory :

Paton and Rang in 1965 proposed that the most important factor determining drug action is the rate at which drug-receptor combination takes place.

Therefore, the rate theory suggests that the pharmacological activity is a function of the rate of association and dissociation of the drug with the receptor, and not the number of occupied receptors.

At equilibrium, the rates of combination and dissociation of drug-receptor reactions are same and equation (I) can be rewritten as :

$$\frac{K_1 [A] ([r] - [RA])}{[r]} = \frac{K_2 [RA]}{[r]} \qquad ... (2.4)$$

By simple mathematical manipulation from equation (2.3), it can be shown that

Rate of receptor occupation

$$= \frac{K_2}{1 + \dfrac{RA}{[A]}} \qquad ... (2.5)$$

When the response is proportional to the number of receptors occupied, the equation (2.3) of occupation theory is important and when the response is proportional to the rate of receptor occupation rather than to the proportion of receptors occupied, equation (2.5) of rate theory is important.

(c) The Induced-fit Theory of Enzyme-Substrate Interaction :

The induced-fit theory of Koshland was originally proposed for the action of substrates and enzymes. According to this theory the receptor (enzyme) need not necessarily exists in the appropriate conformation required to bind the drug (substrate). As the drug approaches the receptor, a conformational change is induced which orients the essential binding sites. This conformational change in the receptor could be responsible for the initiation of the biological response. e.g., acetylcholine may interact with the regulating protein and alter the normal forces which stabilise the structure of the protein, thereby producing a transient rearrangement in the membrane structure and a consequent change in its ion regulating property.

The receptor was suggested to be elastic and it could return to its original conformation after the drug was released. The drug may also undergo conformational changes.

According to the induced-fit theory, an agonist would induce a conformational change (i.e. intrinsic activity) and elicit a response, but an antagonist would bind without a conformational change (i.e., devoid of intrinsic activity). The macromolecular perturbation theory and the activation aggregation theory are extensions of the induced-fit theory.

(d) Macromolecular Perturbation Theory :

According to this theory, Belleau proposed that interaction of small molecules of drug or a substrate with a macromolecule (such as the protein or a drug receptor) may lead either to specific conformational perturbations (SCP) or to non-specific conformational perturbation (NSCP).

A SCP (specific change in structure or conformation of a protein molecule) would result in the specific response of an agonist i.e. the drug would possess intrinsic activity.

If a NSCP occurs, no stimulant response would be obtained and an antagonistic or blocking action may be produced. If a drug possesses features which contribute to formation of both a SCP and a NSCP, an

equilibrium mixture of the two complexes may result, which would account for a partial stimulant action e.g. alkyl trimethyl ammonium ions. Lower alkyl trimethyl ammonium ions (C_1 to C_6) alter the receptor structure in a specific perturbation, thus stimulating the muscarinic receptor. With a chain of 8-12 carbon atoms, the antagonistic action is observed due to non-specific conformational perturbation while the inter-mediate, heptyl and octyl derivatives act as partial agonists.

(e) Activation-Aggregation Theory :

It was proposed by Changeux and Karlin. According to this theory, even in the absence of drugs, a receptor is in a state of dynamic equilibrium between an activated form (R_o), which is responsible for the biological response and an inactive form (T_o). Agonists shift the equilibrium to the activated form, antagonists bind to the inactive form and partial agonists bind to both conformations. In this mode, the agonist binding site in the R_o conformation can be different from the antagonist binding site in the T_o conformation. If there are two different binding sites and conformations, then this could account for the structural differences in these classes of compounds.

2.4 FORCES INVOLVED IN DRUG-RECEPTOR INTERACTIONS

Drug-receptor interactions involve one or more of the following types of bonding :

(a) Covalent Bonding :

The stability of this type of bond hardly permits the formation of an easily reversible drug-receptor complex. Only when the receptor is inactivated by an irreversible antagonist, there is the formation of covalent bond e.g. acetylcholine-sterases are irreversibly inactivated by a number of phosphate esters. The nitrogen mustards are also irreversible inhibitors of certain receptors.

(b) Hydrogen Bonding :

An important type of bonding between drugs and receptors is a weak and easily broken H-bond. Since many drugs contain hydroxyl, amino, carboxyl and carbonyl groups, they can form H-bonds with the receptors complex. The reduced potency of many sulphur analogues of oxygen-containing drugs has been attributed to the reduced ability of sulphur to form H-bond.

H-bonds are a type of dipole-dipole interaction formed between the proton of a group X-H, (where X is an electronegative atom,) and other electronegative atom (Y) containing a pair of non-bonded electrons. X removes electron density from the hydrogen so it has a partial positive charge, which is strongly attracted to non-bonded electrons of Y. The interaction is denoted as a dotted line, -X-H ... Y-, to indicate that a covalent bond between X and H still exists, but that an interaction between H and Y also occurs.

The hydrogen bond is unique to hydrogen because it is the only atom that can carry a positive charge at physiological pH while remaining covalently bonded in a molecule, and hydrogen also is small enough to allow close approach of a second electronegative atom. The strength of the hydrogen bond is related to the Hammett (σ) constants. There are intramolecular and intermolecular H-bonds; the former are stronger.

(c) Electrostatic Bonding :

The charged ions produced by the drug molecules may be attracted to charged groups within the receptor site. For example, acetyl-choline.

$$X - (CH_3)_3 \overset{+}{N} - CH_2 - CH_2 - OOC - CH_3.$$

The positively charged quaternary nitrogen of acetylcholine may be attracted to the negative charge of an ionised carboxyl group in the receptor site.

(d) Dipole-dipole and Ion-dipole Interactions :

These forces are generally associated along with electrostatic bondings.

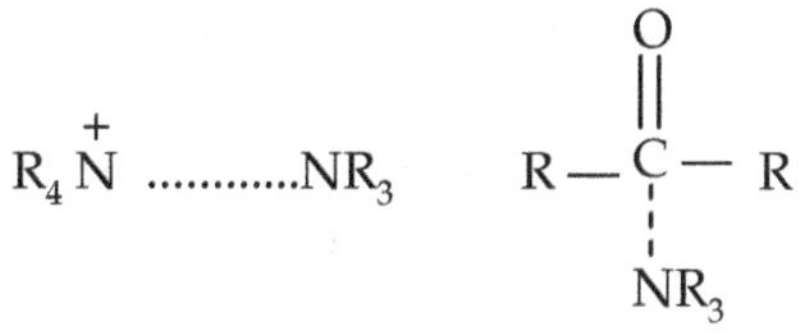

$$R_4 \overset{+}{N} .... NR_3 \qquad R - \overset{\overset{\displaystyle O}{\|}}{\underset{\underset{\displaystyle NR_3}{|}}{C}} - R$$

Ion-dipole　　　　Dipole-dipole

The C-X bonds in drugs and receptors (where X is an electronegative atom) will have an asymmetric distribution of electrons; this produces electronic dipoles. The dipoles in a drug molecule can be attracted by ions (ion-dipole interaction) or by other dipole (dipole-dipole interaction) in the receptor, provided charges of opposite sign are properly aligned. Since the charge of a dipole is less than that of an ion, a dipole-dipole interaction is weaker than an ion-dipole interaction.

(e) Charge Transfer Complexes :

When a molecule (or group) that is a good electron donor comes into contact with a molecule (or group) that is a good electron acceptor, the donor may transfer some of its charge to the acceptor. This forms a charge transfer complex, which, in effect is molecular dipole-dipole interaction. Electron donors contain π electrons, e.g. alkenes, alkynes and aromatic moieties with electron donating substituents or groups that have a pair of non-bonded electrons, such as O, N and S moieties.

Acceptor groups contain electron deficient π orbitals, e.g., alkenes, alkynes and aromatic moieties having electron withdrawing substituents or weakly acidic protons.

(f) Hydrophobic Forces :

In the presence of a non-polar molecule or region of a molecule, the surrounding water molecules orient themselves and, therefore, are in a high energy state than when only the H_2O molecules are around. When 2 non-polar groups, such as a lipophilic group on a drug and a non-polar receptor group, each surrounded by ordered H_2O molecules become disordered in an attempt to associate with each other, this increase in entropy, therefore, results in a decrease in the free energy that stabilises the drug-receptor complex. This stabilisation is known as hydrophobic interaction. It is a reversible type of bonding that liberates energy.

(g) van der Waals or London Dispersion Forces :

van der Waals bonds exist between all atoms, even those of noble gases, and are based on polarizability or the induction of asymmetry in the electron cloud of an atom by a nucleus of a neighbouring atom. Such forces operate within an effective distance of about 0.4 to 0.6 nm and exert an attractive force of less than 2 kJ/mol. Therefore, they are often overshadowed by stronger interactions.

Atoms in non-polar molecules may have a temporary non-symmetrical distribution of electron density which results in the generation of a temporary dipole. As atoms from different molecules (such as a drug and a receptor) approach each other, the temporary dipoles of one molecule induce opposite dipoles in the approaching molecule. Consequently, an intermolecular attraction, known as van der Waals forces results. Thus, every CH_2-CH_2 interaction liberates 0.7 kcal/mol of free energy. e.g. Acetylcholine-sterase combination. In this, methyl groups of acetylcholine are attached to acetylcholinesterase through van der Waals forces.

Table 2.1
Forces involved in drug-receptor interactions

	Bond type	Strength Kcal/mol	Example
1.	Covalent	40 - 140	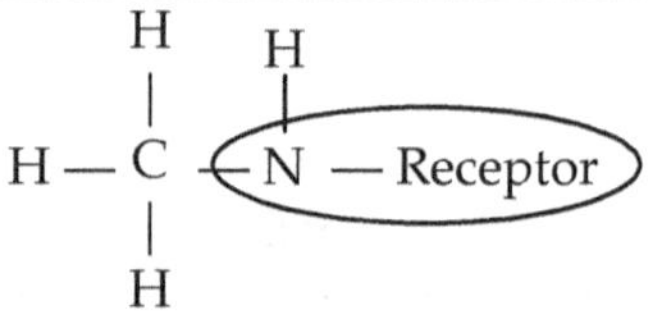
2.	Ionic (in solution)	5 - 10	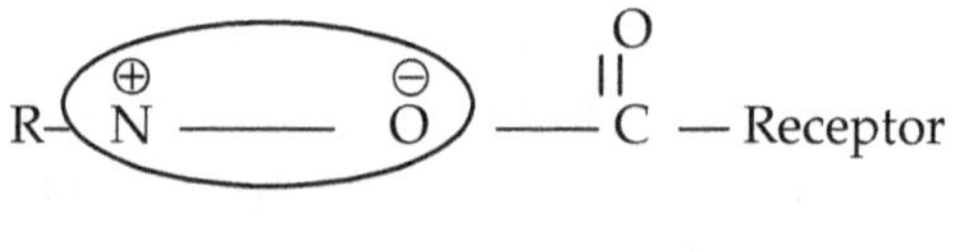
3.	Hydrogen	1 - 7	
4.	Dipole - dipole	1 - 7	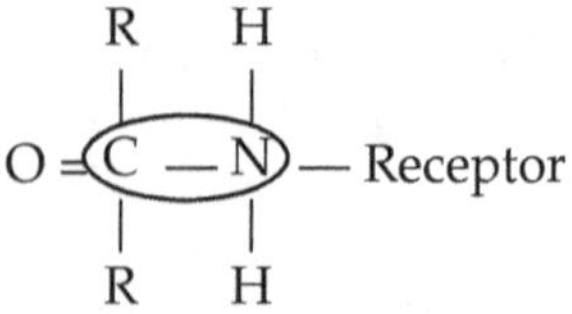
5.	Hydrophobic	1	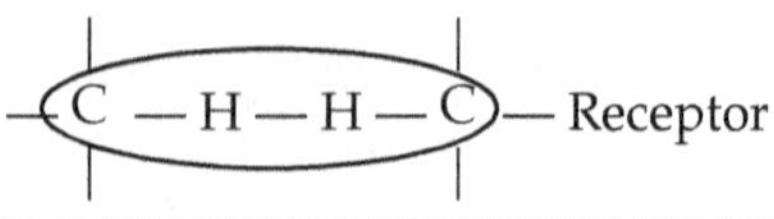

2.5 FACTORS AFFECTING THE DRUG-RECEPTOR INTERACTIONS

The basis of attempts to design compounds of similar biological activity not only involves the presence of common functional groups in compounds but also such groups should be in same specific spatial relationship to each other. This consideration has led to the study of following important factors which affect the drug-receptor interactions.

(1) Isosterism :

Groups of atoms which impart similar physical or chemical properties to a molecule due to similarities in size, electronegativity or stereochemistry are referred under the general term of isostere. For example, the molecules N_2 and CO, both possessing 14 total electrons and no charge show similar physical properties. Examples of isosteric pairs which possess similar steric and electronic configurations are : sulphonamide ($SO_2 NR^-$) and the carboxylate (COO^-) ions, ketone (C = O) and sulphone (SO_2) groups; Divalent ether (– O –), sulphide (– S –), amine (– NH –) and methylene (– CH_2 –) groups. Although dissimilar electronically, they are sufficiently alike in their steric nature to be frequently interchangeable in drugs.

Applications in Structure-Activity Relationship :

(a) Compounds may be altered by isosteric replacement of atoms or groups in order to develop analogues or to act as antagonists to normal metabolites. e.g.,

(i)

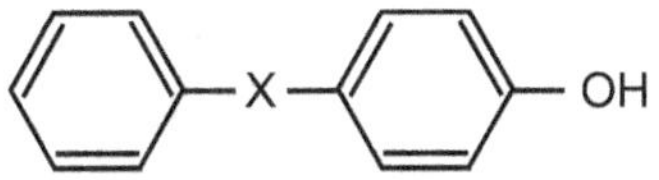

Antibacterial

X = S, Se, O, NH, CH_2,

(ii)

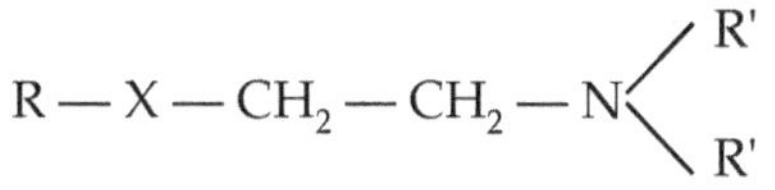

$$R - X - CH_2 - CH_2 - N {\Large\diagdown}_{R'}^{R'}$$

Antihistamines : X = O, NH, CH_2

Cholinergic blocking agents;

X = – COO –, – CONH –, – COS –

(b) When a group is present in a part of a molecule where it may be involved in an essential interaction or may influence the reactions of neighbouring groups, isosteric replacement sometimes produces analogues which act as antagonists. In the field of antineoplastic agents. e.g.,

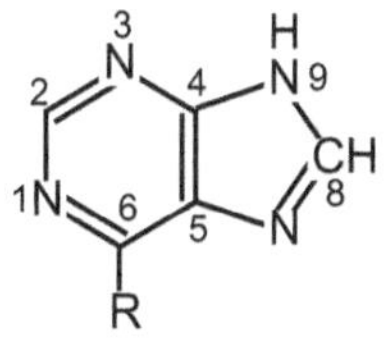

Adenine NH_2 ⎫
Hypoxanthine OH ⎬ – Metabolites
6-mercaptopurine SH – Antimetabolite

On the similar lines, the hydroxyl group of folic acid, if replaced by the amino group leads to aminopterin, an antagonist useful in the treatment of certain types of cancer.

(2) Steric Features of Drugs :

In order to evoke the pharmacological action, a drug must approach the receptor and fit closely to its surface; hence a drug must possess a high degree of structural specificity or stereoselectivity to initiate a response at a particular receptor. e.g. in diethylstilbestrol, only trans-diethylstilbestrol is estrogenic while cis-isomer is almost inactive. Just like geometric isomers, in certain rigid systems (where rotation around the bonds is difficult), conformational isomers also show significant differences in biological activity due to differences in affinity as well as intrinsic activity to the receptor.

In open chain compounds, all possible conformations are not equally manifested by the compounds (due to steric complications) at all times. Hence, by virtue of the ability of such compound to interact in a different and unique conformation with different biological receptors may result in multiple biological effects e.g. Acetylcholine may react in its extended conformational form with the muscarinic receptor and in quasi-ring form, may react with nicotinic receptor.

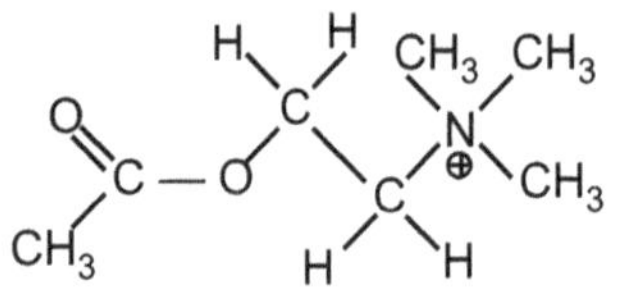

Acetylcholine in extended conformation

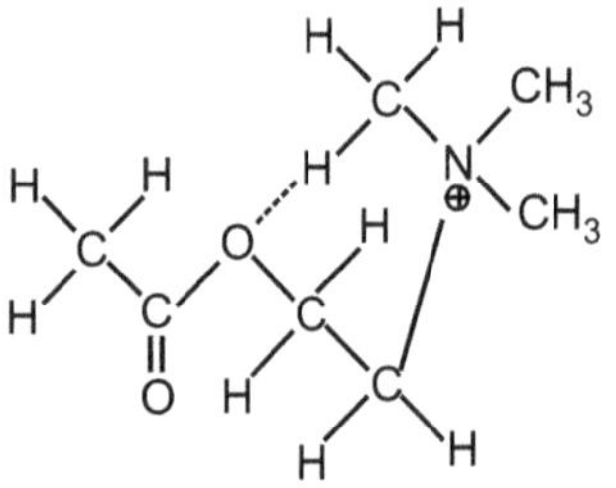

Acetylcholine in Quasi-ring conformation

Fig. 2.3

(3) Optical Isomers and Biological Activity :

Stereochemistry, enantiomers, symmetry, asymmetry and chirality are important concepts that help us to understand the therapeutic and toxic effects of drugs. The word 'chiral' is derived from the Greek word *cheir* which means 'hand'. A chiral drug consists atleast one asymmetric carbon atom and has two enantiomers. Although each enantiomer has identical chemical and physical properties, individually they may interact differently with receptors, enzymes and proteins in the body. A number of mechanisms (e.g. metabolism, protein binding, clearance) in the body can be stereoselective which may account for pharmacokinetic differences among enantiomers.

Formulation factors such as the rate of dissolution, melting point, powder flow characteristics and solubility are all different for the racemate and to be taken into account to ensure bioequivalence of the formulations.

Because the isomers have different three dimensional structures, they have different affinities for receptors and enzymes which are also three dimensional. This explains the reason for the different therapeutic and toxicological properties exhibited by different enantiomers.

Generally one enantiomer is more potent than the other in exhibiting pharmacological response. The more potent enantiomer is called as eutomer and less potent enantiomer is termed as distomer. The ratio of activities of eutomer and distomer is called as 'eudismic ratio' which is a useful parameter to assess the relative potency of the enantiomers. This ratio is normally different at different receptor sites. The logarithm of this ratio is termed as eudismic index (EI).

If two enantiomers of disopyramide are administered independently, they have the same pharmacodynamic and pharmacokinetic profile. If administered together, they have dramatically different pharmacokinetic profiles. This is the result of difference in protein binding.

Table 2.2 : Plasma-protein binding of enantiomers

Drugs	% unbound	
Acidic Drugs :		
Indactinone	R (−) 0.90	S (+) 0.30
Methobarbital	R (−) 2.29	S (+) 0.13
Moxalactam	R (+) 47.00	S (−) 32.00
Pentobarbital	R (+) 36.60	S (−) 26.50
Phenprocoumon	R (+) 1.07	S (−) 0.72
Warfarin	R (+) 1.20	S (−) 0.90

Basic Drugs :		
Amphetamine	(+) 84	(−) 84
Chloroquine	(+) 33	(−) 51
Disopyramide	(+) 27	(−) 39
Fenfluramine	(+) 2.8	(−) 2.9
Methadone	(+) 9.2	(−) 12.2
Propoxyphene	(+) 1.8	(−) 1.8
Propranolol	(+) 12	(−) 11
Tocainide	(+) 86-91	(−) 83-89
Verapamil	(+) 6.4	(−) 11

Anticancer	13.7	15.6	9.4	10.4
Cardiovascular	42.7	46.6	24.8	26.9
Central nervous system	47.7	53.9	8.6	9.0
Dermatological	17.9	18.4	1.3	1.2
Gastrointestinal	43.9	47.2	3.0	3.5
Hematology	16.5	15.4	8.6	9.1
Hormones	20.0	22.0	13.8	14.6
Ophthalmic	7.1	7.4	1.8	2.0
Respiratory	36.5	40.5	5.1	6.1
Vaccines	6.5	7.3	2.0	3.0
Others	39.0	41.9	5.5	5.6
Total	**360.0**	**390.0**	**115.0**	**123.3**

Similarly, the stereoselective clearance affects the plasma half-life of the drug. Upon administration of leucovorin calcium enantiomers, *l*-leucovorin is rapidly cleared from the body and has a plasma half-life of 32 minutes, whereas d-leucovorin is slowly cleared and has a plasma half-life of 45 minutes.

S (-) Timolol is one of the few adrenoceptor blockers marketed as the pure enantiomer used clinically to treat systemic hypertension, angina pectoris and glaucoma. When this form is used topically in eyes for treating glaucoma, severe bronchoconstriction is noticed. In contrast R (+) timolol lowers intraoccular tension without causing significant bronchospasm. R (+) form is therefore safer for treating glaucoma than S (-) form. Similarly humans preferentially metabolise (+) fenfluramine while rats favour the (-) enantiomer.

Table 2.3 (a)

Worldwide sales of single-enantiomer drugs

$ Billions	Total market ($)		Single enantiomer drugs ($)	
	1999	2000	1999	2000
Analgesic	21.5	23.0	1.0	1.3
Antibiotics/ Antifungals	29.3	31.7	23.9	23.9
Antiviral	17.7	19.1	6.2	6.5

Table 2.3 (b)

Pharmacological effects of Racemic drug mixtures

Drug	Biological response	Enantiomer
Terbutaline	Trachea relaxation	(−)
Propranolol	β−blockade	(S)
Amosulalol	α−blockade	(+)
	β− blockade	(−)
Warfarin	Anticoagulation	(S)
Verapamil	Negative chronotropic	(−)
Atenolol	α−blocker	(S)
Nitrendipine	Ca^{++} channel blocker	(S)
Zopiclone	Sedation	(R)
Terfenadine	Antihistaminic	(S)
Albuterol	Antiasthmatic	(S)
Flurbiprofen	Anti-inflammatory	(S)
Ketoprofen	Anti-inflammatory	(S)
Thalidomide	Immunosuppresive	(S)
Tetramisole	Anthelmintic	(S)-form (levamisole)
Propoxyphene	Analgesic	Dextro form
	Antitussive	Laevo form
Tranylcypro-mine	Antidepressant	(−)
	Improvement in performance	(+)
Sotalol	Antihypertensive	(−)
	Antiarrhythmic	(+)

(1) Dexchlorpheniramine is highly stereo-selective; the (S) - (+) - isomer is about 200 times more potent than the (R) - (–) - isomer.

(2) d-Ketamine is a hypnotic and analgesic agent; the *l*-isomer is responsible for the undesired side-effects. In the case of local anaesthetic prilocaine, although both isomers are active, only one isomer contributes to the toxicity.

(3) Both isomers of bupivacaine are local anaesthetics, but only the *l*-isomer shows vaso-constrictive activity. Indacrinone has a uric acid retention side-effect. The d-isomer is responsible for both the diuretic activity and the side-effect while the *l*-isomer acts as a uricosuric agent.

(4) It also, is possible for the enantiomers to have opposite effects. The *l*-isomers of some barbiturates exhibit depressant activity and the d-isomers have convulsant activity. Similarly the d-isomer of the narcotic analgesic picenadol, is an opiate agonist, the *l*-isomer is a narcotic antagonist and the racemate is a partial agonist.

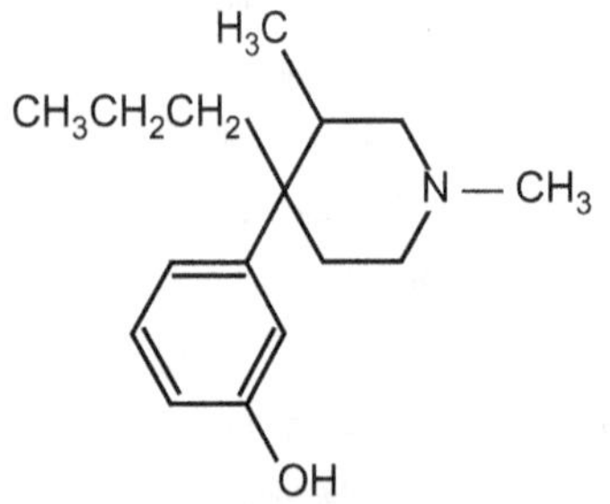

Picenadol

(5) (+) - Butaclamol is a potent antipsychotic, but the (–) isomer is essentially inactive. The eudismic ratio (+/–) is 1250 for D_2-dopaminergic receptor. (–) Baclofen is a muscle relaxant that binds GABA B receptors. The eudismic ratio (–/+) is 800.

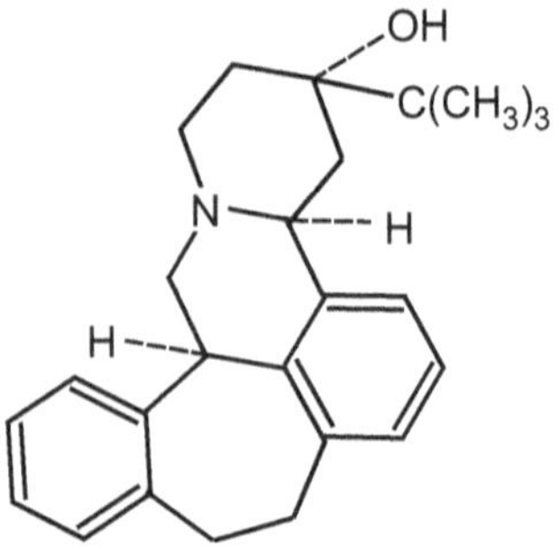

Butaclamol

(6) The eudismic ratio (l/d) for propranolol is about 100. However, propranolol also exhibits local anaesthetic activity for which the eudismic ratio is 1.0. Labetalol, as a result of two asymmetric carbon atoms, exists in four stereoisomeric forms, having the stereochemistries (RR), (SS), (RS) and (SR). This drug has α- and β-adrenergic blocking properties. The (RR) - isomer is predominantly the β-blocker and the (SR) - isomer is mostly the α-blocker. While other 50 % of the isomers, the (SS) - and (RS)-isomers, are almost inactive.

(7) If you consider two enantiomers, such as R-(–) and (S) (+) epinephrine, interacting with a receptor that has only two binding sites (Fig. 2.4), it becomes apparent that the receptor cannot distinguish between them. However, if there are at least three binding sites, the receptor easily can differentiate them. The R - (–) - isomer has three points of interaction and is held in the conformation shown to maximise molecular comple-mentarity. The (S) - (+) - isomer can have only two sites of interaction (the hydroxyl group cannot interact with the hydroxyl binding site, and may even have an adverse steric interaction); consequently it has a lower binding energy.

The chiral interactions help us to discover which parts of the molecule are involved in primary receptor interaction. Chirality may also be used to distinguish different states of activation of ion channel receptors.

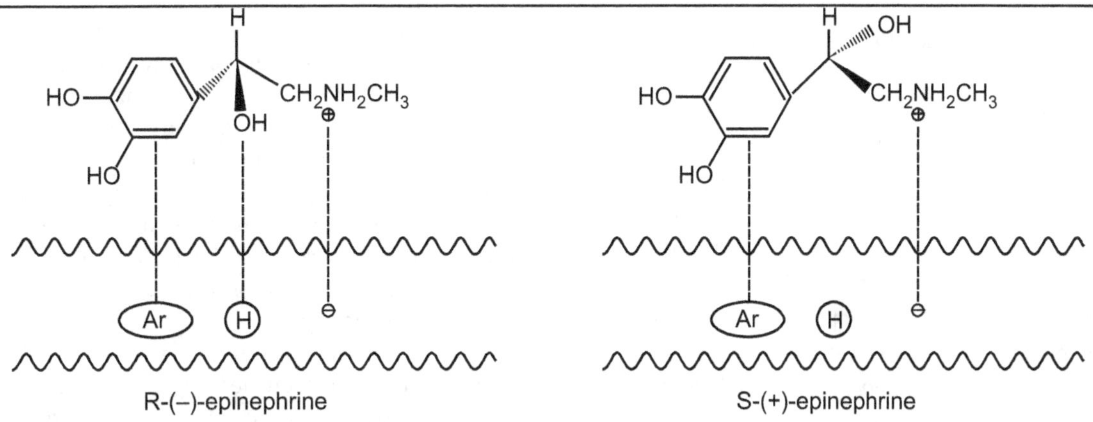

R-(−)-epinephrine   S-(+)-epinephrine

Fig. 2.4 : Effect of stereochemical features on the biological activity

Generally in a recemic mixture, one enantiomer is bioactive while other remains either inactive or possesses different activities. Hence in case of drug containing one asymmetric carbon, administration of a racemic form permits the delivery of 50 % active compound. At present only about 12 % of synthetic chiral drugs are available in pure chiral form in the market while remaining 88 % are sold as racemates.

An effort to make the drug commercially available in pure chiral form, add to the cost of the synthesis. Various options like, to reduce the number of asymmetric centers, replacing asymmetric carbon with nitrogen, adding symmetry to the molecule, are hence used to save this added cost.

When a drug exists in stereoisomeric forms, the rate and routes of metabolism may differ between the enantiomers. The rate of metabolism of two enantiomers would be expected to differ where they form diastereomeric complexes with the metabolizing enzyme. Extra complications may arise because of ability of metabolic processes to interconvert chiral centers.

(4) Conformational Factors :

Various conformations are possible for a flexible drug structure. Besides drug, the receptor sites also exhibit flexible nature and can acquire conformation in adaptation to the mutual effect of drug. However, suitable steric features need to be present in a drug molecule if it is to have significant affinity and intrinsic activity at receptor site. The X-ray crystallographic spectrophotometry is routinely used to determine conformation of a drug molecule while NMR spectra provides information for geometric isomers when the compound is in liquid state.

Optical isomers, particularly diastereoisomers (i.e. compounds with two or more asymmetric centres), exhibit similar chemical reactions but different physical properties. Since the physical properties are important in drug distribution, metabolism and interaction with the receptor, the biological properties of such isomers may also be different.

We may expect from the definition of optical enantiomers (that compounds having identical physical and chemical properties except for their ability to rotate the plane of polarised light) that they may have the same biological activity. However, this is not the case with many of the enantiomers.

Table 2.4 : Stereoisomeric drugs

Cardiovascular Agents :

Acebutolol	Alprenolol	Atenolol
Betaxolol	Bisoprolol	Bopindolol
Bucumolol	Butefolol	Bufuralol
Bunitrolol	Bupranolol	Butofilolol
Carazolol	Carvedilol	Curteolol
Disopyramide	Dobutamine	Indenolol
Mepindolol	Metipranolol	Metroprolol
Nadolol	Oxpranolol	Pindolol
Propranolol	Quinidine	Sotalol
Toliprotol	Verapamil	Xibenolol

Central Nervous System :

Butaclomol	Butorphanol	Buprenorphine
Codeine	Dihydroergotoxine	Dobutamine
Fluoxetine	Ketamine	Lorazepam
Meclizine	Nalbuphine	Nalfename
Naloxone	Naltrexone	Oxaprotiline
Oxymorphone	Phenylpropanol amine	Physostigmine
Chloramphetam ine	Thioridazine	Toloxaton
Tomoxetin	Vasopressin	Viloxazin

Anti-inflammatory and Analgesics :

Beclomethasone	Betamethasone	Cicloprofen
Corticosteroid	Dihydroxy-thebane	Fenbuphen
Fenoprofen	Flurbiprofen	Ibuprofen
Ketoprofen	Indoprofen	Minoxiprofen
Norlevorphanol	Oxycodone	Pirpofen
Stanozolon	Steroids	Suprofen
Triamcinolon		

Anticancer :

Bleomycin	Cytarabine	Doxorubicin
Methotrexate	Mitomycin C	

Antibiotics, Anti-infectives, Antiviral :

Ciprofloxacin	Norfloxacin	Ofloxacin

Genitourinary Hormones :

Benzyl glutamate	Bromocriptine	Butoconazole
Calcitonin	Estradiol	Flurogesterone
Gonadorelin	Ketodesogestrel	
Norgestrel	Prednisolone	
Progesterone	Testosterone	

2.6 SPARE RECEPTORS

In most of the cases, the biological response is a function of total number of receptors that are occupied or activated by drug molecules. But in certain cases, it has been observed that a relatively small fraction of the available receptors, if occupied, may result into the maximal biological response of which, the tissue is capable. Furchgott (1954) showed that only 1% of the ideal receptors have to be occupied in order to get the maximum response. Here the remaining 99% receptors, even if occupied or unoccupied, do not make any difference. Such receptors are known as spare *receptors or reserved receptors.* These receptors are not qualitatively different from non-spare receptors. Myocardium is said to contain a large number of spare receptors. They are not inactive receptors. An agonist can easily turn on the spare receptor to get a response but the maximum effect is attained as soon as the desired number of receptors have been activated.

2.7 SILENT RECEPTORS

The binding sites of any origin, that can retain the drug molecules, without initiating the biological response, are known as *silent receptors* e.g. the adsorption sites on plasma-proteins can be categorised as silent receptors. The binding of drug on plasma-protein does not evoke the response. It delays the release of free drug into the plasma, hence the drug-effect and drug-metabolism. Thus, silent receptor prolongs duration of action of drug.

2.8 MECHANISM OF Ca^{++} - DEPENDENT HORMONE ACTION

The action of a wide variety of hormones and drugs is operated through the Ca^{++} signals, generated by cytosolic Ca^{++} ion concentration. The signal generation leads to the rapid breakdown of membrane inositol phospholipids into inositol triphosphates and diacylglycerol. Inositol triphosphate mobilises Ca^{++} ions from bound Ca^{++} intracellular stores, thus acting as a messenger for the intracellular mobilisation of Ca^{++}. Besides this, Ca^{++} influx is also stimulated to increase cytosolic Ca^{++} ion concentration. The binding of cytosolic Ca^{++} with intracellular Ca^{++} dependent regulatory protein, calmodulin causes initiation of phosphorylation of target enzymes. Another breakdown product, diacylglycerol causes activation of protein kinase C. The latter, independently, initiates phosphorylation of different chain of target enzymes. Thus, the drug-receptor interaction may lead to an increase or decrease in the intra-cellular concentration of either c-AMP or calcium ions, resulting into an activation or termination of dependent biochemical reaction. The biological response thus obtained, is said to be propogated through second messenger system.

Thus, the hydrolysis of a minor membrane phospholipid, phosphatidylinositol 4, 5-biphosphate, by a specific phospholipase C is one of the earliest key events by which more than 100 extracellular signaling molecules are known to regulate functions of their target cells. The hydrolysis produces two intracellular messengers, inositol triphosphate and diacylglycerol. The former induces the release of calcium from internal stores and activates protein kinase C.

Phosphorylation governs activation or deactivation of enzymes. Phenolic group of tyrosine and alcoholic hydroxyl groups of serine and threonine act as the principal sites for phosphorylation. The newly introduced phosphate group avails two negatively charged oxygens through ionization at physiological pH. Phosphorylation thus converts H-bonding tendency of previous hydroxyl groups into strong ionic bonding tendency of phosphate group. The latter forms strong ionic bonds with positively charged residues in the protein, changing the enzyme tertiary structure. This in turns, results in the exposure or closure of the enzyme active site.

Another breakdown product, diacylglycerol causes activation of protein kinase C, which then moves from the cytoplasm to the cell membrane. There it catalyses phosphorylation of various enzymes within the cell leading to variety of responses.

Diacylglycerol is phosphorylated to form phosphatidic acid while inositol-1,4,5-triphosphate is dephosphorylated and then recouple with phosphatidic acid to form phosphoinositol-4,5-biphosphate once again.

The calcium ions activate calcium-dependent protein kinases which in turn phosphorylate and activate cell specific enzymes. Once the inositol triphosphate and diacylglycerol have completed their tasks, they are recombined to form phsophatidylinositol diphosphate.

2.9 NON-RECEPTOR-MEDIATED ACTIONS OF DRUGS

Several drugs do not act by virtue of combination with receptors. They may interact specifically with small molecules or ions that are normally or abnormally present in the body. e.g. –

(a) The chelators or chelating agents form strong bonds with specific metallic cations and form chelate. The therapeutic neutralisation of gastric acid by an antacid (base) is also a good example.

(b) In 'counterfeit incorporation mechanism' techniques, certain drugs which are structural analogues of normal biological constituents may get incorporated into cellular components and biochemical chain reactions of the organism and thereby alter their function. The clinical utility of this technique has already been tried in cancer chemotherapy.

(c) The biological activity of volatile general anaesthetic agents could not be correlated with diversity of their structure which suggests a relatively non-specific biochemical mechanism of action. Since their individual potencies correlate well with their 'oil : water' partition coefficient, their physical properties rather than the concept of drug-receptor interaction enjoy the importance.

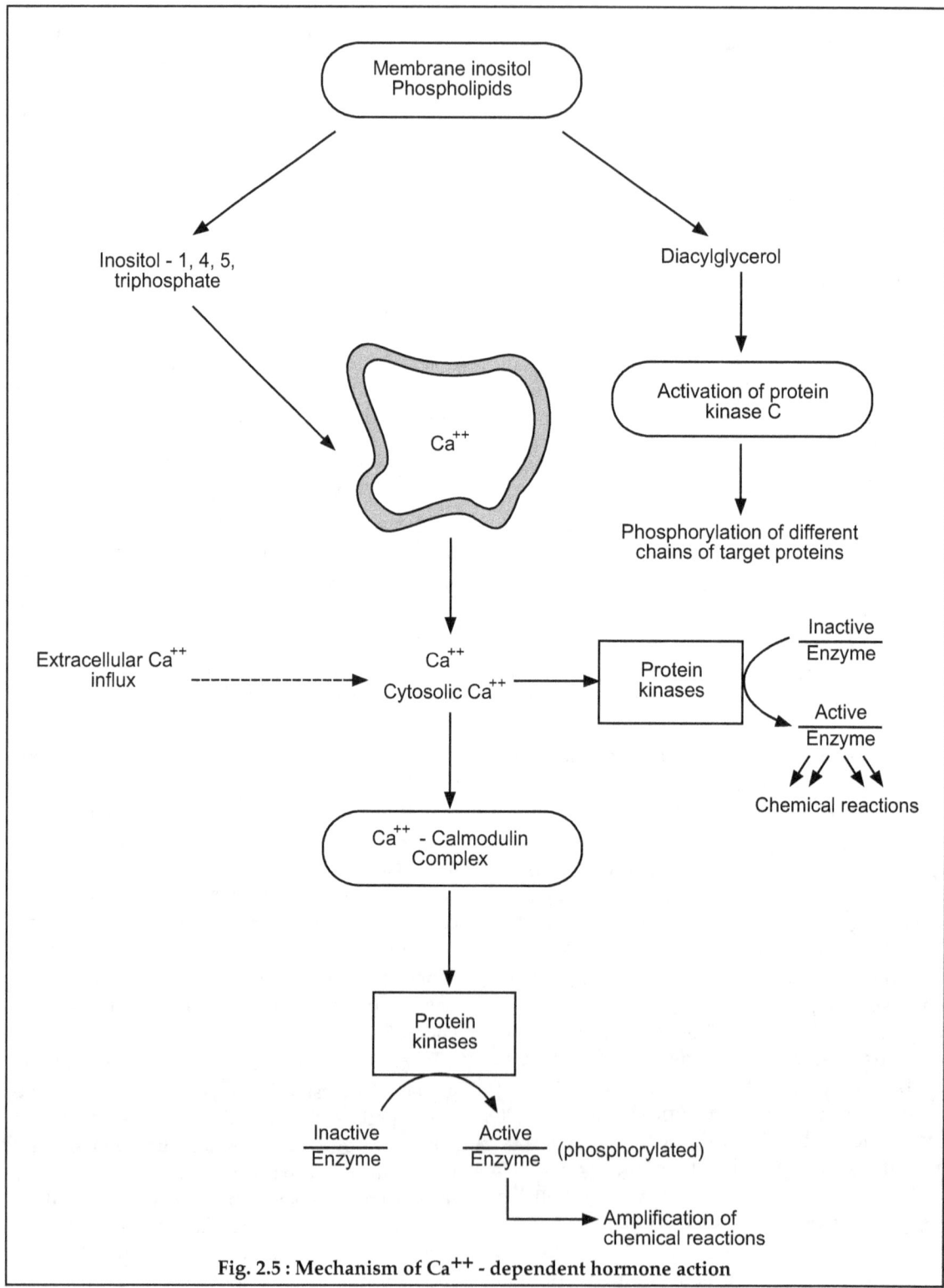

Fig. 2.5 : Mechanism of Ca^{++} - dependent hormone action

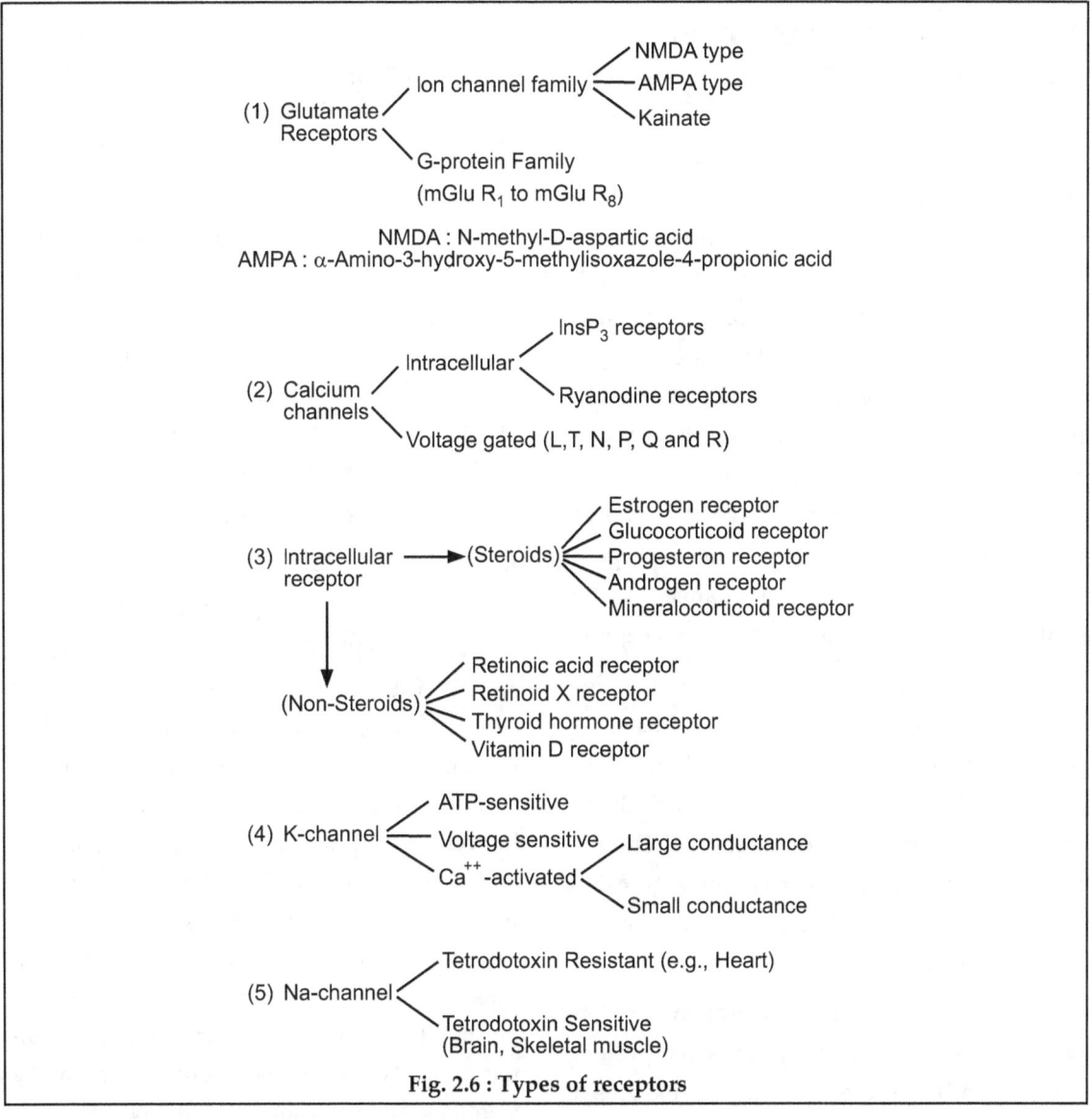

Fig. 2.6 : Types of receptors

The membrane bound ion channels regulate the passage of ions of various types. Ion channels controlled by - (a) chemical messengers are called ligand-gated ion channels. (b) trans-membrane potential of the cell, are called voltage-gated ion channels. In ligand-gated ion channel, receptor glycoprotein changes its shape upon binding with ligand. This leads to opening of ion-channel, a process better known as gating. The receptor glycoproteins are classified by the number of transmembrane domains (2 TM, 3 TM, 4 TM) present in them.

The passage of ions across the cell membrane is dictated by the electrical and chemical gradients that have been established by metabolically driven ion pumps e.g. Na^+/K^+ - ATPase. The influx or efflux of such ions (Ca^{++}, Na^+, K^+, Cl^-) modulates the transmembrane potential which provides the basis of most nervous and neuronal transmission processes. These channels may be modulated by neurotransmitters, nucleotides and inorganic ions.

2.10 SIGNAL TRANSDUCTION MECHANISMS

Signal transduction : It means triggering a biochemical chain of events. It refers to the movement of signals from outside the cell to inside. When extracellular element activates a receptor, it leads to a response through triggering a biochemical chain of events inside the cell. Extracellular receptors are integral transmembrane proteins and make up most of the receptors. They span across the plasma membrane of the cell with one part of the receptor outside and other projects inside of the cell. The ligand binds to the outside region of the receptor inducing a change in the conformation of the inside part of the receptor.

This leads to either activation of enzymes (tyrosine kinase, phosphatases) or release of second messangers (cAMP, cGMP, IP3). Example of extracellular receptors include: G protein coupled (including adrenergic receptors and chemokine receptors), tyrosine and histidine kinase, intergrin, Ligand gated ion channel, etc.

Signal transduction in G protein coupled receptor begins with an inactive G protein coupled with the receptors. Ligand induces a change in receptor conformation to activate the G protein. The activated G protenin binds a molecule of GTP to dissociate from other G protein submits.

All these activated G protein submits detach from the receptor and initiate signalling from many effector proteins such as phosphatases and ion channels. This results in the release of second messanger molecules (like nitric oxide, c-AMP, c-GMP, etc.).

The intracellular receptors (nuclear receptors, cytoplasmic) are soluble proteins localized within their respective areas). Their typical ligands include steroid hormones, derivatives of vitamins A and D.

More complex signal transduction involves coupling of ligand-receptor interactions to many intracellular events. These events include phosphorylations by tyrosine kinases and/or serine/threonine kinase. Protein phasphorylation changes enzymes activity and protein conformations.

Major Signaling Pathway :

(i) MAPK/ERK pathway :

It is also known as the Ras-Raf-MEK-ERK pathway. MAPK (mitogen-activated protein kinases) or ERK (extracellular signal-regulated kinases). This pathway is a chain of proteins in the cell that communicates a signal from the surface receptor to the DNA in the nucleus of the cell by adding phosphate groups to a neighbouring protein. Mutation in one of the proteins in the pathway leads to cancer. One effect of MAPK activation is to alter the translation of mRNA to proteins. It regulates the activities of several transcription factors. In many cell types, activation of this pathway promotes cell division and many forms of cancer are associated with disfunctioning of this pathway.

(ii) c-AMP dependent pathway :

Many enzymes are regulated by covalent attachment of phosphate in ester linkage to the side chain hydroxyl group of a particular amino acid residue, especially serine, threonine or tyrosine. A protein kinase transfers the terminal phosphate of ATP to amino acid hydroxyl group while a protein phosphatase catalyses removal of phosphate group from amino acid hydroxyl group by hydrolysis.

Protein kinas and phosphatases are themselves regulated by complex signal cascades. Protein kinases are activated by Ca^{++}-calmodulin, c-AMP).

(iii) IP$_3$/DAG pathway :

Diacylglycerol (DAG) and inositol 1,4,5-triphosphate are generated by cleavage of phospholipid phosphatidylinositol-4,5-biphosphate. DAG remains bound to the membrane and IP3 diffuses through the cytosol to bind IP3 receptors in calcium channels. This leads to increased influx of Ca^{++} ions. This increased cytosolic concentration of Ca++ leads to a cascade of intracellular changes and responses. DAG and Ca^{++} ions work together to activate various protein kinases to phosphorylate other enzymes, leading to altered cellular activities.

3

ADRENERGIC AGENTS

3.1 INTRODUCTION

The sympathetic nervous system controls various important systems including cardio-vascular, bronchial airway tone, muscular, metabolic etc. It prepares the organism against the conditions of stress, either of physical or physiological origin. In addition to epinephrine, a large number of agents can mimic the responses obtained as a result of stimulation of adrenergic nerves. They bear structural resemblance with the neurotransmitter, epinephrine. Hence, they can be used to mimic or alter the functioning of sympathetic nervous system in several clinical disorders like hypertension, asthma, arrhythmia and various allergic conditions. Majority of these substances contain an intact or a partially substituted amino group and hence, also called as sympathomimetic amines.

These drugs are divided into two broad categories according to their structures.

(a) Compounds with 3, 4-dihydroxy - phenyl nucleus or a catechol nucleus : They are termed as catecholamines.

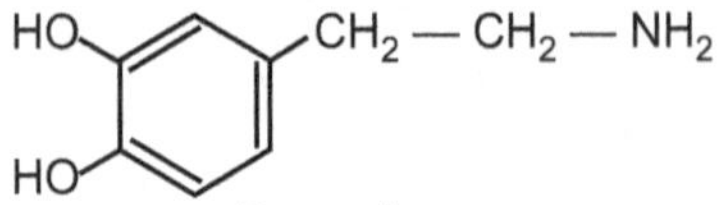

Dopamine

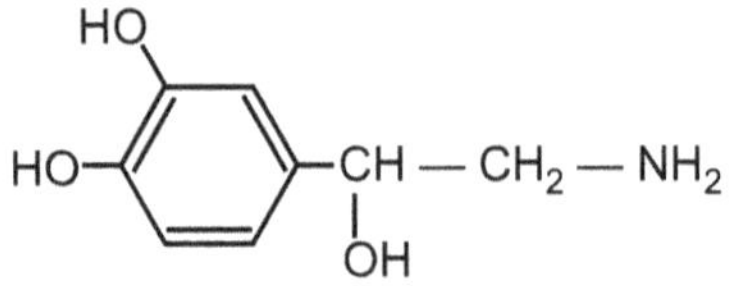

Norepinephrine (Noradrenaline)

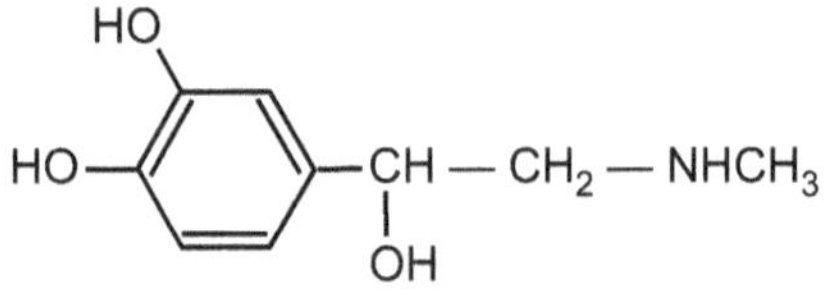

Epinephrine (Adrenaline)

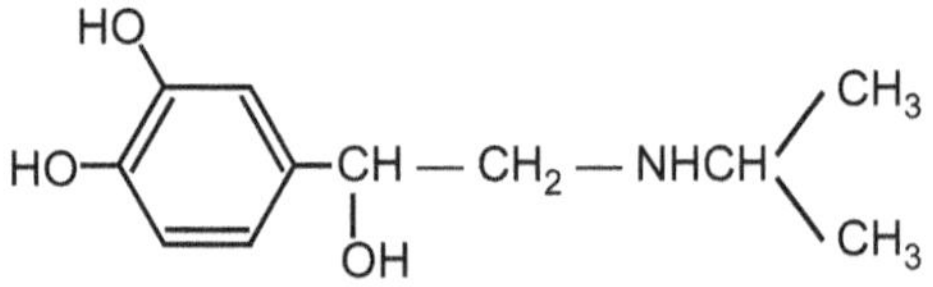

Isoprenaline (Isoproterenol)

(b) Compounds those lack hydroxy groups on phenyl ring : They are termed as non-catecholamines.

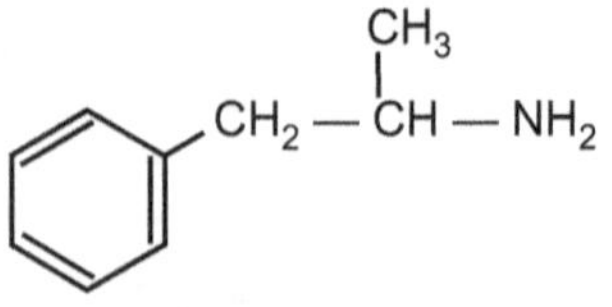

Amphetamine

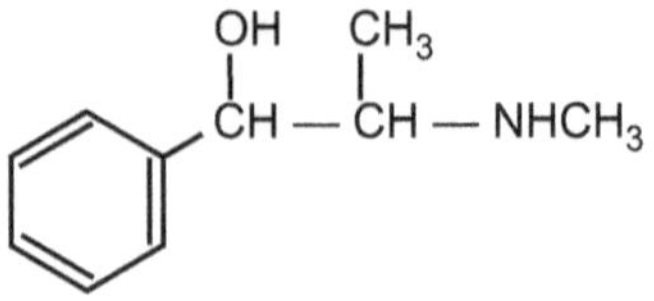

Ephedrine

(3.1)

(a) Catecholamines :

With few exceptions, drugs which act on the adrenergic nervous system, all possess some chemical elements of the endogenous agonist, epinephrine. Epinephrine, norepinephrine and dopamine are the naturally occurring catecholamines. They control most of the familiar responses of the "flight or fight" system.

Norepinephrine is a neurotransmitter present in the sympathetic nerves and in brain. It also serves as a precursor for the synthesis of adrenaline in the adrenal gland. Adrenaline is the hormone of adrenal medulla. A pressor effect exerted by adrenal extracts was observed in 1895. It was first separated from the adrenal medulla by Abel and Crawform (1897) in the form of its polybenzoyl derivative. The active principle was called epinephrine by Abel. One of the laboratories (Japanese chemist, Takamine) engaged in isolation and purification of this pressor constituent, named it as adrenaline. It was first synthesised by Stoltz in 1904.

Catecholamines are prone to easy oxidation to produce ortho quinone like compounds. The development of a pink to brown colour is indicative of oxidative breakdown. Hence, antioxidants such as ascorbic acid or sodium bisulfite may be used to stabilize the solution of catecholamines.

A large number of synthetic amines, structurally related to epinephrine were prepared and evaluated for the activity by Barger and Dale in 1910. They described the activity of these compounds as sympathomimetic. The racemic mixture thus formed, was resolved by Tullar in 1948. Upon resolution, dextro-epinephrine was found to be about one twelfth potent as laevo-epinephrine. Its role as a neurotransmitter in the sympathetic nervous system, was proposed by Elliott in 1904.

Dopamine, a third naturally occurring catecholamine, acts as a neurotransmitter in the basal ganglia of CNS. Dopamine-β-hydroxylase enzyme converts dopamine into norepinephrine. This enzyme is not present in the dopaminergic neuron. Hence, dopamine remains in its original form to carry out the function of neurotransmitter. For example, dopamine acts through dopaminergic neuronal mechanisms to dilate mesenteric and renal vascular beds.

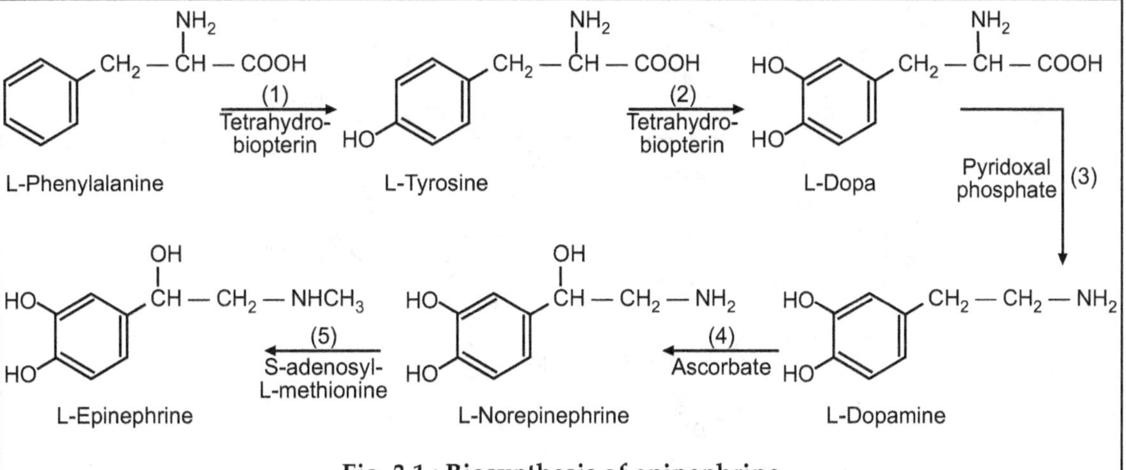

Fig. 3.1 : Biosynthesis of epinephrine

3.2 BIOSYNTHESIS OF NEUROTRANSMITTER

The Fig. 3.1 represents the biosynthetic pathway for norepinephrine and epinephrine in the nerve terminals.

The enzymes which catalyse the intermediate steps of biosynthesis of sympathetic neurotransmitter are denoted by the number present on the arrow. They are listed as below :

Enzymes Participating :

1. Phenylalanine hydroxylase
2. Tyrosine hydroxylase
3. DOPA decarboxylase
4. Dopamine–β–oxidase
5. Phenylethanolamine-N-methyl-transferase.

These enzymes are synthesised within the cell bodies of the adrenergic neurons and are then transported along the axons to their nerve terminals. The activity of tyrosine hydroxylase is low and conversion of tyrosine to DOPA is a rate - limiting step in neurotransmitter synthesis. The remaining enzymes are of generally low specificity. Steps 1 to 3, takes place in cytoplasm. Dopamine, the end product of step 3, then enters into the synaptic vesicles where it is converted into norepinephrine. Norepinephrine thus synthe-sized is then stored inside the nerve endings within the synaptic vesicles.

3.3 SYNAPTIC INTERACTIONS

(1) When the impulse reaches to the nerve terminals, the membrane becomes more permeable for the influx of Ca^{++} ions. This causes the release of neurotransmitter from the synaptic vesicles through exocytosis. The transmitter migrates across the synapse and binds to its receptor sites upon the target organ.

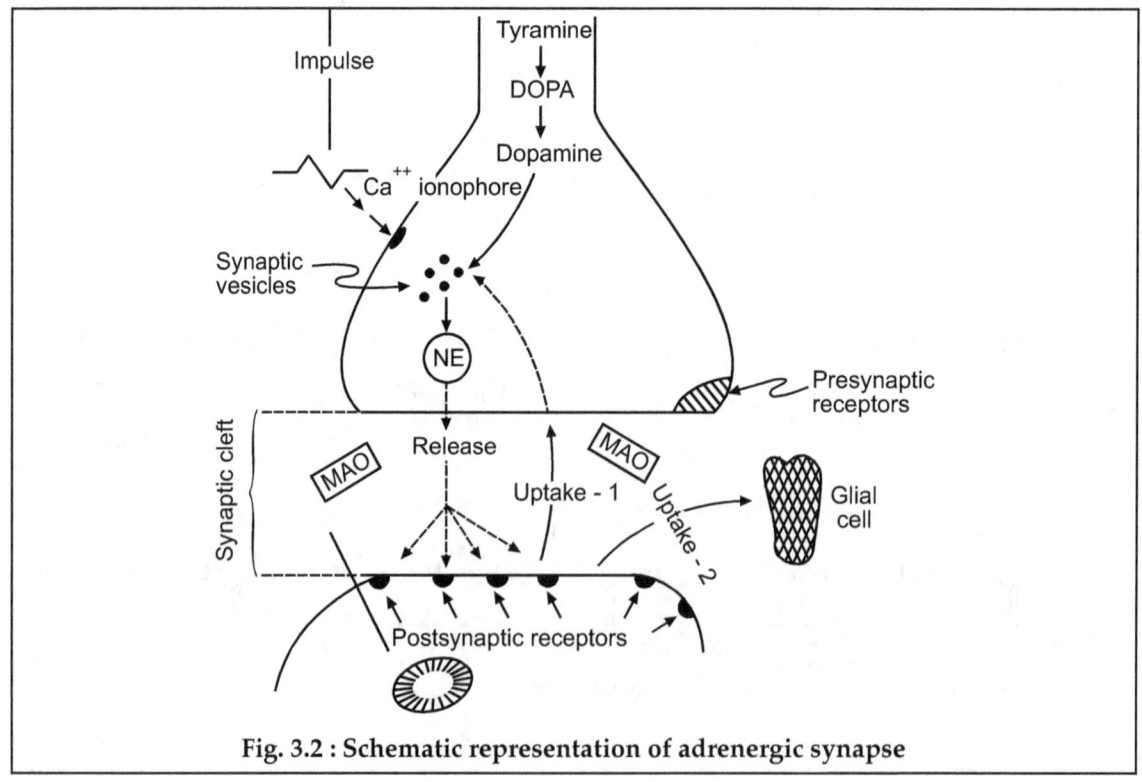

Fig. 3.2 : Schematic representation of adrenergic synapse

The neuro-transmitters being highly flexible molecules, can switch on different receptors to give different biological responses. Hence, body takes care to release them close to their target receptors, then quickly inactivating them to avoid their journey to other receptors.

(2) After its interaction with receptor, norepinephrine may be removed by the following routes :

(a) Norepinephrine is rapidly and efficiently 'reabsorbed' into the neuron i.e. nerve terminals and then into its storage sites. The maximum quantity of norepinephrine is removed in this way. This type of uptake (uptake-1) has strict ionic requirements, being completely dependent on the presence of Na^+ ions (and low concentration of K^+ ions) in the external surrounding medium. Similarly this uptake exhibits high stereochemical selectivity and operates against concentration gradient. Certain drugs like cocaine and imipramine selectively block this neuronal uptake and avail high concentration of norepinephrine in the synaptic cleft.

(b) Extraneuronal Uptake :

In addition to neuronal uptake, there exists a second uptake process of norepinephrine from synaptic cleft to supporting tissues (glial cells). This process is not stereo-selective and is not inhibited by usual inhibitors of neuronal uptake. This extraneuronal uptake is reported to be inhibited by metanephrine and corticosteroids. This extraneuronal uptake can be regarded as transport and metabolism while neuronal uptake is transport and retention of neurotransmitter.

(c) Part of the neurotransmitter may also be lost due to its diffusion across the synaptic cleft :

In the adrenergic synapses, diffusion mechanism is a route of minor importance in removing norepinephrine. The blood vessels, probably stand as an exception where the immediate disposition of released norepinephrine is accompanied largely by a combination of extra-neuronal uptake, diffusion and enzymatic breakdown of neuro-transmitter.

The other routes of removing norepinephrine are metabolic in nature.

For example, norepinephrine through its interaction with cytoplasmic monoamino oxidase (MAO) enzymes, is converted to the corresponding aldehyde which then non-enzymatically get further oxidised. Similarly, catechol-O-methyl transferase (COMT) enzyme methylates the m-hydroxy group of the phenyl ring of the catecholamines, rendering them less active.

3.4 PHARMACOLOGICAL ACTIONS OF CATECHOLAMINES

(1) They exert excitatory effects on smooth muscles present in blood vessels and on salivary as well as sweat glands.

(2) They initiate inhibitory responses on smooth muscles of GIT, bronchial tract and of blood vessels provided to skeletal muscles. Thus, the blood vessels get dilated to supply the skeletal muscles with more blood.

(3) Depending upon the drug employed, the secretion of various endocrine glands either increases or decreases.

(4) They exert excitatory effects on cardiac cells resulting into an increase in force of contraction (i.e. positive ionotropic effect) and an increase in the rate of contraction (i.e. positive chronotropic effect).

(5) The increased level of catecholamines in the CNS leads to respiratory stimulation, alertness, an increase in psychomotor activity and a reduction in appetite.

(6) Catecholamines promote glyco-genolysis both in liver and skeletal muscles and cause a reduction in the production of free fatty acids from adipose tissue.

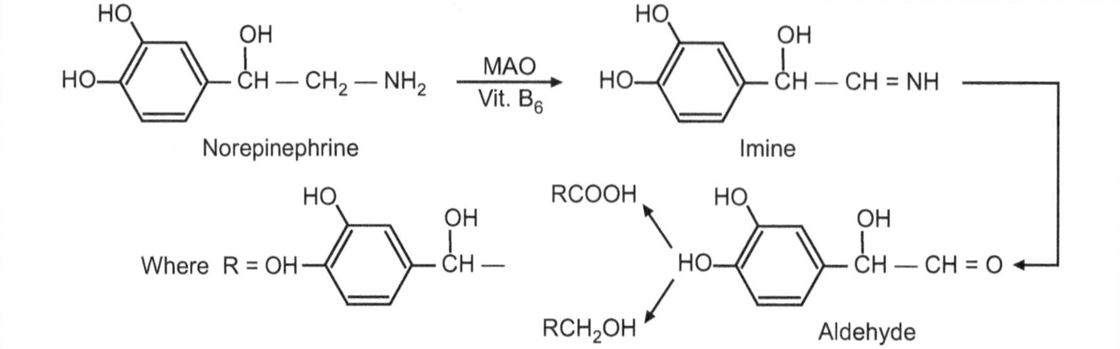

Fig 3.3 : Metabolic inactivation of norepinephrine by monoamine oxidase enzyme

(7) Epinephrine reduces intraocular pressure. Epinephrine bitartrate, dipivefrin and epinephryl borate (complex between boric acid and epinephrine) are preferred preparations used in the treatment of open-angle glaucoma. In the lacrimal fluid, epinephryl borate readily dissociates to release free drug.

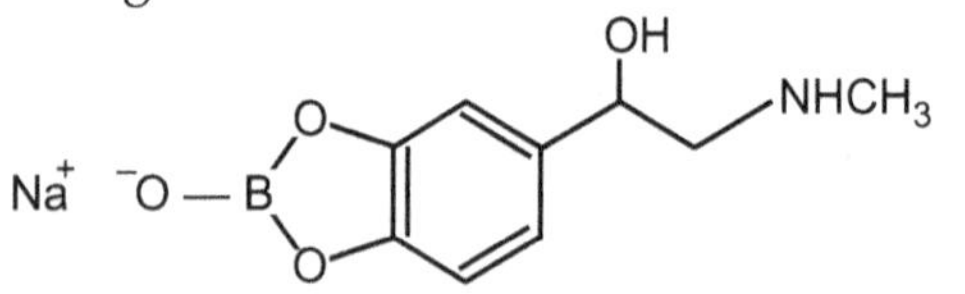

Epinephryl borate

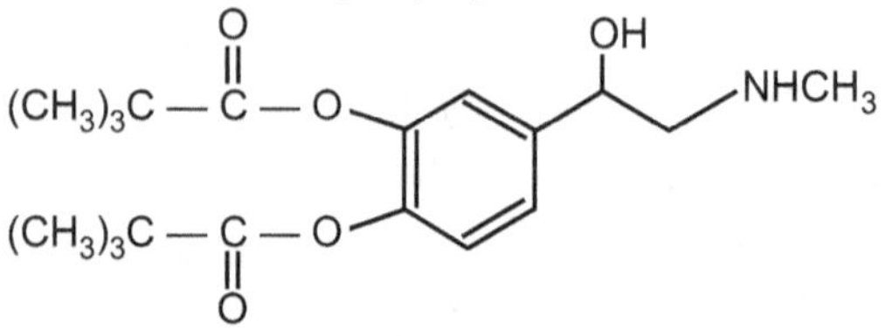

Dipivefrin (Pivalic acid ester)

3.5 METABOLISM

Monoamino oxidase (MAO) and catechol - o-methyl transferase are the main enzymes which metabolise the sympathomimetic drugs. About 60% of the administered dose of epinephrine or norepinephrine in man remains untouched by these main enzymes which then is excreted in its original form or in its conjugated form with sulphuric or glucuronic acid. Conjugation usually occurs at phenolic hydroxyl groups.

The major fraction of natural catecholamines is attacked by MAO and / or

COMT. At periphery, they are preferentially oxidised to the acid and in the CNS, they are reduced to glycol.

Thus, the principal metabolites of norepinephrine (MPOGAL, MOMA and MOPEG) are excreted through urine alongwith a free or conjugated form of unaltered norepinephrine. Of these, 3-methoxy-4-hydroxymandelic acid is the principal metabolite and the estimation of its content in urine can be taken as an index of catecholamine metabolism. On an average, about 70% of metabolised dose of epinephrine or norepinephrine follow metabolism by COMT enzymes while only 20% favour the attack by MAO enzymes.

By using drugs which inhibit these metabolising enzymes, the duration and intensity, of effects can be raised. For example, some agents can specifically block the MAO enzymes and are in clinical use under the name of MAO inhibitors, while only few agents can block the activity of COMT enzymes on circulating catecholamines and did not find clinical applicability. These include pyrogallol and tropolone derivatives.

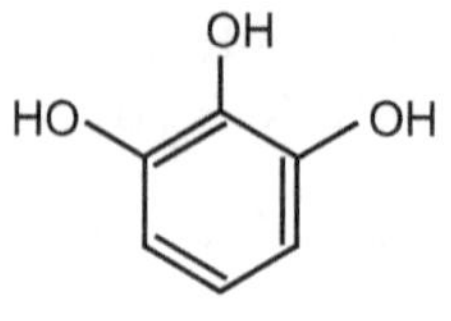

Pyrogallol

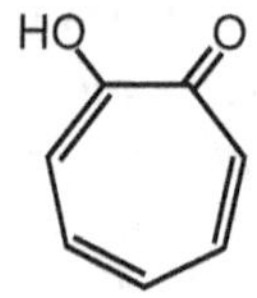

Tropolone

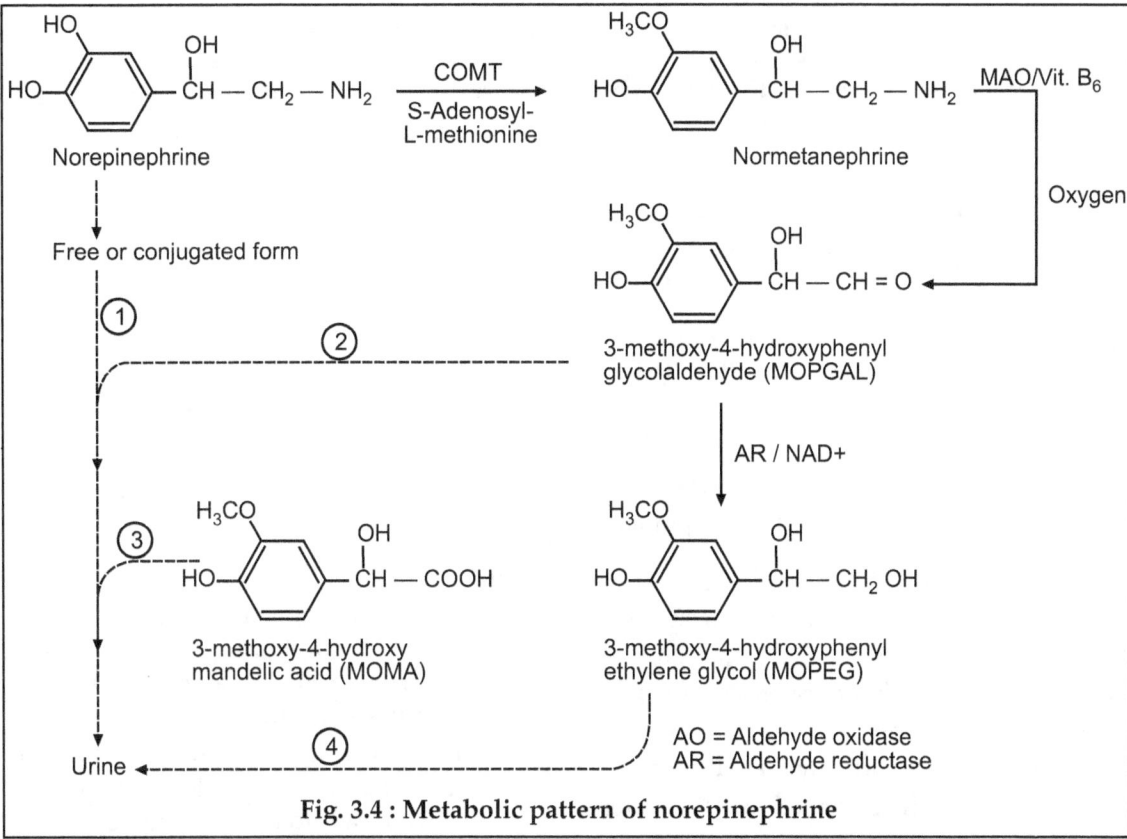

Fig. 3.4 : Metabolic pattern of norepinephrine

3.6 ADRENOCEPTORS

Upon discharge from nerve terminals, norepinephrine reacts with post-synaptic receptor sites to evoke its pharmacological response. In 1948, Ahlquist observed that, the tissues he examined, carried two kinds of adrenergic responses, i.e. alpha and beta responses, as shown in the table 3.1.

Table 3.1 : Results of Ahlquist experiment

Group 1 responses (α-responses)	Group 2 responses (β-responses)
Vasoconstriction	Vasodilation
Contraction of Uterus	Relaxation of Uterus
Contraction of Ureters	Increased rate and force of heart beats
Constriction of Pupil Relaxation of Intestine	

From the table 3.1, it can be easily seen that (with the last response as an exception) α-responses are mainly excitatory in nature while β-responses are inhibitory in nature. In general, inhibitory β-receptors can be activated at quite low concentration of catecholamines than that is needed to activate excitatory α-receptors.

Lands and co-workers in 1967, based on the differences in the cardiac and bronchial responses of the sympathomimetic agents, proposed a further subdivision of the β-receptors into :

(i) β_1-receptors whose activation accounts for cardiac stimulation, lipolysis and intestinal relaxation effects of sympathomimetic drugs, and

(ii) β_2-receptors whose activation accounts for relaxation in vascular bed, bronchial tree, uterus and ureter alongwith metabolic effects of sympathomimetic agents.

Table 3.2 : Distribution of receptor sub-types

β−receptor predominance	α−receptor predominance	α and β
Cardiac cells (β_1)	Blood vessels to	Coronary blood vessels
Metabolic effects	– skin	Skeletal muscle
– lipolysis (β_1)	– visceral region	Blood vessel
– glycogenolysis (β_2)	– brain region	Mucous membrane of alimentary tract
Bronchial muscles (β_2)	– renal region	
Ciliary muscles (β_2)	Intestinal sphincter	
Bladder muscles	Sweat gland	
	Bladder sphincter	
	Dilated pupils	

With an exception of β_2-receptors present in pancreas (which have excitatory response), the activation of most of the β_2-receptors is linked with the inhibitory responses. While the activation of β_1-receptors leads to the excitatory responses in general. The type of response is mainly governed by Ca^{++} ion fluxes at the nerve endings.

On the same line, α-receptors can be categorised into α_1- and α_2-receptors. α_1-receptors are present on post-synaptic receptor sites of smooth muscles of blood vessels and gland cells. While α_2-receptors are present on pre- and post-synaptic sites on the nerve terminals and are also present in the CNS.

An increased prominence of α_2-receptor responses accompanies hypertension and may contribute to the elevated blood pressure. The post-synaptic sites of α_2-receptor include the tissues like brain, uterus, parotid glands and extra-synaptic region at some blood vessels. The pre-synaptic α_2-receptors are present on the nerve terminal. Their activation leads to inhibition of neurotransmitter release (norepinephrine or acetylcholine) through negative feedback inhibitory mechanism.

Their function is :

(i) to govern the release of neurotransmitter, and

(ii) as per need, to alter the rate of synthesis of neurotransmitter.

Thus, the activation of α_2-receptors on the cholinergic nerve terminals within the intestinal wall leads to the inhibition of release of acetylcholine.

Clonidine, yohimbin and α-methyl-nore-pinephrine are more effective agonists on α_2-receptors than α_1-receptors. While phenylephrine, prazosin and methoxamine act prominently on α_1-receptors.

Table 3.3

Effector organ	Receptor responses		
	α	β_1	β_2
Vascular system	constriction	–	dilation
Uterus	constriction	dilation	dilation
Intestine	decreased motility	decreased motility	decreased motility
Heartbeat	–	increased	–
Bronchial muscle	constriction	–	relaxation

Thus in tissues, the overall effect of the adrenergic nerve stimulation depends upon the population of α and β-receptors present in that organ.

For example, in cardiac cells, positive ionotropic and positive chronotropic actions are due to the activation of β-receptors whereas α-receptor activation leads to ectopic excitation induced by sympathetic stimulation.

Further subclassification suggests the presence of four α_1 (α_{1A} to α_{1D}) and four α_2 (α_{2A} to α_{2D}) receptors. In case of β-receptors, the presence of third (β_3) type is postulated. All four α_1-receptors produce vasoconstrictor responses through different biochemical mechanisms for increasing cytosolic free Ca^{++} ions.

Tachyphylaxis or reduced response is a common problem encountered in the prolonged treatment of adrenergic drugs. Upon continuous exposure, the receptors lose their efficiency resulting into decrease in the magnitude of biological response. This is known as desensitisation, refractoriness, down regulation or tachyphylaxis. Various mechanisms are proposed to account for this event.

Thus, tachyphylaxis may be due to following processes :

(a) Feedback regulatory mechanisms governed by cyclic-AMP.

(b) Some receptors may undergo degeneration causing decrease in total number of receptors.

(c) Receptors may be inactivated or blocked due to irreversible phosphorylation, or

(d) The correlation between the receptor and adenylate cyclase may get paralyzed.

Norepinephrine is the most active agent at α-receptor and the latter is least responsive to isoproterenol. The responses mediated through α-receptors are blocked by antagonists like phenoxybenzamine or phentolamine. The excitatory nature of α-receptors and inhibitory nature of β-receptors can easily be seen from the table 3.4.

The β-receptor is most responsive to isoproterenol while the least responsive agent is norepinephrine. The β-receptor mediated responses remain unaffected by the usual α-adrenergic blockers and are blocked by agents like nadolol or timolol.

Table 3.4 : Adrenergic responses

α–receptor mediated responses	β-receptor mediated responses
Vasoconstriction	Vasodilation
Mydriasis	Bronchial smooth muscle relaxation
Release of ACTH	
Uterine myometrial contraction	Uterine myometrial relaxation
Retractor penis contraction	Intestinal smooth muscle relaxation
Seminal vesicle contraction	Positive ionotropic effect on the heart
Pilomotor muscle contraction	
Orbital contraction	Positive chronotropic effect on the heart
Nictitating membrane contraction	
Intestinal smooth muscle relaxation	Hepatic glycogenolysis and Lipolysis

3.7 CLASSIFICATION

Norepinephrine, epinephrine or isoproterenol-like drugs mimic the responses of adrenergic stimulation by acting directly on the receptor sites. While some agents when administered, do not act on the adrenergic receptors. They enter the adrenergic nerve terminals and cause stoichiometric displacement of norepinephrine from the synaptic vesicles. Their pharmacological responses are thus due to this displaced neurotransmitter. The adrenergic agonists can be conveniently divided into :

(a) Direct-acting drugs :

These amines produce their pharmacological responses by their direct action on adrenoceptors. The actions produced are of rapid onset and short-lived. Most of the agents can influence both α- and β-receptors, thus ranging from pure α-agonist (phenylephrine) to pure β–agonist (isoproterenol). The intensity of their effects remains unaffected by the use of reserpine, cocaine or imipramine.

(b) Indirect-acting drugs :

Tyramine does not act directly on the adrenoceptors. The fact that reserpine depletes tissues of norepinephrine (Bertler et al, 1956) indicated that tyramine acts by releasing endogenous norepinephrine. Many sympathomimetic agents exert a large fraction of their effects by releasing (through displacement) norepinephrine from storage sites. The responses of this released norepinephrine are prominently α-receptor mediated, slower in onset and generally long lasting.

Examples of indirect acting drugs include tyramine, amphetamine, etc. These drugs usually lack catechol nucleus. Indirect acting agents have little or no action in reserpinized animals. Cocaine or imipramine also lower the intensity of activity by inhibiting the drug-induced displacement and release of norepinephrine. Since these drugs lack the phenolic hydroxyl groups, the increased lipophilicity imparts pronounced central effects to these drugs. If given repeatedly, tachyphylaxis is likely to occur due to the depletion of norepinephrine stores.

(c) Mixed action drugs :

Many sympathomimetic drugs exert their actions partly by acting directly on the receptor sites and partly by their effect on the norepinephrine release. They are termed as mixed action drugs. Examples include :

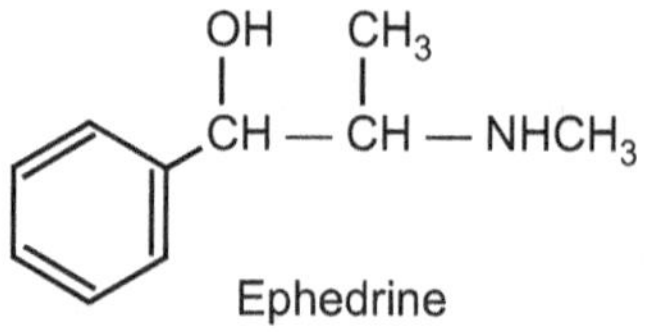

Ephedrine

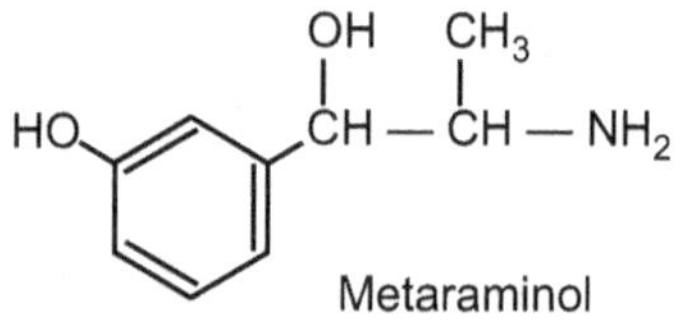

Metaraminol

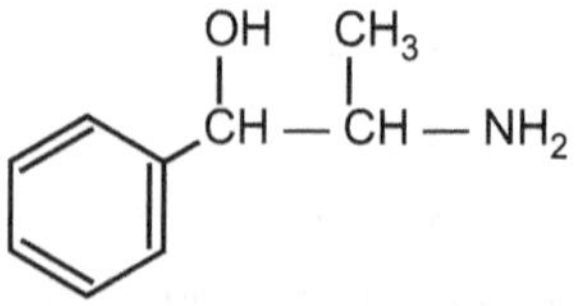

Phenylpropanolamine

They share structural features of both classes. The presence of cocaine, reserpine or imipramine only reduce (and not abolish) the intensity of their effects, where higher doses of these drugs will be needed to produce comparable effects.

Thus if we assume the following skeleton essential for sympathomimetic activity,

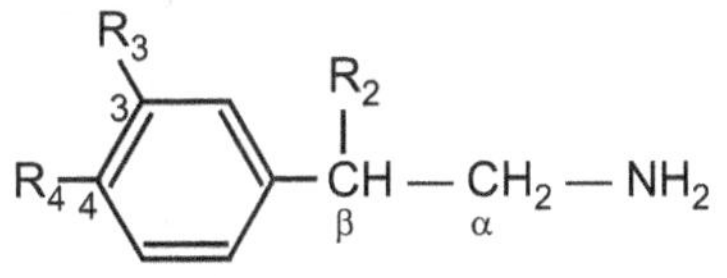

$$R_4 \underset{4}{\overset{3}{\diagdown}} \text{—} \underset{\beta}{CH} \text{—} \underset{\alpha}{CH_2} \text{—} NH_2 \quad (R_3, R_2)$$

then,

(i) Direct-acting drugs will have $R_3 = R_4 = OH$ or OCH_3 and $R_2 = OH$.

(ii) Indirect acting drugs will have only a hydroxyl group at β-carbon atom or no substitution at R_2, R_3 and R_4. They retain the phenylethylamine framework, and

(iii) Mixed action drugs share the structural features of both the above classes.

Thus, examples of direct-acting drugs include :

- norepinephrine (predominantly on α-receptor)
- epinephrine

  (on α, β_1 and β_2 receptors)

  isoprenaline

  (on β_1 and β_2 receptors)

- Tazolol

  (predominantly on β_1- receptor)

- Salbutamol

  (predominantly on β_2 receptor)

- Phenylephrine

  (predominantly on α-receptor)

Prototype of indirect-acting drugs is amphetamine. Prototype of mixed action drugs is ephedrine.

The commonly used alpha blocking agent is dibozane or 1, 4- (bis- 1, 4-benzodioxan-2-yl-methyl) piperazine while the commonly used beta blocking agent is propranolol.

3.8 DESIGN OF DRUGS AFFECTING ADRENERGIC NERVOUS SYSTEM

Development of a new drug can be done in the following areas :

(A) Drugs that affect the biosynthesis of norepinephrine.

(B) Drugs that affect the storage of norepinephrine.

(C) Drugs that affect the metabolism and/or removal of norepinephrine from the area surrounding the receptor.

(D) Drugs that mimic the effects of norepinephrine at the receptor sites (agonists).

(E) Drugs that block the interaction of norepinephrine with the receptor (antagonists).

(F) Drugs that affect post-synaptic regulation of hormone action.

(A) Drugs Affecting Biosynthesis of Norepinephrine :

The key enzyme is tyrosine hydroxylase, which requires a tetrahydrofolate coenzyme, O_2 and Fe^{++} and is quite specific. DOPA-decarboxylase acts on all aromatic amino acids and requires vitamin B_6 as cofactor. Dopamine-β-hydroxylase, located in the membranes of storage vesicles, is a copper containing protein, a mixed function oxygenase that uses O_2 and ascorbic acid. Finally phenylethanolamine-N-methyl transferase located in the adrenal medulla (the main site of adrenaline synthesis) and in the brain, uses S-adenosyl-methionine as a CH_3-donor.

(i) α-Methyl tyrosine effectively inhibits the action of tyrosine hydroxylase in the first step of biosynthesis, which is rate determining step.

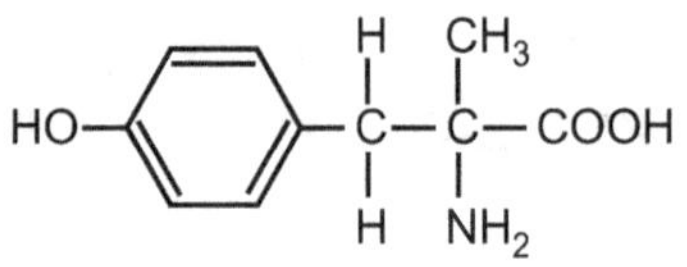

α-Methyl tyrosine

Unfortunately, the compound is not clinically useful.

(ii) DOPA- decarboxylase may be inhibited by α-methyl DOPA. Since the rate of decarboxylation of α-methyl DOPA is considerably slower than that of DOPA, it ties up the enzyme for a longer period of time and acts as an effective inhibitor.

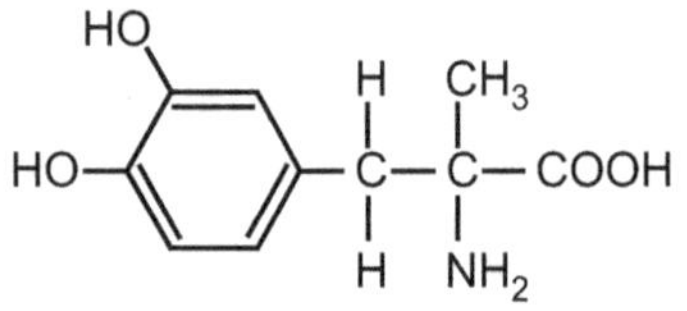

α-Methyl DOPA

(iii) Dopamine hydroxylase may be inhibited by a variety of compounds including disulfiram. Disulfiram inhibits dopamine hydroxylase probably by breaking into 2 molecules diethyldithiocarbamate which forms a chelate with Cu^{++} - ion of enzyme's prosthetic group.

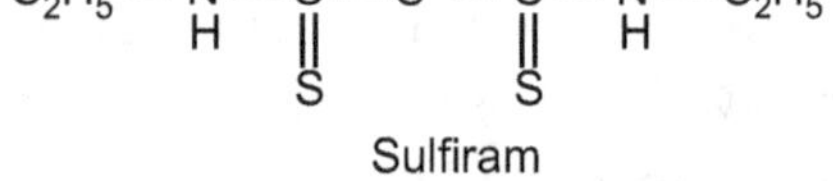

Sulfiram

(B) Drugs Affecting the Release of Stored Norepinephrine (Indirect acting agonists) :

(a) False neurotransmitters : Tyramine, produced by decarboxylation of tyrosine (and especially the β-OH derivative of tyramine, octopamine), can be taken up through the pre-synaptic membrane by the not very selective uptake-1 mechanism. Tyramine then enters the storage granules to a certain extent and

displaces neurotransmitter norepinephrine which, when released causes post-synaptic effects. Octopamine, is taken up even more readily into storage vesicles and is, in turn, released when the neuron fires. As an agonist, it is only about 1/10 active as norepinephrine. Compounds that behave like neurotransmitters of low potency are called as false neurotransmitters.

Rotigotine : It is a non-ergoline dopamine agonist indicated for treatment of Parkinson's disease and restless legs syndrome.

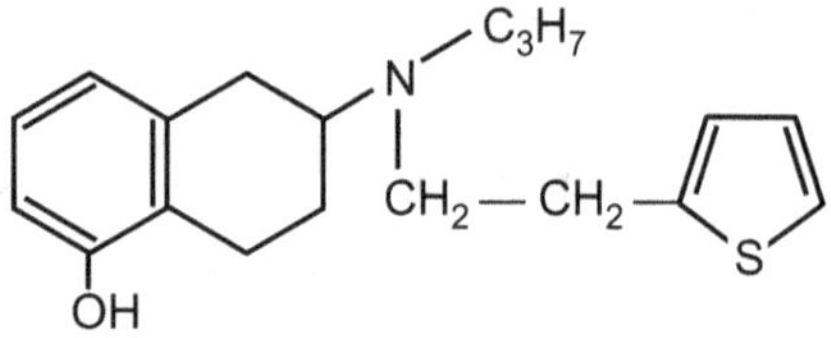

Ropinirole and **Pramipexole** are non-ergoline dopamine agonists used in the treatment of Parkinson's disease and restless leg syndrome.

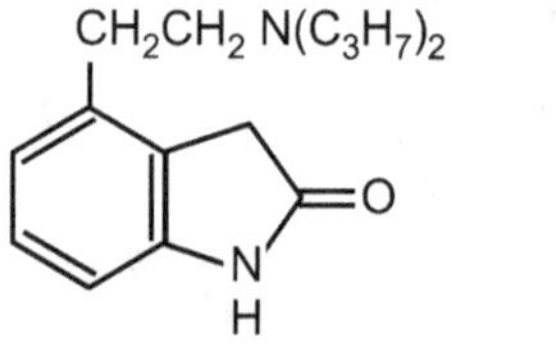

Ropinirole

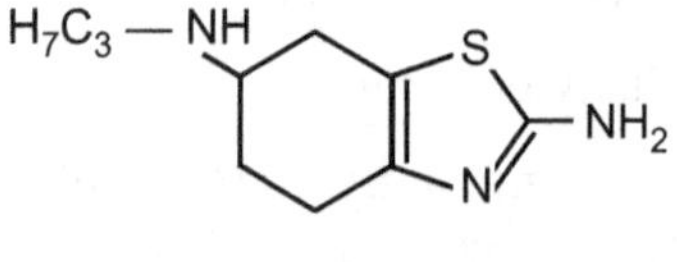

Pramipexole

(b) True uptake inhibitors : They block the amine pump of the reuptake-1 mechanism in central adrenergic, dopaminergic and serotonergic neurons. e.g., tricyclic antidepressant agents.

(i) Cocaine interferes with norepinephrine uptake at the neuron and thus increases the concentration of norepinephrine at the receptor. Reserpine depletes the neuronal storage sites. Released norepinephrine is then metabolised by MAO.

(ii) A number of antihypertensive agents exert their activity by affecting the storage and release of norepinephrine e.g. Bretylium and Guanethidine.

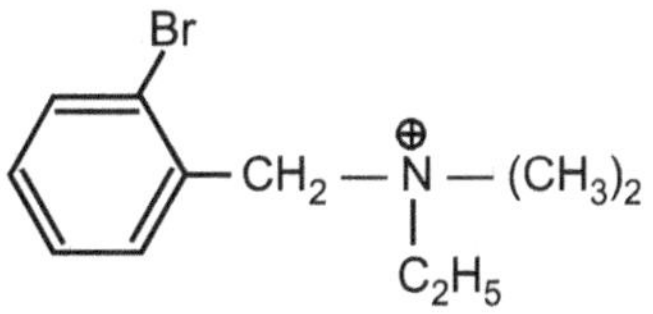

Bretylium

Atomoxetine : It is selective NE reuptake inhibitor. It is used in the treatment of attention deficit hyperactivity disorder.

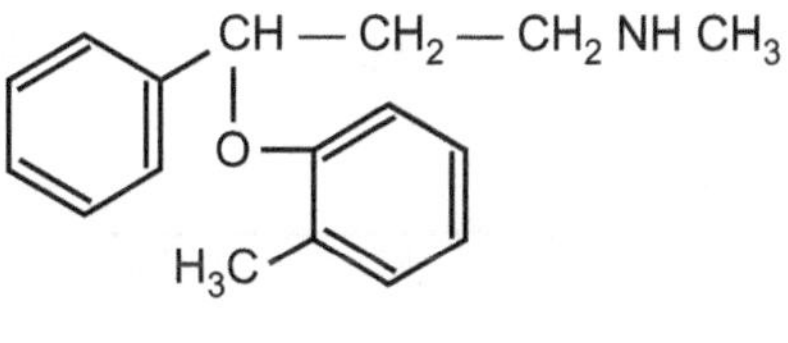

(iii) The following structure is representative of indirect acting drugs.

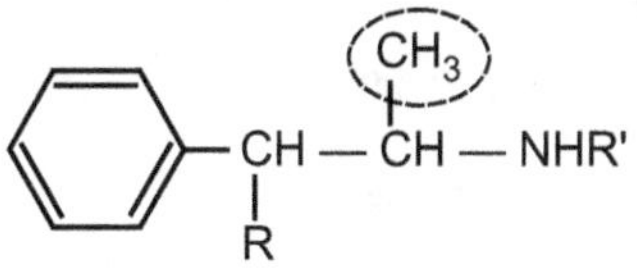

R = H or OH

R' = H, CH_3 or heterocyclic ring

(a) Indirect acting adrenergic agents do not contain phenolic hydroxyl groups at the 3, 4-positions. The lack of these ionic groups increases oral absorption and penetration into CNS.

(b) The encircled methyl group is not present in norepinephrine or its direct acting analogues. It provides increased oral activity, probably by preventing interaction with enzyme that metabolise the direct acting analogues.

(c) The benzylic hydroxyl group may or may not be present in indirect acting compounds. Those without this alcoholic hydroxyl group, are less polar, pass more readily through Blood-Brain-Barrier and demonstrate greater CNS stimulation.

(d) The amino nitrogen may be primary or secondary amine or a part of a heterocyclic ring.

(e) The phenyl group may be replaced by other aromatic group, cycloalkyl group or alkyl group.

In addition to the actions that mimic adrenergic responses, a number of indirect acting adrenergic drugs have an anorexic or appetite depressing action. In attempts to modify the phenylethylamine structure to provide anorexic activity without pronounced CNS stimulation, compounds were prepared in which the amino nitrogen is a part of heterocyclic system, but they failed to separate totally the two effects.

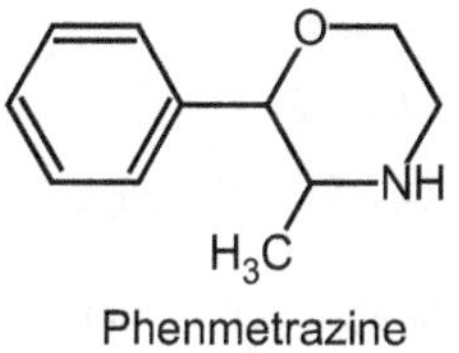

Phenmetrazine

It represents an attempt to produce an appetite suppressant lacking the CNS-stimulant properties of ephedrine or amphetamine.

Table 3.5 : Indirect-acting agonists of norepinephrine

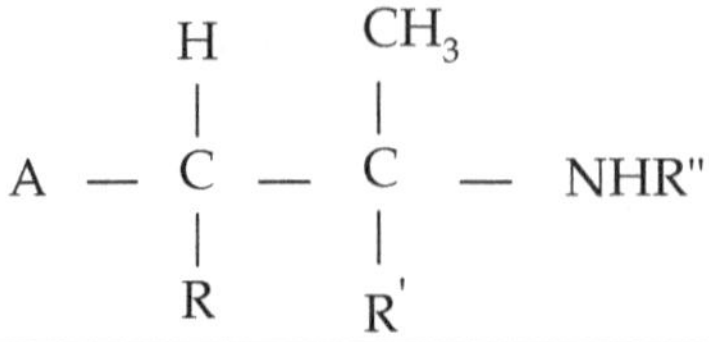

$$A - \overset{\overset{\displaystyle H}{|}}{\underset{\underset{\displaystyle R}{|}}{C}} - \overset{\overset{\displaystyle CH_3}{|}}{\underset{\underset{\displaystyle R'}{|}}{C}} - NHR''$$

Sr. No.	Name	A	R	R'	R''
1.	Phenylpropanolamine	C_6H_5	OH	H	H
2.	Amphetamine	C_6H_5	H	H	H
3.	Methamphetamine	C_6H_5	H	H	CH_3
4.	Phentermine	C_6H_5	H	CH_3	H
5.	Chlorphentermine	$P - Cl\ C_6H_4$	H	CH_3	H
6.	Methoxyphentermine	$P - CH_3\ O\ C_6H_4$	H	CH_3	H
7.	Cyclopentamine	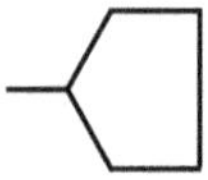 (cyclopentyl)	H	H	CH_3
8.	Propylhexedrine	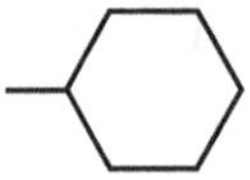 (cyclohexyl)	H	H	CH_3

Nasal decongestants

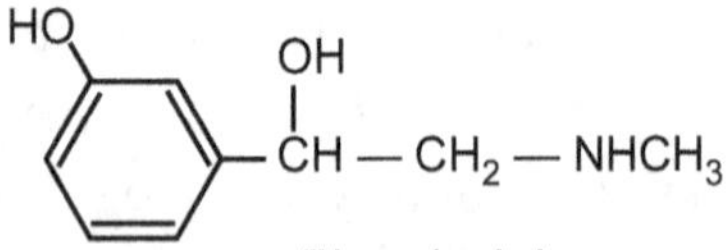

Phenylephrine

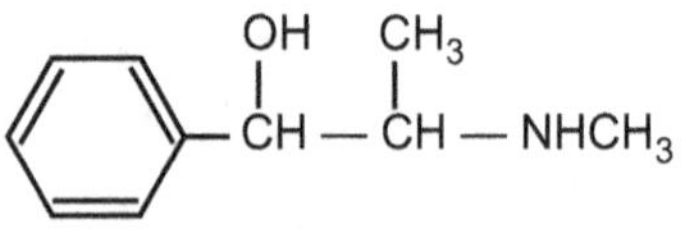

Ephedrine

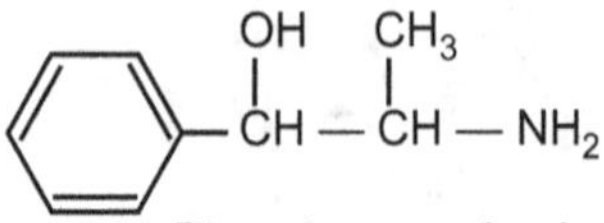

Phenylpropanolamine

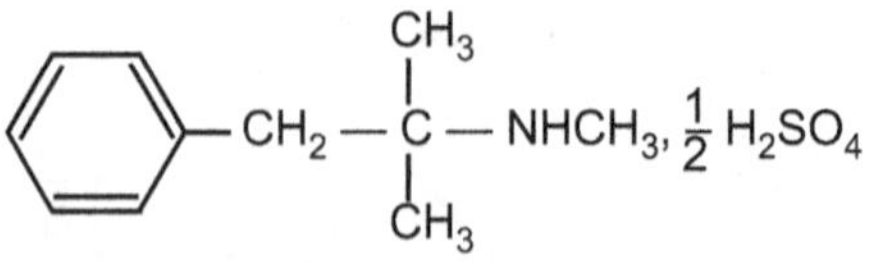

Mephentermine sulphate

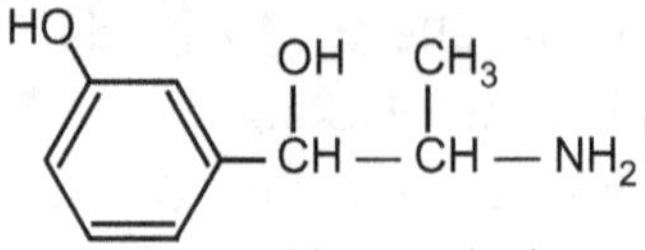

Metaraminol

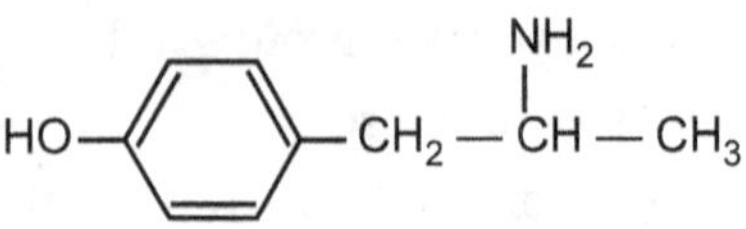

Hydroxyamphetamine

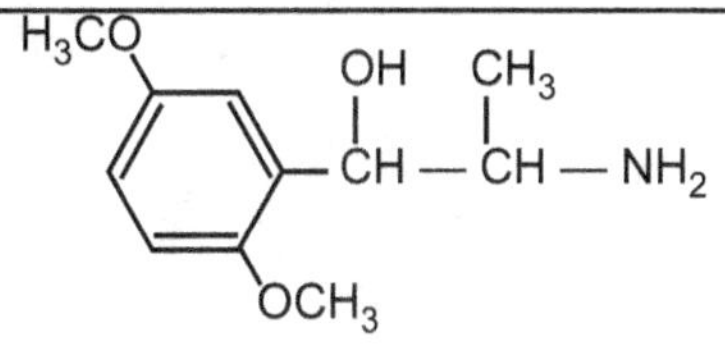

Methoxamine

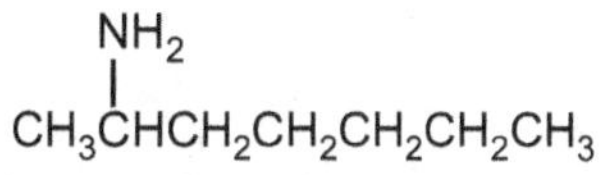

Tuaminoheptane

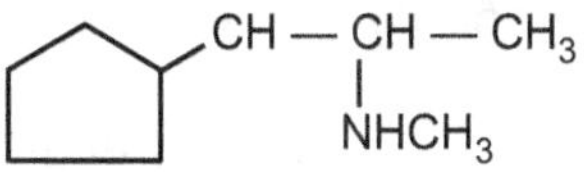

Cyclopentamine

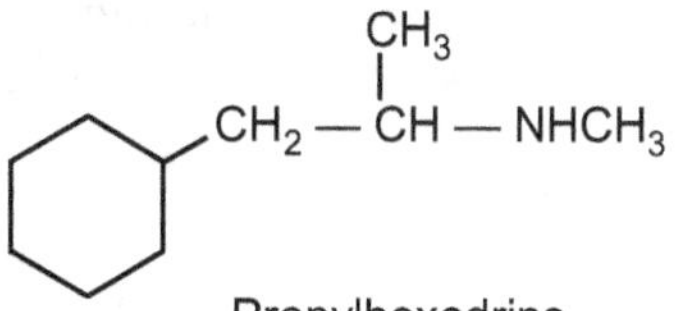

Propylhexedrine

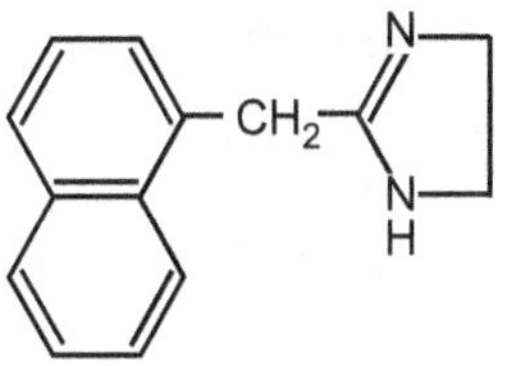

Naphazoline

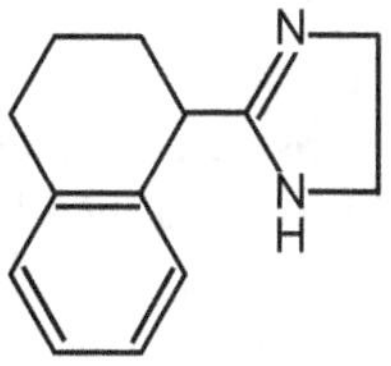

Tetrahydrozoline

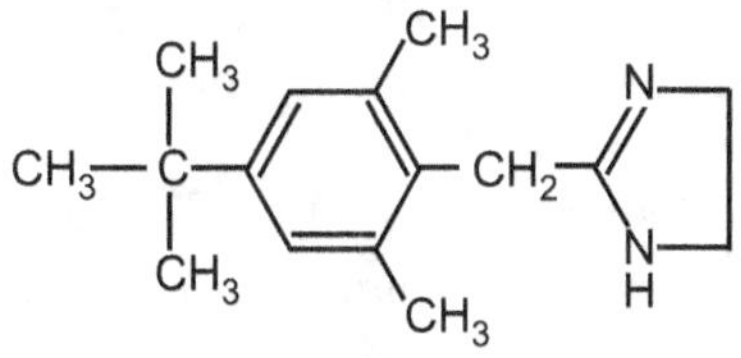

Xylometazoline
(Otrivin, Ciba)

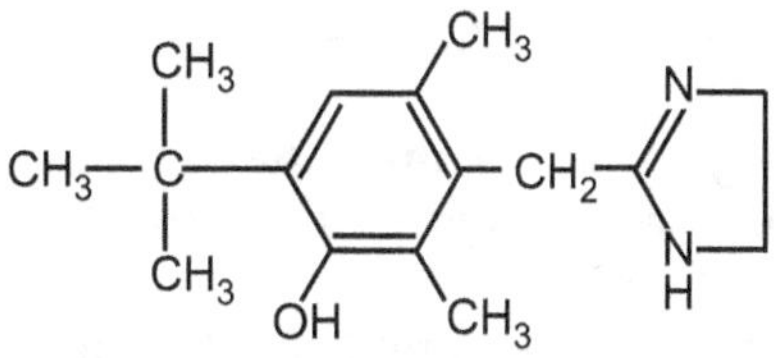

Oxymetazoline
(Nasivion, Merck)

(C) Drugs Inhibiting the Metabolism of Norepinephrine :

MAO oxidises norepinephrine through the removal of two hydrogens to give an imine, using pyridoxal phosphate (vitamin B_6), and then the non-enzymatic hydrolysis of this imine results into an aldehyde.

Inhibition of these enzymes will increase the concentration of norepinephrine at the receptor. Thus, MAO-inhibitors will be useful in the therapy of depression. They are divided into three types.

(a) Hydrazines and hydrazides.

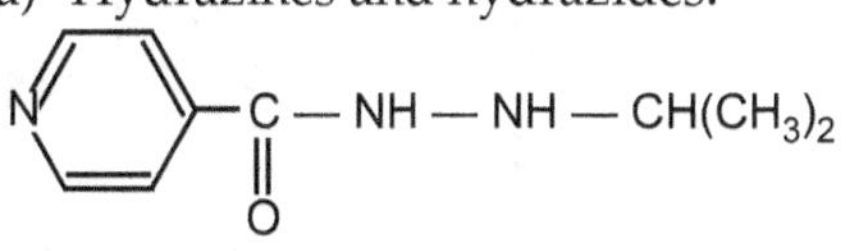

Iproniazid

(b) The rigid analogues of phenylethylamine e.g. tranylcypromine.

(c) Structures not directly related to norepinephrine.

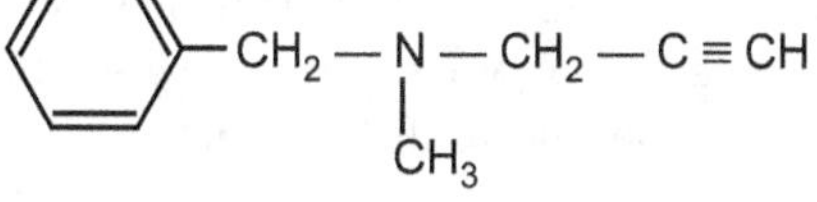

Pargyline

Entacapone : It is a COMT inhibitor, used in the treatment of Parkinson's disease.

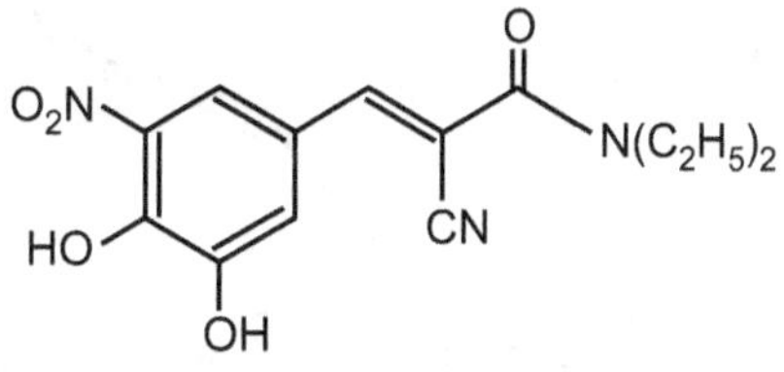

$$\underset{\text{Norepinephrine}}{\text{HO—}\overset{\displaystyle \text{HO}}{\bigcirc}\overset{\displaystyle \text{OH}}{\underset{|}{\text{CH}}} - \text{CH}_2 - \text{NH}_2} \xrightarrow[\text{Vit. B}_6]{\text{MAO}} \underset{\text{Imine}}{\text{HO—}\overset{\displaystyle \text{HO}}{\bigcirc}\overset{\displaystyle \text{OH}}{\underset{|}{\text{CH}}} - \text{CH} = \text{NH}} \xrightarrow{\text{H}_2\text{O}} \underset{\text{Aldehyde}}{\text{HO—}\overset{\displaystyle \text{HO}}{\bigcirc}\overset{\displaystyle \text{OH}}{\underset{|}{\text{CH}}} - \text{CH} = \text{O}}$$

Rasagiline : It is an irreversible inhibitor of MAO used in the treatment of Parkinson's disease.

$$HC \equiv C — CH_2 — NH_2$$

Tolcapone : It inhibits COMT enzyme. It is used in the treatment of Parkinson's disease as an adjunct to levodopa/carbidopa medication.

(D) Drugs that Mimic the Effects of Norepinephrine at Receptor Sites (Direct acting agonists) :

The structural requirements for agonist activity at adrenergic receptors are :

(I) A phenylethylamine parent structure.

(II) 3, 4-dihydroxy substitution on the phenyl ring :

Phenylethylamine structure

Although the catechol group is of major importance for agonist activity, the phenolic groups can be successfully replaced by alkyl or arylsulphonamide functions.

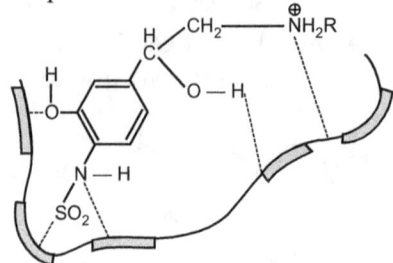

Fig. 3.5 : Schematic representation of binding of sulphonamido analogues of catecholamine

(a) The amino group should be separated from the aromatic ring by two carbon atoms for optimal activity.

(b) Direct acting agonist activity is enhanced by the presence of a hydroxyl group of the correct stereochemical configuration (i.e. laevorotatory) on the β-carbon but is reduced by the presence of a methyl group on α-carbon. The presence of α-methyl group increases the duration of action by making the compound more resistant to metabolic deamination by MAO.

(c) Small substituents (H, CH_3, C_2H_5) may be placed on the carbon without affecting agonist activity significantly.

(d) Small substituents (H or CH_3) may be placed on the nitrogen atom, without affecting agonist activity.

(e) The nitrogen atom must have at least one H-atom.

(f) The highly critical factor in the interaction of adrenergic agonists with their receptor is that of stereoselectivity. Stedman and Easson proposed a three point interaction of the catechol, β-hydroxyl and amino group as shown for norepinephrine.

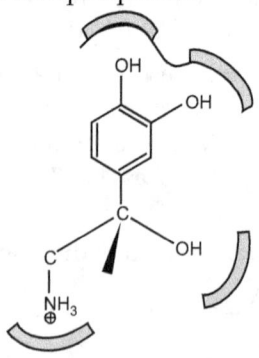

Fig. 3.6 : Representation of the stereoselective three-point binding of norepinephrine

For epinephrine, norepinephrine and related compounds, the more potent enantiomer has the R (-) configuration. None of these compounds (Table 3.5) can be considered totally specific for either receptor and that they interact to some extent with both of the compounds listed in table 3.6. Phenylephrine is the most specific drug acting chiefly at the α-receptor, whereas isoproterenol acts most specifically at the β-receptor.

Ibopamine : It is a sympathomimetic used in opthalmology to induce mydriasis.

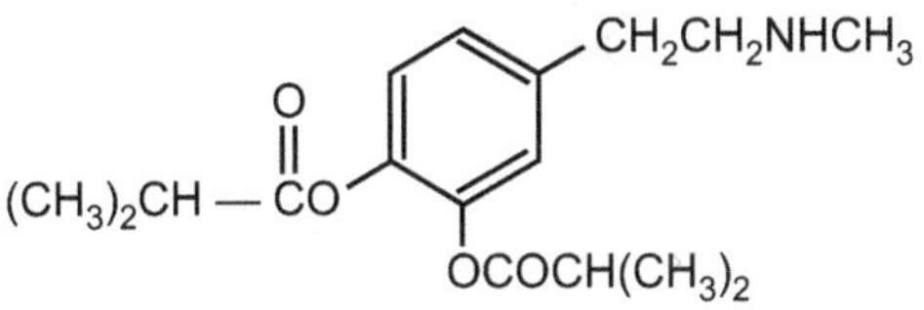

Selective β$_2$ Agonists :

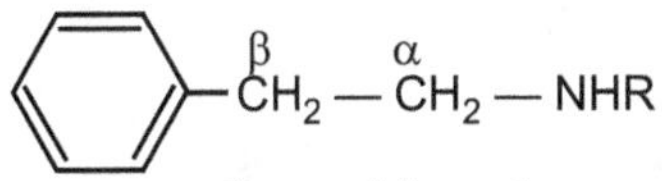

General formula

(i) Only one aromatic hydroxyl group is necessary (usually at the para, but sometimes at meta position).

(ii) An α-methyl or ethyl group is preferred for vascular effects.

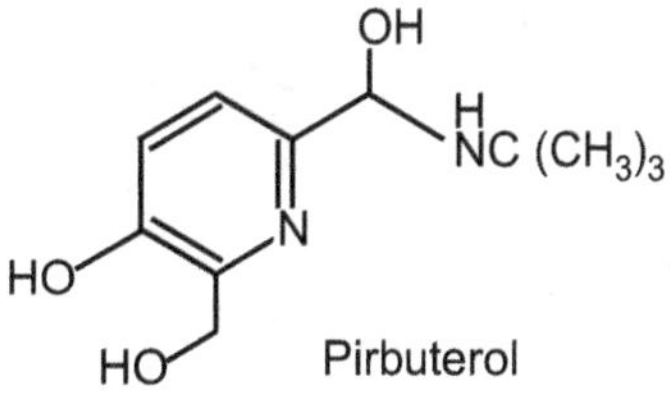

Pirbuterol

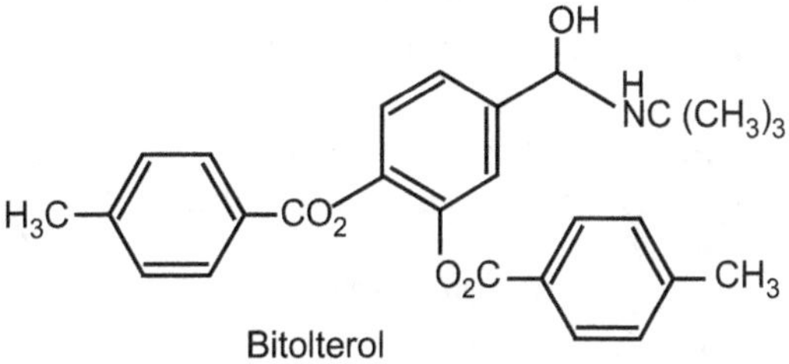

Bitolterol

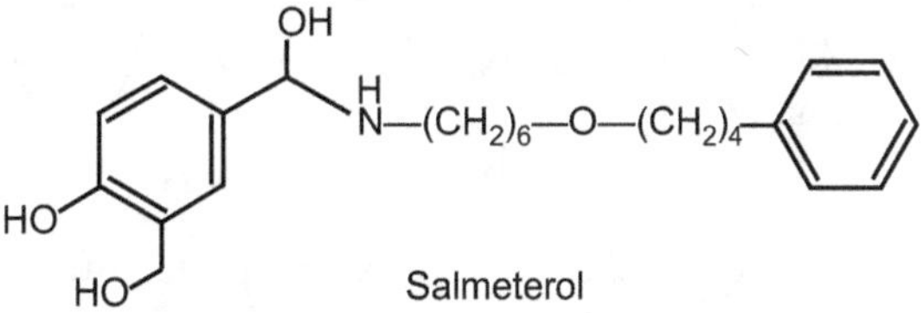

Salmeterol

Table 3.6 : Direct-acting adrenergic agonists

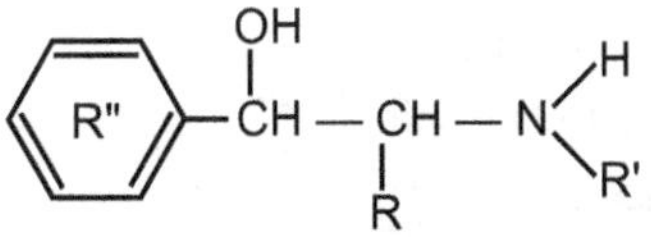

Compound	R"	R	R'	Primary receptor site
1. Norepinephrine	3, 4, – di OH	H	H	α
2. Epinephrine	3, 4, – di OH	H	CH$_3$	β
3. Phenylephrine	3 – OH	H	CH$_3$	α
4. Isoproterenol	3, 4, – di OH	H	– CH (CH$_3$)$_2$	β
5. Isoetharine	3, 4, – di OH	– C$_2$H$_5$	– CH (CH$_3$)$_2$	β
6. Metaproterenol	3, 5, – di OH	H	– CH (CH$_3$)$_2$	β
7. Metaraminol	3 – OH	CH$_3$	H	α

Arformoterol : It is a long acting β-adrenoceptor agonist effective in the treatment of chronic obstructive pulmonary disease.

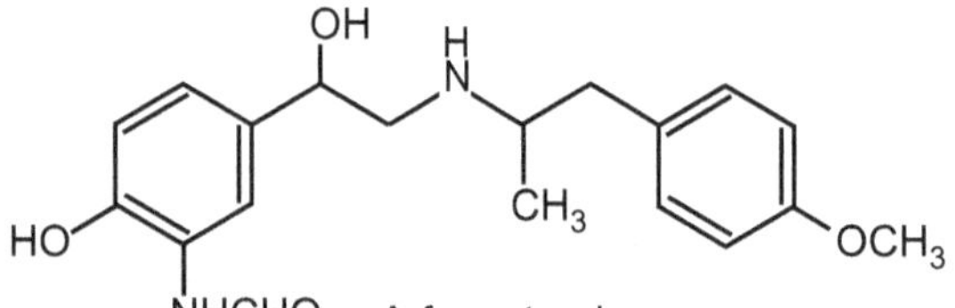

Arformoterol

Two clinically useful compounds of this category are isoxsuprine and nylidrin.

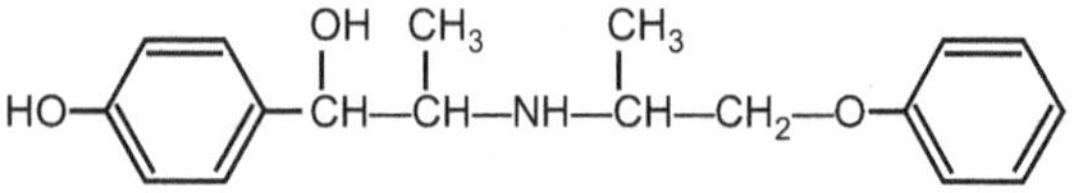

Isoxsuprine

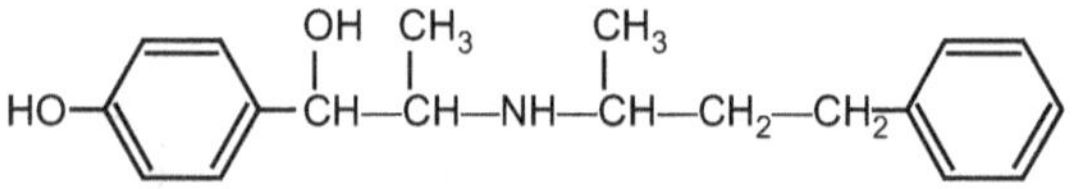

Nylidrin

If the α-CH$_3$ group is dropped, more selectivity for bronchial β$_2$-receptor is obtained. The phenolic groups in nonpinephine are involved in H-bonding to receptor. The COMT enzymes cause metabolic methylation of one of these phenolic groups which accounts for its shorter duration of action. Replacing one of these phenolic groups by a hydroxyethyl group saves the hydroxy group from COMT enzymes without affecting its ability to activate receptor through H-bonding. e.g.

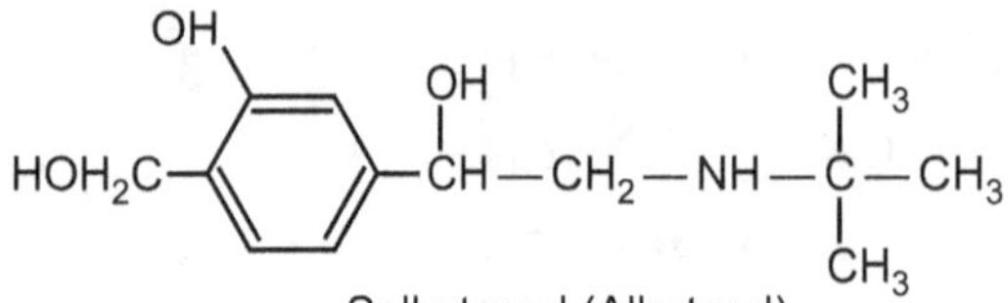

Salbutamol (Albuterol)

Bambuterol : It is a long acting β-adrenoceptor agonist used in the treatment of asthma. It is also a prodrug of terbutaline.

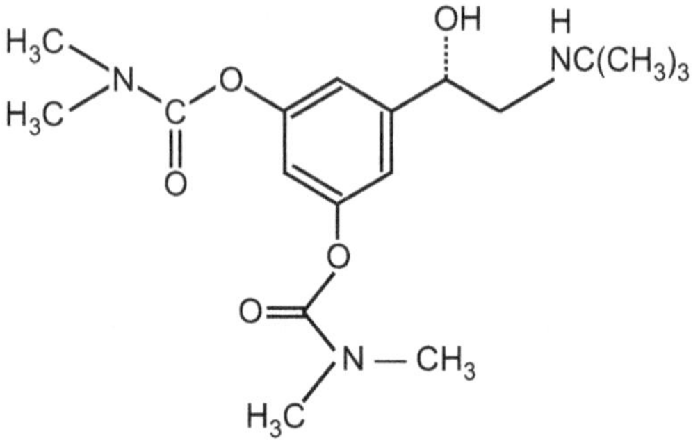

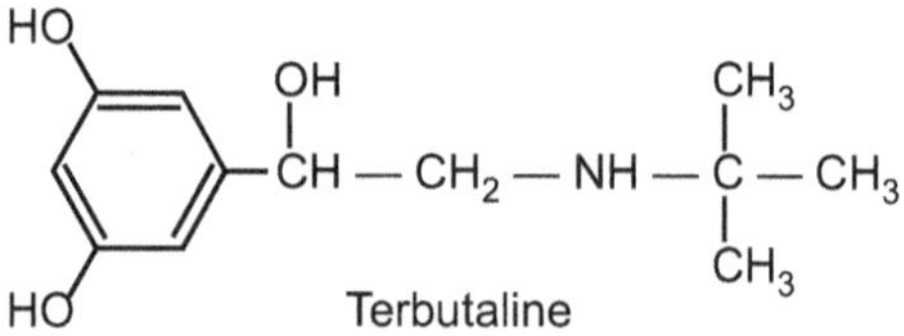

Terbutaline

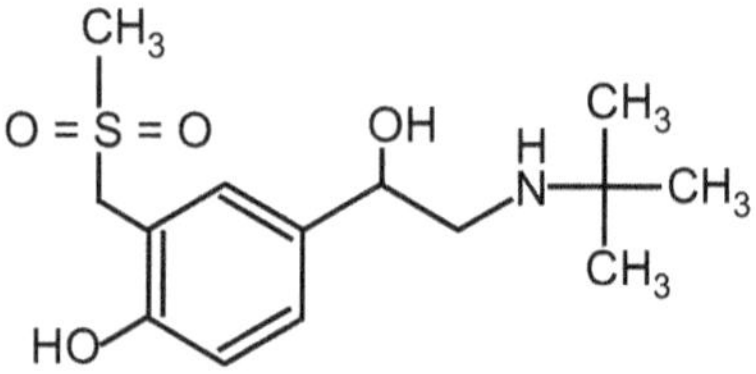

Sulfonterol

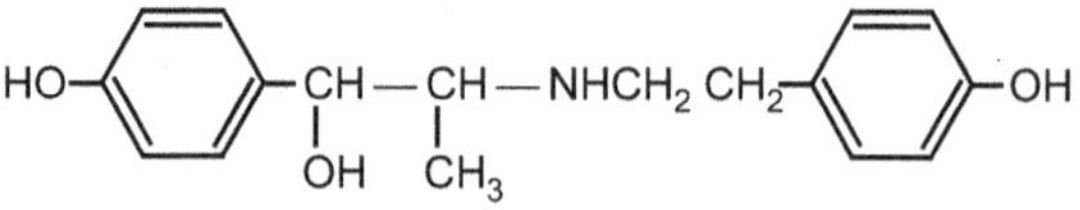

Ritodrine

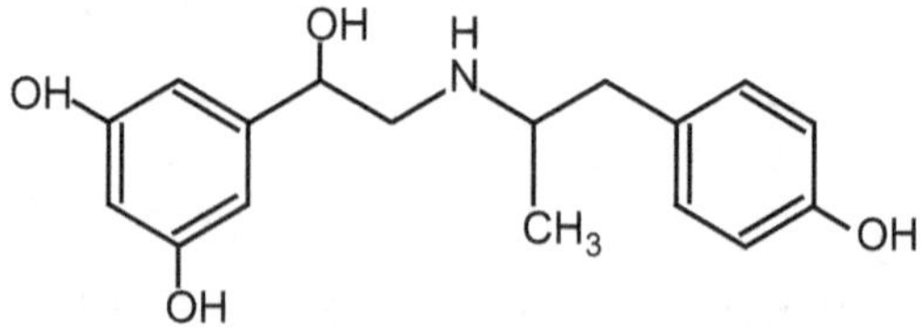

Selective β$_2$-agonist Fenoterol

Salmefamol is 1.5 times more active than salbutamol. It has a longer duration of action.

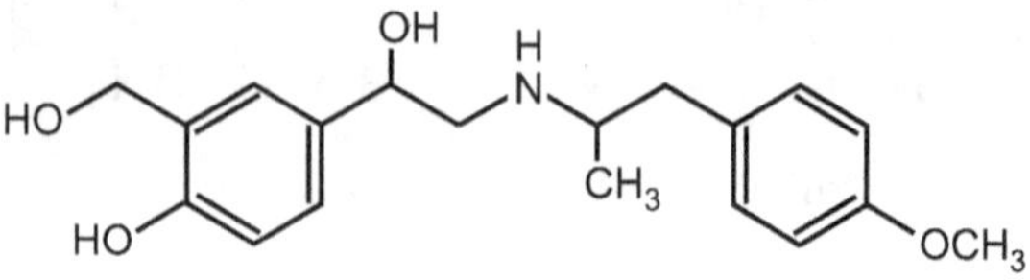

Salmefamol

(E) Drugs that act as α_2-adrenoceptor agonists :

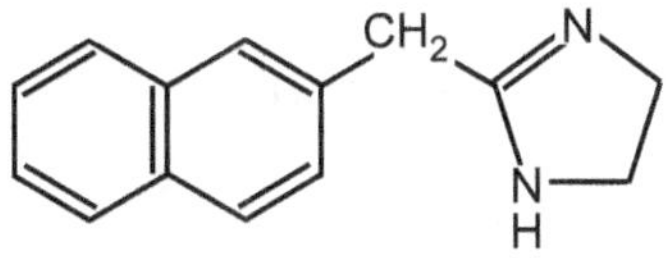

Naphazoline

Brimonidine : It is peripheral α_2-receptor agonist used to treat open angle glaucoma or ocular hypertension.

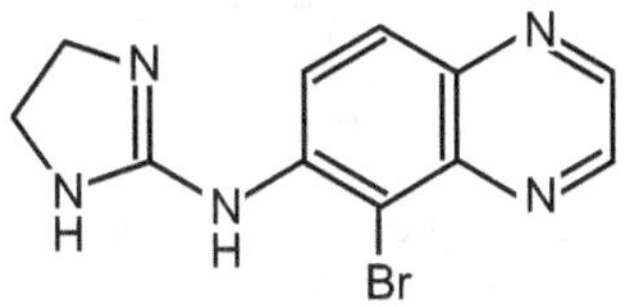

Brimonidine

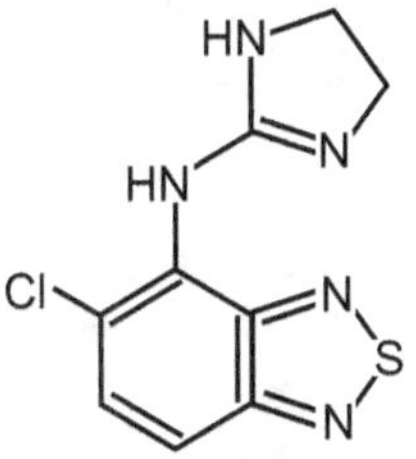

Tizanidine

It is a centrally acting adrenergic α_2-receptor agonist used to treat chronic muscle spasticity conditions, such as multiple sclerosis.

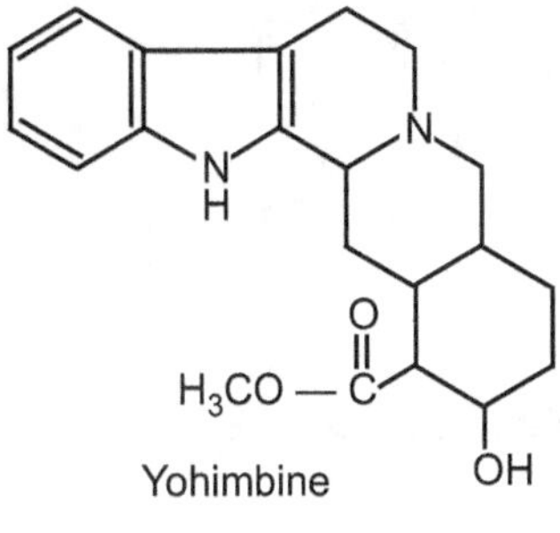

Yohimbine

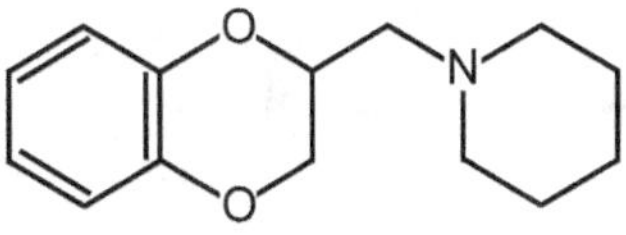

Piperoxan

Clonidine is yet another α_2-adrenoreceptor agonist which is used as a central antihypertensive. It may perhaps act on the baroreceptor (blood pressure) reflex pathway, on cardiovascular centers in the medulla and also peripherally. It abolishes most symptoms of opiate withdrawal and stimulates histamine H_2 receptors. It also acts as antianxiety agent that stimulates α_2-adreno-receptors and therefore decreases norepine-phrine levels.

(F) Drugs that block the interaction of norepinephrine with receptor (antagonists)

Alpha Adrenergic Blockers :

(a) β-Haloalkylamines : These compounds resemble the nitrogen mustard antineoplastic agents and may be represented by the following general formula :

$$R — N — CH_2 — CH_2 — X$$
$$\vert$$
$$R$$

where R = arylalkyl group

X = halogen

The effectiveness is dependent upon the nature of R. e.g., phenoxybenzamine. Dibenzamine [N, N, dibenzyl-N-(β-chloroethyl) amine] was investigated by Nickerson and Goodman as an anti-leukemic nitrogen mustard. Phenoxybenzamine was the outcome of molecular modification of dibenzamine to remove the toxicity.

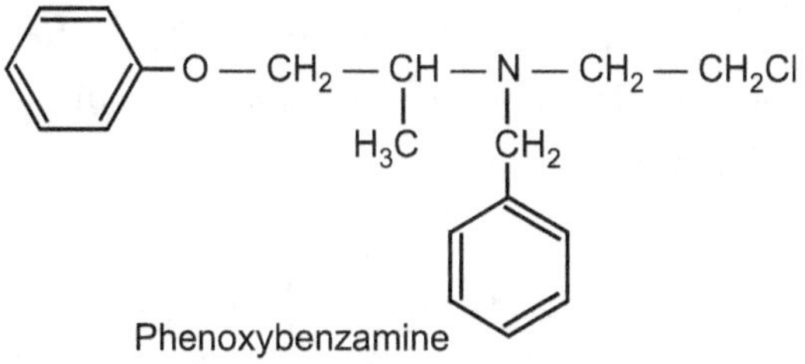

Phenoxybenzamine

The groups attached to the nitrogen are important for transport of the drug to the receptor area and binding to the receptor surface.

The β-haloalkylamines through the formation of an ammonium ion react with a nucleophilic group, present in the alpha receptor, forming a stable and perhaps only slowly reversible covalent bond, as shown in the Fig. 3.7.

Mechanism of Action :

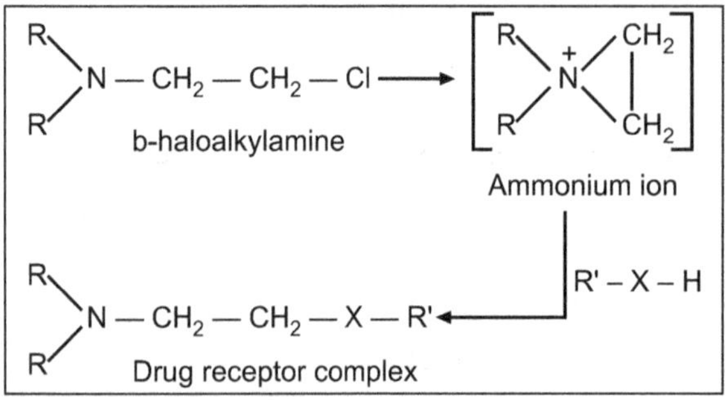

Fig. 3.7

(b) **Ergot alkaloids :** Ergot was recognised as α-adrenergic agent in 1906. The parent compound is Lysergic acid. Ergocristine, ergocryptine, ergocornine and ergonovine which are the derivatives of lysergic acid are found to possess adrenergic blocking action. A number of other amides of lysergic acid have been prepared of which methylergonovine and methylsergide are employed clinically.

(c) **Imidazolines :** Following are the examples of clinically useful agents used in the management of hypertension, i.e. Tolazoline. The encircled portion resembles structurally with norepinephrine

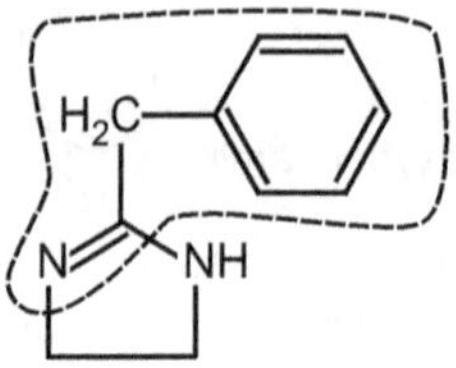

Tolazoline

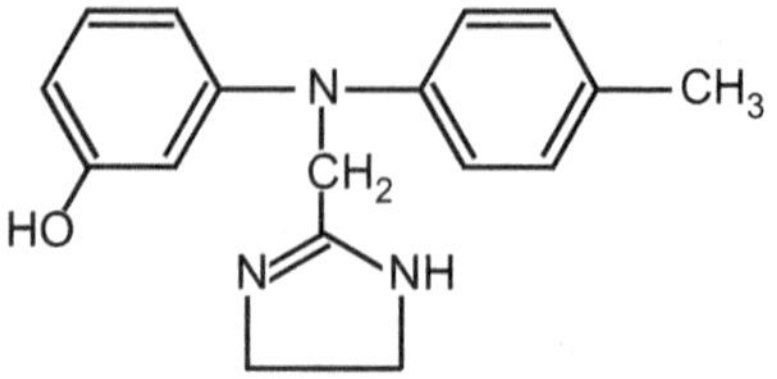

Phentolamine

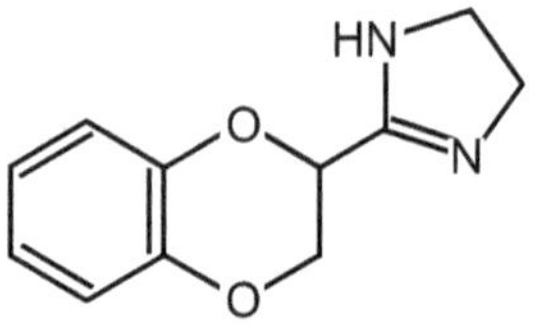

Idazoxan

(d) Other alpha receptor blocking agents include, some benzodioxanes and dibenzazepines. Prazosin, a quinazoline derivative is one of the newer clinically available α-blocking agents.

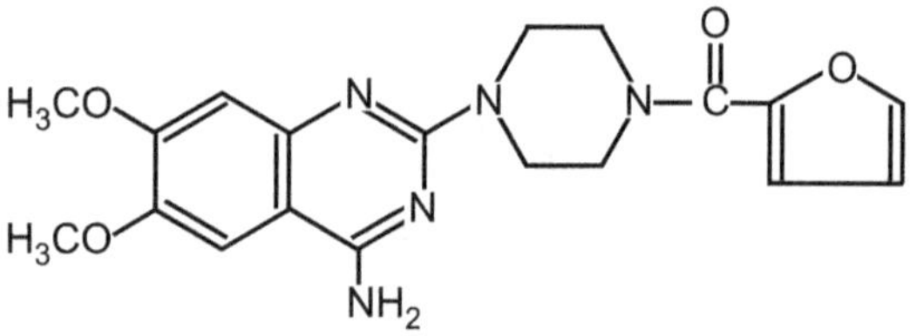

Prazosin

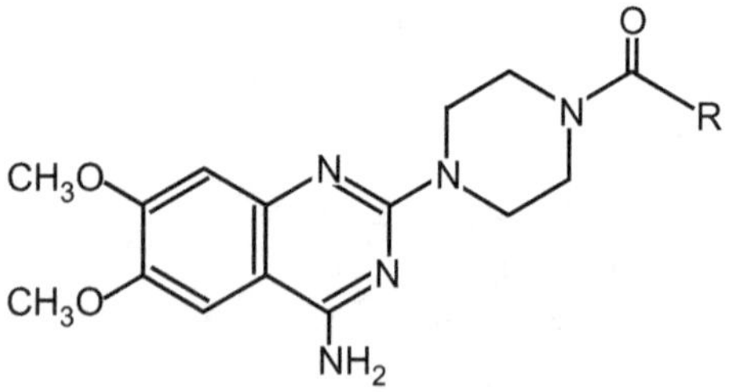

Terazosin R =

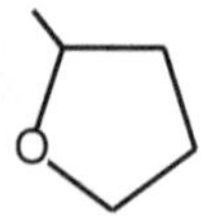

Doxazosin R =

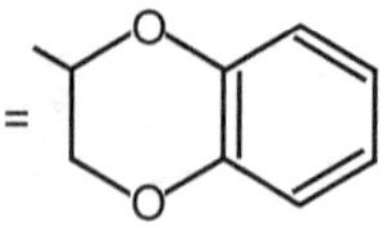

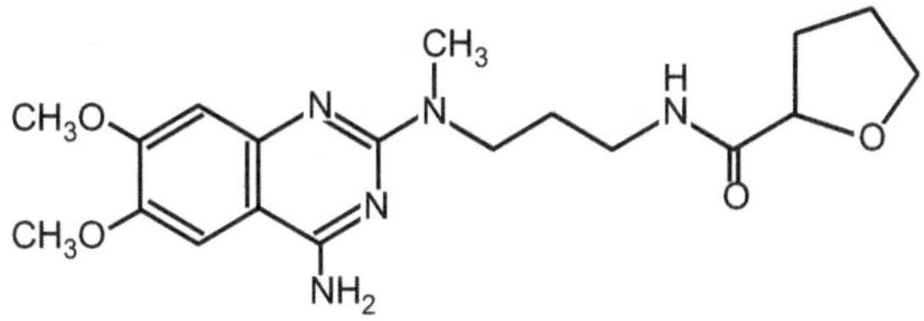

Alfuzosin

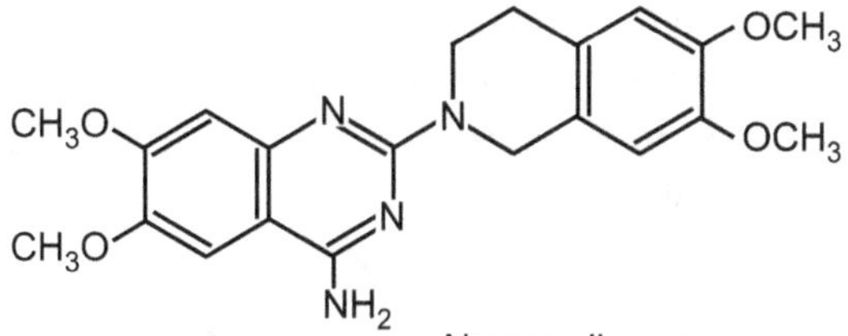

Abanoquil

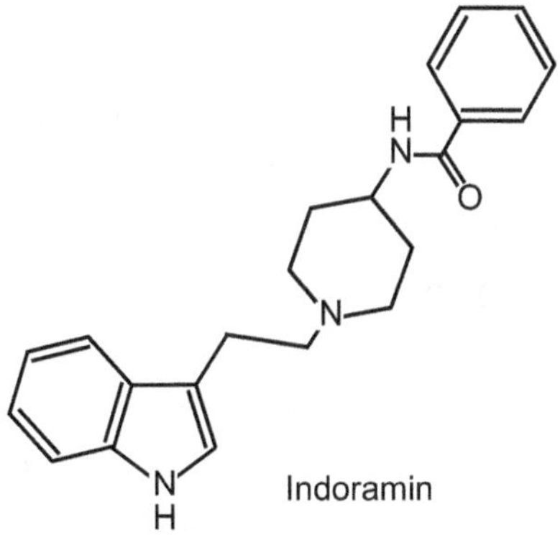

Indoramin

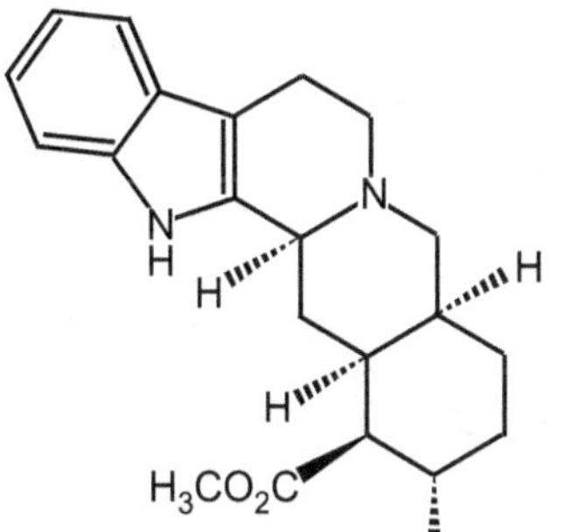

Rauwolscine

Tamsulosin : Selective α_1-blocker. It is used in symptomatic treatment of benign prostate hyperplasia.

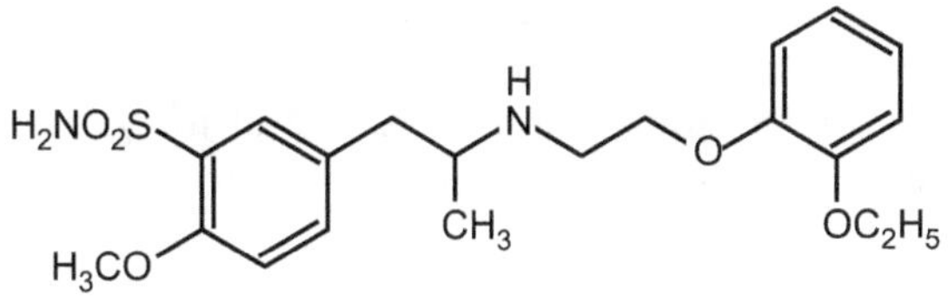

β-Adrenergic Blockers :

Unlike α-adrenergic blockers, the structural requirements for β-adrenergic blockers have been fairly well defined.

SAR : (1) Phenolic OH groups are important for adrenergic agonist activity. Removal of the 4-OH leaves intact only α-agonist activity, (e.g., phenylephrine, methoxamine - both vasoconstrictors used in treating hypotension and nasal congestion), whereas removal of the 3-OH group abolishes both α- and β-agonist activity. The 3-OH group can, however, be replaced by a SO_2NH_2 (soterenol) or a $OHCH_3$–(salbutamol) group. 3-amino compounds can be extremely potent. Replacement of 4-OH group by any such groups leads to an almost total loss of activity and compound may become an antagonist.

(2) The two-carbon side-chain is essential for activity. The benzylic carbon (next to the ring) must have (R) absolute configuration.

(3) The alcoholic OH can be replaced only by an amino or – CH_2OH group.

(4) Small (–H, –CH_3) N-substituents produce α-activity; larger ones [–CH–$(CH_3)_2$, aryl] produce β-activity.

There are two main classes of these agents :

(a) Arylethanolamines

(b) Aryloxypropanolamines

(a) Arylethanolamines : Isoproterenol is a basic structure to yield good β–adrenergic blocking compounds.

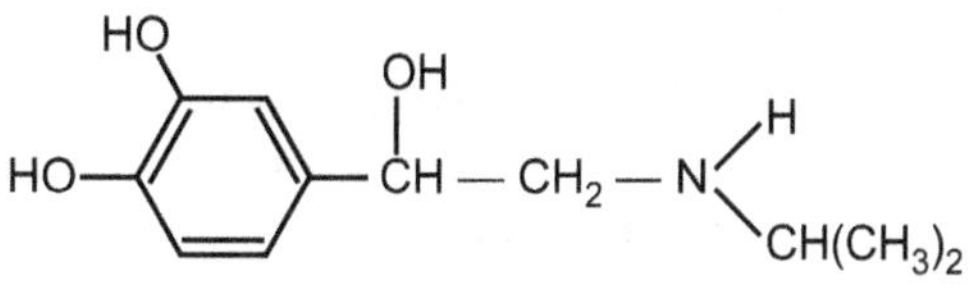

Certain modifications can be made on this basic structure, like,

(i) Replacement of catechol hydroxyl groups with chlorine to give dichloroisoproterenol (DCI), a classic β-blocking agent. It is the first useful β-blocker discovered in 1948. Since DCI is also a partial β-agonist and it cannot be used as a hypotensive agent. DCI turned out to be carcinogenic.

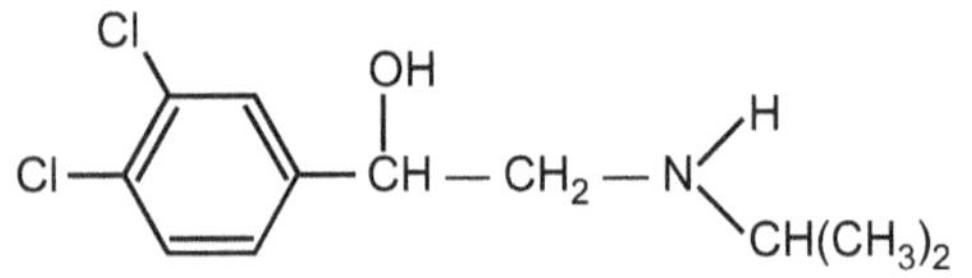

Dichloroisoproterenol

(ii) Replacement of the electron rich hydroxyl groups with an electron rich phenyl at 3, 4 positions gives pronethalol, which is even better β-blocker than dichloroisoproterenol.

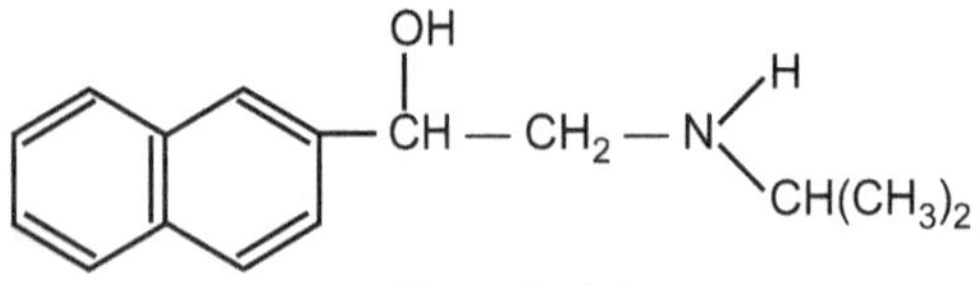

Pronethalol

(iii) **N-Substitution :**

(a) N, N-disubstitute, compounds are inactive.

(b) Alpha-methyl group decreases activity.

(c) Activity is maintained when phenylethyl, hydroxyphenylethyl or methoxyphenyl-ethyl groups are added to amine part of the molecule.

(d) Cyclic alkyl substituents are better than corresponding open chain substituents at nitrogen atom of amine.

(e) Chain length may extend to a total of 4-atoms with or without a terminal phenyl carbon.

(iv) Reduction of one ring to give either of two tetraline analogues did not affect activity.

(v) Converting the aromatic portion to phenanthrene or anthracene was disadvantageous.

(vi) Other derivatives, in which the para-hydroxyl group on phenyl ring is replaced by methylsulphonamide were also prepared, e.g. Sotalol.

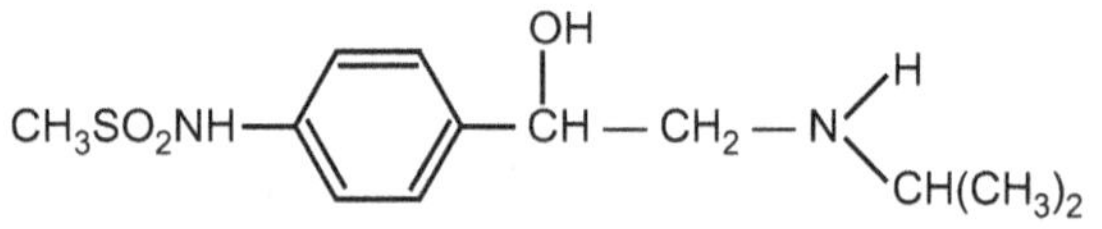

Sotalol

In this series, if the methylsulphonamide group is replaced by nitro, appreciable activity is maintained.

(b) Aryloxypropanolamines :

(1) Pronethalol, an arylethanolamine, was withdrawn from clinical testing because of reports that it caused thymic tumours in mice. However, within two years of this report, Black and co-workers discovered, a potent β-blocker propranolol, a close structural relative of pronethalol.

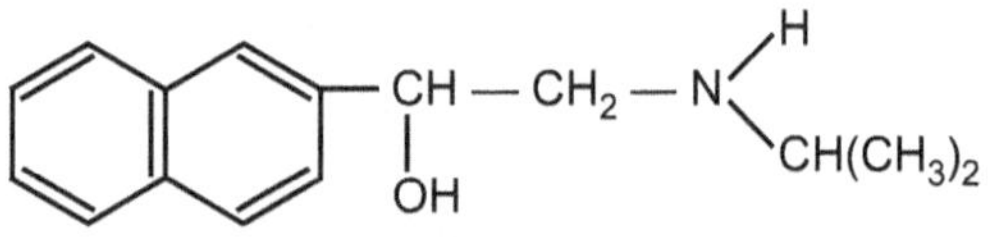

Pronethalol

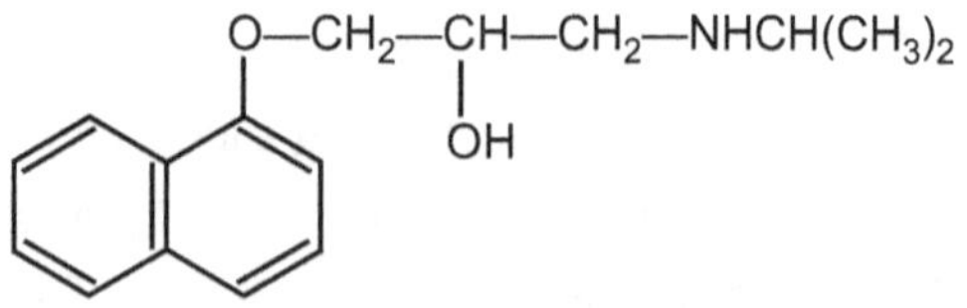

Propranolol (log P = 3.65)

Propranolol is the prototype of the group of β-blocking agents known as aryloxypropranolamines.

A propranolol metabolite of particular interest is 4-hydroxypropranolol, which is a potent β-antagonist.

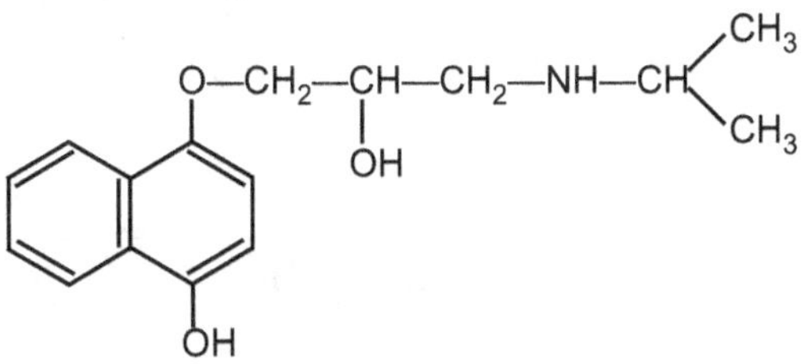

4-hydroxy propranolol

(2) (a) Most derivatives of this series possess various substituted phenyl rings rather than the naphthyl ring. The catechol ring system can be replaced by a great variety of other ring systems varying from phenylether (oxprenolol) and sulphonamides (sotalol) to amides (labetolol), indoles (pindolol, benzpindolol) and naphthalene (propranolol). N-substituents must be bulky to ensure affinity to β-receptors; isopropyl is the smallest effective substituent.

(b) Substitution of CH_3, Cl, OCH_3 or NO_2 groups on the phenyl ring was most favoured at 2 and 3 positions and least favoured at 4 - position.

(c) Alkenyl and alkenyloxy groups in the ortho positions on phenyl ring, provided good activity. e.g. oxprenolol, alprenolol.

These compounds could be considered as ring opened analogues of propranolol.

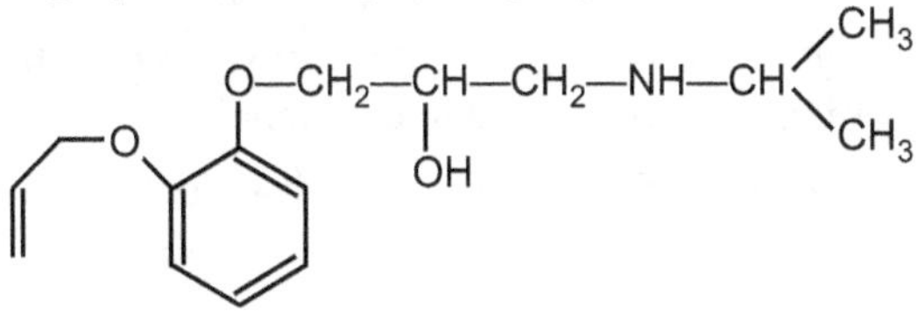

Oxprenolol

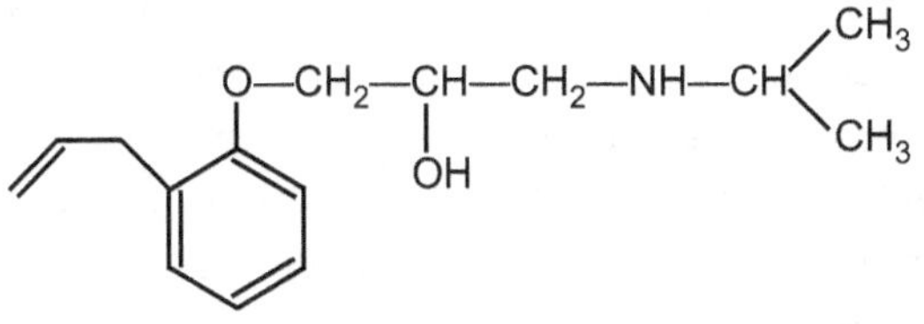

Alprenolol

(d) Longer alkyl chains are less effective but isopropyl or t-butyl, which gives an optimal basicity or nucleophilicity to the amino group for receptor affinity are most preferred.

(3) A major clinical problem with propranolol was its high lipid solubility, which allowed it to penetrate nerve tissue and exert an undesirable cardiodepressant effect in addition to its β-blocking. To avoid this problem, use of polar group (such as methanesulphonamide-$NHSO_2CH_3$) was considered. The prototype of this series of compounds was practolol, which is devoid of the depressant effect of propranolol. It was the first cardioselective $β_1$-antagonist.

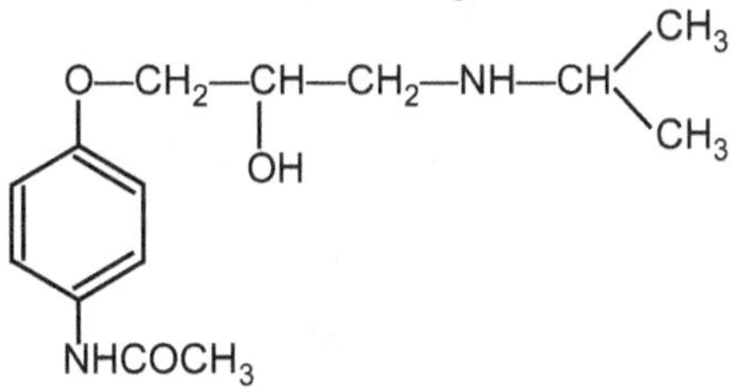

Practolol (log P = 0.79)

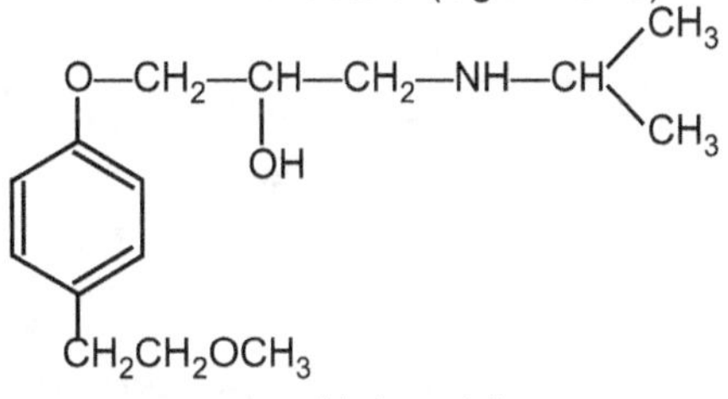

Metoprolol

Other selective $β_1$-blockers under study are :

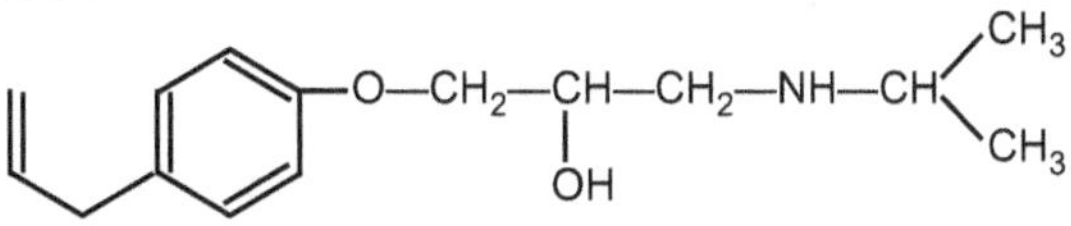

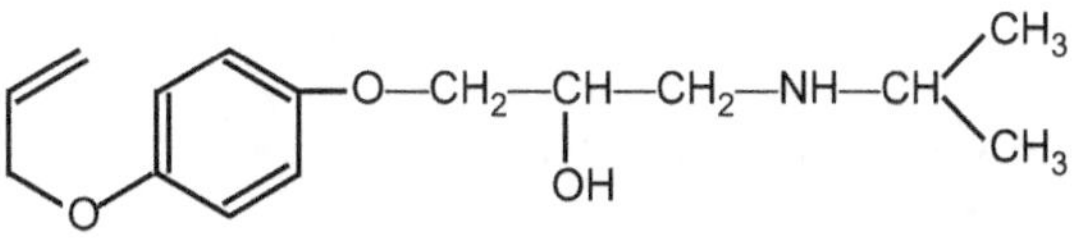

These compounds are characterised chiefly by p-substitution rather than o-substitution.

Selective β_2-Antagonists :

Butoxamine has a selective β_2-antagonistic action. It blocks β_2-receptors present in smooth muscle and in skeletal muscle.

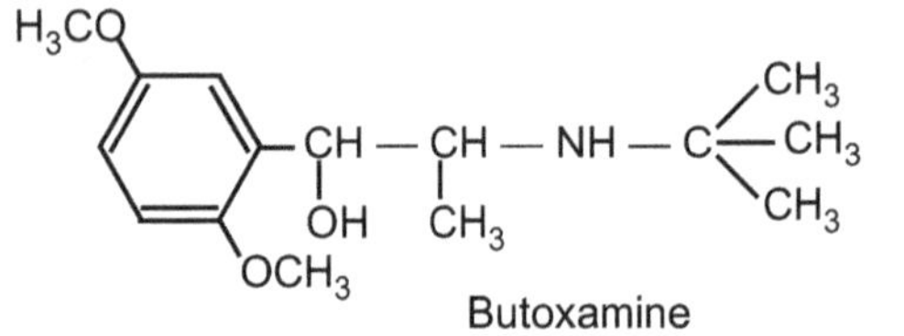

Butoxamine

It is an useful research tool but it does not, at present, have clinical use.

Other compounds which have selective β_2-blocking action, are

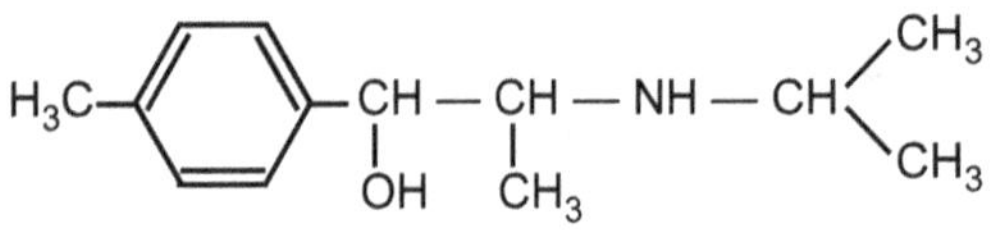

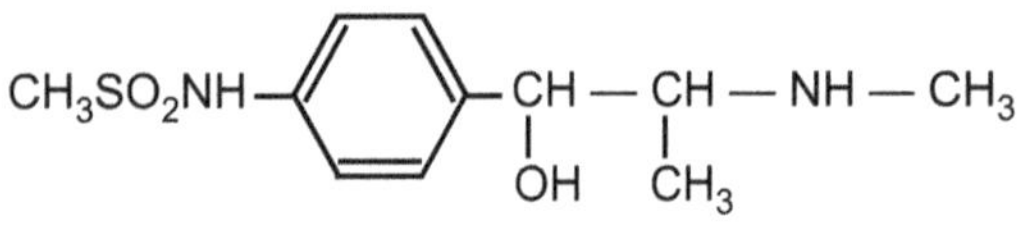

Metalol

Non-selective β-Blockers :

Alongwith alprenolol, propranolol, oxprenolol, other new compounds such as nadolol, timolol and labetolol, also exhibit non-selective β-receptor blocker activity.

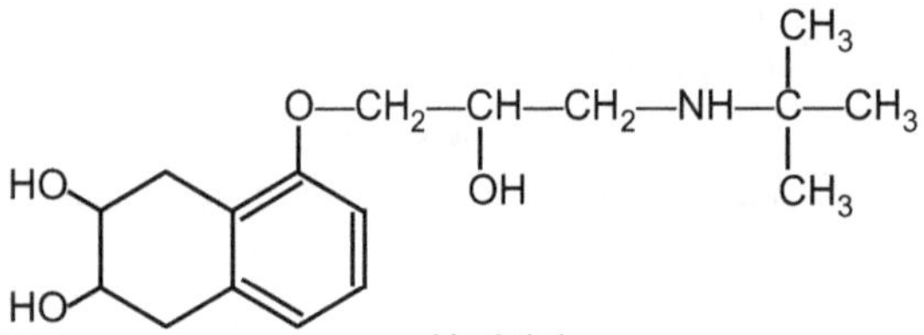

Nadolol

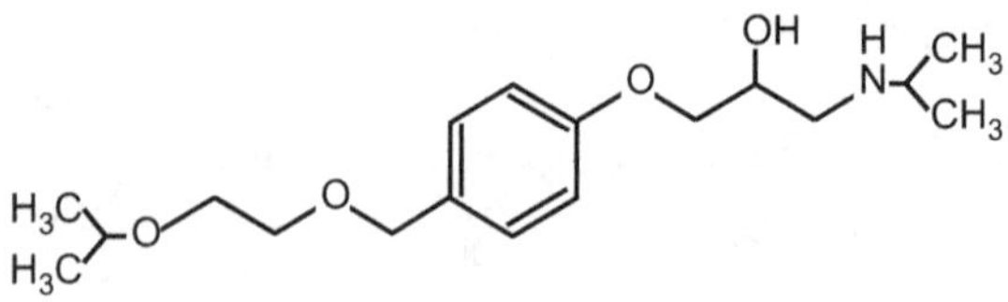

Highly selective β_1-antagonist
Bisoprolol

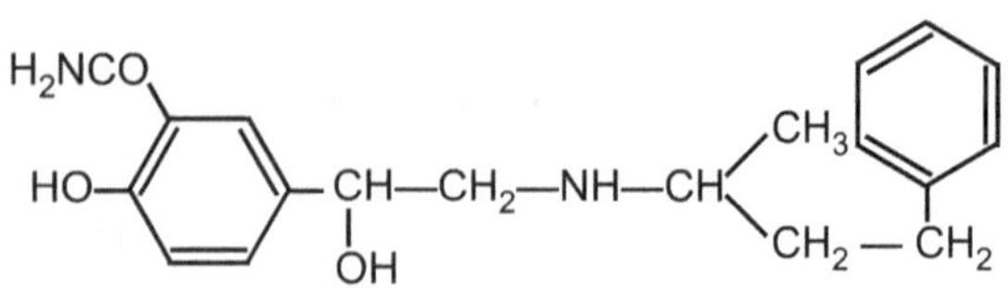

Labetolol

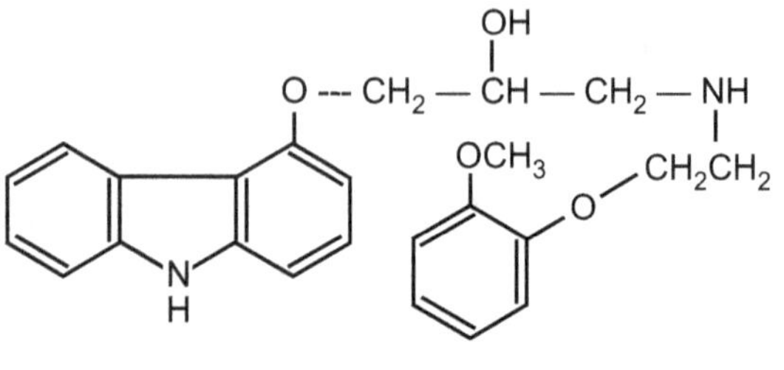

Carvedilol

Labetolol and carvedilol are the examples of non-selective β-blockers with α_1-receptor antagonistic activity.

Another compound having direct vasodilating effects in addition to β-blockage which offers an additional advantage of a reduced peripheral resistance with the original antihypertensive action is :

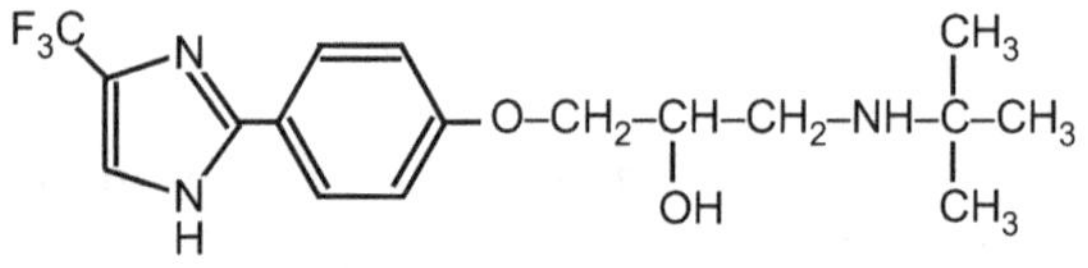

where β-blockers have been resolved, the β-blocking activity has resided with the S-enantiomer. This has the same absolute configuration as the naturally occurring agonists, noradrenaline and adrenaline.

Clinical Significance of β_1-Blockers as Antihypertensive Agents :

It is found that β_1-receptors are predominant in heart (alongwith few β_2-receptors). Stimulation of β_1-receptors therefore, results in an increase in heart rate and increased force of contraction of heart muscles. Therefore, selective β_1-blockers gained a high clinical importance as antihypertensive agents.

Similarly, β_2-receptors are predominant in lungs particularly bronchial muscles (alongwith few β_1-receptors). Hence, selective β_2-blockers will cause bronchial muscles constriction, a case contraindicated in patients suffering from bronchial asthma and hence clinically useless, but can serve as a research tool for a medicinal chemist to develop new, potent, selective β_1-blockers or antihypertensive agents. Cardioselective β-antagonists are drugs that have much greater affinity for the β_1-receptors of the heart than for β_2 receptors in other tissues. Such agents should have two important features : (a) The lack of an antagonist effect on the β_2-receptor in bronchi. This would make β_1-blockers, safe for use in patients who have bronchial asthma. (b) The absence of blockage of the vascular β_2-receptors (which mediate vasodilation), which otherwise leads to vasoconstriction resulting in increased peripheral resistance, an undesirable effect in antihypertensive activity of non-selective β_2-antagonist. Theoretically, one cannot obtain complete cardioselectivity because of the presence of both β_1- and β_2-receptors in cardiac and lung tissues. Hence, on strict pharmacological ground, antihypertensive agents of this category could be expected to raise rather than lower the arterial pressure by blocking the vasodilation-mediated by vascular β_2-receptor. They are antihyper-tensive and act through the following postulated mechanisms :

(1) Inhibition of renin release.

(2) Inhibition of cardiac output (β_1-blockage).

(3) Inhibition of sympathetic output by central action.

(4) Restoration of vascular relaxation response.

(5) Inhibition of the synaptic norepinephrine release.

Receptor Structure :

The most effective compound, acting on alpha receptor is norepinephrine.

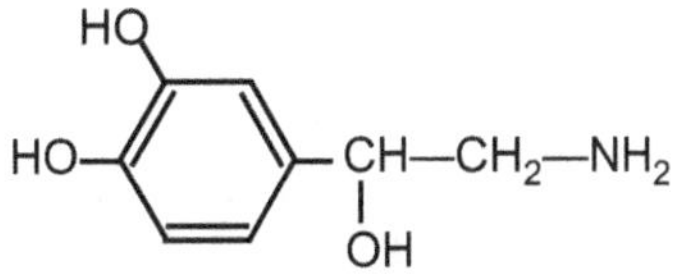

Norepinephrine

The more bulkier the substituents on nitrogen, alpha receptor activity decreases e.g. Isoprenaline.

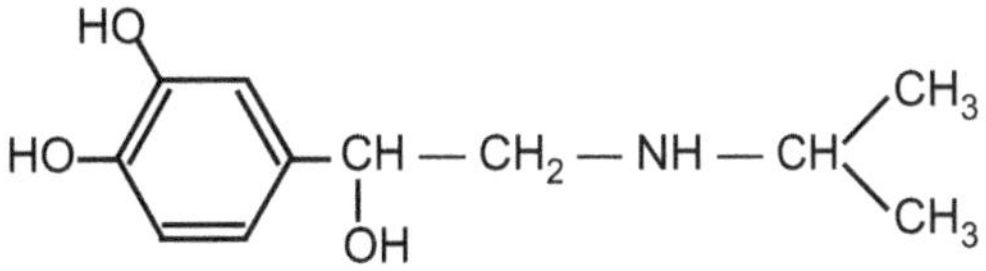

Isoprenaline

α-Receptor :

The α-receptor carries a negatively charged group (probably a phosphate) which will then react with the positively charged ammonium nitrogen.

Bulky substituents present on the nitrogen (as in the case of isoprenaline), would hinder the attack of positively charged cation on phosphate anion. Hence, isoprenaline has less affinity for α-receptors.

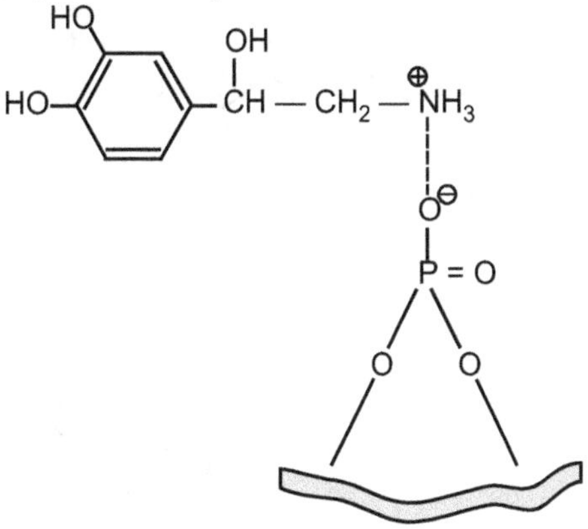

Fig. 3.8 : α-receptor activation

Table 3.7 : Useful β-blocking agents

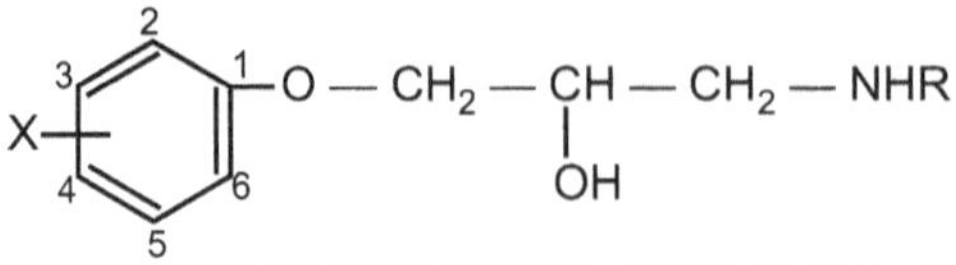

$$X \text{—} \underset{5}{\overset{\overset{2}{\underset{}{}}}{\text{(ring)}}} \text{—} O \text{—} CH_2 \text{—} \underset{\underset{OH}{|}}{CH} \text{—} CH_2 \text{—} NHR$$

Sr. No.	Name	X	R	Selectivity on receptor
1.	Pindolol	2, 3- 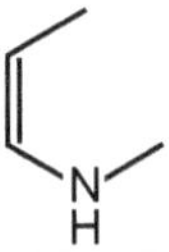 (indole ring)	isopropyl	non-selective
2.	Bunitrolol	2 - CN	t - butyl	non-selective
3.	Nadolol	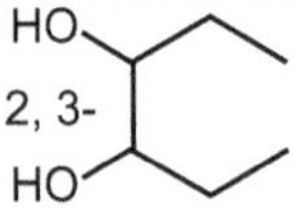 2, 3- (HO, HO cyclohexane ring)	t-butyl	non-selective
3.	Metoprolol	$4\text{-}CH_2CH_2OCH_3$	isopropyl	β_1 - receptor
4.	Atenolol	$4\text{-}CH_2CONH_2$	isopropyl	β_1 - receptor
5.	Acebutolol	$4\text{-}NHCOC_3H_7$	isopropyl	β_1 - receptor
6.	Timolol	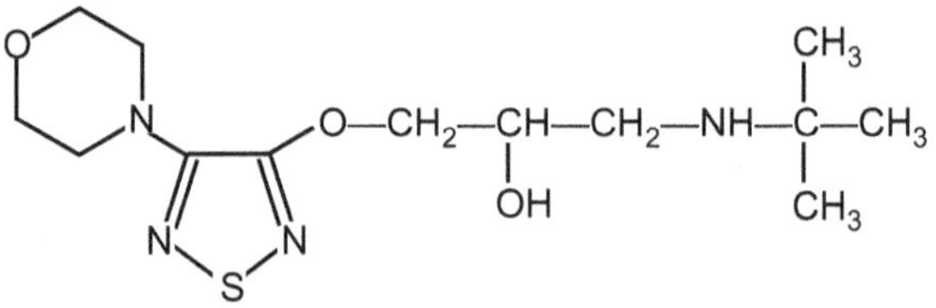		

A new series of selective β_1-blockers replacing N-alkyl groups (e.g. isopropyl, t-butyl) by araalkyl groups was developed which bind to the β_1-receptor through an additional H-bonding interaction.

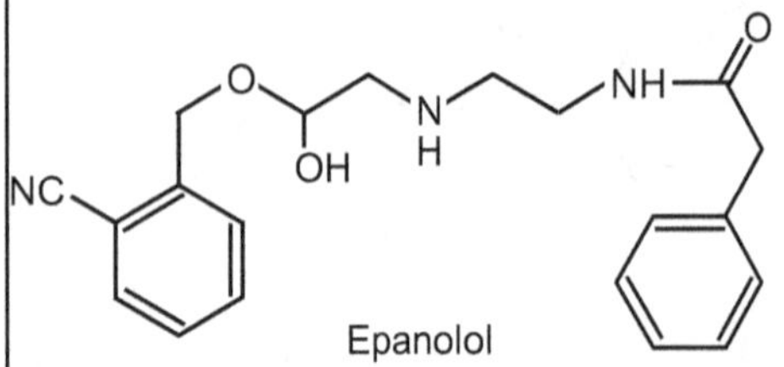

Epanolol

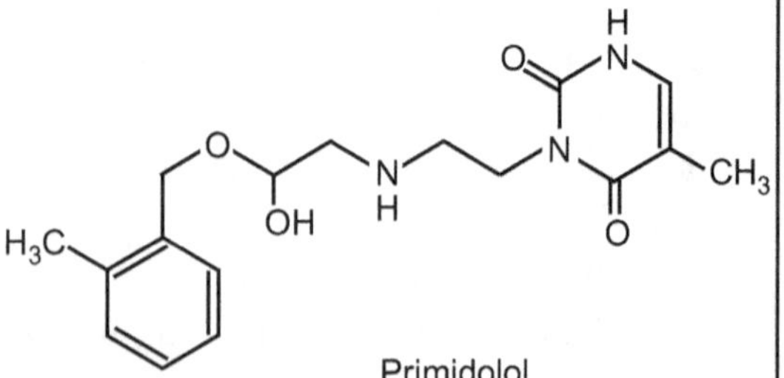

Primidolol

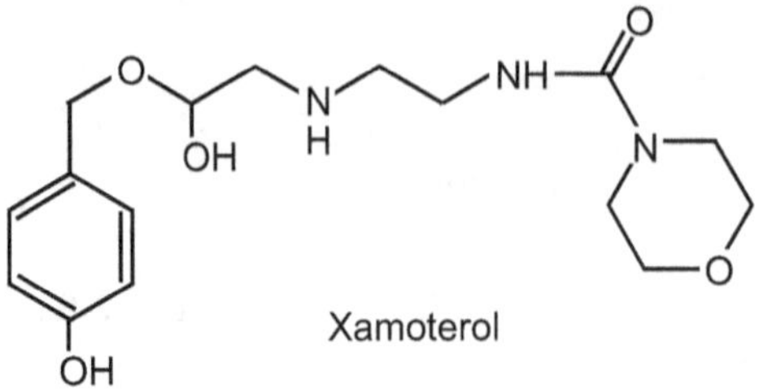

Xamoterol

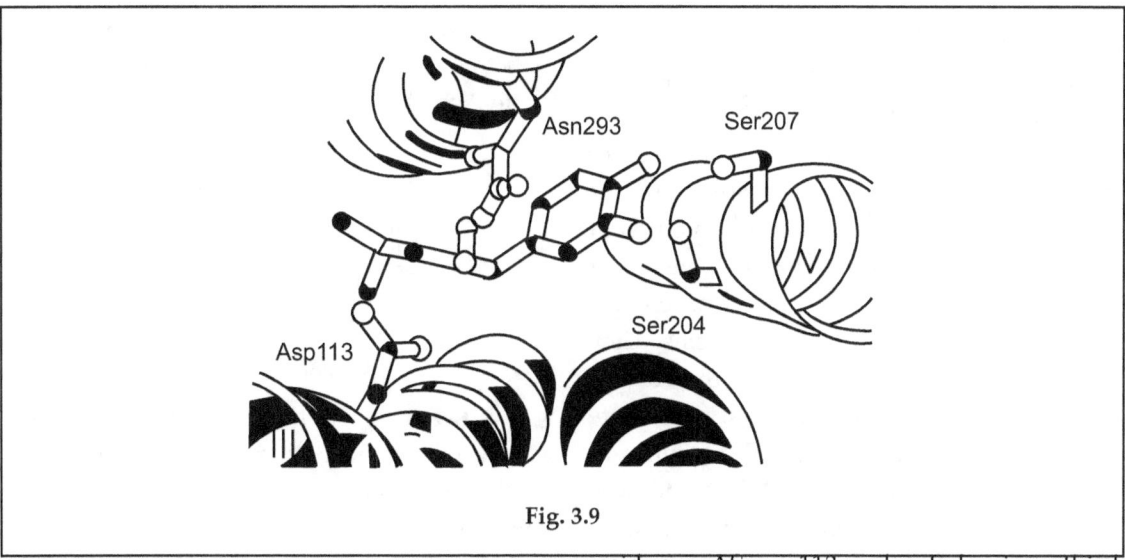

Fig. 3.9

β-Receptor :

The seven α-helices proposed for the β-adrenoceptor are radically arranged around a central "pore" in which the receptor ligands bind. It has been postulated that the phenyl ring of Phe 290 in the sixth transmembrane helix, participate in binding of the aromatic ring of agonist ligands. The m- and p-hydroxyl groups of the catecholamine agonists are postulated to form H-bonds to Ser 204 and Ser 207. The β-hydroxyl group in the side chain may interact with either Ser 165 of transmembrane helix 4 or ASn 293 of transmembrane helix 6. An aspartic acid residue ASp 113, located in third transmembrane spanning helix is required for both agonist and antagonist binding to β-adrenoceptor. The free carboxyl group of this amino acid interacts with the protonated amino group of adrenergic ligand.

Indications of β Blockers :

- Angina pectoris Myocardial infraction
- Thyrotoxicosis Anxiety
- Glaucoma Hypertension
- Cardiac arrhythmias Pheochromocytoma
- Migraine Essential tremors
- Hypertrophic subaortic stenosis

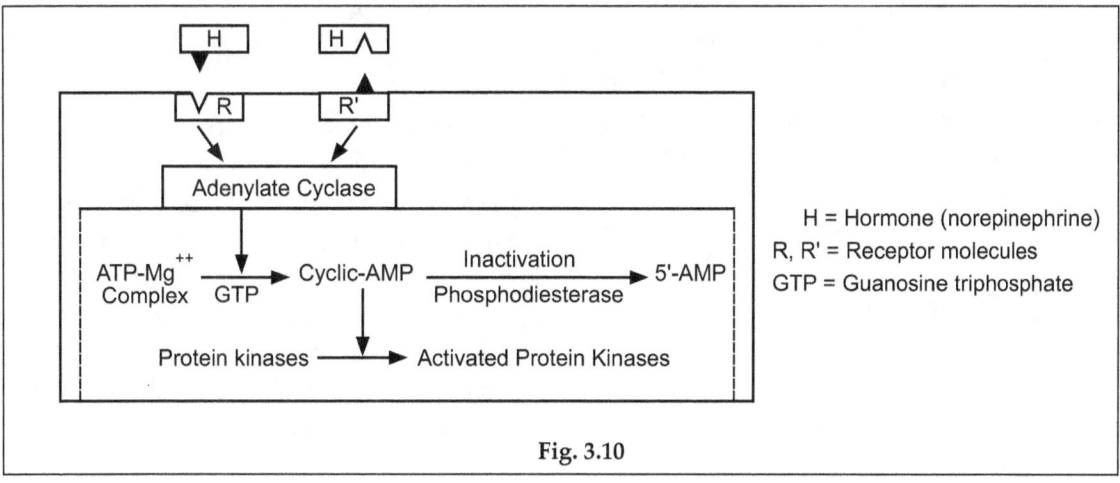

H = Hormone (norepinephrine)
R, R' = Receptor molecules
GTP = Guanosine triphosphate

Fig. 3.10

Post Receptor Binding Events :

Receptors for a number of hormones and autacoids function by regulating the concentration of the intracellular second messenger cyclic adenosine 3', 5'-monophosphate (cyclic AMP) through the stimulation or inhibition of the membrane - bound enzyme, adenylate cyclase. Adenylate cyclase and β-adrenergic receptors are considered to be proteins. They are embedded in lipid matrix of the cellular membrane in such a way that adenylate cyclase faces the intracellular fluid, whereas the receptor faces the extracellular fluid. The activation of adenylate cyclase enzyme leads to the formation of cyclic AMP from Mg^{++} -ATP complex. An additional protein appears to mediate this conversion in guanosine triphosphate (GTP). Similarly, phosphodiesterase enzymes metabolise cyclic AMP to inactive 5' - AMP.

The function of cyclic AMP is to regulate the activity of a class of enzymes, the protein kinases, which activate a wide variety of reactions which are characteristic of β-adrenergic responses e.g. increased cardiac contractility, smooth muscle relaxation, glycogenolysis etc.

Dual-acting Antihypertensive Agents :

Introduction of a known vasodilator moiety into the o-position of a β-blocker, which is known to be sterically undemanding, has given the β-blocker vasodilator prizidolol.

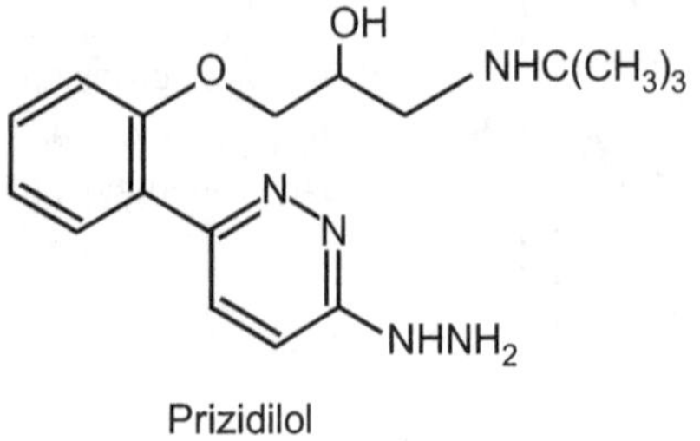

Prizidilol

Isoxaprolol was 16 times more potent than labetolol as a β-blocker and 4-times more potent as an α-blocker.

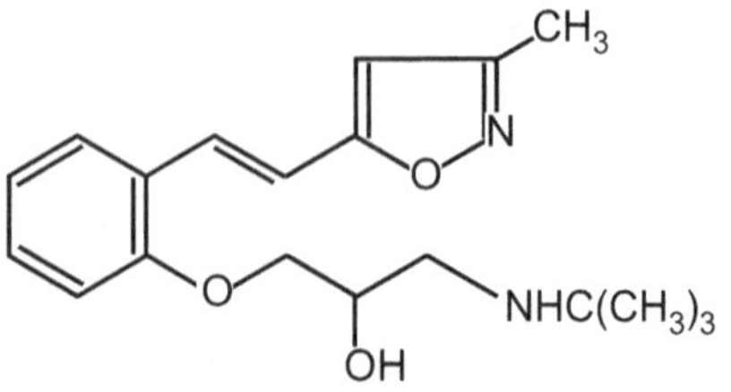

Isoxaprolol

MK-761 (a) was equipotent with timolol as a β—blocker and 3.8-times more potent than hydralazine as a vasodilator, and was not a β_2-agonist.

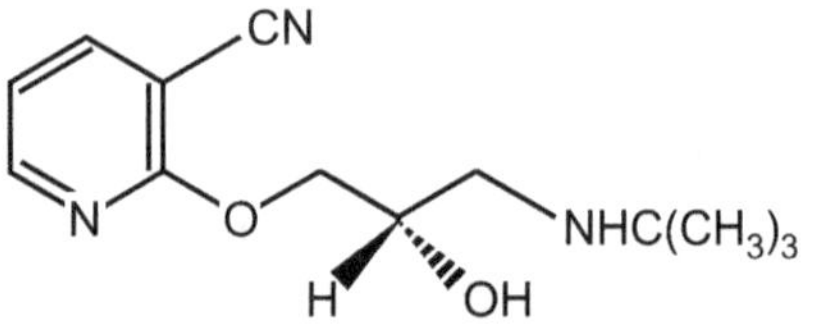

(a)

Although it is not formally described as a combination, β-blocker-nitrate molecule, K 351 (b) clearly owes its vasodilator activity to the presence of the nitrate ester.

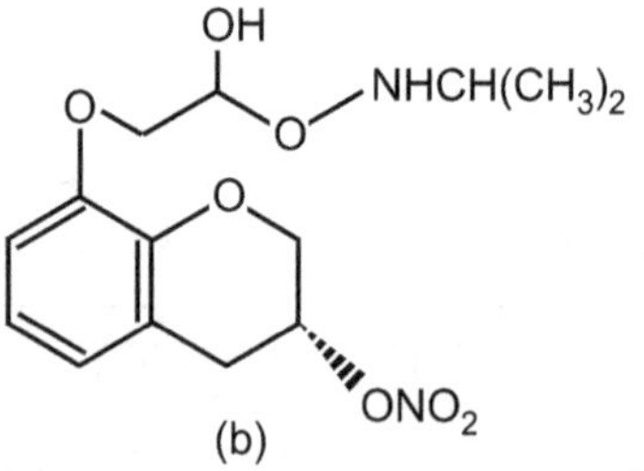

(b)

An extension of the work led to the potent β_2-selective blocker, ICI 118551 (c). A β_2-selectivity ratio of 123 : 1 has been reported from in-vitro studies and greater than 250 : 1 in-vivo. ICI 118551 has no partial agonist activity; it has the same degree of membrane stabilizing activity as propranolol and is currently undergoing clinical evaluation for potential use in migraine and essential tremor.

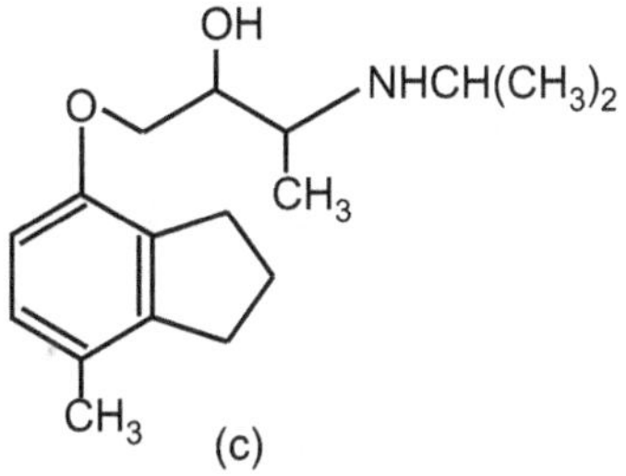

(c)

Spirendolol (LI 32468) (d) is another β_2-selective blocker in clinical trial. It is effective in controlling essential tremor at doses which have no effect on heart rate.

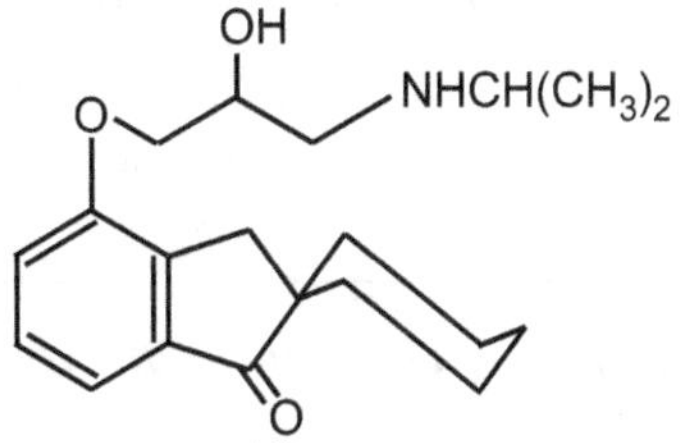

(d)

It was hypothesized that the cardioselectivity was the result of an interaction between the oxygen or sulphur atom and a complementary site on the β-receptor.

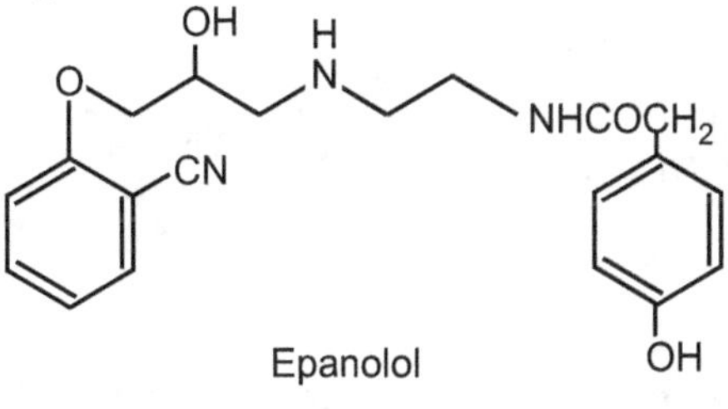

Epanolol

Epanolol (ICI 141292), a cardioselective β–blocker with partial agonist activity, is undergoing clinical evaluation.

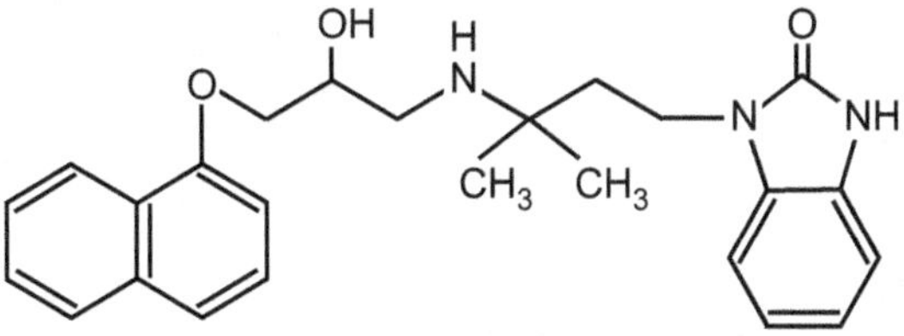

Imidolol

Imidolol is reported to be β-blocker with α–blocking activity.

Structural features of adrenergic receptor subtypes :

The adrenergic receptor subtypes include α_1 (α_{1A}, α_{1B} and α_{1C}), α_2 (α_{2A}, α_{2B} and α_{2C}) and β (β_1, β_2 and β_3). They are all composed of a single polypeptide chain with three intracellular (i), three extracellular (e) and 07 hydrophobic stretches likely to constitute 07 transmembrane domain (tm) spanning the lipid bilayer and they are all coupled to a GTP-binding protein. The α_2-receptor subtype C-terminal regions are shorter than those of the β and much shorter than those of the α_1 subtypes. The human α_2B thus has a 23-residue C-terminus whereas the human α, β C-terminal region is 167 residues long.

Atleast one disulfide bond, probably formed between Cys[106] and Cys[184] in the β_2 receptor has been suggested to be essential for ligand binding by site directed mutageneis. A second disulfide bond may be formed between the Cys[190] are Cys[191] which are only present in the 03 subtypes of β-receptors.

While Asp113, Ser204 and Ser207 which exist in homologous positions in all adrenergic receptors, appear essential for ligand binding, other residues actively participate both in binding and in signal transmission, leading to activation of the a-subunit of the G protein coupled to the receptor. Substitution of these residues results in severe changes in agonist/antagonistic binding potential with the receptor.

Residues composing the amino-and carboxy-terminal segments of the 3rd intracellular loop (i3) appear to constitute the main site of interaction with G proteins.

All adrenergic receptor subtype (except β_3), contain target sites for phosphorylation by protein kinase A. They all occur in the i 3 or carboxyterminal domains close to the sites of G-protein interaction. Absence of these sites prevents agonist promoted desensitization.

Table 3.8 : Comparison of Structural features

Sr. No.	Parameter	α_{1A}	α_{1B}	α_{1C}	α_{2A}	α_{2B}	α_{2C}	β_1	β_2	β_3
01	Chromosome number	5	5	8	10	2	4	10	5	8
02	Protein structure length	515	517	466	450	451	461	477	413	408
03	Glycosylation site (N-terminal)	2	4	3	2	0	2	2	2	2
04	Phosphorylation sites	-	PKA	PKA	PKA β ARK	-	-	PKA β ARK	PKA β ARK	0
05	Prototype tissue	Artery	Heart	-	Brain Platelet	-	Spleen	Heart	Lung	Fat
06	Mechanism of actin	Ca⁺⁺- channel	IP3, DG	IP3 DG	↓cAMP	↓cAMP	↓cAMP	↑cAMP	↑cAMP	↑ cAMP

PKA₁ protein kinase A; βARK, β-adrenergic receptor kinase; IP₃, phosphatidyl inositol triphosphate; DG, diacyl glycerol.

Synthesis

(i) Methyl dopa :

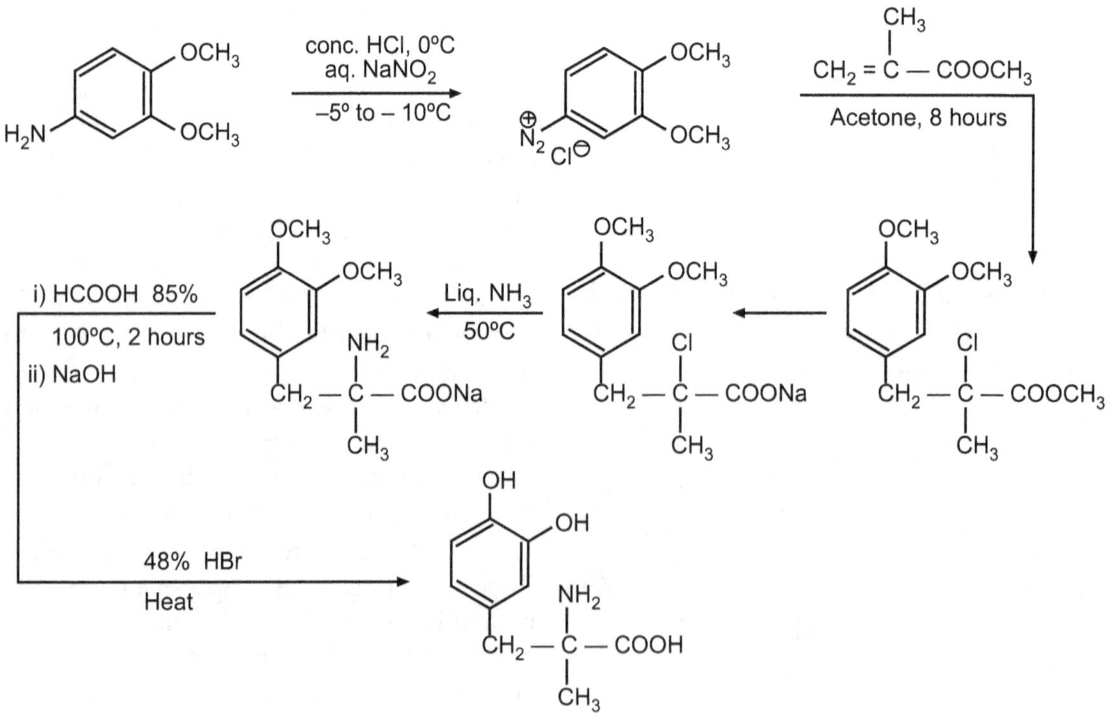

Methyl dopa

(3.29)

(ii) Atenolol :

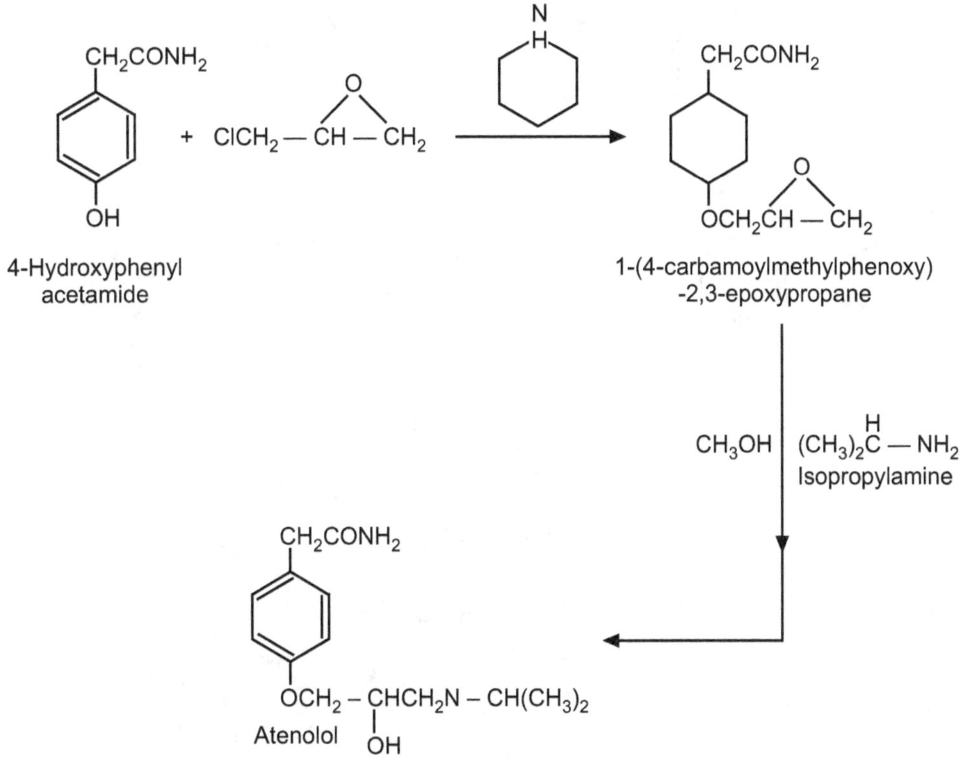

CH2CONH2
OH
+ ClCH2 — CH — CH2
O
N
H
4-Hydroxyphenyl acetamide
1-(4-carbamoylmethylphenoxy) -2,3-epoxypropane
OCH2CH — CH2
CH3OH
(CH3)2C — NH2
H
Isopropylamine
OCH2 – CHCH2N – CH(CH3)2
OH
Atenolol

(iii) Prazocin :

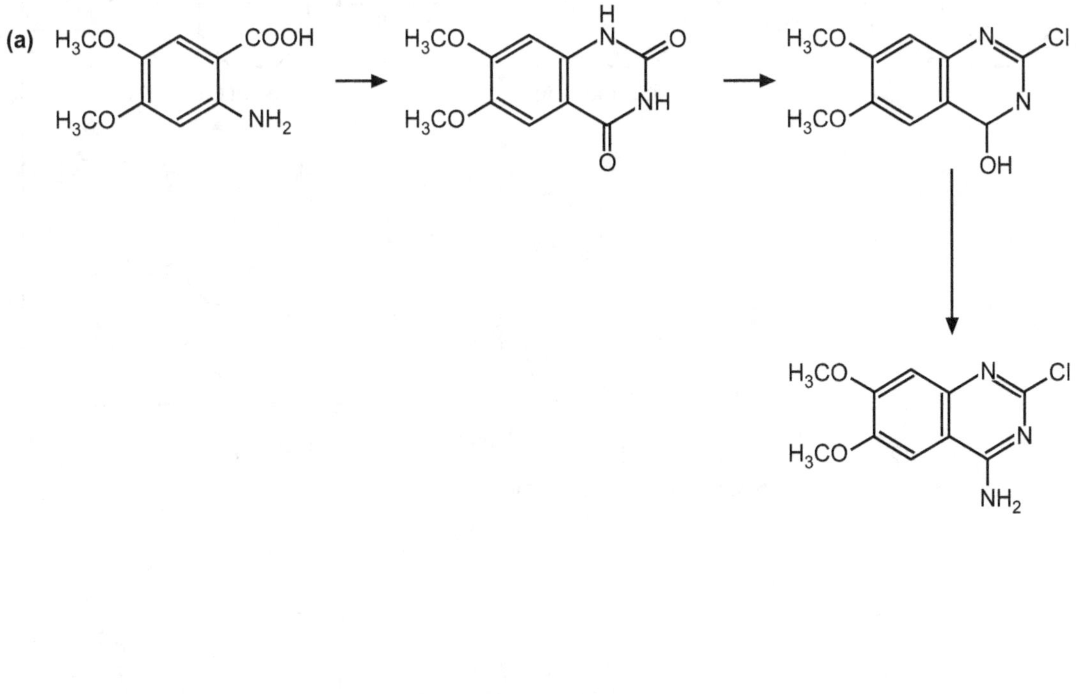

(a)
H3CO
COOH
NH2
NH
O
Cl
N
OH

(b)

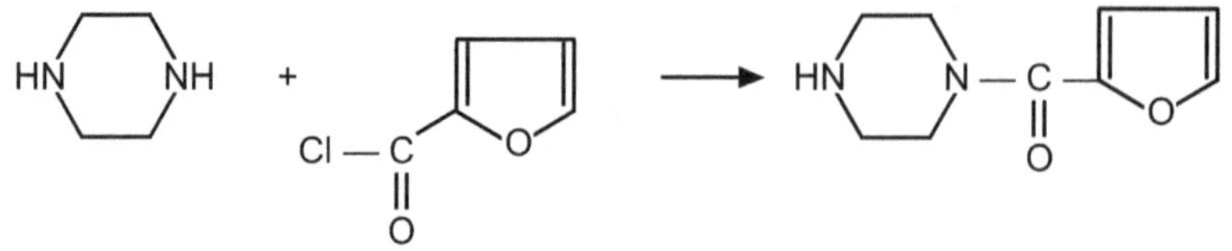

(c)

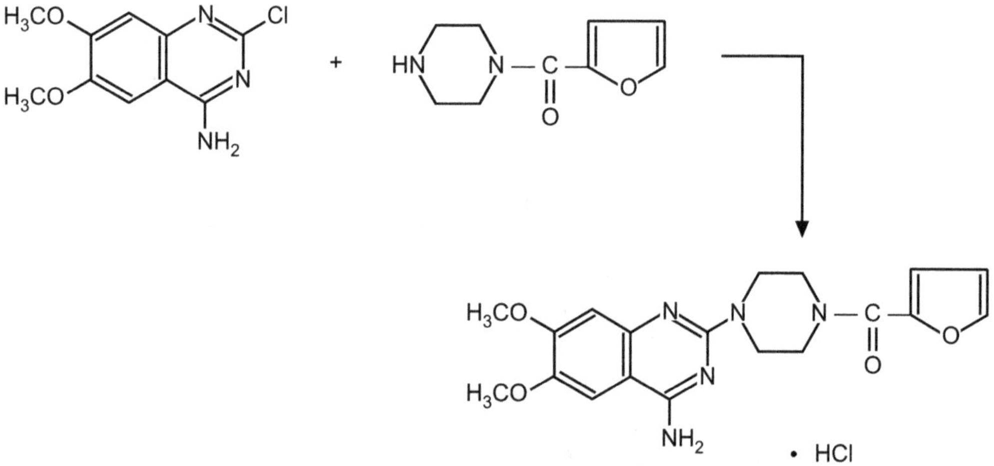

Prazosin hydrochloride

(iv) Guanethidine :

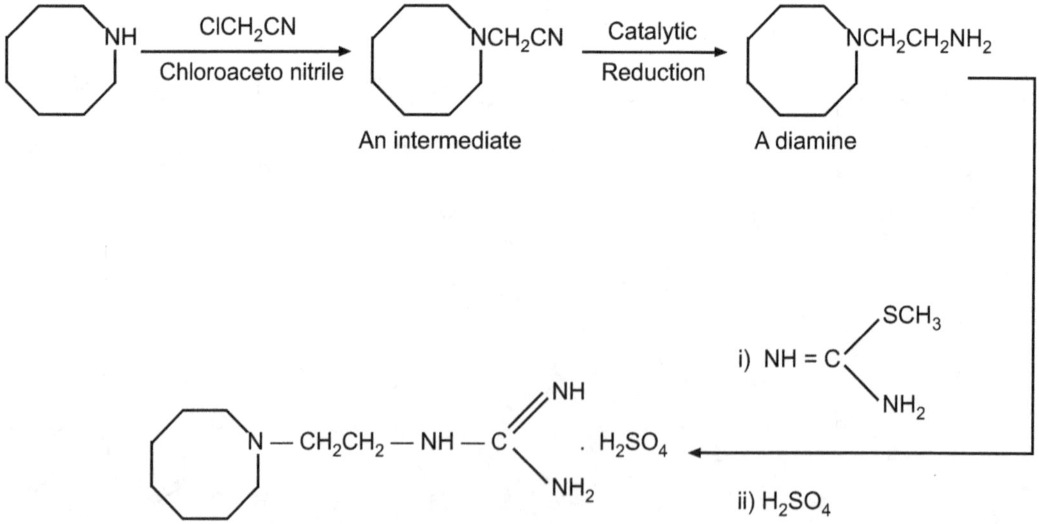

An intermediate   A diamine

i) $NH = C \overset{SCH_3}{\underset{NH_2}{\diagdown}}$

ii) H_2SO_4

Guanethidine monosulphate

(v) Terbutaline :

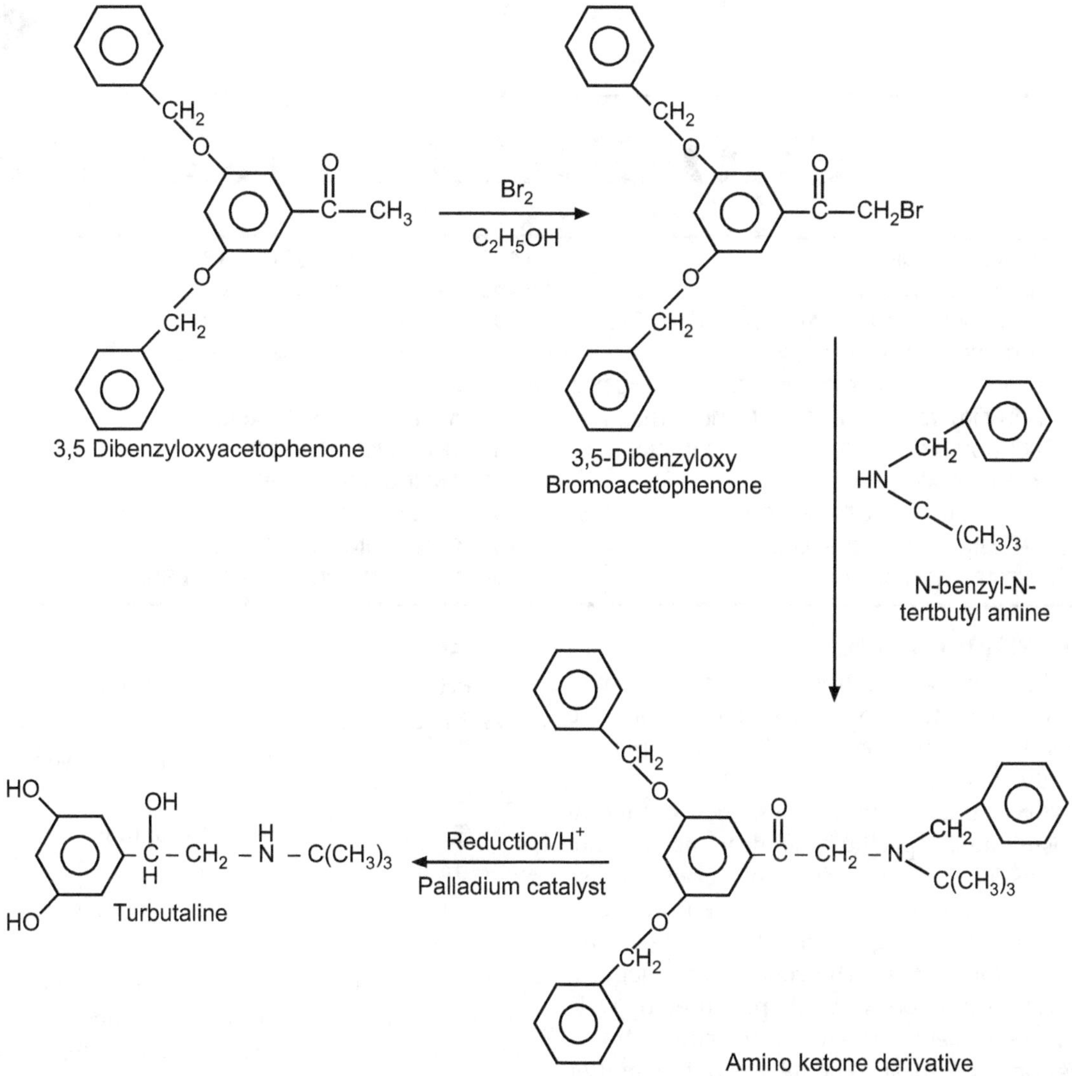

3,5 Dibenzyloxyacetophenone

$\xrightarrow[\text{C}_2\text{H}_5\text{OH}]{\text{Br}_2}$

3,5-Dibenzyloxy
Bromoacetophenone

N-benzyl-N-
tertbutyl amine

$\xleftarrow[\text{Palladium catalyst}]{\text{Reduction/H}^+}$

Turbutaline

Amino ketone derivative

❖ ❖ ❖

4

CHOLINERGIC AGENTS

4.1 INTRODUCTION

Cellular systems for the transduction of external stimuli into intracellular signals are essential components of the plasma membranes.

According to the theory of neurohumoral transmission, specific chemical agents are responsible for transmission of nerve impulse across most synapses and neuro-effector junctions. These agents are known as *neurohumoral transmitters*. The concept of "chemical neurotransmission" was first proposed by Dale and co-workers, instead of "electrical transmission" hypothesis. The release of transmitter substances occurs when the nerve impulse elicits the responses at smooth, cardiac and skeletal muscles, exocrine glands and postsynaptic neurons. These neurotransmitters cross the synapse or the neuro-effector junction to initiate activity in another neuron or in a muscle or a gland cell by interacting with the postsynaptic receptors. A clear understanding of the impulse transmission therefore, is essential to study the pharmacology of the drugs acting on autonomic nervous system.

4.2 NERVOUS SYSTEM

Principally the nervous system may be described as a device of,

(1) receiving information (i.e. sensory input),

(2) processing information (i.e. integration) and

(3) transmitting information (i.e. motor output).

The fundamental unit of a nervous system is the neuron or a nerve cell. Each neuron consists of a nucleus and a cell body i.e., stems (an extensive network of branches), the axon (long process) and the dendrites (short process).

The surface membrane of a neuron consists of a semipermeable layer of lipoproteins. The composition of salt solution inside the membrane is usually different from that on the outside. This is due to differences in the permeability of the membrane to the various ions like Na^+, K^+, Ca^{++}, Cl^-, HCO_3^- etc.

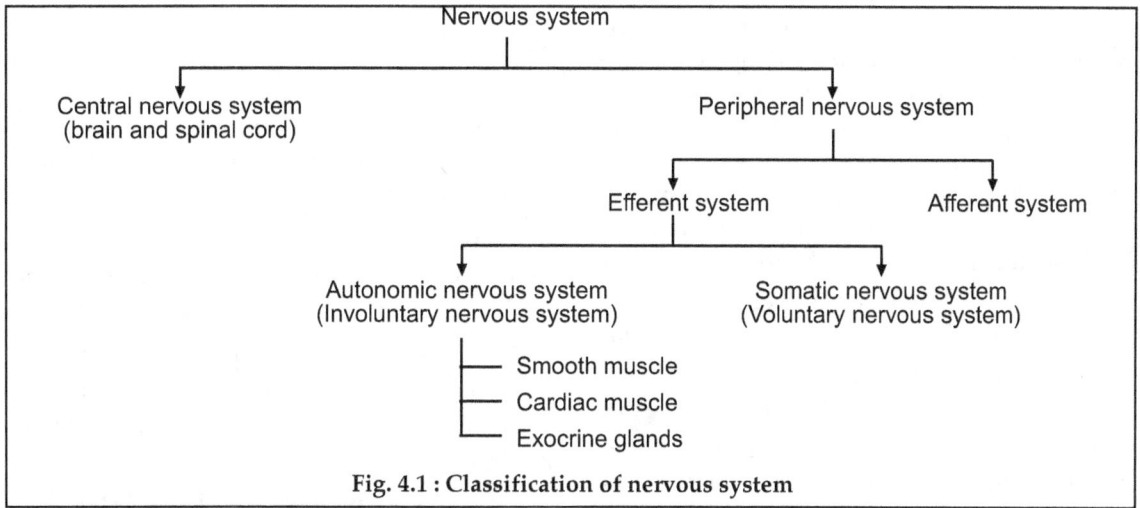

Fig. 4.1 : Classification of nervous system

In the resting state, the inside of neuronal membrane is more negative than the outside. This normal situation is known as resting state or polarised state. When any exogenous stimulus is applied; a change in the electrical activity occurs within the neuron. At the point, where an exogenous stimulus occurs, the inside of neuronal membrane becomes positive than the outside. As a result, local action currents are set up, which have the effect of transferring the area of reversed polarisation to an adjoining region of the nerve while normal resting conditions are re-established in the previously stimulated area.

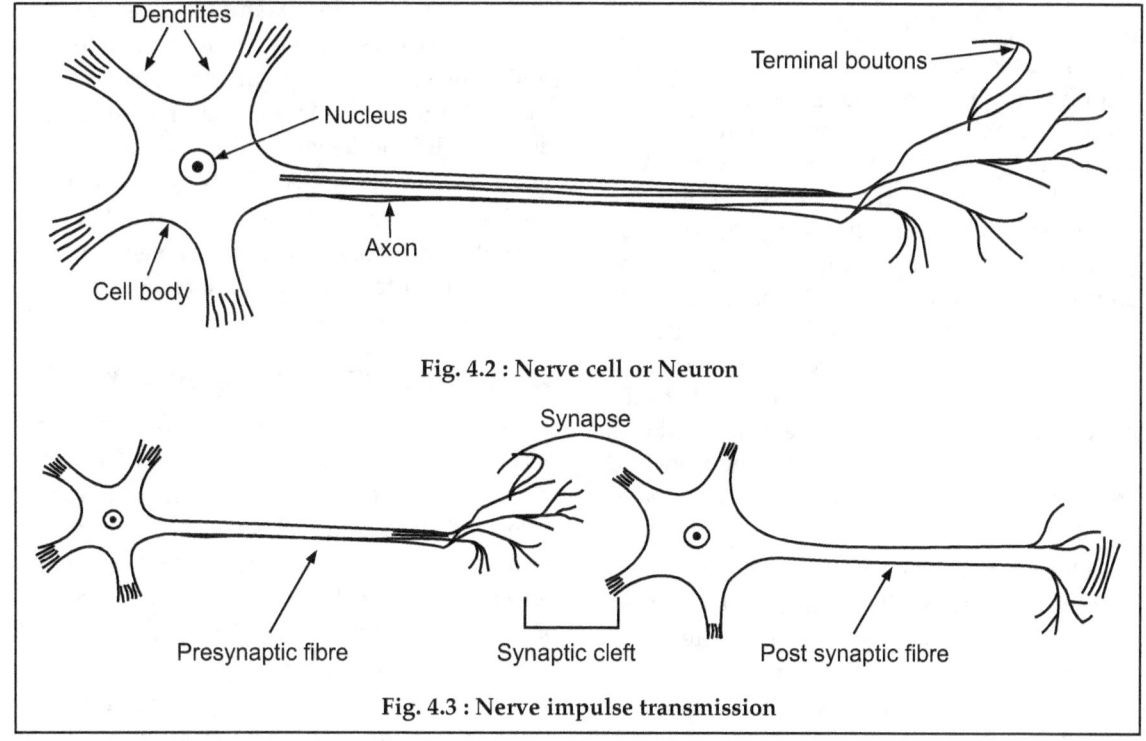

Fig. 4.2 : Nerve cell or Neuron

Fig. 4.3 : Nerve impulse transmission

In this way, the path of reversed polarisation is transmitted along with the nerve. The process is continued until the whole length of the nerve has been visited by the impulse. The nerve impulse, in other words, jumps from one patch to other patch. As soon as this impulse reaches the terminal boutons, it activates the influx of extracellular Ca^{++} ions. These ions, upon their entry in the cytoplasm lead to the release of intracellular Ca^{++} ions from the sacs present on sarcoplasmic reticulum. When the cytoplasmic concentration of Ca^{++} ions reaches a threshold value, the storage granules for neurotransmitter get ruptured and a discrete amount of neurotransmitter is discharged from the presynaptic nerve endings into the synaptic cleft. The synaptic cleft or junctional cleft is generally about $200 - 400A°$ wide but in some blood vessels, it may be as wide as $10,000$ A $°$.

The transmitter, then diffuses across the synaptic space and binds to the receptor sites present on the cell body of post-synaptic neuron. This binding causes conformational changes in these receptors, which in turn, produce a change in ion-permeability of the axon membrane of post-synaptic neuron. As a result, local action currents are set up into the post-synaptic neuron. The post-synaptic axon branches many times upon entering the effector tissue forming a plexus among the innervated cells. The release of neuro-transmitter from post-synaptic nerve terminals into the neuro-effector space then leads to the biological response in a muscle or a gland cell. This synapse between a motor neuron and effector cell is also termed as a neuro-effector junction.

Once the neurotransmitter has interacted with the receptors, it is either removed by active uptake processes back to the terminal boutons of pre-synaptic neuron or by surrounding glial cells where it is destroyed by metabolic deactivation.

4.3 NEURO-CHEMICAL TRANSMITTERS

Following are the examples of chemical agents that act as neuro-chemical transmitters in nervous system.

(a) Aspartic acid, taurine, glycine, gamma amino butyric acid (GABA), and glutamic acid. These can be grouped as amino acids.

(b) Acetylcholine, dopamine, tyramine, norepinephrine, epinephrine, histamine and serotonin (5-HT). These can be grouped as amines.

(c) **Miscellaneous :** Peptide substance P, ATP, c-AMP, c-GMP, prostaglandin E, enke-phalins, neurotensin, cholecystokinin etc.

Neurotransmitters have an ability to initiate the impulse propagation. Certain substances do not initiate the process of impulse transmission but can modify it.

Such substances are termed as modulators of transmission. For example, most of the autonomic drugs act either by mimicking or modifying the actions of the neurotransmitter released by the autonomic fibres at either synaptic cleft or effector cells. Besides this, the nerve cell is provided with a number of feedback control systems which regulate the biosynthesis, release and metabolism of the neurotransmitter and thus exercise a control over the biological response.

4.4 AUTONOMIC NERVOUS SYSTEM

The ANS consists of central and the peripheral components. It is evident from the investigations that elicitation of autonomic reflexes (e.g. blood pressure changes, vaso-motor responses to alterations of body temperature, sweating, constriction of urinary bladder) can occur at the level of the spinal cord. However, integration of many auto-nomic functions occurs at supraspinal levels. Thus, regulation of respiration and blood pressure is integrated in medulla. The hypo-thalamus plays a prominent role in integration of various autonomic functions, e.g. regulation of blood pressure, sleep, emotions, sexual reflexes and carbohydrate-fat metabolism. Posterior and lateral hypothalamic nuclei are connected with the sympathoadrenal system, while anterior and midline nuclei are concerned with parasympathetic functions. The posterio-medial hypothalamus is involved in the modulation of the baro-receptor reflex. The other higher centres involved in the integration of various autonomic functions include the neostratum, limbic system and cerebral cortex.

The autonomic nervous system controls all involuntary actions aimed to maintain the constancy of the internal environment. It provides a homeostasis for the regulation of all metabolic changes which are essential for life. The ANS is termed as the visceral, vegetative or involuntary nervous system. In the periphery, it functions through nerves, ganglia and plexuses and regulates autonomic functions which are not under the conscious control. These include, breathing, regulation of the cardiovascular system, glandular secretions, digestion, body temperature and metabolism. Except skeletal muscles, all innervated organs of the body, are supplied with efferent nerves of ANS, while skeletal muscles are provided with somatic nerves. Thus, ANS is essentially a motor system. The sensory fibres are numerous than autonomic motor nerves and they pass into the cerebrospinal axis via either somatic nerves or various ramifications of ANS without synaptic interruption.

Hypothalamus is a principle control centre for organisation and co-ordination of the autonomic nervous system. The cells of the adrenal medulla constitute an integral part of the ANS, which upon activation, release epinephrine and norepinephrine into the circulation.

4.5 DIVISIONS OF AUTONOMIC NERVOUS SYSTEM

The autonomic nervous system controls tissues, e.g., glands, smooth muscles and cardiac muscles that are not under voluntary control. It consists of two main divisions :

(a) Sympathetic nervous system and

(b) Parasympathetic nervous system.

Both these divisions have essentially opposite actions. The sympathetic nervous system is associated with catabolic effects whereas parasympathetic nervous system is characterised by its anabolic effects.

The principle neurotransmitter present in parasympathetic nerves liberate acetylcholine.

(i) The pre-ganglionic and post-ganglionic fibres of the parasympathetic nerves liberate acetylcholine.

(ii) The pre-ganglionic fibres and some postganglionic fibres (e.g., salivary glands) of sympathetic nerves liberate acetylcholine.

(iii) All autonomic ganglia and skeletal muscle end plate region need acetylcholine as a neurotransmitter to evoke biological response. The end plate is a specialised region of the muscle with which the terminal ramifications of the motor nerve fibres are associated. The ganglionic transmission is a highly complex process and several secondary transmitters or modulators either enhance or diminish the sensitivity of the post-ganglionic cell to acetylcholine.

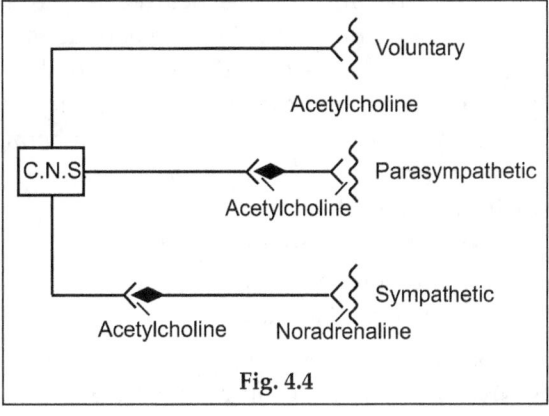

Fig. 4.4

Stimulation of parasympathetic nervous system induces the constriction of the pupils and bronchi, decrease in heart activity and an increase in the activity of the digestive system- salivation and GIT secretions are promoted, the motility of the intestine is increased.

Similarly the principal neurotransmitters present in the sympathetic nervous system include epinephrine (adrenaline), norepinephrine (noradrenaline) and dopamine. The post-ganglionic fibres of the sympathetic nerves with few exceptions, bring about their effects by the liberation of norepinephrine.

Stimulation of the sympathetic nervous system causes dilation of the pupils, acceleration of rate of (positive chronotropic) and the force of (positive inotropic) heart contraction, peripheral vasoconstriction, glycogenolysis, inhibition of intestinal motility and of gastrointestinal secretory activity (except salivary gland).

When the transmitter substance reacts with the post-synaptic receptors, it may produce either excitation or inhibition. The action of the transmitter results in selective increase or decrease of ionic permeability of membrane for ions. In inhibition, there is a negligible change in the ion potential and the fibre remains at near to the resting potential, thereby preventing the fibre to get in an excited position.

The transmitters in the neurons are in a state of flux, being continuously biosynthesised, released and metabolised, thus producing profound changes in the activity of the nerves. The nerves in the peripheral nervous system are classified on the basis of their functions into,

(1) Sensory (afferent) neuron,

(2) Motor (efferent) neuron and

(3) Internuncial neuron.

Sensory neurons transmit impulses from CNS to or towards the muscle or tissues.

Internuncial neurons are located in CNS and they transmit impulses from sensory to the motor neurons.

Many neurotransmitters play an important role in the propagation of the nerve impulse in the sensory neurons. These include substance P, somatostatin, vasoactive intestinal polypeptides and cholecystokinin.

H-Arg-Pro-Lys-Pro-Gln-Gln-Phe-Phe-Gly-Leu-Met-NH$_2$

Substance P

The efferent (motor) nervous system of ANS can be broadly categorised into,

(a) Parasympathetic (or craniosacral) division and,

(b) Sympathetic (or thoracolumbar) division.

This classification is mainly based upon the type of neurotransmitter that predominates in each division.

The cholinergic nervous system consists of pre-ganglionic and post-ganglionic fibres. The pre-ganglionic fibres have their origin in midbrain, medulla oblongata and the sacral part of the spinal cord. Thus, the principal site of control and co-ordination of both sympathetic and parasympathetic nervous system is hypothalamus. The hypothalamus along with cerebral cortex serves as a locus of integration of the entire autonomic nervous system. Hypothalamus also plays an important role in the regulation of gastrointestinal, cardiovascular, sexual, emotional and the functioning of limbic system.

In contrast to other cholinergically innervated organs, the cardiac impulse conduction system (i.e. S-A node, atrium, A-V node and the His-perkinje system) has its own activity where the conduction of impulse can be influenced but not initiated by autonomic nervous system. In cardiac cell, cholinergic influence results into inhibitory response due to hyperpolarization. The hyperpolarization results due to the increased permeability of the axon membrane to potassium ions.

In parasympathetic division, a preganglionic fibre synapses with one or at the most two post-ganglionic neurons. The synapses are located very close to or within the organ innervated. Due to the limited distribution, parasympathetic preganglionic neurons can affect only specific organ and do not influence a wide region of the body. In contrast to this, sympathetic synapses are located in the vertebral and prevertebral ganglia. Hence, a single sympathetic preganglionic fibre may synapse with 60 to 189 post-ganglionic neurons provided to a widely separated regions of the body. Naturally upon activation, sympathetic nervous system can evoke and influence the biological activities of the whole body. The area of functioning of parasympathetic division is thus limited and involves accumulation and preservation of body resources. While sympathetic division regulates body compartments of vital importance and prepares the person in conditions of stress and emergencies. Its stimulation results in a generalised somatic or mass reflex action.

(a) Parasympathetic Nervous System :

Acetylcholine is the neurotransmitter which propagates impulse transmission in the parasympathetic division. Besides this, acetylcholine also functions as a neurotransmitter in,

(i) Motor nerves to skeletal muscles and

(ii) Certain neurons within CNS.

Reid Hunt and Taveau (1906) were first to report the properties of acetylcholine. In 1921, Otto Loewi, a German pharmacologist identified the nervous stimulation of the heart as a chemically mediated event. Loewi then, along with Navratil demonstrated in 1926 that acetylcholine functions as a neurotransmitter in cholinergic nerves. This was later confirmed by Dale and Feldeberg in 1934 on stimulation of vagal fibres to the stomach.

The three important responses mediated by acetylcholine in man or laboratory animals include

1. Contraction of smooth muscles.

2. Cardiac inhibition and

3. Peripheral vasodilation.

Since upon stimulation, parasympathetic nerve fibre liberates acetylcholine, the parasympathetic division is also termed as cholinergic nervous system. The terms cholinergic and adrenergic were first presented by Dale to denote neurons that release acetylcholine and norepinephrine respectively.

Acetylcholine is biosynthesised by the acetylation of choline molecule. Choline itself has a weak parasympathomimetic activity and upon injection, causes a fall in blood pressure. Acetylcholine is about 10,000 times more active than choline molecule.

Acetylcholine is biosynthesised in the nerve terminals as shown in Fig. 4.5.

Active transport mechanisms are involved in picking up choline molecules from the extrasynaptic fluid into the exoplasm. This transport is dependent upon the intracellular concentration of Na^+ and K^+ ions. The choline molecule is acetylated in the cytoplasm by acetyl coenzyme A which is biosynthesised in the mitochondria present in the nerve terminal. The acetylation of choline is catalysed by choline acetyl transferase enzyme. The enzyme is synthesised within the perikaryon and has a molecular weight of about 68,000. In peripheral cholinergic nerves, it is usually present in higher concentrations. As soon as acetylcholine is synthesised, it is sequestered within the synaptic vesicles.

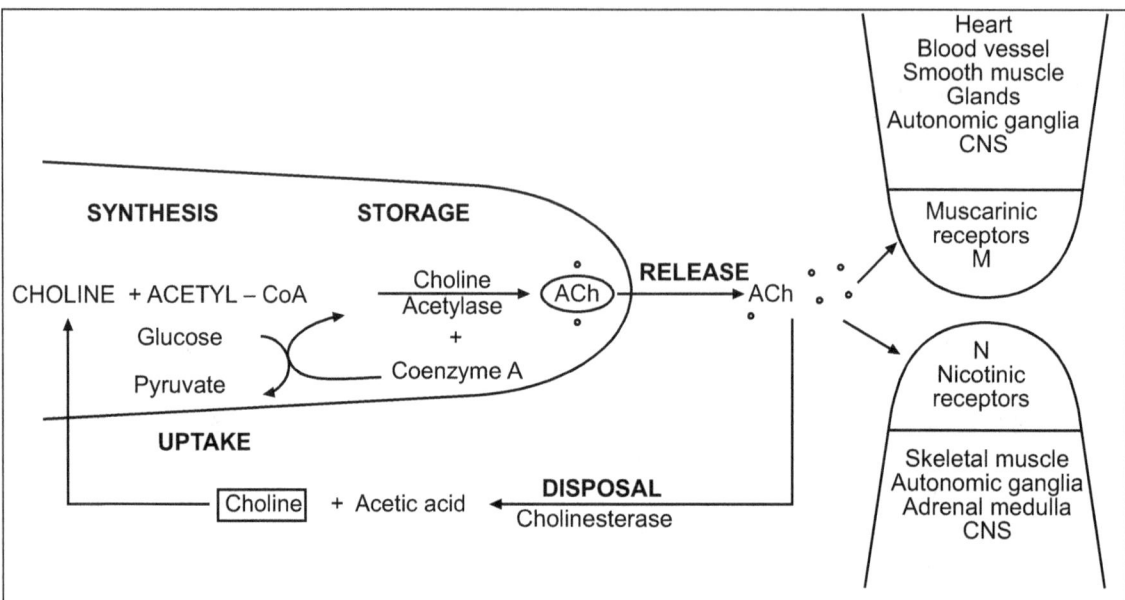

Fig. 4.5 : Biosynthesis of acetylcholine

Site 1 : Acetylcholine synthesis can be blocked by styryl pyridine derivatives such as NVP.

Site 2 : Acetylcholine transport into vesicles is blocked by vesamicol (AH 5183). (±) Vesamicol is a potent inhibitor of vesicular ACh storage with L (-)-Vesamicol being more potent than D(+) - Vesamicol.

Site 3 : Release is promoted by β-bungarotoxin, black widow spider venom, and Ca^{++}. Release is blocked by botulinum toxin, cytochalasin B, collagenase pre-treatment, and Mg^{++}.

Site 4 : Postsynaptic receptors are activated by cholinomimetic drugs and anticholinesterases. Nicotinic receptors, at least in the peripheral nervous system, are blocked by rabies virus, curare hex amethonium, or dihydro-β-erythroidine; n-methylcarbamylcholine and dimethylphenyl piperazinium are nicotinic agonists. Muscarinic receptors are blocked by atropine, pirenzepine, and quinuclidinyl benzilate.

Site 5 : Presynaptic muscarinic receptors may be blocked by AFDX - 116 (an M_2 - antagonist), atropine or quinuclidinyl benzilate. Muscarinic agonists (e.g. oxotremorine) will inhibit the evoked release of acetylcholine by acting on these receptors.

Site 6 : Acetylcholinesterase is inhibited reversibly by physostigmine (eserine) or irreversibly by DFP.

Site 7 : Choline uptake competitive blockers include hemicholinium 3, troxypyrrolium tosylate.

The biosynthesised acetylcholine is stored within the synaptic vesicles immediately inside the membrane of the nerve terminal. Each vesicle is expected to contain about 5,000 - 10,000 molecules of acetylcholine. The number of such vesicles present in the nerve terminal varies in different organs. For example, a motor nerve terminal may contain 300,000 or more synaptic vesicles.

When an impulse reaches to nerve terminal depolarisation causes an activation of calcium ionophore. It allows an influx of extracellular calcium ions which is an essential step for the rupturing of storage vesicles of almost all neurotransmitters. The extracellular calcium then leads to the release of acetylcholine from the vesicles. Four calcium ions are taken up for each molecule of acetyl-choline released. The ruptured synaptic vesicles again re-shape to store fresh neurotransmitter.

The vesicular release of acetylcholine is reported to be inhibited by excess of magnesium ions. The released acetylcholine along with extracellular calcium ions then mobilise intracellular calcium ions from the sacs present on sarcoplasmic reticulum. The increase in the concentration of free intracellular calcium ions then activates calmodulin dependent myosin light chain kinase and phosphorylation of myosin, in turn, creates the conditions that initiate muscle contraction. In general, minimum concentration of calcium ions needed to evoke muscle contraction is estimated to be 10^{-6} mol/litre.

The free acetylcholine present in blood and other tissues, gets quickly hydrolysed by either e-cholinesterase (present in erythrocytes) or s-cholinesterase (present in serum). Upon hydrolysis, acetylcholine is converted into acetic acid and choline molecule.

The cholinesterase enzyme is present in high concentration in the synapses of both, cholinergic and somatic nerves and striated muscle. Hydrolysis occurs in the immediate vicinity of the nerve ending. At the neuro-muscular junction, hydrolysis occurs at the end plate region after acetylcholine has initiated the muscle twitch. In the autonomic ganglia, cholinesterase is usually present in the preganglionic fibre. While serum esterase is present in glial cells, plasma, liver and at other sites.

Cholinesterase enzymes are present in two different forms.

(i) Simple oligomers of a 70,000 dalton catalytic subunit, and

(ii) Elongated forms of complex structure.

The cholinesterases are not very selective enzymes. Both these types hydrolyse a large number of esters, both of, choline and other carboxylic acids. Cholinesterase is one of the most efficient enzyme present in the body. It can hydrolyse about 3×10^5 acetylcholine molecules per mole per minute.

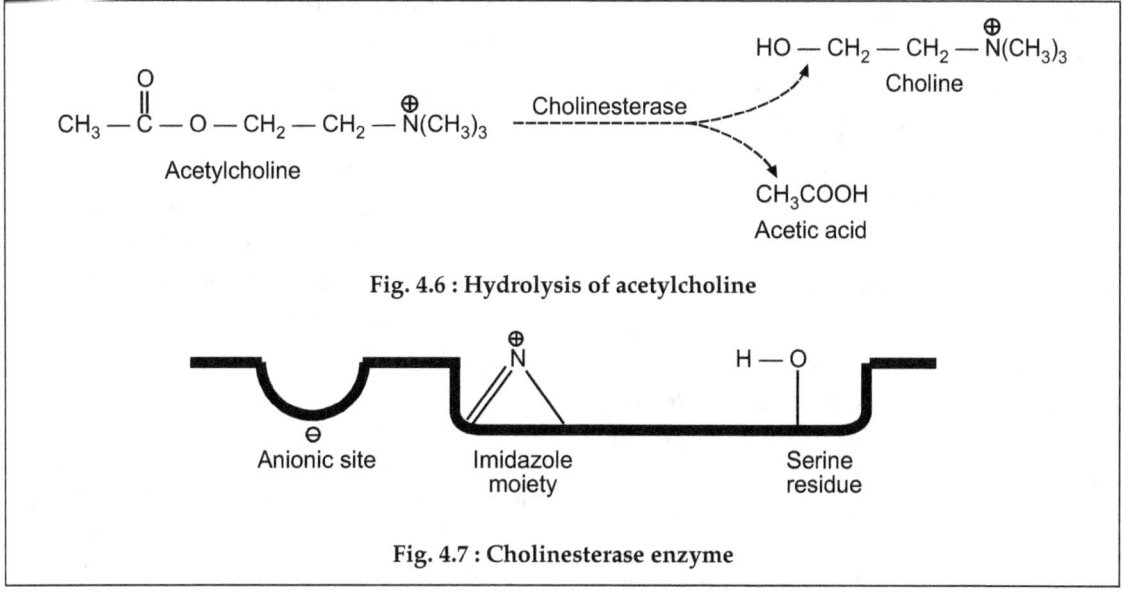

Fig. 4.6 : Hydrolysis of acetylcholine

Fig. 4.7 : Cholinesterase enzyme

During hydrolysis, acetylcholine binds with the enzyme surface through tetrahedral orientation. The tetrahedral intermediate then gets converted first to choline and then to acetic acid.

If the enzymatic hydrolysis of acetylcholine is inhibited, it will lead to prolongation and potentiation of neurotransmitter action. This can be done by the inhibition of cholinesterase enzyme.

Muscarine is a naturally occurring plant alkaloid, obtained from the poisonous mushroom, Amanita muscaria. Its actions on the smooth muscle, cardiac muscles, exocrine glands and its vascular effects are very much alike to that exhibited by acetylcholine.

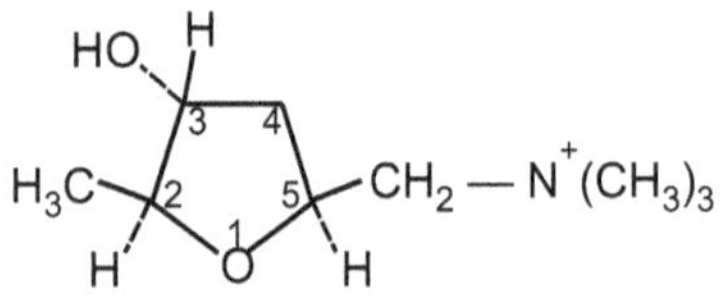

Cis-L–(+) muscarine

Similarly nicotine, yet another alkaloid, mimics the actions of acetylcholine on autonomic ganglia and the adrenal glands. Hence, it was proposed that acetylcholine exhibits some of its action via muscarinic receptors while remaining actions are propagated through the nicotinic receptors.

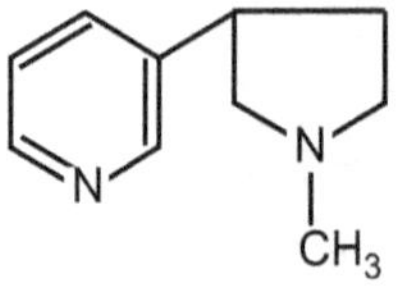

Nicotine

Muscarinic receptors are further subdivided into M_1 (neuronal type), M_2 (cardiac type) and M_3 (smooth muscles/glandular type) depending upon the selectivity of certain agonists and antagonists. The prototype of M_1-selective agonist is the quaternary ammonium compound McN-A343. The corresponding M_1-selective antagonists

are tertiary amine, pirenzepine and the quaternary ammonium compound, o-methoxy-sila-hexocyclium. Pirenzepine is a valuable drug in the treatment of peptic ulcer.

N-Ethyl-guvacine-propargyl ester was found to be a potent partial M_2 agonist in the heart but a competitive antagonist at ileal M3-receptors.

M_2-selective antagonists include pirenzepine derivative AF-DX 116, the alkaloid himbacine and polymethylene tetra-amine methoctamine. M_2-receptor agonists may become useful in lowering heart rate in patients with tachyarrhythmias, whereas M_2-selective antagonists are regarded as promising drugs in the therapy of bradycardia. M_3-selective antagonists are expected to serve as antispasmodics with minor side-effects.

The nicotinic cholinergic receptor is a protein of five sub-units (i.e. α_2, β, γ, δ) having a molecular weight of about 280,000 and is embedded into the cell surface membrane.

The actions of acetylcholine thus, are classified into :

(I) Muscarinic actions :

These include,

(1) Cardiac inhibition

(2) Peripheral vasodilation

(3) Constriction of the eye pupils

(4) Increased salivation and increased flow of secretory glands and

(5) Contractions and peristaltic action on the GIT and urinary tract.

All muscarinic actions are antagonised by atropine.

(II) Nicotinic actions :

Nicotinic receptors occur at striated muscle and at autonomic ganglia. Nicotine first stimulates and then paralyses all autonomic ganglia. The nicotinic actions are thereby involved in the stimulation and maintenance of tone of the skeletal muscle. These actions are not antagonised by atropine. Nicotinic receptors (N_1) at the neuromuscular junction are activated by phenyl-trimethyl-ammonium and are blocked by deca-methonium, succinylcholine and d-tubocurarine. Nicotinic receptors (N_2) in autonomic ganglia are activated by tetramethylammonium and are blocked by hexamethonium and trimethaphan.

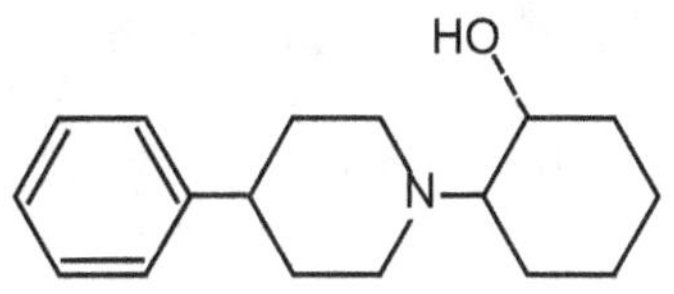

Vesamicol (AH5 183)

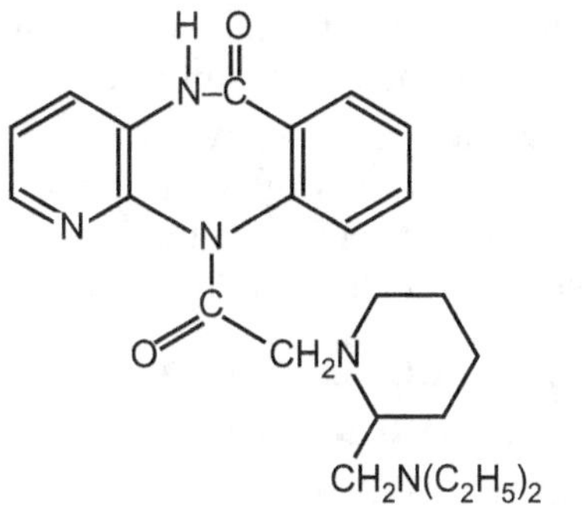

AF – DX 116

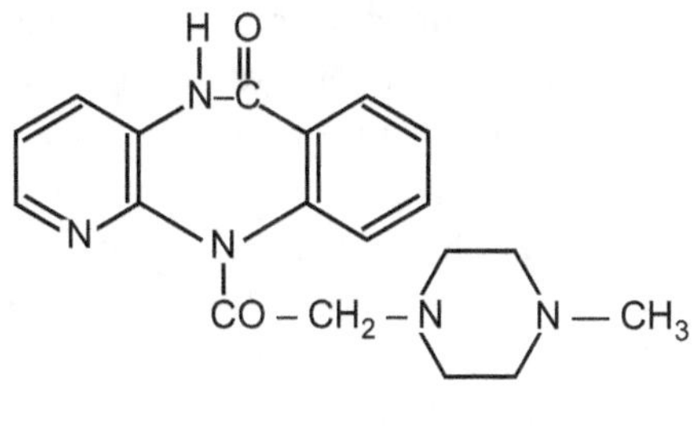

Pirenzepine

Fig. 4.8 : Structures of some drugs that affect the cholinergic nervous system

(b) Sympathetic Division :

Epinephrine, norepinephrine and dopamine are the principle neurotransmitters present in the sympathetic nervous system. In many cases, synaptic transmission may be mediated by the release of more than one neurotransmitter.

Dopamine is a predominant transmitter in the human extrapyramidal system, mesocortical and mesolimbic neuronal pathways. The first evidence for norepinephrine as a principal neuro-transmitter in ANS was given by Euler in 1946. The sympathetic system is distributed to effector cells throughout the body. It is also called as thoracolumber division because the preganglionic neurons of sympathetic nervous system have their cell bodies in the thoracic and lumbar regions of the spinal cord. The sympathetic ganglia are categorised into,

(a) Paravertebral,

(b) Prevertebral and

(c) Terminal.

This classification is based upon their sites of location. The terminal ganglia are few in number and consist especially of those connected with the urinary bladder and rectum.

The sympathetic system is normally active at all times and by stimulating mental alertness, respiration, energy production and heart activity, it prepares the person for 'fight or flight' situation. Receptors for a number of hormones including norepinephrine and autacoids, function by regulation of the concentration of the intracellular second messenger, cyclic adenosine-3', 5'-monophos-phate (cyclic AMP) through the activation of adenylate cyclase. Cyclic AMP was discovered by Suderland and co-workers in 1956.

Epinephrine   Norepinephrine   Dopamine

Epinephrine and norepinephrine catalyse many of the responses of the autonomic nervous system. The biosynthesis of epinephrine occurs in the nerve terminals using tyrosine as a starting material. This scheme of biosynthesis was first proposed by Blaschko in 1939. Phenylalanine is converted to dopamine in cytoplasm via two intermediates. The hydroxylation of tyrosine to DOPA is generally regarded as the ratelimiting step in the biosynthesis of catecholamines. To meet increased demands for norepinephrine, acute regulation mechanisms are available at nerve terminals to activate tyrosine hydroxylase enzyme.

The biosynthesised norepinephrine is stored in the synaptic vesicles or chromaffin granules which are about 0.05 to 0.2 μm in diameter. In these vesicles, catecholamine is present along with ATP in the molecular ratio 4:1. The vesicles may contain other substances like ascorbic acid, enzymes, chromogranin proteins and endogenous peptides. The release of stored norepinephrine requires ATP and magnesium ions and is blocked by reserpine like drugs. The release is effected by the process of exocytosis which is influenced by a number of cytoplasmic proteins. These proteins include : calmodulin, tubulin, neurin (actin-like), and stenin (myosin-like). *l*-Norepinephrine is released almost exclusively at the post-ganglionic sympathetic nerve endings. While adrenal medulla releases a mixture of both, i.e., *l*-norepinephrine and *l*-epinephrine.

After the exocytosis, the neurotransmitter is released into the synaptic cleft. It crosses the synaptic cleft and releases at the adrenergic receptors present at post-synaptic neuron. The action of epinephrine at the myoneural junction is blocked by ergotamine. The transmitter action is terminated by a number of processes. These include,

(a) Re-uptake mechanisms carry the neurotransmitter into the nerve terminals or glial cells.

(b) Part of the neurotransmitter diffuses out into the surrounding tissue fluid and blood circulation where it is metabolised by catechol–o–methyl transferase (COMT) enzymes.

(c) And part of the neurotransmitter is attacked by mono amino oxidase (MAO) enzymes present in the mitochondria of the nerve terminal and it results into the metabolic deactivation of neurotransmitter.

MAO and COMT enzymes are present in almost every vital organ of the body. The highest concentration of these enzymes is reported in brain, liver and kidney.

4.6 ACETYLCHOLINE AND EPINEPHRINE AS NEUROTRANSMITTERS

Acetylcholine and epinephrine are the neurotransmitters of major importance which lead the list of parasympathetic and sympathetic functions respectively. The Fig. 4.9 shows an element of structural similarity between these neurotransmitters.

The replacement of H-atom present on β–carbon of choline molecule by a catechol nucleus results into formation of dimethyl derivative of epinephrine. Thus, by an introduction of catechol nucleus in a choline molecules, the parasympathetic activity is shifted into sympathomimetic activity. Table 4.1 illustrates some points of differences between the sympathetic and parasympathetic divisions of ANS.

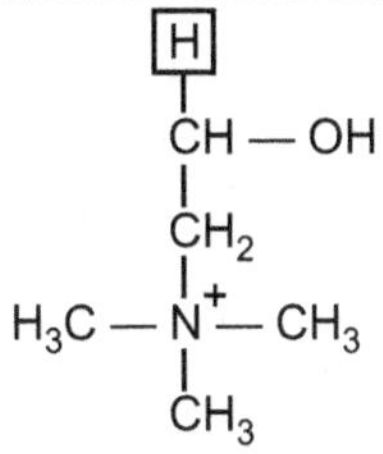

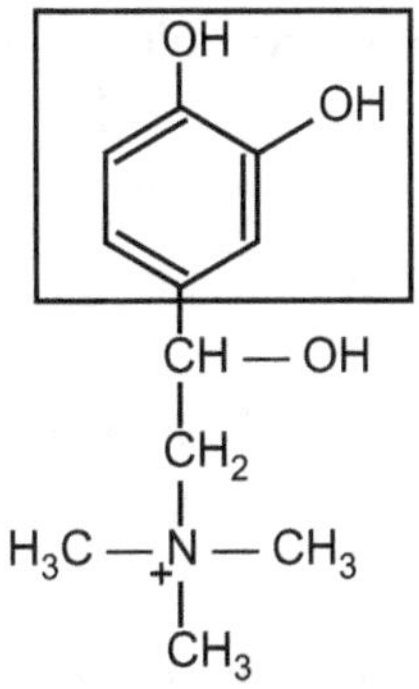

Fig. 4.9 : Structural similarities between epinephrine and choline part of acetylcholine

In most instances, the sympathetic and parasympathetic divisions act as physiological antagonists. Exception is male sexual organ where both divisions act to promote sexual function.

The sympathetic fibres to sweat glands and to certain blood vessels provided to skeletal muscles, release acetylcholine and hence the effect of stimulation of both the divisions at these target sites is similar.

For example, in salivary glands, both divisions upon activation leads to an increase in saliva production.

Some organs are innervated only by sympathetic nervous system. These include, most blood vessels, spleen, sweat glands, etc.

Table 4.1

Sr. No.	Parasympathetic division	Sympathetic division
1.	Craniosacral division.	Thoracolumbar division.
2.	Acetylcholine is a principal neurotransmitter.	Epinephrine and norepinephrine are principal neurotransmitters.
3.	Emerges at segmental level S_2 to S_4 of spinal cord.	Emerges at segmental level T_1 to L_2 or L_3 of spinal cord.
4.	Ganglia are small and suited very close to the organs innervated.	Ganglion contains neurons that are distributed to a number of organs.
5.	Effects are localised and limited and affects only a small region of the body.	Influences a wide region of the body.
6.	It is involved mainly in storage and preservation of body resources.	Prepares the person to face emergency cases.
7.	In rare cases, c-GMP is used as second messenger.	Operates through c-AMP which acts as second messenger.
8.	In the organs, innervated by both these divisions, effects upon stimulation of parasympathetic system is exactly opposite to that obtained after the stimulation of sympathetic system.	

4.7 NEUROTRANSMITTERS PRESENT IN CENTRAL NERVOUS SYSTEM

Along with acetylcholine and norepinephrine, other neurotransmitters which function in the CNS include, dopamine, epinephrine, serotonin, glycine, gamma amino butyric acid, aspartic acid, taurine, histamine, substance P, enkephalins and ATP.

It is usually difficult to establish an identity of any other substance as a candidate to function as neurotransmitter in CNS. Many drugs affect CNS functioning by influencing the release, action or metabolism of the neurotransmitter. In such cases, it can not be judged easily whether the altered CNS pattern is due to involvement of new neurotransmitters or due to modulating effect of drug given. It can be decided by developing such specific agents that will block the specific form of the nervous activity in CNS that was supposed to be operated by the drug which was claimed to be a new neurotransmitter.

Acetylcholine has been searched out in the brain cortex, limbic system, extrapyramidal nuclei and reticular formation. It regulates the senson functions, short term memory, the classical phase of sleep and elimination of hormones, especially vasopressin.

Norepinephrine acts as a neurotransmitter in limbic system, reticular formation, locus coeruleus, hypothalamus and medulla oblongata. It is involved in thermoregulation, memory, motor activity and vegetative functions.

Dopamine is present at higher concentration in the extrapyramidal nuclei and limbic structures. It regulates motor activity, emotional tonus, memory and release of hormones.

Serotonin is a mediator which influences thermoregulation, learning, classical phase of sleep, analgesia and sensory functions. It is present in limbic system, hypothalamus, spinal cord and Raphe nuclei. Lysergic acid diethylamide (LSD) interferes in and reduces serotonin turnover in the brain. This explains the basis of hallucinogenic action of LSD. The depression of serotonin activity results in the inhibition of visual and other sensory inputs.

CNS excitation occurs as a result of the release of excitatory neurotransmitters like acetylcholine, catecholamines, dopamine, glutamic acid etc. Similarly CNS depression arises either due to,

(a) Inhibition of the release of CNS excitatory neurotransmitter, or

(b) Release of inhibitor, neurotransmitter which then stimulates inhibitory responses. The inhibitory neurotransmitters include, serotonin, glycine, taurine and gamma-amino butyric acid (GABA).

Glycine :

It acts as an inhibitory neurotransmitter predominantly in the reticular formation. Strychnine appears to antagonise selectively the glycine responses but fails to antagonise the effects mediated by GABA.

Taurine :

It uniformly depresses the functioning of CNS except the cortex where it has very weak depressant action.

GABA :

Though it has widespread depressant action on the various regions of CNS, its main sites of action involve local interneurons in the brain and presynaptic sites within the spinal cord. Its presence in brain was first reported in 1950.

Table 4.2 : Some of the neurotransmitters present in CNS

$CH_3 - \overset{\overset{\textstyle O}{\|\|}}{C} - O - CH_2 - CH_2 - \overset{\oplus}{N} - (CH_3)_3$ Acetylcholine	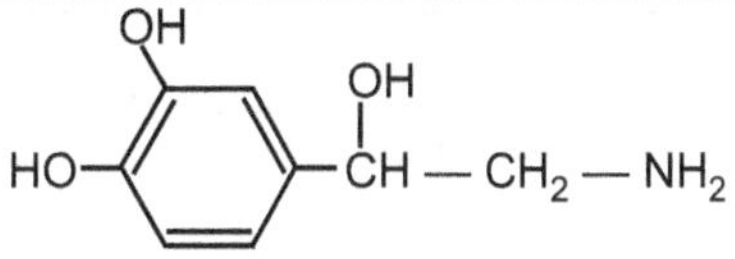 Norepinephrine
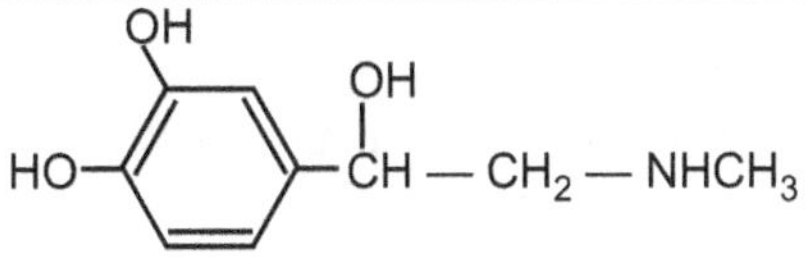 Epinephrine	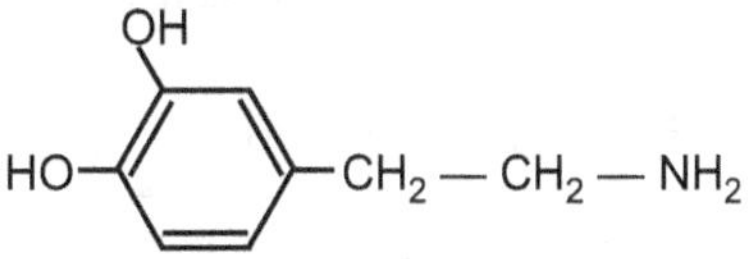 Dopamine
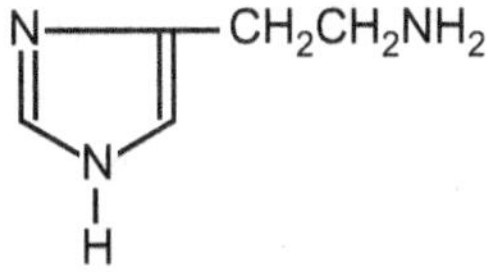 Histamine	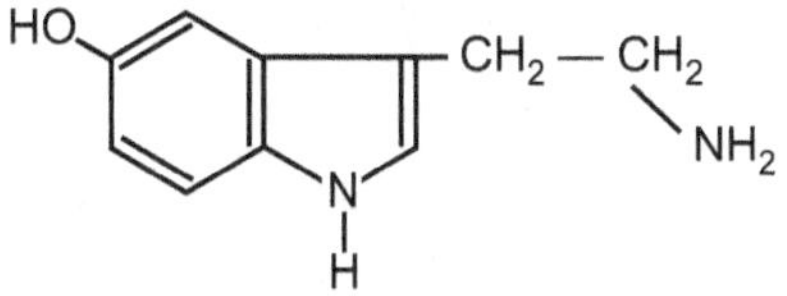 5-Hydroxytryptamine (Serotonin)
$NH_2 - CH_2 - COOH$ Glycine	$H_2N - \overset{\overset{\textstyle}{\underset{\textstyle COOH}{\|}}}{CH} - CH_2 - COOH$ Aspartic acid
$H_2N - \underset{\underset{\textstyle COOH}{\|}}{CH} - CH_2 - CH_2 - COOH$ Glutamic acid	$H_2N - CH_2 - CH_2 - CH_2 - COOH$ γ- Amino butyric acid
H – Tyr – Gly – Gly – Phe – Met – OH Methionine enkephaline	H – Tyr – Gly – Gly – Phe – Leu – OH Leucine enkephaline
H – Arg – Lys – Pro – Pro – Gln – Gln – Phe – Phe – Gly – Leu – Met – NH$_2$ Substance P	

Many drugs lead to excessive CNS stimulation (convulsant action) mainly due to the blockade of inhibitory nerve-channels mediated by GABA. For example, the action of benzodiazepines is linked with the potentiation of the functions of receptor-chloride ionophore systems that are regulated by GABA. The activation of chloride ionophore causes influx of chloride ions which causes the hyperpolarisation of the nerve tract.

4.8 ACETYLCHOLINE

Acetylcholine was first synthesised by Baeyer in 1867. In general, stimulation of parasympathetic nervous system induces constriction of pupil and bronchi, decrease in heart activity and an increase in the activity of digestive system i.e. salivation and other GIT secretions are promoted. Motility of the intestine is also increased.

Chemical Features of Acetylcholine :

$$H_3C-\overset{\overset{O}{\|}}{C}-O \mid CH_2-CH_2 \mid \overset{\oplus}{N}\begin{matrix} CH_3 \\ CH_3 \\ CH_3 \end{matrix}$$

| Acetyl group | Ethylene bridge | Quaternary ammonium cation (onium group) |

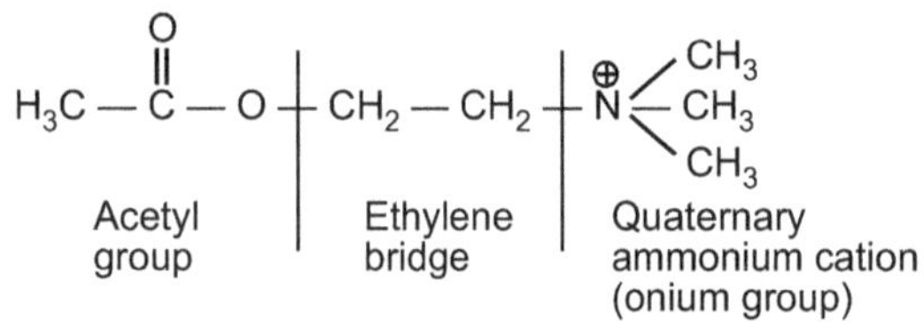

Fig. 4.10 : Acetylcholine

Following are some of the important chemical features of acetylcholine molecule :

(i) Chemically it is an ester of acetic acid and choline, an amino alcohol.

(ii) On the structural basis, it offers three sites for molecular modifications :

(a) acetyl group,

(b) ethylene bridge and

(c) quaternary ammonium group.

(iii) The quaternary ammonium group (i.e. onium group) is linked by an ethylene bridge to an ester group.

(iv) Acetylcholine is stable in acidic solutions but it is very unstable in alkaline media.

(v) Free acetylcholine present in the tissue fluids and circulation, is rapidly hydrolysed to acetic acid and choline molecule by choline-sterase enzyme.

(vi) Acetylcholine exhibits some of its actions via G-protein coupled muscarinic receptors while remaining actions are propagated through nicotinic receptors.

Muscarinic receptors are also reported to be present at cortical and subcortical site within the CNS and in autonomic ganglia. Nicotinic actions at autonomic ganglia are antagonised by hexamethonium and related drugs whereas at neuromuscular junction of skeletal muscle, they are antagonised by tubocurarine. At nicotinic receptor sites, acetylcholine produces stimulant effects in small doses whereas large doses of acetylcholine lead to receptor inhibition.

Pharmacological Actions :

(a) Cardiovascular System :

If acetylcholine is injected intravenously, the muscarinic effects of acetylcholine are predominantly seen on cardiovascular system. These effects include :

(i) Vasodilation.

(ii) Decrease in the force of heart contraction

(negative chronotropic effect)

(iii) Decrease in the force of heart contraction (negative inotropic effect).

Low doses acetylcholine are sufficient to produce vasodilation including the pulmonary and coronary vasculature. This is brought about mainly by the stimulation of muscarinic receptors present in the endothelial cells of vasculature. The vasodilatory effect of acetylcholine on peripheral vasculature is very marked but is quickly terminated. The latter two effects of acetylcholine can be observed only in higher doses. In heart, cholinergic innervation is provided mainly to the sinoarterial node, atrioventricular node and the atrial muscles. The activation of this innervation leads to an increase in the permeability of cardiac fibres to potassium resulting into a decrease in the activity of S-A node.

The effects of acetylcholine on cardio-vascular system just described, sometimes may be reversed by the release of catecholamines from the adrenal medulla and from sympathetic ganglia. This release may be due to the stimulation of nicotinic cholinergic receptor sites present in these organs.

(b) Smooth Muscle :

At moderate doses, acetylcholine stimulates the muscarinic receptors present on the smooth muscles of GIT, urinogenital and respiratory tract, and eye resulting into contraction of these muscles. The increased muscle tone of GIT may lead to nausea and vomiting. The lacrimal, salivary, gastric, pancreatic, and sweat glands are also stimulated. The motility of gall bladder and bile ducts is also increased.

The stimulatory effects of acetylcholine can be explained on the basis of an increase in the permeability of the muscle cell to Na^+ and Ca^{++} ions which results into a depolarisation of the cell membrane. When acetylcholine reacts with the post-synaptic receptors, it may produce either excitation or inhibition. The action of the transmitter results in selective increase or decrease of ionic permeability of membrane. The ratio of permeability for K^+ to that of Na^+, if increased may lead to hyperpolarisation (as in cardiac cells) and if decreases, may cause depolarisation (as in smooth muscle cells). For example, high concentration of acetylcholine may lead to the complete heart block due to hyperpolarisation.

Thus, enhanced permeability to monovalent cations, an increase in the concentration of intracellular calcium ions, an increase in the concentration of guanosine - 3', 5'-monophosphate (cyclic GMP) or the inhibition of adenylate cyclase enzyme are some of the mechanisms associated with muscarinic receptor stimulation. Investigations in the role of c-GMP started from 1960. It is widely distributed in the tissues. It is present at higher concentration in cerebellum and particularly in retina.

Due to the quaternary cationic nature, acetylcholine, at low doses, can not readily reach the skeletal muscles embedded by the fatty layers. Hence at low doses, the nicotinic actions of acetylcholine are not prominent. At large doses, acetylcholine can stimulate nicotinic receptors present in both, sympathetic and parasympathetic ganglia.

Acetylcholine is poor therapeutic agent since it gets easily hydrolysed by cholinesterase enzyme. Clinically, its use as acetylcholine chloride, is restricted in ophthalmic surgery to obtain rapid and complete miosis during cataract removal. For this purpose, 0.5 to 2.0 ml of 10 mg/ml solution of acetylcholine chloride can be applied locally.

Structure-Activity Relationship :

(i) Any change in the ethylene bridge may affect the chemical stability of acetylcholine molecule.

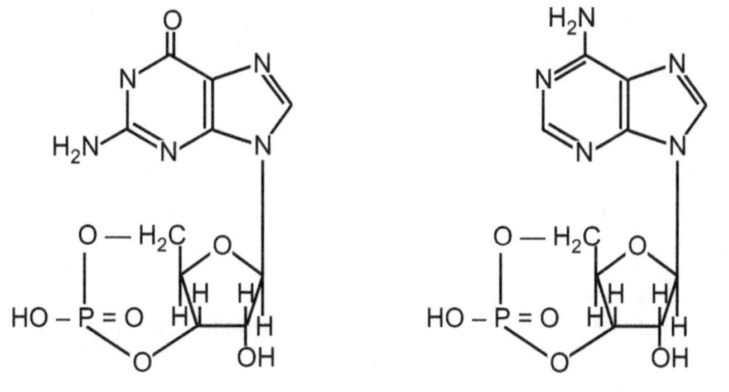

Cyclic GMP   Cyclic AMP

Fig. 4.11 : Important cyclic nucleotides

(ii) A cationic ammonium group is essential for the manifestation of both muscarinic and nicotinic receptor activities. If one or more of the methyl groups on nitrogen atom are replaced by hydrogen or ethyl group, both activities are reduced.

(iii) The quaternary nitrogen atom itself may be replaced by arsenic, antimony, phosphorus or sulphur atom without the loss of all acetylcholine-like activities.

(iv) Ing in 1949 proposed that for maximal muscarinic activity, there should be not more than four atoms between the nitrogen and terminal C-atom.

(v) If bulky substituents are placed on the terminal C-atom of acetyl group, through a firm binding and 'Umbrella effect,' these substituents block the access of acetylcholine to the receptor. This results in the antimuscarinic activity. Examples include, benzilylcholine, tropylcholine etc.

(vi) Carbachol and acetyl-β-methylcholine are the cholinergic agonists acting chiefly at muscarinic receptors while propionylcholine and acetyl α-methylcholine act chiefly at nicotinic cholinergic receptors.

4.9 CYCLIC ANALOGUES OF ACETYLCHOLINE

Muscarine is a cyclic analogue of acetylcholine, devoid of nicotinic receptor activity. It has a quaternary ammonium group but does not possess an ester function. Hence, it is not enzymatically metabolised by cholinesterase enzyme. This explains its long duration of action. If administered in sufficient concentration, it reaches the CNS by crossing blood-brain barrier and evokes cortical arousal.

The following structures, along with the rigid size requirements for the esters of choline, also indicate steric and conformational requirement for optimal fit on the muscarinic receptors.

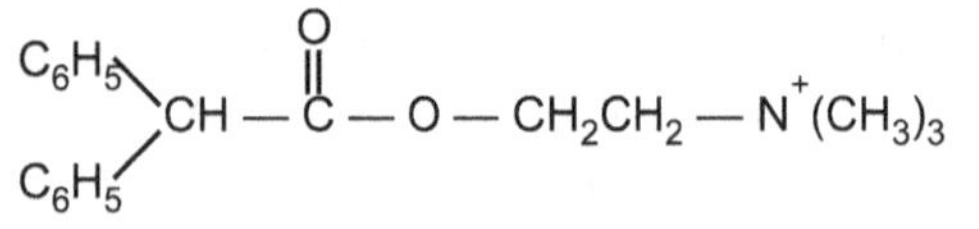

Benzilylcholine

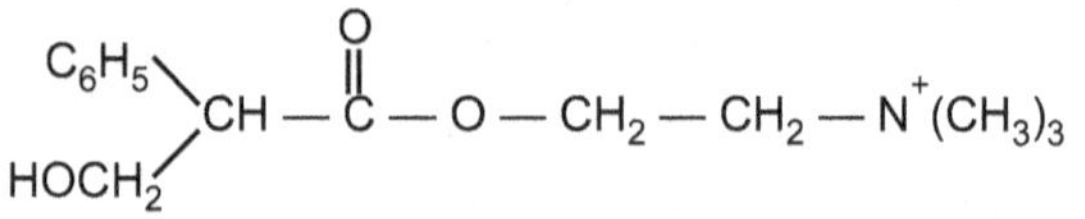

Tropylcholine

Cyclic analogues of acetylcholine :

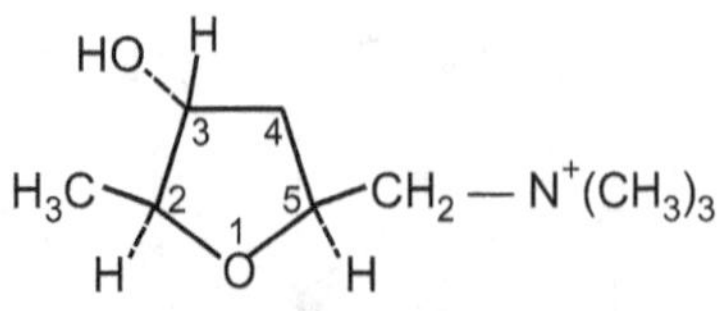

Cis-L-(+) muscarine

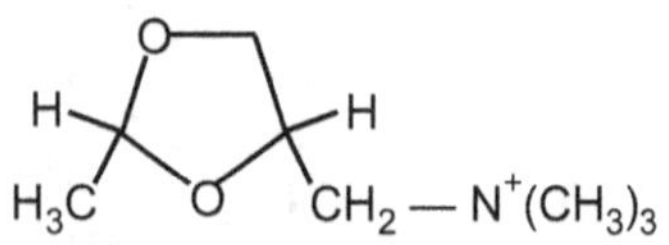

2-methyl-4-trimethyl ammonium - methyl-1,3-dioxolone

Fig. 4.12

For example, Acetyl–β–methyl choline adopts following conformation.

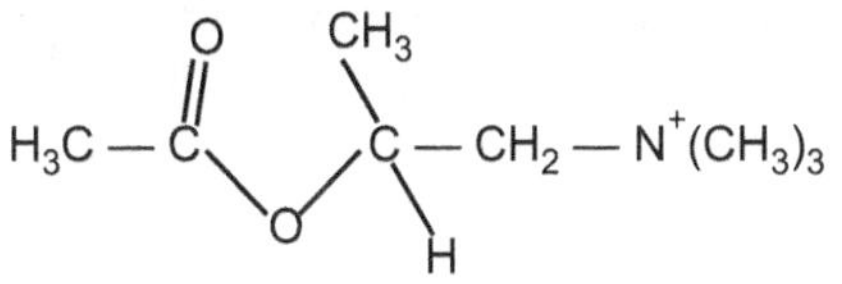

$$H_3C - \overset{\overset{O}{\|}}{C} \diagdown \underset{\underset{H}{|}}{O} \diagup \overset{\overset{CH_3}{|}}{C} - CH_2 - N^+(CH_3)_3$$

Acetyl-β-methylcholine

4.10 CHOLINERGIC RECEPTORS

From the SAR studies, the structure of a cholinergic receptor is predicted as shown in the Fig. 4.13.

The negative charge at the anionic site of the receptor may result from the ionisation of a dicarboxylic amino group (i.e., aspartic or glutamic acid) present in the receptor. The quaternary ammonium group forms an electrostatic bond with this anionic site. The ester or other group capable of forming H-bond interacts at the esteratic site through H-bonding.

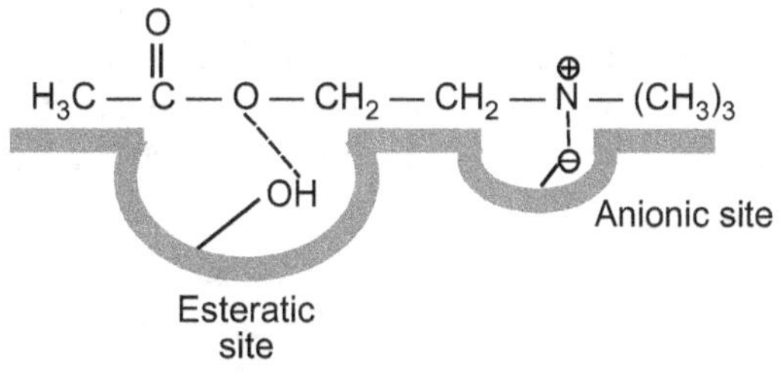

$$H_3C - \overset{\overset{O}{\|}}{C} - O - CH_2 - CH_2 - \overset{\oplus}{N} - (CH_3)_3$$

Anionic site

Esteratic site

Fig. 4.13 : Cholinergic receptor

Since the tissues containing muscarinic receptors are extremely complex, binding studies between acetylcholine analogues and cholinesterases were made. They indicate that the methyl groups present on N-atom along with the terminal methyl group are bound to the receptor by both hydrophobic and van der Waal's forces. This binding assures a close fit of the molecule to the receptor as shown in Fig. 4.14.

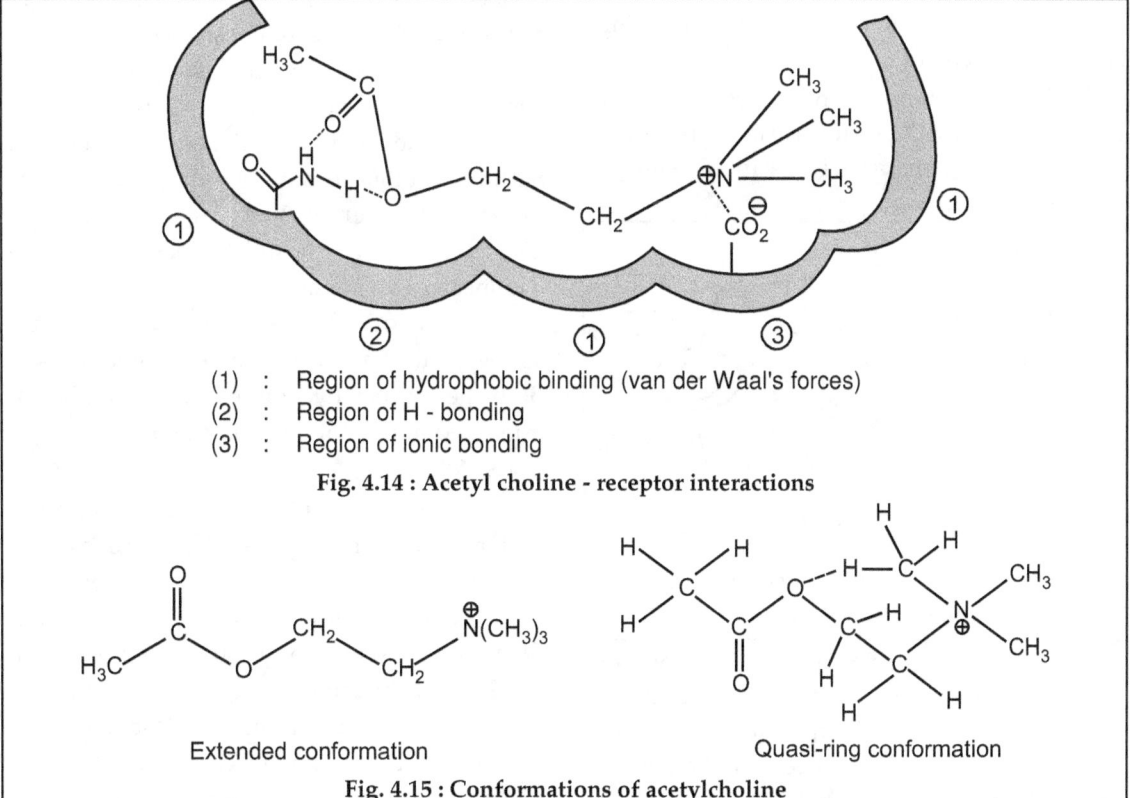

(1) : Region of hydrophobic binding (van der Waal's forces)
(2) : Region of H - bonding
(3) : Region of ionic bonding

Fig. 4.14 : Acetyl choline - receptor interactions

Extended conformation

Quasi-ring conformation

Fig. 4.15 : Conformations of acetylcholine

But, due to the free rotation around most of its covalent bonds, acetylcholine can exist in a large number of conformations. The following two structures represent extremes in all such possible conformations (Fig. 4.15).

The structure of any drug can be categorised into an essential part (necessary for better intrinsic activity) and supporting part (necessary for better affinity and pharmacokinetic properties). The supporting structure also helps to bring the essential structure in the correct three-dimensional arrangement with respect to the receptor surface.

The essential as well as supporting structures, both differ in their conformations as regard to the action of acetylcholine on muscarinic and nicotinic receptors. For example, acetylcholine is present in an extended conformational form when it fits on muscarinic receptor while it adopts quasi ring conformation when it acts on nicotinic cholinergic receptors.

While in another hypothesis, Beckett proposed that, the muscarinic receptors contain one anionic and two cationic sites as shown in Fig. 4.16.

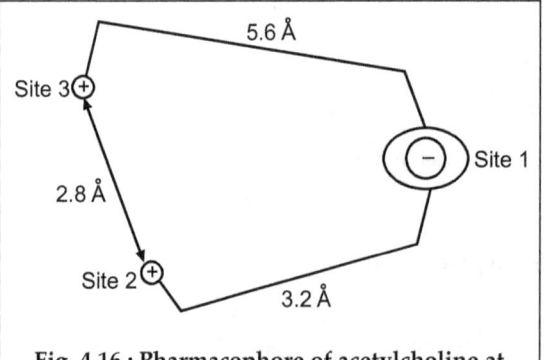

Fig. 4.16 : Pharmacophore of acetylcholine at muscarinic receptor site

The anionic binding site (site 1) accommodates the quaternary nitrogen of muscarine. The site 2 or a H-bonding site is for ether oxygen of muscarine or acetylcholine while the site 3 can interact with the carbonyl group

of acetylcholine or the ether oxygen of dioxolone or with the alcohol group of muscarine as shown in Fig. 4.17. Although acetylcholine has three reactive sites, only two sites are necessary for the various actions of the compound.

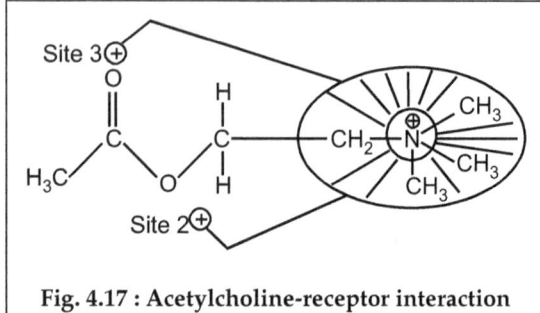

Fig. 4.17 : Acetylcholine-receptor interaction

4.11 METABOLISM OF ACETYLCHOLINE

The free acetylcholine present in the blood and other tissues, gets quickly hydrolysed by either e-cholinesterase (present in erythrocytes) and s-cholinesterase (present in the serum). Dale (1914) first proposed the concept of enzymatic destruction of acetylcholine in the blood and other tissues. Serum cholinesterase is also known as butyrocholinesterase while e-cholinesterase is also termed as acetylcholinesterase. The cholinesterases are not very selective enzymes. A number of other s-cholinesterases share some of the properties of e-cholinesterases. Both these types hydrolyse a large number of esters, both, of choline and of other carboxylic acids.

The basic unit of the enzyme is a tetramer with a molecular weight of 320,000; each of the protomers contains an active site. Normally, three such tetrameric units are linked through disulphide bonds to a 50 × 2 nm stem. Analysis of the amino acid composition of the enzyme shows that it bears a close similarity to the acetylcholine receptor in its high proportion of acidic amino acids.

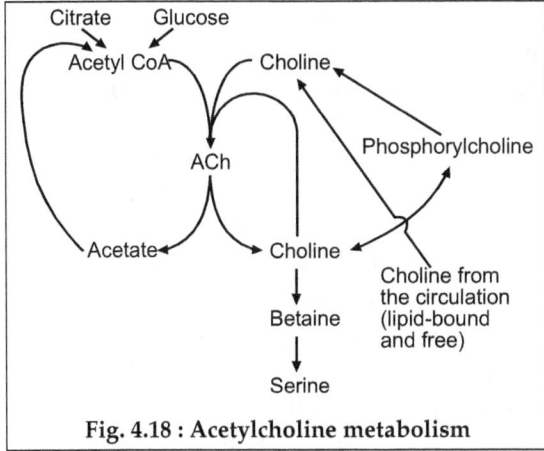

Fig. 4.18 : Acetylcholine metabolism

4.12 CHOLINOMIMETICS OR CHOLINERGIC AGONISTS

The cholinomimetics have as their primary action the excitation or inhibition of autonomic effector cells that are innervated by post-ganglionic parasympathetic nerves. They differ from acetylcholine in,

(1) their selectivity on muscarinic and nicotinic receptors.

(2) their chemical stability.

(3) their resistance to hydrolysis by cholinesterases and

(4) their duration of action.

On the structural basis, the cholinomimetic agents can be divided into,

(a) Acetylcholine and several synthetic choline esters.

(b) Naturally occurring and synthetic alkaloids.

(c) Cholinesterase inhibitors or anticholinesterases and

(d) Ganglionic stimulants.

The last two categories do not act at post-ganglionic cholinergic effector sites and produce their effects by acting in an indirect way.

Structure-Activity Relationship

(a) Modifications of the Onium (Quaternary ammonium) Group :

(i) The trimethylammonium group is the optimal functional requirement for activity, although following are the exceptions.

Pilocarpine

Arecoline   **Nicotine**

(ii) Phosphonium, sulphonium, arsenonium or substances larger than methyl on the nitrogen, had less activity and not used clinically.

(b) Modifications of the Ethylenic Bridge :

(i) In studying a series of n-alkyl tri-methyl ammonium salts, Ing noted that for maximal muscarinic activity, there should be not more than four atoms between the nitrogen and terminal carbon atom. This rule was referred to as five atom rule.

(ii) Replacement of the hydrogen atoms of the ethylenic bridge by alkyl groups produces far less active compounds except when a single, methyl group is placed either at α or β to the quaternary nitrogen atom.

(iii) The presence of a methyl group β to the quaternary nitrogen atom increases the muscarinic activity, e.g. Methacholine.

The high selective muscarinic action is due to orientation of methyl group of methacholine in the same position as a methylene group in muscarine.

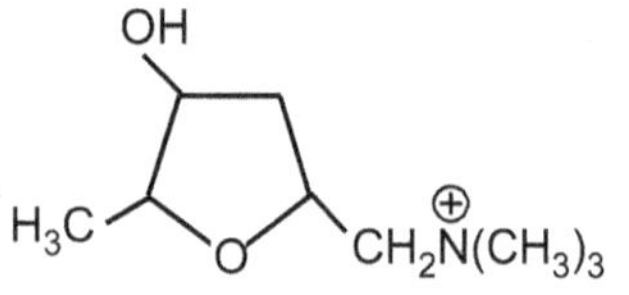

Muscarine

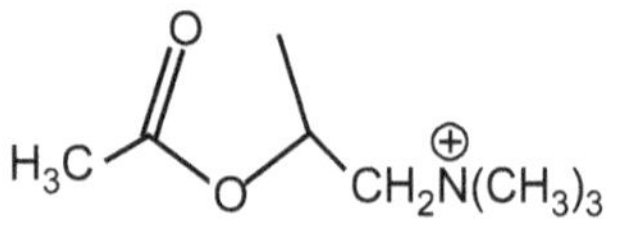

(S) - Methacholine

Moreover the added methyl group hinders the attack of esterase enzyme, thus slows down enzymatic hydrolysis.

(iv) A methyl group alpha to the nitrogen increases nicotinic activity e.g. Acetyl Methyl-choline.

(c) Modifications of the Acyl Group :

(i) When the acyl group is substituted by its higher homologues (i.e. the propionyl, butyryl etc.), less active compounds are formed.

(ii) Choline esters of aromatic or higher molecular weight acids are cholinergic antagonists rather than agonists.

(iii) When the terminal methyl group is replaced by – NH_2 group, the resulting compound, (the carbamic acid ester), however, is a potent cholinergic agent with both muscarinic and nicotinic activities.

Bethanechol chloride

Carbachol chloride

Carbachol is certainly stable to hydrolysis and has the right size to fit the cholinergic receptor. The carbamic acid ester of β-methylcholine is also a stable therapeutic agent. The measured interprosthetic distances

in acetylcholine are 7.0 Å ketone oxygen to methyl and 5.3 Å ether oxygen to methyl. Obviously, the interprosthetic distances for acetylcholine, methacholine, carbamino-ylcholine, and urecholine are the same. Apparently, if the interprosthetic distances are optimal, the receptors on the cell do not differentiate between ether, ketone, ester, or acetyl oxygen atoms.

(iv) In carbachol, the terminal methyl group of acetylcholine is replaced by -NH_2 group, while size of the molecule remains the same as that of acetylcholine. So it becomes apparent that the size of the molecule may be more important to its activity than the acyl group present. Similarly, the ether oxygen appears to be of primary importance for high muscarinic activity. As a result of such reasoning, ethers of choline and alkylamino-ketones were examined for activity.

$$CH_3 - CH_2 - O - CH_2 - CH_2 - N^+ (CH_3)_3 \ Cl^-$$

choline ethyl ether
(High muscarinic activity)

$$CH_3 - CH_2 - O - \overset{\overset{\displaystyle CH_3}{|}}{CH} - CH_2 - N(CH_3)_3$$

β- methylcholine ethyl ether
(High muscarinic activity)

(v) The reduced biological activity of compounds in which oxygen is replaced by sulphur (e.g. thiomuscarine) suggests the presence of H-bonding or dipole-dipole interaction between the drug and the receptor because sulphur atom has a less ability to form H-bonds with the receptors.

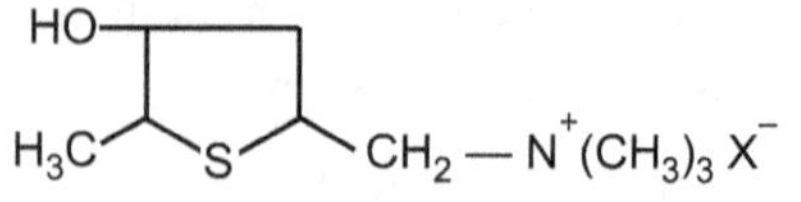

Thiomuscarine

(vi) The concept that the ester i.e. carbonyl or other group is not essential for activity but may enhance it by increasing the affinity of the molecule for the receptor was confirmed by a study of the muscarinic properties of N-alkyltrimethyl ammonium salts.

$$CH_3 - (CH_2)_n - N^+ (CH_3)_3\ X^-$$

N-alkyl trimethyl ammonium salts

Compounds in this series showed muscarinic activity when n = 1, 2, 3 or 4. Compounds with groups larger than pentyl were partial agonists and those with groups larger than heptyl were antagonists. This appears to believe the hypothesis that size rather than functional groups is necessary for the intrinsic activity.

Adverse Reactions :

All synthetic choline esters should never be administered by intravenous route. They are usually administered preferably by oral or by subcutaneous route. The usual side-effects include, salivation, vomiting and severe gastrointestinal cramps.

Contra Indications :

These synthetic derivatives of acetylcholine are contraindicated in patients suffering from peptic ulcer, bronchial asthma, hypotension, presence of organic urinary tract or gastrointestinal obstruction.

4.13 ANTICHOLINESTERASE

The cholinesterase enzyme terminates the biological activity of acetylcholine by hydrolyzing acetylcholine into acetic acid and a choline molecule, thus limiting the turnover time of acetylcholine to 150 microseconds. The hydrolysis of acetylcholine occurs through deacetylation reaction which is catalysed by cholinesterase enzyme.

The cholinesterases present in the human body can be broadly categorised into,

(a) Acetylcholinesterase or e-cholinesterase or true cholinesterase or specific cholinesterase and

(b) Butyrocholinesterase or s-cholinesterase or pseudo cholinesterase or non-specific cholinesterase.

The specific or acetylcholinesterase is found in R.B.C., in the brain and other nerve tissues. It is present in high concentration on presynaptic sites, post-synaptic membrane sites and at motor nerve end plate regions of cholinergic nervous system. At presynaptic sites, its role is to regulate the acetylcholine levels in cholinergic nerve terminals. It is also located in autonomic ganglia and certain cholinergic synapses in the CNS. The non-specific or butyrocholinesterase is present in plasma, glial cells, intestine and other organs. The cholinesterases present in different species or organs sometimes bear basic differences and need not be identical.

These enzymes are mainly located in the outer basement membrane of the synapses and in the neuromuscular junctional cleft. They are also reported to be present in the cisternae of the endoplasmic reticulum.

Sometimes cholinesterase enzymes have been located in such regions where they can not claim the role of 'acetylcholine-killer'. In such cases, they are supposed to be tied up with some independent activities like,

(a) to control the membrane permeability and

(b) to control the blood level of fatty substances.

Cholinesterase inhibitors, as the name indicates, increase the concentration of the acetylcholine at the receptor sites by inhibiting its metabolism by cholinesterases, resulting into prolongation and potentiation of acetylcholine activity at both, muscarinic and nicotinic receptors. They do so mainly through competitive antagonism and hence often resemble with acetylcholine in structure.

The unhydrolysed acetylcholine accumulates and exerts its actions. Hence, cholinesterase inhibitors are also termed as indirectly acting cholinomimetic agents.

The activation of muscarinic receptors results into various muscarinic effects which include miosis, contractions of smooth muscles, diarrhoea, vasodilation, bradycardia, nausea, vomiting, salivation, perspiration, lacrimation etc. All these effects can be blocked by administration of muscarine blocker like, atropine.

The activation of nicotinic receptors by high levels of accumulated acetylcholine results into generalised muscle twitching followed by the muscle weakness and ganglionic stimulation. The activation of nicotinic receptors present in the autonomic ganglia and adrenal medulla leads to the release of catecholamines which may further alter the cardiovascular function.

Some anticholinesterases have an independent direct cholinomimetic action of their own while some may cause neuromuscular blockade. The toxic effects of some drugs may be due to their in-vivo metabolism to toxic metabolites.

4.14 STRUCTURAL FEATURES OF CHOLINESTERASE ENZYME

Cholinesterase constitutes an example of one of the most effective enzyme systems present in the body. It is a tetramer having a molecular weight of about 3,20,000. The cholinesterase molecule consists of three important sites namely, anionic, cationic and esteratic site. The anionic site is formed by an ionised gamma-carboxylate group of a glutamic acid residue and is stereospecific. The cationic site possesses hydroxyl group probably that of tyrosine residue. While the esteratic site consists of two imidazole groups (Im$_1$ and Im$_2$) from histidine moieties and a serine residue.

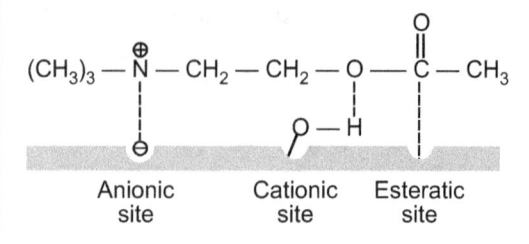

Anionic   Cationic   Esteratic
site   site   site

Fig. 4.19 : Possible interactions between acetylcholine and cholinesterase enzyme

The process of hydrolysis of acetylcholine, thus occurs in the following steps :

(i) The imidazole group Im$_2$, of histidine, accepts a proton from a serine hydroxyl group at the esteratic site, creating a strong nucleophile while OH - from tyrosine just serves as binding site to ether oxygen of the acetoxy group of acetylcholine.

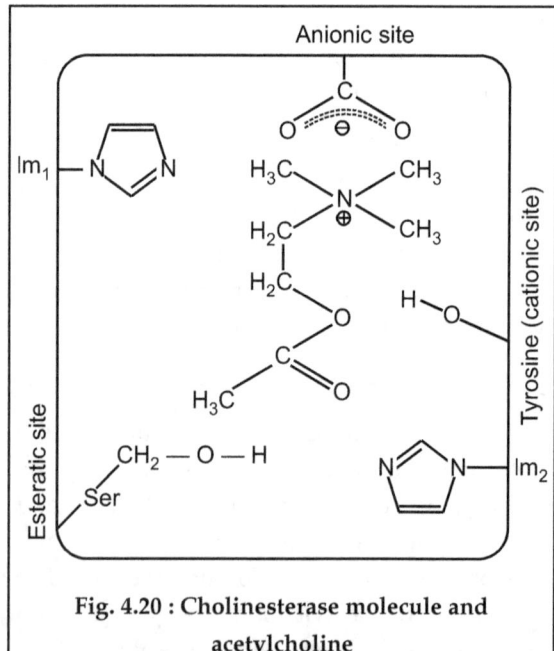

Fig. 4.20 : Cholinesterase molecule and acetylcholine

(ii) The anionic site of the enzyme binds with the quaternary nitrogen of the acetylcholine through both ionic and hydrophobic forces. The latter binding force is provided by the presence of three methyl groups which are present on the nitrogen. The activated serine, being a strong nucleophile, then attacks on the C-atom of carbonyl group of acetylcholine resulting into a tetrahedral intermediate. This intermediate is very short-lived and its collapse results into the release of choline molecule, leaving the acetylated serine residue on the enzyme.

(iii) The choline molecule readily dissociate from the anionic site, since it is bound only by van der Waals forces and hydrophobic forces. The acetyl group, however, forms a covalent bond with the nucleophilic group (activated serine residue) of the enzyme. The acetylated enzyme then undergoes a conformational change which brings the acetylated serine in close proximity to the second imidazole (Im_1) residue. In presence of a water molecule, the second imidazole residue catalyzes hydrolysis of acetylated serine to give acetic acid and serine residue. This step is rate limiting step which occurs at a very rapid rate and the enzyme is thereby efficiently regenerated back.

The cholinesterase enzyme from a purified sample of OX red blood cell is found to hydrolyse 3×10^5 molecules of acetylcholine per minute.

4.15 CLASSIFICATION OF ANTICHOLINE-STERASES

The anticholinesterases are classified into :

I. reversible anticholinesterases

II. irreversible anticholinesterases.

(I) Reversible Anticholinesterases :

They bear a structural resemblance to acetylcholine, hence capable of combining with the anionic and esteratic sites of cholinesterases and receptors as well. They have a great affinity for active sites but no intrinsic activity. This produces the temporary inhibition of the enzyme. In contrast to other reversible cholinesterases, edrophonium forms reversible complex only with the anionic site and hence has a shorter duration of action.

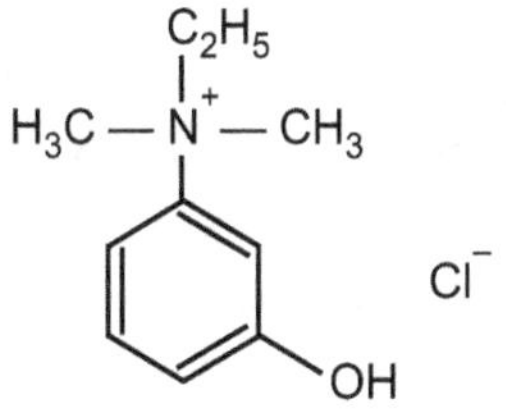

Edrophonium chloride

These can further be divided into :

(a) Naturally occurring : e.g. physostigmine

(b) Synthetic : e.g. Neostigmine, pyridostigmine, ambenonium, miotine, demacarium, edrophonium and benzpyrinium.

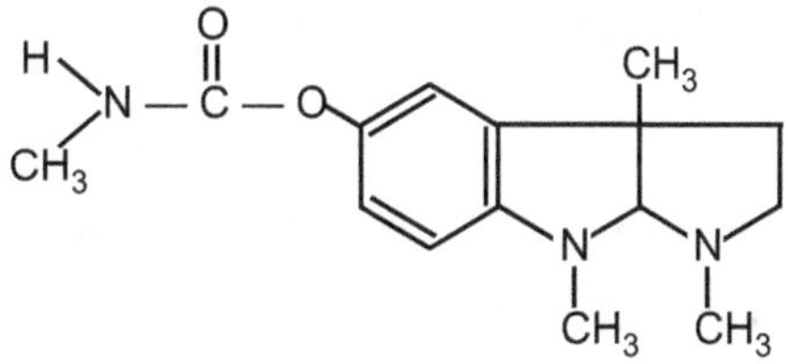

Physostigmine

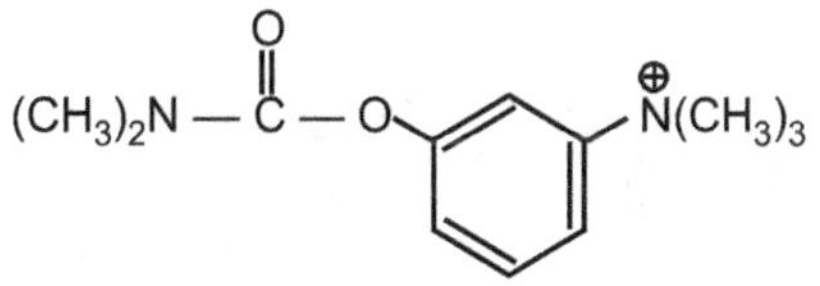

Neostigmine

In neostigmine, increased stability to hydrolysis is achieved by using a dimethyl carbamate in place of methyl carbamate group. Because of charged nitrogen, neostigmine can not cross the blood-brain barrier and cause CNS side-effects.

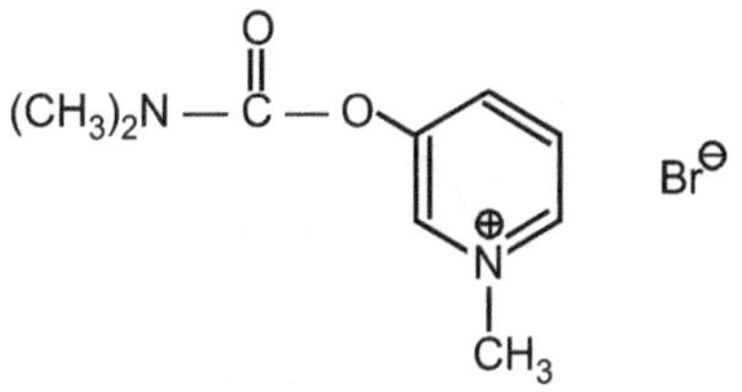

Pyridostigmine bromide

Patients with Alzheimer's disease present with progressive impairment of memory and cognitive functions such as a lack of attention, disturbed language function and an inability to complete common tasks. Although the exact defect in the central nervous system has not been elucidated, evidence suggests that a reduction in cholinergic nerve function is largely responsible for the symptoms.

Rivastigmine (1997) : It is a cholinesterase inhibitor used for the treatment of mild to moderate dementia associated with Parkinson's disease.

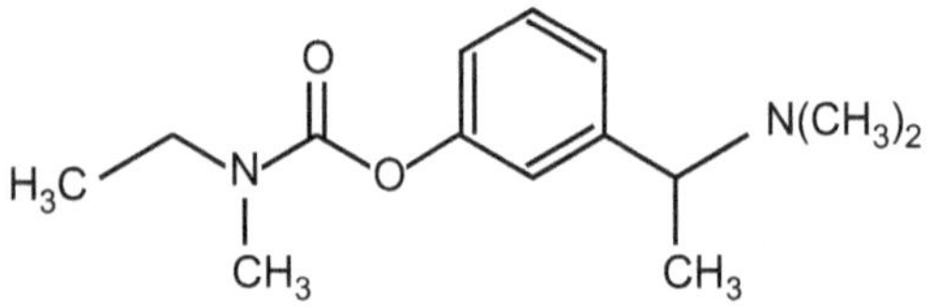

Donepezil : It is centrally acting revesible cholinesterase inhibitor used in the palliative treatment of mild to moderate Alzheimer's disease.

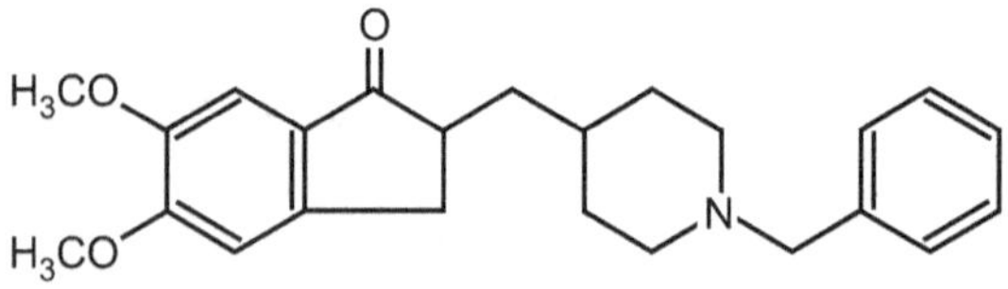

Galantamine : It is an alkaloid obtained synthetically or from the bulbs and flowers of Galanthus caucasicus. It is a reversible cholinesterase inhibitor and also is nicotinic receptor modulator. It is used in the treatment of mild to moderate vascular dementia and Alzheimer disease.

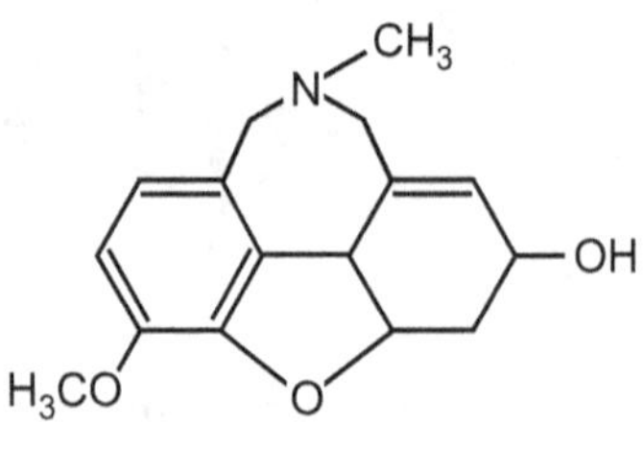

Tacrine : It is the first centrally acting reversible cholinesterase inhibitor approved for the treatment of Alzheimer's disease.

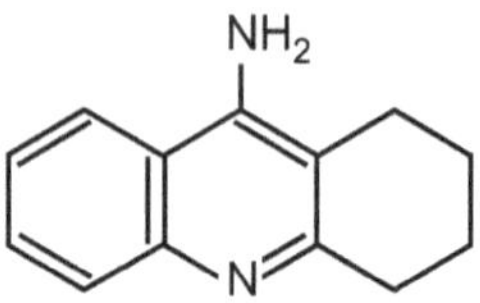

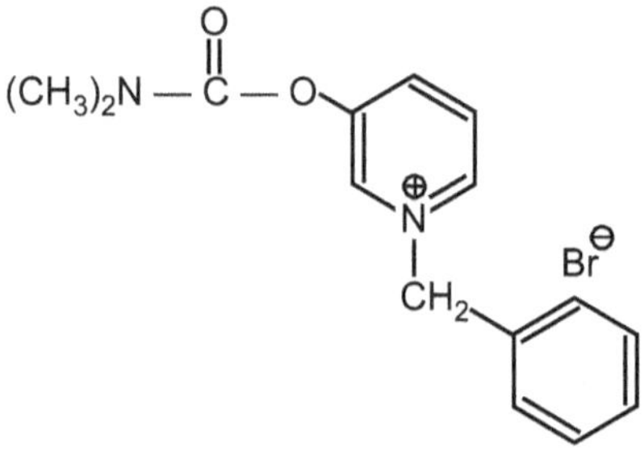

Benzpyrinium bromide

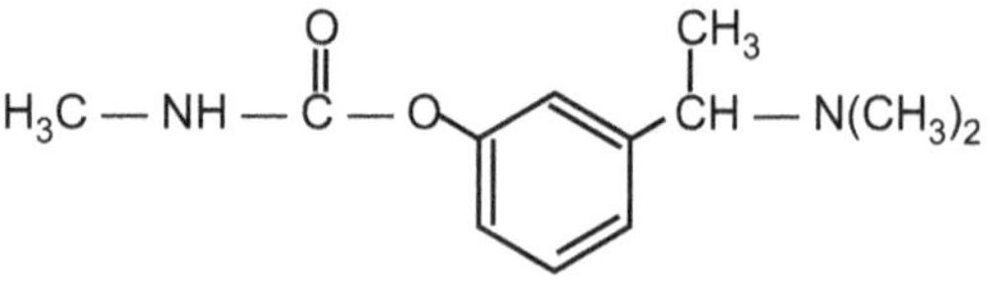

Miotine

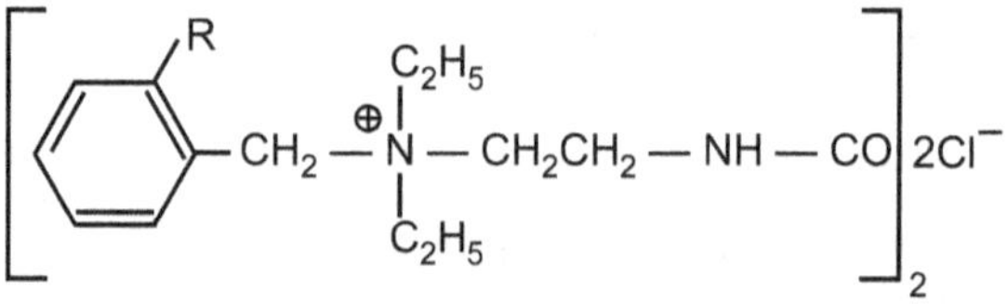

R = – Cl; Ambenonium chloride
R = – OCH$_3$; Methoxyambenonium chloride

Structure-Activity Relationship :

(i) The distance across the ether oxygen and nitrogen atom is approximately same as that between the ether oxygen and nitrogen atom in acetylcholine.

(ii) The two heterocyclic rings of physostigmine are not essential for anticholinesterase activity. During hydrolysis, the phenolic fragment of this drug is eliminated, leaving the carbamoyl group attached to the enzyme. The rate of hydrolysis of carbamoyl group is about 60 times less than the rate of hydrolysis of acyl group of acetylcholine.

(II) Irreversible Anticholinesterases :

Organophosphorus compounds combine only with esteratic site of cholinesterases and the esteratic site is phosphorylated. The hydrolysis of this phosphorylated site, however, is extremely slow which produces a long term inhibition of cholinesterases. In contrast to other organophosphorus compounds, echothiophate forms complex with both anionic and esteratic sites and hence is much more potent.

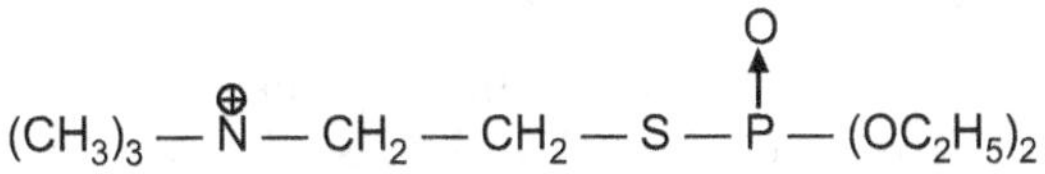

$$(CH_3)_3 - \overset{\oplus}{N} - CH_2 - CH_2 - S - \overset{\overset{O}{\uparrow}}{P} - (OC_2H_5)_2$$

Echothiophate

A number of phosphate, pyrophosphate and phosphonate esters apparently react irreversibly with cholinesterase by forming phosphate ester with the esteratic site. Because the rate of hydrolysis of the phosphorylated enzyme is measured in hours, these compounds have long duration of action. These compounds esterify the serine residue in the cholinesterase enzyme. The hydrolysis rate of the phosphorylated serine is extremely slow and hydrolysis to the free enzyme and phosphoric acid derivative is so limited that the inhibition is considered irreversible.

The following are the examples of organophosphorus compounds which are irreversible anticholinesterases.

$$(C_2H_5O)_2 - \overset{\overset{O}{\uparrow}}{P} - O - \overset{\overset{O}{\uparrow}}{P} - (OC_2H_5)_2$$

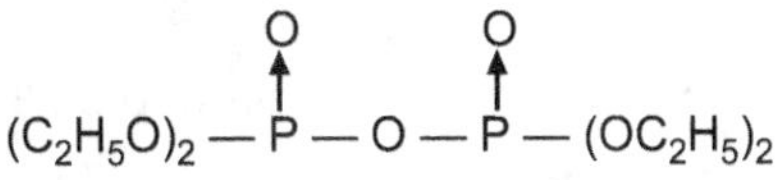

Tetraethyl pyrophosphate

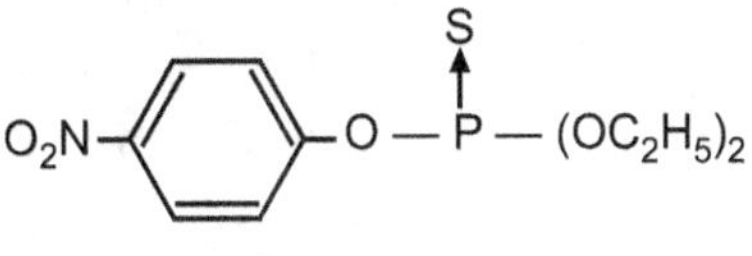

Parathion

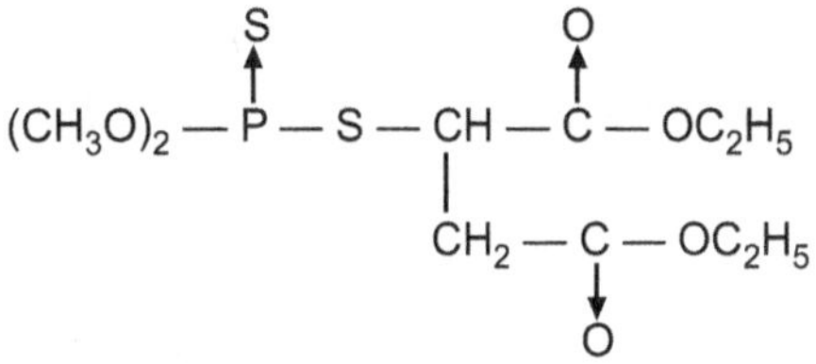

Melathion

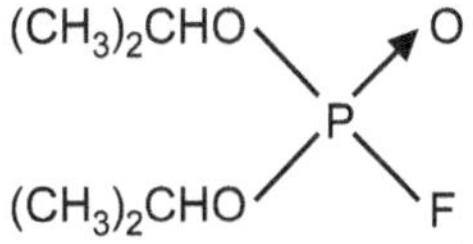

Isofluorphate

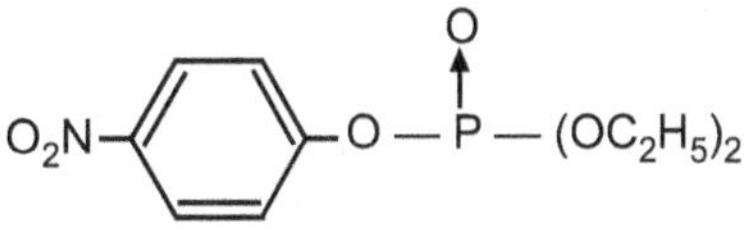

Paraoxon

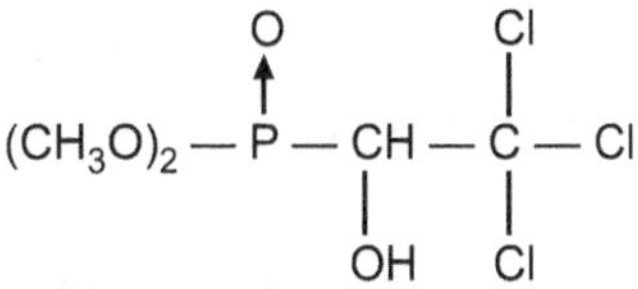

Dipterex

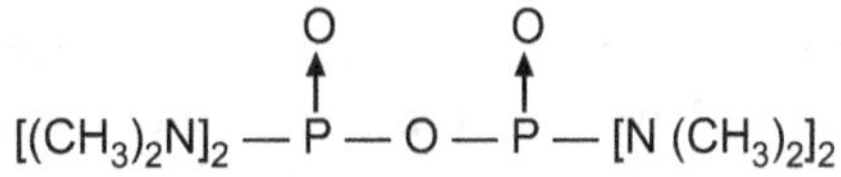

$$[(CH_3)_2N]_2 - \overset{\overset{O}{\uparrow}}{P} - O - \overset{\overset{O}{\uparrow}}{P} - [N(CH_3)_2]_2$$

Schradran

$$(CH_3)_2CH - O - \overset{\overset{O}{\uparrow}}{\underset{F}{P}} - O - CH(CH_3)_2$$

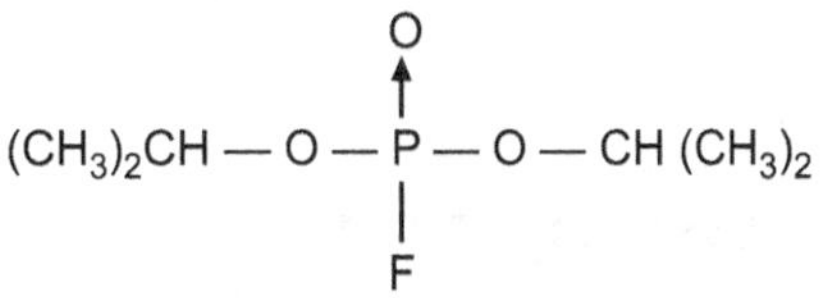

Di-isopropylfluorophosphate

Structure-Activity Relationship :

A general formula for these compounds is as follows :

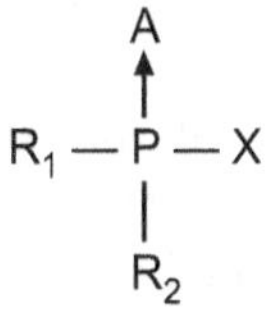

$$R_1 - \overset{\overset{A}{\uparrow}}{\underset{R_2}{P}} - X$$

where　R_1 = alkoxyl

　　　R_2 = alkoxyl, alkyl or tertiary amine.

　　　X = A good leaving group,

e.g. F, CN, thiomalate, p-nitrophenoxy.

(i) A is usually oxygen or sulphur, but may also be selenium. When A is other than oxygen, biological activation is required before compound becomes effective.

(ii) X is good leaving group when the molecule reacts with the enzyme.

(iii) The R moiety imparts lipophilicity to the molecule and contributes its absorption through skin.

(iv) In alkoxy series, compounds which contain fluorine are more active than those containing iodine or other radical.

These organophosphorus compounds are nerve poisons and used as :

(1) Nerve gases in warfare.

(2) As agricultural insecticides in which the death of insects can be attributed to the inactivation of their acetylcholinesterases.

(3) In the treatment of glaucoma.

These compounds are very toxic to humans and must be handled with extreme caution. Toxic symptoms are nausea, vomiting, excessive sweating, salivation, miosis, bradycardia, low blood pressure and respiratory difficulty that is usually the cause of death.

4.16 THERAPEUTIC USES

The reversible cholinesterase inhibitors find their clinical uses mainly due to their following basic properties :

(1) They activate muscarinic receptors by accumulating acetylcholine at the receptor sites.

(2) Activation of nicotinic receptor sites leads to stimulation, followed by depression or paralysis of skeletal muscles.

(3) Activation of muscarinic receptors in the CNS leads to stimulation followed by depression of the centrally governed cholinergic effects.

The cholinesterase inhibitors are recommended under following condition,

(i) in glaucoma, in which high intraocular pressure can lead to permanent damage to the optic disk, resulting in blindness,

(ii) in myasthenia gravis : They increase the acetylcholine concentration and excitation of the neuromuscular junction. Disease is characterised by muscular weakness and abnormal fatigue that patients can not even keep their eyes open. These drugs increase the strength and endurance, and

(iii) as curare antidotes because the increased acetylcholine levels displace the blocker more readily.

4.17 ANTIDOTES FOR NERVE GASES

When an irreversible cholinesterase is used, it combines with cholinesterase and the OH group of the serine gets phosphorylated. It was usually considered that water in body fluids attacks the phosphorylated serine residue and causes its hydrolysis. But the rate of hydrolysis is very slow and that a more effective agent was required for rapid hydrolysis i.e. it involves the administration of a better nucleophile than water to attack the phosphorus atom and thereby eliminate or liberate the enzyme back to its original form, as shown below :

(1) Enzyme-Ser $-$ CH$_2$ $-$ OH $+$ N $-$ atom of

$\downarrow$ imidazole (Im$_2$)

           of histidine

Enzyme $-$ Ser-CH$_2$ $-$ O$^{\ominus}$ $+$ HN-imidazole (Im$_2$)

(2) Enzyme $-$ Ser-CH$_2$ $-$ O$^{\ominus}$ $+$ RO $-$ $\overset{\overset{O}{\|}}{P}$ $-$ OR

$\downarrow$ irreversible

       cholinesterase

Enzyme $-$ Ser-CH$_2$ $-$ O $-$ $\overset{O}{\overset{\uparrow}{P}}(OR)_2$

Phosphorylated serine residue
of cholinesterase enzyme

(3) Enzyme – Ser-CH$_2$ – O – $\overset{\overset{O}{\uparrow}}{P}$ – (OR)$_2$

+ Nu (better nucleophile)

Enzyme – Ser-CH$_2$ – O – $\overset{\overset{O}{\uparrow}}{\underset{\oplus}{P}}$ – (OR)$_2$

Rapid
hydrolysis   Nu

Enzyme – Ser-CH$_2$ OH + Nu – $\overset{\overset{O}{\uparrow}}{P}$ – (OR)$_2$

Regenerated enzyme

The effective antidotes for irreversible anticholinesterases developed are as follows :

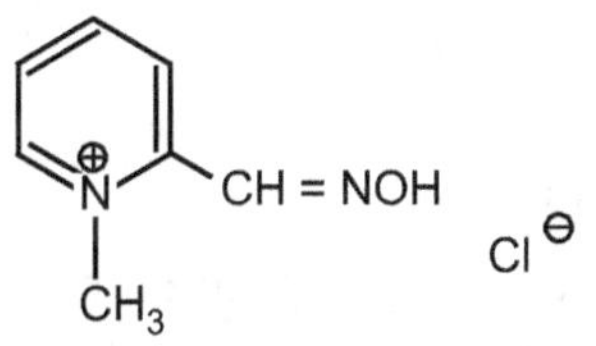

2-pyridine aldoxime methchloride
(Pralidoxime chloride)

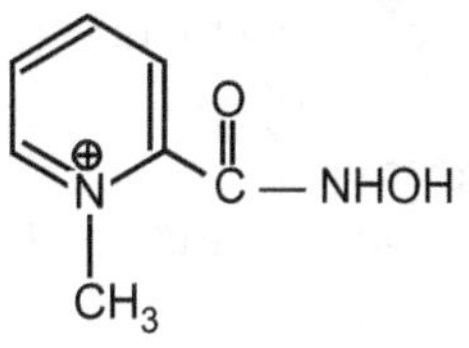

2-Pyridine hydroxamic acid
methiodide

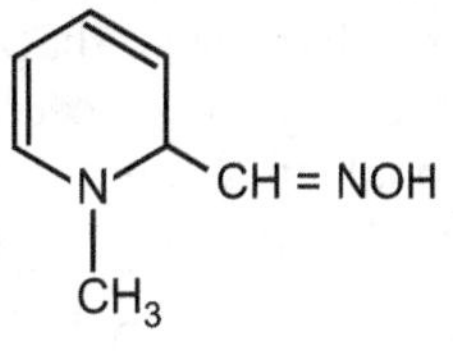

Dihydro 2-Pyridine aldoxime methiodide

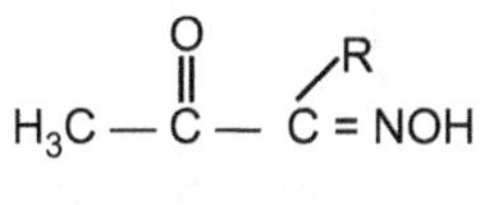

$H_3C — \overset{\overset{O}{\|}}{C} — \overset{\nearrow R}{C} = NOH$

R = – CH$_3$; Diacetylmonoxime

R = – H; Pyruvaldoxime

Hydroxamic acid or aldoxamine part of the structure is known for zinc (metalloenzymes) binding properties.

To potentiate the action of 2-PAM, atropine is also used along with it. Atropine acts as competitive antagonist for the accumulated acetylcholine at muscarinic sites.

The effectiveness of the oximes as antidotes is not entirely attributed to their reactivating action on cholinesterases. They may also alter the distribution of the inhibitor, diverting it to the liver as well as exerting a curare like action sufficient to effect a partial relief to the neuromuscular blockade.

Limitations of Oximes as Antidotes :

(i) These reactivators (antidotes) are only effective if they are given immediately before or soon after the exposure to the inhibitor. The phosphorylated enzyme undergoes a fairly rapid process, called as 'ageing' (which probably involves the loss of an alkyl part of alkoxy group) as a result of which it becomes resistant to the action of the antidote.

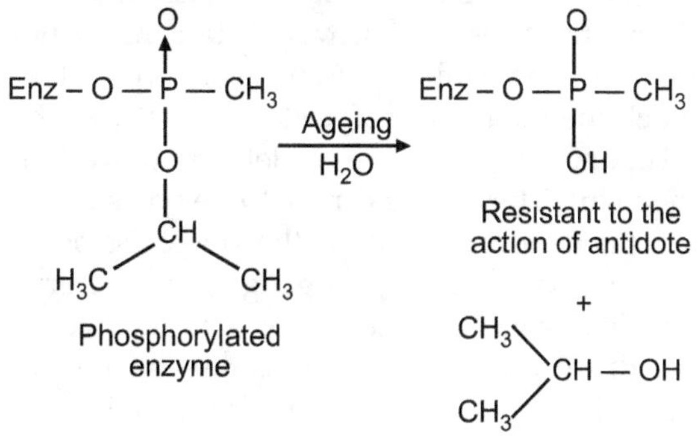

(ii) The reactivators are not very successful in restoring cholinesterase activity in CNS.

(iii) They are not effective against all organophosphorus compounds, the toxicity of few of which is actually increased by the oximes.

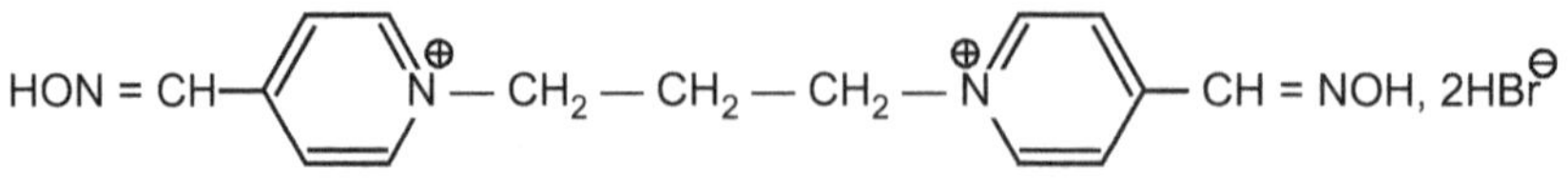

1, 3 bis (pyridinium - 4 - aldoxime) propane dibromide

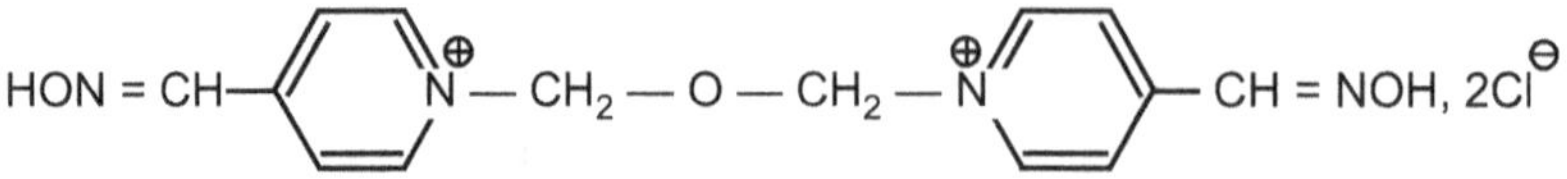

Obidoxime chloride (Toxogenin)

Parasympatholytics or Antispasmodics or Cholinergic Blocking Agents :

They are anticholinergic drugs that inhibit the effects of acetylcholine released from postganglionic parasympathetic nerve endings. They block muscarinic actions of acetylcholine including smooth muscle contractions and exocrine gland secretion. Atropine is the prototype of this class.

Two obvious approaches are there, to treat the conditions characterised by overstimulation of cholinergic nerves.

(i) Use of agents that inhibit the synthesis or release of acetylcholine.

(ii) Use of agents that block the acetylcholine from reacting with the receptors.

Compounds that inhibit acetylcholine synthesis have been discovered but have not proved to be clinically useful while drugs that block the interaction of acetylcholine with the receptor, however, are widely employed in medicine. These drugs are of three types :

(a) Those who block the transmission at parasympathetic post-ganglionic nerve terminals e.g. Atropine.

(b) Those who block transmission, at sympathetic and parasympathetic ganglia e.g. hexamethonium.

(c) Those who block neuromuscular junctions in skeletal muscles e.g. d-tubocurarine. Such compounds should have the opposite effects of cholinergic agonists and their administration should be characterised by decreased secretion of saliva and gastric juices, decreased mobility of GIT and urinary tract (antispasmodic) and dilation of pupil.

Because of their ability to relax smooth muscle, they are referred to as antispasmodic. Such compound should have an affinity for cholinergic receptor but should lack intrinsic activity.

The interaction of atropine with muscarinic receptors was found to be loose and reversible.

Classification :

Chemically, antispasmodic drugs are classified as :

1. Atropine and its synthetic analogues
2. Synthetic aminoalcohol esters
3. Aminoalcohol ethers
4. Aminoalcohols
5. Aminoamides
6. Papaverine and its synthetic analogues
7. Miscellaneous agents.

Structure-Activity Relationship :

(A) Anticholinergic compounds may be considered as chemicals that have some structural similarity to acetylcholine but contain additional substituents which enhance their binding to the cholinergic receptors.

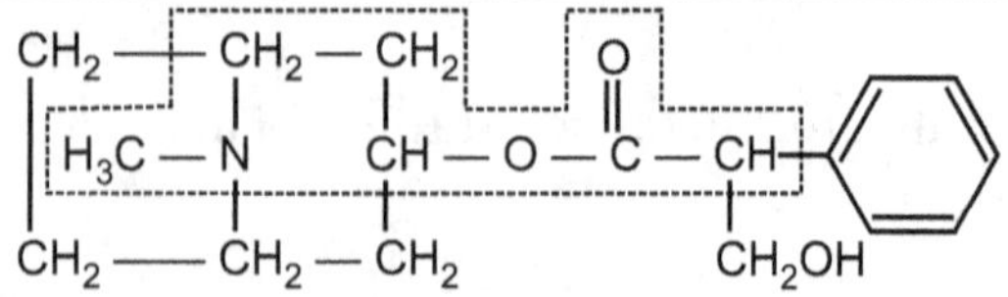

Fig. 4.21 : Atropine

The circled portion of atropine molecule reveals the segment resembling with acetylcholine.

Atropa belladonna was named by Linnaeus in 1753, after Atropos, the eldest of the three Fates of Greek mythology and the one whose duty was to cut the thread of life. "Belladonna" does refer to an Italian name ("handsome woman") for the plant, which was used by Venetian ladies to give them "sparkling eyes". The greater molar potency of atropine helps it to block several moles of acetylcholine. The umbrella-like atropine molecule may mechanically or electrostatically inactivate adjacent receptors on the cell surface so that these receptors are also unavailable for acetylcholine or other parasympathomimetic stimulants. Atropine and scopolamine are esters of tropic acid with the complex organic bases *tropanol* (*tropine*) and *scopine*, respectively. Scopine differs from tropanol only by the oxygen bridge between C-6 and C-7. The alkaloid atropine was first isolated by Mein and also by Geiger and Hesse in 1832. Ladenburg, who, in 1880, produced the semisynthetic derivative homatropine, which is still widely used.

Scopolamine (Hyoscine)

The action of scopolamine differs from that of atropine in one important respect : when given by injection, in ordinary doses, scopolamine, in addition to its cholinergic blocking effect, exerts a powerful sedative or hypnotic action.

To reduce CNS side-effects, quaternary salts of atropine like, ipratropium (bronchodilator) and atropine methonitrate (to lower GI tract motility) are used clinically.

(B) Since acetylcholine and atropine both are acetic acid ester of aminoalcohol, many substituted acetic acid esters of amino alcohols were prepared and evaluated for biological activity. Such esters of phenylacetic acid had little activity. Similar esters of diphenyl acetic acid are found therapeutically useful.

R = alkyl group

Therefore, the minimum structure necessary for pure antagonistic activity is :

where

R = hydroxyalkyl, alkyl, cycloalkyl or heterocyclic

R' = alkyl

(i) In the above general formula, the antagonist may contain larger groups than methyl on the nitrogen atom. In general, these groups should not be larger than butyl, if the compound is to be an effective antagonist.

(ii) The nitrogen atom in an antagonist need not be always quaternised. Since the pH of the receptor is acidic, this amino group gets protonated and carries a positive charge that interacts with the anionic site of the receptor.

(iii) The acyl group in an antagonist, is always larger than the acyl group in acetylcholine. The larger acyl group ensures that the compound is not a partial agonist.

(C) The acetylcholine molecule does not cover all the area of receptor. The area of a receptor, which is not covered by a acetylcholine molecule appears to be chiefly hydrophobic in nature. Hence, hydrophobic substituents increase the affinity of the antagonist by binding to this area. However, this area is not uniform in its hydrophobic nature. The fact that esters of triphenyl acetic acid have low potency can be justified only if the hydrophobic area does not accommodate binding by a third phenyl ring.

(D) The high potency of esters and amides of tropic acid result from their ability to H-bond with a suitable group on the receptor, surrounded by the hydrophobic area.

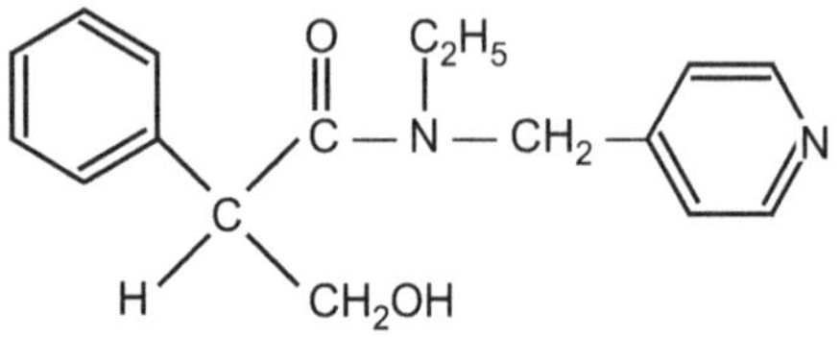

Tropicamide

It is used to produce mydriasis and cycloplegia.

(E) Since a number of alcohols, esters and ethers resembling choline are less potent than acetylcholine, but still demonstrate appreciable agonist properties, it might be expected that the addition of two large groups to these molecules would produce cholinergic blocking agents. The reasoning was correct and yielded therapeutically useful compounds.

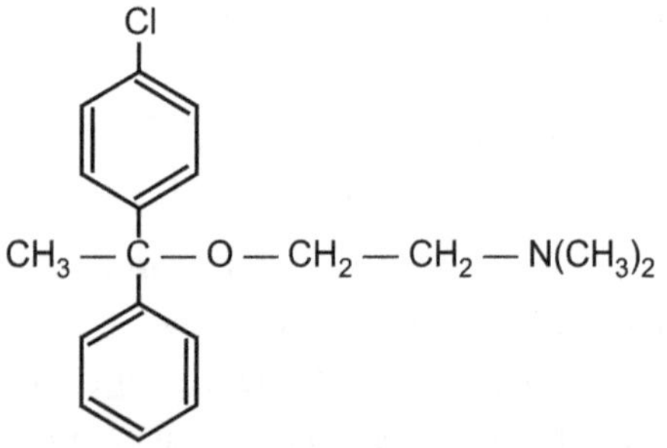

Chlorphenoxamine

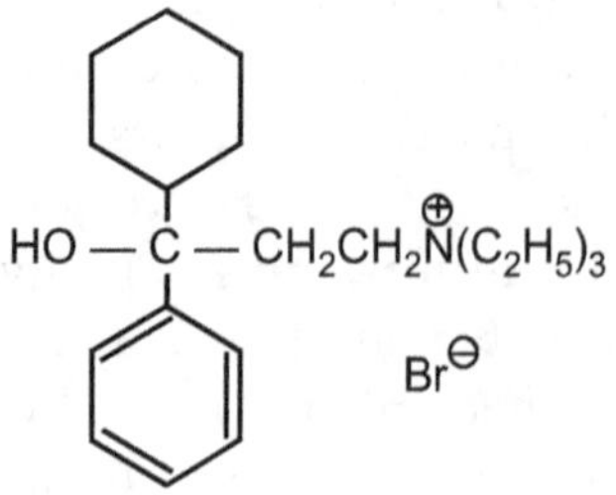

Tridihexethyl bromide

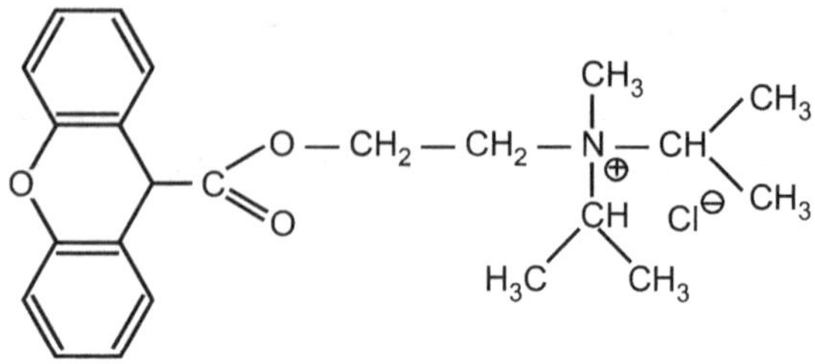

Propantheline chloride

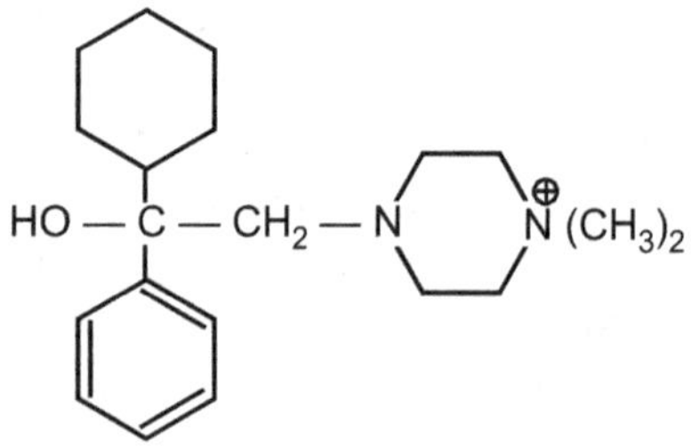

Hexocyclium

Fesoterodine : It is an antimuscarinic agent used to treat-over active bowel. It is a prodrug converted by plasma esterases to active metabolite, 5-hydroxymethyl toiterodine.

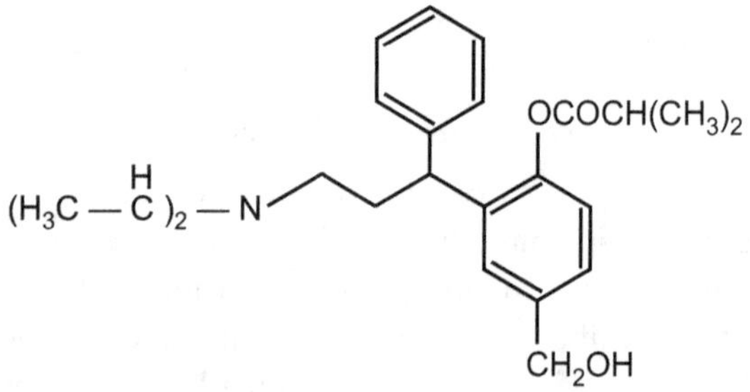

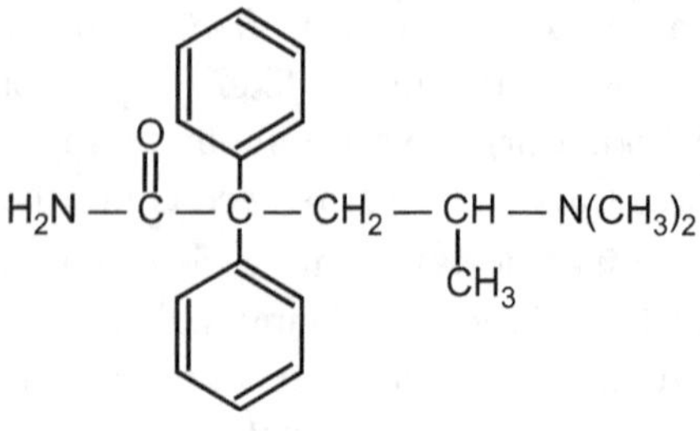

Aminopentamide

This is an indication for the need of at least one portion of the molecule to have the space occupying, umbrella like shape which leads to firm binding at the receptor.

(F) Size alone, is not the sole criteria for potent blocking agents. The special arrangement or the stereochemical features of the molecule are also important presumably because of a good fit of its prosthetic group with the receptor site.

Mode of Action :

The main difference in cholinergic and anticholinergic agents appears to be the size of the acyl group.

$$R - \overset{\overset{\displaystyle O}{\displaystyle \|}}{C} - O - CH_2 - CH_2 - N\,(R)_2$$

In cholinergic compounds R = small group.

In anticholinergic compound R = large group.

The large (alkyl or aryl) group may not only increase the affinity of the blocking agent but through an 'Umbrella effect' may also block the approach of acetylcholine to the receptor.

Adverse Effects : Adverse effect of the antispasmodic drugs are dose dependent and include dry mouth and skin, flushing, tachycardia, pupillary dilatation with blurred vision, cerebral excitement and delirium. The quaternary ammonium compounds may also cause postural hypotension and impotence because of their ganglionic blocking effects.

Uses : The anticholinergic drugs have been widely used in the treatment of peptic ulcer disease and irritable bowel and functional disorders, including diarrhoea. The

main contraindications to anticholinergic drug use are narrow angle glaucoma, pyloric outlet obstruction and reflux oesophagitis.

Bellaeu's Concept of Enzyme Perturbation :

This concept views that the receptor alters its conformation to fit the acetylcholine or its agonists. Since it is bound to the membrane, it sufficiently changes membrane structure to alter the transport of ions through the membrane to generate muscle contraction.

The applicability of this concept is further enhanced by the fact that as the size increases in the series of compounds with cholinergic activity, there is not an abrupt change from cholinergic to anticholinergic activity.

$$[\text{e. g. } CH_3(CH_2)n N^+ (CH_3)_3]$$

when   (1) n = 1 to 4, potency increases

        (2) n = 5 to 7, partial agonists

        (3) n = more than 7, compound is antagonist.

Bellaeu's concept can be represented as shown in Table 4.3.

In this table, compound 1 (ACh) can exactly fit on the receptor to provide orientation favourable for agonist activity. Some molecules like compound 2 and 3, when in an unfavourable orientation [i.e. 2(a) and 3 (a)] exhibit antagonistic activity, while remaining molecules can assume a conformation i.e. 2 (b) and 3 (b), that will fit on the receptor to give an orientation favourable for agonist activity. Therefore, the combined effect is being partial agonist. Molecule 4 is too large to fit the receptor in such a way as to provide a favourable conformation. It acts totally as an antagonist.

Table 4.3 : Belleau's concept of enzyme perturbation

Favourable Orientation	Unfavourable orientation
1 ACh	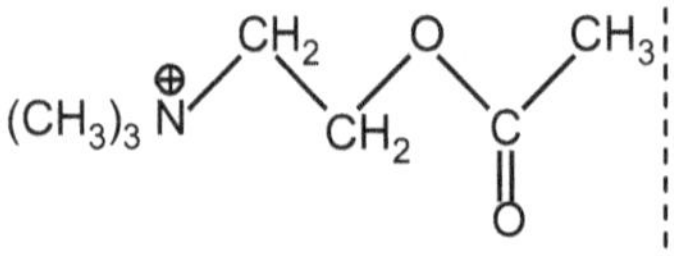
2 (a) 5	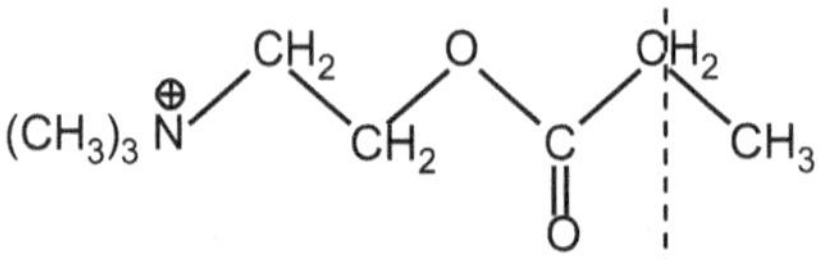
(b) 5	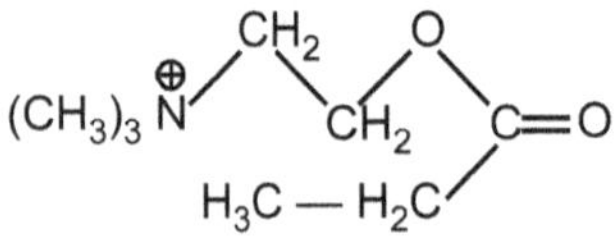
3 (a) 6	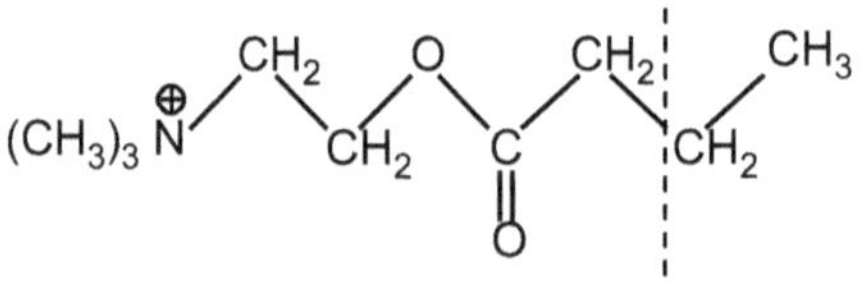
(b) 6	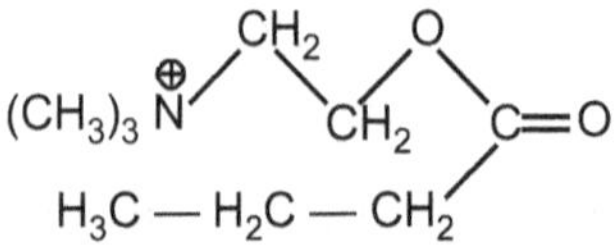
4 9	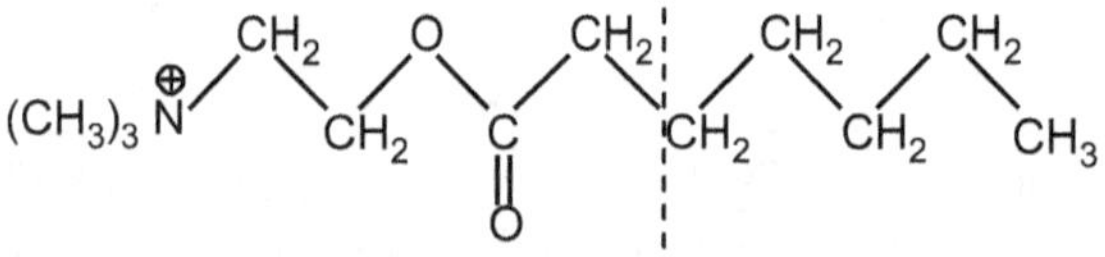

Table 4.4 : Compounds with cholinergic blocking action

$$R - \overset{\overset{\textstyle O}{\|}}{C} - O - CH_2\,CH_2 - R_1$$

R	R_1	Names
(1)	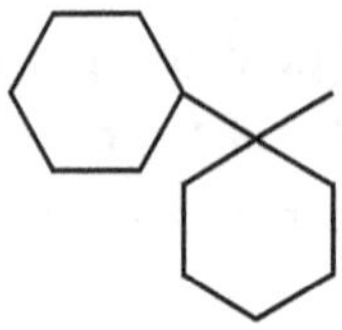 $-\,N\,(C_2H_5)_2$	Dicyclomine

Contd...

(2)	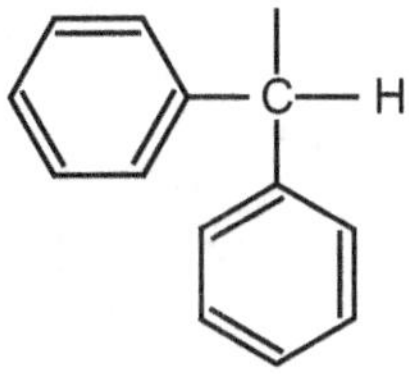	$- N (C_2H_5)_2$	Trasentine
(3)	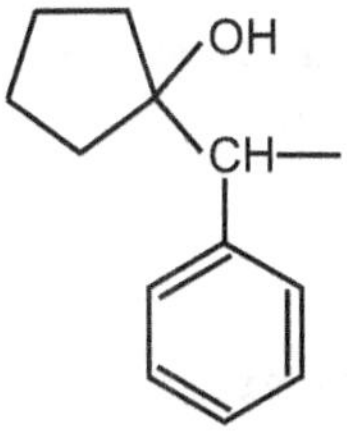	$- N (CH_3)_2$	Cyclopentolate
(4)	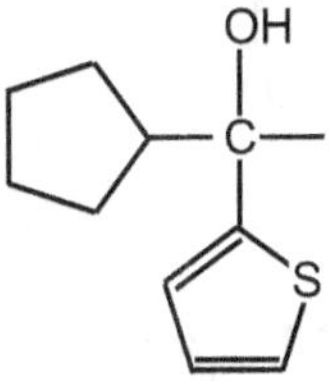	$\overset{CH_3}{\underset{\oplus}{- N}} - (C_2H_5)_2$	Penthienate
(5)	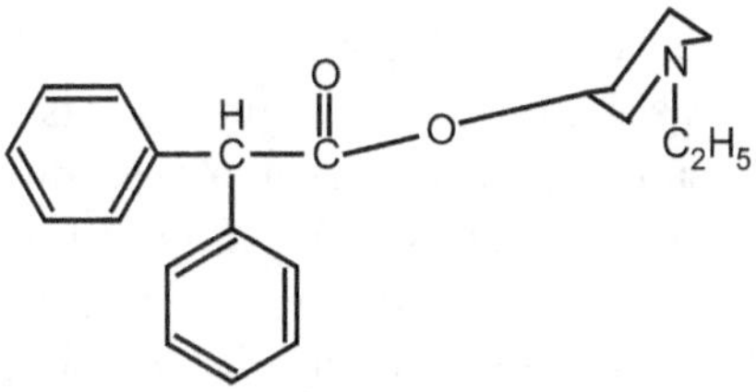		Piperidolate
(6)	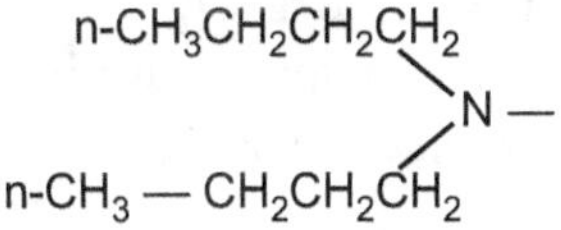	$\overset{C_2H_5}{\underset{\oplus}{- N}} - (CH_3)_2$	Dibutoline

Clinically Useful Antispasmodic Agents

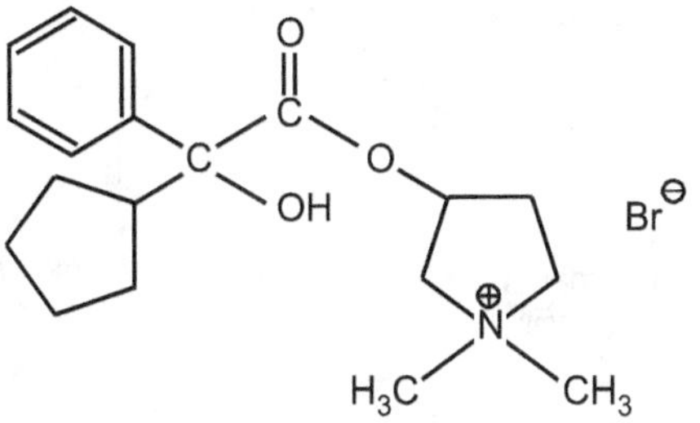

Glycopyrrolate

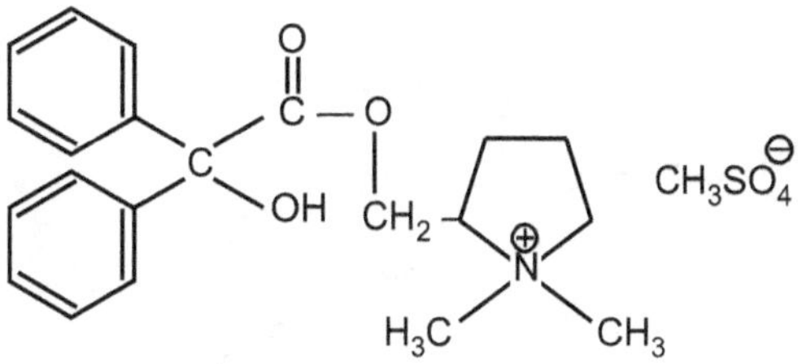

Poldine Methylsulphate

Papaverine and its Synthetic Analogues :

This is a group of antispasmodic agents that do not act by interfering with cholinergic nerve transmission.

Papaverine

Ethaverine

Methantheline; R = – C₂H₅
Propantheline; R = isopropyl

Isopropamide

Dioxyline

Tetrahydropapaverine

Alverine

Neupaverine

Mechanism of Action :

Since cholinergic nerve stimulation increases peristaltic movements of GIT (spasmodic), adrenergic nerve stimulation will produce antispasmodic effect through the stimulation of β-adrenergic receptors. Cyclic-AMP (cyclic-3', 5'-adenosine monophosphate) is the active factor which is a product of the response of β-adrenergic receptors. Papaverine and its analogues are inhibitors of phosphodiesterase, an enzyme that destroys cyclic-AMP.

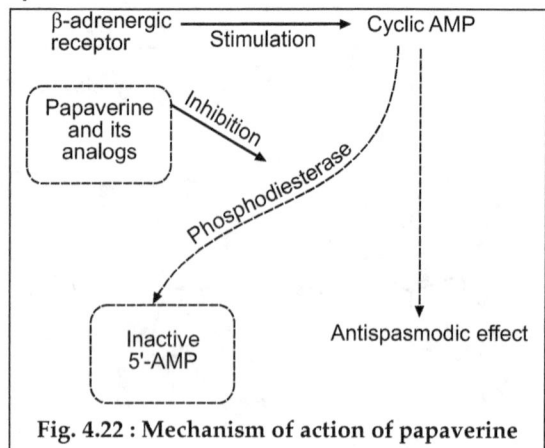

Fig. 4.22 : Mechanism of action of papaverine analogues

Chemical structures of AChE inhibitors and nicotinic agonists under investigation as therapeutic agents in Alzheimer's dementia :

(a) AChE inhibitors :

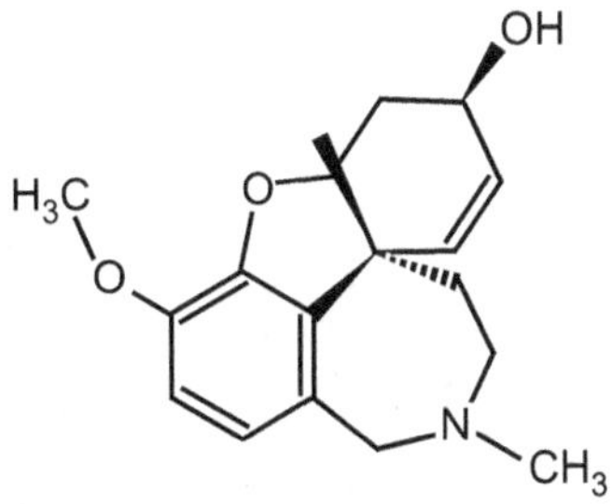

Galanthamine

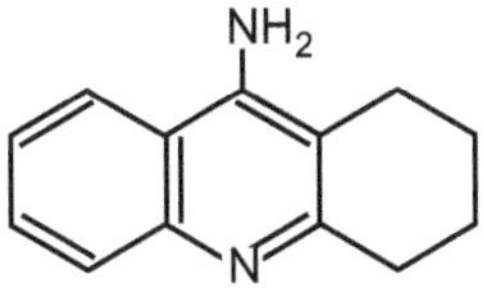

Tacrine

Tacrine hydrochloride is a reversible cholinesterase inhibitor, used in the treatment of mild to moderate Alzheimer's dementia.

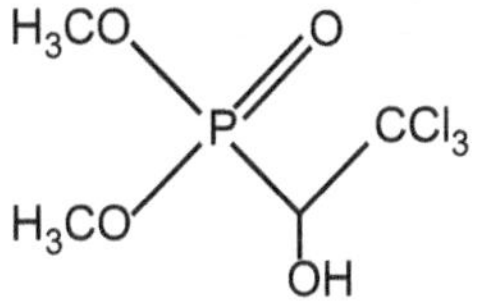

Metrifonate

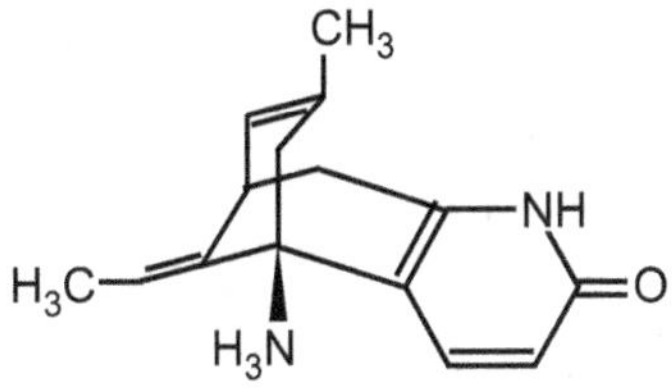

Huperzine A

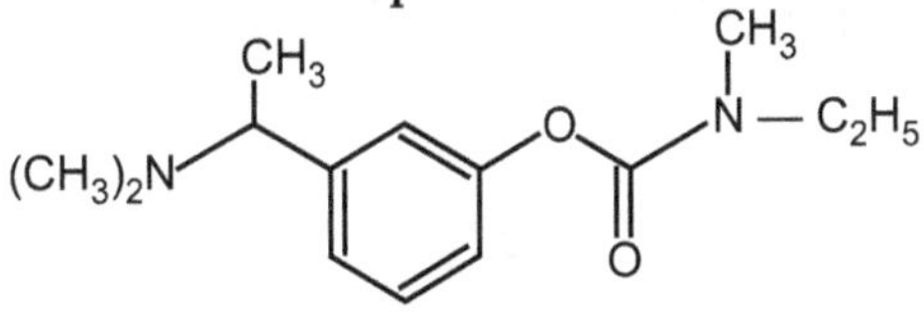

Rivastigmine

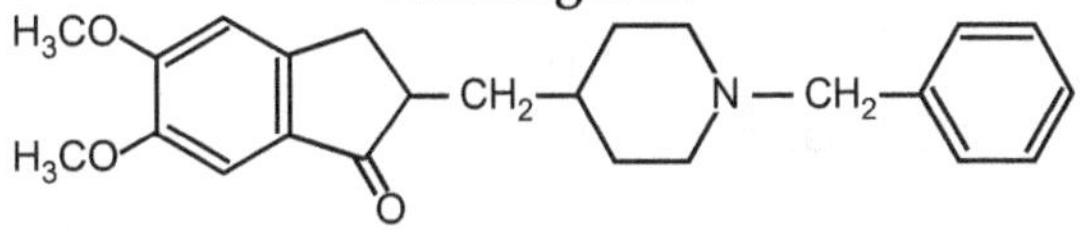

Donepezil

It is a reversible non-competitive centrally acting cholinestrase inhibitor.

Nicotinic and muscarinic agonists :

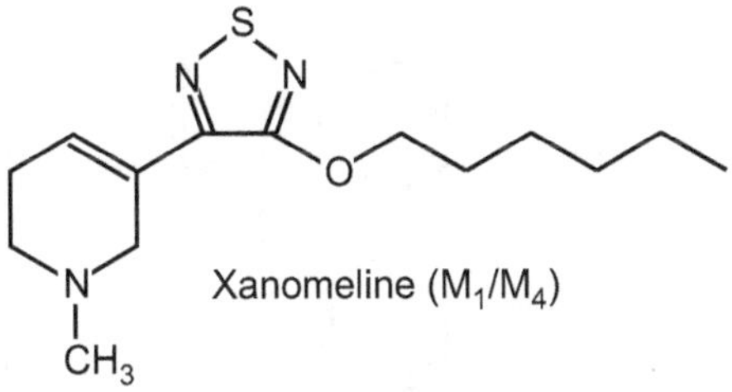

Xanomeline (M_1/M_4)

Varenicline (2006) : It is nicotinic receptor partial agonist. It may be used to treat smoking addiction. **Cevimeline** is a parasympathomimetic and M_3 – muscarinic agonist. It stimulates salivary gland, therby alleviating dry mouth.

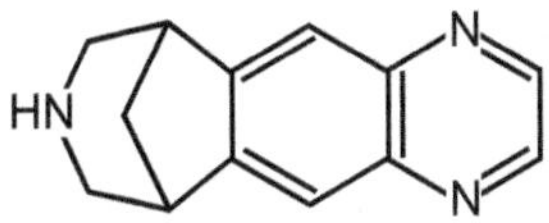

Varenicline

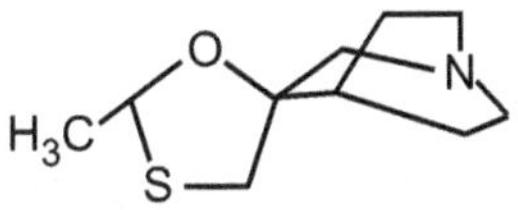

Cevimeline

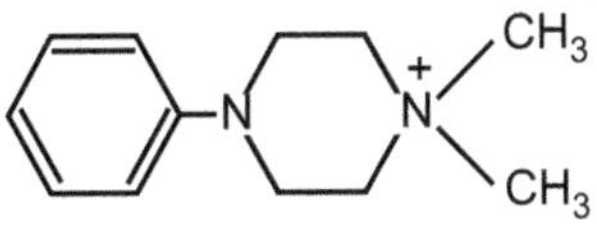

1, 1-Dimethyl-4
phenylpiperazinium (N_2)

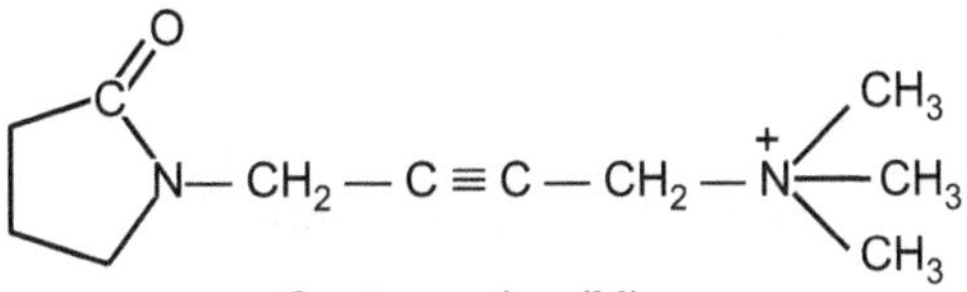

Oxotremorine (M)

Nicotinic antagonists :

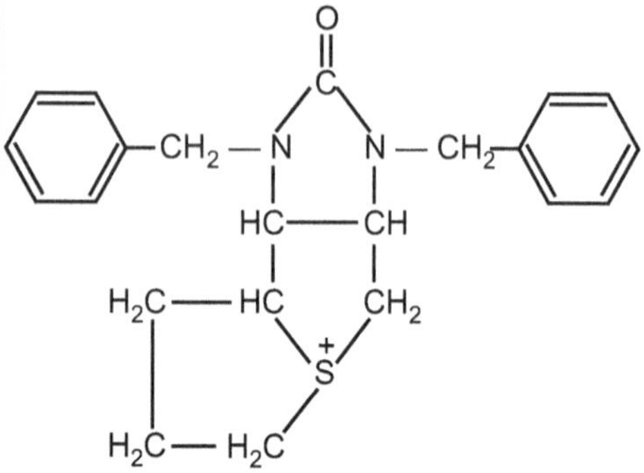

Trimethaphan (N$_2$)

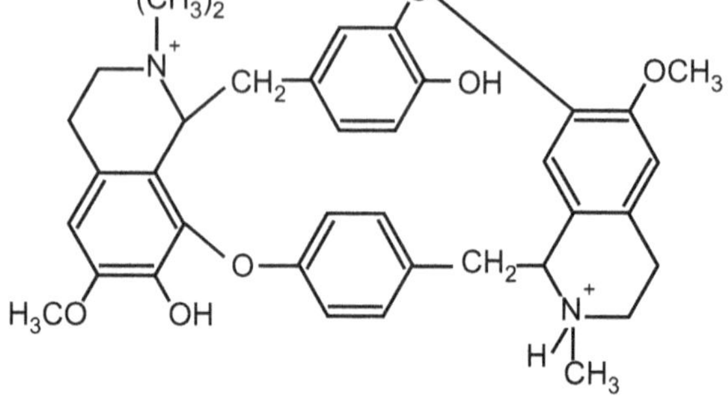

d-Tubocurarine

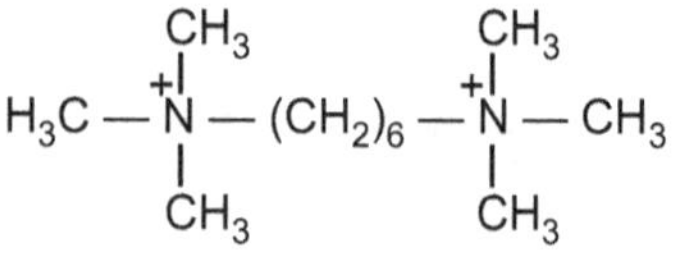

$$H_3C - \overset{\overset{\displaystyle CH_3}{+|}}{N} - (CH_2)_6 - \overset{\overset{\displaystyle CH_3}{+|}}{N} - CH_3$$
$$\underset{CH_3}{|}\underset{CH_3}{|}$$

Hexamethonium (N$_2$)

$$H_3C - \overset{\overset{\displaystyle CH_3}{+|}}{N} - (CH_2)_{10} - \overset{\overset{\displaystyle CH_3}{+|}}{N} - CH_3$$
$$\underset{CH_3}{|}\phantom{- (CH_2)_{10} - }\underset{CH_3}{|}$$

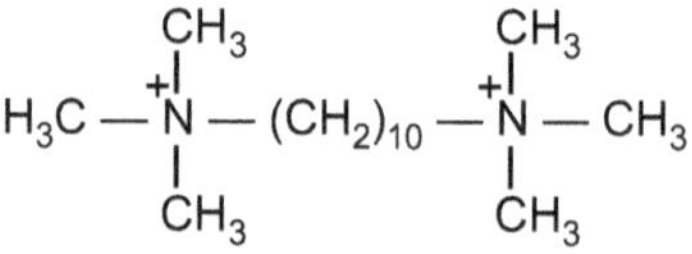

Decamethonium (N$_2$)

Muscarinic antagonists :

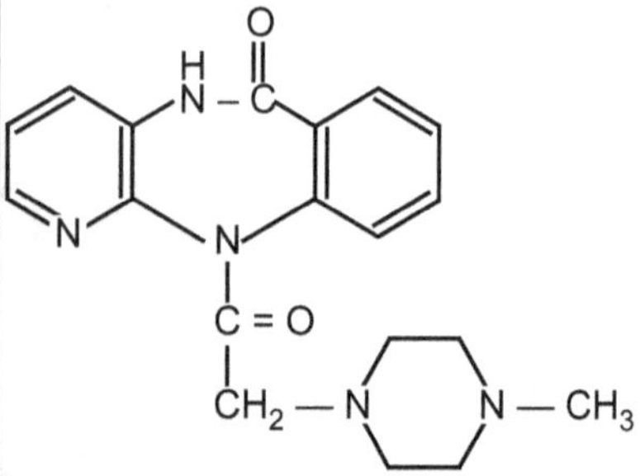

Pirenzepine (M$_1$)

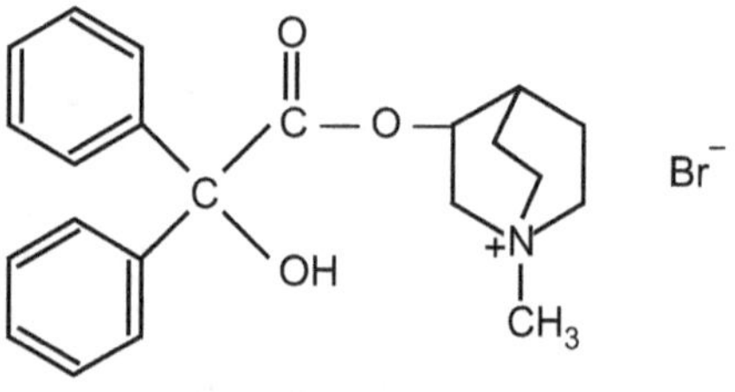

Clidinium bromide (M$_3$)

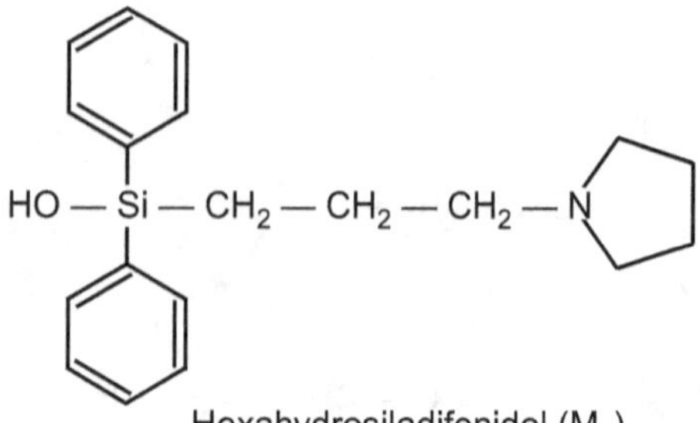

Hexahydrosiladifenidol (M$_3$)

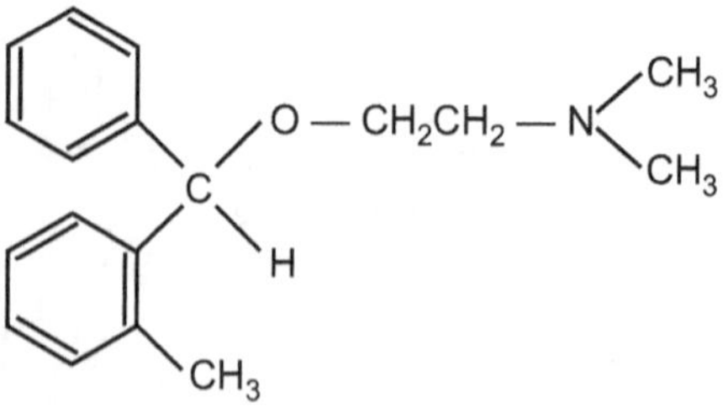

Orphenadrine (M$_1$)

4.18　URINARY ANTISPASMODIC (M₃-ANTAGONISITS)

Flavoxate : It has antimuscarinic activity in addition to direct muscle relaxant action. It is used to treat urinary bladder spasms.

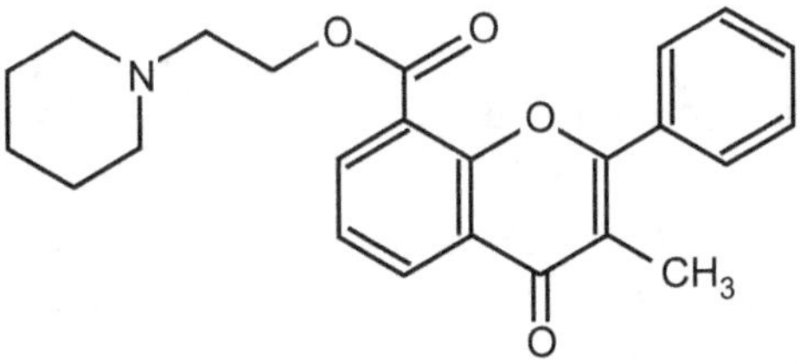

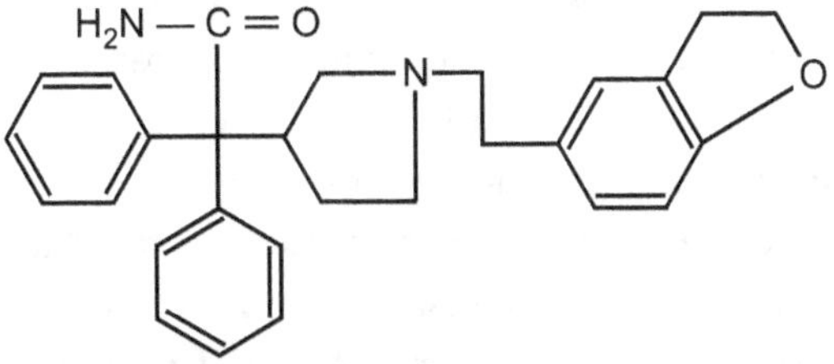

Darifenacine
(M₃ - antagonist urinary antispasmodic)

Solifenacin : It is a competitive muscarinic (M₃) receptor antagonist. It is used as urinary antispasmodic to reduce smooth muscle tone in the urinary bladder.

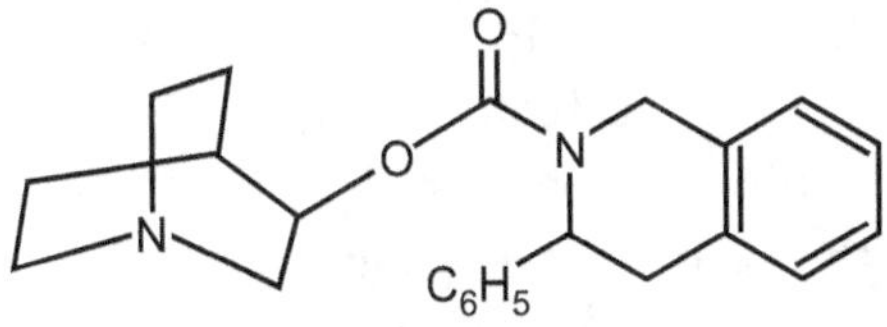

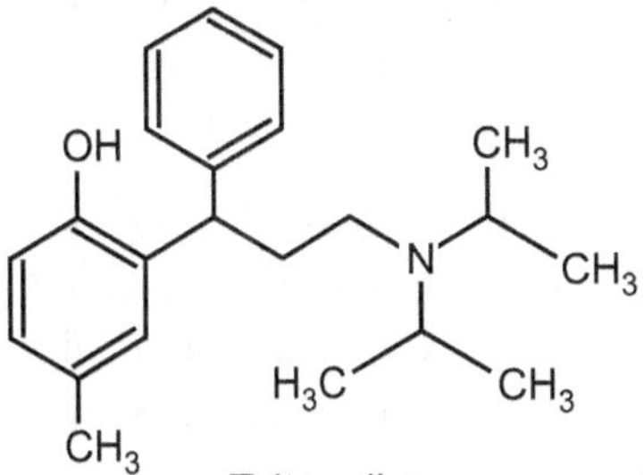

Tolterodine
(antimuscarinic urinary antispasmodic)

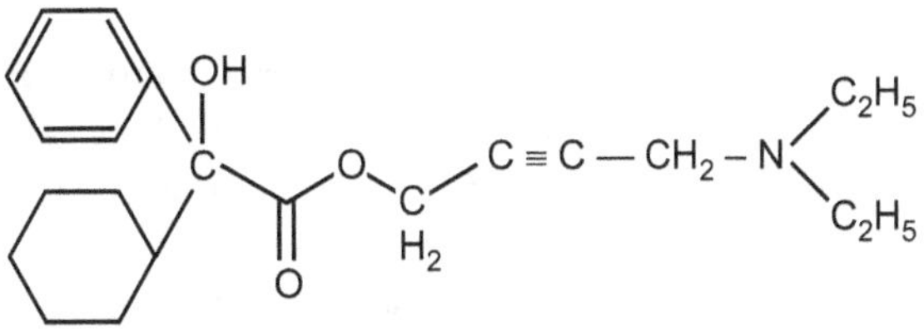

Oxybutynin
(antimuscarinic urinary antispasmodic)

Tolterodine is a selective M₃ antagonist and is considered to be the drug of choice for hyperactive bladder. This condition is characterized by frequent and involuntary urination. The drug is better tolerated than oxybutynin. **Fesoterodine** is a related drug with similar activity.

Darifenacin : It is M₃ – muscarinic receptor blocker, used to decrease the urgency to urinate in overactive bladder.

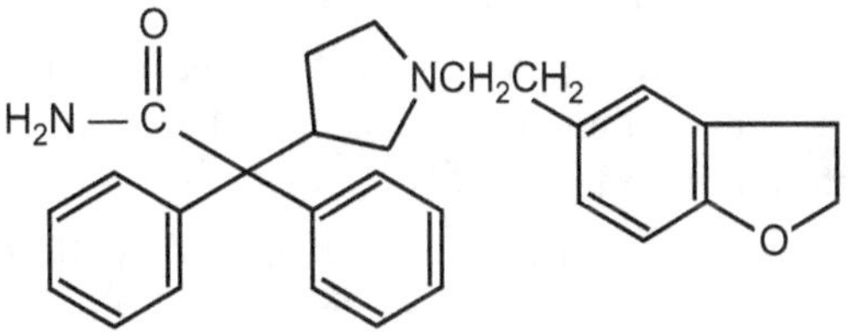

Trospium chloride : It is a urinary antispasmodic used for the treatment of overactive bladder.

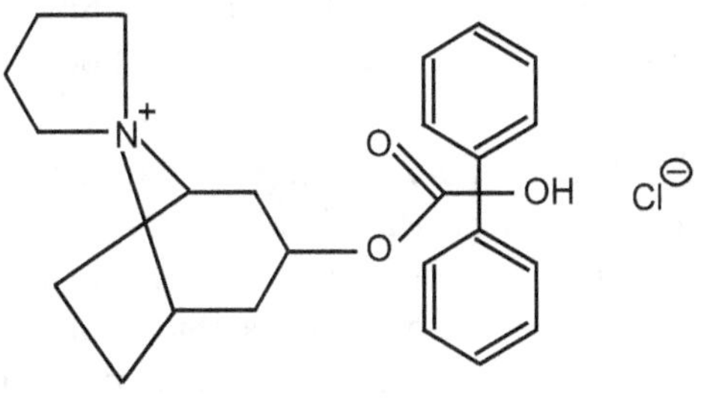

4.19 GANGLIONIC BLOCKERS

The balance, co-ordination and control of muscle movement and muscle tone is governed by the autonomic ganglia in the regions of mid-brain, cerebellum and spinal cord. Like in neuromuscular transmission, acetylcholine plays the role of main neurotransmitter also in autonomic ganglionic transmission. This is supported by the fact that d-tubocurarine, a neuromuscular blocking agent, can also cause the blockade of ganglionic transmission. In addition, there are several points of similarity between ganglionic and neuromuscular transmission. For example, the transmission in parasympathetic ganglia obeys the same presynaptic to postsynaptic cell relationship as that is seen in neuromuscular junctions. In most of the cases, however, transmission through autonomic ganglia is quite complex and may involve neurons interposed between the pre and post synaptic components. These neurons are therefore termed as interneurons.

In general, following categories of drugs can alter the transmission through the autonomic ganglia.

(a) drugs which inhibit either synthesis or storage of acetylcholine. Hemicholiniums is an example of this category.

(b) drugs which reduce or prevent the release of acetylcholine from preganglionic nerve fibers. Example is botulinus toxin.

(c) drugs which inhibit metabolism of acetylcholine by blocking cholinesterase enzymes. Example is physostigmine and

(d) drugs which potentiate or inhibit the interaction of acetylcholine with postganglionic receptor sites.

For better understanding of the action of various drugs which alter the transmission through the autonomic ganglia in either ways, a concise report about the events taking place during ganglionic transmission is presented below.

GANGLIONIC TRANSMISSION

The ganglionic synapse retains many of the characteristic features of neuromuscular synapses. However in sympathetic ganglia and some parasympathetic ganglia, a dopaminergic neuron is present in the region of synaptic cleft. The muscarinic receptors present on interneuron are activated by the acetylcholine released from preganglionic nerve ending. This, results into release of catecholamines (i.e., noradrenaline, adrenaline or dopamine) from the interneuron which then activate the postsynaptic α-adrenergic receptors. Thus, the dopaminergic interneuron if activated, results into characteristic catecholamine fluorescence spectrum and hence the interneuron may also be termed as a small intensity, fluorescent cell (SIF). At many places, its role is assigned to be of modulator of ganglionic transmission.

In neuromuscular junction, the end-plate region comprises only of nicotinic cholinergic receptors but in autonomic ganglia, both types i.e., muscarinic and nicotinic receptors are located on the postganglionic fiber. The post-ganglionic cell body also possesses receptor sites for autacoid (e.g., angiotensin, bradykinin, serotonin or histamine) which are brought near to the ganglionic membranes through circulation. Depending upon the type of autacoid reacting, these receptor sites may give rise to excitatory or inhibitory type of responses and modulate the ganglionic transmission.

The released acetylcholine thus reacts with muscarinic and nicotinic receptor sites present on the cell body, and with muscarinic receptor sites of SIF cell. The stimulation of nicotinic receptors leads to the generation of fast excitatory post-synaptic potential (fast EPSP).

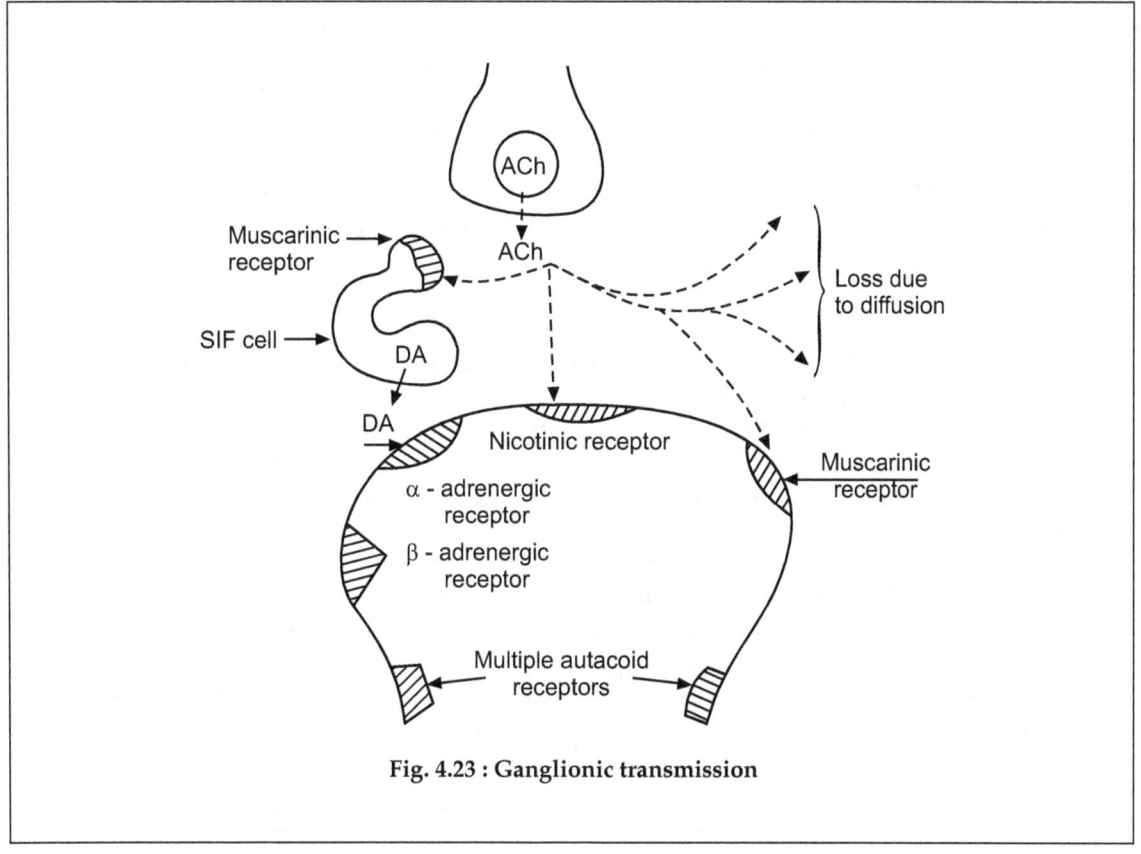

Fig. 4.23 : Ganglionic transmission

The events involved in fast EPSP are essentially similar to that which occur in neuromuscular junction. The release of catecholamine from SIF cell activates α–adrenergic receptor located on postganglionic cell body and leads to release of cyclic AMP. The accumulation of cyclic AMP in the ganglia causes a change in membrane permeability resulting into hyperpolarization of the cell. This hyperpolarization is responsible for the development of a slow inhibitory post synaptic potential (slow IPSP). A part of the acetylcholine released from the preganglionic nerve terminal, comes in contact with the muscarinic receptors present on the postganglionic cell-body, resulting into activation of these receptor sites. As a consequence, there is a release of cyclic GMP which is responsible for a slow excitatory post-synaptic potential.

Thus, the use of specific blockers of muscarinic and α-adrenergic receptors will alter secondary events like slow EPSP and slow IPSP but could not affect the fast EPSP.

The generation of fast EPSP is primary event and will only be influenced by drugs that block specifically nicotinic actions of acetylcholine.

Table 4.5 : Ganglionic versus neuromuscular transmission

Ganglionic transmission	Neuromuscular transmission
1. Post ganglionic membrane possesses various types of (muscarinic, nicotinic, α- and β- adrenergic, etc.) receptors.	1. The end-plate region possesses only nicotinic receptors.
2. Ganglionic post-synaptic potential is more complex and consists of three phases : Fast EPSP, slow IPSP and slow EPSP.	2. End-plate potential is a simple partial depolarization. No such subsidiary mechanisms exist.
3. Cholinesterases (ChE) are present in preganglionic fibre and prevent further release of neurotransmitter.	3. Most ChE are concentrated at the end-plate region.
4. Diffusion and not the enzymatic hydrolysis is an important mechanism for terminating transmitter's action in ganglia.	4. Enzymatic hydrolysis is the most important mechanism for termination of ACh-action.
5. Hence anti-ChE agents are less effective at ganglionic synapses.	5. Anti-ChE agents are effective agents, employed to reverse the paralysis produced by anti-depolarizing substances.

Thus, ganglionic transmission consists of three sequentially followed mechanisms, as listed below :

(a) Fast excitatory post-synaptic potential (Fast EPSP) : This is the primary pathway which causes rapid depolarization of the postganglionic membrane due to the opening of ion-channel with an inward sodium ion current. The events and mechanism are essentially same as that in neuromuscular transmission. An action potential is generated when the initial EPSP attains a critical amplitude. The activation, in the similar fashion of multiple synapses, is required before transmission becomes effective.

In multiple synapses subsidary pathways are necessary to amplify or suppress the excitatory post-synaptic potential. They prove a device to limit the ganglionic stimulation. These include

(i) Slow inhibitory post-synaptic potential (slow IPSP) : This results due to hyperpolarization of post ganglionic sites by the activation of α-adrenergic receptor sites. The catecholamine released from SIF cell is mainly responsible for this.

(ii) Slow excitatory post-synaptic potential (slow EPSP) : This phase arises by accumulation of cyclic GMP due to the activation of post-ganglionic muscarinic sites. Cyclic GMP decreases K^+ conductance and causes slow EPSP.

GANGLIONIC STIMULANTS

Ganglionic stimulating agents can be categorised into :

(a) Drugs which stimulate ganglionic nicotinic receptors : These agents, including nicotine itself, do not have clinical applications. The stimulation of postganglionic nicotinic receptors lead to a rapid depolarization alongwith the generation of a fast excitatory post-synaptic potential. Their ganglionic stimulatory action is rapid in onset and can be blocked by competitive or non-depolarizing ganglionic blockers.

(b) Drugs which stimulate postganglionic muscarinic receptors : Muscarine, methacholine, McN-A-343 and reversible anticholinesterases are the examples of this category. They activate the postganglionic muscarinic receptor sites and give rise to slow EPSP. It takes a considerable period of time to attain critical amplitude which is necessary to evoke action potential. Hence, the excitatory effects of these drugs on ganglia are slow in onset and can be blocked by atropine-like drugs.

Ganglionic stimulation is mainly brought about by drugs which stimulate post-ganglionic nicotinic receptor sites. Beside this, they may stimulate the nicotinic receptors present on various other organs and produce a response of complex nature. For example, during their use

(i) Signs of adrenergic nervous system stimulation can be seen due to the release of adrenaline and noradrenaline from adrenal medulla and sympathetic nerve terminals.

(ii) Contraction of skeletal muscle may be observed due to their action on nicotinic receptors present at end-plate region of skeletal muscles.

(iii) Nausea and vomiting are the common side-effects observed due to the activation of nicotinic chemoreceptors in the aortic arch and carotid bodies and

(iv) Both excitatory and inhibitory types of responses arise due to activation of nicotinic receptors that are located in the CNS.

Nicotine, an alkaloid obtained from leaves of Nicotina tobacum, is a prototype of this series. The actions of other ganglionic stimulants are qualitatively similar to the actions of nicotine and bear only quantitative differences. Hence, a brief review of various actions of nicotine is presented below.

NICOTINE

It is one of the few natural liquid alkaloids. Its isolation from the natural source is first reported in 1828 by Posselt and Reiman. Demonstration of ganglion as it's site of action was given in 1889 by Langley and Dickinson. The biological effects produced by nicotine are generally of complex nature due to the simultaneous activation of nicotinic receptors located at different organs. Hence, the ultimate response at any one system represents the summation of both stimulant and depressant actions of nicotine.

Lobeline, a nicotine analogue was isolated from dried leaves of Lobelia inflata. Wieland in 1915, successfully isolated crystaline α-Lobeline which is the chief constituent of lobelia. Lobeline is less potent than nicotine in its pharmacological actions. Besides this, some synthetic compounds are also employed to cause ganglionic stimulation. These include tetramethyl ammonium (TMA) and 1,1-dimethyl-4-phenyl piperazinium (DMPP).

Pharmacology of nicotine : The alkaloid, at low doses, stimulates and at high doses depresses the functioning of many organs. This type of activity is known as biphasic action.

(a) Nicotine exerts a biphasic action at autonomic ganglia on adrenal medulla (i.e. discharge of catecholamines) and neuro-muscular junction.

(b) Like acetylcholine, nicotine also stimulates a number of sensory receptors.

Table 4.6 : Ganglione stimulants

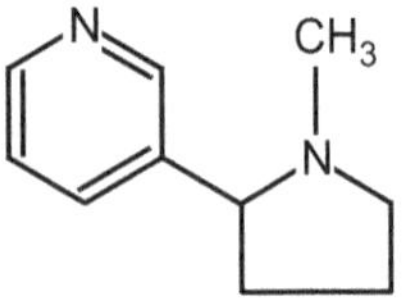

Nicotine

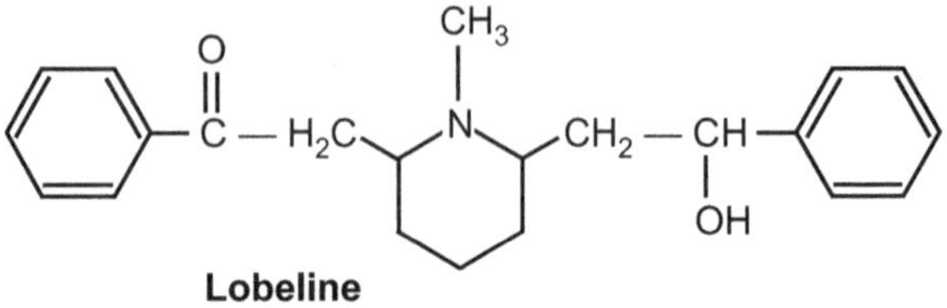

Lobeline

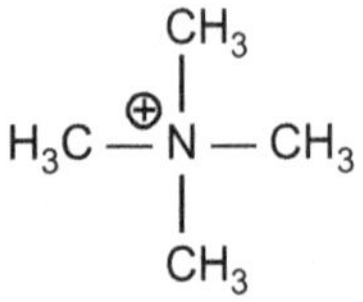

Tetramethyl ammonium (TMA)

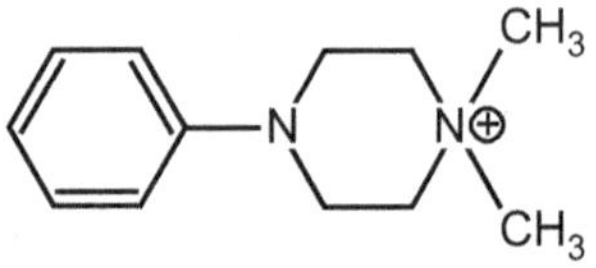

1,1 dimethyl- 4-phenyl piperazinium (DMPP)

(c) The effects on respiratory system are mainly central in origin. For example, in low doses, nicotine activates chemoreceptors located in aortic arch and respiratory centers. High doses of alkaloid cause direct stimulation of respiratory centers alongwith a generalized CNS stimulation. While in toxic doses, it causes CNS depression followed by death due to respiratory paralysis. The failure of respiration is due to the inhibition of respiratory centers in the brain stem as well as to a depolarizing blockade of neuromuscular junction of respiratory muscles.

(d) It causes the release of antidiuretic hormone from pituitary gland.

(e) Cardiovascular effects of nicotine are mainly due to the activation of

(i)   sympathetic ganglia,

(ii) adrenal medulla

(iii) sympathetic nerve endings and

(iv) chemoreceptors of aortic and carotid bodies. The ultimate or overall effects of nicotine administration results in vasoconstriction, tachycardia and increase in blood pressure.

(f) GIT : The overall increase in the tone and muscle activity in GIT is mainly due to the combined activation of parasympathetic ganglia and cholinergic nerve endings.

(g) Exocrine glands : Nicotine first stimulates and then depresses the secretions of bronchial tract and salivary gland.

Nausea, vomiting and diarrhoea are seen as the side-effects after systemic absorption of nicotine and lobeline. They are caused due to central and peripheral actions of these alkaloids. They are readily absorbed from the mucous membranes of oral cavity, GIT and respiratory system. Liver serves as the main site of metabolism but the drug also undergoes metabolism in lung and kidney. Cotinine and nicotine-1'-N-oxide are the principal metabolites excreted through urine alongwith unchanged fraction of administered dose of nicotine. Half-life of nicotine, administered parenterally or by inhalation is estimated to be two hours, during which, it can readily cross blood-brain-barrier and placental barrier.

In 1913, Marshall, first reported the ganglionic biphasic action of tetraethyl ammonium (TEA). The synthetic analogue, DMPP is about 3-4 times more potent than nicotine. Both the synthetic analogues do not cause ganglionic blockade except when given in large intra-arterial doses.

GANGLIONIC BLOCKERS

Various drugs which exert blocking activity at autonomic ganglia can do so by

(i) acting presynaptically and affecting the neurotransmitter synthesis, release and re-uptake,

(ii) acting postjunctionally and

(a) initially stimulating the ganglia by an ACh like action and then blocking the ganglia by a persistent depolarization. Blokade occur due to desensitization of cholinergic receptors sites. These agents are known as depolarizing ganglionic blockers.

(b) blocking the ganglionic transmission either by inhibiting competitively the interaction between ACh and its receptor sites or closing the channel when it is open. These agents are known as competitive ganglion blocking agents.

(a) Depolarizing ganglionic blockers: Nicotine itself, is an example of this class. In small doses, nicotine stimulates all autonomic ganglia. But, if given in larger doses or during prolonged administration, nicotine causes an initial repetitive stimulation phase followed by blockade of ganglionic transmission due to persistant depolarization. The desensitization of the cholinergic receptor sites present on postganglionic cell-body is the main reason of ganglionic blockade. Beside nicotine, many drugs possess variable degrees of ganglionic blocking activity as a side-effect. The members of this class are not used clinically for this purpose.

(b) Competitive ganglionic blocking agents : It is a class of clinically employed ganglionic blockers. The fact that d-tubocurarine blocks the transmission of impulses in neuromuscular junction by competitively inhibiting the ACh-receptor interaction, stimulated the development of this series. The competitive ganglionic blocking action of hexamethonium, a prototype of this series was first reported by Paton and Zaimis in 1949. This is followed by development of other synthetic ganglion-blockers. The blocking action of hexamethonium is mainly due to its ability to occlude or to close the ion-channel which was opened due to ACh-receptor interaction. This leads into a reduction in the duration of current flow resulting into ganglionic blockade. While trimethaphan acts as competitive antagonist of ACh and blocks the receptor sites on post-ganglionic surface. Thus, the initial EPSP does not develop.

Hexamethonium, Azamethonium and pentolinium are the members of a series of bis-quaternary ammonium salts. Pentolinium has a longer duration of action than hexamethonium. The report about the effectivity of triethylsulfonium salts as ganglionic blockers, led to the development of trimethaphan. It has a very short duration of action; hence it is available only for parenteral administration (50 mg/ml). Trimethaphan, in high doses, can stimulate the release of histamine resulting into a direct vasodilation. Hence, it should be used with caution in patients with asthma or allergy. Another agent, mecamylamine was developed and studied in mid-1950s. Soon after, it was released into the market. It is as potent as hexamethonium but less potent than pentolinium, in its ganglionic blocking activity. Due to its nonquaternerized nature, it is well absorbed and distributed in various body compartments. It is able to penetrate the CNS and placental barriers. It is excreted unchanged by kidney. The main side-effects of mecamylamine include tremors, mental confusion, mania and depression, all of central origin. Pempidine is a newly introduced ganglionic blocker having simple structure. In larger doses, pempidine controls the release of acetylcholine from the preganglionic nerve terminals.

ABSORPTION, FATE AND EXCRETION

Most of the important agents of this category are quaternary or bis-quaternary ammonium salts. Hence, their absorption remains poor and unpredictable. Once absorbed, they are mostly retained in the extracellular space. They are not affected much by metabolizing enzymes and get excreted through urine in almost unchanged form.

SIDE EFFECTS

The side effects associated with their use are mainly due to their unselective blocking action and include, nausea, vomiting, dry mouth, anorexia, decrease tone and motility of GIT, xerostomia, anhydrosis, cycloplegia and postural hypotension. These side effects sufficiently disturb the patient and limit their chronic use.

THERAPEUTIC USES

(a) Because they reduce the level of sympathetic activity, they were once widely used in the treatment of hypertensive cardiovascular disease. Since the mechanism governing transmission in all autonomic ganglia remains same, their unselectivity of action leads to numerous side-effects. Hence they are now totally replaced by more selective and less toxic β_1-adrenergic blockers.

(b) They are used to produce controlled hypotension to minimize blood loss during plastic, neurological and opthalmic surgery or in operative procedures where extensive skin dissection is needed. Trimethaphan is a drug of choice due to its short duration of action. The hypotension can easily be reversed within few minutes of stopping the drug administration.

(c) Trimethaphan, pentolinium and mecamylamine can be used in the management of autonomic hyperreflexia or autonomic neurovegetative syndrome. This syndrome results due to excessive catecholamine discharge by the injuries of upper spinal cord. For the treatment α-adrenergic blockers can also be employed.

LIMITATIONS

(i) During prolonged administration, tolerance may develop and to achieve the same intensity of pharmacological response, one has to increase the dose of the drug.

Some patients, however, may show hypersensitive responses when exposed to the treatment of these drugs.

Table 4.7 : Pharmacological actions of hexamethonium related drugs

System	Effects of ganglionic blockade
Salivary glands	decrease in the salivary secretion (xerostomia)
Sweat glands	decrease in perspiration (anhydrosis)
GIT	reduction in tone and motility
Urinary bladder	urine retention
Ciliary muscle	paralysis of accommodation (cycloplegia)
Iris	pupil dilation (mydriasis)
Arterioles	vasodilation, increase in peripheral blood flow, hypotension.
Veins	vasodilation, decreased venous return.
Heart	decreased cardiac output, tachycardia.

4.20 NEUROMUSCULAR BLOCKERS

Spasticity is a condition which is characterized by exaggerated resting tone of a muscle. Muscle hypertonus is usually accompanied by an increased resistance to passive stretch. The skeletal muscle relaxants are used to relieve muscular spasticity. Spasticity may be caused by musculoskeletal or spinal cord trauma, brain lesions or brain diseases. Regardless of the cause, spinal cord region is the site for the mechanisms involved in the expression of spasticity.

Neuromuscular blocking agents may find clinical utility in :

(a) Surgery and in intensive therapy units where they are used to provide muscular relaxation.

(b) Convulsions e.g. electroconvulsion therapy, where they are used to prevent injury due to the violence of the fit. For example, in status epilepticus, tetanus or in the case of convulsant drug poisoning, neuromuscular blocking agents are used with mechanical respiration when other means are insufficient.

(c) Various orthopedic procedures where they help in correction of dislocations and the alignment of fractures.

(d) Neuromuscular blockers of short duration of action, are used to facilitate intubation with an endotracheal tube and have been used to facilitate laryngoscopy, bronchoscopy and esophagoscopy in combination with a general anaesthetic agent.

Acetylcholine produces its spectrum of biological activities by acting either on muscarinic cholinergic receptors or nicotinic cholinergic receptors. The actions of ACh on autonomic ganglia and skeletal muscles are thus due to activation of nicotinic receptors. These structures are stimulated by small doses of ACh and get depressed if ACh is administered in larger doses. Since nicotine also evokes same response on these systems, this action is referred to as the ganglionic or nicotinic action of acetylcholine.

The main source of nicotine is the plant, Nicotiana tabacum from potato family. The alkaloid is present in varying quantities (1-8%) in the dried tobacco leaves, in combination with malic and citric acids.

Pharmacology of Nicotine :

(a) In GIT, the alkaloid stimulates musculature and the activity of secretory glands.

(b) It depresses cardiac activity. Small doses of alkaloid cause an increase in blood pressure while in larger doses, it causes decrease in blood pressure.

(c) Both, autonomic ganglia and skeletal muscles are stimulated by small doses and paralysed due to larger doses of nicotine. Nicotine leads to repetitive excitation (fasciculation) followed by block of transmission in the neuromuscular junction. This results in neuromuscular paralysis.

Neuromuscular Transmission :

The skeletal muscles are supplied with somatic efferent nerves. Depending upon the skill and delicateness of function assigned to skeletal muscle, the main nerve is linked with other nerves. For example, the nerve controling the functioning of larger muscles of limb is interconnected with less number of other nerves while the nerve controlling a delicate function needs interconnections with several nerves to exercise fine control.

The axon loses its myelin sheath when the nerve comes in close contact with the muscle fiber and gets bifercated into several fine branches which penetrate the muscle cell membrane. The region of contact of the terminals of these branches with the muscle membrane is known as 'neuromuscular junction'.

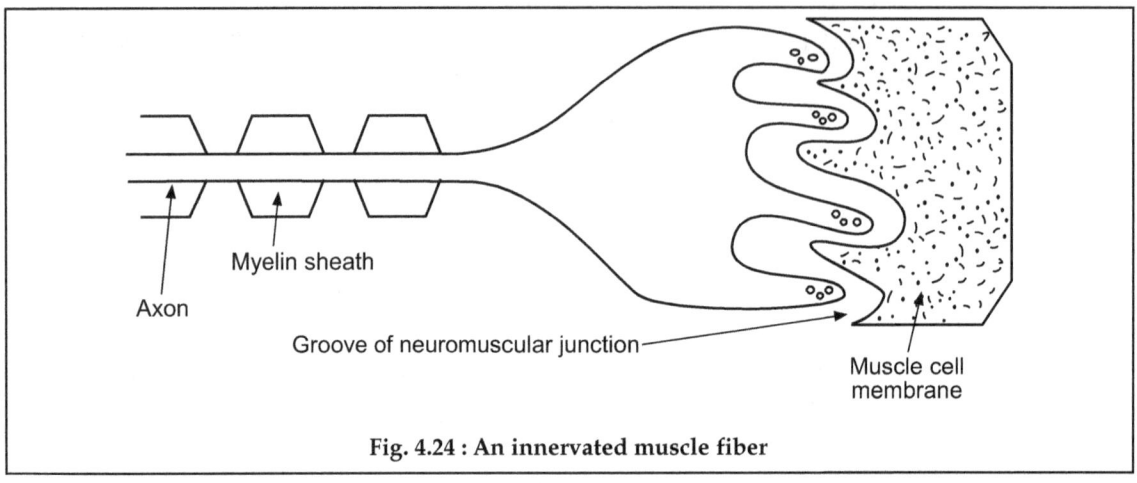

Fig. 4.24 : An innervated muscle fiber

The surface of muscle fiber that is near to the nerve terminals and is encircling the nerve terminal is known as 'end-plate' region which carries the sites for nicotinic receptors and cholinesterase enzyme. The gap between the nerve terminal and end-plate region is about 50 mm wide and may be termed as synaptic cleft.

The process is just similar to neurotransmission in other synapses. When the motor nerve is stimulated, an action potential is generated by the exchange of potassium and sodium ions. It travels along the length of the axon and reaches to nerve terminals. The activation of Ca^{++}-ionophore leads to influx of extracellular calcium into the nerve terminal. In response to Ca^{++}- influx, many storage vesicles get ruptured and release ACh into the synaptic cleft. The ruptured vesicles immediately reform and store the newly biosynthesized acetylcoline.

The released ACh then reacts with nicotinic receptor sites present in the junctional folds of end-plate region and causes opening of ion-channels resulting into development of local, graded currents in the membrane of muscle-fiber. These are termed as end-plate currents. They are generated due to increased inward Na^+ and outward K^+ conductances. When their summation attains adequate intensity, it can lead to excitation of the muscle which is followed by contraction of the skeletal muscle. The bound ACh is then hydrolysed by cholinesterase enzymes present in junctional folds to choline and acetate. This entire process of muscle contraction is completed within 2-3 m sec. and maintains its uniformity if repeated many times per second.

Nicotinic Cholinergic Receptors :

In vertebrate skeletal muscle, the end-plate region comprises of about 0.1 % of the total cell-surface. The end-plate region bears the sites for nicotinic cholinergic receptors. Recent studies revealed the structure of a nicotinic receptor. It consists of five subunits in the ratio of $\alpha_2 \beta \gamma \delta$. Only α-subunits are found to possess binding sites for ACh. These α-subunits have molecular weight of 40,000 daltons each while β, γ and δ subunits are 50,000; 60,000 and 65,000 daltons. These subunits are arranged in the cylindrical fashion (with a diameter of about 8 nm) leaving some space within them, to form an open channel like interior. The nicotinic receptors usually occur in pairs linked by a disulfide bridge between the delta sub-units.

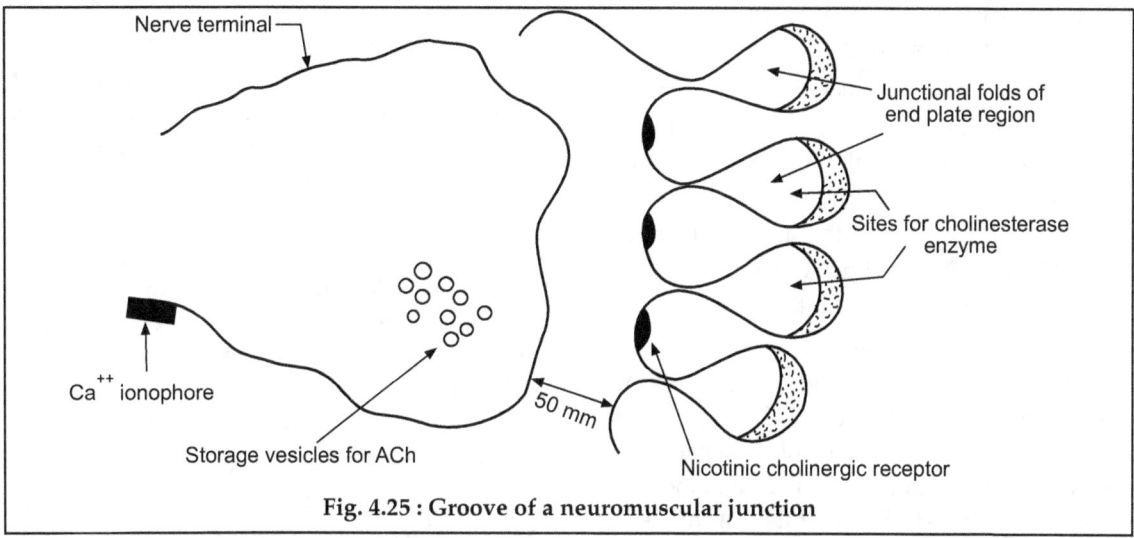

Fig. 4.25 : Groove of a neuromuscular junction

The receptor concentration in the end-plate region appears to be 8-10 thousand/μm^2. The binding of ACh to the receptor surface results into the opening of the ion-channel. The channel life-time depends mainly on the intrinsic properties of the drug used. For example, ACh-induced receptor activation leads to opening of ion-channel for about 1m sec. Anticholinesterase drugs prevent the degradation of ACh and extends its biological life. This results into increase in survival period of ACh. In such case ACh will repetitively bind with the receptor and will cause repetitive ion-channel opening. Tetraethylammonium and 4-aminopyridine are the examples of drugs which increase the neuronal ACh release by prolonging duration of action potential at nerve terminal.

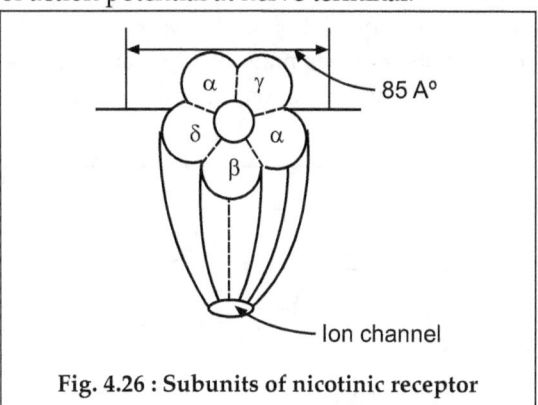

Fig. 4.26 : Subunits of nicotinic receptor

Due to this, the number of vesicles which undergo rupture, increases, resulting into more ACh release into neuromuscular junction. The bursts of miniature end-plate currents cause repetitive contractions of the skeletal muscle.

Classification :

Various neuromuscular blocking agents act by interferring with

(a) synthesis or release of ACh

(b) ACh-receptor interaction.

Hence, they can be classified accordingly into :

I. Drugs that depress ACh junctional concentration

(a) by inhibition of its synthesis or

(b) by inhibition of release.

II. Drugs that prevent the action of released ACh on receptors.

(a) by depolarizing the muscle end-plate region or

(b) by inhibiting depolarizing action of ACh.

III. Centrally acting muscle-relaxants.

I. (a) Drugs which inhibit the biosynthesis of ACh :

Choline, an aminoalcohol is needed for ACh biosynthesis. It is transported to the site of synthesis by intracellular transport mechanisms. Triethylcholine and hemicholiniums, due to their structural resemblance with choline, compete with the transport mechanisms and thus decrease the rate of synthesis of ACh.

Hemicholinium, a series of compounds synthesized by Schueler in 1955 compete with choline. Their inhibitory action is reversed by increasing the concentration of choline. The most extensively studied member of this series is HC-3. Both, triethylcholine and HC-3 could not be employed clinically due to their lack of selectivity. They impair the production of ACh in other cholinergic nerves and in brain tissues as well.

(b) Drugs which inhibit the release of ACh :

(i) The influx of extracellular Ca^{++} ions in nerve terminal leads to rupture of synaptic vesicles which release ACh. Hence, there exists a quantitative relationship between the concentration of Ca^{++} ions and amount of ACh released. Naturally neuromuscular block can easily be obtained if ACh enough to generate post-junctional end-plate potential, is not released due to reduction in the amount of Ca^{++} ions. Potassium ions facilitate transmission by enhancing ACh release while magnesium ions have exactly opposite effects.

(ii) **Ion-channel blockers** : Many categories of drugs including, atropine, amino-glycoside antibiotics, local anaesthetics, barbiturates and some psychotropic drugs interfere with ACh-induced opening of an ion-channel. They bind to these receptor sites and cause narrowing of ion-channel passage which results into reduction in the muscle tone. They do not interfere in the release of ACh from prejunctional sites. The anaesthetic agents specifically stabilize the post junctional membrane with weak to moderate potencies and reduce the intensity of current flow. This activity of anaesthetic agents is synergistic with the action of competitive (non-depolarizing) neuromuscular blocking agents.

(iii) **Botulinum toxin** : Clostridium botulinum, an anaerobic organism releases toxins which are categorised into eight antigenically distinct types. Of these, the type A has been identified as the neurotoxic component of botulinum toxin. It has a molecular weight of about 900,000 daltons, of which the two polypeptide chains of about 150,000 daltons have been characterised. It is a potent inhibitor of the ACh release from the nerve terminals. This inhibitory action is effected by locking of the molecular gates through which ACh molecules are released from the nerve terminal into the synaptic cleft. The depression of the release of ACh from the motor nerve terminal results into neuromuscular paralysis. The botulinum toxin can cross blood-brain barrier and exerts its effects on CNS. However, it lacks the ability to cross placental barrier. In the persons affected by botulinum toxin, treatment with anticholine- sterases may improve and restore the strength and functioning of the muscles.

$(C_2H_5)_3 - \overset{\oplus}{N} - CH_2\,CH_2OH$

Triethylcholine

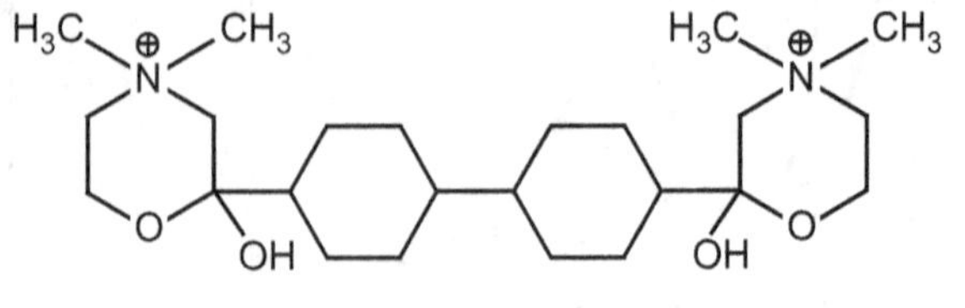

Hemicholinium, HC-3

II. Drugs that prevent the action of released ACh on the receptor sites :

(a) Both depolarizing blocking agents and competitive (non-depolarizing) blocking agents cause neuromuscular blockade by acting on the nicotinic receptor sites present in post-junctional membrane. The depolarizing agents are weak agonists of ACh having greater affinity and weaker intrinsic activity at the receptor sites. They bind to nicotinic receptor and depolarise the post-junctional membrane by opening the ion-channel. Due to their greater affinity, they may cause prolonged depolarization by repeated opening of ion-channels and make further depolarization by endogenous ACh impossible. This repeated excitation leads to muscular fasciculation and the loss of significant quantities of K^+ ions from the muscle cell. The continuous triggering of muscle excitation then causes a block of transmission followed by neuromuscular paralysis. These events can also be seen with very high doses of acetylcholine. Due to prolonged and repeated end-plate depolarization, a time comes when the depolarized area can not generate muscle action potential sufficient to cause muscle contraction.

The action of depolarizing muscle is mani-fested at an early stage by transient muscular fasciculation. This is followed by the paralysis of muscles of fingers and eyes. The larger muscles of limb and trunk are affected. Ultimately respiration ceases due to paralysis of diaphragm. During recovery the muscles regain their strength and function in the reverse order to that of paralysis.

Succinylcholine is the only agent from this category which is used clinically. It has more side-effects than competitive neuromuscular blockers.

(i) Succinylcholine : It was synthesized by Bovet et al in 1949 in order to create synthetic alternatives or substitutes for d-tubocurarine, a natural competitive neuromuscular blocker. As shown in the structure, succinylcholine is a twin structure comprising of two ACh molecules. It has a rapid onset and a short duration of action. It acts on the nicotinic receptors and initiates repeated depolarization of the end-plate region resulting into a brief period of muscle fasciculations. This is phase I which is followed by phase II, inducing neuromuscular blockade if the drug is administered repeatedly.

Succinylcholine has a very short duration of action (5-10 minutes). Its action is terminated due to its rapid hydrolysis by butyrocholinesterases present in plasma and liver. The main metabolite, succinylmonocholine still retains a weak competitive neuromuscular blocking activity. The drug undergoes a two step metabolism as shown in the Fig. 4.26.

The action of succinylcholine can be prolonged by administration of local anaesthetics which block butyrocholinesterase enzymes. The drug does not reach the CNS. Its prolonged administration may lead to an increase in intraoccular pressure due to its contractile action on extraoccular muscles.

Succinylcholine bromide ; R = − CH₃

Suxethonium bromide ; R = − C₂H₅

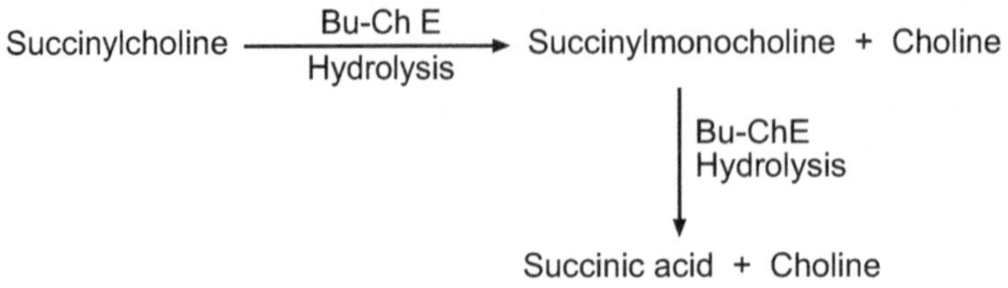

Succinylcholine $\xrightarrow[\text{Hydrolysis}]{\text{Bu-Ch E}}$ Succinylmonocholine + Choline

$\downarrow$ Bu-ChE Hydrolysis

Succinic acid + Choline

Fig. 4.27 : Metabolism of succinylcholine

Adverse effects include muscle fasciculation, muscle ache and pain, hyperkalemia, increase in intraoccular pressure and rise in blood pressure. The latter effect is due to stimulation of autonomic ganglia and not due to histamine liberation. Diazepam may be used to reduce muscle pain and spasm associated with the use of succinylcholine.

Succinylcholine is mainly used to prevent tetanic muscle contraction and for providing general muscle relaxation needed to carry out surgery. Its ethyl analog, suxethonium bromide has similar properties as that of succinylcholine except that it gets hydrolyzed more rapidly than succinylcholine.

(ii) Decamethonium : It is an example of a series of compounds in which a polymethylene chain bridges two quaternary nitrogens. Such a series is known as methonium series and is represented as

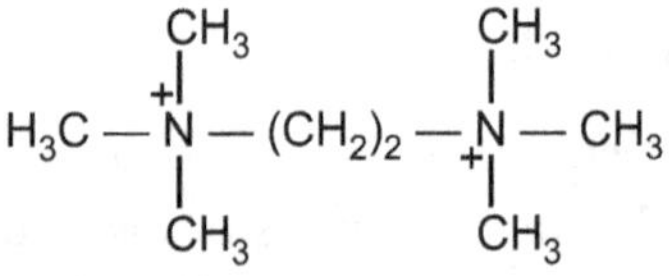

$$H_3C - \overset{+}{\underset{CH_3}{\overset{CH_3}{N}}} - (CH_2)_2 - \overset{CH_3}{\underset{\overset{+}{CH_3}}{N}} - CH_3$$

Methonium series

Decamethonium is an effective neuro-muscular blocking agent. In usual doses, it neither releases histamine nor it blocks autonomic ganglia. Its effectiveness as a depolarizing agent is due to the distance of separation between two quaternary nitrogens which is about 1.4 mm.

This distance correlates closely with the distance covering two adjacent ACh receptors at the end-plate region.

$$(CH_3)_3 \overset{+}{N} - (CH_2)_{10} - \overset{+}{N} (CH_3)_3 ; 2\overset{-}{Br}$$

Decamethonium bromide

It is longer acting and more stable molecule than succinylcholine. It is not employed clinically.

(iii) Carbolonium bromide : It depolarizes the motor end-plate region mainly due to its anticholinesterase activity. Presently, it is not under clinical use.

$$[(CH_3)_3\overset{+}{N} - (CH_2)_2 - O - \overset{\overset{O}{\|}}{C} - NH -]_2 (CH_2)_6; 2\overset{-}{Br}$$

Carbolonium bromide

(b) Drugs that act by inhibiting depolarizing action of acetylcholine :

Acetylcholine released from the nerve terminal, binds to α-subunits of the nicotinic-cholinergic receptor and causes opening of an ion-channel. When the summation of end-plate currents attain adequate level (post-junctional end plate potential), it leads to the excitation of the muscle, followed by contraction.

If the end-plate receptor sites are already blocked by drugs having affinity but not intrinsic activity, endogenous ACh cannot bind to the receptor and hence can not depolarize the end-plate region. This will result into muscle relaxation due to neuromuscular block. Since these agents act competitively with endogenous ACh to occupy receptor sites, such drugs are known as competitive or non-depolarizing or anti-depolarizing or membrane stabilizing agents.

Since they block competitively the transmitter's action on the receptor sites, the post-junctional membrane remains insensitive to the propagated nerve impulse and contraction does not occur. Examples of this category include, d-tubocurarine, Alcuronium, Pancuronium, Gallamine, Atracurium and β-erythroidine, etc. Action of all these compounds can be reversed by increasing the concentration of ACh at receptor sites. This can be achieved by anticholinesterases.

(i) d-Tubocurarine : It is an example of various curare alkaloids which are found in plants of genera Menispermaceae and Strychnos. The term 'Curare' is used to describe various South American arrow poisons which possess neuromuscular blocking alkaloids. Currently d-tubocurarine is obtained mainly from the bark of Chondo-

dendron tomentosum. Since at that time, the native were using bamboo tubes to store the crude preparation, the alkaloid was named as tubocurarine.

The first clinical use of this crude alkaloid was done in 1932 by West to treat spastic disorders. The isolation, structural elucidation and determination of optical activity of the ingredient of the crude preparation was carried out in 1935 by King. Since 1942, its use for promoting muscle relaxation in general anaesthesia was continued on ever-increasing scale. Soon after, metocurine, a synthetic dimethyl analogue of tubocurarine was developed which was found to be three times more potent as muscle relaxant than d-tubocurarine.

Table 4.8 : Competitive neuromuscular blocking agents

(i)

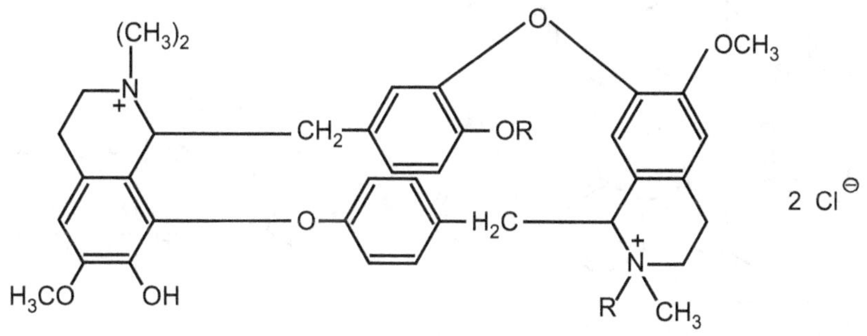

d-Tubocurarine chloride ; R = – H
Metocurine chloride ; R = – CH₃

(ii)

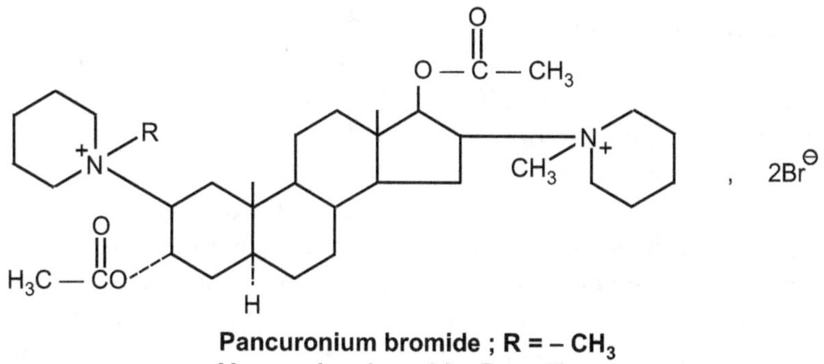

Pancuronium bromide ; R = – CH₃
Vecuronium bromide; R = – H

(iii)

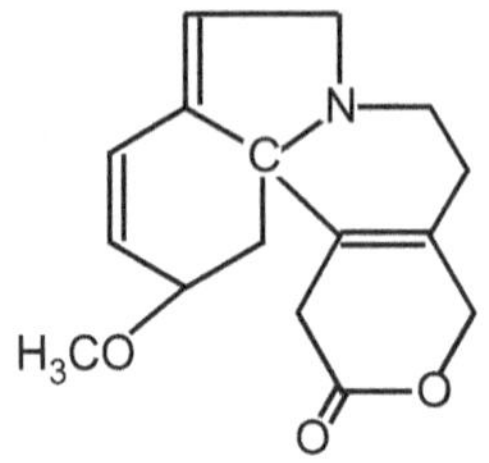

β-erythroidine

(iv)

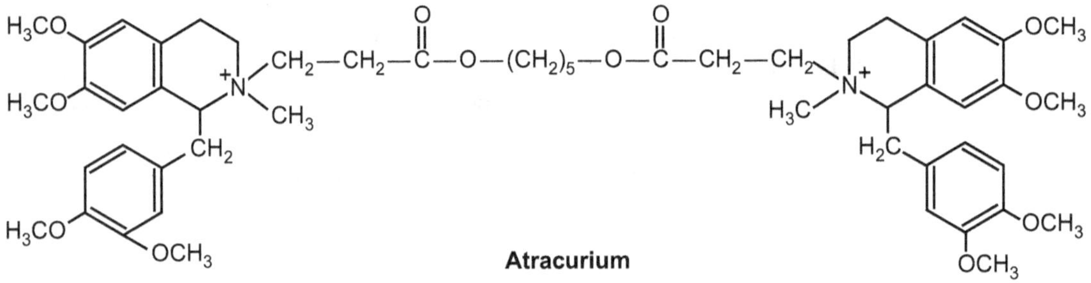

Atracurium

(v)

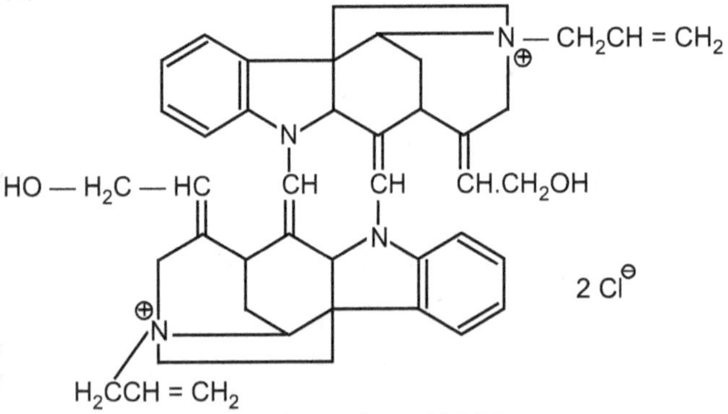

2 Cl$^{\ominus}$

3I$^{\ominus}$

Alcuronium chloride 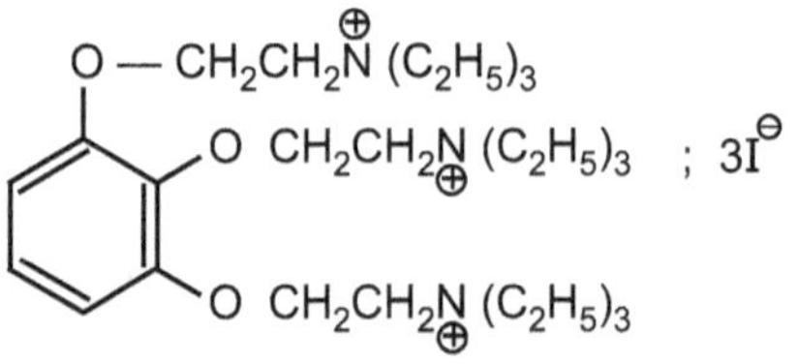   **Gallamine triethiodide**

d-Tubocurarine has a rapid onset of action, if given intravenously. It competitively binds to the end-plate region and reduces the frequency of channel-opening events resulting into flaccid paralysis. At therapeutic doses, it partially blocks the ganglionic transmission. Some of the side-effects of the drug can be explained by its capacity to liberate histamine from the mast cells. (These side-effects include bronchospasm, hypotension, excessive bronchial and salivary secretion, etc.). In larger doses, d-tubocurarine blocks the transmission both at autonomic ganglia and at adrenal medulla resulting into a fall in blood pressure and tachycardia. Histamine release is partly responsible for this hypotensive response. It also decreases the tone and motility of GIT and leads to an increase in intraoccular pressure.

d-Tubocurarine and all other quaternary neuromuscular blockers lack an ability to enter the CNS. Hence, they do not exert central effects in man. They are used as muscle-relaxants in anesthesia mainly due to their peripheral effects at neuromuscular junction. For this purpose, d-tubocurarine chloride is administered 0.2 to 0.7 mg/kg of body weight for an adult either by i.v., or i. m. route. It is commonly used to relax muscles and thus to prevent dislocation and fracture associated with electroconvulsive therapy.

(ii) Gallamine : It is one of the member of a series, synthesized by Bovet and co-workers in 1946 in hope to avail synthetic substitutes for curare alkaloid. It is widely used as competitive neuromuscular blocking agent. It contains three quaternary nitrogens and block the muscarinic receptors of cardiac branches of vagus through atropine like action. This results into an increase in heart rate, blood pressure and develops occasional arrhythmias.

(iii) Pancuronium : This compound first synthesized in 1964 consists of a steroidal nucleus in which acetylcholine part is incorporated. It does not have steroidal activity. It is about five times more potent than d-tubocurarine as a blocker of neuromuscular junction. This activity is potentiated by ether. It has quite less ability to cause histamine liberation.

Vecuronium is a moderately short-acting and a bit potent analog of pancuronium. The structure of vecuronium does lack the 2β methyl group present in pancuronium.

It does not lead to release of histamine. It neither affects autonomic ganglia nor the vagal neuroeffector junctions.

(iv) Atracurium : It is another new synthetic derivative of curare and has intermediate duration of action. It is 3-4 times less potent than pancuronium and its neuromuscular blocking activity is potentiated by halothane. It is metabolized in plasma primarily by hydrolysis of the ester group or by disconnecting both quaternary nitrogens from each other. It possesses a half-life of about twenty minutes and has less ability to cause liberation of histamine.

(v) Dihydro-β-erythroidine : It is a semi-synthetic derivative of β–erythroidine, an alkaloid obtained from E. americana. From various semi-synthetic derivatives of β-erythroidine, the dihydro compound was found to be clinically useful muscle relaxant.

(vi) Baclofen : It is a newly introduced muscle relaxant used in the treatment of spasms associated with disorders that affect spinal cord.

$$H_2NH_2C - \underset{\underset{C_6H_5}{|}}{CH} - CH_2\ COOH$$

Baclofen

Its structure is closely related to that of GABA, an inhibitory neurotransmitter present in CNS. After oral administration, the drug is rapidly absorbed and enters into the CNS where it may inhibit monosynaptic and polysynaptic spinal reflexes. About 35% of the administered drug appears unchanged in urine. It can be used orally in a daily dose of 15 mg to treat spinal spasticity and spasticity associated with multiple sclerosis. If desired, the dose can be progressively increased upto 50 mg.

(vii) Dantrolene sodium : This agent is of special interest mainly due to its unique mechanism of action. It causes muscle relaxation by directly blocking the contractile mechanism of skeletal muscle fiber. It prevents both, the influx of extracellular calcium ions and the release of intracellular Ca^{++} ions from the sarcoplasmic reticulum. This results into blocking of excitation, contraction and coupling of skeletal muscles.

Dantrolene sodium

It is not used as an adjuvent to anaesthesia due to its slow onset and longer duration of action. It has a half-life of 7-9 hours. Generally the drug action is more pronounced on fast muscle fibers than slow muscle fibers. It is metabolised by liver microsomal enzymes and excreted mainly through urine and bile.

It is used orally in a dose of 12-25 mg, once a day, for the treatment of chronic spasticity due to spinal cord injury or multiple sclerosis. In the treatment of malignant hyperthermia, it is usually given intravenously.

Side-effects include drowsiness, diarrhoea, visual disturbances, hallucination and a dose-dependent muscle weakness. Hence it is contraindicated in patients with liver disease or weakness of respiratory muscle.

(viii) Benzodiazepines : Beside having anxiolytic and anticonvulsant activities, some of the benzodiazepines possess muscle relaxant activity. Diazepam, chlordiazepoxide and clonazepam are the most useful agents for the control of flexor and extensor spasms, spinal spasticity and multiple sclerosis. They are usually employed in the dose range of 15-60 mg.

(ix) Some antipsychotic drugs like chlorpromazine and fonazine are also of value in the therapy of muscle relaxation. Fonazine, a phenothiazine derivative causes a non-specific arrest of histamine release.

Structure-Activity Relationship :

(i) The quaternary nitrogen moiety maintains cationic charge in minimally hydrated condition and confers good neuromuscular blocking activity.

(ii) The neuromuscular blockade can also be obtained with non-quaternerized compounds like nicotine.

(iii) Larger alkyl substituents at quaternary nitrogen hinder the attack of the drug molecule at receptor-sites.

(iv) Lipophilicity plays an important role in governing the access of molecule to the muscle membrane. More bulky and rigid molecules generally exhibit competitive type of activity while simple and flexible structure is found to be necessary for depolarizing type of muscle-relaxant activity.

(v) The distance between two quaternary nitrogens in the drug governs the activity. It should be near about 1.2 - 1.4 nm for optimal activity. Gallamine and β-erythoidine are exceptions to this rule. Quaternerization of nitrogen atom in β-erythoidine results in decline of activity.

(vi) The quaternary nitrogen atom can be substituted by arsenium, osmium, sulfonium, phosphonium and platinum with retention of muscle-relaxant activity.

Absorption, Distribution And Excretion :

In general, the quaternary ammonium compounds, due to their ionic nature are poorly absorbed after oral administration. From intramuscular sites, absorption is rapid and regular. Major amount of drug is eliminated through urine. Pattern of metabolism is not uniform in each type. Insignificant amount of the drug administered may be excreted through bile.

Therapeutic Uses :

(i) Muscle-relaxants are employed as an adjuvant in surgical anaesthesia in order to carry out operations with ease. They are administered after the patient is anaesthesized.

(ii) They are used in the treatment of status epilepticus and to reduce painful muscle spasms of tetanus.

(iii) They can be used in various orthopedic operations.

(iv) Some of these agents are used in the treatment of spastic muscle disorders. These disorders involve an increased tone of muscle due to imbalance between the central and spinal control of muscle tone.

(v) d-Tubocurarine is particularly useful in the diagnosis of myasthenia gravis and conditions symbolized by immobility of joints.

Table 4.9

Parameter	Depolarizing agents	Competitive agents
1. Neuromuscular block can be reversed by	Antidepolarizing agents but difficult to reverse	Anit-ChE, K$^+$-ions, adrenaline, depolarizing agent and ephedrine
2. Nature	Partial agonists	Competitive antagonists
3. Muscle twiches	Few muscle twiches followed by a flaccid paralysis	Flaccid paralysis not preceded by muscle twitches
4. Histamine	Do not liberate histamine	Liberate histamine

Toxic Effects :

Respiratory muscles, muscles of the eyes and digits may be attacked by these neuromuscular blockers. If these muscles get paralyzed, the patient may be exposed to fatal effects.

The ability of some competitive muscle relaxant to liberate histamine from the mast cells may lead to prolonged apnea, broncho-constriction and cardiovascular side-effects of these drugs.

The acute toxicity by these drugs can be overcome by the administration of anticholinesterases, adrenaline, potassium chloride or antihistaminics. Artificial respiration proves to be beneficial in recovering the condition of the patient.

Competitive Versus Depolarising Agents :

The following table summarises some of the important points of differences between depolarizing and competitive types of neuromuscular blocking agents.

Centrally Acting Muscle Relaxant :

The muscle relaxants we studied just now, do so by acting peripherally at neuromuscular junctions. Yet another category of muscle relaxants exists which bring out their effects by their action on CNS. Muscle-relaxation is achieved by the suppression of some reflexes involving interneurons, mainly in the region of brain-stem, thalamus and basal ganglia. Hence these agents are also termed as interneuronal blocking agents. The muscle-relaxation is effected without loss of consciousness. In therapeutic doses, these agents do not impair voluntary muscle activity.

Mephenesin, a phenoxypropanediol deri-vative, synthesized in 1945, serves as the prototype of this category of drugs. To minimize the side-effects of mephenesin, its derivatives have been prepared. But instead of muscle-relaxant nature, they proved to be good antipsychotic agents. Surprisingly enough, diazepam an anxiolytic agent used in psychosis treatment, retains the muscle-relaxant activity. It appears therefore that since these drugs cause muscle-relaxation due to their central action, they also might have an action on emotional centres and hence can be useful agents in the treatment of psychotic disorders.

(1) Mephenesin : Berger and Bradley in 1946 prepared a series of glycerol ether derivatives, of which mephenesin is a centrally acting muscle-relaxant having highest activity. It depresses internuncial neurons in the CNS, which are involved in the control and maintenance of tone and movements of muscles. In therapeutic doses, it has membrane-stabilizing and analgesic activities. Muscle-relaxation is accompanied by depression of reflex activity and tremors.

It is administered orally (2-3 g) usually 3-4 times a day. It has a short duration of action. When given intravenously, mephenesin exposes the patient to risks of hypotension, haemolysis and haemoglobinuria. In compa-rison to mephenesin, its carbamate ester has a longer duration of action.

(2) Mephenesin derivatives : In order to increase the potency and minimize side-effects associated with mephenesin, series of compounds bearing structural resemblance with mephenesin have been prepared and were evaluated for their central muscle relaxant activity but vary in their capacity to produce sedation and analgesia, and their duration of action. These include methocarbamol, carisoprodal, phenyramidol, phenoglycodol, chlorzoxazone and chlormezanone. The latter two drugs can also be used as anxiolytics. Some of the above mentioned agents, due to their sedative property, (e.g., phenaglycodol) also find place in anticonvulsant therapy.

Nefopam has a benzoxazocine structure and is developed as cyclized analogue of diphenhydramine. It lacks antihistaminic activity. Its muscle relaxant activity may be due to its interference with serotonergic transmission.

Therapeutic Uses :

(i) Due to their centrally located site of action, these agents can be used to treat spasticity in spinal cord injury and multiple sclerosis.

(ii) As peripheral neuromuscular blockers, these agents can be employed as an adjunct for induction of anaesthesia.

(iii) Drugs having prominent anxiolytic action (e.g., diazepam and lorazepam) can be used to relieve muscle tension and pain in stress and anxiety.

The usual dose of centrally acting muscle relaxants varies according to the disorders and the agent chosen for its treatment. Generally for relaxing the muscles, the dose for following agents can be used

Diazepam   – 10 mg i.v.
Chlordiazepoxide – 50 to 100 mg i.v./i.m.
Mephenesin   – 1.2 g per day orally
Meprobamate – 1.2 g – 1.6 g per day orally

Table 4.10 : Some centrally acting muscle-relaxant

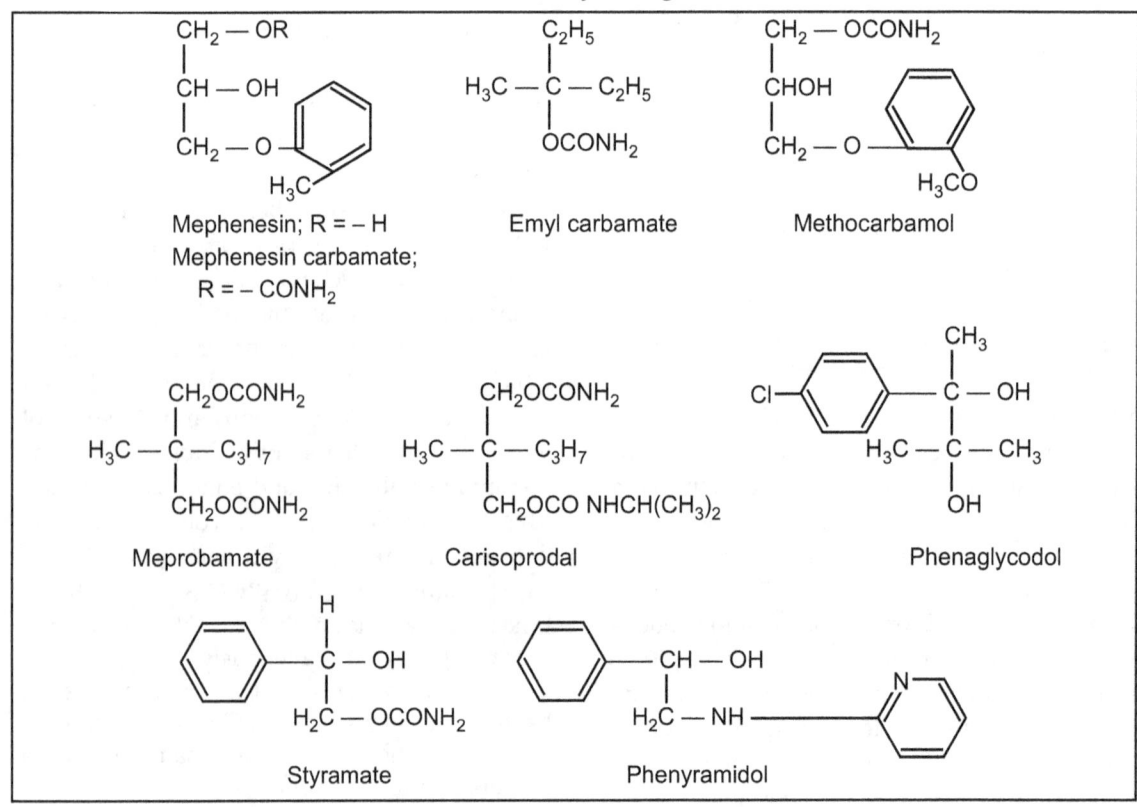

Mephenesin; R = – H
Mephenesin carbamate; R = – CONH$_2$

Emyl carbamate

Methocarbamol

Meprobamate

Carisoprodal

Phenaglycodol

Styramate

Phenyramidol

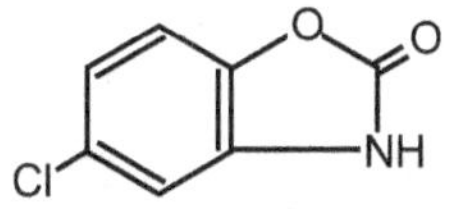

Chlorzoxazone

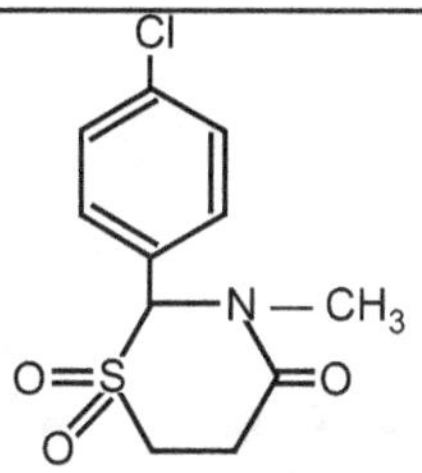

Chlormezanone

Synthesis

(i) Carbachol chloride :

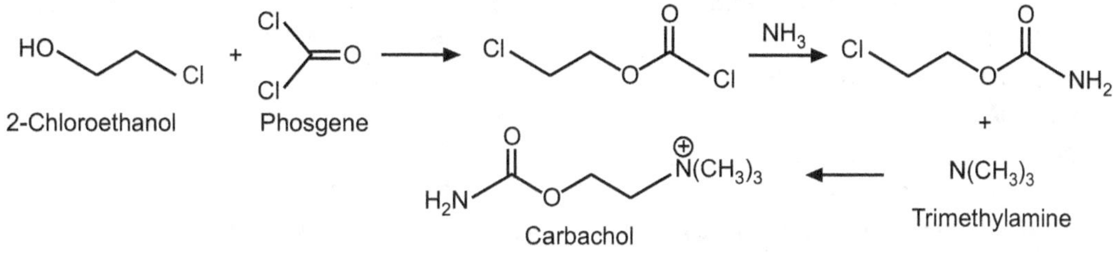
2-Chloroethanol
Phosgene
NH_3
Trimethylamine
Carbachol

(ii) Dicyclomine hydrochloride :

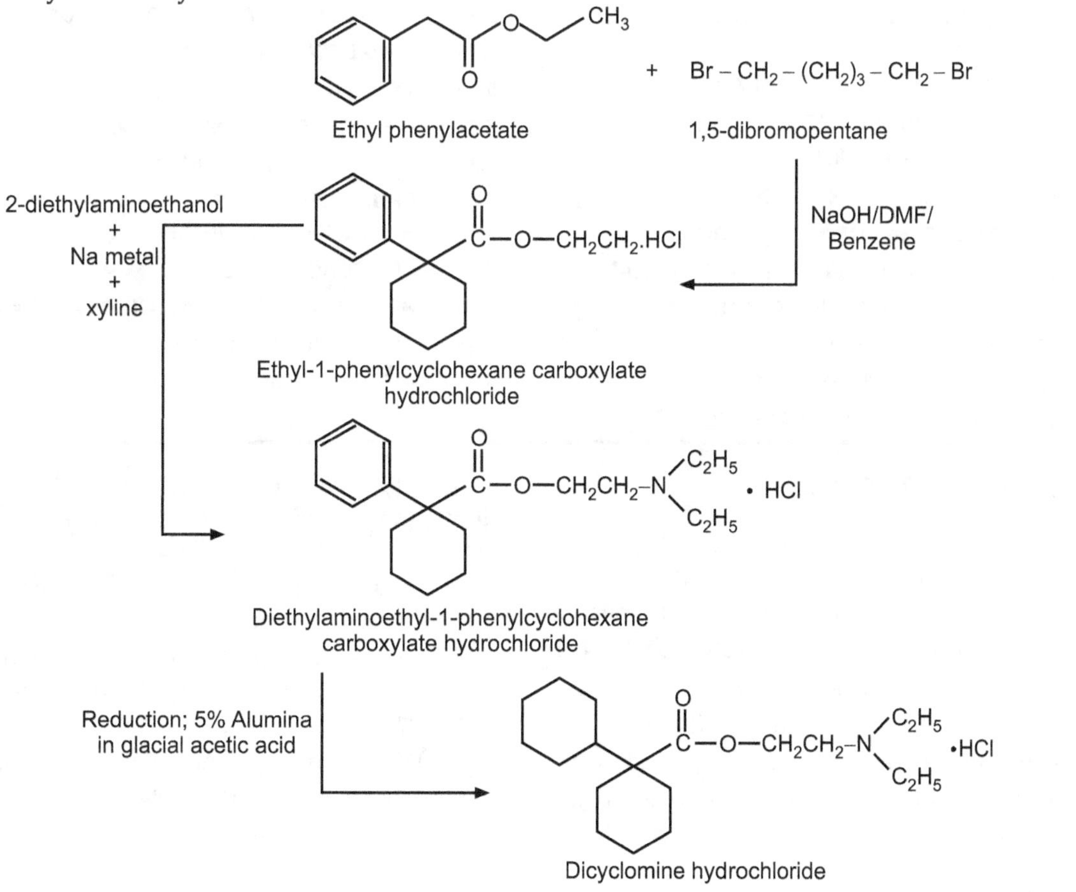
Ethyl phenylacetate
$Br - CH_2 - (CH_2)_3 - CH_2 - Br$
1,5-dibromopentane
NaOH/DMF/
Benzene
2-diethylaminoethanol
+
Na metal
+
xyline
Ethyl-1-phenylcyclohexane carboxylate hydrochloride
Diethylaminoethyl-1-phenylcyclohexane carboxylate hydrochloride
Reduction; 5% Alumina in glacial acetic acid
Dicyclomine hydrochloride

❖❖❖

5

CARDIOVASCULAR DRUGS

5.1 INTRODUCTION

One need not stress upon the importance of cardiovascular system in the body. A major pharmacological action of a number of clinically used agents is merely due to their influence over cardiovascular system. Much advances have been witnessed in cardiovascular therapy over the past 20 years. For convenience of discussion, these drugs may be classified as,

(a) Positive inotropic agents : e.g., dobutamine, digitalis glycosides, amrinone etc.

(b) Vasodilators : e.g., minoxidil, prazosin, hydralazine etc.

(c) Drugs altering Renin-Angiotensin-Aldosterone system : e.g., captopril, saralasin, enalapril etc.

(d) Calcium ion channel blockers : e.g., nifedipine, verapamil, diltiazem etc.

(e) Antiarrhythmic agents : quinidine, lidocaine, bretylium etc.

(f) Beta-adrenoceptor blocking agents : propranolol, labetalol, oxprenolol etc.

(g) Centrally acting antihypertensive agents : e.g. clonidine, methyldopa, guanabenz etc.

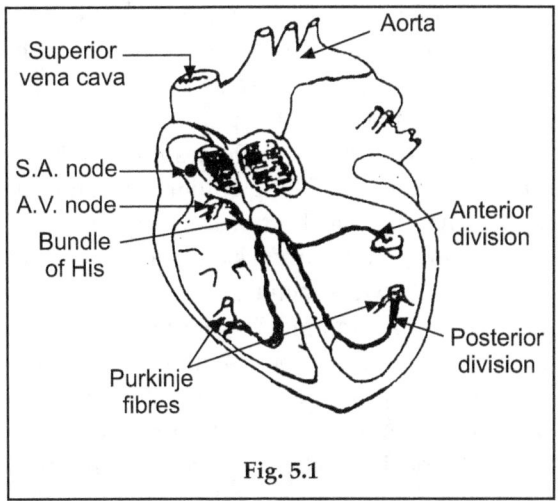

Fig. 5.1

To understand the effects of these drugs on the cardiovascular system, an understanding of normal heart functioning and propogation of cardiac impulse will be beneficial. The above figure represents essential elements of cardiac impulse propogation.

The sino-atrial node cells possess an intrinsic ability of their own to generate and to propogate an impulse. The S.A. node is a specialised muscle which is self-excitatory. Hence, it is known as normal pacemaker. It sends out impulses rhythmically to the surrounding tissue in order to cause atrial contraction (atrial systole). The impulse thus generated by S.A. node, spreads through the atria and finally reaches atrioventricular node (A-V node).

A.V. node lies at the junction of atria and ventricles. The adjoining region of A.V. node is made up of non-conductive tissue while A.V. node possesses the capacity to conduct an impulse slowly and functions as a delay circuit. It thus acts as a "filter" of atrial

impulses. The S.A. node is concerned with the rate of sinus rhythm while A.V. node acts as a controlling centre for ventricular contractions.

The signal generator (S.A. node) continuously initiates the impulses in a co-ordinated fashion which are received by A.V. node. The latter, after a short delay, sends an excitation wave (impulse) through the bundle of His and Purkinje system to the ventricular muscles, resulting into ventricular contraction (ventricular systole). Due to the large muscle mass, the ventricular conduction system is more elaborate where Purkinje fibres serve as final conducting components. The rate and force of ventricular systole is influenced by both, extrinsic factors, such as level of catecholamines and intrinsic factors like, the length of fibres, just before contraction.

The cardiac muscles are also innervated by both, sympathetic and parasympathetic nerves in order to control and cause the impulse generation to take place in a co-ordinated fashion. The tone of autonomic nervous system thus has prominent influence on ventricular rate. For example, adrenergic nerve stimulation (as under the conditions of strain or stress) causes increased heart rate (positive chronotropic effect) and increased force of contraction (positive inotropic effect). While vagal stimulation leads to increased filtration of atrial impulses through A.V. node resulting into suppression of both, rate and force of heart contraction. Following its release from the vagous nerve acetylcholine first interacts with M_2 muscarinic receptors that slow heart rate, in part, by activating a cardiac potassium channel through a signal transduction mechanism involving G protein coupled receptors. This leads to cardiac pacemaker cell hyperpolarization, thus slowing the heart rate. An enhanced vagal activity at A.V. node appears to originate from several sites in nervous system such as - central vagal nuclei, nodose ganglion and autonomic ganglion.

5.2 MYOCARDIAL CELL

Sarcomere (myocardial cell) is the functional contractile unit of cardiac muscle. Each cell is characterized by the presence of one central nucleus, and a number of mitochondria and many myofibrils aligned along the cell's axis. The whole contractile process is supported by ATP. Mitochondria are the principle sites for energy generation where it is converted into creatine phosphate and ATP through the process of oxidative phosphorylation. Creatine phosphate functions as reserved depot of energy. The events necessary for the contraction of myofibrils are initiated by the operation of Na^+-K^+- ATPase pump. The energy needed for this process is released during hydrolysis of ATP by Mg^{++}- activated myofibrillar enzyme known as myosin ATPase. However, this enzyme cannot function in the absence of calcium ions.

The whole process of cardiac contraction involves active participation of

(a) Na^+-K^+-ATPase pump,

(b) the release of calcium sequestered upon the sarcoplasmic reticulum, and

(c) activation of actin-myosin tension generating system.

5.3 ACTIN-MYOSIN TENSION GENERATING SYSTEM

Actin consists of twisted long strands, each of which is made up of actin monomers. These two strands are twisted around tropomyosin. While at regular intervals of about 400 A°, troponin is bound to these filaments as shown in the Fig. 5.2.

Troponin has three sub-centres :

1. Centre that prevents an interaction between actin and myosin is known as troponin I.
2. Centre that binds the troponin to the tropomyosin is known as troponin T.
3. While the third centre binds with calcium released from the endoplasmic reticulum.

The myosin filament possesses very high affinity for actin. The globular sub-unit of myosin have a site for ATPase activity. The troponin-tropomyosin system inhibits the interaction between actin and myosin, in the absence of calcium ions. The electrical impulse pushes out calcium ions sequestered in the nearby cisternae into the myofibrils. The calcium binds with troponin resulting into initiation of interaction between actin and myosin. Calcium ion also allows the combination of ATP with the ATPase site present on the globular part of myosin. It thus facilitates the energy release needed for contraction of the muscle.

Relaxation phase is characterized by disposal of calcium from vicinity of myofibrils back into cisternae through active transport. The energy needed is provided through the action of ATPase that can pump upto 4 ions of calcium per molecule of ATP consumed. Thus like contraction, relaxation phase also needs ATP. Removal of calcium from the myofibrils results into activation of troponin-tropomyosin inhibitory system which prevents actin-myosin interaction.

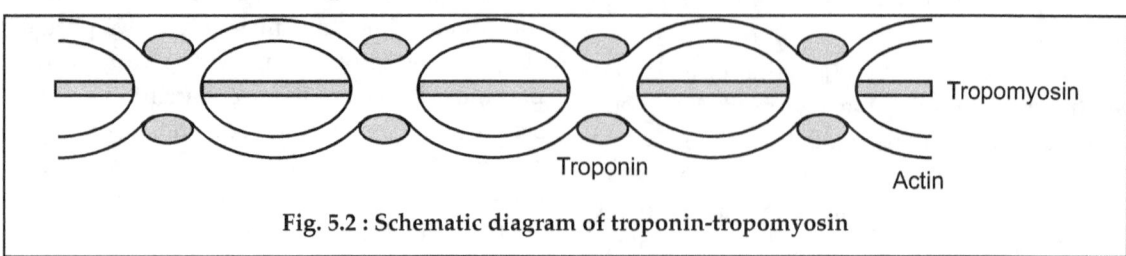

Fig. 5.2 : Schematic diagram of troponin-tropomyosin

5.4 MOLECULAR BASIS OF MYOCARDIAL CONTRACTION

The cardiac cell is surrounded by a lipoprotein membrane, which behaves as if it has aqueous pores in it. Sodium ions are maintained at higher concentration in the extracellular fluid while potassium ions are at higher concentration inside the cell.

Fig. 5.3 : Cardiac cell at resting potential

This unequal distribution (which is against the concentration gradient) of K^+ and Na^+ ions is maintained by the pump system in the sarcolemma of cardiac fibres. This ATP energized membrane pump system (Na^+- K^+ - ATPase pump) actively pushes Na^+ ions out of the cell and K^+ ions into the cell and thus making the cell membrane electrically neutral (resting potential).

When an impulse is initiated by S.A. node. electrical changes start occurring. More K^+ ions leave the cell than the Na^+ ions that enter in it, because of the differences in size of the ions and permeability of cell membrane to these ions. As a result, there is a net loss of positively charged ions from the cell. The inside of myocardial cell remains negative in comparison to its outside (– 90 mV) and the cell is said to be polarized. Since S.A. node has the most rapid intrinsic rate, the transmembrane potential in S.A. node remains – 70 mV during polarization state, while it remains – 90 mV in working muscle cells and non pace-making special conducting tissues (like, Purkinje fibres).

The polarized state of the cell serves as an electrical stimulus which causes conformational changes in the membrane to open ion channels (molecular gates) that selectively allows the permeation of Na^+ ions into the cell. This leads to reduction in intracellular negativity, by which depolarization commences (phase 4).

When this depolarization reaches a certain threshold level (–70 mV), the permeability of the cell membrane (opening of fast ion channels) to Na^+ abruptly increases, allowing more rapid influx of Na^+ as well as Ca^{++} to produce spike action potential (phase 0), resulting into complete depolarization.

This upstroke causes the release of intracellular Ca^{++} ions from the sacs of sarcoplasmic reticulum into the cytoplasm. This rise in the level of free or "activator" calcium within the cell removes the inhibition of troponin-tropomyosin system over the contractile elements and initiates the contraction of cardiac muscle. Contraction of most mammalian hearts is thus initiated by and is proportional to the influx of extracellular Ca^{++} which in turn triggers the release of additional Ca^{++} from the sarcoplasmic reticulum.

Following depolarization, commences the phase of repolarization. It is characterized by removal of free Ca^{++} ions from the cytoplasm back into cisternae. It is an energy consuming process, that occurs in three sub-phases.

(i) A partial abrupt repolarization (phase 1) occurs as a result of closure of the fast sodium ion channels and an influx of chloride ions.

(ii) A prolonged repolarization i.e. plateau region (phase 2) occurs due to much slower K^+ efflux along with the slow influx of Na^+ and Ca^{++} ions.

(iii) Rapid but not abrupt repolarization (phase 3) occurs as a result of the closure of the slow inward channels for Na^+ and Ca^{++} ions and the opening of one or two fast outward channels for K^+.

The extracellular Ca^{++} ions that were influxed during depolarization are driven out (in fact exchanged for extracellular sodium ions) by a transport-system that is governed by concentration gradient and the transmembrane potential. Thus, at the end of repolarization (phase 3), the transmembrane potential is restored back again to – 90 mV but now the intracellular fluid has lost K^+ and gained Na^+.

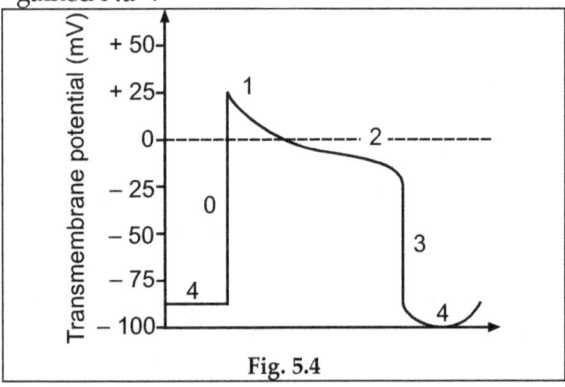

Fig. 5.4

Here Na^+ - K^+ - ATPase pump again plays a role. This pump utilizes ATP to actively transport Na^+ out of the cell and K^+ into the cell to restore normal levels of Na^+ and K^+. The pump transports Na^+ and maintains their respective gradients in a $3 Na^+ : 2 K^+ : ATP$ ratio. It uses energy from hydrolysis of the terminal phosphoryl group of one molecule of intracellular ATP to transport three Na^+ ions outwards and two K^+ ions inwards across the cell membrane against steep electrochemical gradients to restore normal levels of Na^+ and K^+. It is a

dimeric protein with an α-subunit of 100 KD and a β-subunit of 55 KD. The α-subunit contains the ATP hydrolysis subsite, in which aspartate accepts the γ-phosphate of ATP. The function of glycoprotein β-subunit is not clear. The cardiac glycoside binding site, which is partially located on the outside of the α-subunit, inhibits the ATP-driven ion transport and the Na^+ dependent conformational change. The pump system present elsewhere in body has different α-subunits showing different steroid binding capabilities.

Thus, ATP, intracellular Na^+ ions and extracellular K^+ ions may be viewed as substrates and ADP, orthophosphate, extracellular Na^+ and intracellular K^+ ions as products of the enzymatic process. Many low molecular weight, non-steroidal inhibitors of different types have been studied. They are useful for analyzing various properties of Na^+ - K^+ - ATPase rather than being used as a prototype drug.

The enzyme, Na^+ – K^+ -ATPase was discovered in 1957 by Jens Skou in the cell-membrane. It hydrolyses ATP molecule to release the energy necessary for functioning of this pump. The enzyme and the pump, both are tightly bound to the plasma membrane. The hydrolysis of ATP molecule needs the presence of Na^+, K^+ and Mg^{++} ions.

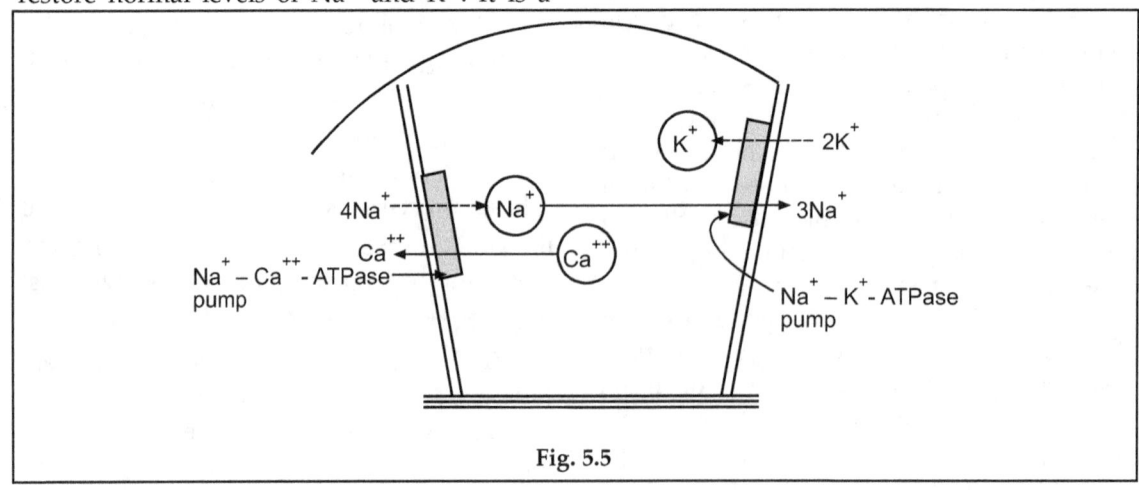

Fig. 5.5

5.5 CARDIOVASCULAR DISEASES

(a) Thromboembolic Diseases :

This group of diseases is characterized by adhesion of platelets to the inner vascular wall resulting into the interference in the functioning of extrinsic or intrinsic blood clotting system. The platelets adhere to the collagen exposed due to an injury to the vascular endothelium. The release of thromboxane A_2 results into vasoconstriction and enhances platelet aggregation. The permanent platelet fibrin clot initiates a series of events that may lead to myocardial infarction (a region with deficient oxygen supply) and to congestive heart failure.

The treatment of myocardial ischemia (deficient O_2 supply) may involve the therapies to improve coronary blood supply. This can be done either by means of drugs such as nitrates or by means of aortacoronary bypass grafts. The myocardial ischemia can also be treated by reducing the heart work-load so that the heart may work efficiently even under deficient O_2 supply. This can be done either by decreasing the pre-load (venous vasodilation) using drugs like nitrates, diuretics etc. or by decreasing myocardial contractility (using drugs like β_1-adrenoceptor blockers). However, the latter approach may result in a decrease in heart rate. Beneficial results may also be obtained by decreasing the after-load of the heart using drugs such as arterial vasodilators or Ca^{++} antagonists. However, any attempt to decrease heart work-load usually results in a decrease in the cardiac output. This limits the patient's capacity to carry out any work.

(b) Congestive Heart Failure :

The force of cardiac contraction is proportional to the degree to which cardiac muscle fibers are stretched. However, the contractile power declines if the muscle fibers are stretched beyond a critical length. This is known as Frank-Starling law of the heart functioning. Under certain circumstance, the activation of neurohumoral system (e.g. increased release of catecholamines, elevation of plasma renin activity or plasma antidiuretic hormone level) may result into increased

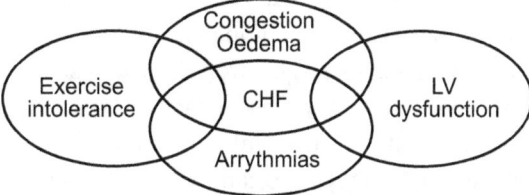

Clinical Syndrome of Heart Failure

blood volume, venous return and end diastolic volume. The heart work-load increases resulting into stretching of muscle fibres beyond that critical length. If such situation remains for considerable period of time, this leads to a progressive decline in the force of heart contraction. Blood accumulates in the heart due to its inability to eject all the blood. So the heart work-load progressively increases resulting into progressive increase in the stretching of muscle fibres and failure of the heart becomes gradually pronounced. The blood starts accumulating into large veins and in the tissues, highly perfused with blood. Thus congestion of both, pulmonary and systemic circulation results into peripheral edema (dropsy) and diminished exercise tolerance. This situation is known as congestive heart failure.

It is characterized by left ventricular dysfunction, reduced exercise tolerance and frequent ventricular arrhythmias.

Usually advanced age, hypertension, diabetes mellitus and ischemic heart diseases contribute to the development of congestive heart failure.

(c) Angina Pectoris :

It is characterized by a discomfort of cardiac origin resulting due to temporary ischemia of the myocardium. The myocardial ischemia results due to deficiency of oxygen during increased metabolic activities. The increased demand for oxygen can not be fulfilled due to coronary vessel constriction. The primary cause of angina is supposed to be atherosclerosis of large coronary arteries. This may lead to reflex vasospasm of coronary arteries that results into sudden, severe substernal pain which often radiates to the left shoulder and along the flexor surface of the left arm. This occurs most commonly with exertion or emotional stress. Breathlessness sometimes occurs along with other discomforts. The duration of anginal episode may vary from 30 seconds to 30 minutes and may be relieved by rest or nitroglycerin. Hypertension and cigarette smoking are amongst the principle etiologies of angina pectoris.

(d) Arrhythmias :

The rhythmic contraction of the heart is possible due to the presence of intrinsic pace makers and conduction tissues in the heart. S.A. node is considered as normal pace maker due to its most-rapid intrinsic rate (60-100/min). Hence, the rhythmic contractions of the heart are due to impulses generated by S. A. node. Therefore, if an impulse is generated from non S. A. node region, that may interfere into S. A node-organized contraction process, leading to arrhythmia.

For the heart to function as an efficient pump, the various contractile units must operate in a co-ordinated and rhythmic fashion. The generation of cardiac impulses in the normal heart is represented in Fig. 5.6. An impulse is generated by S.A. node and its conduction through A.V. node is shown by P wave while its conduction through bundle of His and Perkinje fibres is completed when the wave reaches to point Q.

The ventricular depolarization is indicated by QRS complex while ST segment represents repolarization of ventricles.

An arrhythmia may arise due to abnormality in –

(a) rate, regularity or site of origin of cardiac impulse, or

(b) conduction that causes an alteration in the normal sequence of the atria and ventricles.

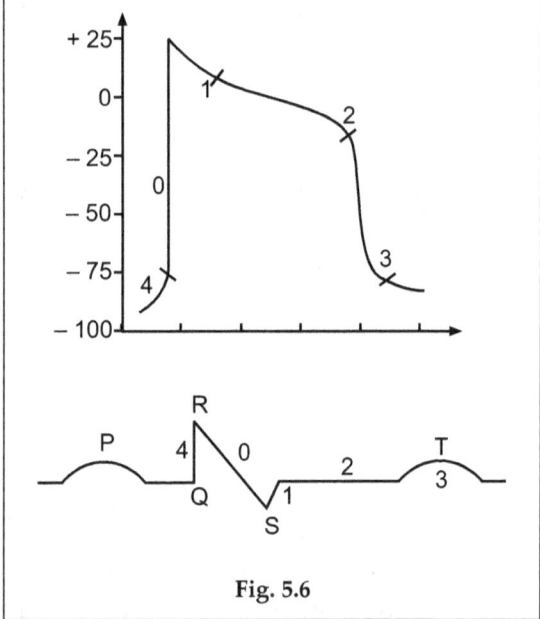

Fig. 5.6

It may be sub-classified as per the rate of beats and its anatomical location as follows :

(i) Sinus tachycardia :

In this, an impulse is generated by S. A. node that spreads through atria and ventricles using normal conducting tissues. It is simply tachycardia (increase in the rate of impulse generation) due to increased S. A. nodal automaticity. Heart rate ranges between 100-180 / min. It usually occurs even in normal individuals under the conditions of exercise, anxiety, stress or fright and ceases as soon as the underlying cause ends.

During myocardial infarction, increase in S.A. node discharge rate may be due to inhibition of vagal suppression or to sympathetic discharge. Efforts to suppress S.A. node rate by producing β-adrenergic blockade (propranolol) can lead to significant depression of myocardial contractility and is a potentially hazardous therapy which should be used with caution.

(ii) Atrial flutter and fibrillation :

The severity of an increased automaticity enhances from tachycardia to flutter and then to fibrillation. Atrial flutter is characterized by rapid atrial firing at a rate of 150-300 beats/min of ectopic origin. Ventricular conduction and contraction remain unaffected due to filtering ability of A.V. node.

In atrial fibrillation, rapid, disorganized atrial rhythm at a rate of 350-600/min occurs due to random and changing firing (automaticity) of ectopic origin. A.V. node plays the role of filter to this rapid firing rate and censors majority of impulses, entering into the ventricular mass. This leads to random and irregular contractions of ventricular muscle fibres. Both, atrial flutter and fibrillation are more prone to occur in persons with advanced age. Atrial fibrillation is sometimes described as 'slow' or 'fast' depending on the ventricular rate. A patient with slow atrial fibrillation in which an effective A.V. node block permits only a small proportion of impulses to pass from the atria to the ventricles may not need treatment. In contrast, fast atrial fibrillation which occurs in patients with an ineffective A.V. node block features rapid and irregular ventricular beats and consequent inefficient filling of the ventricles and inefficient circulation.

(iii) Sinus bradycardia :

It is just opposite to sinus tachycardia and arises due to decreased automaticity (heart rate of less than 60 beats/min) of S.A. node

with no conduction defects. Due to decreased heart rate, both, ventricular filling time and end-diastolic volume also increase. It usually occurs due to either increased vagal activity or decreased efficacy of S.A. node (because of myocardial ischemia).

Bradyarrhythmias are generally caused by tissue damage, a decrease in sympathetic autonomic tone or an increase in parasympathetic tone mediated by the vagus nerve. Increased vagal tone causes AV block of varying degree which reduces the rate of impulses reaching the ventricles. Immediate treatment is normally to decrease vagal tone with intravenous atropine which will decrease AV block and increase SA rate. If atropine is ineffective, intravenous adrenaline or isoprenaline may be used. The only oral treatment available for bradycardia is slow-release isoprenaline which is not generally satisfactory.

(iv) Sick sinus syndrome :

It is a type of bradycardia (decreased automaticity) of no fixed etiology. Abnormalities in both, impulse generation and conduction system are witnessed. Electrolyte or endocrine imbalances may contribute to its development. The early symptoms such as, fatigue, dizziness and confusion may become severe upto congestive cardiac failure, if remains untreated.

(v) Atrioventricular block :

It is characterized by reduced impaired A-V conduction. The bundle of His and Purkinje fibres may also come under affected area. Both cardiac (acute myocardial infarction or AV nodal disease) and non-cardiac (enhanced vagal tone) reasons may cause the development of A.V. block.

Premature Atrial Complexes (PAC) :

PACs usually represent the re-entry of a stimulus, arising in S.A. node, which "echoes" back to the atrium, either at the A.V. junctional level or via intra-atrial conduction pathways. Less frequently, ectopic foci may become enhanced and compete with the sinus node pace maker.

(vi) Premature ventricular contractions :

Here S.A. nodal automaticity is not altered but additional impulses are generated from local tissues in the ventricular region. The development of ectopic foci in ventricular mass may be pronounced with the presence of cardiac disease. Certain drugs (e.g., catecholamines, methylxanthines) may also increase the frequency of its occurrence.

(vii) Paroxysmal (recurrent) supraventricular tachycardia (PSVT) :

The AV junction is not a single electrical circuit but can be envisioned as being divided into parallel pathways (much like separate strands in a multicable electrical conduit). The parallel A.V. junctional pathways may have dissimilar recovery times and, if challenged by a premature atrial stimulus, one limb may be accommodating and allow its transmission; the other may not be fully recovered and as a

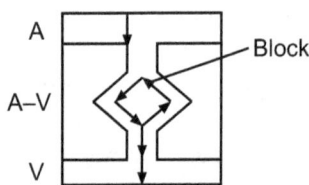

result, the antigrade signal is blocked. The initial stimulus may then pass retrograde through the blocked limb and re-enter in the A.V. junction with each circular passage stimulating the ventricles and usually atria as well. The majority of regular supraventricular tachycardias are not due to the discharge of an ectopic foci but rather due to re-entry of a premature stimulus in the A.V. junction (A.V. nodal re-entry).

It is characterized by the appearance of narrow QRS complexes with a heart rate of 150-250 beats/min. The principle etiologies include re-entry and increased automaticity of atrial ectopic focus. Lidocaine is the preferred agent for the rapid control of ventricular tachycarda.

(viii) Re-entry :

The electrical system of the heart consists of intrinsic pace makers and conduction tissues. An impulse is generated in S. A. node and it is conducted in bundle of His and Purkinje system through A. V. node in antegrade (towards ventricles) direction. Since the surrounding tissue is refractory in nature, an impulse terminates in Purkinje fibres. Thus, the conduction system is large enough so that the conduction pathways are repolarized before the next sinus impulse arrives at A.V. junction.

Due to the development of premature atrial impulse from any ectopic focus or due to partial or complete block in conduction, an impulse after causing ventricular contraction, travels in retrograde (towards atria) direction. Thus, the impulse may continue around the obstacle to establish re-entry circuit. The disturbances in conduction can be partial or complete (delay or complete block) or can be unidirectional or bidirectional and may occur with or without re-entry or circus movement.

(ix) Ventricular flutter :

It is characterized by the ventricular rate of 150-300 / min generated due to rapid and regular firing from ectopic foci of ventricular origin. If remains untreated, ventricular flutter may be converted into a more severe form, i.e. ventricular fibrillation.

(x) Ventricular fibrillation :

It is characterized by the ventricular rate of 150-500/min generated in rapid and random fashion from ectopic foci present in ventricular mass. The co-ordination between the ventricular contractile elements is lost which results into disorganised and random ventricular contractions. This leads to irregular and ineffective pumping of blood from the heart.

5.6 CARDIAC GLYCOSIDES

Cardiac glycosides are the example of positive inotropic agents (i.e. which increase the force of myocardial contraction). These positive inotropic agents are classified into :

(a) Cardiac glycosides

(b) β- adrenoceptor agonists, and

(c) Bipyridine derivatives.

All these agents act by increasing. the amount of intracellular calcium ions resulting into more forceful contraction of cardiac muscles. However, they differ in the chemistry, mechanism of action and specific side-effects. All positive inotropic agents have the dose-dependent peripheral; vascular effects, ranging from vasoconstriction (digitalis glycosides) to vasodilation (bipyridine derivatives). Except bipyridine derivatives, these agents also exhibit considerable arrhythmogenic potential.

Cardiac glycosides are naturally occurring drugs which are present in the glycoside forms, in a wide variety of plants and in a non-glycosidic form, in the poison of toad. In plants, the leaves of Digitalis purpurea (purple foxglove) and Digitalis lanata (cohite foxglove) contains digoxin, digitoxin and deslanoside while seeds of various species of stropanthus are the source of stropanthin (S. kombe) and ouabain (S. Ianata). Helleborus species and squill (the freshly dried bulb of Urginea maritima) are botanical sources for other glycosides like scillaren A.

Cardiac glycosides are the drugs that increase the force of contraction of heart muscles without increasing the oxygen consumption. Since they exert a positive inotropic effect without involving more expenditure of energy, they are called as cardiotonic agents.

Chemistry :

Since the clinically used agents from this class (digoxin, digitoxin) are derived from the plants of the genus Digitalis, these cardiotonic glycosides are collectively termed as digitalis glycosides. These glycosides can also be obtained through synthetic routes, but the cost of production is very high. Hence, they are mainly obtained from the plant source. In some plants, the cardiac glycosides occur in the form of their precursors, which are themselves glycosides along with a molecule of sugar. e.g. proscillaridin A. About 500 different cardiac glycosides from both, animals and plant sources are documented in literature. Cardiotonic glycosides are the conjugation products of a sugar and a non-sugar portion called as genin or aglycone. An aglycone is a steroidal nucleus having a 5- or 6-membered lactone ring attached at C-17 position. The lactone ring is usually unsaturated having Δ α, β structure. The satu-ration or loss of cyclic nature of the lactone ring results into decreased biological response. The aglycone portion may have structural resemblance to steroidal sex hormones and adrenocorticoids. However, it differs from endogenous steroidal hormones in having unusual cis-fusion of rings C and D. The glycosidic linkage occurs through C-3 hydroxyl group. This C-3 hydroxyl group of aglycone has been treated with many organic acids, xanthines and other reagents in order to get semisynthetic derivatives.

The aglycone structures of different cardiac glycosides have been shown in the table 5.1. All aglycones exhibit similar set of pharmacological actions. It is the attached sugar moieties that play an important role in governing duration of action, partition coefficient, absolute potency and protein binding properties of glycosides. It also inhibits an enzyme induced metabolic change in the aglycone configuration.

At a time, the aglycone portion may combine with 1 to 4 molecules of sugar. The sugar attached through glycosidic linkage may be mono-, di-, tri- or tetrasaccharide.

5.7 PATHOPHYSIOLOGY OF HEART FAILURE

According to the Frank Starling mechanisms, the degree of force of heart muscle contraction is governed by the extent of ventricular muscle stretching. It does not apply to all degrees of muscles stretch. If the myocardial fibre is stretched beyond critical length, instead of an increase in force of contraction, a fall in contraction force results. A failing heart does not pump blood efficiently enough to meet the body's needs for oxygen and nutrients due to reduced power of contraction. Blood starts accumulating in the heart due to poor efficiency of the heart. The resulting progressive increase in end-diastolic volume leads to gradual increase in heart failure. The body's compensatory mechanisms get activated to cause increased sympathetic tone, elevation of plasma renin and plasma antidiuretic hormone activity. The manifestations of failing heart include :

(a) Stimulation of sympathetic nervous system, innervated to S. A. node resulting into vasoconstriction, tachycardia and sweating. These are largely the compensatory body mechanisms to counterbalance the effects of inefficient and poorly pumping heart.

(b) As a consequence, salt and water retention results into peripheral and pulmonary edema.

Table 5.1 : Aglycone structures of cardiac glycosides

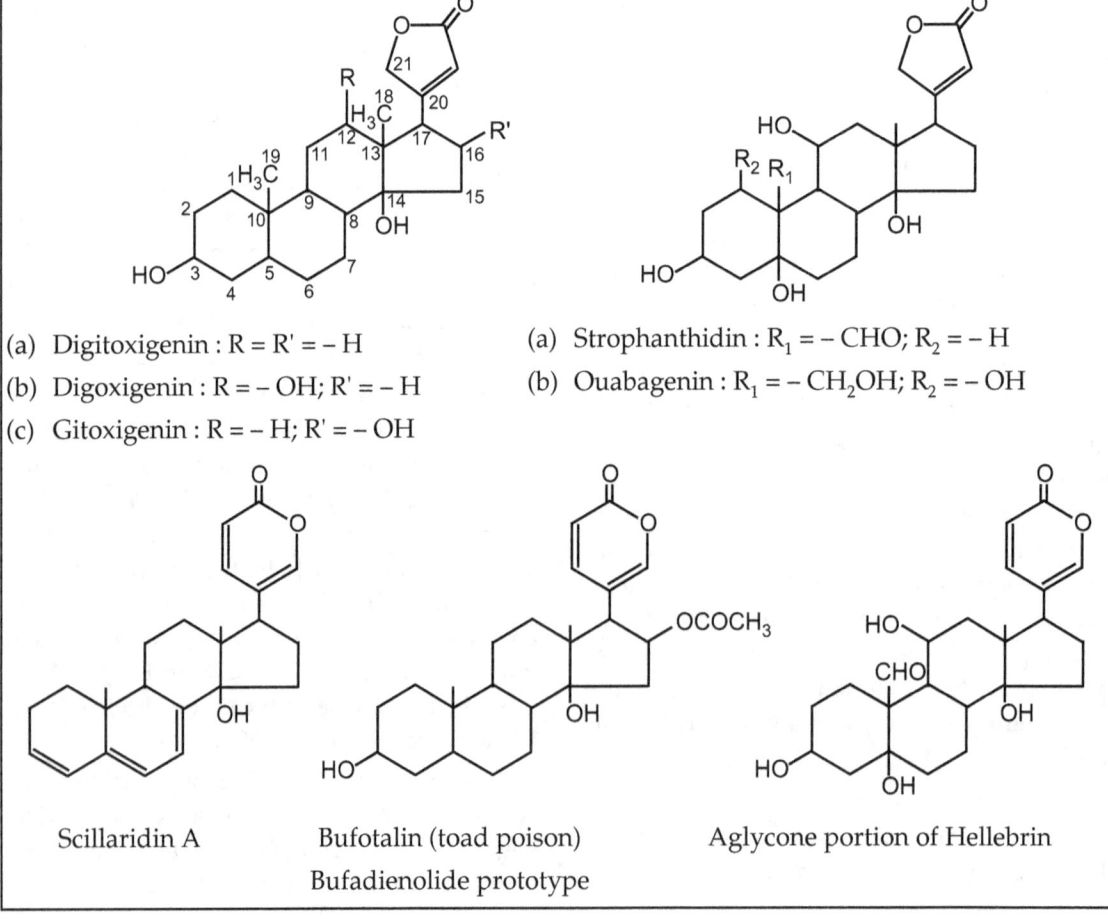

(a) Digitoxigenin : R = R' = – H

(b) Digoxigenin : R = – OH; R' = – H

(c) Gitoxigenin : R = – H; R' = – OH

(a) Strophanthidin : R_1 = – CHO; R_2 = – H

(b) Ouabagenin : R_1 = – CH_2OH; R_2 = – OH

Scillaridin A

Bufotalin (toad poison)

Bufadienolide prototype

Aglycone portion of Hellebrin

(c) Secondary symptoms include easy fatigability, breathlessness and hypertrophy of myocardium.

The main pharmacodynamic property of digitalis is its ability to increase the force of myocardial contraction. The first proof regarding cardiotonic activity of digitalis was given in 1938 by Cattell and Gold. The beneficial effects of the drug in patients with heart failure include increased cardiac output, decreased pre-load, decreased heart size and venous return, increased renal flow and diuresis; all these effects lead to relief of edema and normal heart rate.

The decreased heart size brings the heart under the range of operation of Frank-Starling mechanisms. Renal flow allows the drainage of retained edema fluid. The renal sodium ion excretion is increased due to competitive antagonism at mineralocorticoidal receptor because of structural resemblance.

Chemistry of Aglycone Part :

(1) In digitalis glycosides : The anellation of the A - B and C - D rings is cis (Z), the 3 - OH is axial (β), and all of these steroids carry a 14β-OH group. The C-17 side chain is an unsaturated lactone ring. The sugar part, binding to the 3-OH, is a tri or tetrasaccharide consisting mainly of digitoxose and glucose.

(ii) Strophanthin aglycone has a 5β-OH group in addition to other hydroxyls, upto a maximum of 6 in ouabain. The 19-CH_3 is replaced by an CHO or 1° alcohol and the sugars are the unusual rhamnose or cymarose.

(iii) The squill aglycones carry a six-membered lactone ring with two double bonds. None is used because of high toxicity.

(iv) The lactone ring is not essential. The coplanar side-chains instead of a ring have even higher activity.

(v) The activity of a compound depends to a great extent on the position of the 23rd-carbonyl oxygen, which is held quite rigidly by ring D and the double bond.

(vi) Removal of the sugar portion allows epimerization of the 3β-OH group, with a decrease in activity and an increase in toxicity due to changes in polarity.

Compounds having digitalis activity fall into four categories, depending upon their mode of action.

(I) Inotropic and Na^+ – K^+ - ATPase inhibitors :

    e. g, (a) Cardenolides

        (b) Bufadienolides

        (c) Cardenolide-3-bromo acetate.

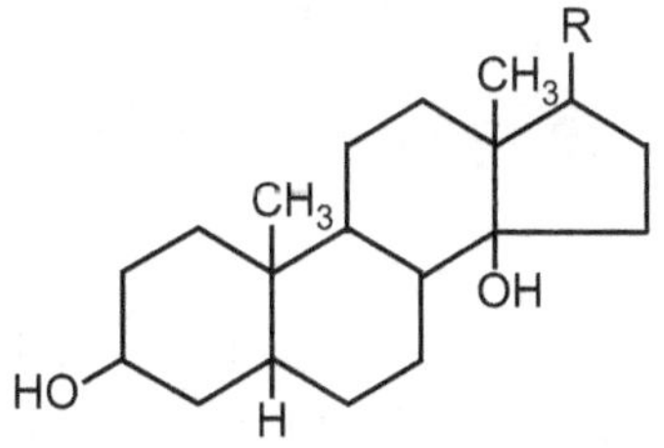

Active compounds : where

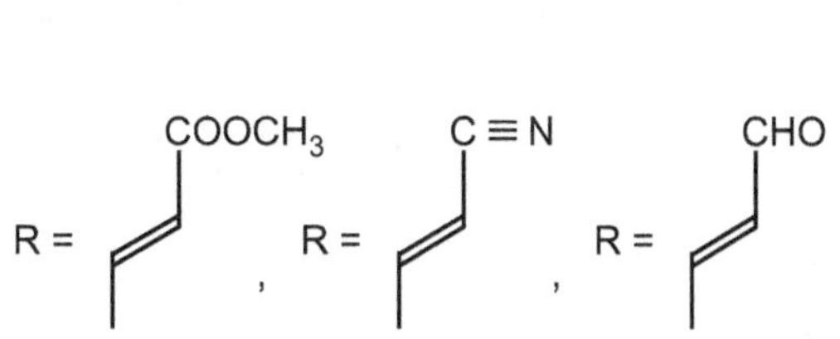

Compounds with moderate activity: where

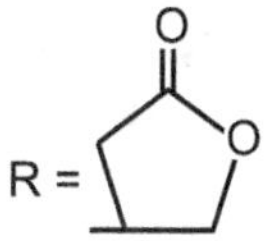

Compounds with marginal activity: where

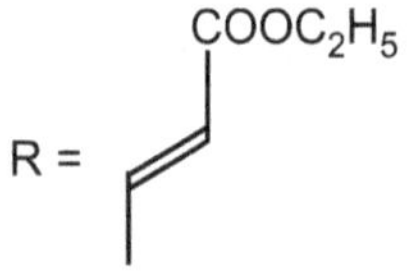

$$R = \quad \text{(structure with COOC}_2\text{H}_5\text{)}$$

COOC$_2$H$_5$

Inactive compounds : where

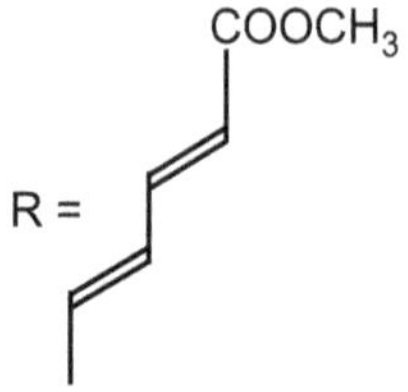

$$R = \quad \text{(structure with COOCH}_3\text{)}$$

COOCH$_3$

(II) Inotropic but not Na$^+$ – K$^+$-ATPase inhibitors :

e.g., catecholamines. caffeine, veratrum alkaloids, etc.

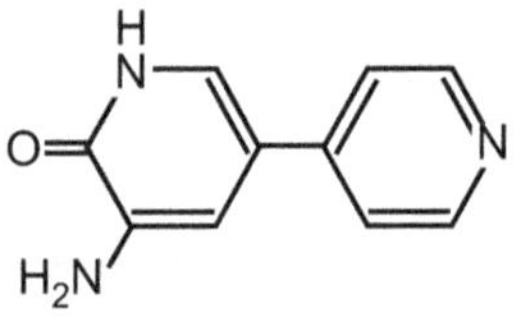

Amrinone

(III) Na$^+$ – K$^+$ - ATPase - inhibitors but not inotropic :

e.g. sodium azide, -SH blocking reagents, mersalyl, fatty acids, diisopropyl fluorophosphate and some steroidal alkylating agent e.g.,

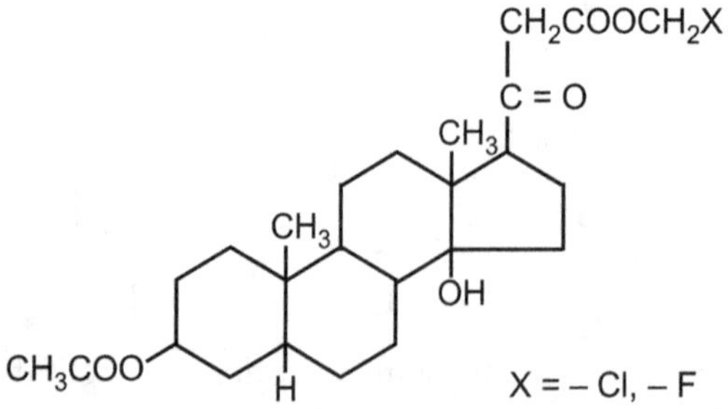

CH$_2$COOCH$_2$X

C = O

CH$_3$

CH$_3$

OH

CH$_3$COO

H

X = – Cl, – F

(IV) Na$^+$-K$^+$-ATPase inhibitors but inotropic activity is uncertain :
e.g., chlormadinone acetate.

Structure - Activity Relationship :

Since cardiac glycosides comprise of
(a) A genin or aglycone portion and
(b) A sugar portion, the SAR studies of these agents are based on the separate SAR investigations on both these portions.

(I) Genin or Aglycone Portion :

(A) C-17 side chain :

The substitutions at C-17 of the genin portion of cardiac glycosides are generally of two types

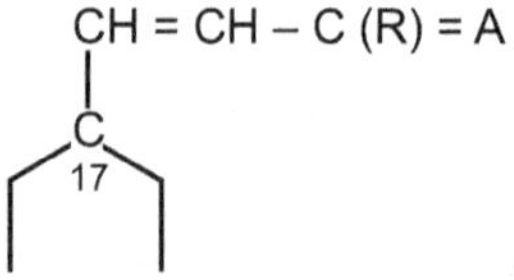

$$CH = CH - C (R) = A$$

C

17

Where A may be oxygen or nitrogen.

(ii) A five or six-membered lactone ring.

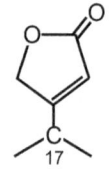

Butenolides 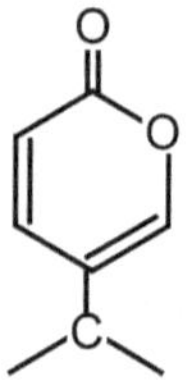   Pentadienolides

In both these types of C-17 substituent, there is a double bond conjugated with a carbonyl oxygen.

(a) Reduction of C-17 side chain double bond results into decreased activity.

(b) In the side chain

$$- CH = CH - (CR) = A,$$

where A may be a hetero atom, activity falls if 'R' is larger than – OCH$_3$. It is generally a hydrogen or small alkyl group.

(c) The compounds having

$$- CH = CH - CH = NH,$$ side chain (A = N)

at C-17, exhibit higher activity.

(d) If the conjugation system in C-17 side chain is extended (i. e. – CH = CH – CH = CH – CH = A), activity abolishes.

(e) Since H-bonding (which takes place between the side-chain and K^+-binding site of $Na^+ - K^+$-ATPase enzyme) determines the degree of $Na^+ - K^+$-ATPase inhibition, the molecule's dipole is an important parameter.

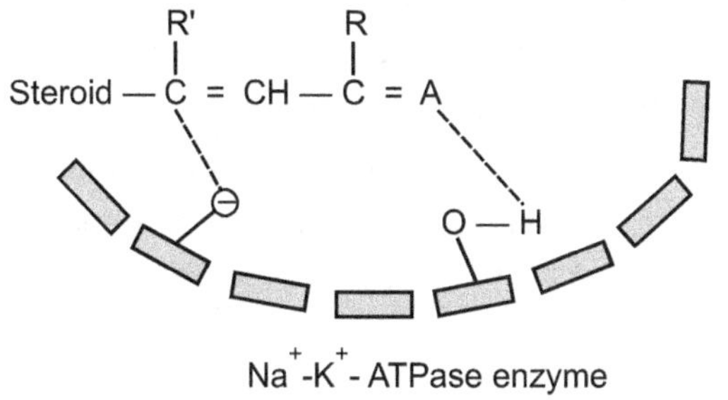

$$Na^+-K^+- \text{ATPase enzyme}$$

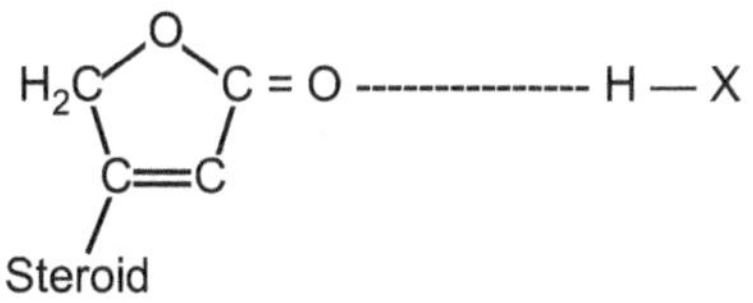

Where, $X = K^+$ binding site on $Na^+ - K^+$-ATPase enzyme.

(f) With the help of PROPHET computer system from National Institute of Health, the most stable conformation of each of variety of genin was superimposed graphically with the digitoxigenin, a cardenolide prototype. It is found that the distance between the position of particular carbonyl oxygen (or nitrile nitrogen), relative to digitoxigenin serves a nearly perfect index of its activity.

(B) Steroid nucleus :

(a) Lactone ring at C-17, as shown by Thomas is essential for activity.

(b) Since some compounds, not having C-14 hydroxyl group, have been shown to exhibit more activity, than corresponding C-14 hydroxy derivatives, C-14 hydroxyl group does not seem to be essential for activity.

(II) Sugar Portion :

Though the sugars are not directly involved in cardiotonic activity, their attachment to the steroid (at C_3) contributes greatly to both pharmacodynamic and pharmacokinetic parameters of the cardiac glycosides. Since the free genins are more rapidly absorbed and more widely distributed than the corresponding glycosides, this leads to their rapid metabolism to give less active 3-epimers, followed by rapid excretion via sulphates and glucuronides formation at free C-3 OH group. The free genins therefore are quite unstable as therapeutic agents. Pharmacodynamically, the genins are usually less potent than their glycosidic forms and show rapid onset and reversal of enzyme inhibitions. In contrast to this the glycosides form very stable complexes with $Na^+ - K^+$-ATPase enzyme. Replacement of the sugar moieties with nitrogen containing side chains gives potent analogs of digitalis e.g. N-(4'-amino-n-butyl) 3-amino acetyl derivative of strophanthidine has about 60 times greater affinity towards $Na^+ - K^+$-ATPase enzyme than the parent genin. H-bonding is the principal interaction involved between sugar and enzyme. Particularly 3-OH and 5-CH_3 groups seem to be binding group in 2, 6-desoxy sugars.

The compounds given in table 5.2 clarify these points of SAR.

5.8 MECHANISM OF ACTION

Digitalis glycosides are effective in cardiac failure, regardless of the etiological reason. The positive inotropic effect of digitalis is manifested in both, normal and failing hearts, although in the former, the increased output may be terminated by its direct vasoconstrictive effects. Digitalis appears to have no indirect effect on mitochondria or on the uptake of any energy yielding substrates (i. e., either ATP or creatinine phosphate). Nor does it have any direct effects on the contractile elements within the sarcoplasm. It does not appear to reverse any biochemical defects associated with heart disease. The intracellular concentration of Na^+ and K^+ are maintained by the activity of $Na^+ - K^+$-

ATPase pump. The hydrolysis of ATP by Na^+ - K^+ – ATPase system provides energy necessary for the operation of pump. The most probable explanation for the direct positive inotropic effect of cardiac glycosides is their ability to inhibit the membrane bound Na^+-K^+-ATPase pump. This inhibition results in impairment of active transport of Na^+ and K^+. The first well documented proof about the pump inhibitory activity of cardiac glycosides was provided by Repke and Portius in 1963.

The Na^+- K^+-ATPase is the prominent binding site for digitalis. It blocks membrane bound Na^+ – K^+ -ATPase in all tissues. But since it has a high affinity for heart muscles, it gets accumulated mainly in the left ventricles and conducting system. It binds with the external surface of the enzyme resulting into suppression of the active transport of Na^+ and K^+ ions. As a result, there is a gradual increase in intracellular Na^+ ions and extracellular K^+ ions. Cardiac fibres possess a mechanism for

Table 5.2

Replacement of the lactone ring of Digitoxigen with open chain moieties having steric and electronic resemblance to the lactone.

	R	Relative Potency	
		+ve inotropic effect	Inhibition of $Na^+ – K^+ – ATPase$
(1)	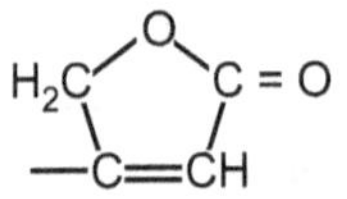 H_2C $C=O$ $-C\!=\!CH$ (lactone ring)	100	100
(2)	$-CH=CH-\overset{OCH_3}{\underset{\vert}{C}}=O$	50	130
(3)	$-CH_2CH_2-\overset{OCH_3}{\underset{\vert}{C}}=O$	Inactive	Inactive
(4)	$-CH=CH-\overset{OH}{\underset{\vert}{C}}=O$	Inactive	Inactive
(5)	$-CH=CH-CH=CH-\overset{OCH_3}{\underset{\vert}{C}}=O$	0.4	3.0
(6)	$-CH=CH-\overset{OC_2H_5}{\underset{\vert}{C}}=O$	3	9
(7)	$-CH=CH-C\equiv N$	70	110
(8)	$-CH=N-NH-\overset{NH_2}{\underset{\vert}{C}}=O$	Inactive	Inactive

exchange of intracellular Na^+ ions with extracellular Ca^{++} ions. The increased intracellular Na^+ concentration activates this mechanism resulting into an increase in net influx of extracellular Ca^{++} ions, which in turn then causes the release of additional intracellular Ca^{++} ions from the stores in sarcoplasmic reticulum to activate contractile force. An elevation in the level of free intracellular Ca^{++} is also due to the drug's individual ability to interfere with Ca^{++} binding on sarcoplasmic reticulum. Thus, the positive inotropic effect of these glycosides is due to an increase in automaticity and excitability of myocardial muscle fibers.

The activity of Na^+-K^+-ATPase pump is regenerated due to the dissociative effect of increased extracellular K^+ ions on the drug - enzyme attachment. Even though the blockage of Na^+ - K^+ - ATPase pump seems to be the main mechanism through which digitalis glycosides exert their positive inotropic effect, many other ATPase inhibitors (such as actinomycin, quinidine, oligomycin, sodium azide, sulfhydryl blocking agents) fail to exhibit the expected positive inotropic effect on the heart. On the other hand, catecholamines (i.e. isoprenaline) have considerable cardiotonic actions but have very short biological half-life.

Besides this, acidosis, hypoxia, cardiac ischemia and decreased renal perfusion are some of the factors that bring down the efficacy of Na^+- K^+ - ATPase pump.

5.9 OTHER EFFECTS OF DIGITALIS GLYCOSIDES

Besides their ability to inhibit the functioning of Na^+- K^+-ATPase pump, digitalis exerts some of its actions through its effect on autonomic nervous system and on vascular smooth muscles. For example,

digitalis has a vasoconstrictor action on the vascular smooth muscle. The changes in the circulation brought about by digitalis are mainly reflection of reflex alterations in A.N.S. functioning. It also changes the heart sensitivity to the vagal and sympathetic neuro-transmitters.

At low to moderate doses, digitalis exerts a negative chronotropic effect mainly due to the increased vagal activity and direct depressant action on the conducting tissue (A. V. node). Digitalis also increases refractory period of both, atrial and ventricular muscle. Thus, the depression of conducting tissue accompanied with increased refractory period may protect ventricles from excessive bombardment in atrial arrhythmias due to increased filtration through A.V. node. But this may lead to bradycardia and in toxic doses, even heart block. In addition, the presence of delayed afterpolarization due to low conduction velocity can slow and impair impulse propogation giving rise to reentrant rhythms.

In S.A. node, the rate of generation of impulse is decreased by mainly parasympathetic activation. The atrial myocardium however, remains almost unaffected at therapeutic concentrations of digitalis. A decrease in atrial action potential duration and effective retractory period is mainly due to the predominance of vagal tone. However high concentration of digitalis can decrease the excitability of all cardiac tissues. Digitalis-induced arrhythmias may result due to an enhanced sympathetic activity from the effect of digitalis on medulla oblongata. These arrhythmias can be treated by β-adrenergic blockers.

At the level of A.V. node, digitalis induces slow conduction and increased refractory period. Below this level, the effects on ventricular myocardial fibers are mainly exerted through Perkinje system. In all myocardial region, the only region which is strongly influenced by sympathetic tone is His-Purkinje system. It is least sensitive to the changes in vagal activity. In this region a decrease in refractoriness (i.e. shortening of action potential duration) is observed.

In summary, the most important hemo-dynamic effect of digitalis is its positive inotropic action which results in decrease in heart size leading to increased cardiac output with increased efficiency of the heart. Thus, it is an effective drug in congestive cardiac failure. It may also lead to cardiac arrhythmias due to increase in myocardial excitability and automaticity. The vagal tone predominance usually results into :

(a) Decrease in atrial refractory period (increased atrial conduction velocity may convert flutter into fibrillation).

(b) Delay in conduction of impulses through A.V. node.

(c) Bradycardia.

The fluid in peripheral edema is drained out due to diuretic action of digitalis. This action is due to -

(i) Increased cardiac output with increased renal perfusion, and

(ii) Direct action upon the distal renal tubule by exerting competitive antagonism with aldosterone (due to structural similarity).

5.10 PHARMACOKINETIC PARAMETERS

Digoxin and digitoxin are the most commonly prescribed agents. Both are readily absorbed from GIT. However, to a considerable extent, digoxin is inactivated (to form 2 - hydroxydigoxin) by intestinal microflora while digitoxin is extensively (92-95%) absorbed. Certain drugs like, kaolin, antacids may interfere with the absorption.

These glycosides possess relatively large volume of distribution (VD). This accounts for their slow distribution in the body compartments. Digitoxin is extensively (79.5%) bound to plasma proteins while digoxin is also significantly (20-25%) bound to plasma proteins. Skeletal muscles, heart, kidneys and RBCs are the body tissues where most of the administered dose of cardiac glycosides get concentrated.

Digoxin has fairly rapid onset of action when administered intravenously while digitoxin is usually not given by i.v. route due to its slow onset of action. It has the longest duration of action, if used orally. Intramuscular route is not preferable for the administration of these drugs due to the induction of severe pain and muscle necrosis.

Other less commonly used cardiac glycosides include ouabain, lanatoside C and deslanoside. The latter acts as a precursor of digoxin in the body. All these drugs are poorly absorbed from GIT and are usually administered intravenously. Liver serves as the principal site of metabolism for all these glycosides. Digitoxin and digoxin are metabolized to relatively inactive dihydrodigoxin by hepatic microsomal enymes. Hence in case of toxicity, the rate of metabolism can be increased by giving metabolic enzymes inducers like, phenobarbital or phenylbutazone.

Other metabolic mechanisms involve cleavage of glycosidic linkage. The free genin portion is then excreted in the form of glucuronide. Part of the genin portion is also reported to undergo epoxidation.

The half-life of digoxin is estimated to be about 35-40 hours. It readily crosses placenta. Its metabolites (i.e., dihydrodigoxine, digoxigenin, dihydrodigoxigenin) are primarily eliminated in urine. The rate of elimination of cardiac glycosides is very slow which, if not taken into consideration, may result into drug intoxication due to its accumulation. Hence, the cardiac glycosides are usually administered orally in two stages. The patient is treated with an initial dose of the drug to get therapeutic response. This dose administration, is known as 'initial digitalization or loading dose'. The therapeutic response obtained through digitalization is further maintained by a low dose schedule which is known as 'maintenance dose'.

5.11 THERAPEUTIC USES

(A) Congestive Cardiac Failure :

The positive inotropic effect of these glycosides causes the heart to contract more strongly and efficiently. The beneficial effects of these drugs in patients with heart failure include: increased cardiac output, decreased heart size and venous pressure, diuresis and relief of edema. The reduction in myocardial oxygen demand decreases the intensity of compensatory sympathetic nervous system which results in a decrease in systemic arterial resistance and venous tone. However digitalis treatment is not effective when :

(a) Heart failure is associated with very high preload or after load. In such cases the use of diuretics (which lower down blood volume and ventricular filling pressure) and/or vasodilators (which reduce preload, and after load) is given more weightage.

(b) Chronic treatment is required. This is due to a loss in therapeutic efficacy through development of significant tolerance to drug action. In such case vasodilators and/or inhibitors of angiotensin converting enzyme (saralasin, captopril) are the drugs of choice used along with digitalis or a diuretic.

(B) Atrial Arrhythmias :

At therapeutic doses, cardiac glycosides have a protective action upon the ventricles. This action is exerted by increasing the vagal tone and by a direct. depressant action upon A.V. conduction. This results into an increased 'filtering' of the impulses which are generated at relatively higher rate during atrial arrhythmias. The reduction in conduction velocity and an increase in refractory period protect the ventricular muscles from excessive stimulation. Atrial arrhythmias where digitalis finds clinical use, include-atrial flutter, atrial fibrillation and paroxysmal atrial tachycardia.

However, the glycosides are contraindicated in patients having hypokalemia, hypercalcemia, impaired renal function or ventricular tachycardia. Quinidine or procainamide are better drugs to treat ventricular tachycardia.

5.12 ADVERSE EFFECTS

The cardiac glycosides have a low therapeutic safety margin. Consequently the adverse reactions are quite frequent and can be severe in toxic doses. These adverse reactions are mainly due to –

(i) An increased parasympathetic tone.

(ii) A loss of intracellular potassium (hypokalemia)

(iii) An increased intracellular Ca^{++} concentration. The cardiac effects of digitalis glycosides are much complicated due to unusual combination of -

(a) Decreased A.V. conduction and increased refractory period due to enhanced vagal activity, and

(b) Increased abnormal or ectopic automaticity due to drug's direct effect.

Digitalis glycosides are used to treat a diseased heart. Due to the combination of above two effects, such a diseased heart easily get attacked by arrhythmias or A. V. block occurred due to an exaggeration of depressant action on conduction. Digitalis in high dose, is likely to induce the development of almost every known cardiac arrhythmia. The infarcted myocardium serves as a site to develop ectopic foci which is responsible for the occurrence of both atrial and ventricular tachycardia. It is better to discontinue drug therapy under such conditions.

5.13 DIGITALIS INTOXICATION

The large volume of distribution (VD), low rate of elimination (longer duration of action), the concurrent effects of the glycosides on A.N.S. and on peripheral vascular smooth muscles (besides their action on $Na^+ - K^+$-ATPase pump) and hypokalemia (in patients receiving diuretics along with digitalis) are the factors that provoke the sensitivity of the patient towards digitalis intoxication. The low therapeutic index of these drugs necessitates careful clinical observation of the patients during the period of initial digitalization. Hence, extreme caution is to be observed when they are given intravenously. Both hypokalemia and hypercalcemia sensitize myocardium to the glycoside action. In such a condition, a decline in resting membrane potential, brings the cell quite near to their threshold value for generating an impulse. This explains the basis of digitalis-induced extrasystoles during the therapy. An adequate potassium intake should always be maintained in the therapy when hypokalemia is reported. The hypokalemia, if remained uncorrected, may lead to the tachyarrhythmias in digitalis overdose (due to decline in resting membrane potential). Hence, if a diuretic is needed in patients receiving digitalis, then potassium sparing diuretics are to be used.

However, in toxicity signs due to conduction impairments (i.e. A.V. block), potassium intake may provoke the digitalis toxicity. Hence, it is contraindicated in cases of A.V. block. Under such conditions vagolytic agents are useful.

An enhancement of automaticity by digitalis is the probable reason behind the drug induced atrial arrhythmias. Any antiarrhythmic drug can be used to suppress atrial arrhythmias due to digitalis toxicity.

A considerable fraction of orally administered digoxin is inactivated (to 2 - hydroxydigoxin) by intestinal microflora.

Hence in the patient receiving digoxin along with an antibiotic, the extent of absorption of active drug suddenly increases. This leads to appearance of toxic effects of digoxin in therapeutic dose level.

5.14 TREATMENT OF INTOXICATION

(1) Digitalis glycosides have very poor therapeutic index. In case of digitalis intoxication, the therapy should be immediately discontinued so as to lower down the plasma concentration of the drug.

(2) The patient should be evaluated to trace out hypokalemia if diuretics are concurrently administered. The plasma potassium level may be maintained in the upper normal level by giving potassium either orally or intravenously. The increasing extracellular K^+ ion concentration may produce the stimulatory effect on $Na^+ - K^+$-ATPase pump, there by decreasing the binding of digitalis with the pump system. The suppression of ectopic beats and abnormal rhythms (due to the drug induced automaticity) are other beneficial effects of potassium intake. However its administration is contraindicated in the presence of diminished cardiac conduction (e.g., sinus bradycardia, A.V. block). In such conditions atropine like drugs may improve the functioning of heart by suppressing the underlying cause (i.e., increased vagal tone).

(3) Digitalis increases the automaticity and excitability of myocardial fibres. In toxic doses digitalis may induce severe atrial arrhythmias. Many antiarrhythmic agents (e.g., propranolol, phenytoin, lidocaine) along with potassium salts can be used in suppressing digitalis induced atrial arrhythmias.

(4) In severe life-threatening digitalis intoxication (accidental or attempted suicides), above treatment may not be effective to get immediate response. In such cases, specific glycoside antibodies administration leads to rapid recovery of the heart functioning. Digitalis specific fab antibody fragments were first evaluated for their effectiveness in humans in 1976. Like other antibodies, however their use is accompanied by emergence of allergic reactions in sensitive patients. This limits their use in patients with pre-allergic history.

5.15 ALTERNATIVES TO DIGITALIS THERAPY

The low margin of safety and inherent toxicities associated with the use of digitalis glycosides, led to the search for development of group of agents having positive inotropic effect. There was an increasing tendency to use vasodilators (hydralazine, prazosin, nitrates), diuretics or cardiac stimulants (β-adrenergic agonists) to reduce the preload and/or after load of the failing heart. However, adrenergic drugs have a shorter duration of action while vasodilators may not be the primary drugs of choice in all the cases. Out of available alternatives to digitalis, bipyridine derivatives are of special interest due to the combination of both positive inotropic property and vasodilatory effect in one compound. Examples from this class include, amrinone and milrinone.

Amrinone

Milrinone

Chemically, amrinone is 5-amino (3', 4-bipyridine) - 6 (1 H) - one, while milrinone is a 2-methyl, 5-carbonitrile derivative of amrinone. Both these agents can be used orally as well as intravenously. Milrinone is considerably more potent but has relatively shorter duration of action than amrinone. Their use in congestive heart failure is mainly due to their positive inotropic and vasodilatory effects. The mechanism of the positive inotropic effect of amrinone differs from that of conventional positive inotropic agents. Since their efficacy is not decreased by the use of adrenergic blockers, the direct activation of adrenergic receptor is not their mechanism of action. Probably the mechanism may be related to an increase in intracellular concentration of c-AMP by inhibition of phosphodiesterase enzymes, (however, several agents that inhibit these enzymes, do not exert a positive inotropic effect). The increase in c-AMP then lowers the rate of influx of Ca^{++} ions resulting into vasodilation. The net effect is reduction in the afterload. The positive inotropic effect makes these agents useful in the treatment of congestive cardiac failure, where their inotropic effect is additive to that of cardiac glycosides.

Liver serves as the principal site for metabolism. About six metabolites of amrinone have been identified. Its use in the chronic treatment is not advisable due to serious adverse effects. Amrinone during long term use may induce immunologic abnormality. This along with long term inhibition of phosphodiesterase enzyme may contribute for the appearance of adverse effects. These effects include nausea, vomiting, abdominal cramps, diarrhea, fatigue and reversible thrombocytopenia, headache, fatigue and hepatotoxicity. Hence, its daily dose should not exceed 10 mg/kg.

Milrinone is quite a safe drug. Its use is not associated with most of the adverse effects seen in amrinone therapy. However efficacy of the drug appears to be age dependent.

Other drugs having positive inotropic effects include dopamine, dobutamine (β_1-agonist), ephedrine and pirbuterol. Pirbuterol is a β-adrenergic agonist having both, a positive inotropic and vasodilatory effect. The positive inotropic effect of catecholamines is due to a resultant increase in the intracellular Ca^{++} concentration that is brought about by the drug induced changes in c-AMP level. However in many cases, inotropic effect and c-AMP level may be dissociated.

9. Coronary flow is increased with dobutamine in proportion to myocardial oxygen consumption with little change in oxygen extraction. Dobutamine significantly increases oxygen delivery by 48.5 % and oxygen consumption by 22%.

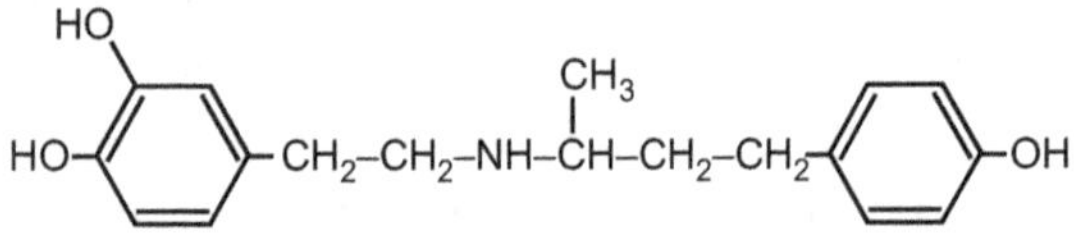

Dobutamine

Dobutamine has a unique combination of positive inotropic effects, enhancing contractility and arterial vasodilation, reduced afterload and enhancing perfusion. Thus it acts as both, inotropic agent and vasodilator.

Since the extracellular calcium is important in deciding the force of heart contraction, attempts were also made to design specific camera molecules for Ca^{++} ions which will introduce more extracellular Ca^{++} ions into the cell. X 537-A is such an agent developed by Holland et al in 1975. Since the pacemaker activity is less dependent on Ca^{++} ion concentration and requires different ionic basis than the myocardial cell, this increased influx of Ca^{++} ions results in positive inotropic effect without associated tachycardia. However a decrease in apparent Ca^{++} sensitivity of the contractile proteins may occur in response to a fall in intracellular pH and rise in cytoplasmic levels of inorganic phosphate and creatine phosphate.

5.16 ANTI-ARRHYTHMIC AGENTS

Normal synchronous mechanical activity of the heart depends upon a specific sequence of electrical activation for all myocardial cells during each beat, beginning first at the SA node and ending with depolarization of the ventricle.

Thus an arrhythmia may arise because of alteration in,

(1) Automaticity

(2) Conduction, and

(3) Refractory period of the myocardial cells.

Abnormalities of heart rate are included among the arrhythmias even though the actual rhythm of the beat is not necessarily disturbed in these conditions.

Origin of Arrhythmia :

The generation of cardiac impulses in the normal heart is usually confined to specialised tissues that spontaneously depolarize and initiate the action potential. These cells are located in the right atrium and are referred to as the sino atrial node (S. A. node) or pacemaker cells. When the impulse is released from the S.A. node, excitation of the heart tissue takes place in an orderly manner by a spread of the impulse throughout the specialised automatic fibres in the atria resulting in contraction of the atria. A. V. node functions as a delay circuit and conducts this impulse slowly to the bundle of His and finally, through the Purkinje fibre network in the ventricles, resulting into ventricular contraction. The P wave represents atrial depolarization and the QRS complex represents ventricular depolarisation. The interval between the two (PR interval) is the time taken to conduct the beat through the AV node and is lengthened in AV block. The T wave denotes ventricular repolarization, and the QT interval denotes the time between depolarization and polarization of the ventricles. A prolonged QT predisposes to torsades de pointes (i.e. a fast ventricular rhythm with polymorphic QRS complexes). The events are represented in following figure.

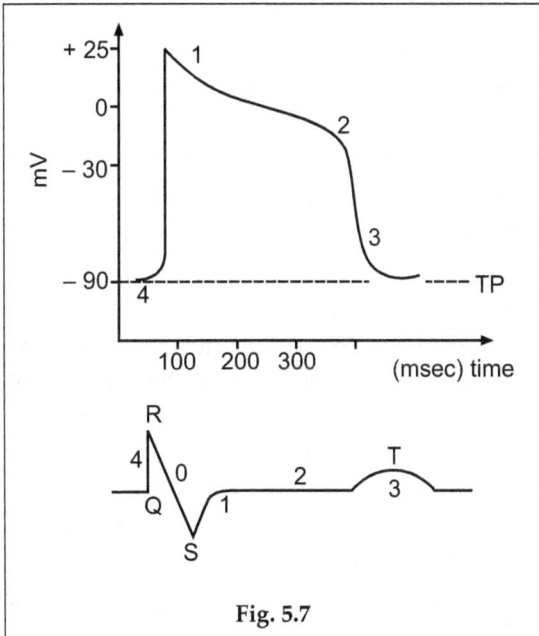

Fig. 5.7

Though the spontaneous electrical depola-rization of the S.A. node (pacemaker) cells is independent of the nervous systems, these cells are innervated by both sympathetic and parasympathetic nerves, which may cause an increase or decrease in the heart rate, respectively. Other special cells in the normal heart, which possess the property of automaticity (secondary pacemaker) may

influence cardiac rhythm when the normal pacemaker is suppressed or when pathological changes occur in the myocardium to make these cells the dominant source of cardiac rhythm (ectopic pace makers), especially when myocardial cell damage occurs because of localized myocardial disease (infarction) or from digitalis toxicity, excessive vagal tone, excessive catecholamine release from sympathomimetic nerves to the heart, or even high catecholamine plasma levels. If the SA node is prevented from operating normally, the AV node will usually take over as pacemaker or, if both are inactive, the ventricular conducting tissues will serve as pacemaker. Whenever the SA node is not the controlling pacemaker, the heart beat is less well co-ordinated and this may result in inefficient pumping with an increase in energy expenditure to maintain an adequate circulation or ineffective pumping with an inadequate circulation. The development of automaticity in these secondary pacemaker cells (e.g., special atrial cells, A.V. nodal cells, bundle of His or / and Purkinje fibres), may lead to cardiac arrhythmias.

In summary, SA node cells depoiarize quickly and thus control the heart rhythm. The impulses are conducted from the SA node across the atria to the atrioventricular (AV) node and then down the bundle of His to the Purkinje fibres and the ventricles. This is termed as sinus rhythm. The cardiac arrhythmias may arise from abnormalities in either impulse formation or impulse conduction or by both. These reasons may be brought about in several ways :

(1) An infarction may cause the death of pacemaker cells or of conducting tissue.

(2) A cardiac tissue disorder, e.g. fibrosis or rheumatic fever, or a multisystem connective tissue disorder, e.g. sarcoidosis, disrupts the conduction network.

(3) Sympathetic or parasympathetic control changes, e.g. stress, anxiety, exercise or smoking.

(4) Hypothyroidism, hyperthyroidism, hypo adrenalism, hyperkalaemia and hypokalaemia or other electrolyte disturbances may predispose to arrhythmias.

Abnormality in an impulse formation (automaticity) gives rise to changes in heart rate and to the development of ectopic (abnormal) beats, originating in secondary pacemaker cells. While disturbances in conduction can be partial or complete (delay or block), can be unidirectional or bi-directional and can occur with or without re-entry or circus movement.

Thus, all cardiac rhythms can be described in terms of the rate origin and pattern.

(a) Rate related arrhythmias : Tachycardia and bradycardia.

(b) Origin related arrhythmias : Sinus, atrial, nodal, supraventricular, re-entrant and ventricular.

(c) Pattern related arrhythmias : Ectopic, premature contraction, paroxysmal, flutter, fibrillation block, and torsades de pointes.

What has been described as "circus move-ment" or, more recently, "macro-reentry" occurs when a wave of excitation travels around an anatomical obstacle, an anatomical loop, or along functional pathways.

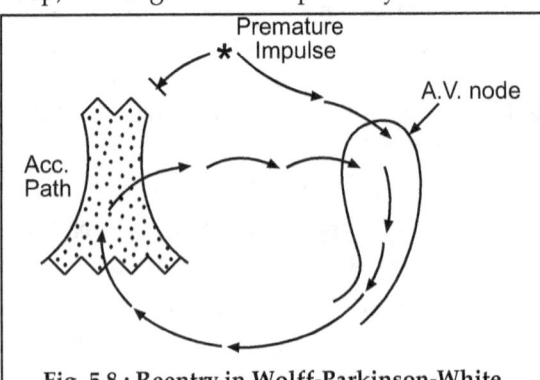

Fig. 5.8 : Reentry in Wolff-Parkinson-White syndrome

Macro-reentry arrhythmias have been demonstrated in tissues with slow response action potentials (i.e., A.V. node, S.A. node) as well as in those with clearly separate parallel pathways possessing different electro-physiological characteristics (i.e. paroxysmal atrial tachycardia associated Wold-Parkinson - White preexcitation syndromes).

Signs and symptoms of arrhythmias may include dizziness or collapse because of poor blood supply to the brain : shortness of breath due to poor oxygenation; angina associated with a poor coronary circulation and/or increased cardiac workload arising from a tachycardia, and weakness and palpitations.

Chemistry and Classification :

The major antiarrhythmic drugs were introduced into medicine as either antimalarial anticonvulsants or local anesthetics and it was only by chance that their antiarrhythmic properties were discovered.

Treatment of cardiac arrhythmias has been empiric in the past because the electrophysiologic mechanisms involved in the initiation and perpetuation of the majority of abnormal cardiac rhythms were unknown. This required a knowledge of the complete pharmacology of the antiarrhythmic agents as well as complete electrophysiologic knowledge of arrhythmogenesis.

Electrophysiologic studies on antiarrhythmic agents in normal and diseased tissue have revealed effects on impulse formation (pacemaker activity), intramyocardial conduction, and/or recovery of electrical excitability. Most antiarrhythmic agents suppress abnormal pacemaker activity but produce little effect on normal pacemaker activity until toxic concentrations are attained.

Antiarrhythmic drugs may reduce the rate of rise of action potential as well as magnitude of voltage charge during the upstroke (phase 0) of action potential. Membrane responsiveness (change in membrane potential to applied depolarizing current) may be diminished and threshold potential may be decreased by antiarrhythmic agents. They may slow recovery of electrical excitability and alter the relationship between membrane potential during repolarization and recovery of excitability.

Antiarrhythmic agents can be divided into atleast 4 groups based on what is known as their elcctrophysiologic actions, as originally suggested by Vaughn-Williams and coworkers.

Class I : Local Anaesthetic Drugs :

The major electrophysiologic effect of this class of drugs is a reduction in the maximum rate of myocardial cell depolarisation during phase 0 of the action potential without any effect on the resting membrane potential.

Accordingly the various antiarrhythmic drugs are classified as :

(IA) Membrane - depressant drugs (depressant of electrophysiological properties of myocardial cells)

e.g., Quinidine
　　　Procainamide
　　　Diisopyramide

(IB) Drugs which facilitate impulse conduction and shorten refractory period while depressing automaticity

e.g., Lidocaine
　　　Phenytoin
　　　Mexiletine
　　　Tocainide
　　　Aprindine

(IC) Flecainide
　　　Encainide
　　　Lorcainide
　　　Propafenone

(II) β-adrenergic blockers

e.g., Alprenolol
　　　Atenolol,
　　　Metoprolol
　　　Practolol
　　　Propranolol, Pindolol

(III) Amiodarone
　　　Bretylium
　　　D-Sotalol

(IV) Selective Ca^{++} antagonists

e.g., Nifedipine
　　　Verapamil
　　　Diltiazem

(V) Miscellaneous agents
　　　Atropine
　　　Neostigmine
　　　Edrophonium

Anticholinergic drugs such as tricyclic antidepressants or atropine may remove vagal control and cause tachycardia.

In the presence of these agents, conduction velocity is decreased and the threshold for excitability (current required for cellular depolarization) is increased. Repolarization and recovery of excitability must proceed to a greater extent before another impulse can be initiated because of drug-induced decrease in depolarizing current. This results in an increase in the effective refractory period (ERP). The major drugs with class I actions are quinidine, procainamide, lidocaine, flecainide, encainide, lorcainide, propafenone, phenytoin and disopyramide.

Phenytoin is a blocker of sodium channels and shortens the action potential in heart muscle cells and therefore - according to Vaughan - Williams classification - it is a member of class Ib antiarrhythmic drugs. Side effects including CNS complaints (ataxia, nystagmus, confusion) are major drawbacks of phenytoin treatment. One direction of research led to the change of phenytoin character from acidic to basic i.e. ropitoin, active in various types of arrhythmia models after oral and intravenous administration.

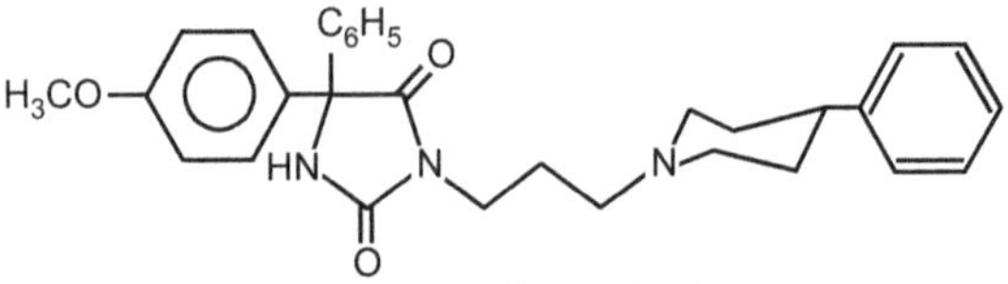

Ropitoin

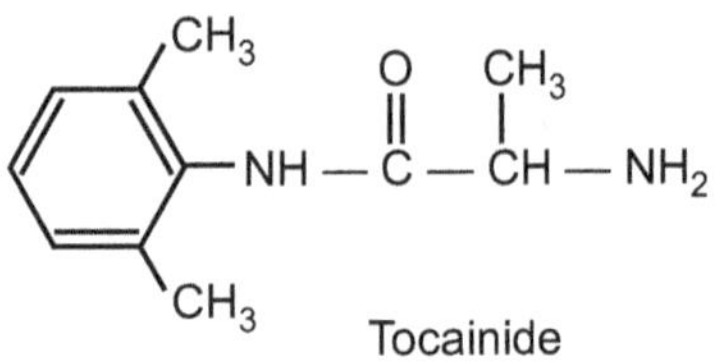

Tocainide

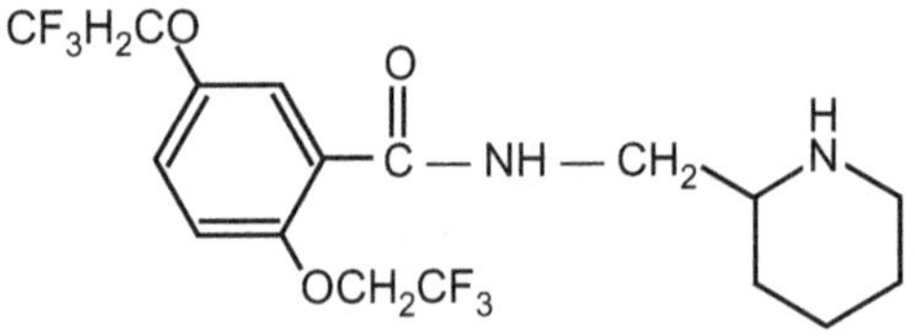

Flecainide

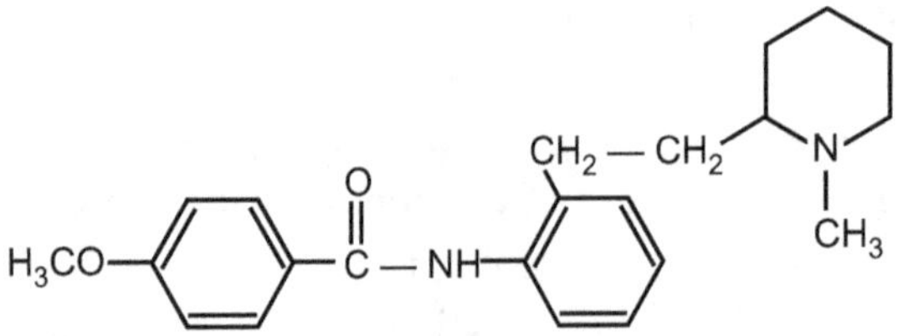

Encainide

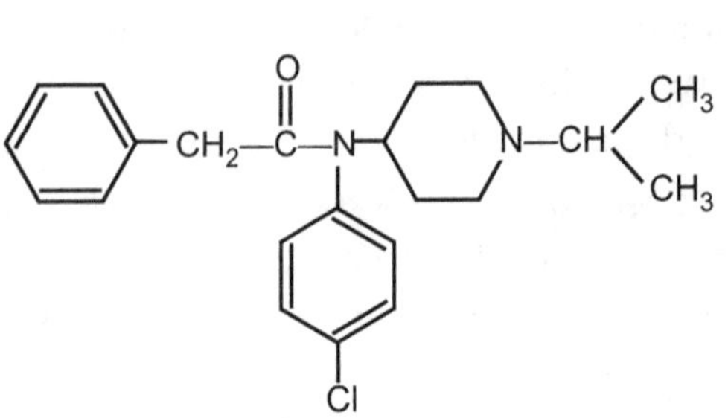

Lorcainide

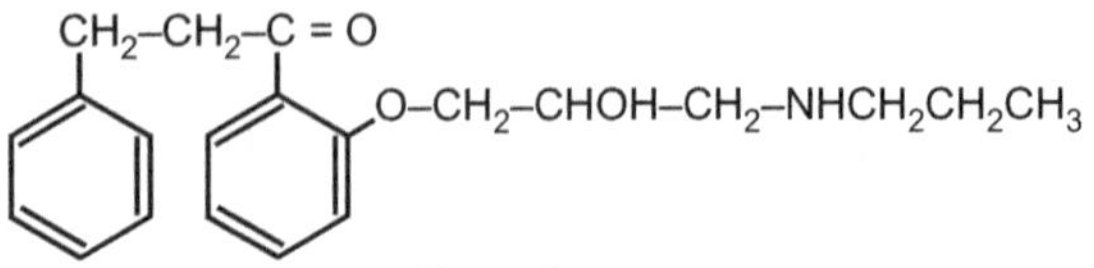

Propafenone

Class I : β-adrenergic Blocking Agents :

Local increase in catecholamine activity that accompany centrally mediated sympathetic nervous system discharge or myocardial ischemia can be associated with sufficient local enhancement in automaticity so that competing rhythms and ectopy emerge. β-Blockers can suppress this type of automaticity and can also produce direct depressant effects on the myocardial cell membrane.

Class III : Agents that Prolong the Action Potential Duration :

The class III anti-arrhythmic drugs are pharmacologically and chemically diverse group of compounds that have ability to prolong action potential duration and hence refractory period of cardiac tissues. Bretylium is a prototype. These agents share the common property of prolonging both action potential duration and the effective refractory period. Bretylium and amiodarone supress cardiac catecholamine effects that result from sympathetic nerve stimulation. The most impressive action of this class has been their ability to suppress ventricular tachycardia and/or ventricular fibrillation. D-solatol lacks the non-selective β-blocking activity of racemic sotalol.

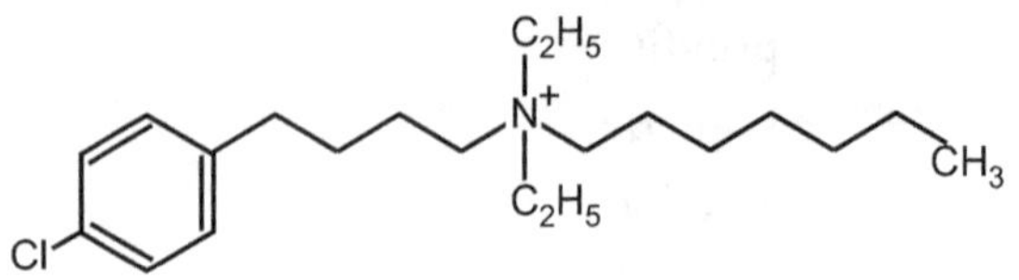

Clofilium

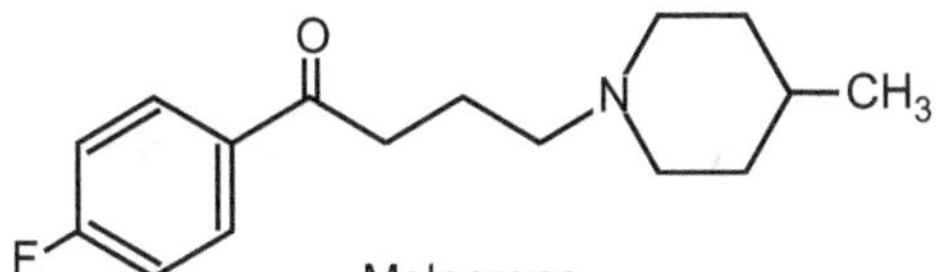

Melperone

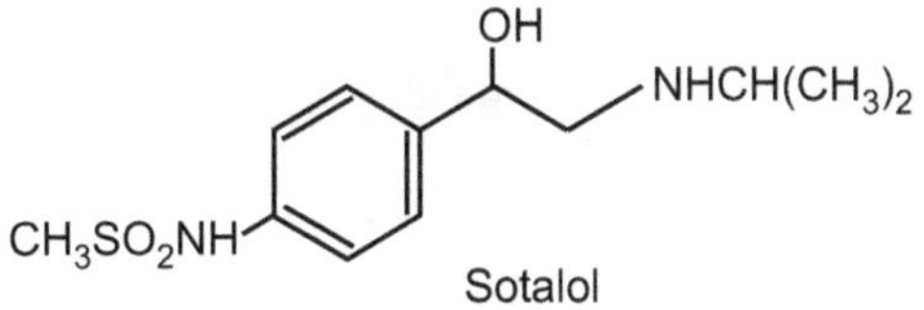

Sotalol

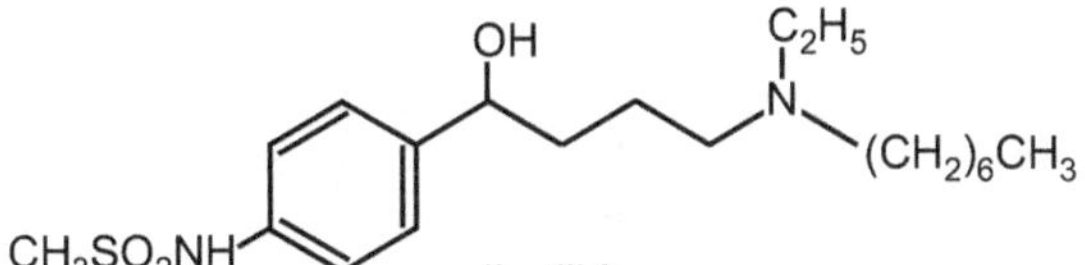

Ibutilide

Ibutilide : It is a class III antiarrhythmic agent. It acts by induction of show inward sodium current, which prolongs action potential and refractory period of myocardial cells.

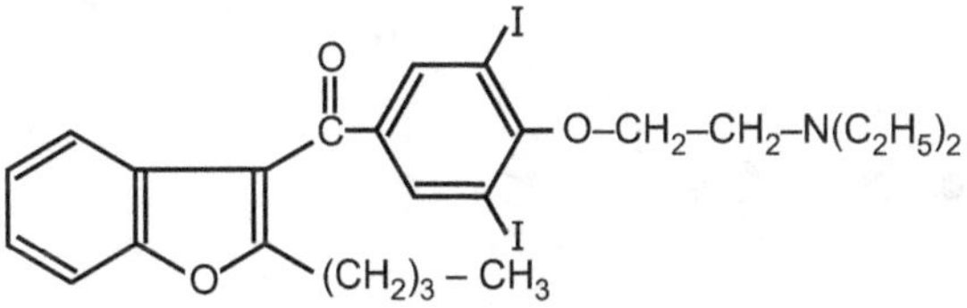

Amiodarone

Dronedarone : It is a potassium channel blocker related to aminodarone used in the treatment of cardiac arrhythmias.

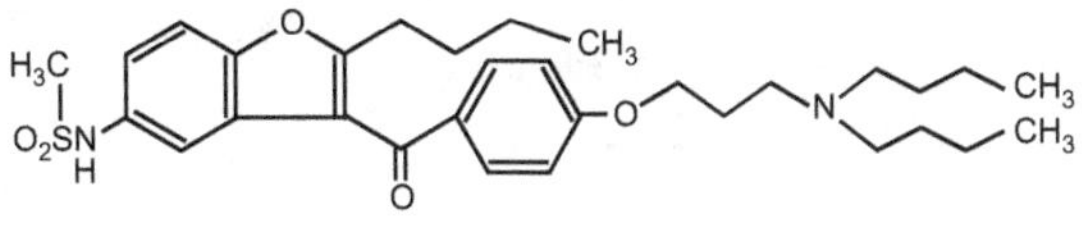

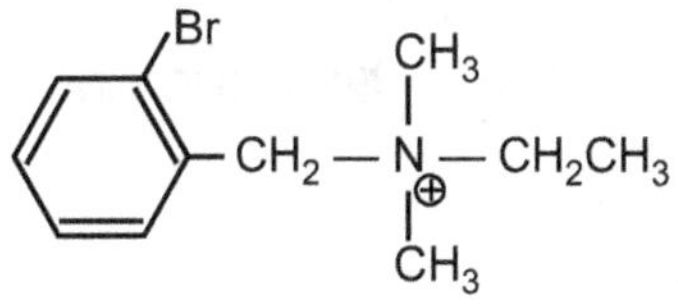

Bretylium

Amiodarone is a benzofuran derivative initially developed in 1962 as antianginal agent due to its ability to increase coronary blood flow and to decrease myocardial oxygen demand. Increase in action potential duration is its major electrophysiological effect. It has structural similarities to thyroxine. Similar increases in action potential duration are seen in hypothyroxidism. It prolongs the action potential duration in atrial and ventricular muscle as well as Purkinje fibres without altering resting membrane potential or auto-maticity. It has antifibrillatory activity and reduces ventricular fibrillation. It also blocks calcium ion channels resulting into additional vasodilation activity.

Moricizine : It is a phenothiazine derivative with class 1c antiarrhythmic properties. It is extensively metabolized and may have pharmacologically active metabolites.

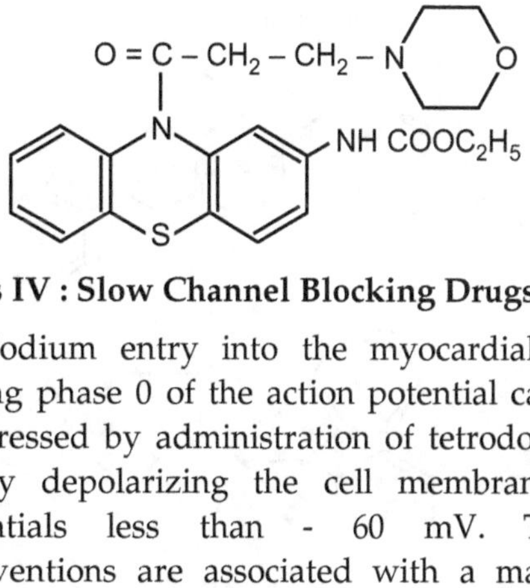

Class IV : Slow Channel Blocking Drugs :

Sodium entry into the myocardial cell during phase 0 of the action potential can be suppressed by administration of tetrodotoxin or by depolarizing the cell membrane to potentials less than - 60 mV. These interventions are associated with a marked decrease in the slope for phase 0 of the action potential. These slowly rising action potentials have been associated with marked reduction in conduction velocity, unidirectional block, reentry and also with the appearance of spontaneous automaticity. Clinical use of these drugs has shown them to be effective in controlling ventricular response rates to supraventricular arrhythmias, presumably via depressant effect on slow response potentials involved in A.V. nodal conduction. Reentrant rhythms within A.V. node, such as paroxysmal atrial tachycardia are also suppressed, probably by similar mechanisms. Ventricular arrhythmias have not been effectively suppressed by these agents.

New and Experimental Antiarrhythmic Drugs :

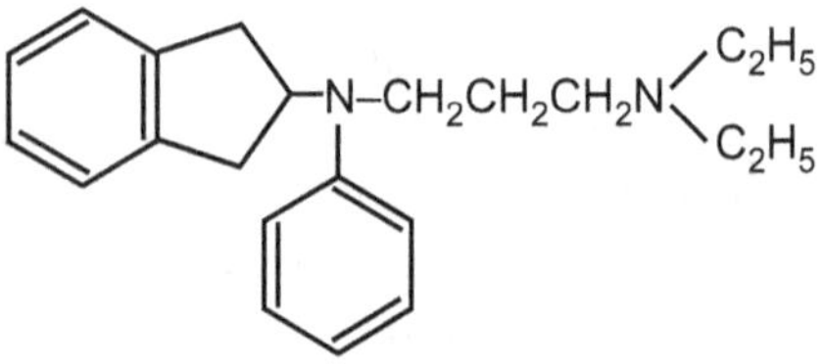

Disopyramide

Aprindine

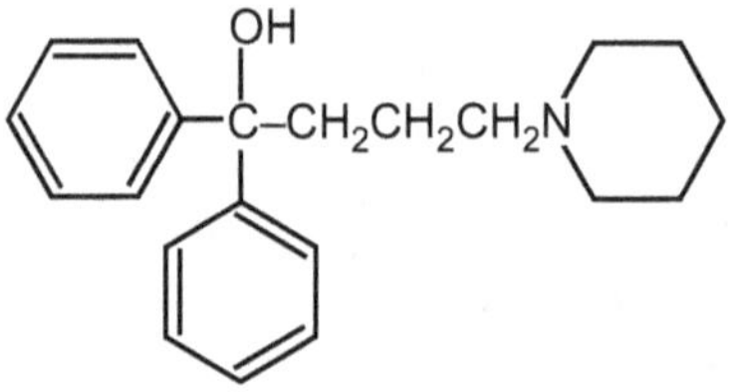

Phenytoin

Diphenidol

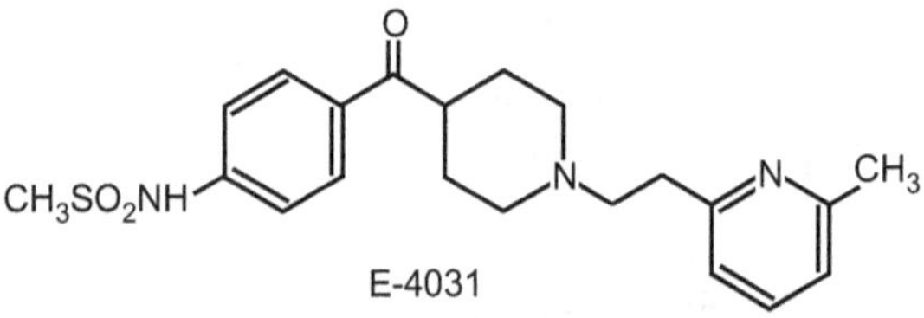

Almokalant

E-4031

MK-499

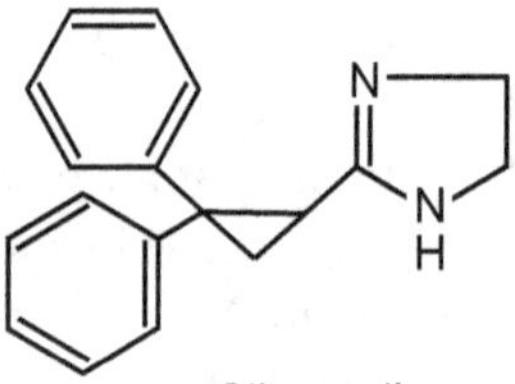

Cibenzoline

It has an active metabolite namely desethylamiodarone.

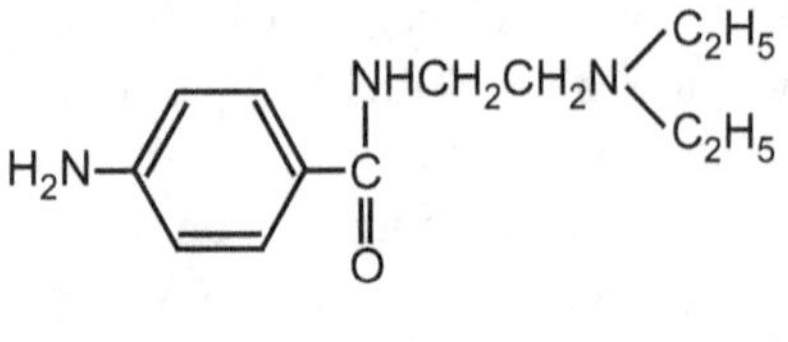

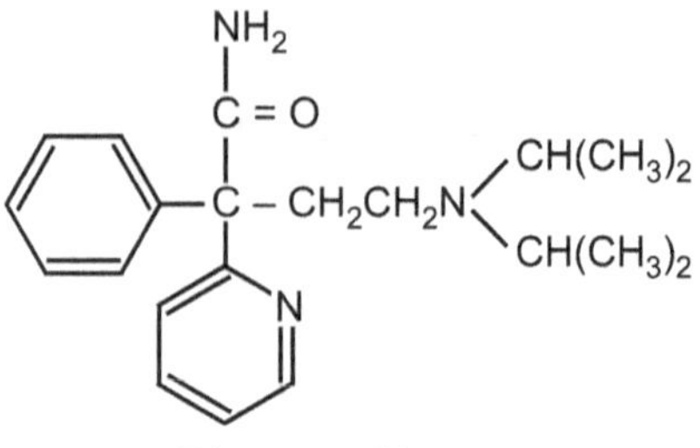

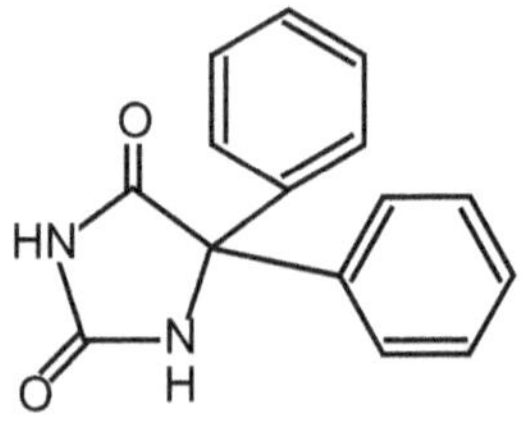

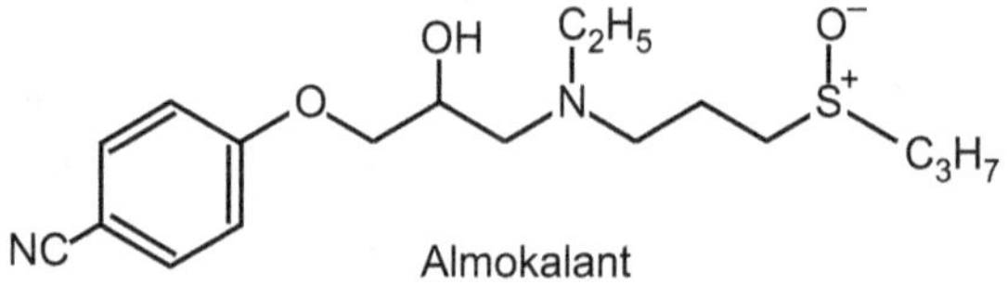

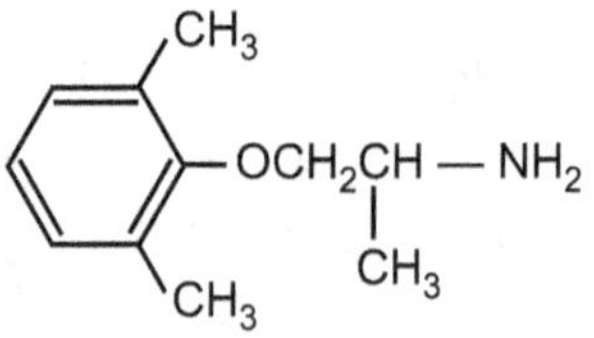

Mexiletine

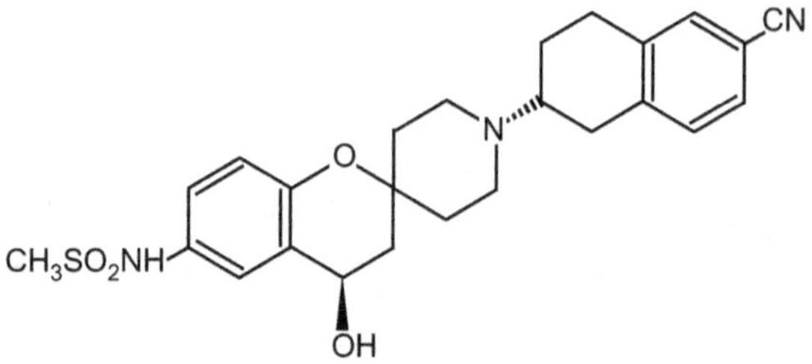

Procainamide

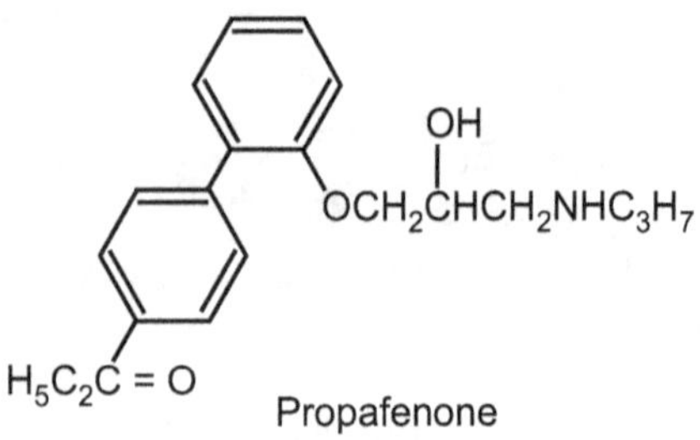

Propafenone

5.17 ANTI-ANGINAL DRUGS

The word 'angina' (from the Greek verb meaning, 'to choke') is used to describe the pain or discomfort of cardiac origin which results due to temporary ischemia of the myocardium; that means the flow of blood is inadequate to maintain the metabolic demands of heart for oxygen and nutrients.

The heart normally extracts almost all the available oxygen from blood, hence the heart must therefore meet its increased metabolic demands for oxygen (in exercise or stress) by increasing the rate of coronary blood flow.

Angina is caused by the coronary vessel constriction which prevents this increase in blood flow. Reflex vasospasm of coronary arteries appears to be a primary cause of angina and it may be (but is not necessarily) superimposed on atherosclerotic coronary artery disease.

Angina is generally manifested by sudden, severe, pressing substernal pain, which often radiates to the left shoulder and along the flexor surface of the left arm. Breathlessness sometimes occurs along with other discomforts.

In 1910, Osler stated that "spasm or narrowing of a coronary artery or even of a branch, may so modify the action of a section of the heart that it works with disturbed tension. Coronary vasospasm does occur in the vicinity of proximal atherosclerotic lesions leading to reversible, but often complete, coronary occlusion.

Recent data suggests that both exercise-induced and cold induced coronary spasm may also be α–receptor mediated. Indeed, ergonovine maleate, an ergot alkaloid with α-receptor agonist properties, has been widely used as a provocative test for coronary spasm. Cholinergic drugs such as methacholine can precipitate coronary spasm and atropine is an effective spasmolytic agent. It is possible that, under the influence of circulating catecholamines, platelets are sensitised to thrombin facilitating the release of TXA_2, which has marked platelet aggregating and vasoconstrictor properties. Because of its potent vasoconstrictor activity, thromboxane A_2 coming from platelets or endothelial cells may be considered as the main cause of vasospasm seen in Prinzmetal's angina.

Factors Shown to Precipitate Coronary Vasospasm

Pharmacologic factors	Physical factors
α-adrenergic agonists	Exercise
β-adrenergic antagonists	Cold
Ergot alkaloids	Hyperventilation
Noradrenaline, alcohol	
Cigarette smoking	

The third possibility is that one of the many local vasoactive substances found in the heart e.g., adenosine, lactate and histamine may be involved in either the initiation or termination of coronary spasm.

Types of Angina Pectoris :

Three different types of anginal attacks have been recognized. This categorization is based upon the differences in the cause and symptoms. These types of angina include,

(a) Classical angina : This type of anginal attack occurs mainly due to physical exertion or mental stress and hence it is also known as angina of efforts. In most of the cases atherosclerotic coronary artery disease is also a contributing factor.

(b) Unstable angina : In this type, atherosclerotic coronary artery disease is the prominent cause. The characteristic feature however, is that the attack is accompanied by vasospasm.

(c) Prinzmetal's or varient angina : Both the above types of anginal attacks can be relieved by rest. However varient anginal attacks may be seen at rest, usually in the morning. This is an example of anginal attack seen in patients who are free from atherosclerotic coronary stenosis.

Biochemical and Metabolic Aspects of Ischemia :

Since the myocardial energy requirements are extensive, mitochondria comprise between 25 - 50% of myocardial mass. ATP production per mole of glucose metabolised is tenfold greater with aerobic compared to anaerobic metabolism. Thus, although brief intervals of anoxia or ischemia may be tolerated during which anaerobic glycolytic metabolism can supply some ATP, more prolonged intervals can not be tolerated because of inability of anaerobic intermediary metabolism to produce ATP fast enough to sustain the energy supply required for myocardial viability.

Under conditions in which substrate availability may be limited, but O_2 supply is adequate (e.g., with profound hypoglycemia), myocardial metabolism becomes dependent on utilisation of endogenous substrate stored in the form of glycogen, triglycerides and other moieties serving as depot sources for substrate. Endogenous triglycerides can supply fatty acid for catabolism when substrate availability is limited. However, fatty acid metabolism requires oxidation. Since the most common cause of substrate limitation is ischemia, and since the limited availability of substrate is accompanied by impaired oxidative capability, fatty acids released from endogenous triglycerides accumulate in the cytosol as acyl esters with potentially noxious effects on myocardial membranes.

In ischemic myocardium, contractility is impaired virtually instantaneously, despite the relatively slower deteriorating of myocardial intermediary metabolism and the comparably slow decline of high-energy phosphate stores. This may be manifested in its extreme form by production of so called stone-heart. Prolonged ischemia results in mitochondrial swelling with a decrease in mitochondrial matrix density and the appearance of amorphous granules thought to contain lipids. Swelling is a reversible feature but deposition of granules in the matrix is among the earliest morphological criteria of irreversible injury. Thus, despite the persistence of some electron transport function, oxidation of pyruvate coupling of respiration to synthesis of ATP and suppression of latent mitochondrial ATPase are markedly impaired.

Myocardium obtains energy from substrate catabolism and transduces it to mechanical energy utilised in contraction, thereby fulfilling the functional requirements of heart as a pump. Under physiological conditions, metabolism of free fatty acid fulfills 60 to 90% of myocardial energy requirements. Thus, production of ATP under aerobic conditions is dominated by free fatty acid oxidation.Approximately 140 moles of ATP can be synthesized from one mole of a long chain fatty acid. Under physiological conditions, fatty acids extracted by myocardium are metabolised primarily by β-oxidation within mitochondria. However, during brief intervals of ischemia, uptake continues but oxidation is inhibited; the result is accumulation of cytosolic fatty acids some of which are deposited in triglyceride.

The citric acid cycle refers to a series of reactions that sequentially oxidise 2-carbon units (acetyl CoA) derived from glycolysis or fatty acid oxidation. The cycle is responsible for generating most of the ATP derived from substrate metabolism. Under physiologic aerobic condition, one turn of cycle results in production of 12 moles of ATP and liberation of 2 moles of CO_2 per mole of acetyl CoA catabolized. Glycolysis (glucose metabolism) occurs in cytoplasm while fatty acid oxidation occurs in mitochondria.

Accumulation of noxious metabolites appears to contribute to the accelerating impairment of myocardial metabolism and ultrastructural integrity. Fatty acyl CoA esters inhibit activity of adenine nucleotide translocase, an enzyme involved in transport of ATP from mitochondria to cytosol. Increased concentrations of acyl CoA, coupled with the increased concentrations of acyl CoA, coupled with the increased concentrations of glycerol phosphate, promote synthesis of triglycerides by virtue of the mass action effect. Accumulation of neutral fat is therefore observed in myocardium subjected to repeated ischemia. The acyl esters themselves, and possibly other metabolites such as Iysophosphatides, accumulate in the ischemic tissue and may contribute to loss of membrane integrity.

Kallikrein is a serine protease enzyme which acts to form the potent vasodilator, bradykinin. It has an important mediatory action in the local control of cardiac and renal function. Bradykinin acts as an endogenous mediator of cardioprotection. In patients, activation of the plasma Kallikrein-kinin system has been identified during myocardial ischemia.

The most common symptom is chest pain which occurs either at rest or with exercise. Ischemic pain may result from a sudden decrease in coronary blood flow (e.g., coronary thrombosis or spasm) and/or from the inability to increase coronary blood flow sufficiently to meet an increment in myocardial O_2 demand as occurs during exercise (e.g., severe coronary narrowing due to atherosclerosis). Such pain may occur in the absence of coronary occlusive disease when coronary perfusion pressure is low (e.g. hypotension) or when oxygen demands are greatly elevated (e.g., aortic stenosis)

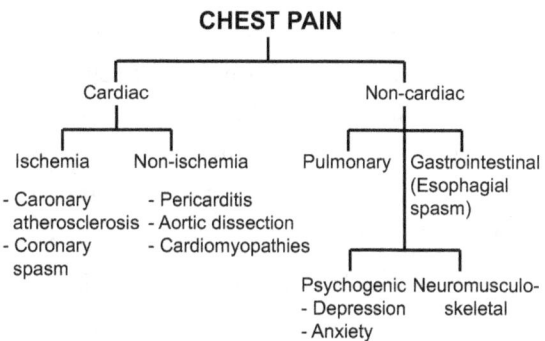

Established independent coronary risk factors include increasing age, male sex, hypercholesterolemia, cigarette smoking, diabetes and hypertension.

Potential risk factors include, Obesity, lifestyle, family history of premature coronary artery disease, Type A personality, hypertriglyceridemia and hyperuricemia.

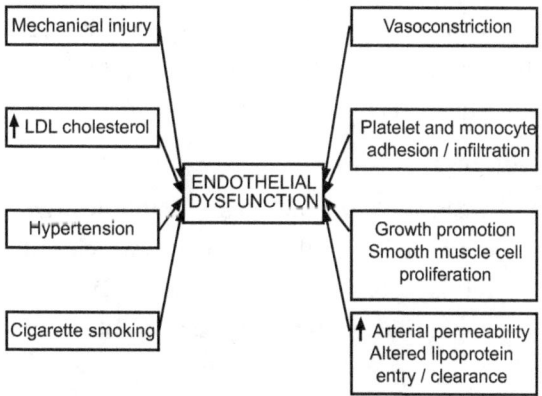

Classification of Antianginal Drugs :

Drugs employed for the treatment of angina pectoris include :

(i)　Nitrates and nitrites

(ii)　Xanthines (aminophyllines)

(iii)　Nicotinic acid and its derivatives

(iv)　Papavarine

(v)　β-adrenergic blockers

(vi)　MAO inhibitors

(vii)　Miscellaneous

Nitric oxide has been identified as a mediator in a vast array of physiological processes such as endothelium dependent relaxation. neuro transmission and cell mediated immune responses (i.e. macrophage induced cytotoxicity).

Nitric oxide is a potent local vasodilator. A ubiquitous enzyme in endothelium, nitric oxide (NO) synthetase, forms NO from the N-guanidino terminal of L-arginine and molecular oxygen. Nitric oxide stimulates guanylate cyclase to increase c-GMP which in vascular smooth muscle dilates blood vessels and inhibites platelets. The NO generation by nitro-prusside is an accepted mechanism in systemic vasodilation.

Both nitrates and nitrites exhibit same pharmacological action. Nitrates convert themselves into nitrites and hence both are collectively termed as nitrites.

Nitrates :

- Mechanism of nitrates → nitrates gets dinitrated in the smooth muscles to release NO → activates cGMP → dephosphorylated myosin light chain kinase → relaxation occurs.

- All nitrates undergo extensive first pass metabolism except isosorbide mononitrate.

Nitrites bring about relaxation of smooth muscle particularly of post capillary vessels (like veins and venules). They do not have a direct action on capillaries as capillaries do not have smooth muscles, but this action takes place via relaxation of precapillary spinctures which are responsible for inflow of blood in capillaries.

General Measures :

Certain general measures are indicated in the treatment of anginal patients to reduce the cardiac work load and to prevent further arterial degeneration.

The load on the heart can be reduced by,

(1) Correcting any obesity by avoiding heavy meals.

(2) Avoiding situations that lead to stress.

(3) Lowering of plasma levels of cholesterol and triglycerides.

(4) Avoiding excess of exercise and excess of work.

Treatment of Angina Pectoris :

(i) Etiology must be corrected first e.g. anemia, syphilis etc.

(ii) Administration of glycerol trinitrate (nitroglycerin) before exercise.

(iii) Disciplined life to prevent the chances of attack and reduction in weight is beneficial.

(iv) For prophylaxis longer acting nitrates should be employed.

(v) Short acting nitrite agents are useful in case of nitroglycerine tolerance.

(vi) Use of sedative in anxious patients.

(vii) Reducing smoking habit.

(viii) Prophylactic use of β–blockers in frequent attacks.

(ix) Anticoagulants in severe conditions of angina.

(x) Surgical procedures.

Nicotinic acid in larger doses influences lipoprotein ratio, decreasing the concentrations of very low and low-density lipoproteins but has not effect on HDL-cholesterol complexes. Acipimox, a new pyrazine derivative is 20 times more active than nicotinic acid.

Mechanism of Action of Antianginal Drugs :

These agents cause redistribution of coronary blood flow to the ischemic regions of the heart and also reduce myocardial oxygen demand. This latter effect is produced by a reduction in venous tone due to vasodilation effect and a pulling of blood in the peripheral veins that results in a reduction in ventricular volume, stroke volume and cardiac output. It also causes reduction in peripheral resistance during myocardial contractions. The combined vasodilatory effects cause a decrease in cardiac work load and reduction in oxygen consumption or demand.

Combination Therapy :

Nitrites, β-adrenoceptor blocking agents and calcium channel blockers are the prominent categories of antianginal drugs. Each of them act by different mechanisms. For example, nitrites preferably reduce preload and calcium channel blockers reduce afterload of the heart. While β–blocking agents decrease the rate and force of heart contraction. Hence if the drugs from two different categories are used concurrently, the effective minimum dose for each drug can be minimized.This will result into reduction in frequency and intensity of adverse effects of the drugs used.

Table 5.3 : Clinically used antianginal drugs

(I) Nitrites and Nitrates :

(a) Nitrites :

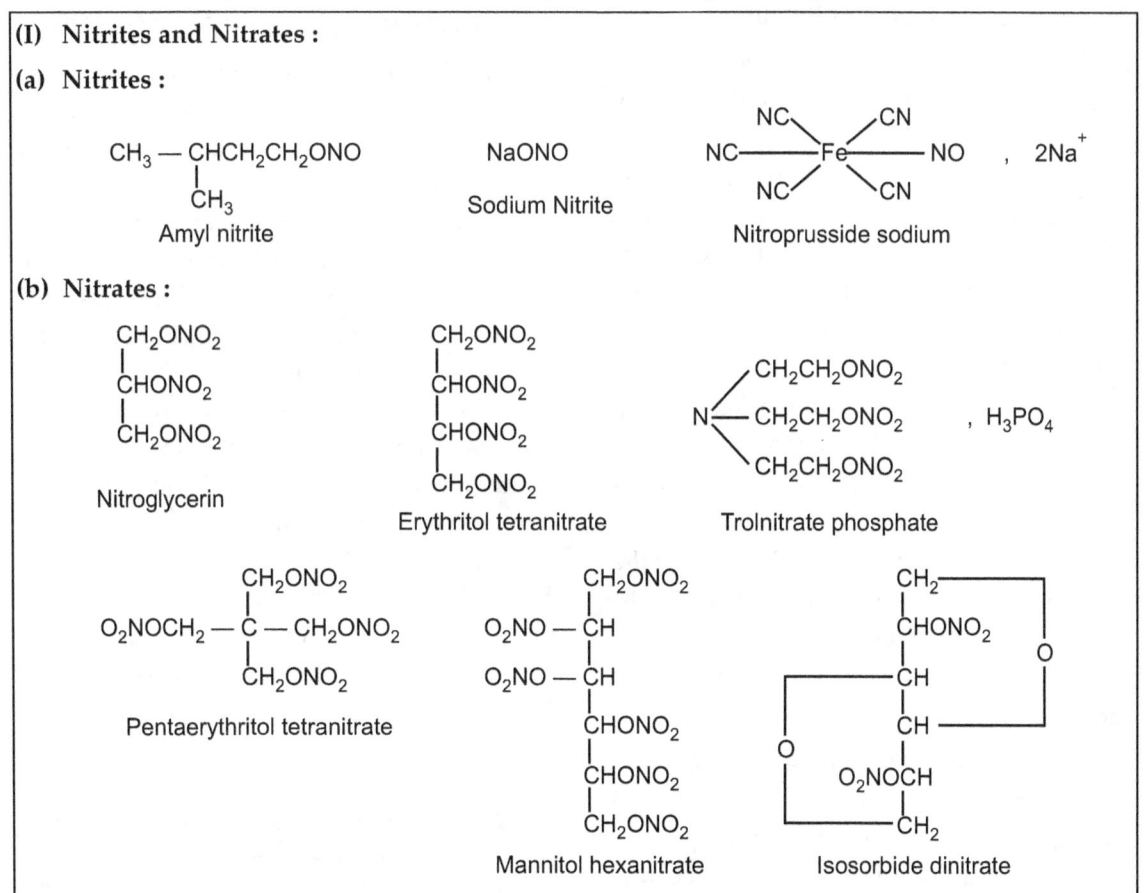

Amyl nitrite　　　　　Sodium Nitrite　　　　　Nitroprusside sodium

(b) Nitrates :

Nitroglycerin　　Erythritol tetranitrate　　Trolnitrate phosphate

Pentaerythritol tetranitrate　　Mannitol hexanitrate　　Isosorbide dinitrate

(II) Miscellaneous Antianginal Drugs :

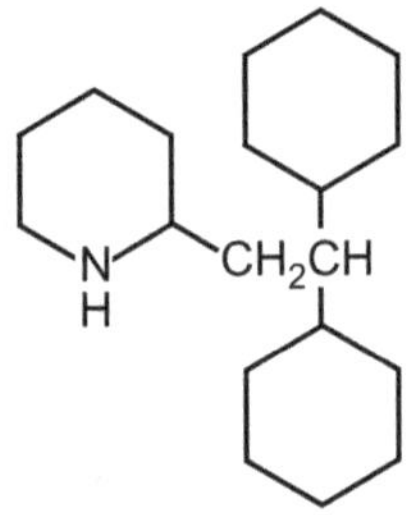

Perhexilene

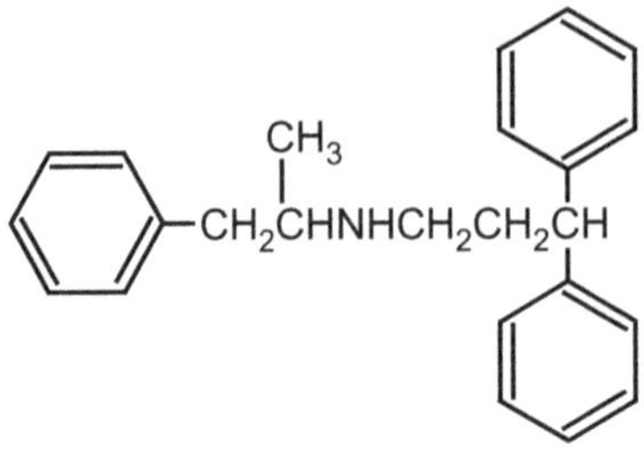

Prenylamine

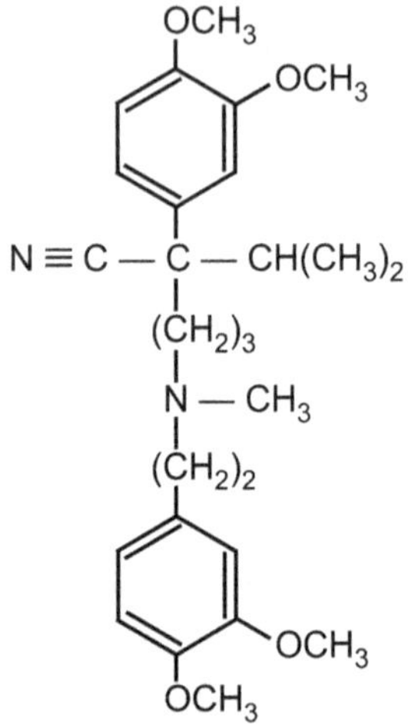

Verapamil

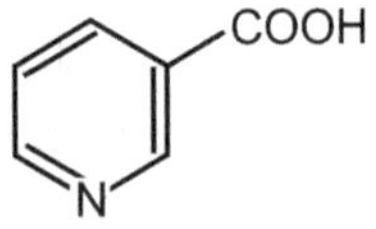

Nicotinic acid

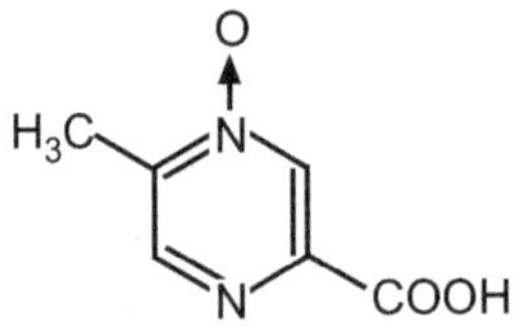

Acipimox

For example, if used individually :

(a) Nitrite therapy will induce reflex tachycardia and an increase in the force of heart contraction.

(b) β-blocking agents induce constriction of coronary arteries due to unopposed α-adrenoceptor activation. Similarly they depress myocardial contraction process, resulting into a decrease in rate and force of heart contraction, and

(c) In calcium channel blockers, except nifedipine, other members depress S. A. node, A.V. nodal conduction and ventricular functioning.

Thus, nitrites can be combined together with β–blocking agents where mutual benefits are reflected in inhibition of :

(i) coronary vaso constriction by nitrites and

(ii) reflex tachycardia by β-blocker.

If β-blocker is to be combined with calcium channel blocking agent, nifedipine is a drug of choice because it lacks myocardial depressant activity.

5.18 ANTI-HYPERTENSIVE AGENTS

Blood pressure is a biophysical parameter which is closely related to the mechanisms that control perfusion or irrigation of blood to various tissues. The normal systolic/diastolic blood pressure of a healthy adult person are supposed to be 120/75 - 85 mm Hg. A highly complex regulatory system operates for perfusion of blood into various tissues. The fluctuations in the vascular environment are nullified through the activation of baro- and chemoreceptors which maintain the blood pressure at a constant value. Blood pressure is only a part of mechanism that controls the perfusion of blood through the various tissues. The elevated blood pressure may cause death through certain deleterious effects like stroke (i.e., damage to cerebral blood vessels), heart failure and kidney failure.

Mosaic Model :

The body has to provide a limited amount of blood to a great variety of areas, all with different demands. This necessitated the presence of the highly complex sensing

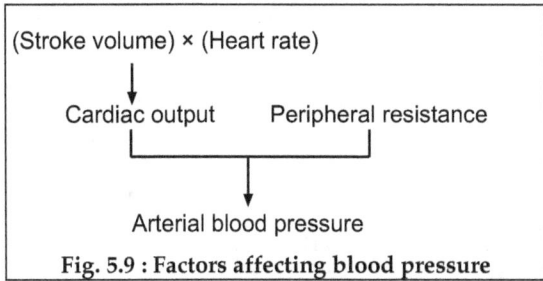

Fig. 5.9 : Factors affecting blood pressure

devices widespread through the body to warn of change. They may be baroreceptors that inform the brain of changes in blood pressure or chemoreceptors that acknowledge the changes in environmental chemical composition. All such components of the regulatory system work in equilibrium with each other.

Many mechanisms operate in equilibrium with each other in order to maintain a constant blood pressure. These mechanisms include, central mechanism, peripheral adrenergic activation, baro and chemoreceptor, cardiac output, viscosity of blood, renin-angiotensin aldosterone system, vascular factors, blood volume etc. The mutual functioning of all these hemodynamic mechanisms in equilibrium with each other appears to be like a mosaic, as represented in the figure 5.12.

Hypertension results due to disturbances in these hemodynamic mechanisms which is reflected through increased peripheral vascular resistance and high diastolic blood pressure.

The vascular fluctuations in the circulation are communicated and controlled by baro and chemoreceptors. The baroreceptors are pressure sensitive receptors located in the walls of heart and blood vessels e.g., carotid sinus and aortic arch receptors. When there is a fall in blood pressure in carotid sinus, it stimulates sympathetic nervous system resulting into vasoconstriction and an increase in blood pressure. On the other hand, an increase in blood pressure activates these baroreceptors resulting into arterial dilation thus opposing a tendency for permanent hypertension. The loss of this inhibitory activity of baroreceptors may lead to moderate hypertension. While chemoreceptors which are also located in vessel wall are sensitive to changes in oxygen content of the blood. They induce vasoconstriction in order to compensate any fall in oxygen concentration in blood. The effects of activation of the baro and chemoreceptors are mediated through the release of renin which then initiates the activation of angiotensin - aldosterone system. Renin (molecular weight 42,000) is a proteolytic enzyme that catalyses the formation of active pressure hormone, the angiotensin.

Its presence in the kidney was first discovered in 1898. It was named 'renin' by Bergman due to its renal origin. Kidney is the rich source of renin where it is stored in the granular juxtaglomerular (JG) cells in the walls of the afferent arterioles, in the form of prorenin (a zymogen with a molecular weight of 63,000). The prorenin in turn, is obtained by intracellular proteolysis of an inactive precursor, preprorenin. Both prorenin and preprorenin are also present in plasma.

Renin - Angiotensin system is an important part of the homeostatic mechanisms in the body. It get activated by decreased blood volume, low renal pressure (baroreceptors in renal afferent arterioles) and low sodium ion concentration in the plasma (chemoreceptors in renal afferent arterioles). It regulates the electrolyte balance by controlling aldosterone secretion by adrenal cortex.

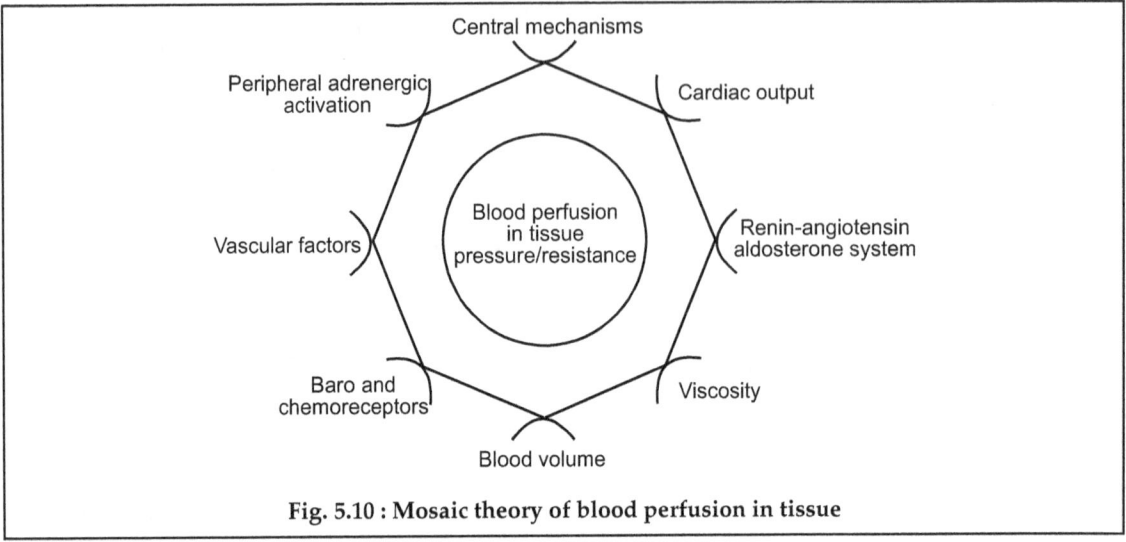

Fig. 5.10 : Mosaic theory of blood perfusion in tissue

The components of renin-angiotensin system are present in many other tissues. Prostaglandins also are found to stimulate the release of renin in response to inflammatory stimuli. For example, PGI_2 (prostacyclin), through its vasodilating action, activates the baroreceptors and stimulates the renin release. Similarly the IG cells are directly innervated by central sympathetic nerves. Hence, under the conditions of strain and stress, the sympathetic stimulation may lead to the hypertension due to the activation of renin-angiotensin system. The renin-angiotensin system then regulates the blood pressure and plasma sodium at normal level by exerting generalized vasoconstriction and inducing aldosterone release.

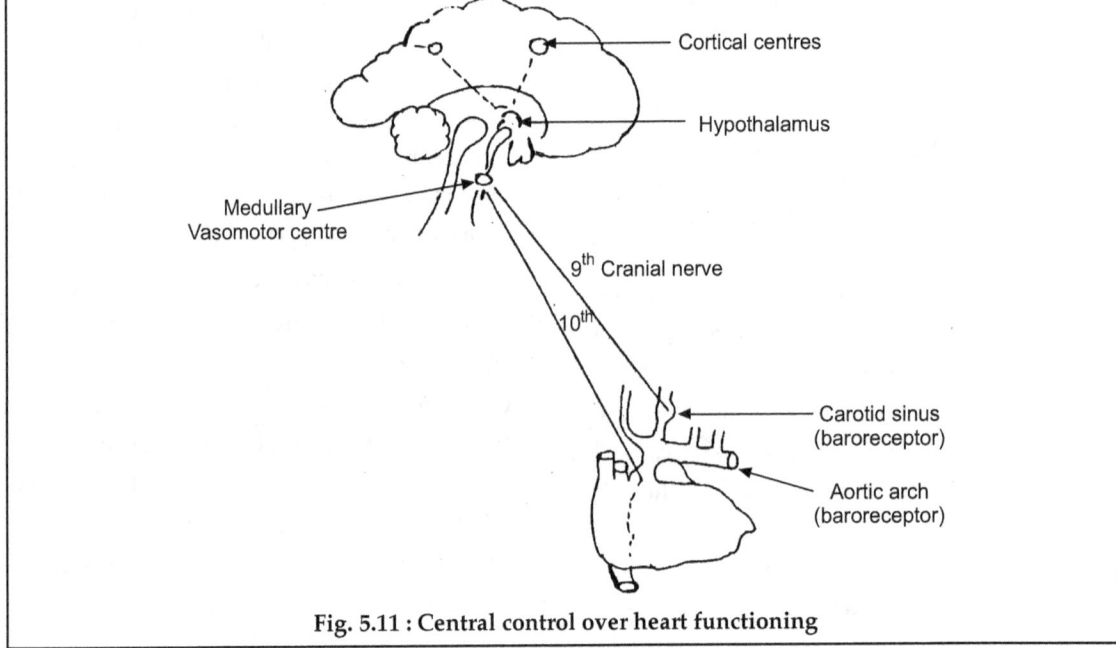

Fig. 5.11 : Central control over heart functioning

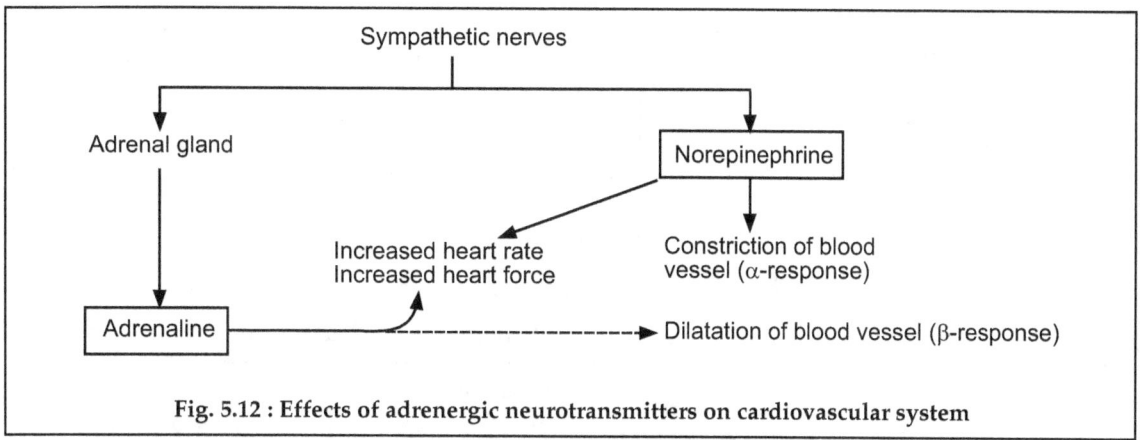

Fig. 5.12 : Effects of adrenergic neurotransmitters on cardiovascular system

Hence, antihypertensive agents which act at adrenergic terminal, may act by various mechanism like,

(i) Interfering with the synthesis of noradrenaline and forming false neurotransmitter, e.g., methyldopa.

(ii) Increasing the metabolism of free noradrenaline.

(iii) Inhibiting the release of noradrenaline at post ganglionic adrenergic nerve terminal e.g., bretylium.

(iv) Inhibiting reentry of noradrenaline into storage sites e.g., reserpine.

(v) Antagonising noradrenaline at receptor sites, e.g., α and β adrenergic antagonist.

The term hypertension is generally defined as a pathologically elevated systemic arterial pressure. In this disorder, the small arterioles appear to be under excessive sympathetic nervous system stimulation which causes arteriolar constriction and increased peripheral resistance to the tissue capillaries and venous circulation resululting into increased blood pressure. Due to the variable nature of the systolic blood pressure, the term hypertension usually refers to an abnormal elevation in diastolic pressure. For practical guidance, usually the systolic/diastolic blood pressure above 160/95 is considered to be a state of hypertension.

When the hypertension is due to the symptoms of definable causes, such as renal artery stenosis (i.e., pathological condition of kidney which restricts the blood flow through the renal artery), pheochromocytoma (a hypertensive condition caused by the release of large amount of catecholamines due to tumors in the adrenal medulla) or an endocrine disorder like aldenomas (excessive secretion of aldosterone by the adrenal cortex), it is referred to as secondary hypertension. Secondary hypertension may be classified as neurogenic, renal, endocrine and cardiovascular. When the cause of hypertension cannot be clearly defined, it is classified as essential hypertension. In the presence of essential hypertension, the primary cause in most of the patients is increased vascular resistance.

Essential hypertension is of two types : gradual (benign) and accelerated (malignant).

Along with other factors like, hypercholesterolemia, diabetes and smoking, hypertension is an important contributory risk factor for the development of arteriosclerotic cardiovascular diseases. Usually in men, hypertension is more common before the age of 45-50 years. After this age, it is more common in women.

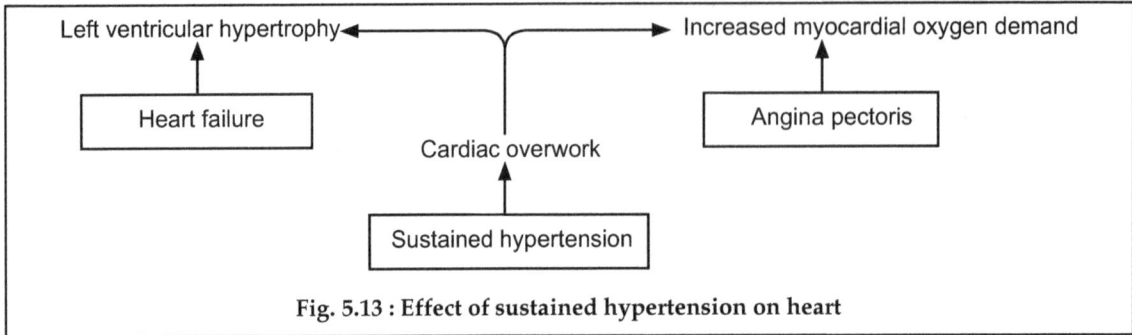

Fig. 5.13 : Effect of sustained hypertension on heart

Sustained hypertension may seriously affect the functioning of vital systems like cardiovascular system, central nervous system and renal system. In heart, the increased systemic pressure leads to an increase in the cardiac workload. The resulting cardiac overwork then becomes a prominent cause of left ventricular hypertrophy.

The sustained hypertension may disturb the functioning of central nervous system resulting into vertigo, dizziness, occipital headaches, dimmed vision, vascular occlusion and hemorrhage while in kidneys, renal arteriosclerotic lesion of the afferent and efferent arterioles develop, resulting into renal failure.

5.19 ETIOLOGY OF HYPERTENSION

The various factors which contribute to less or more extent to the state of hypertension can be classified as -
(a) Neural factors
(b) Hormonal factors
(c) Electrolyte factors
(d) Vessel wall factors, and
(e) Genetic factors.

(a) Neural factors : Stress or emotions causing excessive sympathetic outflow from the brain may result into an increased cardiac output and elevated peripheral resistance. The overproduction or incomplete destruction of sympathomimetic amines may further contribute to the elevated peripheral resistance. The abnormal levels of noradrenaline, adrenaline, dopamine and serotonin may play a peripheral as well as a central role in activation of vasomotor tone. Usually agents which block the effects of sympathomimetic amines are useful to treat hypertension caused by neural factors.

(b) Hormonal factors : Renin, a proteolytic enzyme found primarily in the kidney is released in response to lowered perfusion pressure and low sodium states of the circulating blood. It catalyses the conversion of angiotensinogen to angiotensin I (decapeptide). The latter is rapidly converted in the plasma by a chloride activated enzyme (primarily in the lungs) to angiotensin II (octapeptide). Angiotensin II has three fold action.

(i) It constricts the arterial network to increase peripheral resistance.

(ii) It slowly triggers the release of aldosterone which in turn, increases sodium retention and plasma volume.

(iii) It causes an excessive release of catecholamines from adrenal medulla and from peripheral sympathetic nerves, resulting into an increase in cardiac output. The renin-angiotensin-aldosterone system thus affects all three primary factors which can cause hypertension, like
(a) Blood vessel constriction,
(b) Increased blood volume, and
(c) Increased cardiac output.

Though elevated renin-angiotensin levels appear to play a critical role in severe hypertension, other hormones and vasopressor substances may sometimes be important like arachidonic acid metabolites, prostaglandins, corticoids, kinins, vasopressin and some yet unidentified hormones. Prostaglandins (PGA, PGE) for example, cause a fall in blood pressure and renal dilation. They also initiate the release of renin by a central effect on the vagus.

(c) **Electrolyte factors :** The inability of the kidney to excrete an adequate daily amount of salt and water results into abnormal retention of salt and water in the blood which causes an increase in the blood volume. The net result is an increase in the workload on the heart. The blood potassium and blood selenium level may also play an etiological role in hypertension along with other dietary and environmental factors.

(d) **Vessel wall factors :** The vascular smooth muscles are highly sensitive to changes in the cardiac output. Hence, increased perfusion pressure due to increased cardiac output leads to structural changes (like wall thickening and hypertrophy of vasculature) in the blood vessels. The direct acting vasodilators, hence may be of value in this type of hypertension.

(e) **Genetic factors :** The increased sensitivity and susceptibility to various etiologic factors (which are mentioned above) by off-springs of hypertensives underlies the importance of hereditary factors in hypertension.

5.20 CLASSIFICATION

All currently available antihypertensive drugs act mainly by interfering with normal hemostatic mechanisms and this provides a useful basis for the classification of these drugs.

They are classified as :

[A] **Drugs affecting sympathetic tone :**

(i) Drugs that alter central sympathetic activity e.g., methyldopa, clonidine.

(ii) Drugs that act as adrenergic neuron blockers, e.g., guanethidine, reserpine.

(iii) Ganglionic blocking drugs e.g., trimethaphan.

(iv) α-adrenoceptor blocking agents e.g., prazosin, phentolamine.

(v) β-adrenoceptor blocking agents e.g., propranolol, atenolol.

[B] **Vasodilators :**

(a) *Direct vasodilators :*

(i) Arterial dilators e.g., hydralazine

(ii) Balanced vasodilatores e.g., minoxidil.

(b) *Calcium channel blocking agents e.g., nifedipine*

[C] **Agents acting on renin-angiotensin system :**

(i) Renin inhibitors

(ii) Angiotensin antagonists e.g., saralasin.

(iii) Angiotensin converting enzyme inhibitors. e.g., captopril, enalapril.

[D] **Diuretics :**

(i) Thiazides e.g., hydrochlorothiazide

(ii) Loop diuretics e.g., furosemide

(iii) Potassium sparing diuretics e.g., triamterene.

[E] **Central depressants :**

5.21 GENERAL CONSIDERATIONS

These drugs produce their hypotensive action by affecting the biosynthesis, storage, uptake, release, metabolism and adrenoceptor activation by sympathomimetic amines.

Agents acting at both, central sites (reserpine, guanethidine) and at peripheral sites (cardioselective β_1 - antagonists) are included in this class. The adverse effects include increased renin secretion and development of tolerance. Other effects include sedation, dry mouth and depression.

The lowering of blood pressure by drugs like methyldopa and clonidine is brought about probably by stimulation of central presynaptic α_2-adrenoceptors, thereby reducing the release of efferent sympathetic traffic from CNS.

Prototype examples from each cardiovascular category

Discovery	Prototype	Category
1957	Chlorothiazide	Diuretic
1959	Bretylium	Neuronal blocker
1960	α methyl dopa	Dopa decarboxylase inhibitor
1964	Furosemide	Loop diuretic
	Propranolol	Beta blocker
1966	Clonidine	Alpha-2 agonist
1968	Atenolol	Beta-1 blocker
1971	Nitedipine	Calcium channel blocker
1977	Captopril	ACE inhibitor
1978	Lovastatin	HMG CoA reductase inhibitor
1981	Disopyramide	Antiarrhythmic
1989	Losartan	Angiotensin II receptor antagonist

Guanethidine may be considered as a representative example of the drugs that depress the functioning at adrenergic neurons. Drugs in this class appear to act by more than one mechanism. These agents mainly act by causing a gradual depletion of catecholamine stores from central and peripheral adrenergic nerve endings resulting into reduced sympathetic tone. Unlike clonidine, the therapy with reserpine and methyldopa is usually associated with extrapyramidal side-effects.

Alpha adrenoceptors are subclassified as postsynaptic α_1-adrenoceptors and presynaptic α_2-adrenoceptor. The α_1-receptors are predominantly present in smooth muscle cells of arterial walls. While α_2- receptors are present on the presynaptic adrenergic neurons and exert inhibitory influence over the release of norepinephrine.

Activation of postsynaptic α_1-receptors leads to arterial vasoconstriction resulting into an increase in peripheral vascular resistance. Hence α_1-adrenoceptor blocking agents can be clinically used as antihypertensive agents. Examples include, prazosin, trimazosin and indoramin. They appear to exert vasodilatory effect through the blockade of α_1-adrenoceptors. Prazosin is the first member of this class, reported in 1974 followed by trimazosin. Both are quinazoline derivatives. They mainly affect the venous vascular bed but become more balanced during long term treatment. They affect to varying degree, the functioning of renin-angiotensin system resulting into sodium and fluid retention. They tend to produce tolerance if used chronically. They are mainly used in the treatment of hypertension and heart failure.

β-adrenoceptors are mainly present in heart, pulmonary vessels, vessels supplying blood to skeletal muscles and are also involved in glycogenolysis and lipolysis. The β-adrenoceptor blocking agents act by the competitive inhibition of the effect of catecholamines on β-adrenoceptors. Previously it was proposed that the antihypertensive effect of these drugs results due to a downward suppression of functioning of baro-receptors. But now the antihypertensive effect of β-adrenoceptor blocking agents is explained in the following lines.

(a) Decreased renin release occurs due to inhibition of β_1-receptors while renal plasma flow and rate of glomerular filtration are reduced by blockade of β_2-receptors.

(b) Decreased norepinephrine release occurs from the postganglionic sympathetic nerves due to the blockade of presynaptic β-receptors.

(c) Central mechanism has been proposed for some lipophillic β-blockers, and

(d) The cardioselective β_1-blockers act by exerting a reduction in rate and force of heart contraction. However such cardioselectivity is of relative nature and is seen only at low doses.

Due to interference in glycogenesis, these drugs may cause hypoglycemia like symptoms during chronic treatment.

Dichloroisoproterenol was the first β-blocker introduced in 1960s. All β-adrenoceptor blockers are analogues of adrenoreceptor agonist, isoproterenol.

The β-blockers compete with agonist molecules at three principle reactive sites. They are characterized by a substituted aromatic ring and a side-chain.

The nature of aromatic substituent affects receptor activation ability (i.e. intrinsic activity) while the side-chain appears to govern affinity of these antagonists for the β-adrenoceptors. Usually affinity is proportional to chain-length. The configuration of asymmetric carbon atom is crucial to define the pharmacological activity of the compound. The aromatic substituents also govern the lipophilicity of the compounds and thus their central effects.

Due to the presence of asymmetric - carbon atom in the side-chain, these compounds usually exist as pairs of enantiomers. The laevoisomers are much more potent (50 – 100 times) β-blockers than their dextroisomers. Except timolol (laevoisomer), all other β-blockers are available commercially in the form of their recemic mixture.

Dichloroisoproterenol, due to its weak antagonistic property was soon replaced by pronethalol. But it was also withdrawn from clinical testing because of reports that it caused thymic tumours in mice. However soon after, propranolol, a close structural relative of pronethalol, was developed. It is a non-selective β-blocker, having almost negligible intrinsic sympathomimetic activity (ISA) and is considered now as a prototype of

β-blocker series. It was then followed by atenolol, acebutotol, metoprolol, pindolol, oxprenolol, labetalol, sotalol, timolol, nodolol, practolol and tolamolol.

Practolol was found to induce mucocutaneous reactions while tolamolol was reported to initiate animal tumour development. For these reasons, both these drugs have been withdrawn from clinical use.

The relative lack of postural hypotension and sexual disfunctioning coupled with good therapeutic index are the added advantages of β-blockers over other antihypertensive agents. The membrane stabilizing or *'quinidine like"* effect associated with certain β-blockers (e.g., propranolol) do not play any significant role at the doses needed for their antihypertensive action.

The β_2-receptors are predominantly present in lung, particularly in bronchial muscles. The β_1 to β_2- receptor percentage in human lung is estimated to be nearly 30 : 70. Hence, β-blockers besides exerting their antihypertensive action, may antagonise lung β_2-receptors causing bronchial constriction, a case contraindicated in hypertensive patients suffering from bronchial asthma. The ratio of cardiac to lung activity has been evaluated for propranolol (2 : 1), practolol (15 : 1) and for atenolol (200 : 1). Atenolol and metoprolol are the examples of cardioselective β_1-antagonists that have much greater affinity for β_1-receptors in the heart than the β_2-receptors present in other tissues.

While non-selective β-antagonists (e.g. propranolol) are mainly reserved for the treatment of migraine and tremor. The elevated peripheral resistance is the main cause behind most of the hypertensive cases. Vasodilators act by inducing vascular smooth muscle relaxation, thereby normalizing the elevated peripheral resistance which is the main hemodynamic abnormality in this condition.

The drawback of vasodilator therapy is the reflex activation of compensatory mechanisms such as sympathetic activation (resulting in an increase in the heart rate and cardiac output) and activation of renin-angiotensin-aldosterone system (resulting into increased extracellular fluid due to salt and water retention). The latter effect is much pronounced with hydralazine and diazoxide that cause mainly arterial dilation. This elevation of plasma renin activity and reflex tachycardia induced by vasodilators can be minimized by concurrent administration of a diuretic along with β-adrenoceptor blocking agent.

Vasodilation can be brought about by using -

(a) Pure vasodilators e.g., hydralazine, minoxidil.

(b) Indirect vasodilators :

(i) α_1-adrenoceptor blocking agents and

(ii) Angiotensin converting enzyme inhibitors.

Renin is a proteolytic enyme involved in the synthesis of a decapeptide, angiotensin I. The latter is converted to an octapeptide, angiotensin II by a peptidyldipeptide hydrolase (converting enzyme) in the vascular endothelial cells and epithelial cells of the proximal tubule and small intestine. The converting enzyme is a metalloenzyme (Zn^{++}) and requires the presence of chloride ions. Its activity is suppressed by hypoxia. Angiotensin II is a potent vasoconstrictor and initiates the release of aldosterone. It also independently controls Na^+ transport by epithelial cells in the gut and kidney.

Thus, activation of renin - angiotensin aldosterone system leads to vasoconstriction and hypertension. Hence, drugs that antagonise the effect of renin, angiotensin or aldosterone can be used in the treatment of systemic hypertension, congestive cardiac failure and pulmonary hypertension. The drugs from this class can be subcategorized as -

(a) Renin antagonists

(b) Aldosterone antagonists,

(c) Angiotensin—II antagonists, and

(d) Converting enzyme inhibitors.

At present, renin antagonists do not have therapeutic potential while aldosterone antagonists may principally be used as diuretic agents. Saralasin is an example of angiotensin II competitive antagonist while captopril (1977) is an example of orally effective converting enzyme inhibitor.

Sodium retention and consequent fluid retention usually serve as the initiating factors in hypertension. Certain antihypertensive drugs (e.g. adrenergic neuron blocking agents, vasodilators) could not retain their efficacy due to reflex activation of plasma renin. In such cases diuretics can bring about impressive results by suppressing renal tubular reabsorption of sodium, thus reducing the blood volume and the cardiac output. They exert antihypertensive action by promoting the loss of salt and water through the kidneys. However they too, are not free from adverse effects and may induce reflex renin activation and metabolic changes like, hypokalemia, alkalosis, hyperglycemia and hyper uricaemia. Sexual dysfunction is also reported due to long term treatment with diuretics.

From the forgoing discussion, it becomes clear that none of the above categories qualifies the test for ideal antihypertensive agent. Their efficiency is largely paralyzed due to emergence of compensatory reflex mechanisms in the body. For example, vasodilators lead to reflex tachycardia and elevation of plasma renin activity while sympatholytics gradually lose their effectiveness due to fluid retention. The sympatholytics can abolish reflex tachycardia associated with vasodilator therapy while the fluid retention caused due to sympatholytics and vasodilators can be effectively neutralized by the use of diuretics. Such a combination of a sympatholytic, vasodilator and a diuretic agent presents most effective antihypertensive treatment where very low incidences of side-effects result due to comparatively low doses of each of the three components.

5.22 DRUGS AFFECTING SYMPATHETIC TONE (SYMPATHOLYTICS)

(i) Drugs that Alter Central Sympathetic Activity :

(a) **α-methyldopa** : Tyrosine and DOPA are the principal intermediates in the biosynthesis of catecholamines in the body. Drugs having structural resemblance with these intermediates will then, naturally compete with the enzymes which convert these intermediates into norepinephrine. α-methyltyrosine and α-methyldopa are the examples of drugs developed through this concept. Both get acted upon by enzymes instead of tyrosine and DOPA resulting into false neurotransmitters instead of norepinephrine, which have less potency than norepinephrine.

Since the rate of decarboxylation of α-methyldopa is considerably slower than that of DOPA, it ties up the enzyme, DOPA decarboxylase for longer period of time and is effective inhibitor of the biosynthesis of norepinephrine. Instead of norepinephrine, methyl norepinephrine is formed which has weak central as well as peripheral actions. Thus, pressor response to adrenergic stimuli is reduced.

α-methyldopa

Since it is a potent agonist at presynaptic α_2-receptors in the CNS, it causes an inhibition of further release of central sympathetic outflow. This central mechanism is now recognized as the main site of action of methyldopa and the concept of *'false neurotransmitter'* responsible for peripheral effects is considered as a secondary mechanism of action. Methyldopa is one of the oldest and commonly used antihypertensive agents. Its antihypertensive effect results from a decrease in peripheral vascular resistance without affecting cardiac output. Its use is also suggested in the treatment of malignant carcinoid and pheochromocytomas. It is an antihypertensive agent of choice in pregnant women and children. The plasma level of the drug can not be correlated with its antihypertensive effect since the action is due to its metabolite (α-methyl norepinephrine) and not due to the drug. The drug gradually loses its efficacy due to weight gain and fluid retention.

(b) Other α_2-adrenoceptor agonists :

Guanabenz

Clonidine

In the beginning of 1960s, Helmut Stable, while working on decongestive imidazolines, (e.g., tolazoline, phentolamine) observed that the imidazoline nucleus is connected with an aromatic ring by a methylene bridge. With previous research works, he found out that replacement of –CH$_2$– by –NH– group may lead to increase in decongestive activity. The resulting compounds when tested by Dr. Wolf who administered a few drops of 0.3 % solution to Mrs. Schwandf for common cold, it was found far less interesting than its potent antihypertensive activity. The compound (clonidine) was then developed for this new indication and was introduced in therapy in 1966.

Cardiovascular activity and blood pressure are centrally governed mainly by hypothalamus, the nucleus tractus solitarii and the nucleus of vagus nerve. Catecholamines are the principal neurotransmitters in this region except at vagus nerve. Clonidine is a potent agonist of presynaptic inhibitory α$_2$-adrenoceptors. By activating these receptors, it reduces the sympathetic traffic from the CNS.

The inhibition of sympathetic function results in corresponding dominance of parasympathetic tone resulting into bradycardia. Clonidine is α$_2$-agonist. It stimulates both, central and peripheral α$_2$-receptors resulting into reduced norepinephrine release. It lowers down mild to moderate hypertension by reducing vasomotor tone. It has a number of chlorpromazine like actions which indicates the presence of multireceptor sites for its action.

Introduction of two chlorine atoms in the 2- (arylimine) imidazolidine molecule proved important for the activity of clonidine, as -

(a) two substituents at ortho position forced the molecule into a non-planar conformation with the two rings approximately perpendicular to each other so as to meet the steric requirements to fit α-adrenoceptor.

Norepinephrine can assume several conformations in its interactions with α-receptor, clonidine can alter its conformation

much less readily because of the presence of two chlorine atoms at ortho position preventing free rotation of 2 rings. This contributes to better complimentary fit at α-receptor.

(b) two chlorine atoms also make the molecule sufficiently lipophillic to cross BBB.

Norepinephrine is the prototype of agents acting on α-receptors. The α-adrenergic effects of clonidine may be explained on the basis of structural overlap between clonidine and norepinephrine. According to Pullman and Coubcils, the distance between cationic N$^+$ and center of aromatic ring of nor-epinephrine is between 5.1 - 5.2A°, while nitrogen is situated between 1.2 - 1.4 A° above the plane of aromatic nucleus.

Nor-epinephrine

Clonidine

It is believed to inhibit both, nor-adrenergic and 5-HT-nergic neurons in the brain. It also brings about reduction in plasma and urinary catecholamines, renin activity and urinary aldosterone in hypertensive patient. It is also capable of activating the central H$_2$-receptors. Because of its excellent penetration into CNS, clonidine preferentially stimulates brain α$_2$-adrenoceptors that decrease the cardiovascular activity. In contrast, norepinephrine which is distributed mainly peripherally, increases cardiovascular activity.

Other examples of drugs belonging to this class include guanabenz, guanfacine and piperoxan.

(ii) Drugs that Act as Adrenergic Neuron Blockers :

(a) Guanethidine : A number of antihypertensive agents exert their activity by affecting the storage and release of norepinephrine. This is achieved by inhibition of Ca^{++} - influx into the nerve terminal. Examples include, bretylium, guanethidine and xylocholine. Guanethidine may be considered as representative of drugs that depress the function of postganglionic adrenergic nerves. It utilizes the same transport system which is involved in re-uptake of norepinephrine into the nerve terminals and reaches in the nerve. Upon accumulation in adrenergic nerve fibers, it induces a gradual depletion of catecholamine intraneuronal storage sites and itself acts as a false neurotransmitter and released by nerve stimulation resulting into a decreased pressor response. The effects of guanethidine are cumulative over long-term treatment.

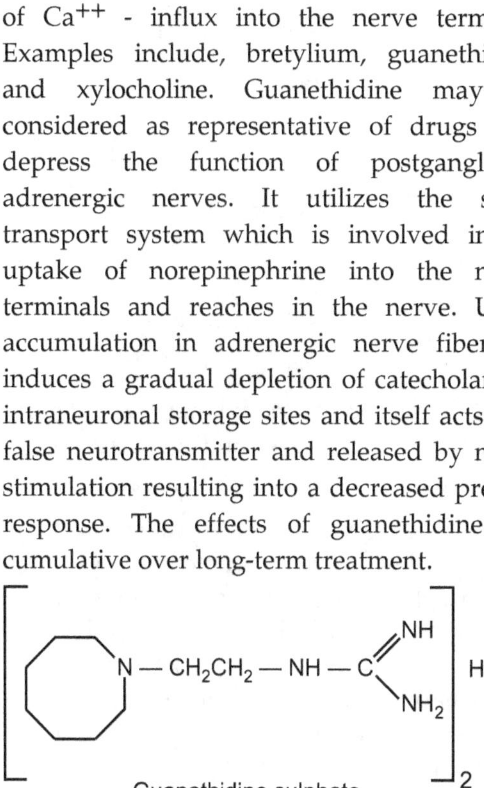

Guanethidine sulphate

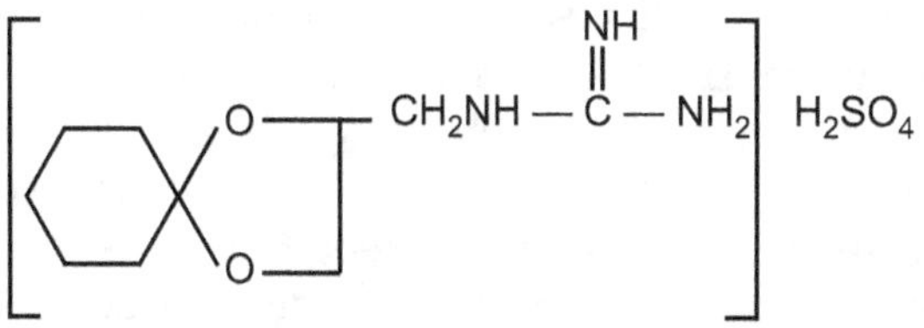

Guanadrel sulfate

(b) Reserpine : It is an example of rauwolfia alkaloids obtained from the roots of Rauwolfia serpentina from Apocynaceae family. Once, reserpine was one of the most favoured antihypertensive agents. Due to its moderate potency and a high incidence of adverse effects, it is rarely used today as an antihypertensive agent. Its parenteral administration in the emergency treatment of severe hypertension brings down the blood pressure in a smooth and gradual fashion.

(iii) Sympathetic Ganglion Blocking Drugs :

In sympathetic ganglia, the release of norepinephrine from the interneuron activates the postganglionic α-adrenergic receptors resulting into characteristic catecholamine response. The ganglionic stimulation may lead to the release of adrenaline and noradrenaline from adrenal medulla and sympathetic nerve terminals. The ganglionic blocking agents can reduce the level of sympathetic activity. Hence, they were once widely used in the treatment of hypertensive cardiovascular disease. Since mechanisms governing transmission in all autonomic ganglia remains same, their non-selectivity of action leads to numerous side-effects. Hence, they are now totally replaced by more selective and less toxic β_1-adrenoceptor blocking agents.

The development of antihypertensive agents from this category began with observation that tetraethyl ammonium chloride transiently lowered blood pressure in hypertensive patients by inhibiting transmission of nerve impulses through sympathetic ganglia. When a series of quaternary ammonium compounds was designed, higher members (e.g. decamethonium) exert curare like paralysis of muscles while lower members (e.g. hexamethonium) produced ganglion blocking action. The drawbacks of antihypertensive ganglionic blocking agents include inconsistent fluctuations in blood pressure, poor oral absorption and side-effects associated with sympathetic and parasympathetic blockade. It was thought that fluctuations in blood pressure and severity of side-effects would be due to poor oral absorption of these agents. This led to the development of mecamylamine which is a secondary amine permitting complete oral absorption. However mecamylamine also failed to improve therapeutic effectiveness. The structures of mecamylamine and pempidine led to the idea of preparing guanidines, alkyl guanidines and arallyl-alkyl guanidines. Guanithidine, bretylium and bethanidine are the outcome of these efforts. Recently introduced examples from this category include,

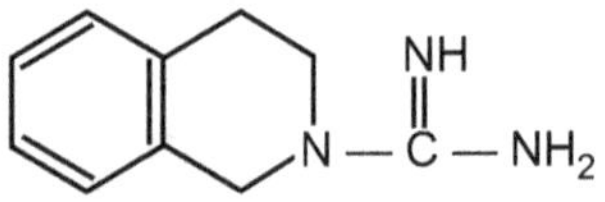

Debrisoquine

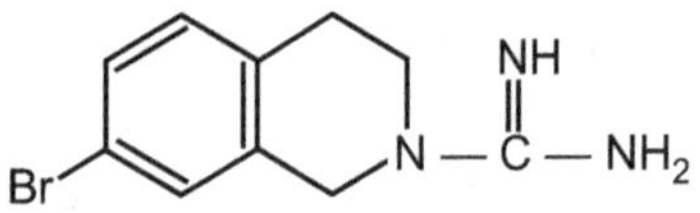

Guanisoquine

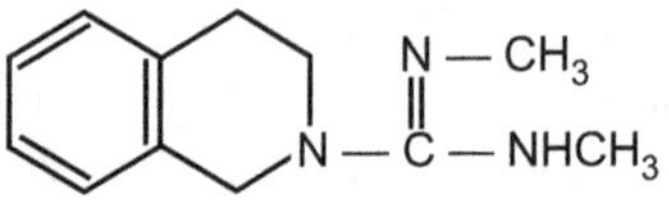

P-4746

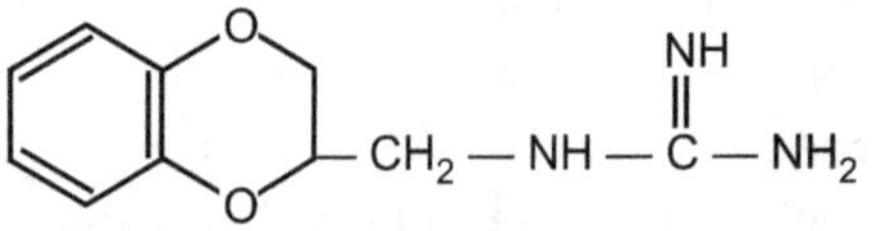

Guanoxan (Pfizer)

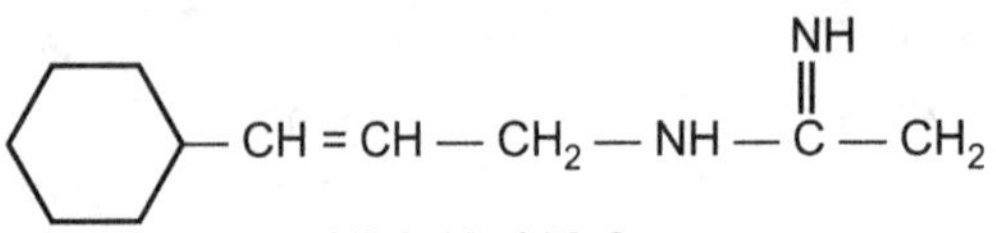

CIBA 13, 686-Su

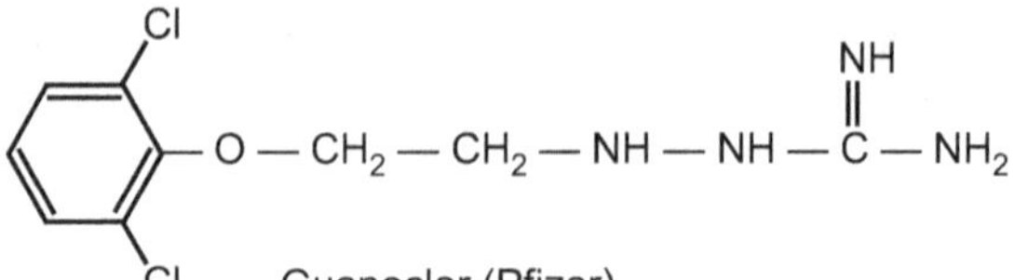

Guanoclor (Pfizer)

Cyclic guanidines (Triazines) :

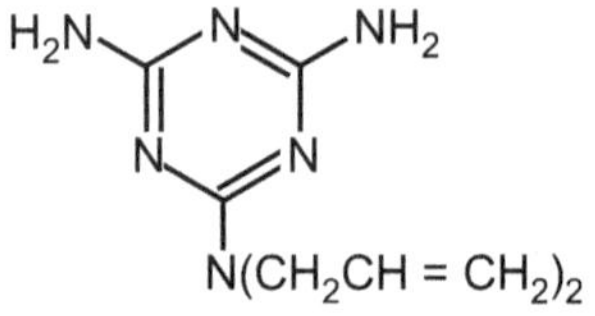

U-7220

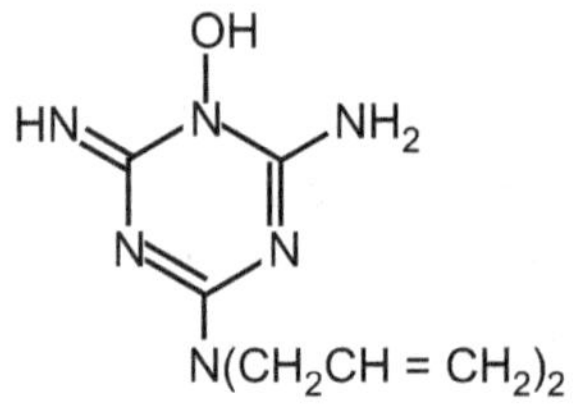

U-20, 388

Both are potent peripheral vasodilators. U - 20388 also possesses antidiuretic activity.

(iv) Adrenoceptor Blocking Agents :

The adrenoceptors are categorized as postsynaptic α_1-adrenoceptors and α_2-adrenoceptors. α_1-receptors are present on smooth muscles of blood vessels and gland cells while α_2-receptors are present on pre and post-synaptic sites on the nerves and are also present in the CNS. The activation of postsynaptic α_1-receptors leads to vasoconstriction while the activation of presynaptic α_1-receptors present on the nerve terminals leads to inhibition of neurotransmitter release. Thus, α_1-adrenoceptor blockers (i.e., vasodilation results, hence also called as indirect vasodilators) or α_2-adrenoceptor agonists will have a potential of antihypertensive action. For example, prazosin and methoxamine act on α_1-receptors while the antihypertensive action of clonidine and α-methyl-norepinephrine is due to their α_2-agonistic property.

α_1-adrenoceptor antagonists :

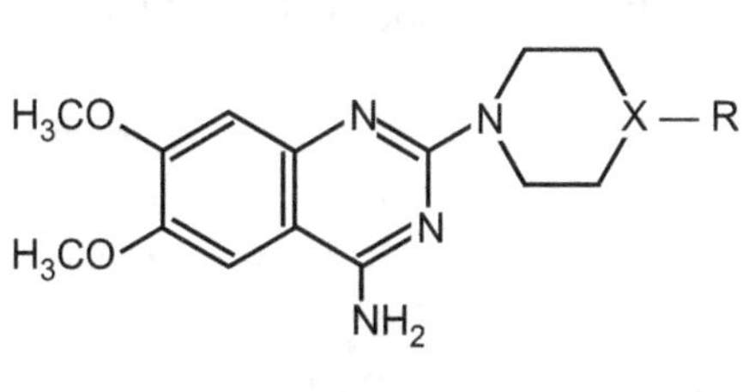

	X	R
(1)	N	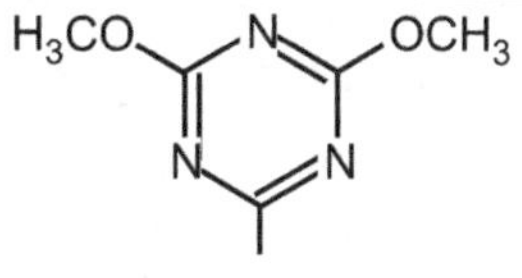
(2)	CH	$CH_2CONHC_2H_5$

(a) Quinazoline derivatives :

While investigating toxicity of antimalarial compounds, Moe et al. in 1949 found that various quinolines produced appreciable anti-α-adrenergic effects. As a result, a series of 6, 7-dimethoxy quinolines was synthesized in Norwich laboratory. The potent hypotensive agents include.

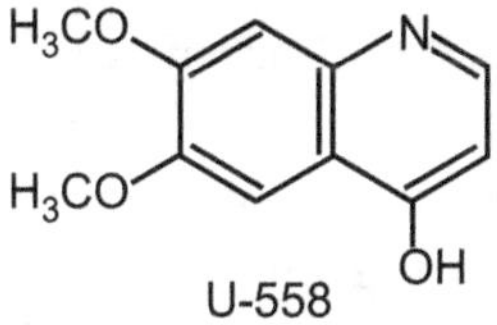

U-558

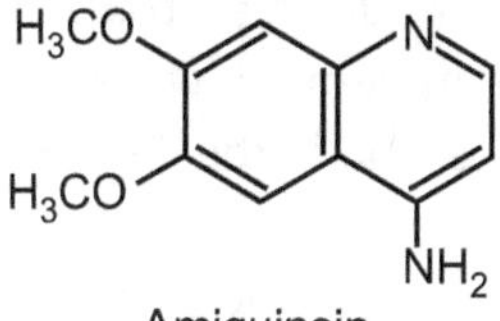

Amiquinsin

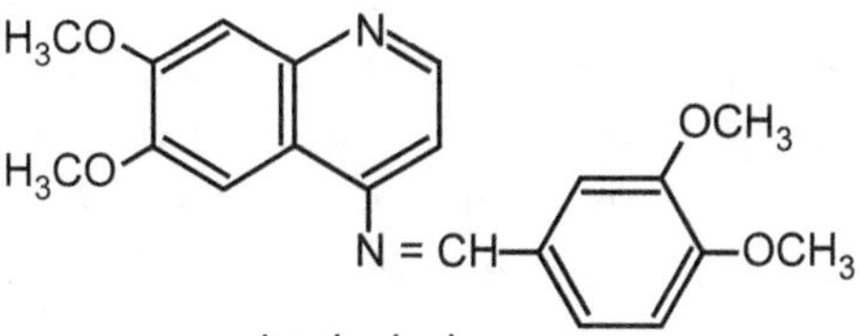

Leniquinsin

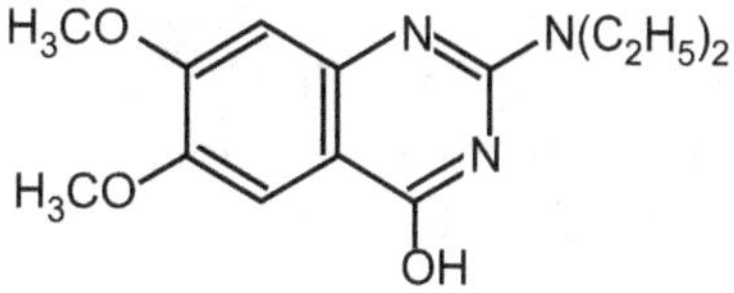

XV

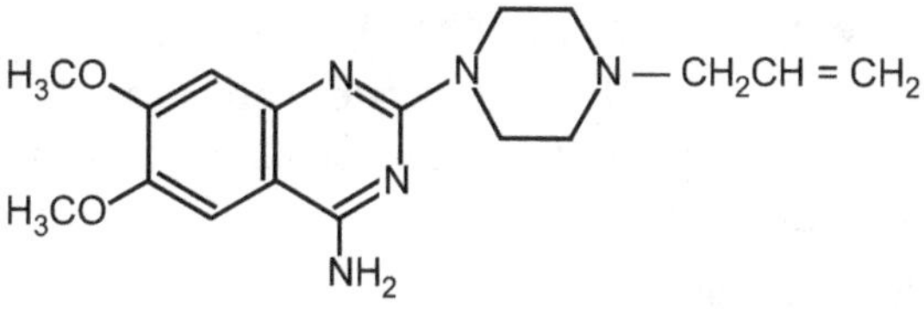

Quinazosin

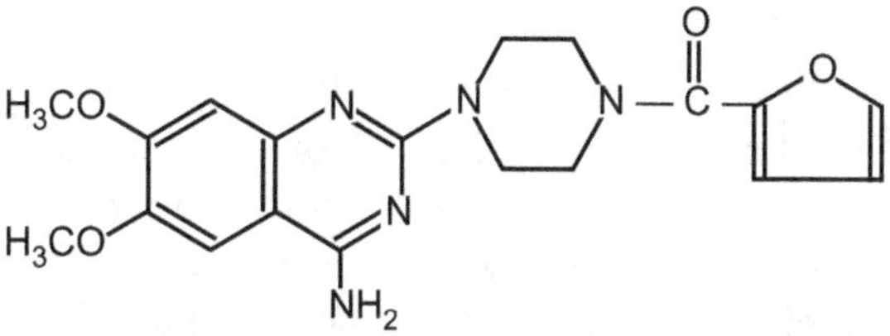

Prozosin

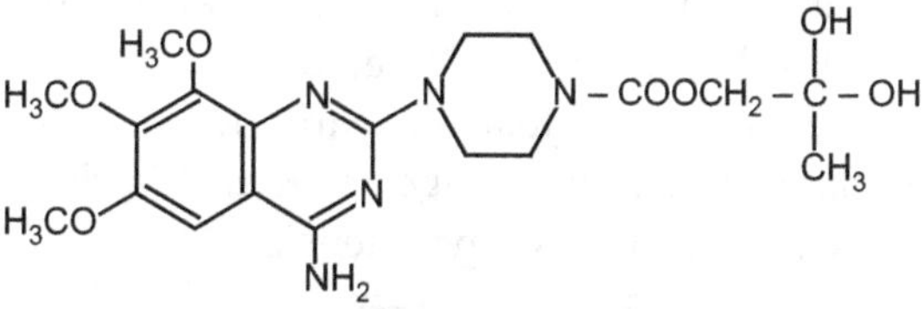

Trimazosin

Prazosin (1974) exerts its antihypertensive action by blocking postsynaptic α_1-adrenoceptor resulting into vasodilation of the arterioles. In therapeutic doses it does not affect the cardiac output and heart rate. No other pharmacological action is reported. The decreased arterial vascular resistance and reduction in arterial and venous tone are the effects mainly due to vasodilation caused by blockage of vascular α_1-receptors. Hence, α_1-blockers are also termed as indirect vasodilators. Its use is accompanied by modest tachycardia (blockade of inhibitoty presynaptic α_2-receptors) and low level of plasma renin - (α_1- blocking effect).

Like prazosin, trimazosin is a quinazoline derivative. Chemically it is 2-hydroxy-2-

methylpropyl 4 - (4 - amino -6, 7, 8 - trimethoxy - 2 quinazolinyl) - 1 piperazine carboxylate monohydrochloride. It is a less potent α_1-blocker than prazosin, otherwise pharmacologically similar to prazosin. Indoramin is yet another example of vascular α_1-receptor blocking agent. Chemically it is 1 [2 - (3 - indolyl) ethyl] derivative of 4 - benzamido piperidine and resembles with the structure of procainamide.

(b) Phentolamine :

The pharmacology of a large series of 2 substituted imidazolines was first studied by Hartmann and Isler in 1939. In addition to α_1-receptor blocking activity, these agents enjoy to varying degrees, sympathomimetic, parasympathomimetic, histamine like, antihistaminergic, MAO and cholinesterase inhibitory activities. The dominance of any of the above properties can be effected by the structural changes in the basic skeleton. Phentolamine and tolazoline are the examples of clinically employed agents from this class, in the management of hypertension.

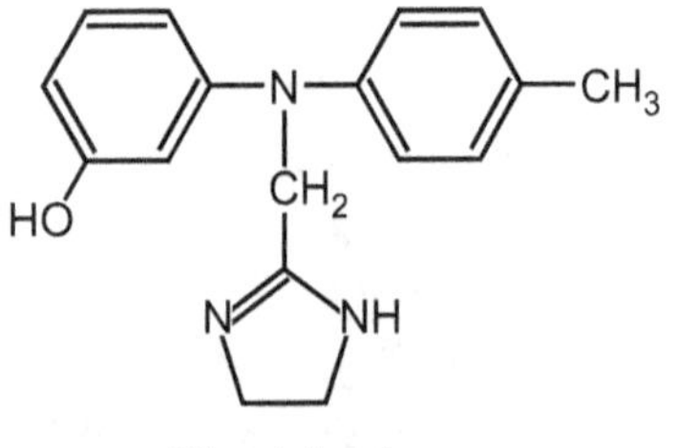

Phentolamine

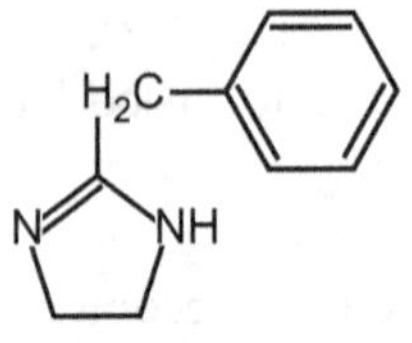

Tolazoline

(v) β-adrenoceptor Blocking Agents :

Mills (1958 Eli Lily Pharmaceuticals) confirmed Ahlquist conclusion. He prepared the dichloro analog of isoprenaline (i.e. DCI) which inhibited the relaxation of bronchial smooth muscles along with the cardiac muscles elicited by isoprenaline. That was the first β-adrenoreceptor blocking agent (β-blocker). It also has a partial agonism as it causes stimulation. But it was not clinically used. Vasodilators were not successful in increasing the O_2 supply to heart. So other possibilities were needed to be explored. The first promising proposition to treat angina effectively was put by Black. He proposed to reduce demand of O_2 of the heart by blocking the effects of sympathetic stimulation. Black concentrated his efforts in obtaining a specific β-blocking agent without stimulant properties of DCI and performed screening test for these types of activities for 18 months. But the success eluded him and crowned his colleague Stephenson who synthesised Pronethalol which was the first clinical β-blocking agent. But in 1963 this compound was withdrawn from the clinic as it exhibited the toxic symptoms (Thymic-tumours) in animals. But it generated quite a lot of attention towards the research to optimize the β-antagonist activity which still continues.

The concept of β-adrenergic blockade was pioneered in 1960's. Researchers who were studying the effects of aryl ring and aryl substitution in the molecule tried to modify the ethanolamine chain itself by Inter alia, the introduction of linking group between aryl ring and ethanolamine chain. After lots of linking groups tried, the best linking group come out to be oxymethylene. It's first analog, propranolol which is the most widely used β-blocker now and is 10 to 20 times potent than its parent compound Pronethalol and quite interestingly BDH workers published papers regarding the anesthetic properties of series of aryloxypropanol amines before the discovery of DCI. This series also included the N-propyl analogue of propranolol, which later emerged as a β-adrenergic blocker.

Cardio-Selective Blockade :

Lipophilicity ensures the transfer across bloodbrain barrier as brain is mostly made up of lipids. This could also lead to CNS side effects of β-blockers e.g. propranolol. Hydrophilicity can minimise these CNS side effects as first reported with Sotalol in 1964. This inspired Crowther, Howe and Smith's work on the synthesis of oxypropanol amine analogs and Smith successfully synthesised the corresponding acetamido compound from readily available para acetamido phenol. This compound was named Proctalol. But the most important characteristics of proctalol was found little later which gave birth to a new era of cardio selective blockade. It was shown that proctalol blocks only the cardiac β-receptors (β_1) and not the vascular receptors (β_2). Thus, proctalol got the first place in the history of cardio selective β_1-blockers. It also opened the gate for treatment of patients with coexisting asthma (though not absolutely) with β_1-blockers.

It also showed minimum side effects on CNS. It has a log P of 0.79 while propanolol has log P of 3.65 (partition coefficient of 4500 : 1). Due to all these virtues practalol was launched in 1970 as the first cardio selective β-blocker. But it had to be withdrawn after several years of clinical use due as its toxic manifestation in some patients like skin rashes, ophthalmic problems, some leading to blindness and severe peritonitis.

Hull and his coworkers came with the next major break through by introducing a methylene group between amide function and aromatic ring. The first compound atenolol is as potent as propranolol and it is also a cardio selective β-blocker.

Metaprolol was next to come when Carlson independently prepared this paramethoxy ethyl compound.

Acebutotol is yet another β-blocker. Its non-selectivity of action is attributed to the generation of an active but non-selective metabolite. Tolamolol was recently developed selective β_1-blocker. Like pronethalol, it was withdrawn from the clinical use because of its ability to induce tumor in animal testings. Nadolol is yet another example of long-acting β-blockers. Like atenolol, it is excreted largely in unchanged form through urine.

All these cardio selective compounds are more hydrophilic than propranolol and their cardio selectivity can be attributed to the fact that β_1-receptors are hydrophilic while β_2-receptors are lipophillic. Another explanation for this cardio selectivity according to other researcher is the additional interaction of a para substituent possibly via H-bond formation with a complimentary site on β_1 and not on the β_2-receptors.

Unlike α-adrenoceptor blocking agents, the β-adrenoceptor blockers exhibit structural similarity with isoprenaline or norepinephrine. Hence structural requirements of these agents have been fairly well defined. This structural similarity of β-adrenoceptor blockers with isoprenaline (agonist) imparts :

(i) A greater specificity of action. These agents act more selectively on β-receptors and do not interfere with cholinergic, histaminergic or serotonergic responses and

(ii) Some degree of sympathomimetic intrinsic activity. These agents with some exceptions, still retain sympathomimetic properties and can be termed as partial adrenergic agonists. Due to their partial agonist nature, they have less ability to induce bradycardia, pulmonary obstruction and rebound hypertension, in comparison to other antihypertensive agents.

It is important to note that the β-blocking effect and intrinsic sympathetic activity do not run opposite to each other. A potent β-blocking agent (e.g., pindolol) may still retain a high intrinsic sympathetic activity. This is probably because the functional groups involved in receptor blockade may in certain cases be quite different from the functional groups involved in receptor activation.

Similarly their structural resemblance with local anesthetics, enable these agents to exert a membrane stabilizing effect or a quinidine like action e.g., propranolol. This property justifies their use to treat cardiac arrhythmias.

β-receptor responses are largely of relaxant nature. The major exception to this generalization is the cardiac β_1-receptors, stimulation of which increases the rate and force of heart contraction. Therefore, selective β_1-adrenoceptor blocking agents gained high clinical importance as antihypertensive drugs.

The cardioselective β_1-blockers act through the following postulated mechanism :

1. Inhibition of renin release.
2. Reduction of cardiac output.
3. Inhibition of synaptic norepinephrine release, and
4. Restoration of vascular relaxation responses.

On the basis of their relative affinity for β-receptor sub-types, these agents can be categorized into three classes.

(a) Non-selective β-blockers :

e.g., propranolol, pindolol, alprenolol, nadolol, bunolol, sotalol, timolol, oxprenolol, penbutolol etc.

(b) Selective β_1-blockers :

e.g. acebutolol, atenolol, metoprolol, practolol, tolamolol, pafenolol etc.

(c) Selective β_2-blockers :

These agents do not find any clinical utility. Butoxamine is a somewhat selective β_2-antagonist.

Table 5.4 : β-blocking agents

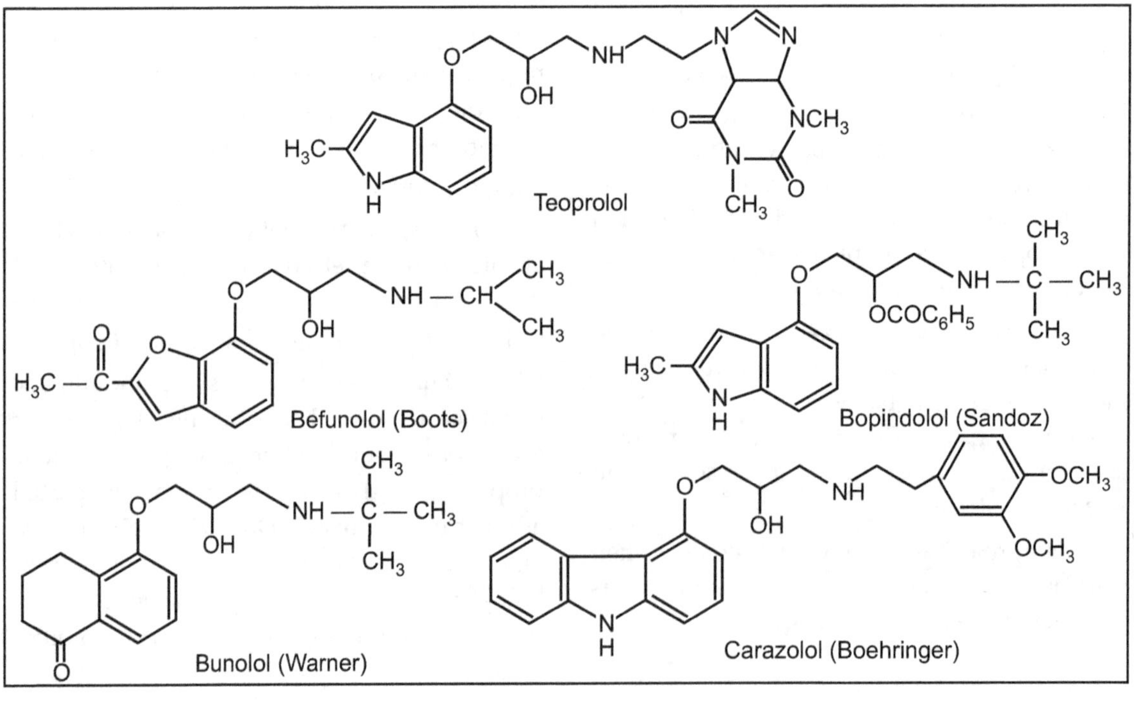

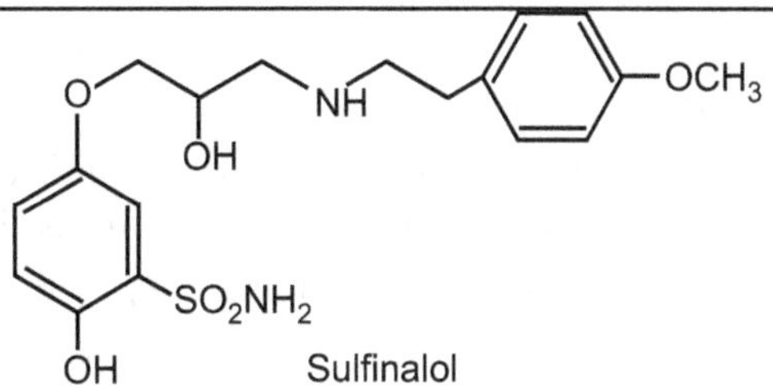

Sulfinalol

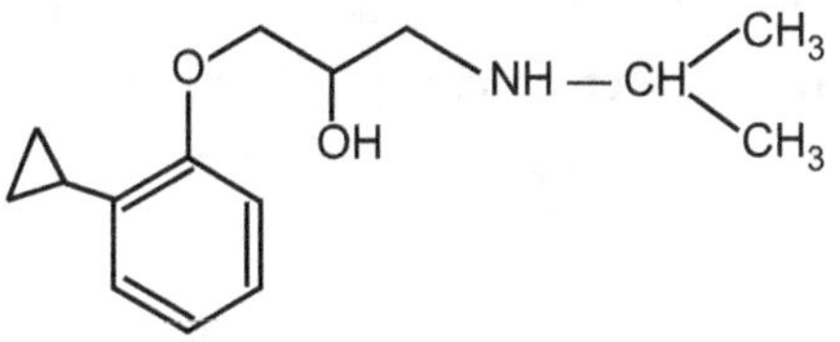

Procinolol (Diamant)

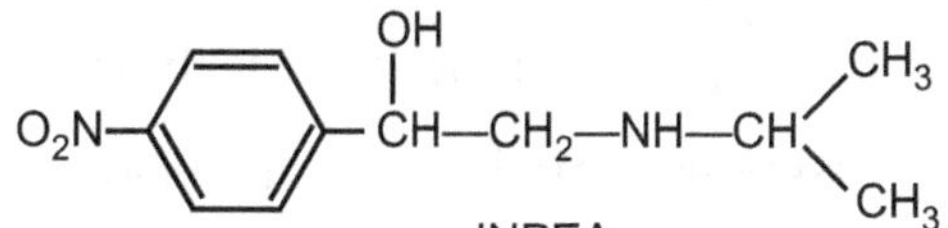

INPEA

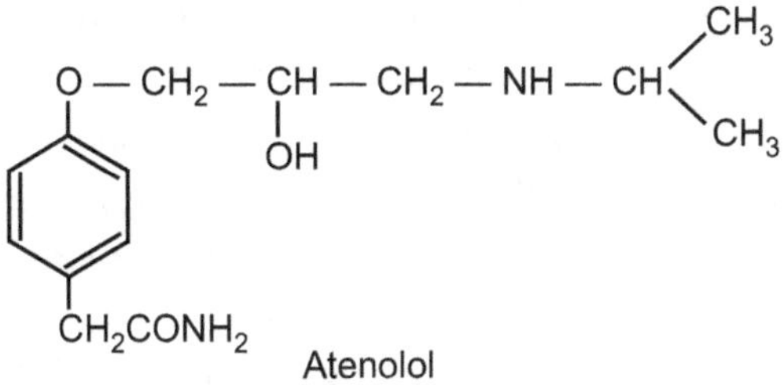

Atenolol

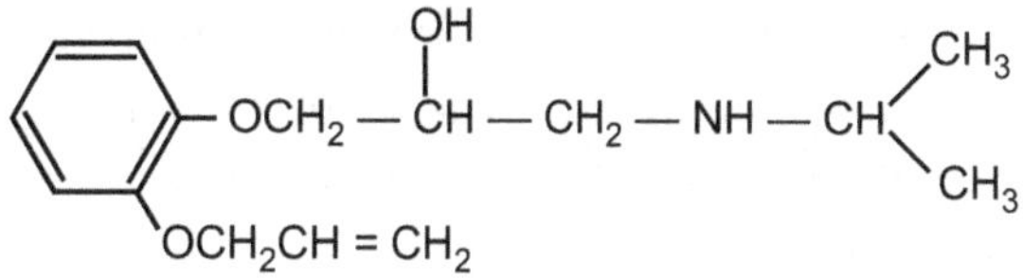

CIBA

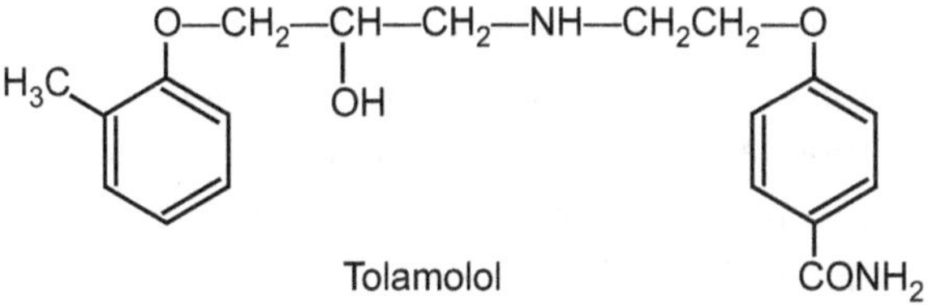

Tolamolol

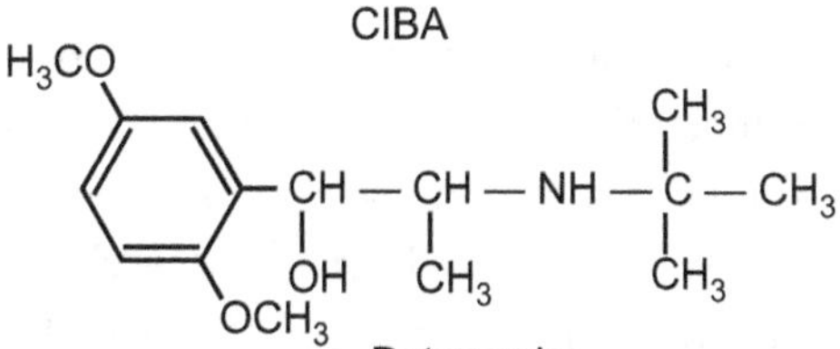

Butoxamine
(selective β_2-blocker)

5.23 VASODILATORS

The elevated peripheral vascular resistance is the main cause behind most of the hypertensive conditions. Vasodilators act by dilating the arterioles by which there is a fall in blood pressure without interfering with the functioning of sympathetic nervous system. The α_1-adrenoceptor blocking agents (indirect vasodilators) bring about vasodilation by interfering with sympathetic functioning. The vasodilators are sub-classified as :

(a) Direct vasodilators :

(i) Arterial vasodilators e.g., hydralazine, and

(ii) Arterial and venous vasodilators : e.g., sodium nitroprusside.

(b) Indirect vasodilators :

e.g., α_1-adrenoreceptor blocking agents.

When heart failure is absent, vasodilator therapy usually results in a drop in cardiac output, whereas in the presence of left ventricular failure, cardiac output is improved. This response relates not only to more favourable afterload conditions on failing (heart) left ventricle but to the highly important circulatory actions of vasodilators on the venous bed as well. Afterload may be defined as 'the force, or stress developed in the ventricular wall during cardiac ejection'.

If the resting muscle length (preload) is held constant increasing the afterload (weight) will decrease both the extent and velocity of muscle shortening, whereas reducing the afterload will decrease the extent and speed of muscle shortening. If the preload and inotropic state are held constant, increasing the afterload will increase both the speed and extent of left ventrical wall shortening, whereas reducing the afterload will be both of these variables.

Agents used for Afterload Reduction (Vasodilators) :

Commonly employed vasodilators include :

(a) **Intravenous :** Sodium nitroprusside, phentolmine, nitroglycerine.

(b) **Oral :** Isosorbide dinitrate, hydralazine, prazosin. These drugs tend to have little or no direct effect on myocardial contractility.

(c) **Calcium channel blockers :** Voltage-dependent calcium channels mainly regulate transmitter release or muscle contraction. They are structurally related to sodium channels and include L-(long lasting), T-(transient), N-(neuronal), P-(Purkingje cells), Q-, and R-types. The L-type exists in neuronal tissue as well as in skeletal and cardiac muscle. This type is sensitive to dihydropyridines. The L-type Ca^{++} channels are hetero-oligomeric and composed of α_1-, α_2-, β-, δ- and γ-subunits. The α_1-subunit provides the binding site for the L-channel blockers. Examples include, verapamil, nifedipine, diltiazam etc. The calcium channel blockers, unlike direct vasodilator cause dilation of coronary arteries and markedly affect the automaticity, conduction velocity and refractory period in myocardial cells. While direct vasodilators have little direct effect on the heart functioning in therapeutic doses. Like antispasmodic agents they principally act through direct musculotropic effect resulting into the relaxation of peripheral vascular smooth muscles. The clinically used vasodilators in the treatment of hypertension are shown in table 5.5.

Table 5.5 : Clinically used antihypertensive agents

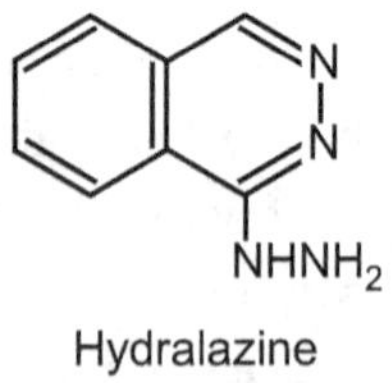

Hydralazine

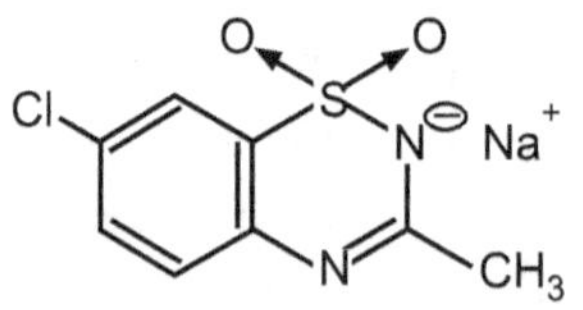

Sodium Diazoxide

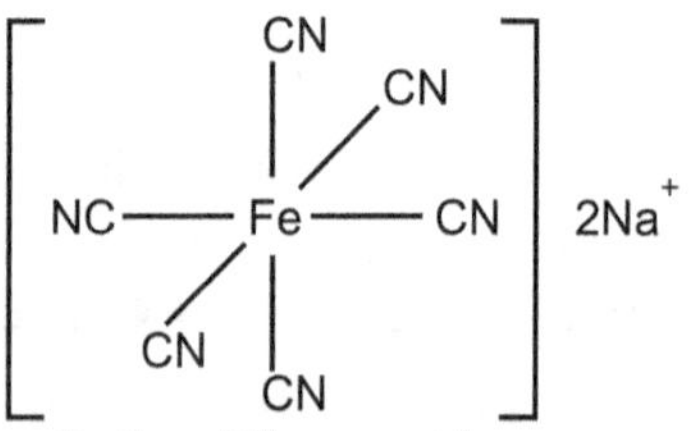

Sodium Nitroprusside

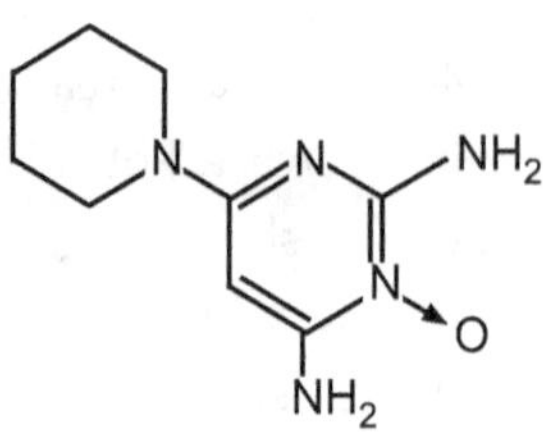

Minoxidil

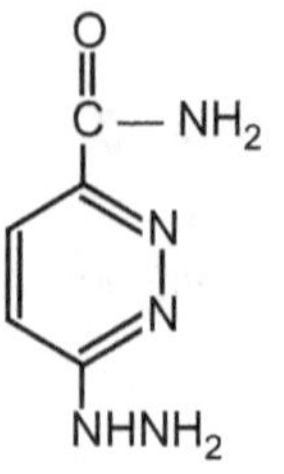

Hydracarbazine

Calcium channel blocking agents :

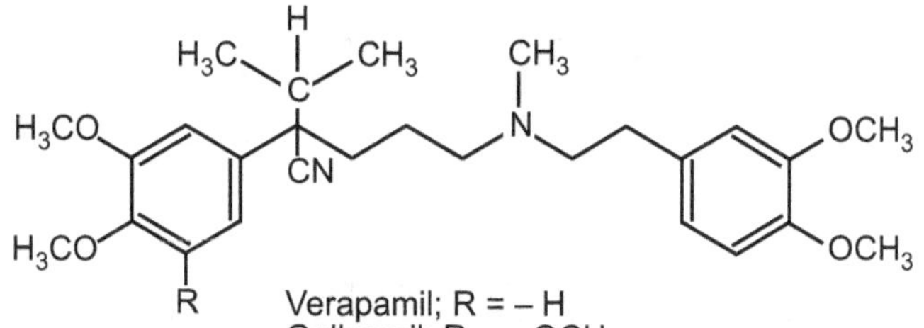

Verapamil; R = – H
Gallopmil; R = – OCH$_3$

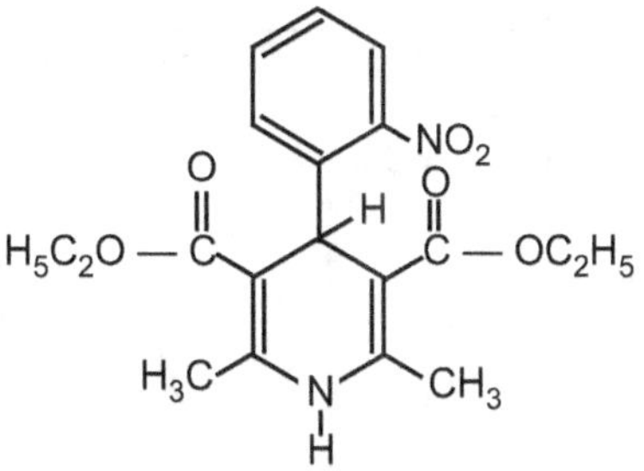

Nifedipine

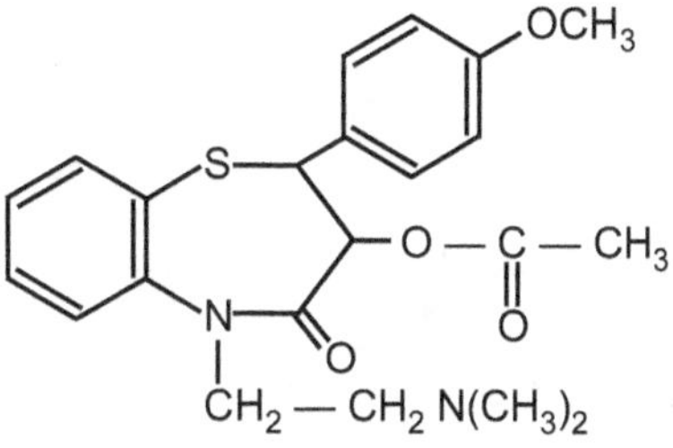

Diltiazem

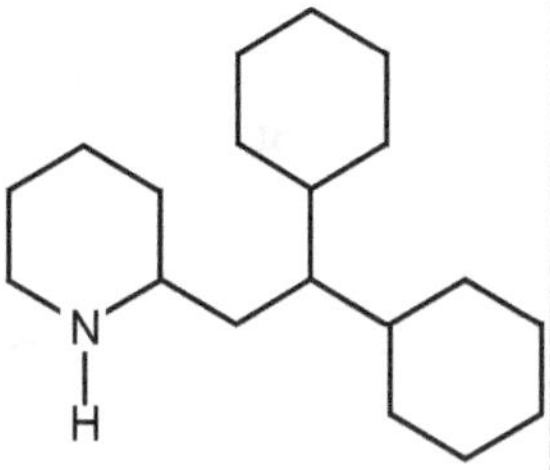

Perhexiline

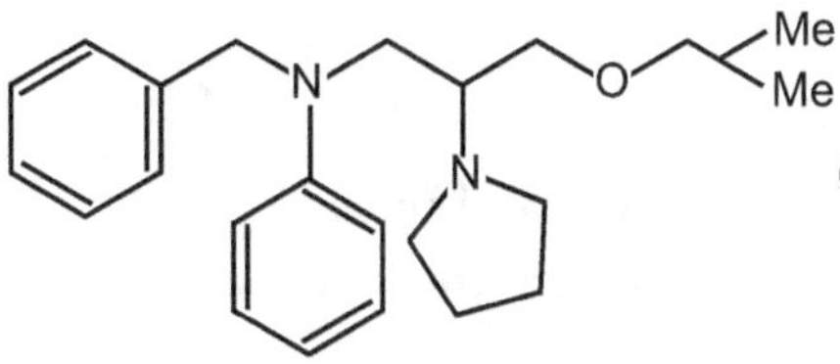

Bepridil

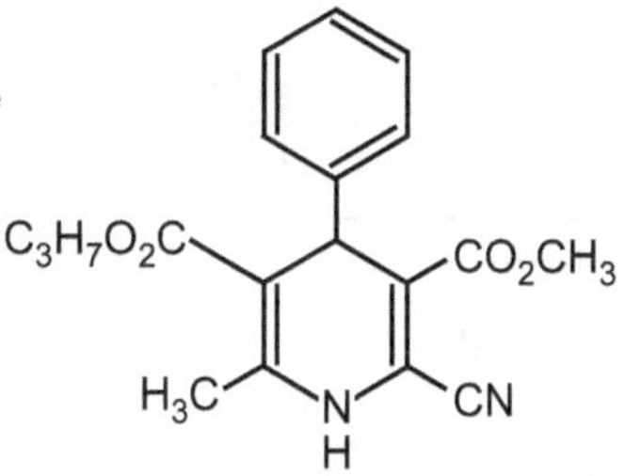

Nivaldipine

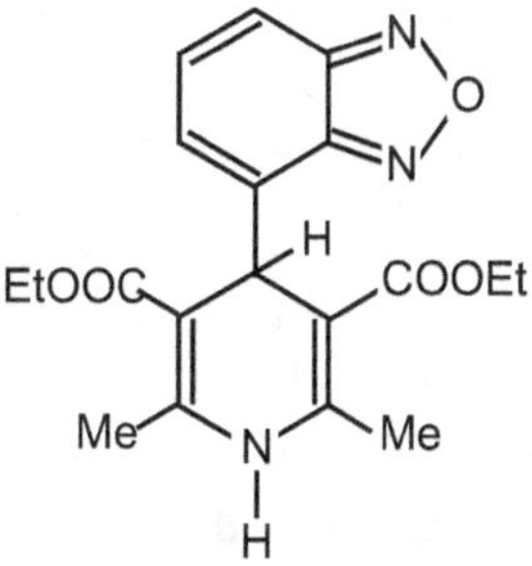

PY 108 - 068

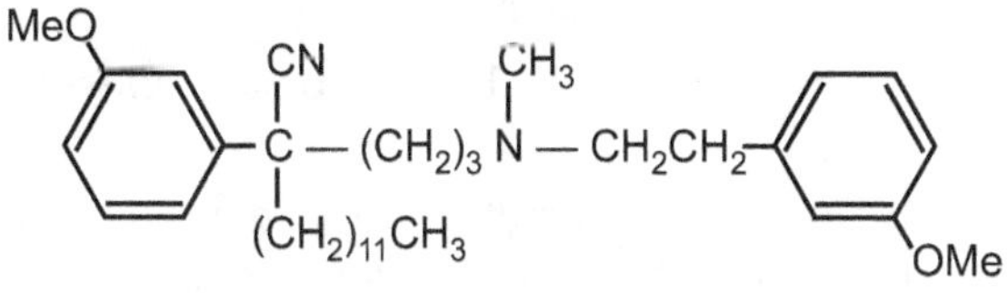

Anipamil

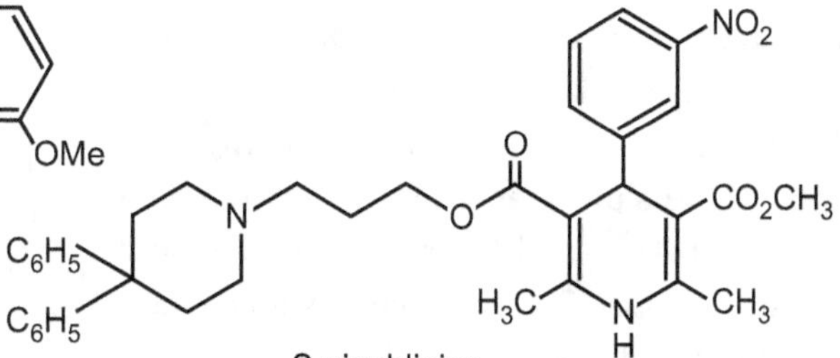

S-niguldipine

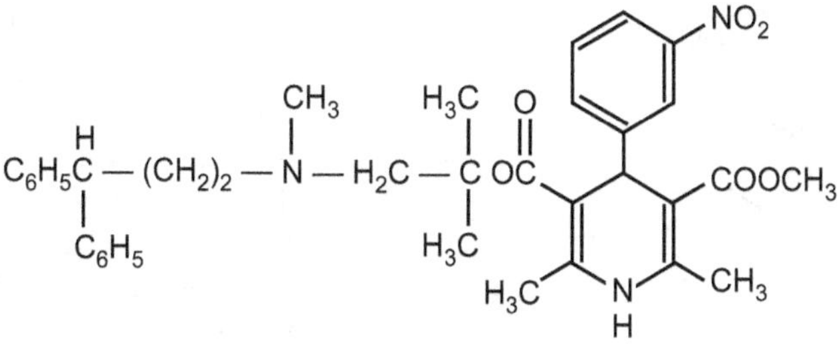

Lercanidipine

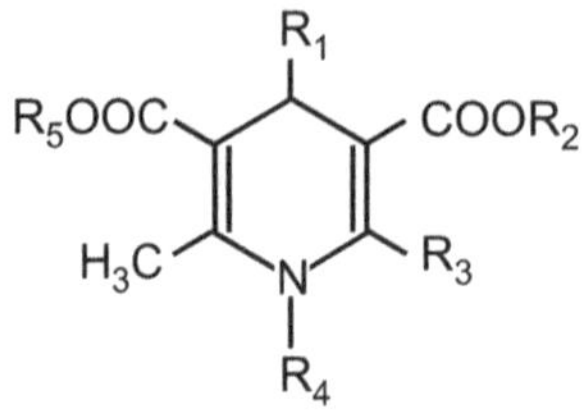

1, 4-dihydropyridines

Name	R_1	R_2	R_3	R_4	R_5
1. Nimodipine	$3\text{-}NO_2C_6H_4$	$- CH(CH_3)_2$	CH_3	H	$CH_2CH_2OCH_3$
2. Nisoldipine	$2\text{-}NO_2C_6H_4$	CH_3	CH_3	H	$CH_2CH(CH_3)_2$
3. Lacidipine	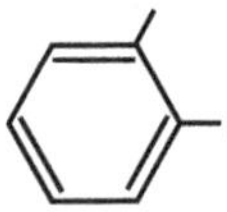 (2-substituted phenyl) $-CH=CH-COO-t\,Bu$	C_2H_5	CH_3	H	C_2H_5
4. Nicardipine	$3 - NO_2C_6H_4$	$- (CH_2)_2- \overset{\displaystyle CH_3}{\overset{\displaystyle \vert}{N}}CH_2C_6H_5$	CH_3	H	CH_3
5. Felodipine	2, 3-dichlorophenyl	$- C_2H_5$	CH_3	H	CH_3

Nitrendipine, a dihydropyridine calcium channel blocker structurally related to nifedipine, inhibits the movement of calcium through the "slow channel" of cardiac and vascular smooth muscles, thus inducing peripheral vasodilation with consequent reductions in elevated blood pressure. The high affinity binding sites for 1, 4 - dihydropyridines have been identified in the region of the slow channel in the sarcolemma of cardiac tissues and brain. Binding to these sites is stereospecific, saturable, reversible and competitive with other dihydropyridine derivatives.

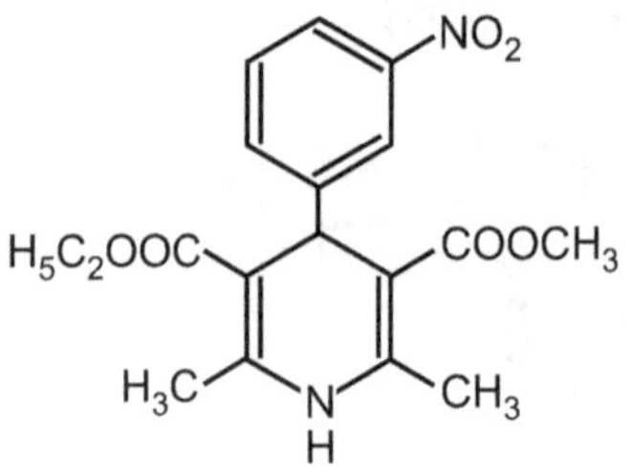

Nitrendipine

SAR of 1, 4 - dihydropyridines :

The following features are essential for activity.

(a) 1,4 - dihydropyridine skeleton,

(b) a secondary nitrogen in dihydropyridine ring,

(c) an aromatic or heteroaromatic C_4-substituent.

In this aromatic substituent, further substitution at ortho position is more effective than at meta position,while para substitution results in inactive compound. The electron withdrawing groups are more favoured than electron-releasing groups.

Certain steric hindrance in ortho position is required to fix the dihydropyridine structure in favourable conformation in which the aromatic group is approximately perpendicular to dihydropyridine ring.

Calcium channel blockers have negative inotropic effects. Therefore, the conditions of many patients with CHF deteriorates when treated with these agents.

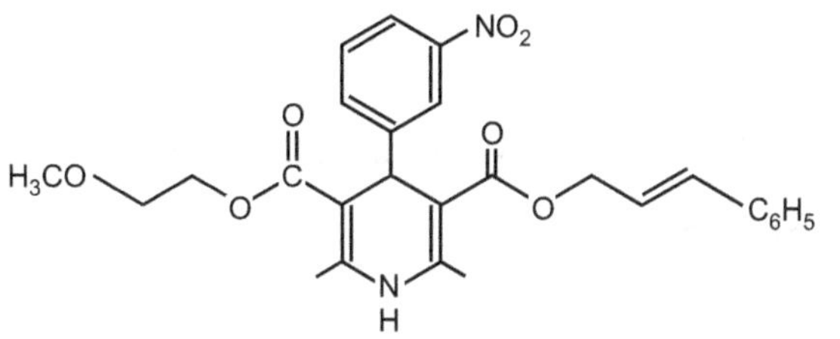

Cilnidipine

Efonidipine : It is a dihydropyridine calcium channel blocker.

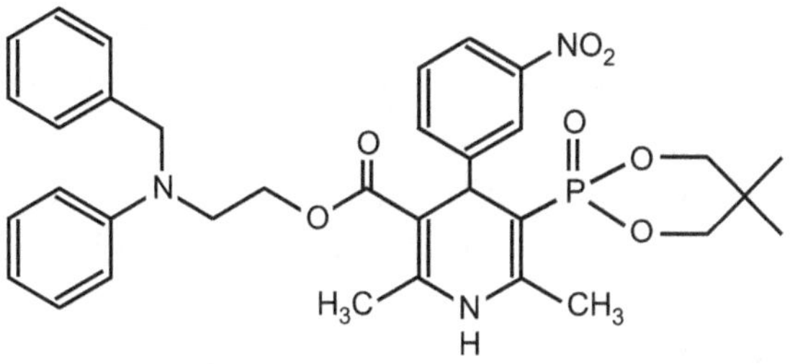

Clevidipine (2008) : It is to be given intravenously for reduction of blood pressure when oral therapy of other dihydropyridine calcium channel blocker is not feasible or not desirable.

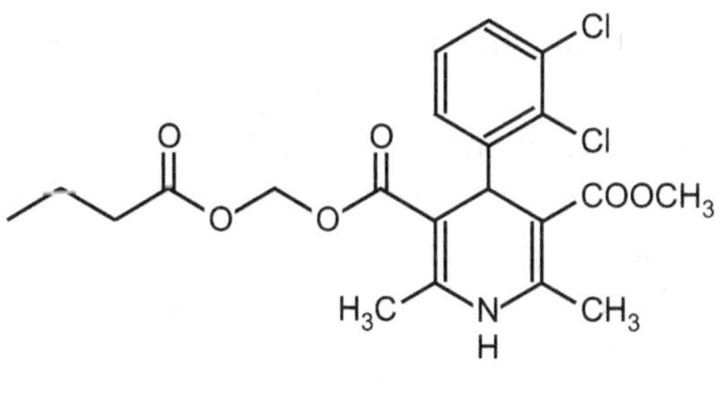

5.24 AGENTS ACTING ON RENIN-ANGIO TENSIN SYSTEM

Renin (molecular weight + 42,000) is a proteolytic enzyme, which is produced and stored in the granules of the juxtaglomerular cells in the walls of the afferent arterioles of the kidney. Upon release into the renal arterial blood stream, renin catalyses the conversion of angiotensinogen (inactive precursor) into angiotensin-I. Angiotensinogen is a circulating alpha - 2 - globulin with 14 - amino-acids. It is synthesized in liver and is circulated in the plasma.

Some renin inhibitors have reached clinical trials, but further development has been limited by poor bioavailability.

Angiotensin - I (decapeptide), which has less intrinsic activity is converted to more active form, angiotensin - II (octapeptide) by angiotensin converting enzyme. Angiotensin - II is one of the most potent vasoconstrictor agent. The renin angiotensin system is an important part of homeostatic mechanisms in the body. It works to maintain the blood pressure at the normal level. It also regulates the electrolyte balance by controlling aldosterone biosynthesis and release from adrenal cortex. Similarly, the juxtaglomerular cells are directly innervated by central sympathetic nerves. Hence, under the conditions of strain and stress, the sympathetic stimulation may lead to hypertension due to the activation of renin angiotensin system.

Angiotensin converting enzyme (ACE) inhibitors, widely used to treat hypertension and concomitant renal diseases and congestive heart failure, block the enzymatic conversion of angiotensin I to angiotensin II, the final effector of the renin-angiotensin system. The potential benefit of angiotensin II antagonists has been demonstrated using the peptide saralasin, which is a specific angiotensin II inhibitor. However the poor bioavailability of this agent has driven a search for orally active non-peptide compounds. In consequence, losartan was recently marketed for the treatment of hypertension.

Angiotensins are the potent vasoconstrictors. They tend to increase the peripheral vascular resistance. The angiotensin-induced release of aldosterone increases the sodium ion retention in plasma, resulting into an increase in plasma volume. The overall result of all these effects is hypertension. Hence, one can expect that angiotensin antagonists would be effective antihypertensive agents. This expectation was proved to be correct by the development of saralasin (1971) and captopril (1977), each being the member of two distinct classes. Saralasin, losartan, valsartan, eprosartan and saprisartan are the examples of competitive antagonist of angiotensin - II, while captopril is inhibitor of angiotensin converting enzyme (ACE) which leads to decrease rate of angiotensin - II synthesis.

(a) Saralasin :

It is a substituted analog of angiotensin - II, designed by Pals et al in 1971, which acts by competitively blocking the angiotensin receptor sites.

Sar - Arg- Val - Tyr - Val - His - Pro- Ala

Saralasin

In the structure of angiotensin – II, the phenylalanine at position 8, is replaced by alanine (results into decreased intrinsic activity) and sarcosyl is substituted at NH_2 - terminal (in order to increase the resistance to enzymatic hydrolysis by aminopeptidases) to yield saralasin molecule. It does not cross blood brain barrier and is retained in the vascular and extracellular fluid compartments to block angiotensin receptor sites. This results into decreased peripheral vascular resistance and blood pressure. An increase in blood pressure at initial stage of therapy may be due to the partial agonistic nature of the drug. In some cases a rebound hypertension after drug withdrawal may be seen which is due to sudden increase in plasma renin activity.

(b) Captopril :

Angiotensin converting enzyme (ACE) is known to be inhibited by a non-apeptide BPF 9α (bradykinin potentiating factors) present in the venom of pit viperus. This non-apeptide is termed as teprotide and has quick onset of action but lacks oral effectiveness. This lack of oral effectiveness was overcome by introduction of captopril at the Squibb laboratories by Cushman, Ondetti and co-workers in 1977 which is structural relative of teprotide. It was marketed as antihypertensive agent in 1980 in the treatment of severe hypertension.

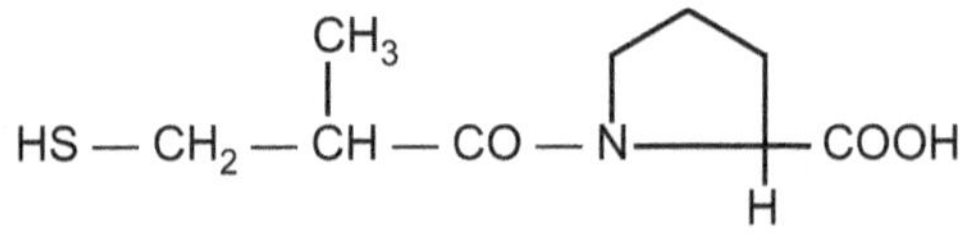

(mer) captopril

Among the angiotensin II antagonists, telmisartan is the most lipophilic compound with a partition coefficient log P = 3.2 (n-octanol/buffer at pH 7.4). Due to its physico-chemical properties, telmisartan shows excellent oral absorption and tissue penetration.

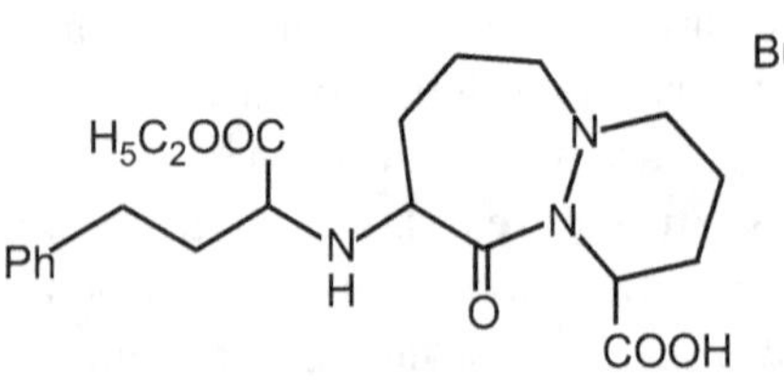

Cilazapril (Hoffmann-La Roche) 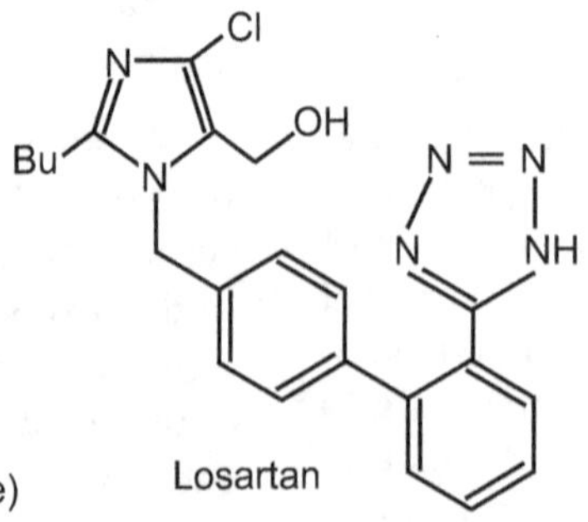   Losartan 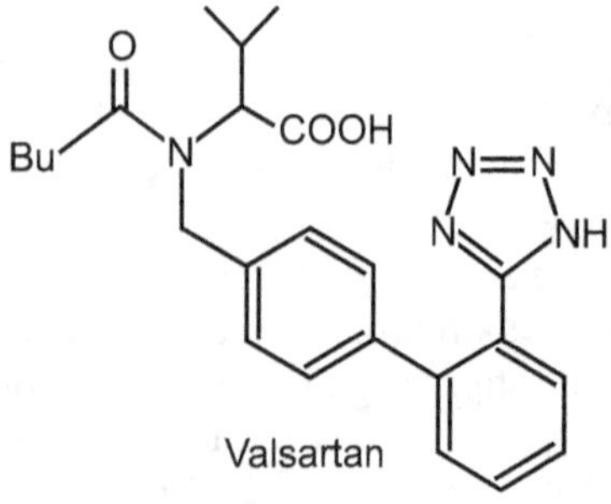   Valsartan

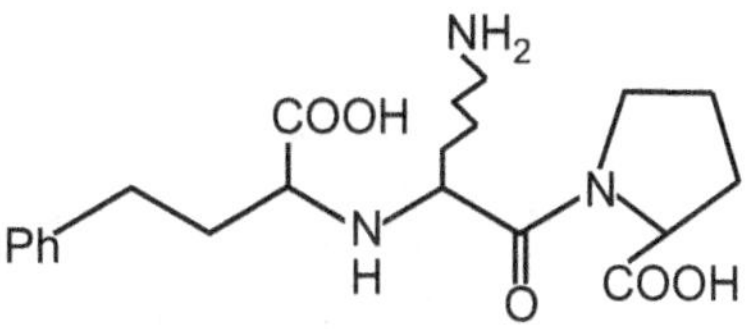

Lisinopril (Merck)

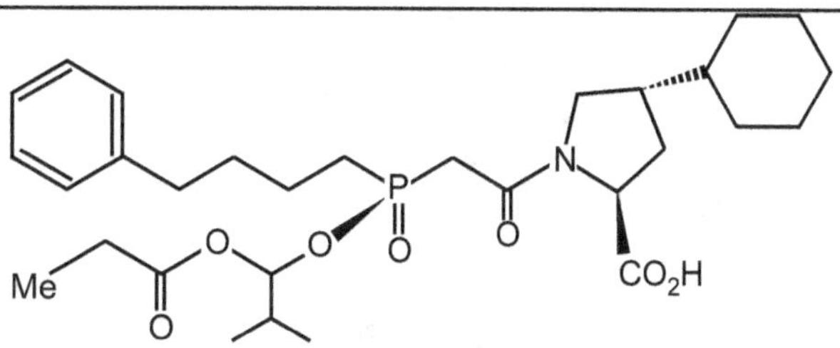

Fosinopril (Bristol - Myers Squibb)

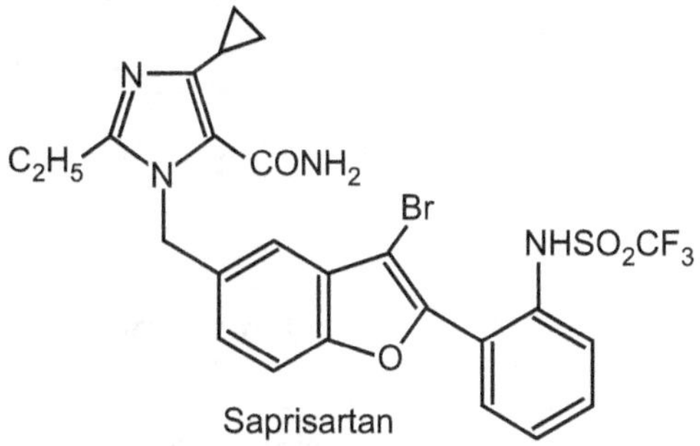

Saprisartan

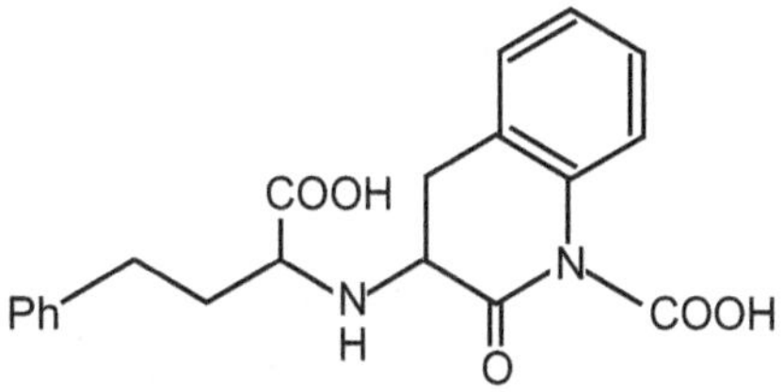

Benzapril (Ciba-Geigy)

Angiotensin II inhibitors :

Losartan

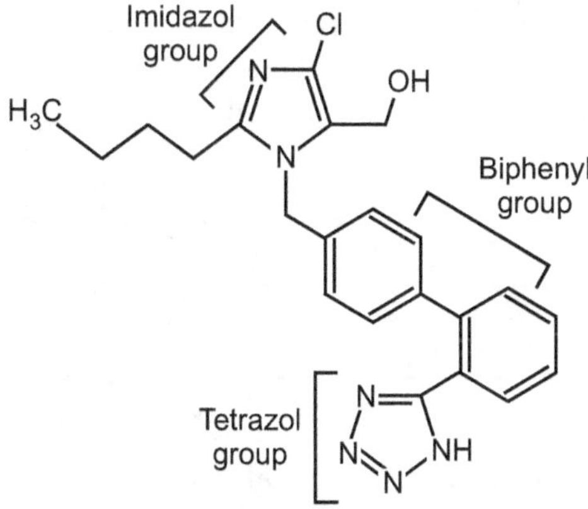

Imidazol group

Biphenyl group

Tetrazol group

Exp 3174

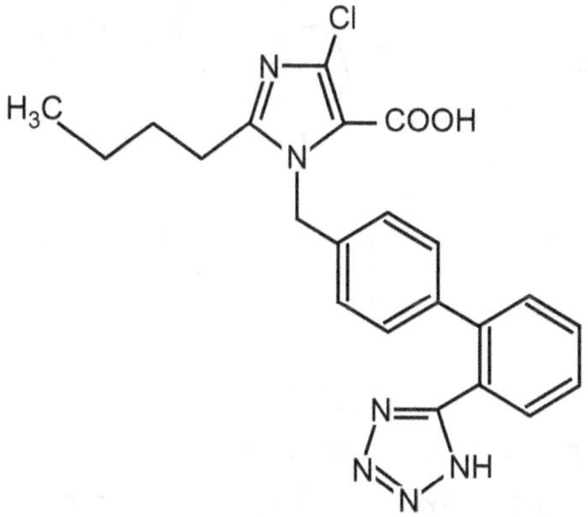

Telmisartan

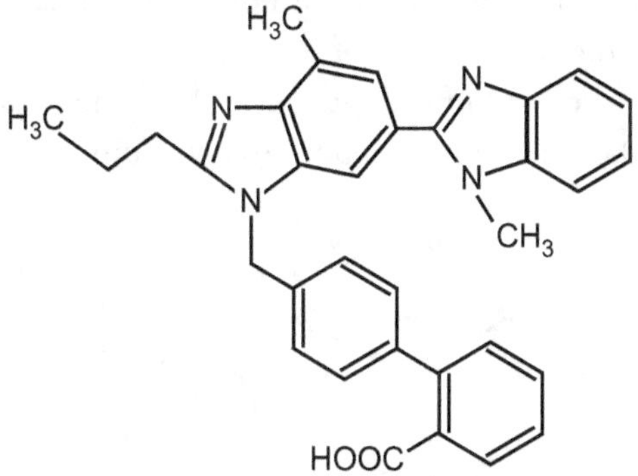

Irbesartan

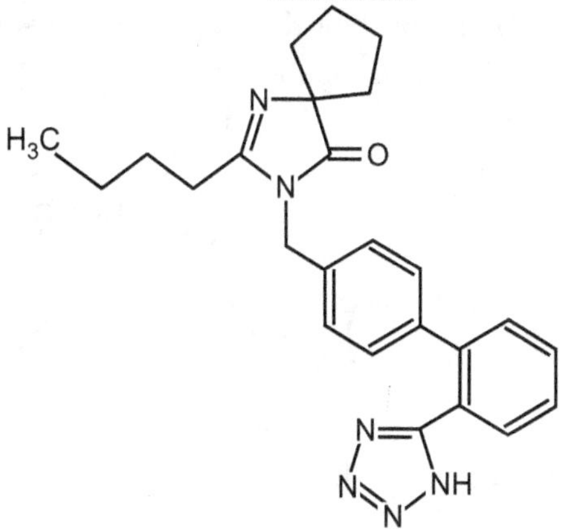

Candesartan

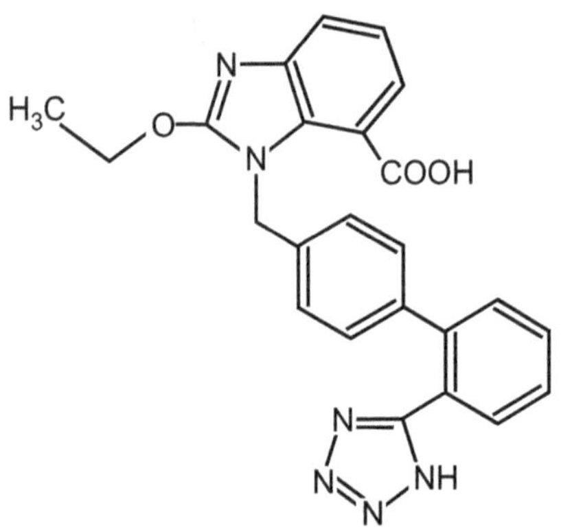

Valsartan

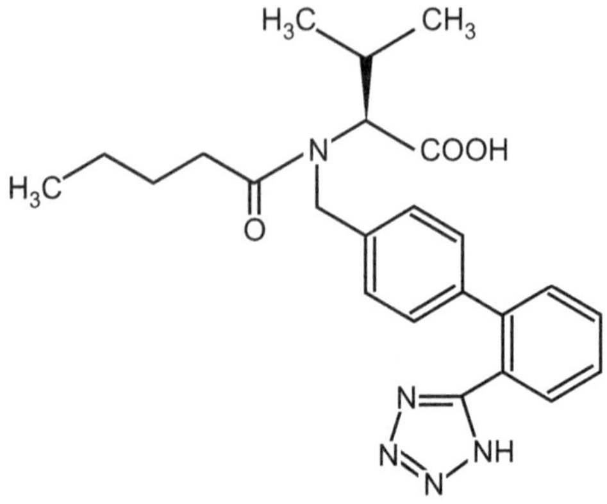

Eprosartan

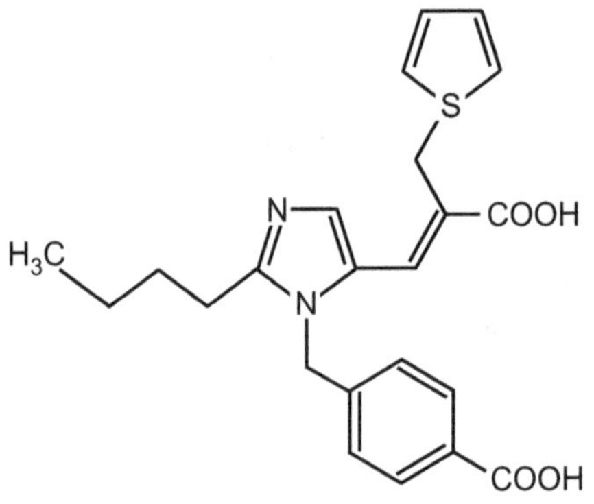

Olmesartan

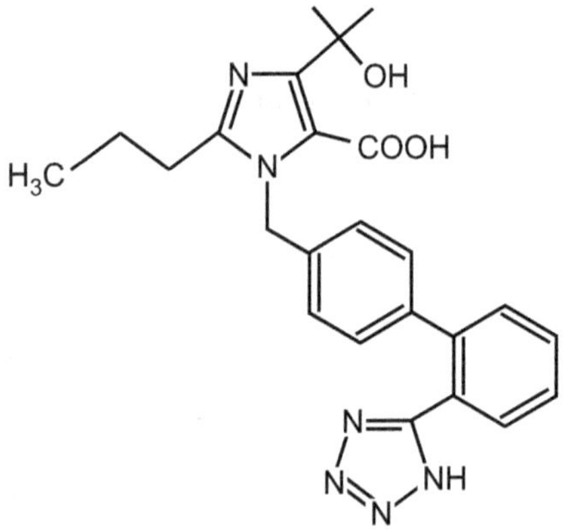

(c) Enalaprilic acid (enalapril) :

Enalapril was developed by Merck Sharp and Dohme and introduced in 1984. It has similar pharmacological effects, mechanism of action and therapeutic uses as that of captopril. Like captopril, it does contain a *"proline surrogate"*.

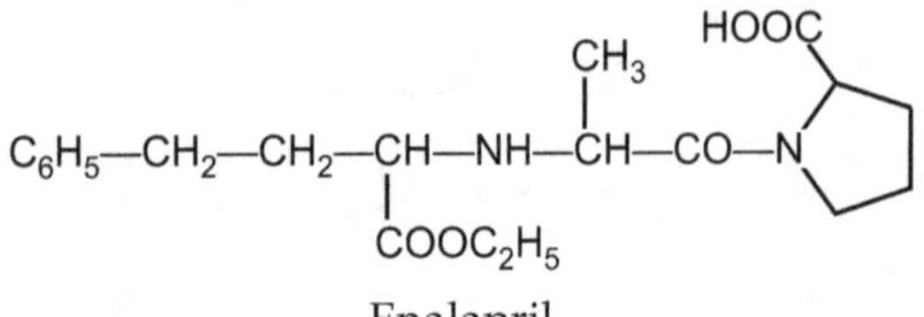

Enalapril

(monoethyl ester of enalaprilic acid)

Lisinopril, a lysine derivative of enalaprilate is an oral long acting ACE-inhibitor. Following oral administration, it does not appear to be bound to other serum proteins. It does not undergo metabolism and is excreted unchanged entirely in the urine. Its plasma half life is about twelve hours.

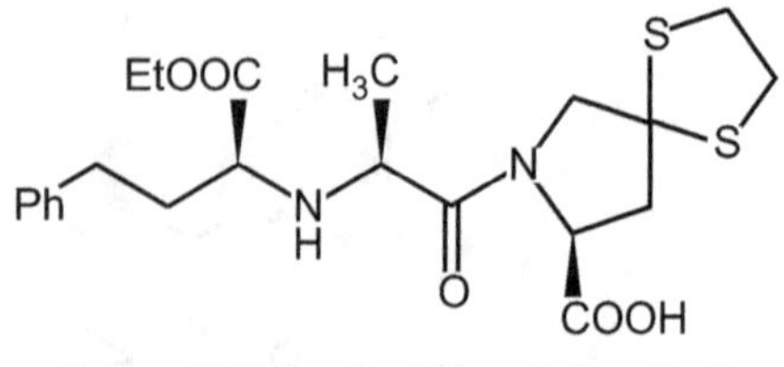

Spirapril (Schering-Plough Sandoz)

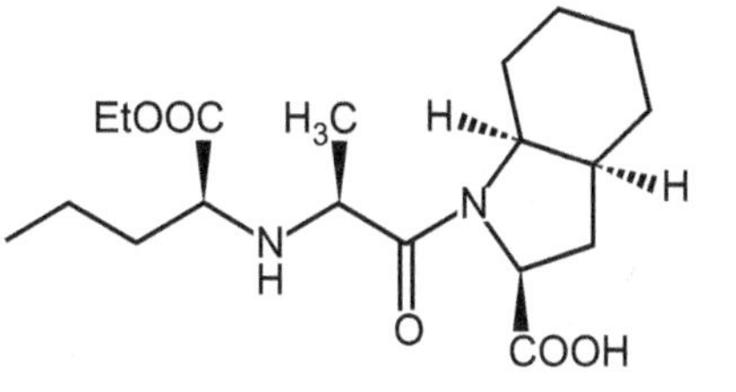

Perindopril (Servier)

Trandolapril : It is an ACE inhibitor used to treat high blood pressure.

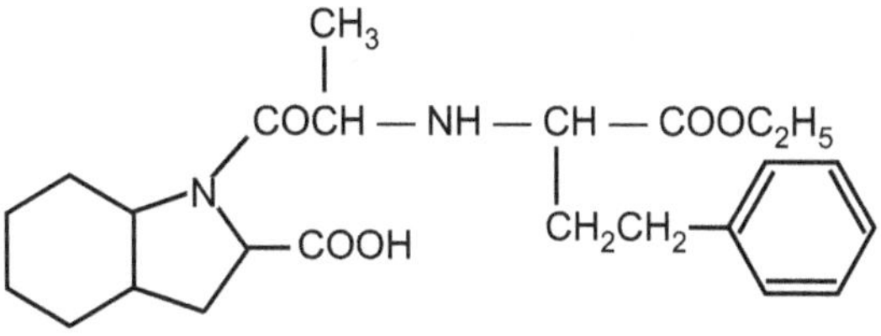

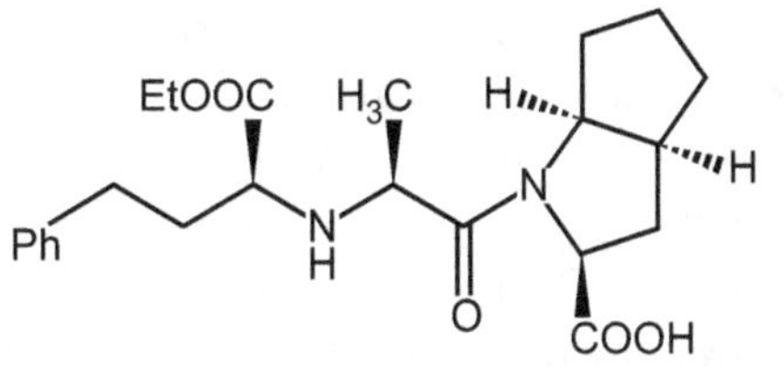

Ramipril (Hoechst)

It acts by suppressing renin-angiotensin-aldosterone system. It is indicated in the treatment of all grades of hypertension in different age groups. It is used alone as initial therapy or concomitantly with other classes of anti-hypertensive agents.

Quinapril : It is a prodrug. It is converted to its active metabolite, quinoprilat in the liver. It is ACE-inhibitor used in the treatment of hypertension and congestive heart failure.

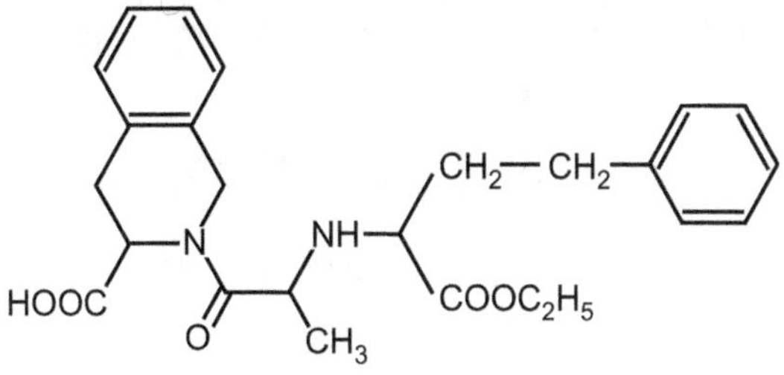

Imidapril : It is an ACE inhibitor used to treat hypertension and chronic heart failure.

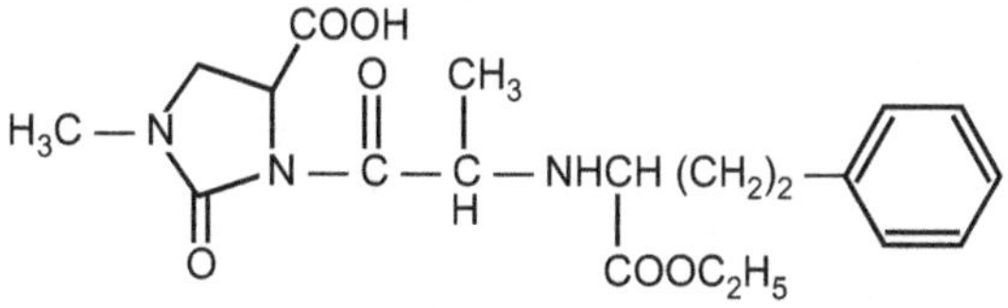

ACE-inhibitors are generally considered as the first step in drug therapy for congestive heart failure. If these can not be tolerated because of side-effects, then a combination of hydralazine and nitrates should be tried. If this combination fails to yield favourable results, then digitalis is started followed by diuretics.

(d) Aldosterone antagonists :

Antagonists of renin and aldosterone have also been developed to cause deactivation of renin angiotensin system. However renin antagonists possess poor therapeutic applicability while aldosterone antagonists are clinically used as diuretic agents.

Aldosterone, deoxycorticosterone and hydrocortisone are potent antidiuretic mineralocorticoids. Spiranolactone an aldosterone antagonist is a steroidal derivative having a lactone ring in the spiro arrangement at 17th position.

Due to the structural similarity, it competitively inhibits the binding of aldosterone with its receptors.

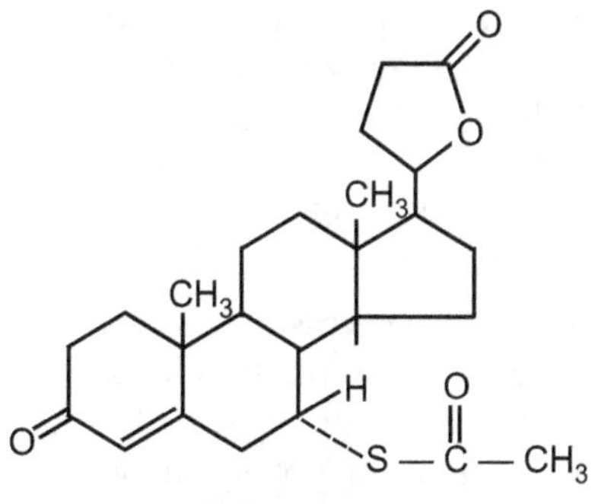

Spiranolactone

Eplerenone : It is an aldosterone antagonist. It is used as an adjunct in the management of chronic heart failure. It is a K^+ - sparing diuretic.

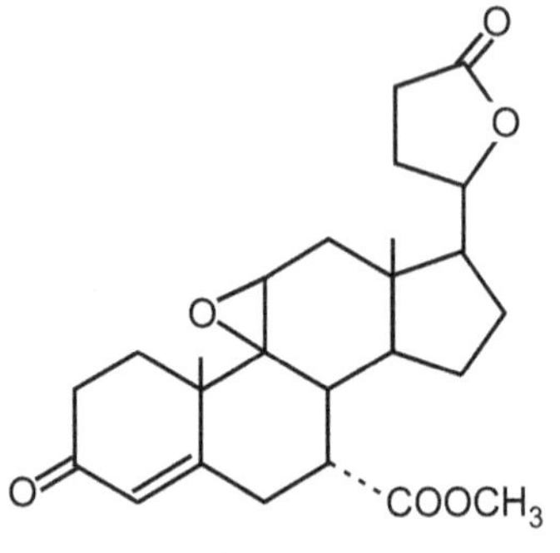

5.25 DIURETICS

Diuretic agents are usually effective in the treatment of edemas of cardiac, hepatic, renal or pulmonary origin. Some of these agents also possess mild antihypertensive activity and may be used in the treatment of hypertension with or without edema. The mean arterial pressure falls due to reduction in plasma volume and cardiac output. While a modest rise in plasma renin activity and renal vascular resistance occurs through reflex activation. Out of several classes of diuretics, agents from

 (a) thiazide diuretics

 (b) loop diuretics, and

 (c) potassium sparing diuretics

classes are usually used to increase effectiveness of primary antihypertensive agents. Thiazides are more effective antihypertensive agents than loop diuretics, while potassium sparing agents are often used as an adjunct (adjunct to long term thiazide therapy where they potentiate the diuresis and reduce the loss of potassium.) The loop diuretics (e.g., furosemide, ethacrynic acid) are reserved when thiazides fail to give expected results.

The novel successors of loop diuretic furosemide include piretanide and etozolin which possess high specificity for NaCl transport, minimum potassium ion excretion and prolonged duration of action.

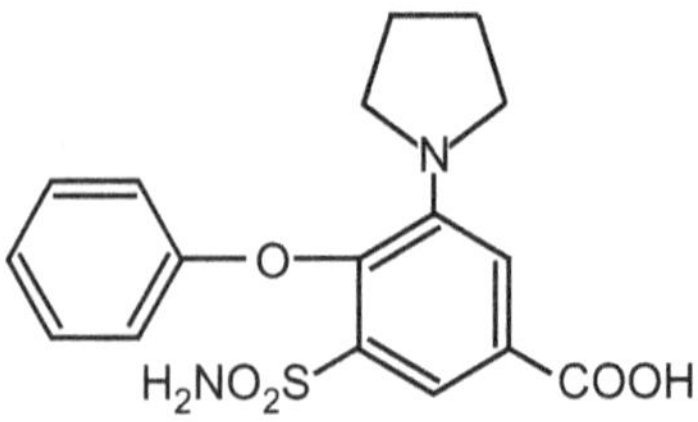

Piretanide

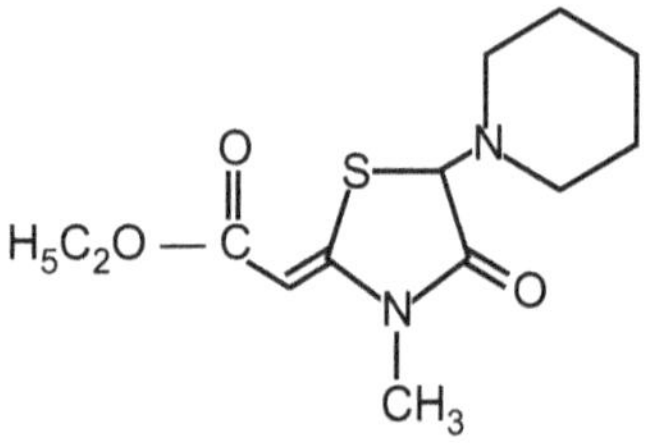

(+) Etozolin

Loop diuretics such as furosemide are the first choice in therapy of CHF. The dose should be gradually increased to limit symptoms and physical signs of edema. An alternative strategy is to occasionally use supplemental agents such as metolazone to maintain control of symptoms.

Chronic excessive doses of diuretics can worsen cardiac failure and contribute to symptoms of fatigue through electrolyte disturbances and dehydration.

Electrolyte imbalances such as hypokalemia, and hypomagnesemia can predispose the patient to arrhythmias.

Symptoms of fainting or dizziness on standing may indicate a need to review diuretic or vasodilator therapy.

5.26 CENTRAL DEPRESSANTS

A meprobamate analogue, mebutamate, lowers blood pressure by exerting depressant effect on the vasomotor centers of brain stem.

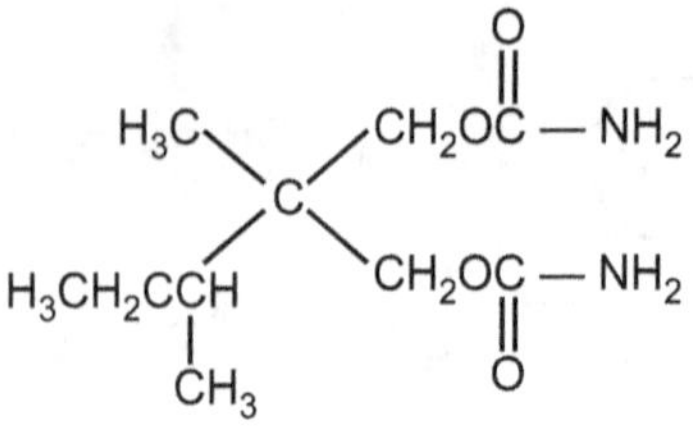

5.27 ATRIAL NATRIURETIC PEPTIDE (ANP)

Blood pressure and fluid volume homeostasis are critically dependent on regulatory peptides, such as angiotensin II which has vasoconstrictive properties, and atrial natriuretic peptide (ANP) which induces diuresis, natriuresis and a slight vasodilation. Nesiritide is a recombinant form of brain natriuretic peptide. It is a potent vasodilator used in the treatment of CCF. ANP is inactivated by neutral endopeptidases (NEP). The simultaneous inhibition of ACE and NEP may prove to be an efficient way of treating various cardiovascular diseases. Mixanpril is an example of such a dual inhibitor.

The physiological functions of ANP include,

(a) vasodilation,

(b) increased GFR and salt-water excretion (diuretic) and

(c) inhibition of the release of angiotensin - II, aldosterone and vasopression.

ANP is derived from a precursor protein produced by cardiac atrium and at lower levels by other tissues. Since ANP receptors were found to be located in smooth muscles of vascular, renal and other tissues, ANP may be considered as a potential lead to develop drugs useful in the treatment of heart failure, renal failure and oedematous conditions. The effects are expected to be mediated through guanylate cyclase.

The parent precursor, ANP preprohormone consists of 151 amino acids. ANP molecule consisting of 28 amino acid residues with numbers 99 to 126, is cleaved from the precursor. A 17 membered ring structure, necessary for biological activity is formed due to a disulfide linkage between cysteine 105 and cysteine 122.

Mixanpril : It is an orally active dual inhibitor of neutral endopeptidase and angiotensin converting enzyme. It is useful in the treatment of chronic hypertension and cardiac failure.

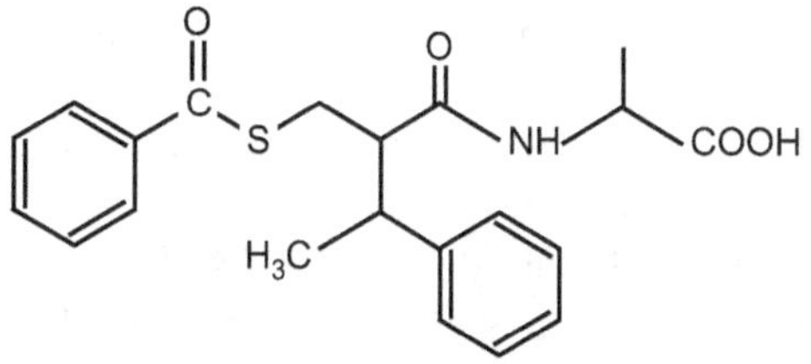

Atrial natriuretic peptide (ANP) was isolated in 1981 by De Bold, Sonnenberg, et al and was characterized as a factor for the control of hemostasis.

Treprostinil : It is a synthetic analogue of prostacyclin (PGI$_2$). It is indicated for the treatment of pulmonary arterial hypertension.

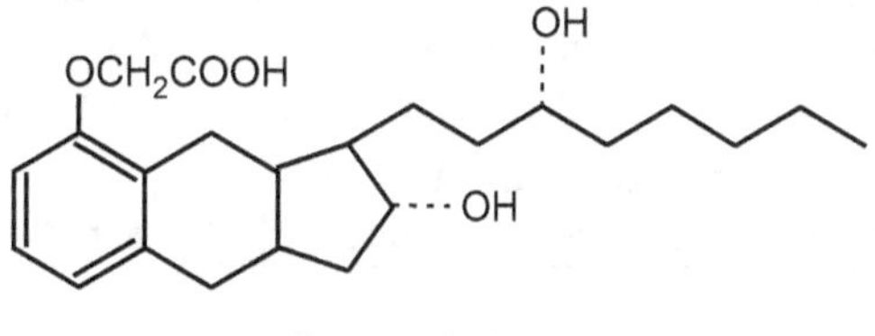

Treprostinil

Trimetaphan : This sulfonium ganglion blockers has a limited use in clinical practice (as i.v. infusion) to induce controlled hypotension in surgery to reduce bleeding.

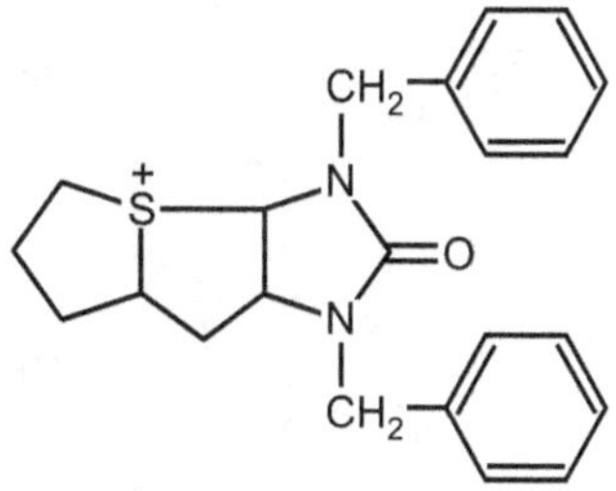

Chlorisondamine : It is nicotinic acetylcholine receptor antagonist that produces both neuronal and ganglionic blockade. It has been used as an anti-hypertensive agent.

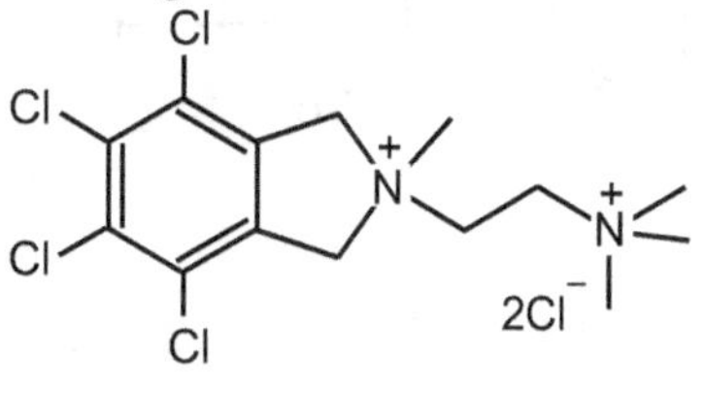

5.28 POTASSIUM CHANNEL MODULATORS

A number of drugs seems to modulate membrane K^+ - channels. Potassium channel activators cause an outward movement of K^+ ions.

The inside membrane potential becomes negative resulting into hyperpolarization. Since depolarization is not possible in such case, Ca^{++}- and Na^+ - ion channels do not open. Thus, the contractile machinery of cardiac smooth muscles remains relaxed resulting into antihypertensive effect. Relaxation of vascular smooth muscles leading to vasodilation also occurs by the same mechanism.

Nicorandil produces a marked increase in coronary blood flow. A negative inotropic effect is observed at therapeutic concentrations. Besides increasing outward membrane K^+ conductance in vascular smooth muscles, nicorandil activates guanylate cyclase, resulting into reduced intracellular Ca^{++} concentration.

All the examples given in the table below do not share the common parent skeleton. For example, the parent skeleton in BRL 34915 is β-ethanolamine, in nicorandil it is nicotinic acid and aminopyridine in pinacidil.

Cromakalim, nicorandil and pinacidil relax bronchial smooth muscles. Hence, these drugs may have potential as novel anti-asthmatic agents.

Cromakalim is the first antihypertensive agent shown to act exclusively through potassium channel activation. It increases the outward movement of potassium ions through channels in the membranes of vascular smooth muscle cells, leading to its relaxation. Cromakalim is an outcome of an effort to dissociate β-blockade activity from antihypertensive activity. The molecule was designed to put conformation restriction in the flexible open chain β-blocking agents.

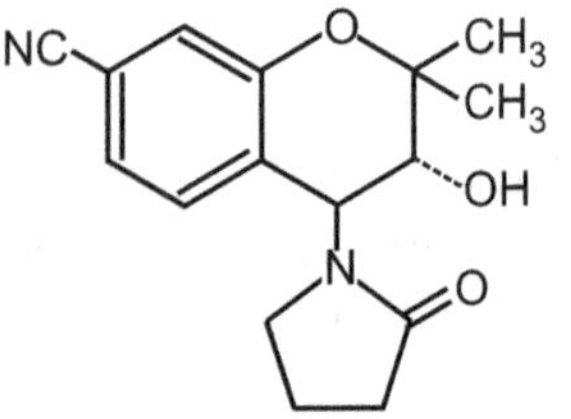

BRL 34915 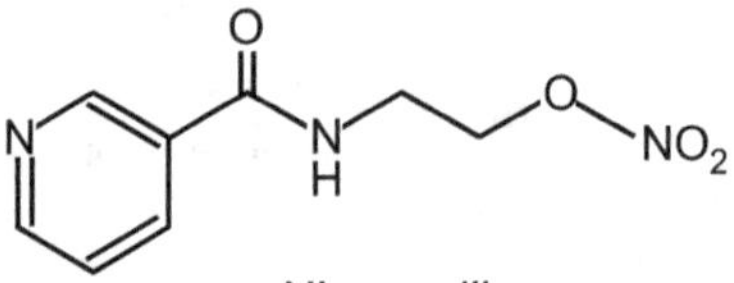   Nicorandil 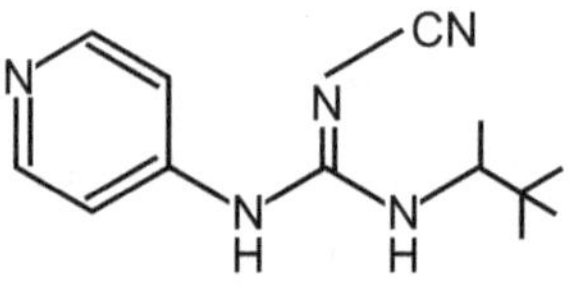   Pinacidil

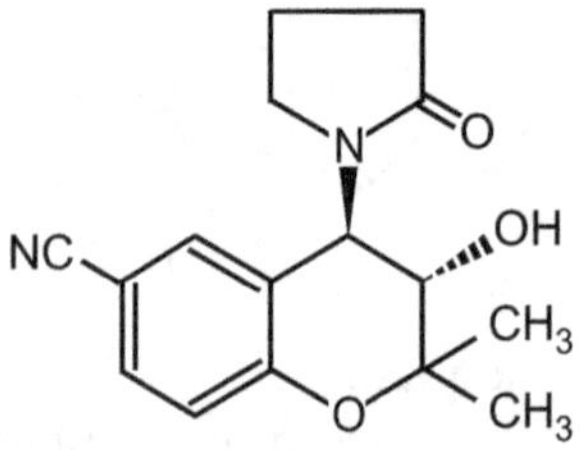

Cromakalim 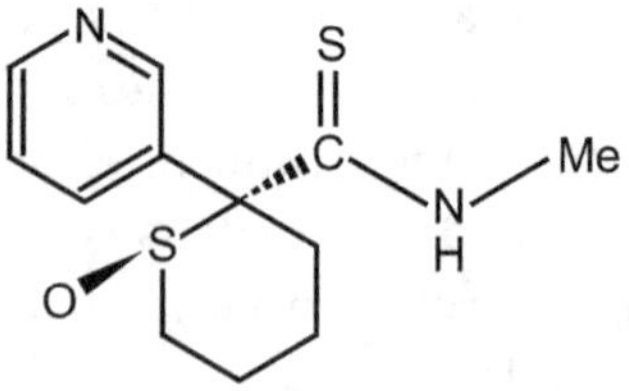   Aprikalim

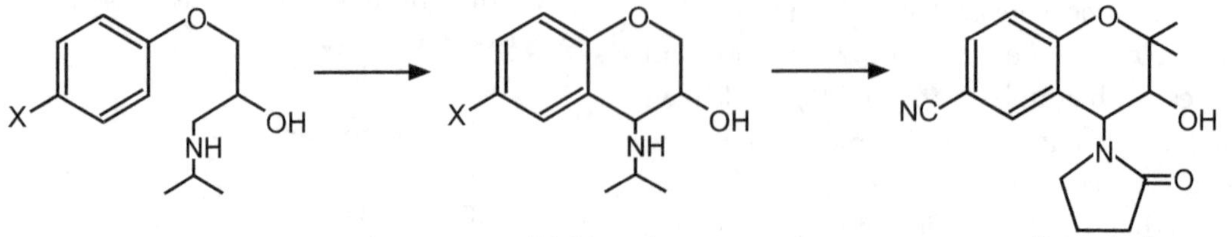

β-blocking agents   Rigid analog   Cromakalim

Table 5.6 : Side effects of commonly used categories of antihypertensive agents

Category	Side effects	Category	Side effects
Diuretics	Incontinence, muscle weakness, confusion, dizziness, gout	Digitalis glycosides	Anorexia, nausea, visual disturbances, diarrhoea, confusion, deterioration or social withdrawal
ACE inhibitors	Hypotension, dizziness, cough, taste disturbance, sore throat, rashes, tingling in hands, joint pains	Potassium salts	Gastrointestinal disturbances, swallowing difficulty, diarrhoea, tiredness, limb weakness.
Nitrates	Headache, hypotension, dizziness, flushing of face/neck GI upset		

Structures of Renin Inhibitors

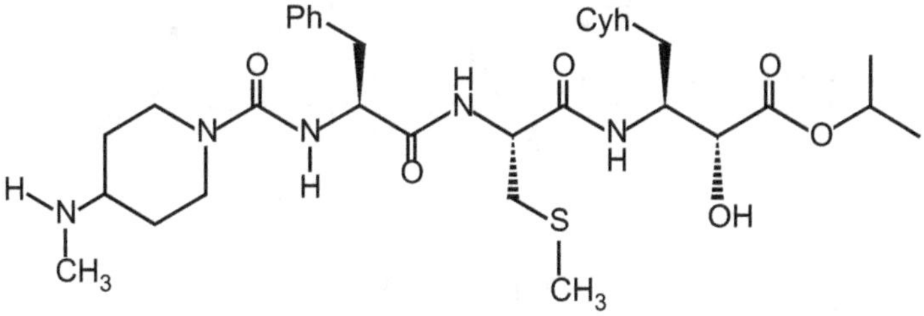

CP - 108, 671

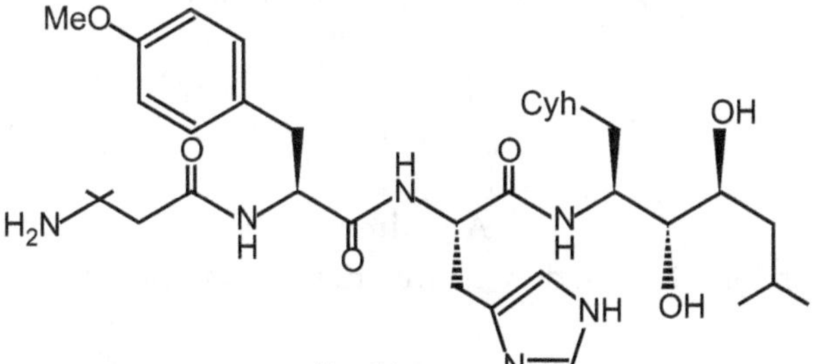

Enalkiren

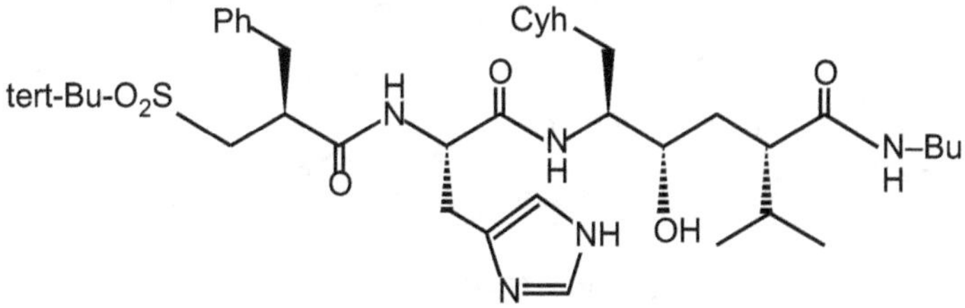

CGP 38560A

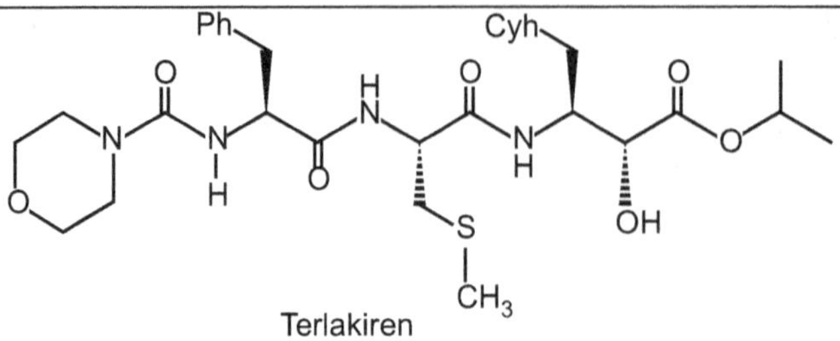

Terlakiren

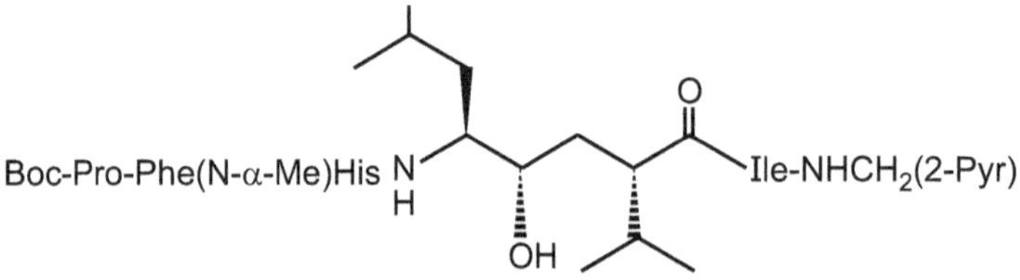

Boc-Pro-Phe(N-α-Me)His

Ditekiren

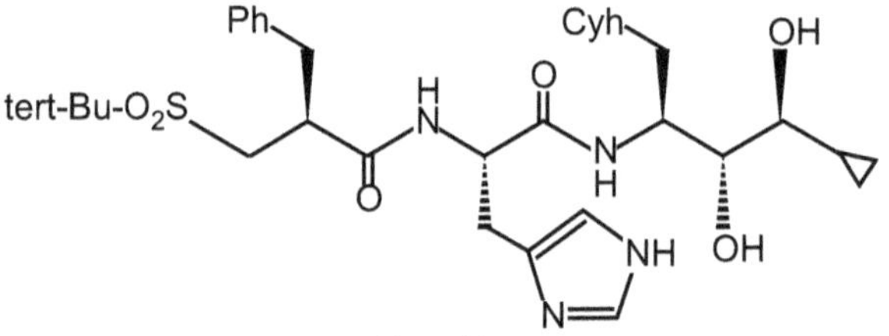

Remikiren

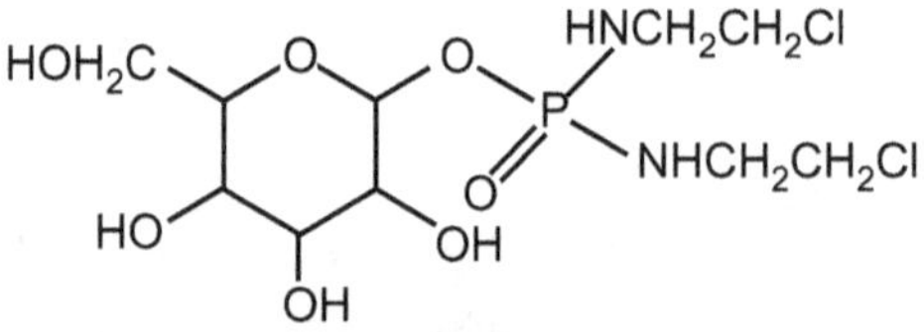

Aliskiren

(It is a renin inhibitor used in the treatment of essential hypertension.)

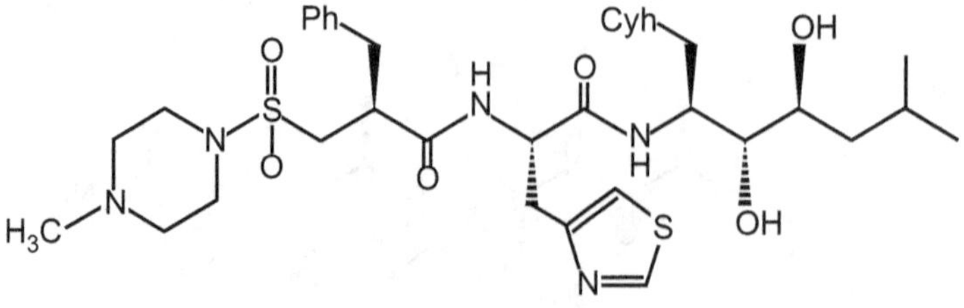

Zankiren (A-72517)

Cyh = cyclohexyl; 2-Pyr = 2-pyridinyl; 3-Pyr = 3-pyridinyl

Structures of dual acting hybrid antihypertensive agents

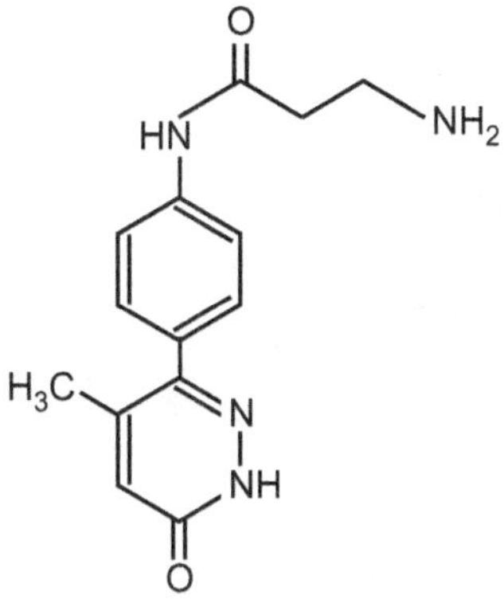

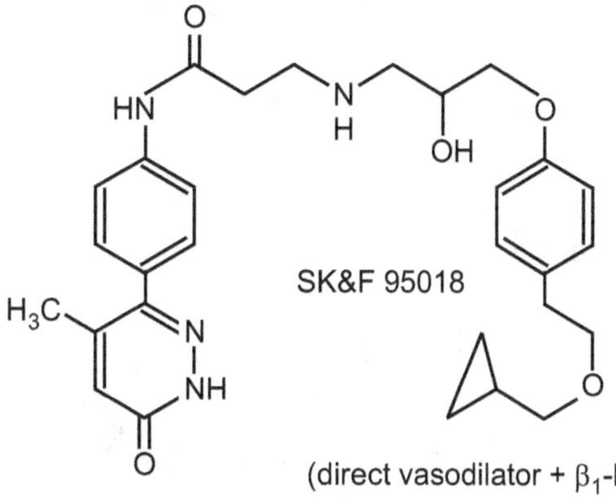

SK&F 95018

(direct vasodilator + β_1-blocker)

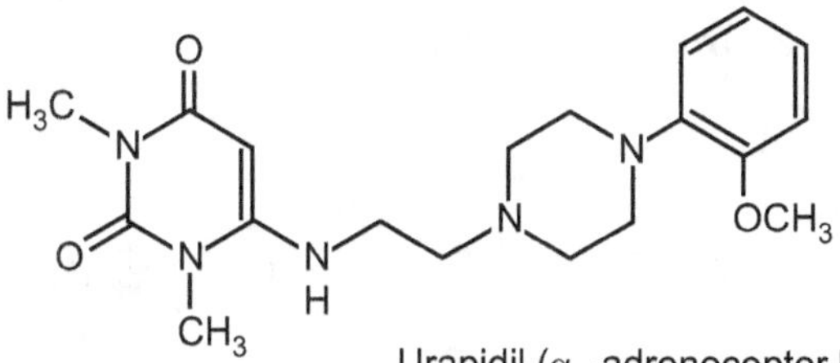

Urapidil (α_1-adrenoceptor blocker +5-HT-agonist)

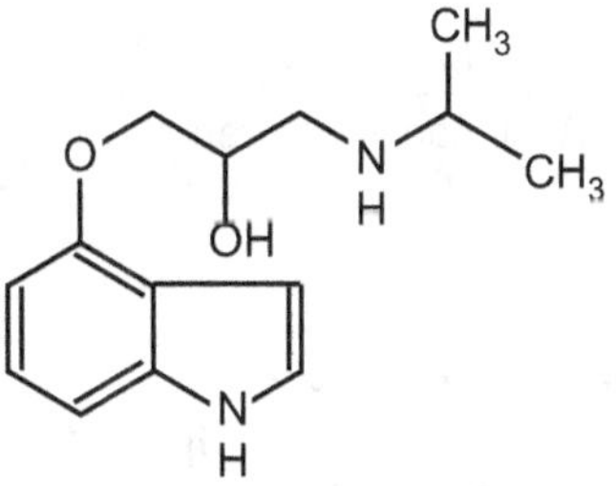

Pindolol

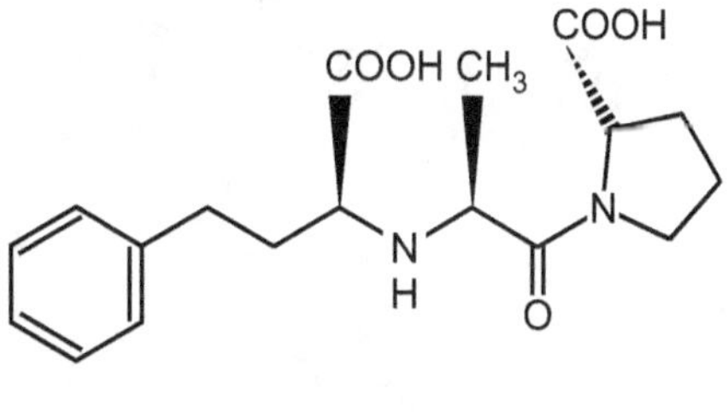

Enalapril

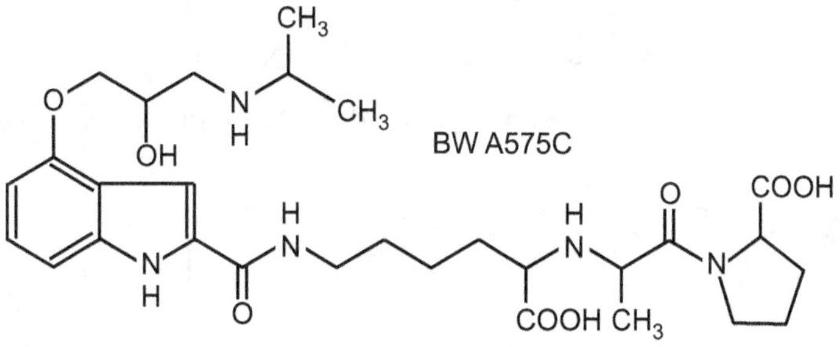

BW A575C

Hybrid of Pindolol and Enalapril

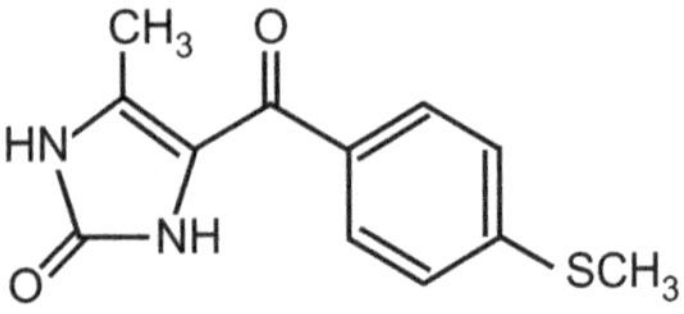

Enoximone

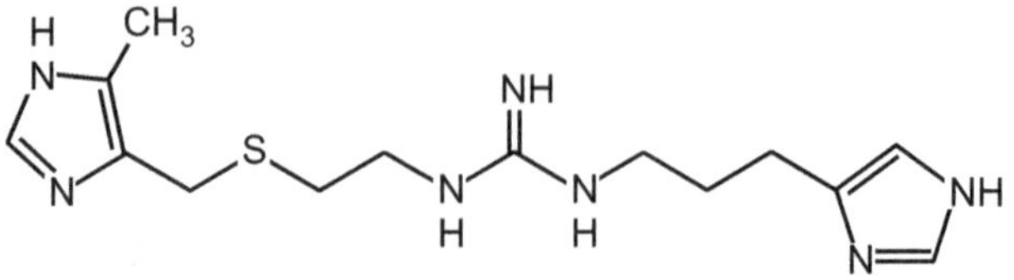

Impromidine

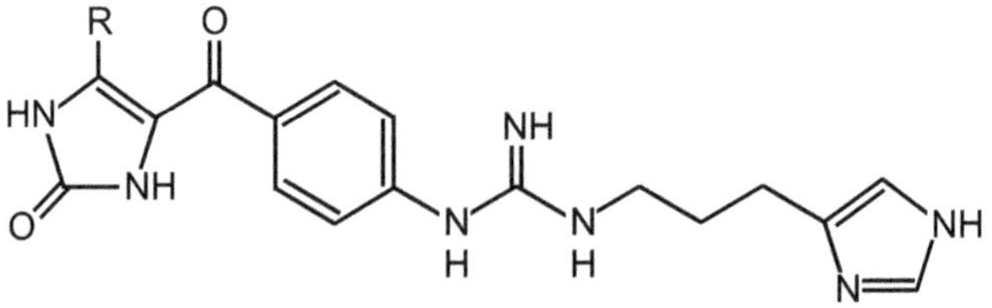

Hybrid of Enoximone and Impromidine

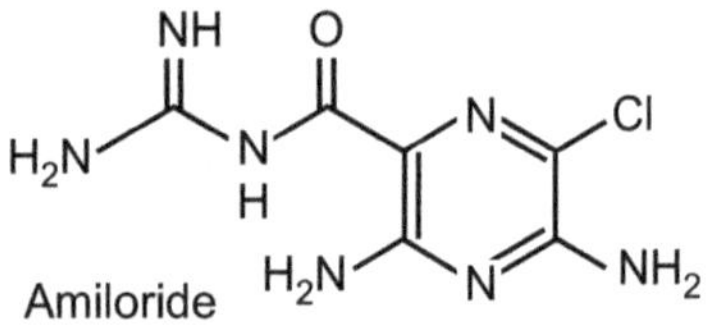

Amiloride

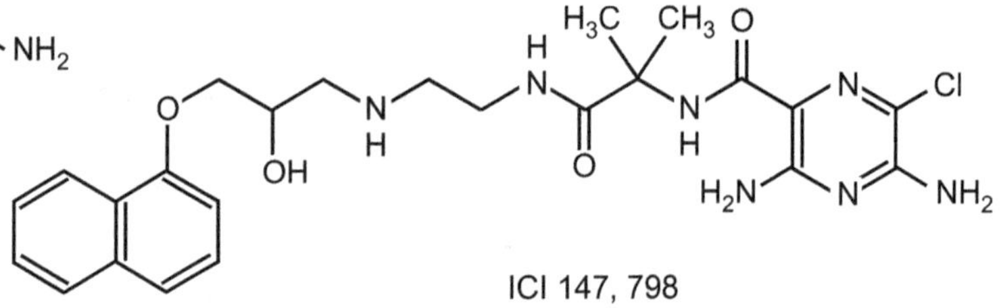

ICI 147, 798
(Amiloride + Propranolol)

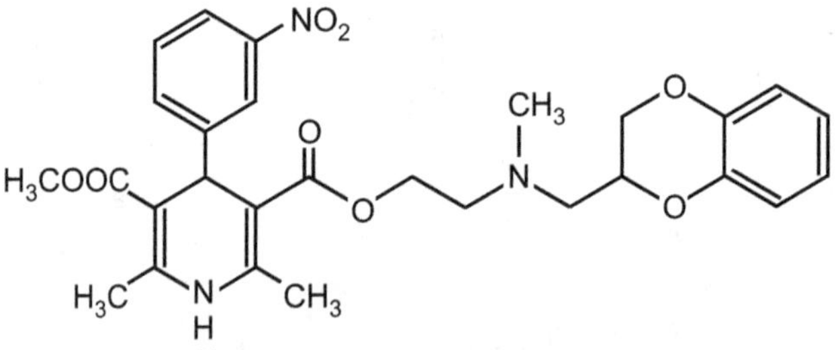

(Ca^{++} - channel blocker + Benzodioxan)

Nebivolol : It is a β_1-receptor blocker with nitric oxide potentiating effect used in the treatement of hypertension.

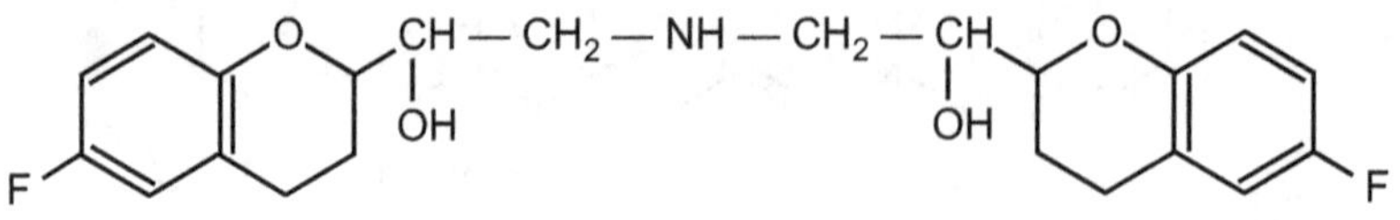

Nebivolol

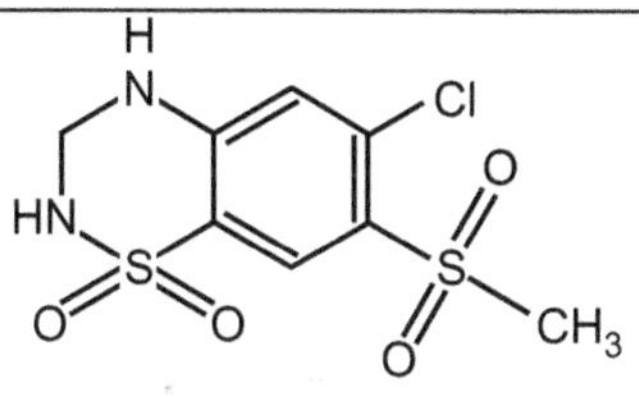

Hydrochlorothiazide

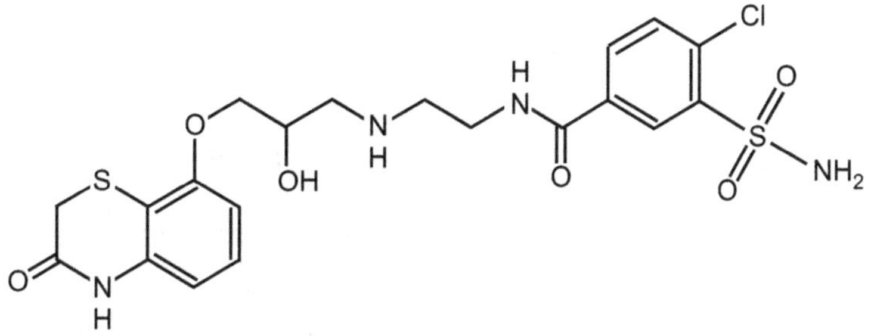

Diuretic + β_1-blocker

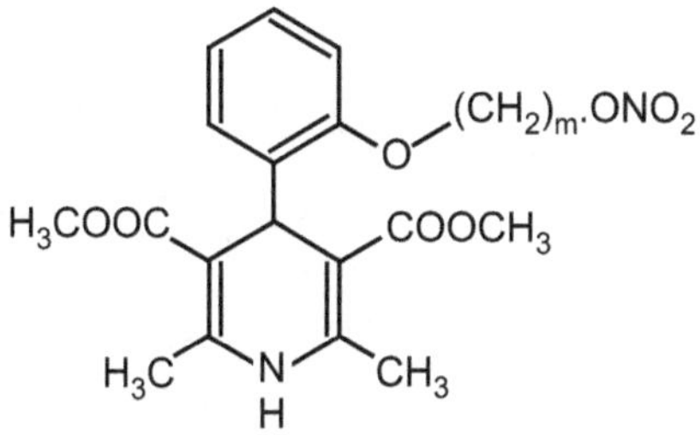

(1, 4-dihydropyridine
+ nitrate ester)

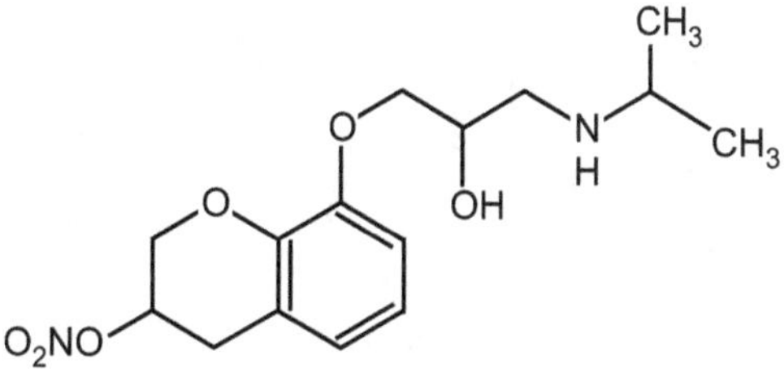

$(CH_2)_m \cdot ONO_2$

Nipradilol

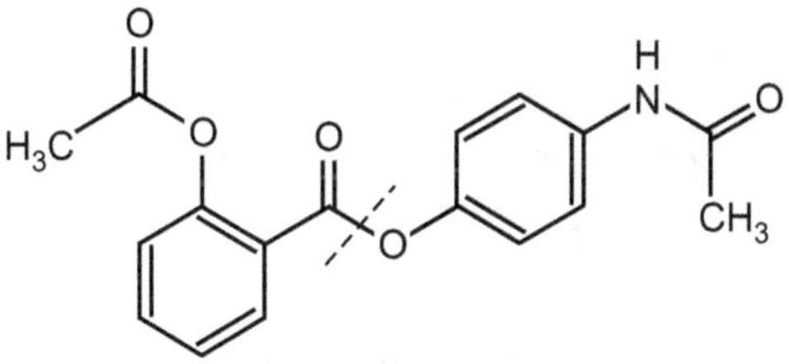

Benorilate

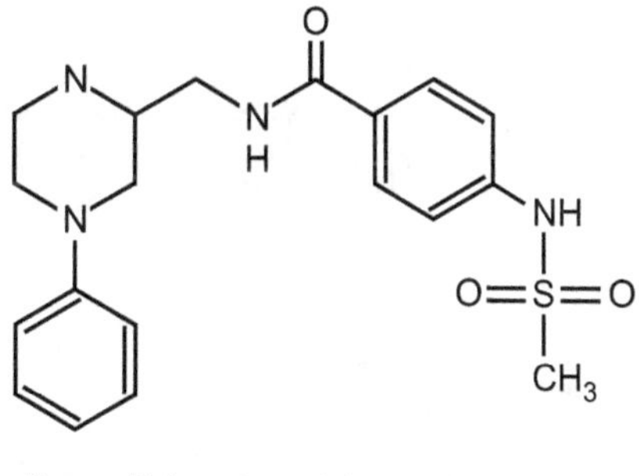

Sematilide + 1-arylpiperazine derivative

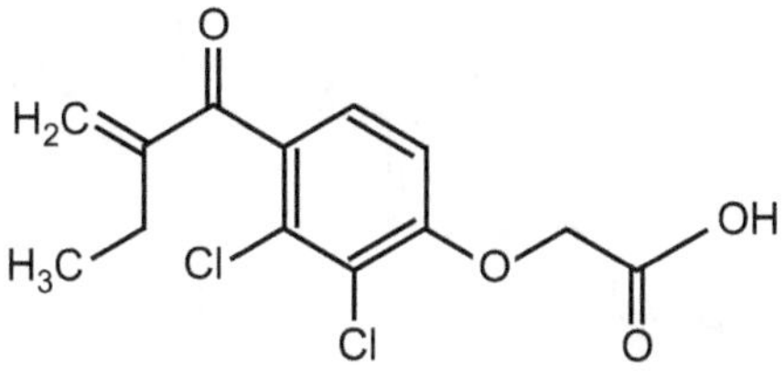

Ethacrynic acid

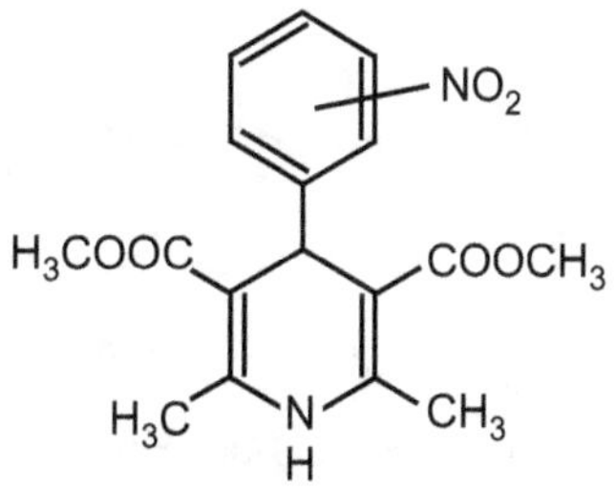

Nifedipine analogue

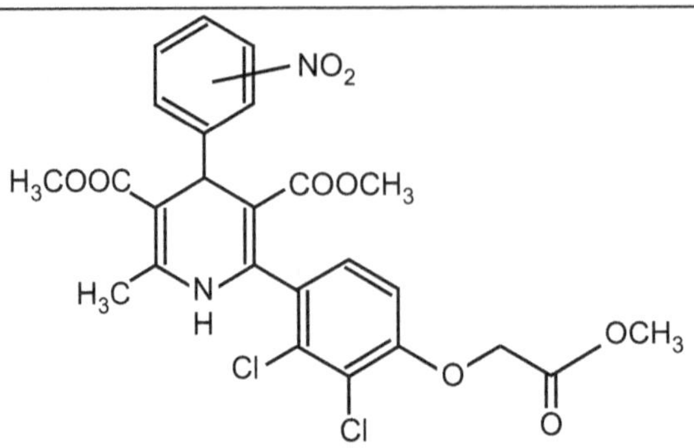

Vasodilator + Diuretic

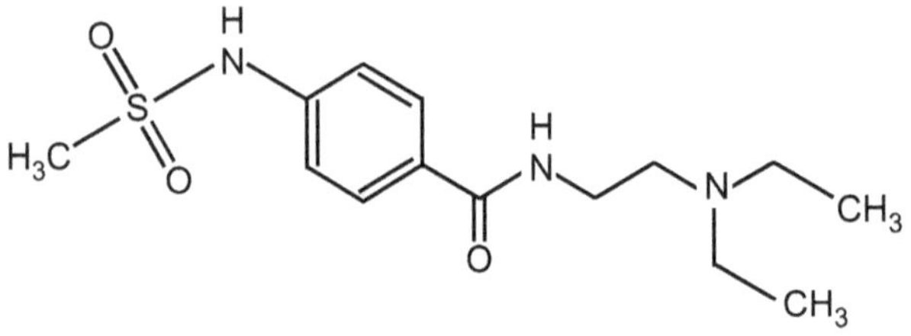

Sematilide

K$^{\pm}$ channel Blocker

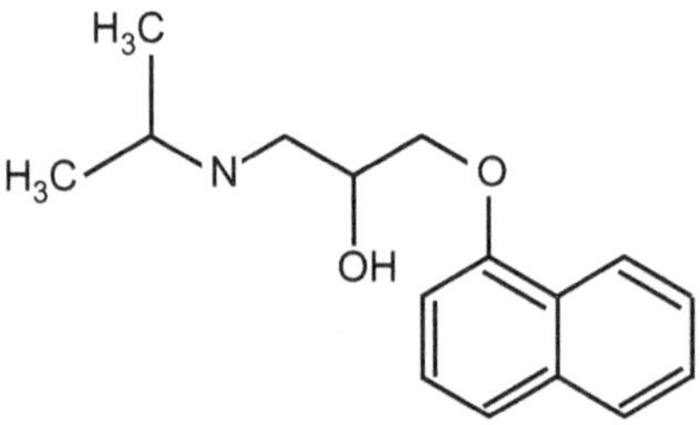

Propranolol

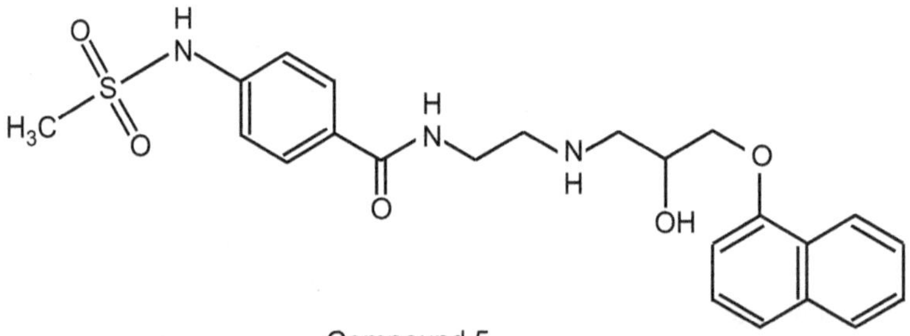

Compound 5
(Potassium channel blocker + β$_1$ - blocker)

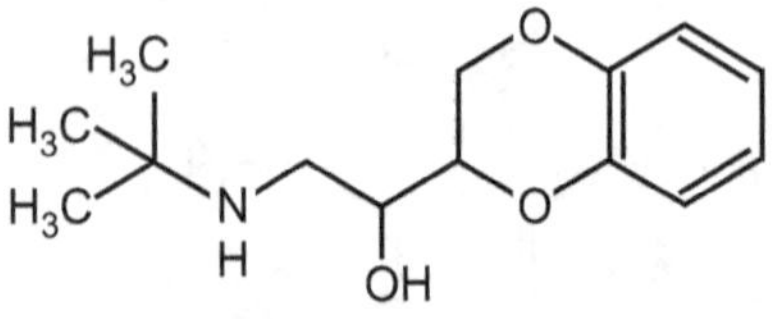

Benzodioxane β-blocker

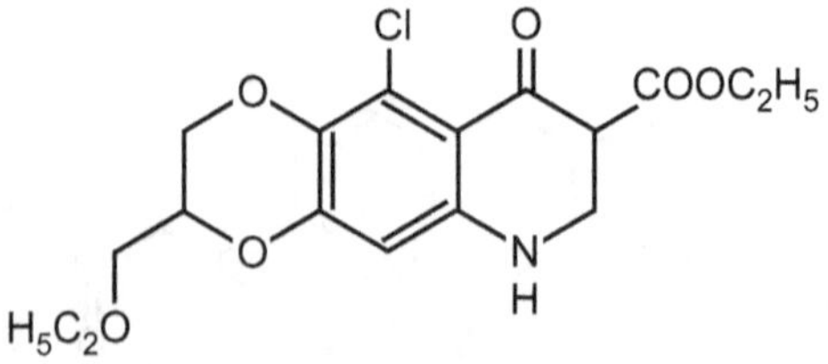

Quincarbate

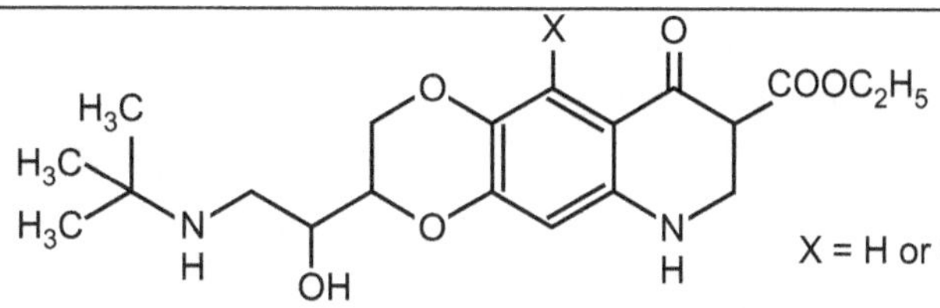

X = H or Cl

Diuretic + β-blocer

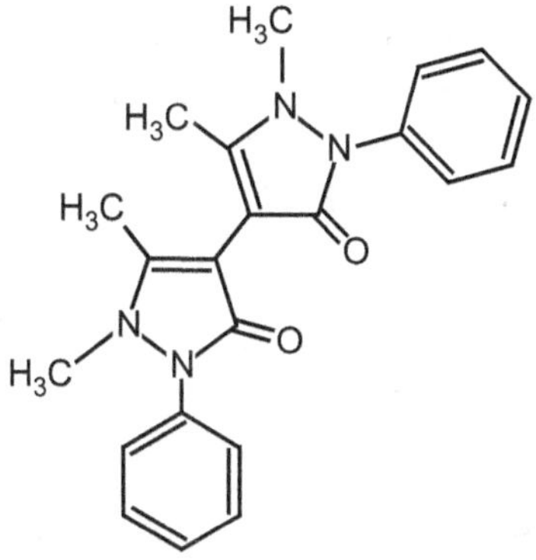

Forbisen

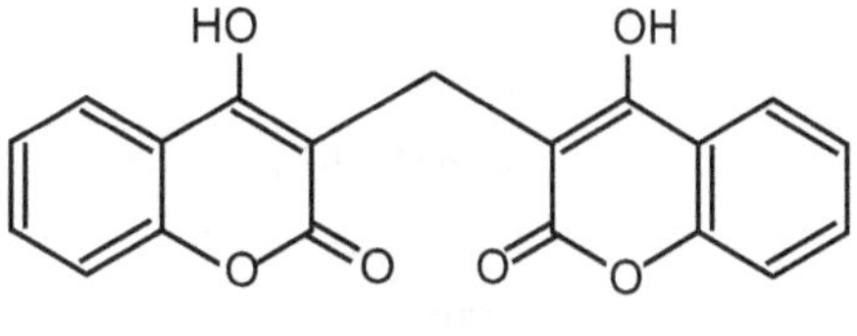

Dicoumarol

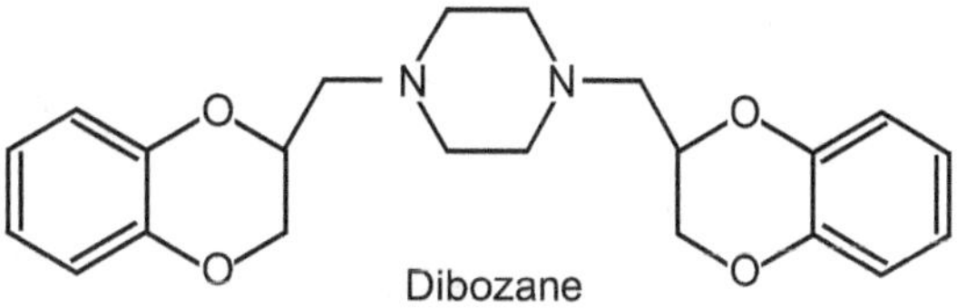

Dibozane

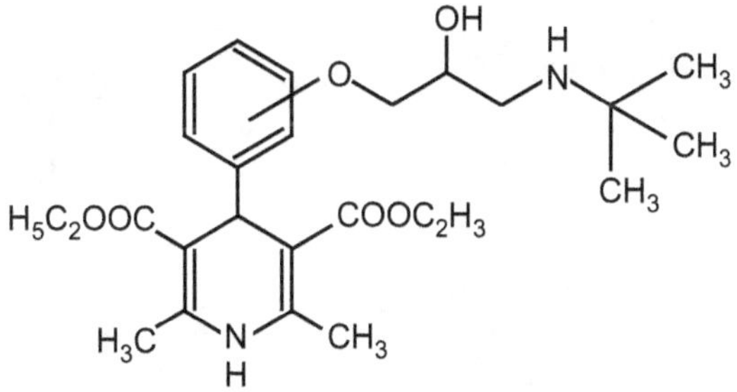

Vasodilator + β$_1$-blocker

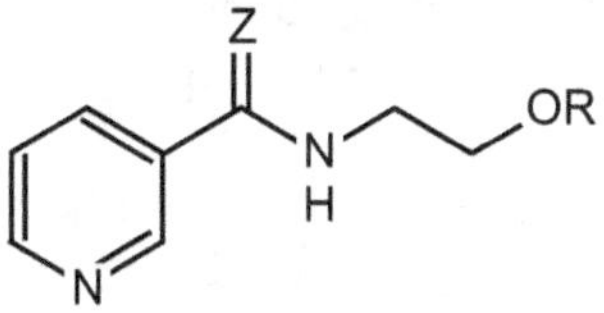

KRN2391	Z = NCN; R = NO$_2$
Ki 3315	Z = NCN; R = H
Nicorandil	Z = O; R = NO$_2$

Vasodilator + Potassium channel activator

Levosimendan : It is a positive inotropic agent with vasodilatory activity. It is used for inotropic support in acutely decompensated severe congestive heart failure.

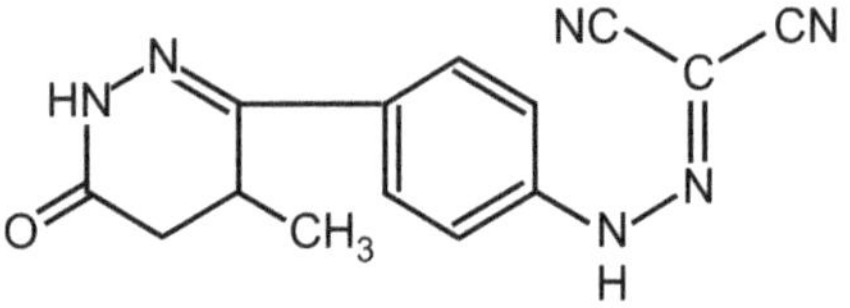

Levosimendan

Fausidil : It is a potent Rho-kinase inhibitor and vasodilator. It is used in the treatment of cerebral vasospasm and stroke victims.

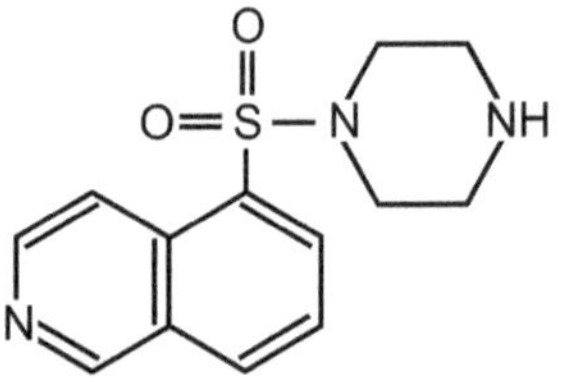

Fausidil

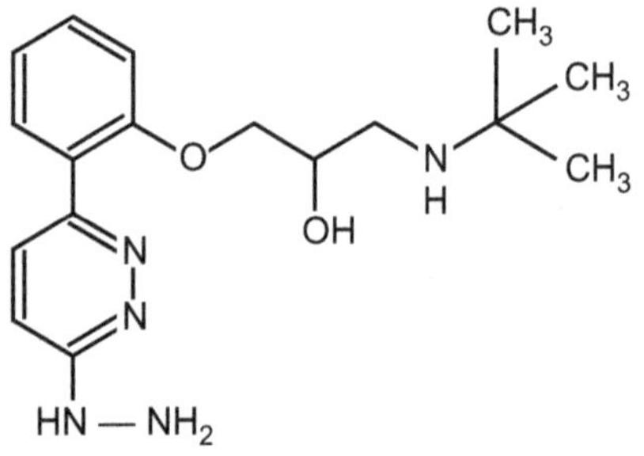

Prizidilol

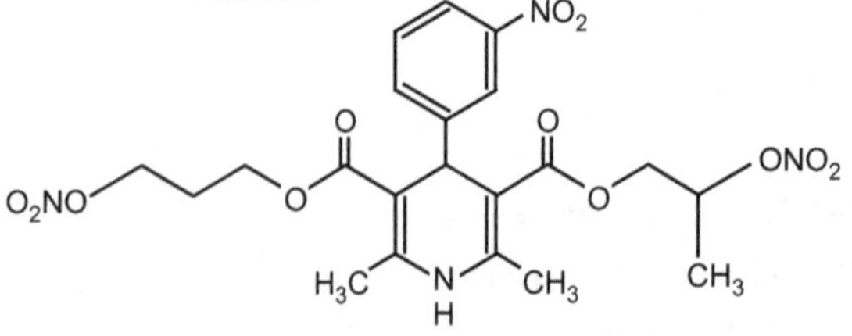

CD – 349

Bosentan : It is a competitive antagonist of endothelin, a substance that narrows blood vessels and elevate blood pressure. It is mainly used for the treatment of pulmonary hypertension.

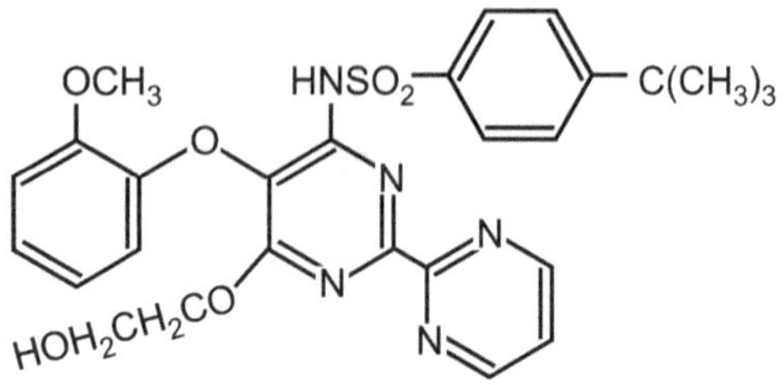

Bosentan

Flunarizine : It is a non-selective Ca^{++}-channel blocker with calmodulin binding properties and histamine H_1-blocking activity. It is used in the prophylaxis of migraine, occlusive peripheral vascular disease and as adjunct in the therapy of epilepsy.

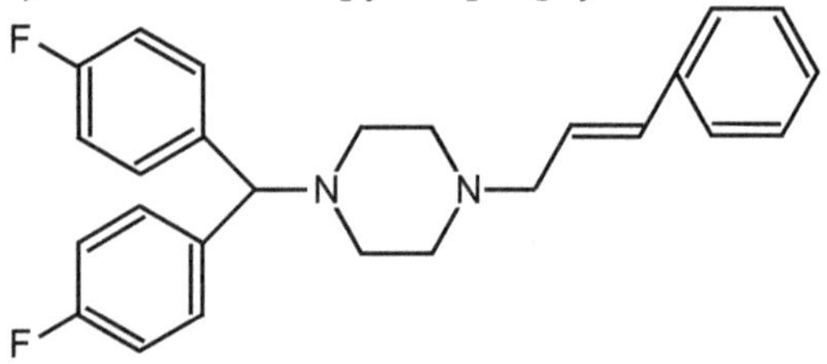

Flunarizine

Fenoldopam : It is a benzazepine derivative which acts as a peripheral D_1 receptor partial agonist. It is used as an antihypertensive agent.

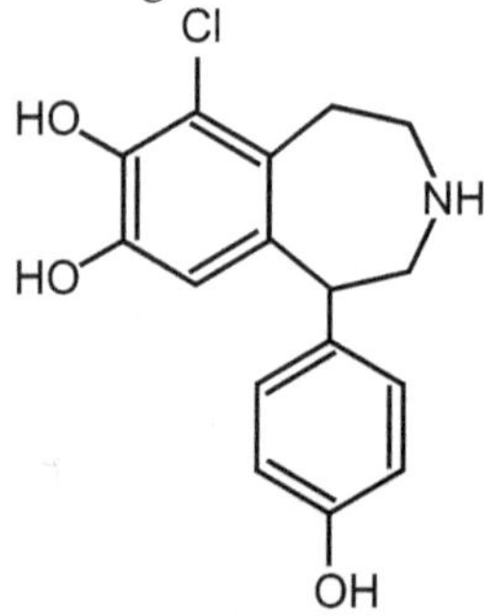

Fenoldopam

Dorzolamide : It is a carbonic anhydrate inhibitor used to lower intraocular pressure in open angle glaucoma and ocular hypertension. It is the **first drug resulted from structure based drug design.**

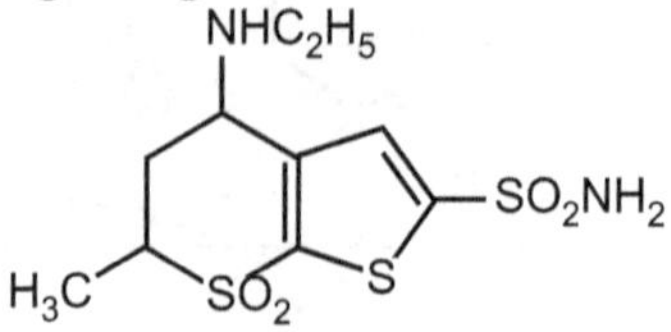

Dorzolamide

5.29 LIPID LOWERING AGENTS

Carbohydrates, proteins and fats are the body fuels which provide necessary energy for growth, maintenance and functioning of various organs in human body. Besides acting as the major form of energy storage, fatty acids are also involved in the formation of cell membranes. For example, phospholipids are the essential constituents of a variety of cell membranes. Plasma cholesterol can be freely utilized in the synthesis of various endogenous steroids and nerve cell membranes. Except plasma cholesterol, rest of the body lipids are catabolised to give carbon dioxide and water as end products, while bile acids are the ultimate end products of cholesterol catabolism. Only a small fraction of these bile acids is excreted through faeces while rest is reabsorbed by the enterohepatic circulation. The shedding of epithelial cells from the gut and skin offers the major route of cholesterol excretion. Atherosclerosis, thrombosis, myocardial infarction and pancreatitis are the clinical manifestations of elevated plasma lipid level. The term, hyper-lipidemia denotes an elevated plasma cholesterol and / or plasma triglyceride level while the term, hyper-lipoproteinemias are the conditions in which there is elevated plasma concentration of cholesterol or triglyceride containing lipoproteins. The term lipoprotein was first coined in 1929 by Macheboeuf of Pasteur institute to denote lipoidal macromolecular complexes.

5.30 TYPES OF LIPOPROTEINS

There are separate mechanisms for the transport of lipids from exogenous (i.e. dietary origin) and endogenous (i.e. of hepatic origin) sources. The dietary triglycerides are hydrolysed to monoglycerides and free fatty acids by pancreatic lipase in the intestinal lumen. These dietary triglycerides and cholesterol are trapped by chylomicrons which are large lipoprotein particles having diameter ranging 80 - 500 nm. Lipoproteins contain a hydrophobic lipid filled core surrounded by a monolayer of amphiphilic lipids and specific proteins i.e. apoproteins. The hydrophobic core acts as the storage package for triglyceride and cholesteryl esters. Apo-proteins are categorised into 5 types, like A, B, C, D and E. Almost 6 classes of lipoproteins are identified in the human body which are involved in the transport of lipids from their sites of absorption and synthesis to the tissues where they are utilized. Size, density and the nature of apoprotein in the lipoprotein are the probable points utilized in the classification of lipoproteins. They are categorised as :

(a) Chylomicrons :

These are the largest species of triglyceride rich lipoproteins which are involved in the transportation of dietary fat from gut. These are secreted into the lymph and contain apoprotein A and B-48.

(b) Very low density lipoproteins (VLDL) :

These are globular particles synthesized in the liver having diameter of 30-80 nm. They contain apoproteins B, C and E. They are involved in the transport of endogenous lipid from liver to the plasma.

(c) Intermediate density lipoproteins (IDL) :

These are the lipoproteins obtained when the triglyceride content of VLDL are partially digested in capillaries by the action of extra-hepatic lipoprotein lipase. They have a diameter of 20 - 35 nm.

(d) Low density lipoproteins (LDL) :

Due to further action of lipoprotein lipase on IDL in the circulation, most of the remaining triglyceride content of IDL is digested resulting into the loss of apoproteins

C and E from their structure. The density of particle is increased and diameter is brought down to 18 - 28 nm. These particles are now termed as LDL which consist of cholesterol, phospholipid and apoprotein B - 100. LDL also contains B - 74 and B - 26. They have longest plasma half-life of about 1.5 days amongst the lipoproteins.

LDL Particles are finally delivered to hepatic and certain extrahepatic tissues for further lysosomal degradation to release the cholesterol which can be utilized in cell membrane formation.

(e) High density lipoproteins (HDL) :

This is a group of heterogeneous lipoproteins having low lipid content. A further subclassification in HDL is based upon density value of these particles. HDL apparently enhances the removal of cholesterol from the arterial wall. Hence, chances of development of atherosclerotic lesions are more when HDL value falls below normal. While the elevated levels of VLDL, IDL and LDL are always correlated with increased risk of atherosclerosis.

5.31 LIPOPROTEIN TRANSPORT MACHINERY

Chylomicrons are the lipoproteins that trap the dietary triglycerides and cholesterol from the intestinal lumen and cross the intestinal mucosal cells to enter into circulation. In the adipose tissue and muscle, the chylomicrons are partly digested by lipoprotein lipase enzymes present in vascular endothelium resulting into fatty acids (i.e., hydrolysis products of triglycerides).

These fatty acids then enter into underlying adipocytes or muscle cells where re-esterification to triglycerides occurs. The newly formed triglycerides are carried by the lymph and then by the blood to various body tissues for either storage or for utilization as a source of energy.

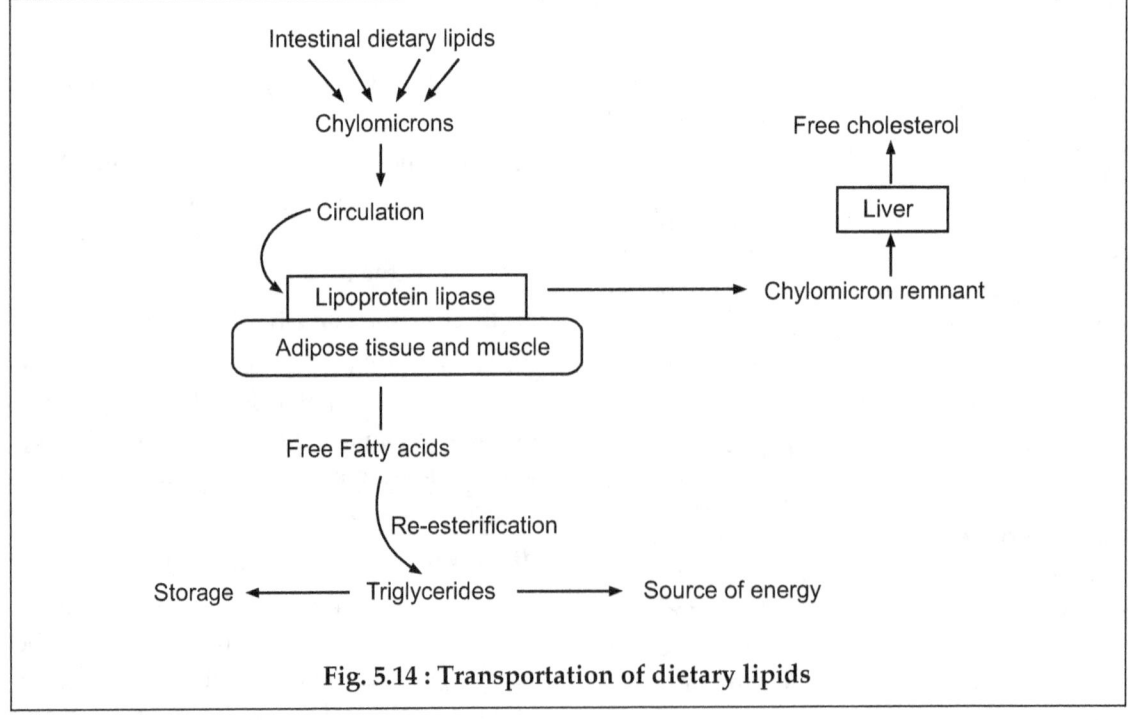

Fig. 5.14 : Transportation of dietary lipids

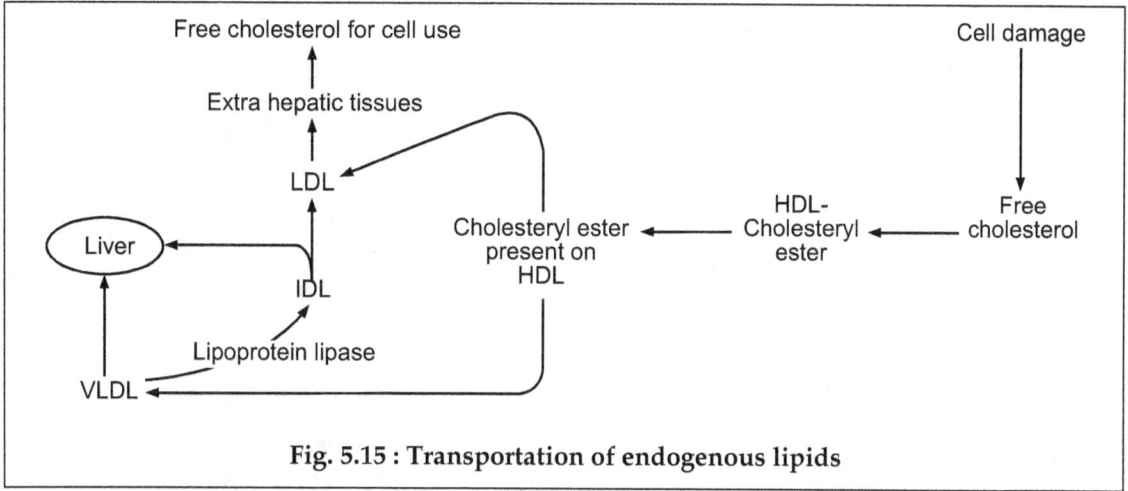

Fig. 5.15 : Transportation of endogenous lipids

The remaining small fraction of triglyceride in the partly digested chylomicrons (now termed as chylomicron remnant, diameter 30 - 50 nm) is digested by hepatic lysosomal enzymes to generate free cholesterol. The transportation of endogenous (hepatic origin) lipids is quite similar to the transportation of exogenous (dietary) lipids. Liver releases triglycerides and cholesterol into circulation by packing them into the core of very low density lipoproteins (VLDL). Due to the partial digestion of VLDL by lipoprotein lipase enzymes present in the vascular endothelium, VLDL is then converted into intermediate density lipoprotein (IDL). Some of IDL particles are recycled through liver to get back VLDL while rest of them are further digested to give low density lipoproteins (LDL).

These particles may be taken up by lysosomes present in the hepatic cells by the activation of LDL-receptors bound to the cell surfaces. The LDL particles thus taken up by receptor mediated endocytosis, is digested to liberate free cholesterol for cell use. Hence, an elevation in the level of circulating LDL particles may be seen in defective LDL-receptor mechanisms.

Some LDL particles are also taken up in certain extrahepatic tissues by receptor mediated endocytosis process to release free cholesterol. Thus, LDL particles in the circulation act as the storage depot for major amount of body cholesterol.

The cholesterol released during the degeneration of cells in tissue damage is taken up by high density lipoproteins (HDL) where re-esterification with long chain fatty acid occur. The resulting cholesteryl esters are then handed over to VLDL or LDL particles by cholesteryl ester transfer protein in plasma. These VLDL or LDL particles loaded with cholesteryl esters, then deliver their content into the liver. Thus, cholesterol conservation is maintained.

5.32 HYPERLIPOPROTEINEMIA

Hyperlipoproteinemia is usually characterized by elevated plasma concentration of VLDL (mostly triglycerides) and / or of LDL (mostly cholesterol). The condition may arise mainly due to inherent genetic defect in the catabolism of various lipoproteins or due to presence of such diseases which induce generalised metabolic disturbances.

Accordingly, hyperlipoproteinemia may be categorised as :

(a) Primary Hyperlipoproteinemia :

Here the genetic abnormalities in the person are usually responsible. If it arises due to single gene defect, it is known as monogenic hyperlipoproteinemia. While if multiple gene defects along with non-genetic factors (i.e. obesity, high fat-riched diet) are involved, then it is known as multifactorial or polygenic hyperlipopro-teinemia. Examples of primary hyperlipoproteinemia include -

(i) Abetalipoproteinemia :

It is an inherited genetic disorder chara-cterised by the absence of chylomicrons, VLDL and LDL. The deficiency of all these apobeta-lipoproteins leads to deficiency of vitamin E and malabsorption of triglycerides.

(ii) Familial lipoprotein lipase deficiency disorder :

As the name indicates, it is a familial (i.e., genetic) deficiency of lipoprotein lipase enzyme.

(iii) Familial type III hyperlipo-proteinemia (dysbeta-lipoproteinemia) :

The E-3 and E-4 isoforms of apolipoprotein E are absent resulting into an accumulation of remnant particles in the plasma.

(iv) Familial hypercholesterolemia :

Due to deficiency of LDL - receptor sites on the cell membrane, hepatic catabolism of LDL-particles decreases. This leads to elevation in the plasma LDL levels.

(b) Secondary Hyperlipoproteinemia :

Elevated levels of VLDL, IDL and LDL particles are seen under certain diseased conditions. For example, diabetes mellitus, uremia, corticosteroid excess, hypothyroidism, chronic alcoholism, nephrosis, glycogen storage abnormalities, acromegaly, obesity etc. induce metabolic abnormalities and increase the risk factor for atherosclerosis. The elevated levels of VLDL and / or LDL particles, hence can be brought to normal range by treating these underlying secondary causes along with the dietary control. Dietary therapy is always the beneficial step for all lipoprotein disorders which minimizes the concentration of lipids in the plasma and it should be strictly observed even if drug therapy has begun.

5.33 DRUG THERAPY OF HYPERLIPOPROTEINEMIA

Atherosclerosis, ischemia and acute pan-creatitis are some of the clinical manifestations of hyperlipoproteinemia. During elevated levels of triglycerides (in the range of 300 - 800 mg/dl) and plasma cholesterol (about 150 - 200 mg/dl), the risk factor for above diseases is likely to increase. It is the elevated level of VLDL and / or LDL particles which is responsible for it. However, the elevated HDL particles (which participates into transport of excess plasma cholesterol into liver) offers safeguard against above conditions and leads to decrease in the risk of coronary atherosclerosis. Diet and weight control are the first line treatment of all patients with high cholesterol or triglyceride blood levels (hyperlipidaemia). However, there are patients who do not respond adequately to non-drug management.

Various drugs used in the treatment of hyperlipoproteinemia may act either by lowering the plasma level of VLDL or LDL particles. Persons with elevations of both VLDL and LDL levels may require combination therapy. These drugs show synergistic effect when used in the combination therapy. On occasions, combination treatment with reduced doses of both drugs is more effective than a single agent with fewer adverse effects.

Table 5.7 : Some clinically used lipid lowering agents

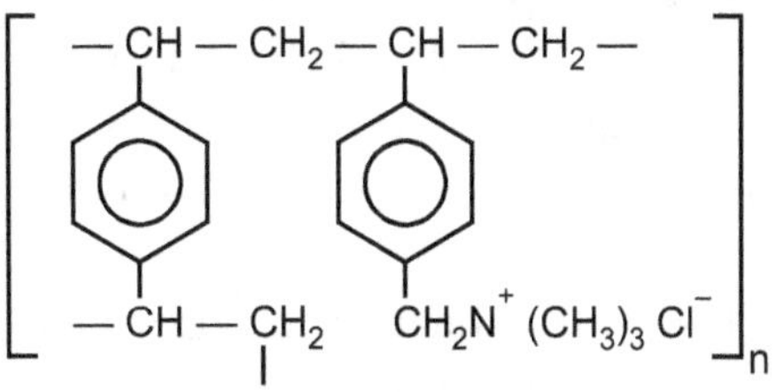

Cholestyramine Resin

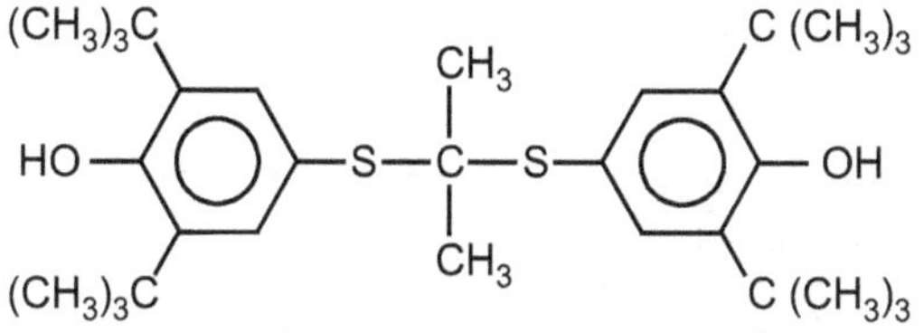

Probucol

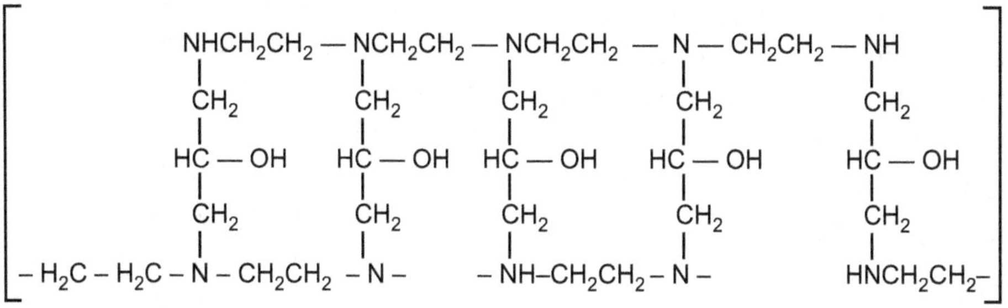

Colestipol

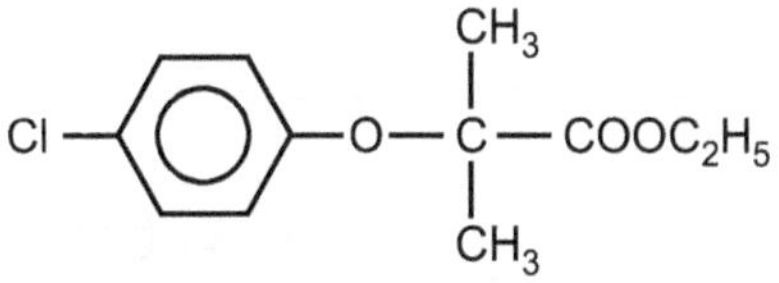

Clofibrate (Ethyl clofibrate)

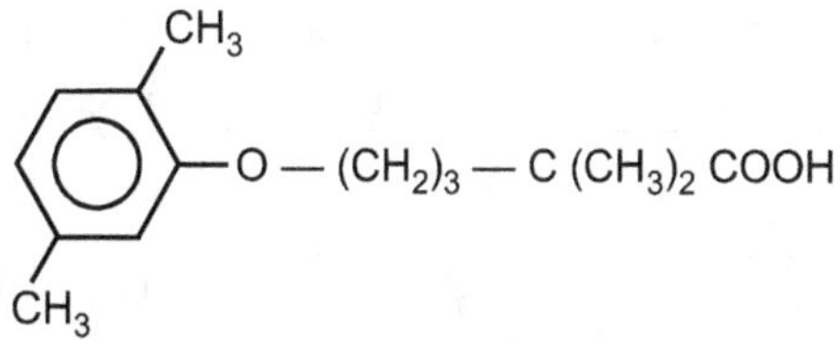

Gemfibrozil

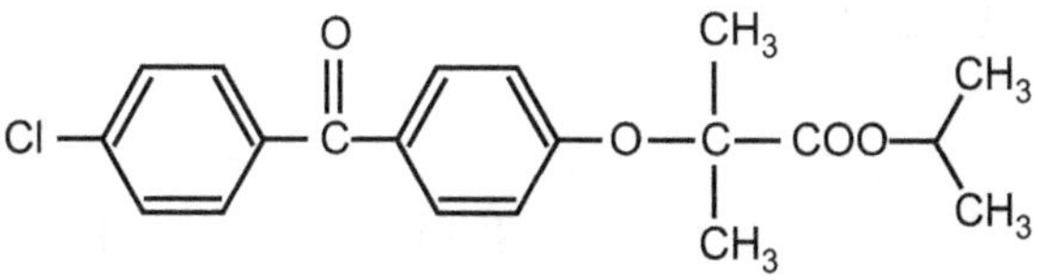

Fenofibrate (2005)

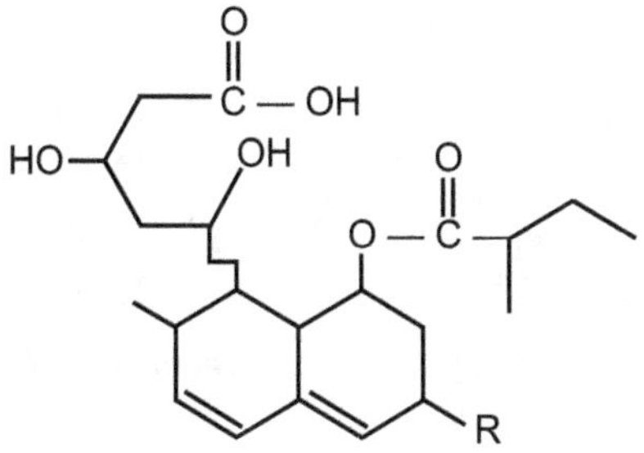

Compactin : R = – H

Mevinolin : R = – CH$_3$

Various drugs used in the treatment of hyperlipoproteinemia may be categorised as,

(A) drugs that act by lowering the plasma LDL level,

(B) drugs that act by lowering the plasma VLDL level,

(C) drugs that act by lowering both, LDL and VLDL level, and

(D) miscellaneous lipid lowering agents.

Since LDL level is primarily related with cholesterol liberation, category A drugs affect mostly cholesterol. Similarly, category B drugs affect mostly triglycerides.

[A] Drugs that Act by Lowering the Plasma LDL Level :

(i) Probucol :

It is highly lipophilic sulphur containing bis-phenol compound. It lowers the plasma LDL level by increasing the rate of LDL removal from the plasma. It also causes lowering of HDL particle level by suppressing the synthesis of apoprotein A - 1 fraction of HDL particles. Major limitation of probucol is its high lipophilicity due to which it is retained in adipose tissues of the body. Hence, its lipid lowering effects are observed for months even after the discontinuation of drug therapy. Most of the drug is eliminated in the bile and faeces. The common adverse effects of probucol include nausea, flatulence, abdominal pain, diarrhoea, eosinophilia and angioneurotic edema. It is contraindicated in pregnancy and in cardiac dysfunction.

It is very poorly soluble in water and only about 1 to 10% of 1 g dose is absorbed from GIT. Since probucol is lipophilic it associates with lipids in the diet and is absorbed along with them and transported by chylomicrons and VLDL through lymphatics to the systemic circulation.

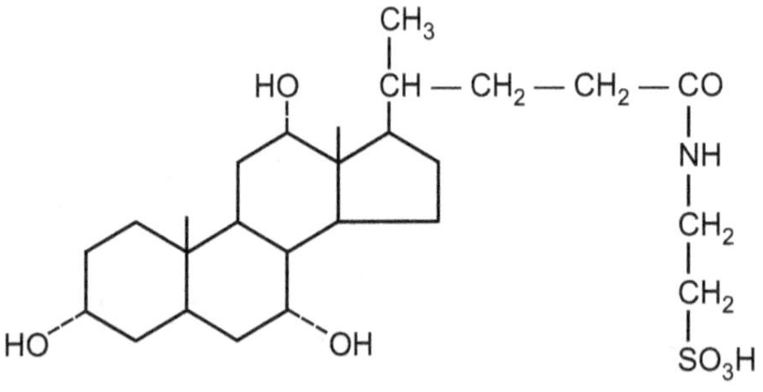

Taurocholic acid

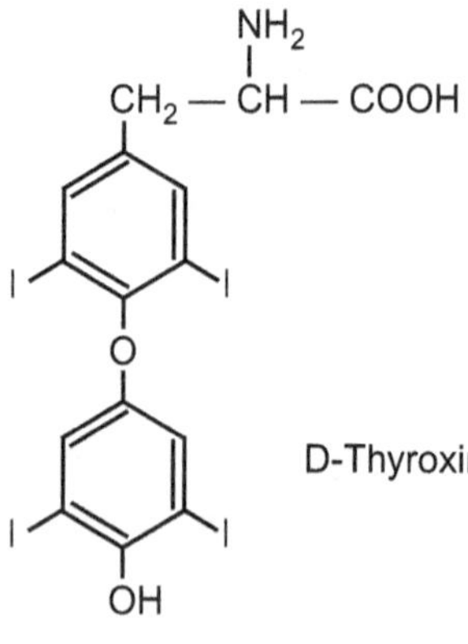

D-Thyroxine

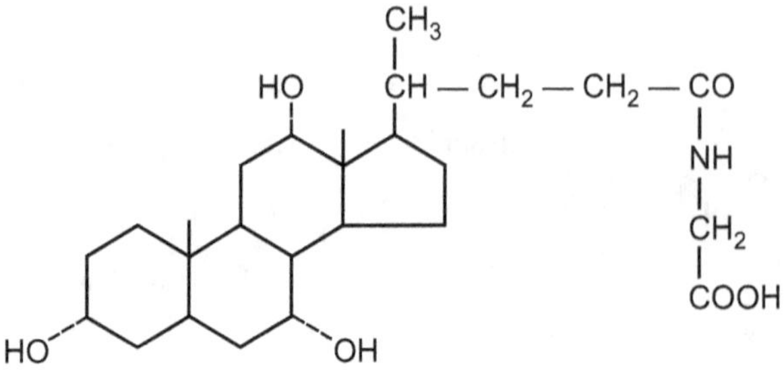

Glycocholic acid

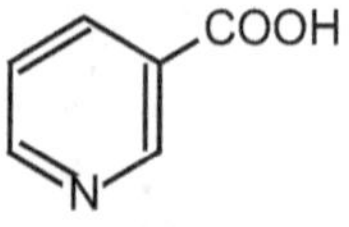

Nicotinic acid

(ii) Dextrothyroxine :

There exists an inversely proportional relationship between plasma levels of cholesterol and thyroxine. This observation led to the clinical introduction of d-thyroxine as lipid lowering agent. It increases the hepatic catabolism of LDL and thus lowers the plasma concentration of LDL particles. In therapeutic doses, d-thyroxine still retains hypercalorigenic effect which is reflected in the increased cardiac function. This situation invites cardiac arrhythmias and anginal attacks.

(iii) Bile acid - binding resins :

Bile acids are the metabolic end-products of cholesterol which are released into the intestine. Major fraction (about 98%) of bile acids released into the gut is reabsorbed through the enterohepatic circulation and suppresses the microsomal hydroxylase enzyme involved in the conversion of cholesterol to the bile acids. Thus, due to enterohepatic reabsorption of the bile acids further catabolism of cholesterol is suppressed. Bile acids, through their emulsifying effect, also enhance the absorption of dietary lipids from the gut lumen. If the concentration of gut bile acid is lowered down by promoting their excretion in the faeces (and by inhibiting their enterohepatic reabsorption), naturally it will be reflected into :

(a) increased conversion of cholesterol to bile acids coupled with a compensatory increase in the rate of hepatic cholesterol synthesis. The latter needs an increased hepatic uptake and catabolism of circulation LDL particles. The overall result will be lowering of plasma LDL level and

(b) deficient absorption of dietary lipids into the circulation. This leads to decrease in plasma lipid concentration.

Cholestyramine and colestipol are the examples of bile acid-binding resins which form a sort of non-absorbable complex with bile acids due to the presence of quaternary nitrogen in their structure. Thus, these drugs promote their elimination from the gut and inhibit their reabsorption into the circulation. The fecal excretion of bile acids in fact, has been shown to increase 30 folds by these drugs.

Both these drugs cholestyramine and colestipol HCl are high molecular weight, water insoluble anion exchange resins. Since these resins carry a positive charge and bile salts carry a negative charge, both bind together to form relatively stable complexes in the intestinal lumen. This drain on the bile acid pool stimulates increased synthesis of bile acids in the liver from cholesterol, thus depleting the hepatic stores of cholesterol. These agents stimulate VLDL production in the liver and hence may increase triglyceride concentrations. In patients who have both raised plasma cholesterol levels and raised triglyceride levels it may be necessary to combine the use of resins with nicotinic acid or clofibrate.

Both these drugs are the examples of anion exchange resins and remain undigested and non-absorbable in the GIT. Hence, the drugs are considered safest antilipidemic agents due to the lack of systemic effects. They are used only in the patients who have elevated LDL levels. They are favoured in the treatment of type II hyperlipoproteinemia. In the treatment of familial hypercholesterolemia, usually a combination of cholestyramine and nicotinic acid gives better results. Besides bile acids, these resins also bind with other drugs due to their anionic nature. Thus, absorption of thyroxin, vitamin C, digitalis glycosides, iron, and warfarin is reported to be impaired by these resins.

The adverse effects include nausea, abdominal pain, flatulence, constipation, acidosis and hypoprothrombinemia. They are contraindicated during the pregnancy.

Colesevelam : It is a bile acid sequestrant administered orally. It is used to reduce low density lipoproteins.

(iv) β - Sitosterol :

It is a plant sterol. Due to the structural similarity with cholesterol, this agent impedes the absorption of dietary cholesterol and produces a moderate reduction in cholesterol level. Its low efficacy and high cost decrease its popularity as lipid lowering agent.

Ezetimibe : It lowers cholesterol by decreasing cholesterol absorption in intenstine.

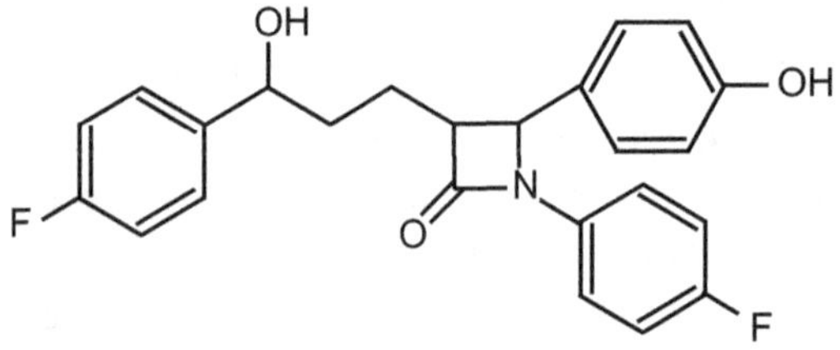

[B] Drugs Acting by Lowering the Plasma VLDL Level :

(i) Clofibrate :

A series of esters of p-chlorophenoxy-isobutyric acid has been prepared out of which clofibrate was found to lower the plasma lipid level more efficiently. Several derivatives of clofibrate are also in clinical use. They include bezafibrate, ciprofibrate, fenofibrate and etofibrate. Etofibrate is an ethylene glycol diester of nicotinic acid and clofibric acid.

Clofibrate is reserved for the treatment of type III hyperlipoproteinemia and hypertriglyceridemia which do not respond to other drugs.

The mechanism of action of clofibrate is not well defined. Various proposed mechanisms include :

(a) Stimulation of lipoprotein lipase enzyme activity.

(b) Increased cholesterol excretion.

(c) Inhibition of hepatic cholesterol synthesis.

(d) Increased intravascular catabolism of VLDL and IDL to LDL.

(e) Inhibition of hepatic VLDL synthesis.

(f) Increase in the plasma thyroxine concentration by clofibrate - induced displacement of thyroxine from albumin.

Due to displacement ability of clofibrate anion exerted on plasma albumin, potentiation of activities of many drugs (which are bound to albumin) can be seen during clofibrate therapy. Such drugs include sulfonylureas, coumarin and indandione anticoagulants.

Clofibrate is well absorbed from GIT. In the circulation, the ester linkage is hydrolysed to release p-chlorophenoxyisobutyric acid which then binds to plasma albumin. The acid metabolite is mainly excreted in the urine along with its glucuronide.

It hydrolyses to clofibric acid which is the active form. Following oral administration, maximum plasma concentration is usually attained with 3-6 hours. Clofibric acid is highly protein bound (93-98%) and has half-life of 13-17 hours. It is used in the management of a condition in which cholesterol rich VLDL and chylomicron remnant particles accumulate in the plasma (type III hyperlipidaemia).

Adverse effects include. nausea, diarrhoea, skin rash, weakness, muscle cramps, impotency and myopathy. The drug is contraindicated during pregnancy and in patients with impaired renal or hepatic functioning.

(ii) Gemfibrozil :

It is a structural relative of clofibrate synthesized in 1968. It was introduced in 1981 in the treatment of hypertriglyceridemia. Besides lowering the plasma VLDL level, gemfibrozil also exerts additional beneficial effect by raising the plasma concentration of HDL upto 20% or greater.

It effectively lowers plasma triglycerides and apoprotein B production in the liver. It stimulates lipoprotein lipase activity, which results in increased clearance of triglyceride rich particles. It is sometimes used in combination with bile acid binding resins.

Its pharmacological actions, pharmacokinetics and mechanisms of action are similar to clofibrate. In addition to the adverse effects seen with clofibrate, this drug also induces musculoskeletal pain, anemia, blurred vision and leucopenia upon chronic administration. Due to its enhancement effect on gallstone formation, gemfibrozil is contraindicated in patients with renal dysfunction or disease of gallbladder.

[C] Drugs that Lower the Plasma Level of both, VLDL and LDL :

(i) Nicotinic acid :

Its use in the treatment of hyperlipoproteinemia was first made by Altschul in 1955. It brings about hypolipidemic action by decreasing lipolysis and by promoting hepatic storage of lipids. It also enhances the activity of lipoprotein lipase resulting into low circulating VLDL level. Since VLDL acts as the precursor for most of the circulating LDL, the low VLDL level results into low level of circulating LDL. Nicotinamide, however, lacks hypolipidemic activity. In many cases, nicotinic acid is coadministered along with bile acid binding resin to get better results.

In body, nicotinic acid undergoes extensive metabolism resulting into formation of various metabolites, such as nicotinamide, nicotinuric acid, methyl nicotinamide, N-methyl - 2-pyridone-3-carboxamide and N-methyl - 2 - pyridone-5-carboxamide. These metabolites are mainly excreted in the urine along with some unchanged nicotinic acid.

Nicotinic acid has a long list of adverse effects. These include vomiting, diarrhoea, peptic ulcer, jaundice, hyperpigmentation, dry skin, postural hypotension, and cutaneous vasodilation (flushing) specifically in the upper part of the body. Gouty arthritis may develop due to the drug-induced elevation in the plasma uric acid level. It is contraindicated during pregnancy. Due to too many adverse effects of nicotinic acid, it is less frequently used alone in the treatment of hyperlipoproteinemia.

[D] Miscellaneous Lipid Lowering Agents :
(i) HMG CoA reductase inhibitors :

Hypercholesterolemia is considered to be one of the major risk factors for atherosclerosis which often leads to cardiovascular, cerebrovascular and peripheral vascular diseases. The cholesterol was found to be responsible for the thickening of the arterial walls and thus decreasing the radius in the arteries which leads in most cases to hypertension and increased risk of occlusive vascular diseases. The HMG-CoA (3-Iiydroxy-3-methylglutaryl-CoA) reductase inhibitors, called statins, inhibit cholesterol synthesis in the body and that leads to reduction in blood cholesterol levels, which is thought to reduce the risk of atherosclerosis and diseases caused by it.

In the 1950s Dawber revealed the correlation between high blood cholesterol levels and coronary heart diseases. HMGR was found to be the rate-limiting enzyme in the cholesterol biosynthetic pathway.

In 1978, Alfred Alberts and colleagues at Merck Research Laboratories discovered a new natural product in a fermentation broth of *Aspergillus terreus*, with a good HMGR inhibition. They named the product mevinolin or lovastatin.

By blocking the HMGR enzyme statins inhibit the synthesis of cholesterol via the mevalonate pathway. The end result is lower LDL (Low Density Lipoprotein), TG (Triglycerides) and total cholesterol levels as well as increased HDL. One of the main design objectives of statin design is the selective inhibition of HMGR in the liver, as cholesterol synthesis in non-hepatic cells is needed for normal cell function.

The essential structural components of all statins are a dihydroxyheptanoic acid and a ring system with different substituents. The statin pharmacophore is modified hydroxyglutaric acid component, which is structurally similar to the endogenous substrate HMG CoA and the mevaldyl CoA transition state intermediate.

It has also been shown that the HMGR is stereoselective and as a result all statins need to have the required 3R,5R stereochemistry.

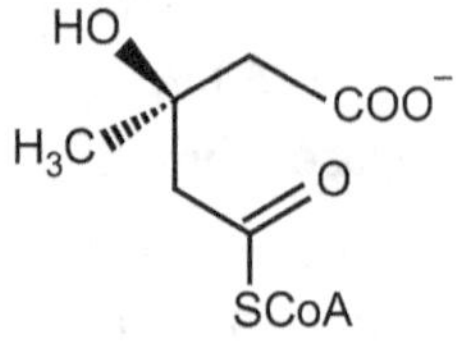

HMG CoA 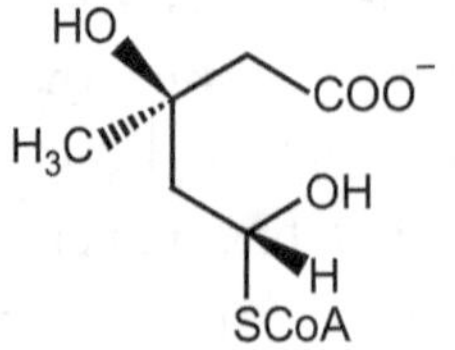　　　　**Movaldyl CoA transition state intermediates**

Compactin was first isolated from the cultures of Penicillium species in 1976 by Endo while mevinolin (or monacolin K) was isolated from the cultures of Aspergillus and Monascus species.

These drugs bring about specific, reversible and competitive blockage of HMG CoA reductase enzyme leading to decreased hepatic cholesterol synthesis. This induces an increased rate of hepatic uptake and catabolism of circulating LDL. Thus, the levels of total and LDL-cholesterol are significantly reduced.

The pharmacokinetic data is not available in man. In animals, however, these drugs are well absorbed and extensively metabolised, primarily in the liver.

About two thirds of body cholesterol is synthesized in the liver and intestine and 1/3 is supplied from diet. On a low cholesterol diet, the liver of a healthy adult synthesizes about 800 mg of cholesterol daily, which replaces that lost in the faeces.

The rate limiting step in the synthesis of cholesterol is the enzyme HMG-CoA reductase. The HMG - CoA reductase inhibitors can selectively and competitively inhibit the action of this enzyme, thus reducing body's ability to synthesize cholesterol. A search for the inhibitors of this enzyme led to the isolation of mevinolin (lovastatin) from the fungi Monascus ruber and Aspergillus terreus.

Rosuvastatin : It is a HMG-CoA reductase competitive inhibitor used to treat high cholesterol level and to prevent CVS disease.

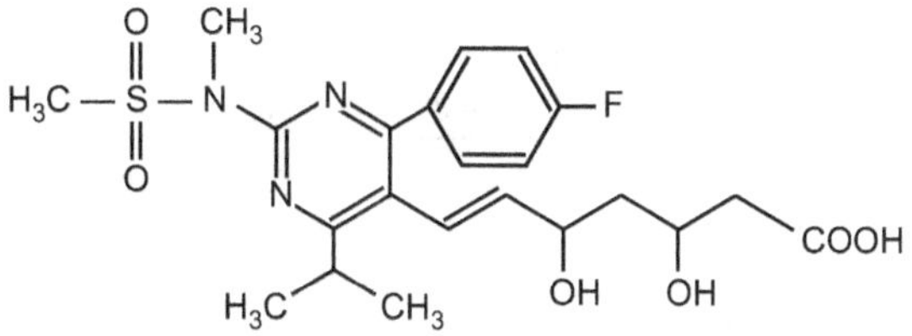

Atorvastatin (1985) : It was first synthesized by Bruce Roth at Pfizer.

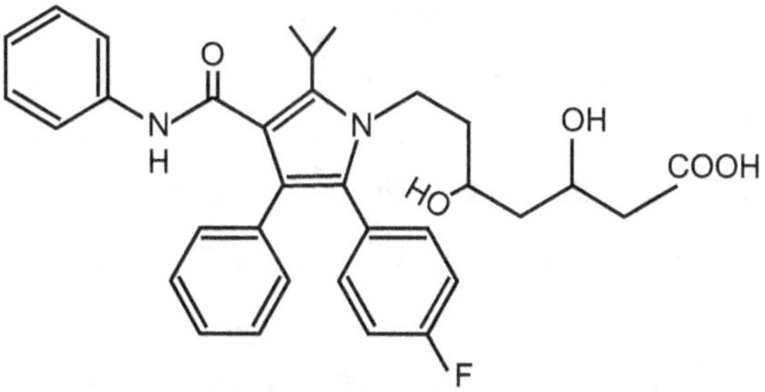

Three statins, lovastatin, simvastatin and pravastatin, have been extensively studied. Simvastatin is a prodrug, the eliminating half-life of which is relatively short (1-3 hrs), but duration of enzyme inhibition is much longer.

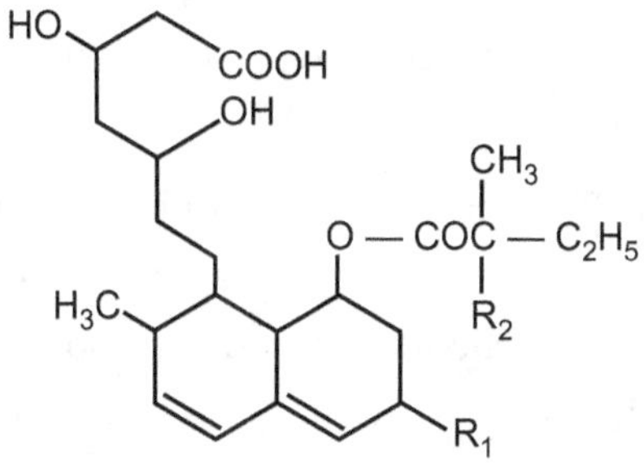

Type1 Statins :

    (i) Lovastatin : $R_1 = - CH_3$; $R_2 = H$

    (ii) Simvastatin : $R_1 = - CH_3$;

                          $R_2 = - CH_3$

    (iii) Pravastatin : $R_1 = - OH$; $R_2 = H$

Type 2 Statins:

- Fluvastatin
- Cerivastatin
- Atorvastatin
- Rosuvastatin

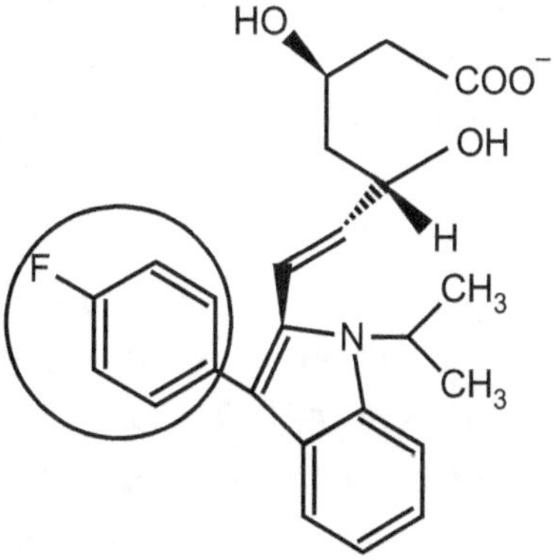

Fluorophenyl group
of type 2 statins

Adverse effects are few and of mild nature. Like other hypolipidemic drugs, HMG – CoA reductase inhibitors are contraindicated during pregnancy.

(i) Fenofibric acid (Fenofibrate) : It is used alone or in conjunction with statins in the treatment of hypercholesterolemia and hypertriglyceridemia.

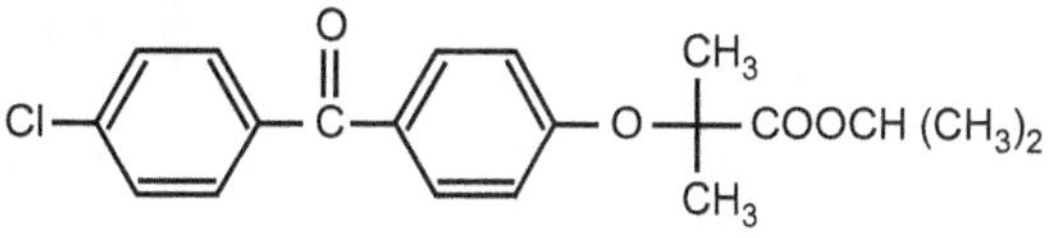

Comparative efficiency and pharmacology of the statins. (Drug)	Reduction in LDL-C (%)	Increase in HDL-C (%)	Reduction in TG (%)	Reduction in TC (%)	Protein binding (%)	T1/2 (h)	Hydrophilic	IC$_{50}$ (nM)
Atorvastatin	26 – 60	5 – 1 3	17 – 53	25 – 45	98	13 – 30	NO	8
Lovastatin	21 – 42	2 – 10	6 – 27	16 – 34	>95	2 – 4	NO	NA
Simvastatin	26 – 47	8 – 16	12 – 34	19 – 36	95 – 98	1 – 3	NO	11
Fluvastatin	22 – 36	3 – 11	12 – 25	16 – 27	98	0.5 – 3.0	NO	28
Rosuvastatin	45 – 63	8 – 14	10 – 35	33 – 46	88	19	YES	5
Pravastatin	22 – 34	2 – 12	15 – 24	16 – 25	43 – 67	2 – 3	YES	44

(ii) Neomycin : It is an aminoglycoside antibiotic. It exerts hypolipidemic activity only in oral administration while if given parenterally, neomycin does not reduce the plasma level of LDL.

The poor absorption upon oral administration of neomycin indicates that its site of action is in GIT. The adverse effects (like, ototoxicity, nephrotoxicity) seen during parenteral administration of neomycin, are not reported to occur with oral use of the drug.

(iii) Acipimox : Acipimox is a synthetic derivative of nicotinic acid and like nicotinic acid, it acts by inhibiting adipose tissue lipolysis (hydrolysis of lipid esters). It appears to produce less flushing and GI-intolerance than nicotinic acid at normal doses (250 mg 2-3 times/day). It is about 20 times more active than nicotinic acid.

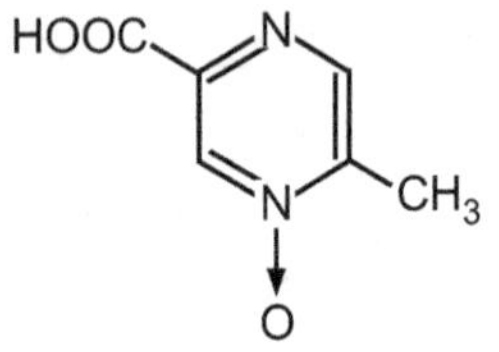

Acipimox

(iv) Metformin : Chemically it is N, N-dimethyl biguanidine. It has no effect on cholesterol biosynthesis but it affects the lipoprotein composition. It produces about 50% reduction in the serum triglyceride level.

It is also a hypoglycemic agent and lowers blood glucose level.

(v) Other agents having hypolipidemic activity include, sucrose polymers, eicosapen-taenoic acid, propranolol and pindolol. Similarly estrogens also interfere in the fat metabolism resulting into a decrease in plasma

LDL concentration and an increase in plasma HDL concentration. These metabolic effects of estrogens are partly opposed by progestin.

(vi) Bile acids (i.e., glycocholic and tauro-cholic acids) are derived from cholesterol by oxidation to cholic acid and then conjugation with glycine (glycocholic acid) or with taurine (taurocholic acid).

Table 5.8

Protein	Molecular weight	Lipoprotein	Function	Effect
ApoAI	28,000	HDL, chylomicrons	Activates enzyme LCAT	Reverse cholesterol transport
ApoAII	16,000	HDL, chylomicrons	Structural role	
ApoB100	555,000	LDL, VLDL	Recognition of receptor	Delivery of cholesterol to cells
ApoB48	250,000	Chylomicron	Recognition of receptor	Delivery of dietary cholesterol to liver
ApoCI	6,000	Chylomicron, VLDL	Structural role	
ApoCII	7,000	Chylomicron, VLDL, HDL	Activates LPL	Triglyceride breakdown
ApoCIII	7,000	Chylomicron, VLDL, HDL,	Structural role	
ApoD	21,000	HDL	Cholesterol ester transfer	Reverse cholesterol transport
ApoE	34,000	Chylomicron, VLDL, HDL	Recognition of receptor	Cholesterol transport

5.34 ANTICOAGULANTS

Two distinct pathways contribute to the formation of the blood clot. When the protein factors present in the circulation provide the whole cause and completion of the clotting process, the clot is said to be effected by the intrinsic system. While, when the blood coagulation is activated by the factors which are not originated from the circulating blood (e.g, tissue thromboplastin), the clot is said to be due to the extrinsic system. Agents used to modify the stages of clotting process may act by :

(i) potentiating the natural inhibitory elements of clotting process e.g, heparin,

(ii) reducing the rate of synthesis of vitamin-K dependent clotting factors e.g., warfarin, and

(iii) potentiating fibrinolytic mechanisms e.g, streptokinase, urokinase etc.

Various conditions contribute to bleeding disorders. These include thrombocytopenia (i.e. low platelet count), hemophilias (i.e, genetic defect in the synthesis of clotting factors. In some cases, certain clotting factors are totally missing from the plasma of the patient) etc. These bleeding disorders may lead to the clot formation (i.e., thrombus) in the artery or vein or even in the heart chamber. Thromboembolism is the next stage in which reduced blood flow occurs at sites quite distinct to the point of thrombus. Myocardial infarction, peripheral arterial emboli, deep venous thrombosis and pulmonary embolization are some conditions where anticoagulant therapy is generally needed. Many compounds prevent the availability of calcium ions during coagulation process. These include soluble salts of citrate, oxalate, fluoride or EDTA. All these compounds can be used as in-vitro anticoagulants. The clinically used anticoagulants fall under two categories :

    (i)   Heparin, and

    (ii) Oral anticoagulants.

5.35　HEPARIN (Parenteral Anticoagulant)

Heparin occurs intracellularly especially concentrated in the basophil cells found in the circulating plasma. Its discovery was reported by Howell in 1922. It was first isolated from liver. Hence it was named as heparin. It is widely distributed in the tissues, particularly in the lungs and liver.

Jorpes in 1937 established its chemical composition and the first clinical use of heparin was also documented in the same year. Chemically it is a heterogenous group of highly electro-negative water soluble straight-chain mucopolysaccharides.

It is a polymer consisting of alternate units of two disaccharides (i.e, D-glucosamine - L - iduronic acid and D-glucosamine - D - glucuronic acid) in addition to sulfuric acid. Besides this, 1 : 1 additional residues of glucuronic acid and fewer residues of N-sulfated glucosamine per heparin molecule are also reported in the structural analysis. Because of its acidic properties, heparin may also be called as 'heparinic acid'.

Commercially heparin is mainly obtained from bovine lung or porcine intestinal mucosa. In most of the samples, the number of repeating disaccharide units per molecule ranges from 6 to 15. Hence, its molecular weight also ranges from 8,000 to 50,000. The commercial samples of heparin may differ in their degree of polymerization and sulfation but biologically all heparins are almost equivalent. In clinical practice, heparin may be used during and after various types of surgery to reduce or to prevent intravascular clotting and thrombosis.

Enoxaparin : It is a low molecular weight heparin used as an anticoagulant to prevent and treat deep vein thrombosis or pulmonary embolism.

Pharmacological Properties :

    (i) As an anticoagulant, heparin is effective both in-vivo and in-vitro. After its administration, several clotting factors are neutralized by heparin and antithrombin III factor. Heparin neutralizes thromboplastin by forming an inactive complex with it, while in the absence of heparin, anti-thromin III factor has an ability to neutralize thrombin but at quite slow speed. Heparin induces some conformational changes in the antithrombin III molecule, thus making it highly active.

Hence, in the presence of heparin, the molecule of antithrombin III can neutralize thrombin and several other clotting factors (IXa, Xa, XIa, XIIa and kallikrein) at much faster rate by forming inactive complexes with these clotting factors. Thus, heparin may act as a catalyst in the neutralization of these clotting factors by antithrombin III factor.

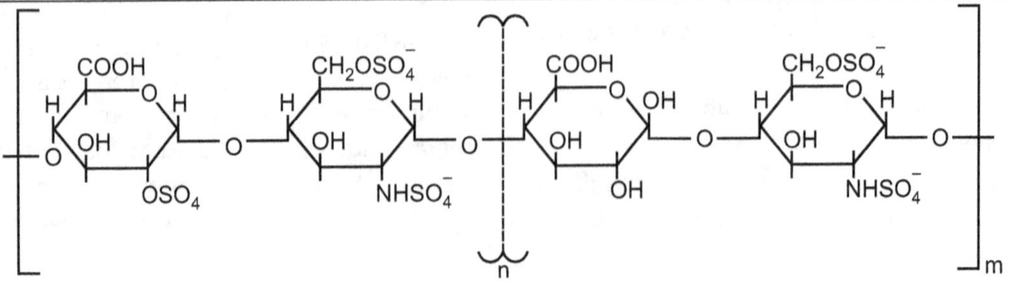

Fig. 5.16 : Polymeric nature of heparin structure

(ii) During hyperlipemia, the plasma triglyceride level increases. The enzyme, lipoprotein lipase is responsible for the hydrolysis of these triglycerides into fatty acids and partial glycerides. These products are then metabolized by extrahepatic tissues. Heparin activates lipoprotein lipase. Thus, it helps to reduce hyperlipemia by lowering of plasma triglyceride level.

Pharmacokinetics :

Heparin is poorly absorbed (less than 15%) from GIT after oral administration mainly because of its polyanionic character (polarity), large molecular size and its instability in the gastric juice. Since its oral or sublingual administration is not effective, it is given parenterally. Because of its acidic properties, it induces local trauma followed by hemotonia formation, if it is administered intramuscularly.

Hence, when low dose of heparin is required, it is usually administered subcutaneously or at intrafat sites. When large dose of heparin is required (as in pulmonary emboli), the intravenous route is favoured.

Heparin is significantly bound (95%) to plasma proteins. It is partially metabolized in the liver by the enzyme, heparinase. The metabolite, uroheparin has slight antithrombin like activity. The plasma half-life of heparin is estimated to be about one hour at a dose of 100 units/kg. However it is dose-dependent. For example, as the dose of administered heparins increased to 400 units/kg, the plasma half-life also reaches to about 2 hours. In hepatic cirrhosis or renal dysfunctioning, the half-life of heparin becomes significantly longer. Heparin neither crosses the placental barrier nor it appears in the milk of lactating mothers.

Adverse Effects :

Heparin itself is of low toxicity and is an excellent anti-coagulant for short-term therapy. However, due to its commercial production from animal tissues, it may induce allergic reactions, specifically when given in high doses. Heparin also retains an inherent property to induce platelet aggregation. This may lead to thrombocytopenia in some patients.

The major adverse reaction in heparin therapy is haemorrhage. The specific heparin antagonist, protamine (low molecular weight, positively charged heparin) may be used to neutralise heparin in cases of severe hemorrhage. Hence, heparin therapy is contra-indicated in patients having intracranial hemorrhage, thrombocytopenia, severe hyper-tension, history of allergy or who consume large amount of ethanol.

Argatroban : It is a direct thrombin inhibitor used to treat thrombosis in patients with heparin-induced thrombocytopenia.

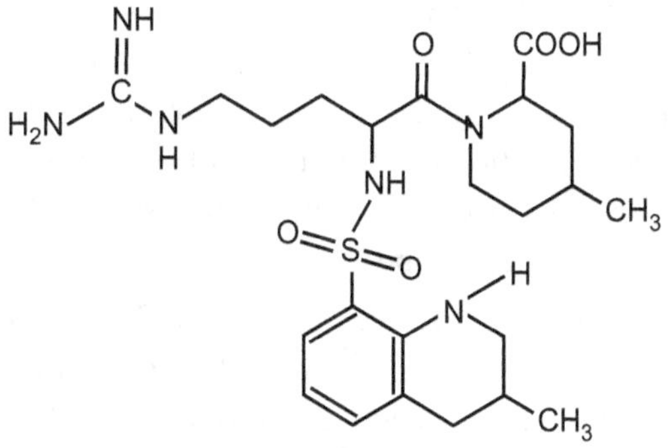

Lepirudin : It is an **anticoagulant** that functions as a direct thrombin inhibitor. It is a recombinant hirudin derived from yeast cells. It may be used when heparin is contra-indicated because of heparin-induced thrombocytopenia.

Aprotinin : It is the basic pancreatic trypsin inhibitor (Bovine BPTI) used to reduce bleeding during heart and liver surgery. It slows down fibrinolysis. It is withdrawn in 2008.

Argatroban : It is a direct selective thrombin inhibitor. It is a non-heparin anticoagulant shown to both normalize platelet count in patients with HT and prevent formation of thrombi.

Heparin is an excellent anti-coagulant for short-term therapy of 10-15 days. Oral anti-coagulants then can be used to extend the anti-coagulant effect for desired period.

Heparin Antagonists :

Severe hemorrhage may occur in patients receiving high dose of heparin. Protamine sulfate can be used in such cases to antagonise the effect of heparin. Protamines are strongly basic proteins of low moleculer weight. They were isolated from the sperm or mature testes of the fish belonging to the family Salmonidase.

Protamine sulfate is usually administered intravenously to neutralise heparin by forming inactive complex with it. Dyspnea may develop, if the rate of infusion of protamine is rapid. An excess of protamine sulfate has anti-coagulant property.

Heparin may be used as an anticoagulant in surgical procedures and in the treatment of myocardial infarction and venous thrombi or thromboembolism.

5.36 ORAL ANTICOAGULANTS

The first orally effective anticoagulant was bishydroxy-coumarin. Isolated in 1939 by Link, its structure was established in 1940. In 1941, it was used clinically as the first orally effective anticoagulant (dicoumarol).

Thereafter it has been used clinically for years in patients with a tendency of thrombus formation.

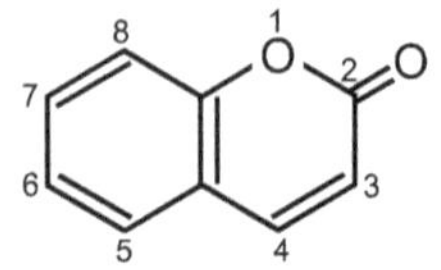

Coumarin nucleus

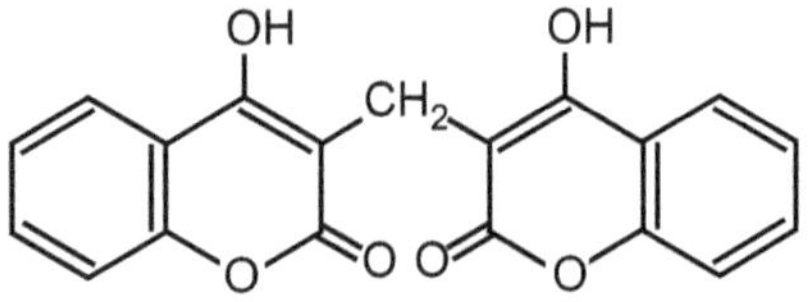

Dicoumarol

Dicoumarol itself has drawbacks as therapeutic agent mainly due to its poor and irregular absorption. Many analogs have been prepared. All these are water insoluble and possess either 4-hydroxycoumarin nucleus (coumarin derivatives) or indan - 1, 3 - dione nucleus (indandione derivatives). The latter are less preferred due to their greater toxicity. Some of these agents (e.g. phenprocoumon, warfarin) contain asymmetric carbon atom in their structure and commercially they are marketed as recemic mixtures. Usually the l - or S (–) - isomers are more potent anticoagulants than are the d - or R (+) isomers.

All these agents differ from each other in onset and duration of their anticoagulant action. Coumarins do not have in-vitro activity. They exert in-vivo effect after a period of 1 - 2 days. Their effects last long. Coumarins suppress the synthesis of clotting factors (pro-thrombin, factors VII, VIII and IX) in the liver which results in the gradual decline in the concentration of clotting factors and hence a slow onset of action.

Whereas the long duration of action may be due to the time taken by liver to accumulate again, enough concentration of clotting factors.

Mechanism of Action :

Vitamin K appears to be related to the important quinone coenzymes called as ubiquinones. Since the oral anti-coagulants have close structural similarity with vitamin K, they exert anticoagulant activity by acting as non-competitive antagonists of vitamin K.

The activation of prothrombine involves formation of γ-carboxyglutamic acid residues which are important for entrapment of calcium ions. Calcium ions are needed at almost every stage to activate the clotting factors.

The carboxylation process of prothrombine in hepatic microsomes is catalysed by vitamin K where the vitamin gets converted to its hydroquinone form. In normal circumstances, the inactive hydroquione form gets reconverted to the active vitamin K form by NADH-NAD$^+$ system.

Table 5.9 : Clinically used oral anticoagulants

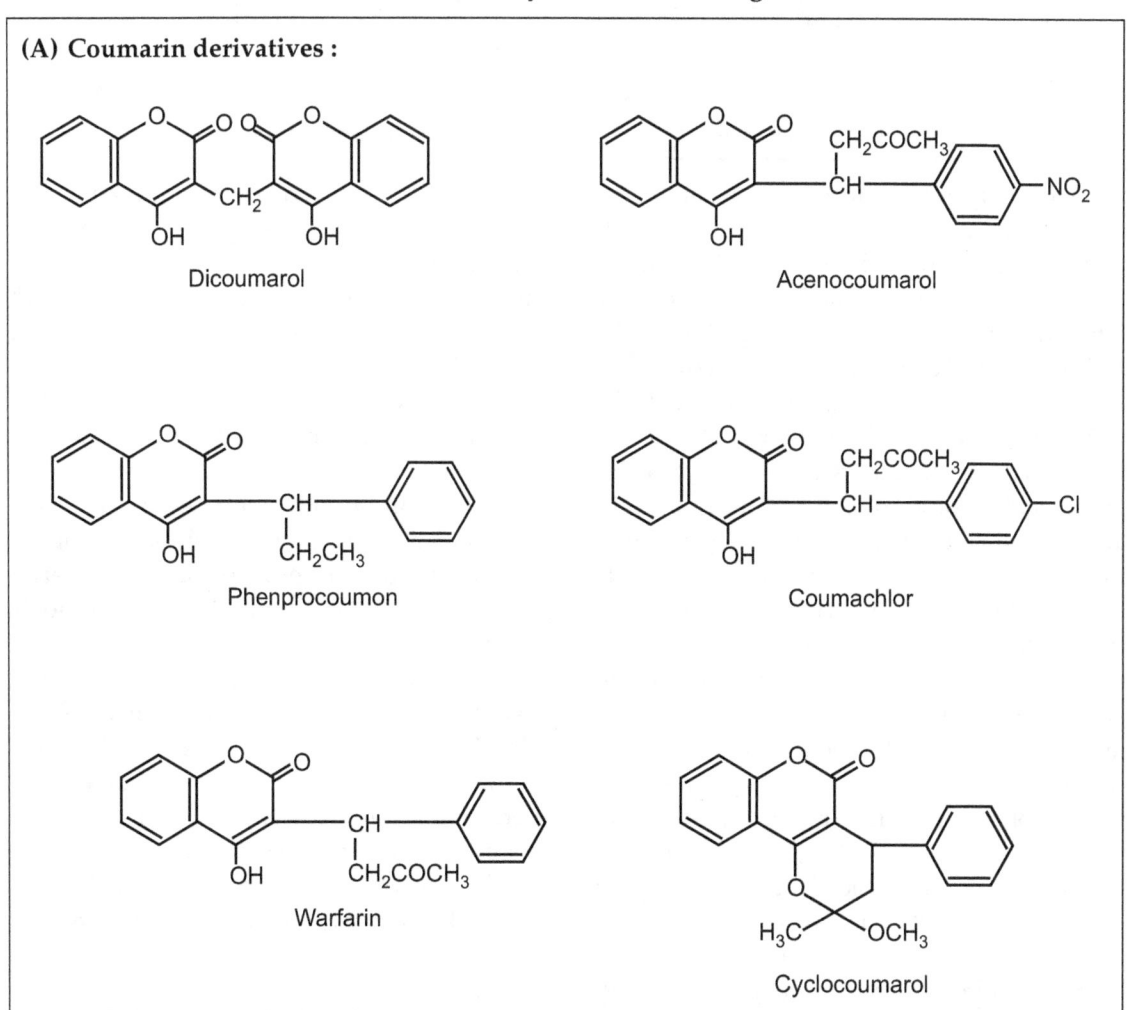

(A) Coumarin derivatives :

Dicoumarol

Acenocoumarol

Phenprocoumon

Coumachlor

Warfarin

Cyclocoumarol

(B) Indandione derivatives :

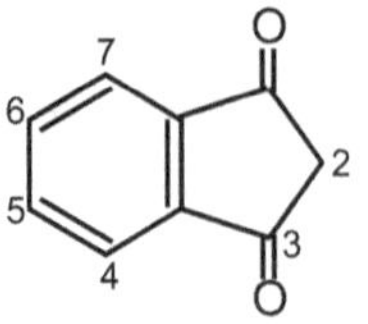

1, 3 - Indandione

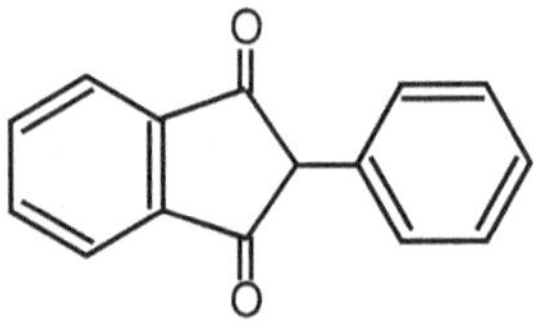

Phenindione

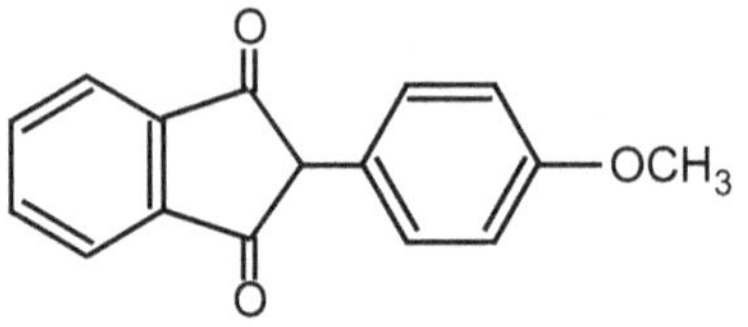

Anisindione

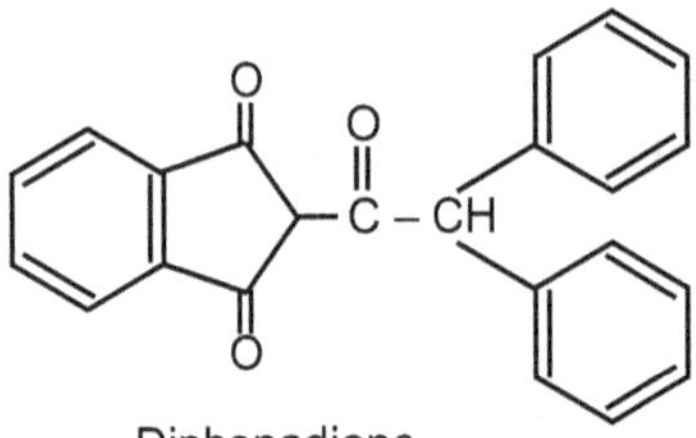

Diphenadione

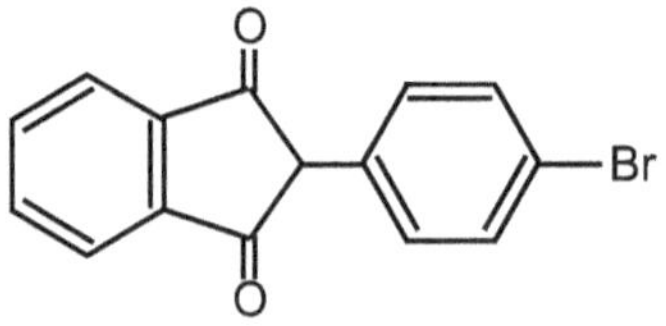

Bromindione

The orally active anticoagulants inhibit the conversion of inactive vitamin K hydroquinone to the active vitamin K form. This leads to the accumulation of inactive vitamin K hydroquinone and depletion of the active vitamin K form in hepatic tissues. The oral anticoagulant agents thus prevent the hepatic synthesis of the biologically active forms of the vitamin K-dependent clotting factor, mainly prothrombin and factors VII, IX and X. The clotting time is prolonged due to the formation of structurally incomplete clotting factors. However, the onset of therapeutic efficacy can be seen only after existing plasma concentration of prothrombin and other vitamin K-dependent clotting factors have been declined. The vitamin K-dependent clotting factors have plasma half-life as follows : Factor II (60 hours), VII (6 hours), IX (24 hours) and X (40 hours). Hence, all these drugs show a long delay (about 3 - 5 days) in their onset of action. The rate of onset is independent of the size of the dose. The longer duration of their anticoagulant activity is mainly due to the long time required by the hepatic microsomal enzymes to convert coumarins into inactive hydroxylated metabolites. The mechanism of action and uses of indandione derivatives are similar to coumarins.

Pharmacokinetics :

Warfarin sodium is usually administered in the form of its racemic mixture. It is completely and rapidly absorbed from GIT. In the circulation, it is extensively bound (about 99%) to the plasma proteins. Unlike heparin, warfarin and phenindione do not have dose-dependent plasma half-life. Warfarin has the plasma half-life of about 35 days. The more potent leavo-isomer of warfarin is metabolised (ring hydroxylation) in the liver to 7-hydroxy warfarin while the dextro-isomer is metabolized by side-chain reduction to a secondary alcohol. The formation of a 6-hydroxy warfarin from both isomers is also reported. All these hydroxylated metabolites are inactive and partly undergo glucuronidation.

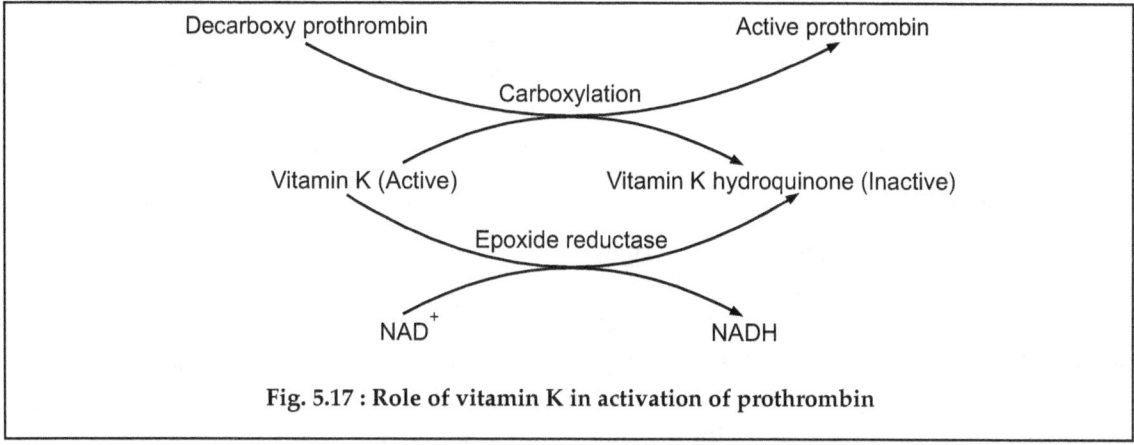

Fig. 5.17 : Role of vitamin K in activation of prothrombin

They are excreted through urine and stools. Under many pathophysiological conditions, the response of a patient to oral anticoagulant therapy may be altered. For example, deficient bile secretion (decreased absorption of dietary vitamin K from GIT), oral antibiotic treatment (decreased vitamin K synthesis by the intestinal microflora), hepatic diseases (decreased rate of synthesis of clotting factors), all these conditions lead to increased response to oral anticoagulant therapy. However during pregnancy, the activity of some clotting factors (i.e., VII, VIII, IX and X) enhances, leading to decrease in the patient's response to oral anticoagulant therapy. Both, warfarin and dicumarol can cross placental barrier and can induce fetal and placental hemorrhage in therapeutic doses.

Due to their slow onset of action, usually heparin is administered first and the anti-coagulant effect is then maintained by oral anticoagulant drugs.

Adverse Effects :

The safest and commonly used drugs are warfarin and bishydroxy coumarin. Side-effects of coumarin include rash, nausea, vomiting, jaundice, leukopenia and thrombocytopenia. Minor hemorrhage during the therapy may be corrected by discontinuing the therapy. In the cases of overdoses, excessive bleeding and long prothrombin time may be treated by intravenous use of vitamin K or its synthetic derivatives such as menadiol diphosphate. Prothrombin itself may be given in the form of plasma or plasma concentrates if immediate treatment of overdoses is required.

Untoward effects with indandione anti-coagulants include leukopenia, hepatitis, agra-nulocytosis and renal tubular necrosis. These drugs are less preferred than coumarins due to their greater toxicities. Their use is advocated only in patients who can not tolerate coumarins.

Oral anticoagulants are contraindicated in bleeding disorders, ulcers, local anaesthesia, hepatic or renal diseases.

5.37 ANTI-THROMBOTIC DRUGS

Thrombus is a physical occlusion of blood vessel lumen due to formation of solid mass consisting of platelets, fibrin, red cells and white cells in the arterial or venous circulation. If part of this thrombus in the venous circulation breaks off and enters the right heart, it may be lodged in the pulmonary arterial circulation causing pulmonary embolism. This is reflected in sudden shortness of breath and dull central chest pain. It may increase the risk of unconsciousness. The peripheral arterial occlusion in the arterial circulation may result either in the lower limbs or in the cerebral circulation. In a large deep venous thrombosis which prevents venous return, the leg may become discoloured and oedematous. The deep vein thrombosis is the common cause of pain, swelling and tenderness of the leg.

The blood platelets play an important etiological role in the pathogenesis of athero-sclerosis, thrombosis, thromboembolism and stroke. The reactivity of platelets, the activity of leucocytes, the coagulation of blood and regulation of blood vessel tone and permeability are in turn governed by the vascular endothelium. These functions are mediated by the release of certain bioactive substances by the endothelial cells which include prostacyclin, nitric oxide, platelet activating factor, plasminogen activator, endothelium derived hyperpolarizing factor, endothelium derived contracting factor and also enzymes that can activate or degrade vasoactive hormones.

Platelets bind to the collagen in the vessel wall and promote other platelets to adhere. The process is stimulated by ADP released by already adhered platelets. Arachidonic acid, thrombin and collagen are the other inducers. Collagen is the fibrous protein of connective tissue and the most abundant protein in the human body. Collagen is involved in platelet adhesion, activation and homeostasis. It occurs in a variety of forms where type III collagen is more potent stimulant of platelet aggregation than other types. Platelets thus play a critical role in the recognition of vascular injury, formation of effective hemostatic plugs, retraction of clots and wound healing.

Collagen when binds on the surface of the platelet membrane, induces the changes in the activities of platelet membrane cyclic nucleo-tides. These changes in turn lead to phospho-rylation of certain platelet component proteins which may then trigger the release reaction and culminate in aggregation. The platelet aggregation occurs in following steps :

(a) the initial adhesion of platelets to collagen,

(b) the release of the contents of platelets like ADP, Ca^{++}, serotonin, and

(c) the subsequent formation of platelet aggregates under the mediation of released ADP and Ca^{++}. The release of adenosine diphosphate (ADP) from platelet under 'release reaction' may be mediated by c-AMP. Dipyridamole, aspirin and other NSAIDS inhibit platelet release reaction.

It is proposed that the free amino groups of lysine and arginine residues of collagen are critical for the platelet aggregating activity of collagen and the carboxy groups are less important.

The platelet activation inhibitory drugs exert their effects by blocking different activation signalling mechanisms. These drugs may be classified as :

(a) Inhibitors of arachidonic acid meta-bolism, example is aspirin.

(b) Stimulators of adenylate cyclase and guanylate cyclase e.g. nitric oxide.

(c) Phosphodiesterase inhibitors e.g. dipyridomole.

(d) Calcium antagonists e.g. nifedipine.

(e) Agents that alter platelet membrane in order to decrease platelet aggregation e.g. ticlopidine.

Platelet aggregation plays a major role in the pathogenesis of thromboembolic events such as stroke and transient ischaemic attack.

Ticlopidine acts by inhibition of adenosine diphosphate - induced platelet aggregation, although suppression of PAF and thromboxane A_2 and activation of adenylate cyclase may play a contributory role.

Inhibitors of platelet activation are also termed as antiplatelet drugs or antithrombotic drugs. The category includes all such compounds that prevent adhesion, aggregation and secretion of platelets.

Platelets are known to play an important role in both haemostasis and thrombosis possibly by the intermediary formation of prostaglandin derivatives and patients with platelet functional disorders may bleed abnormally.

Dextran inhibits platelet function invivo, has an 'anti-adhesive' effect on vascular surfaces, a weak heparin-like action and rheological effects. However, it may induce renal failure due to accumulation in the proximal tubules and is particularly dangerous when renal perfusion is reduced or renal damage occurs. Antiserotonin drugs such as cyproheptadine may also inhibits platelet function.

Thrombolytic Therapy :

Thrombolytic therapy aims at dissolution of the thrombus by activation of the natural fibrinolytic enzyme system.

Plasmin is an unstable proteolytic enzyme which induces lysis of fibrin and also attacks and depletes fibrinogen and coagulation factors V and VIII. Fibrin and fibrinogen degradation products are produced which have an anticoagulant effect and suppress platelet function making the blood hypocoagulable.

Prostacyclin synthetase is present at higher concentration in vascular endothelium but is lacking in the outer layers of the blood vessel wall. It is also present in non-vascular smooth muscle from the lung, uterus, bladder and intestine but could not be demonstrated in cardiac or skeletal muscles. It is a haem-containing protein of about 52000 dalton. Prostacyclin production proceeds by polarisation of the 9 - 11 endoperoxide and the formation of a 6, 9 epoxy derivative giving rise to a bicyclic structure. This is accompanied by loss of hydrogen from C_6.

Anti-thrombotic Agents :

(1) Platelets are the disc-shaped fragments of bone marrow megakaryocytes circulating in the blood.

(2) Although completely non-sticky in the resting state, platelets become sticky with the slightest stimulation. Platelet aggregation occurs in following four steps :

    (a) development of stickiness

    (b) changes in cell shape

    (c) contraction and release of granule contents, and

    (d) irreversible aggregation.

(3) The chain of events in the platelet activation signalling may include changes in cytosolic pH, alteration in cytosolic calcium levels, Na^+/H^+ exchange, activation of GTP - binding proteins, activation of phospholipases, phosphorylation and stimulation of tyrosine kinase, hydrolysis of phosphatidyl inositol 4, 5 - biphosphate, release of lipid mediators and platelet activating factor. Platelet aggregation inducers, such as thrombin, epinephrine, thromboxane and platelet activating factor exert their effect by interacting with several transmembrane spanning G-protein-coupled receptors.

(4) Blood platelets overactivation play a critical role in the clinical complications in acute myocardial infarction, unstable angina, atrial fibrillation, pulmonary embolism, left ventricular dysfunction and sudden deterioration in peripheral vasculature.

(5) Adenosine diphosphate, thrombin, epinephrine, collagen, arachidonic acid, serotonin and platelet activating factor cause irreversible aggregation of platelets and promote secretion of granule contents.

Arachidonic Acid Liberation :

There are four major phospholipids associated with platelet membranes. They are phosphatidyl inositol (PI), phosphatidyl choline (PC), phosphatidyl ethanolamine (PE) and phosphatidyl serine (PS). Phospholipase A_1 specifically releases the fatty acids from the carbon 1 position, whereas phospholipase A_2 liberates fatty acids esterified at the second carbon. Phospholipase C liberates phosphorylated bases from the diglyceride portion of the molecule. Phospholipase D releases the bases such as inositol, choline, ethanolamine and serine from the phospatidic acid moiety. Activation of phospholipase C results in the hydrolysis of PI and formation of a diglyceride and inositol triphosphate. Action of diglyceride lipase and other lipases produce free fatty acids. In addition to phosphatidyl inositols, phosphatidyl choline and phospha-tidyl ethanolamine also may serve as a source for arachidonic acid. Phospholipase A_2 is a membrane associated enzyme responsible for liberation of arachidonic acid from these phospholipids.

Released arachidonic acid is converted to 12-hydroperoxyeicosatetraenoic acid (12 - HPETE) and 12 - hydroxyeicosatetraenoic acid (12 - HETE) by lipoxygenase, whereas arachidonic acid is converted to cyclic endoperoxides (PGG_2 / PGH_2) by cyclo-oxygenase and to thromboxane by thromboxane synthetase.

Phospholipases are a family of esterases capable of hydrolyzing the glycerophospholipid and liberating relatively low molecular weight proteins (~ 14 KD).

Cyclo-oxygenase Inhibitors : They primarily inhibit the conversion of fatty acid to cyclic endoperoxides. Aspirin inhibits the cyclo-oxygenase enzyme in platelets irreversibly by acetylating the serine (Ser 529) residue. Since platelets lack DNA, they can not resynthesize new enzyme. Therefore, aspirin - exposed platelets lose their ability to make cyclo-oxygenase metabolites permanantly. Once the active drug loses its acetyl group and becomes salicylic acid, it no longer exhibits an inhibitory effect on platelet cyclo-oxygenase.

Vascular tissues produce endoperoxidase from substrate arachidonic acid via cyclo-oxygenase pathways as in platelets. Indeed, platelet endoperoxides (PGG_2/PGH_2) can be utilized by endothelial cells to make vasodilatory prostacyclin (PGI_2). Aspirin also inhibits cyclo-oxygenase in endothelial cells. However, these cells can regenerate new enzymes in a few hours.

Therefore, ideal aspirin therapy envisages a low dose aspirin protocol that can inhibit platelet thromboxane synthesis significantly, sparing the ability of vascular tissue to produce PGI_2. Several studies have demonstrated that acetyl salicylic acid (aspirin) transfers its acetyl group to serine (Ser 529) which blocks the availability of the substrate arachidonic acid to the substrate binding site. N-acetylimidazole acetylates several nucleophilic groups in PG synthetase but does not react with Ser 529. Therefore, the specificity of aspirin to acetylate this group seems to be related to affinity of binding of salicylate moiety to this region of PG synthetase. In a novel study Rao et al demonstrated that ingestion of ibuprofen, which lacks an acetyl group, abolishes the in vivo effect of aspirin, suggesting that both drugs are probably competing for the same binding site on the enzyme. Further studies using dipyridil, a ferrous iron chelator, suggested the importance of heme group in prostanoid synthesis. Based on several in-vitro studies and molecular modelling, Peterson et al suggested a model to explain the heme/arachidonic acid interaction, and how NSAID interferes with this reaction and prevents arachidonic acid oxidation. Inhibitors of PG synthetase, other than aspirin, may interfere with peroxidative activity and formation of tyrosil and arachidonic acid radicals thereby preventing prostanoid synthesis.

Drugs Affecting c-AMP/c-GMP Concentration :

Dipyridamole inhibits the platelet release reaction by blocking phosphodiesterase to increase c-AMP.

Prostaglandins E_1, I_2 and D_2 are potent systemic vasodilators and inhibitors of platelet activation. These compounds, and others that stimulate adenylate cyclase, exert their effect by virtue of their ability to promote the formation of c-AMP. Some of the other compounds that stimulate adenylate cyclase include adenosine, forskolin and cloleonol. In addition, compounds that inhibit c-AMP-phosphodiesterase also contribute to the elevation of intracellular c-AMP. Known examples of this class of compounds include dipyridamole, caffeine, papaverine, theophylline and methylxanthines.

Prostacyclin is the most potent naturally occurring inhibitor of platelet function at present. It is available as a stable freeze dried preparation (Epoprostenol) for administration to humans. The use of prostacyclin is underway in several clinical conditions such as extracorporeal circulation, cardio-pulmonary bypass, renal hemodialysis, peripheral vascular disease, primary pulmonary hypertension, subarachnoid hemo-rrhage, ischemia and transplant preservation.

Another vasodilator that can be effectively used is adenosine. This compound also stimulates adenylate cyclase. Adenosine has been shown to exert an antiaggregatory effect on platelets at 0.3 μ mol/l in blood. This compound can be used alone or in combination with an adenosine uptake inhibitor, dipyridamole (2 μ mol/l). The half-life of adenosine is less than 10 seconds at micromolar concentrations and, therefore, it could be used safely at effective therapeutic concentrations without deleterious effects.

ADP is a platelet activator that is released from red blood cells, activated platelets and damaged endothelial cells. It induces platelet adhesion and aggregation. Ticloepidine and clopidogrel inhibit platelet aggregation induced by ADP. Ticlopidine is widely used to prevent thrombosis during caronary stent placement and in patients with cerebrovascular disease. However it is associated with severe and sometime fatal blood dyscrasias. Clopidogrel has similar pharmacological activity but produces fewer side effects.

Nitrosovasodilators as a class seem to exert their effect by producing nitric oxide (NO), a potent stimulator of guanylate cyclase. This enzyme is found in soluble form in platelets, and is stimulated by carbon monoxide, hydroxyl radicals and nitric oxide. Nitric oxide synthetase is present in a variety of cells including macrophages, neutrophills, endothelial cells and platelets. This enzyme uses L-arginine as substrate and generates nitric oxide and L-citruline as metabolites. Methyl ester of L-arginine is a potent specific inhibitor of NO-synthetase.

Cilostazol : It is a phosphodiesterase-3 inhibitor. It inhibits platelet aggregation and is a direct arterial vasodilator. It is used for the treatment of intermittent claudication.

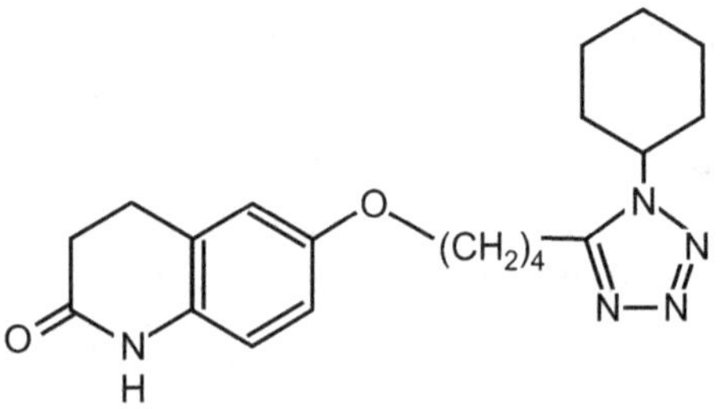

Nitrovasodilators such as nitroglycerine, nitroprusside and Sin - I have been tested effectively in the management of cardiovascular complications.

Argatroban : It is anticoagulant acting as direct thrombin inhibitor. It is used in the treatment of thrombosis in patients with heparin-induced thrombocytopenia. It is an arginine derivative. It is given intravenously and has a half-life of about 1 hour.

Thrombosis may occur due to an increase in the production of aggregating agents such as PGG_2, PGH_2 or TXA_2 or a decrease in production of the naturally occurring inhibitors PGD_2 produced by platelets or PGI_2 produced by blood vessels and that thrombotic episodes may be intensified by local vasoconstriction or vasodilatory actions of some of these agents.

Approaches to prevention or therapy of thrombosis which are based on metabolism of arachidonic acid include :

(a) Inhibitors of cyclo-oxygenase activity : e.g. Aspirin.

(b) Inhibitors of TXA_2 synthetase and antagonists of biological activities of thromboxane A_2 : Several agents have been shown to be selective inhibitors of TXA_2 synthetase. These include imidazole and several of its analogs ; 1' - (isopropyl - 2 - indolyl) - 3 - pyridyl - 3 - ketone; 9, 11 - azoprosta - 5, 13 - dienoic acid. Hydralazine, dipyridamole and diazoxide were also shown to be selective inhibitors of TXA_2 synthetase. Recently 9, 11 - azo - 13 - oxa - 15 - hydroxy-prostanoic acid has been shown to be a potent inhibitor of TXA_2 synthetase as well as an antagonist of TXA_2 and PGH_2.

Tirofiban : It is a non-peptide antiplatelet drug belonging to a class of glycoprotein IIb/IIIa inhibitors. Eptifibatide is yet another antiplatlet drug of the glycoprotein IIb/IIIa inhibitor class. It is a cyclic heptapeptide derived from a protein found in venom of the southeastern pygmy rattle snake.

Prasugrel (2009) : The thienopyridine class of ADP receptor inhibitors include, ticlopidine, clopidogrel, prasugrel. Prasugrel is a potent inhibitor of platelet aggregation.

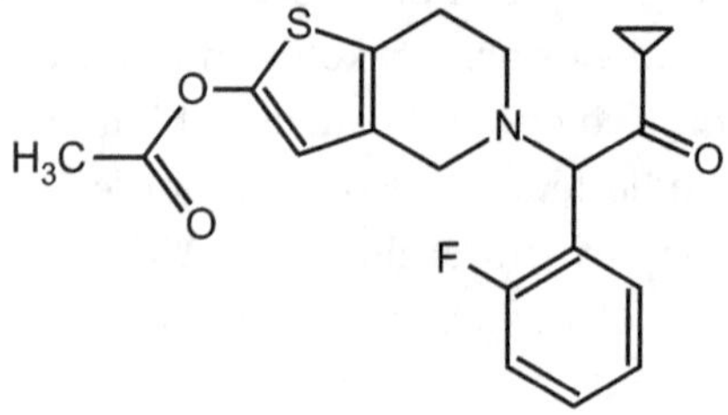

Table 5.10 (a) : Some anti-thrombotic drugs

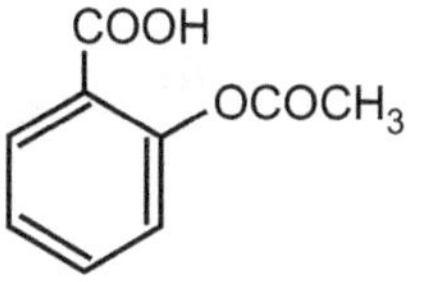

Aspirin

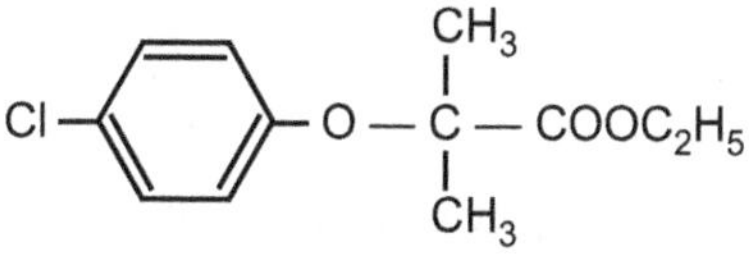

Clofibrate

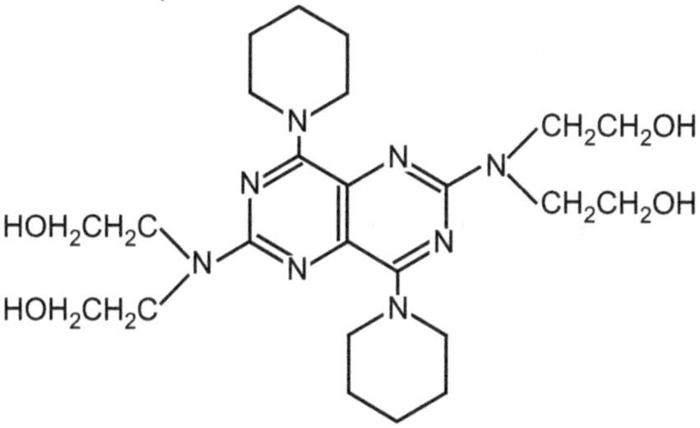

Dipyridamole

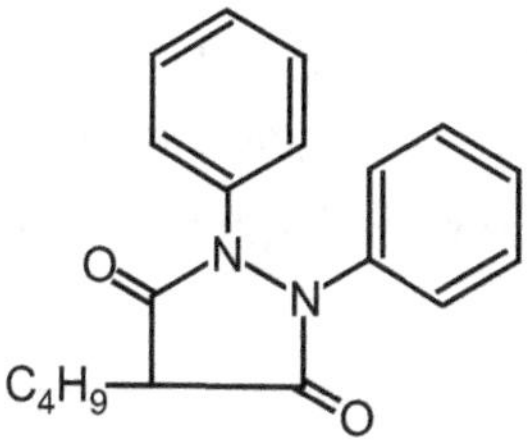

Phenylbutazone

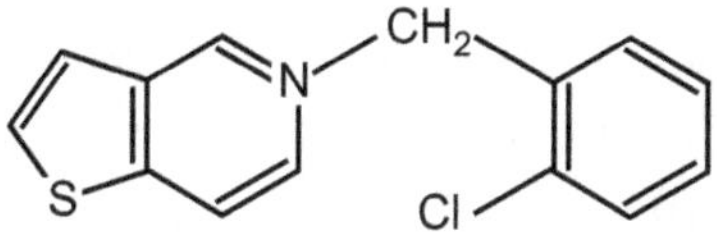

Ticlopidine

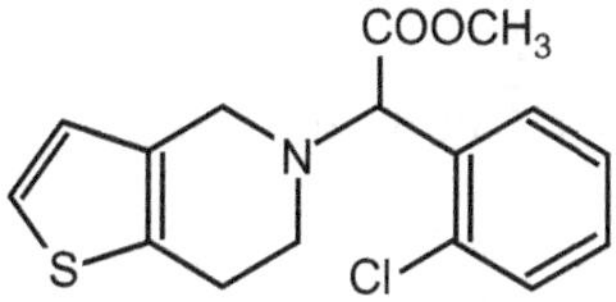

Clopidogrel

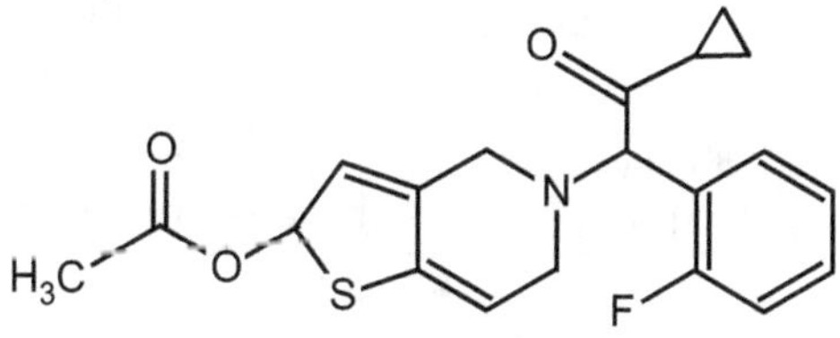

Prasugrel
(Clopidogrel analogue)

Abciximab : It is a glycoprotein IIb/IIIa receptor antagonist mainly used to prevent platelet aggregation and thrombus formation. It is made from Fab fragments of an immunoglobulin.

A number of CVS disorders such as stroke and heartattack are thought to be related to at least in part to an imbalance in synthesis of TXA_2.

Tirofiban : It is a non-peptide inhibitor acting at glycoprotein IIb/IIIa receptors in human platelets. It is an inhibitor of platelet aggregation. It is first drug resulted from pharmacophore based virtual screening lead.

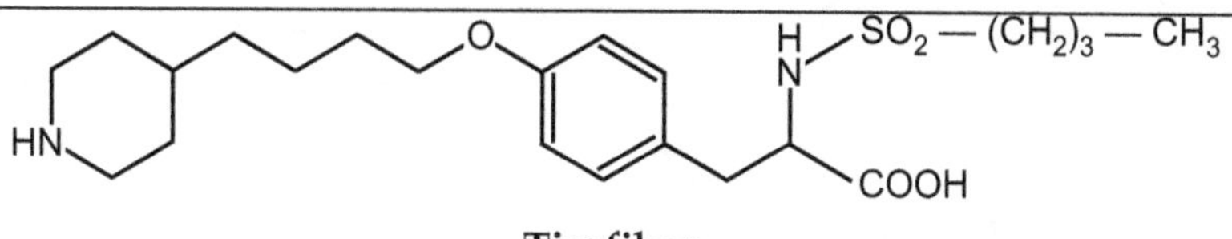

Tirofiban

Table 5.10 (b) : Clinically used Antiplatelet Strategies

Category	Examples
Prostaglandin (PG) synthase inhibition	aspirin, sulfinpyrazone
Blockage of adenosine monophosphate (AMP) breakdown	dipyridamole
Antagonism of adenosine diphosphate (ADP) induced aggregation	ticlopidine, clopidogrel
Thromboxane synthase inhibition	dazoxiben
Thromboxane/endoperoxide receptor antagonism	vapiprost, daltroban, ifetroban
Dual acting thromboxane synthase inhibition/thromboxane receptor blockade	ridogrel, picotamide
Modulation of platelet adenylate or guanylate cyclase	stable prostacyclin analogs (iloprost, ciprostene, cicaprost, beraprost)
Glycoprotein GPIIb/IIIa antagonism	monoclonal antibodies (c7E3 Fab) peptide inhibitors (Integrilin) non-peptide inhibitors (tirofiban, lamifiban etc.)

Vaso-occlusive disorders including unstable angina, myocardial infarction, transient ischemic attacks, stroke and peripheral artery disease remain the major sources of morbidity and mortality. Platelet activation and resulting platelet aggregation play a major role in the pathogenesis of these thromboembolic diseases.

Synthesis

(i) Losartan :

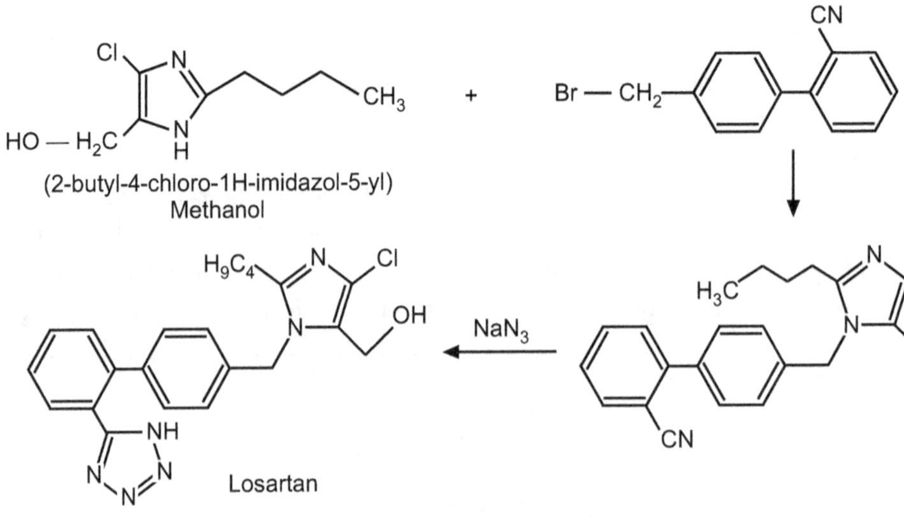

(2-butyl-4-chloro-1H-imidazol-5-yl) Methanol

Losartan

(ii) Clofibrate

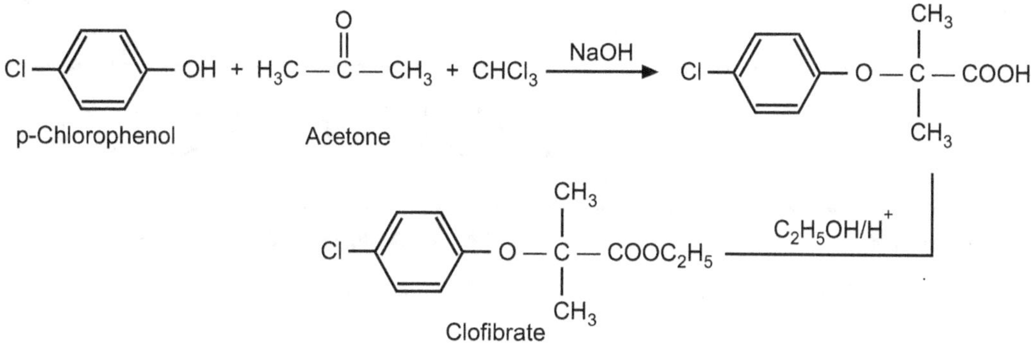

Cl—⟨benzene ring⟩—OH + $H_3C—\overset{\overset{O}{\|}}{C}—CH_3$ + $CHCl_3$ →(NaOH)→ Cl—⟨benzene ring⟩—O—$\overset{\overset{CH_3}{|}}{\underset{\underset{CH_3}{|}}{C}}$—COOH

p-Chlorophenol   Acetone

Cl—⟨benzene ring⟩—O—$\overset{\overset{CH_3}{|}}{\underset{\underset{CH_3}{|}}{C}}$—$COOC_2H_5$ ←(C_2H_5OH/H^+)—

Clofibrate

(iii) Hydralazine :

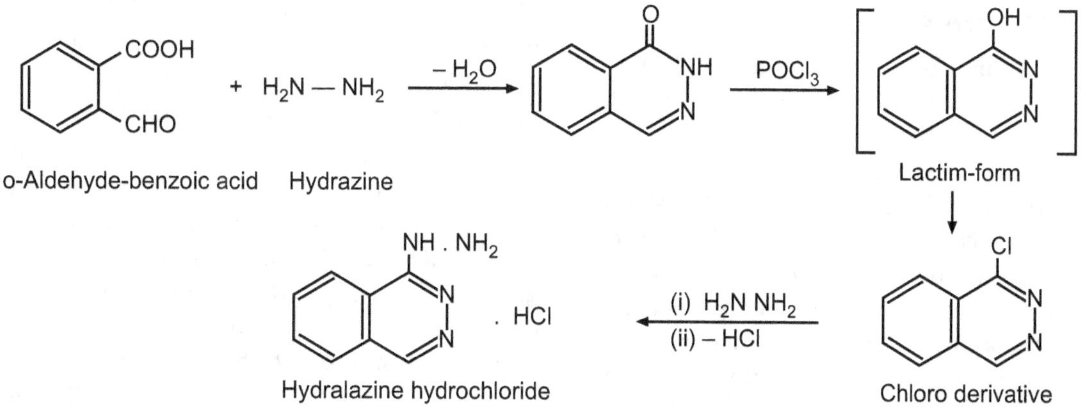

⟨benzene ring with COOH and CHO⟩ + $H_2N—NH_2$ →($-H_2O$)→ ⟨phthalazinone⟩ →($POCl_3$)→ [⟨lactim OH form⟩]

o-Aldehyde-benzoic acid   Hydrazine   Lactim-form

⟨phthalazine with NH·NH_2⟩ · HCl   ←(i) $H_2N\ NH_2$ / (ii) $-HCl$— ⟨phthalazine with Cl⟩

Hydralazine hydrochloride   Chloro derivative

(iv) Captopril :

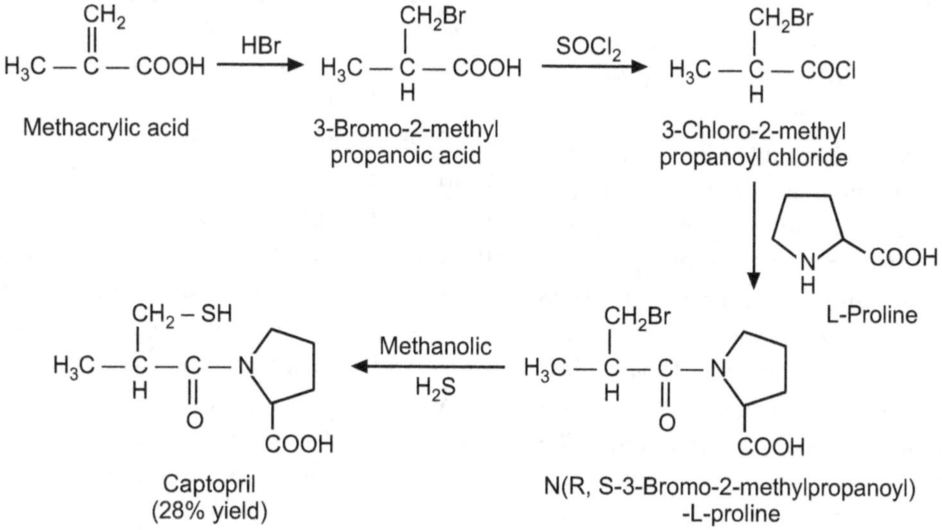

$H_3C—\overset{\overset{CH_2}{\|}}{C}—COOH$ →(HBr)→ $H_3C—\overset{\overset{CH_2Br}{|}}{\underset{\underset{H}{|}}{C}}—COOH$ →($SOCl_2$)→ $H_3C—\overset{\overset{CH_2Br}{|}}{\underset{\underset{H}{|}}{C}}—COCl$

Methacrylic acid   3-Bromo-2-methyl   3-Chloro-2-methyl
                          propanoic acid   propanoyl chloride

⟨pyrrolidine⟩ $\overset{}{\underset{H}{N}}$—COOH

L-Proline

$H_3C—\overset{\overset{CH_2-SH}{|}}{\underset{\underset{H}{|}}{C}}—\overset{\overset{}{\underset{\underset{O}{\|}}{C}}}{}—N$⟨pyrrolidine⟩COOH   ←(Methanolic H_2S)— $H_3C—\overset{\overset{CH_2Br}{|}}{\underset{\underset{H}{|}}{C}}—\overset{\overset{}{\underset{\underset{O}{\|}}{C}}}{}—N$⟨pyrrolidine⟩COOH

Captopril   N(R, S-3-Bromo-2-methylpropanoyl)
(28% yield)   -L-proline

❖❖❖

6

DIURETIC AGENTS

6.1 INTRODUCTION

Depending upon the age and built, body water comprises of about 60 - 70 % of total body weight in the normal person. This body water is distributed in two main compartments - intracellular and extracellular. The latter is valued to be about 15 % of normal body weight. The extracellular fluid is further subdivided into vascular and interstitial space. The porous capillary wall functions as a membrane of selective permeability and allows relatively free passage of water and low molecular weight agents. Large plasma-proteins, blood cells and lipid molecules can not cross the capillary wall. The inter-relationship between vascular and interstitial compartments was first described by *Starling* in 1909.

At the arterial end, there remains a net outward pressure of about 7 mm Hg and fluid passes into the tissue spaces. At the venous end, the net difference is of 10 mm Hg. Tissue fluid moves back into the capillary. This tissue fluid contains various ions, amino acids, glucose and foreign substances. These fluids bathe the organs and tissues of the body and thus create an internal environment. The composition and volume of these body fluids are to be maintained in order to make the internal environment compatible with life processes. This function is served by the kidneys. Kidney carries out this vital function related to the preservation of homeostasis. It is also a principal channel of excretion for many therapeutic agents and their metabolites.

Under resting conditions, in normal adult, about 650 ml of blood visits the kidneys every minute. Of this about 125 ml/min. protein free ultrafiltrate of plasma is formed through glomerulus filtration. Remaining plasma flows through element arterioles to bathe the peritubular surface of the nephron tubules. Out of 125 ml ultrafiltrate, about 80 to 90 % is reabsorbed by the epithelial cells of the proximal tubule. Remaining 10 to 20 % is reabsorbed from Henle's loop and distal tubule. Therefore, out of this 125 ml ultrafiltrate, on an average only 1 ml/min. is excreted as urine.

The accumulation of excessive body fluid in the extracellular compartments of the body is due to the retention of salts. It is generally referred to as edema. Edema may be due to renal abnormal functioning, cardiac failure, pregnancy etc. Diuretic agent corrects this situation by increasing the volume of urine excreted, i.e. causing diuresis. They affect the process of reabsorption of water and alter the renal electrolyte concentration. They are also of value in the treatment of hypertension and diabetes insipidus.

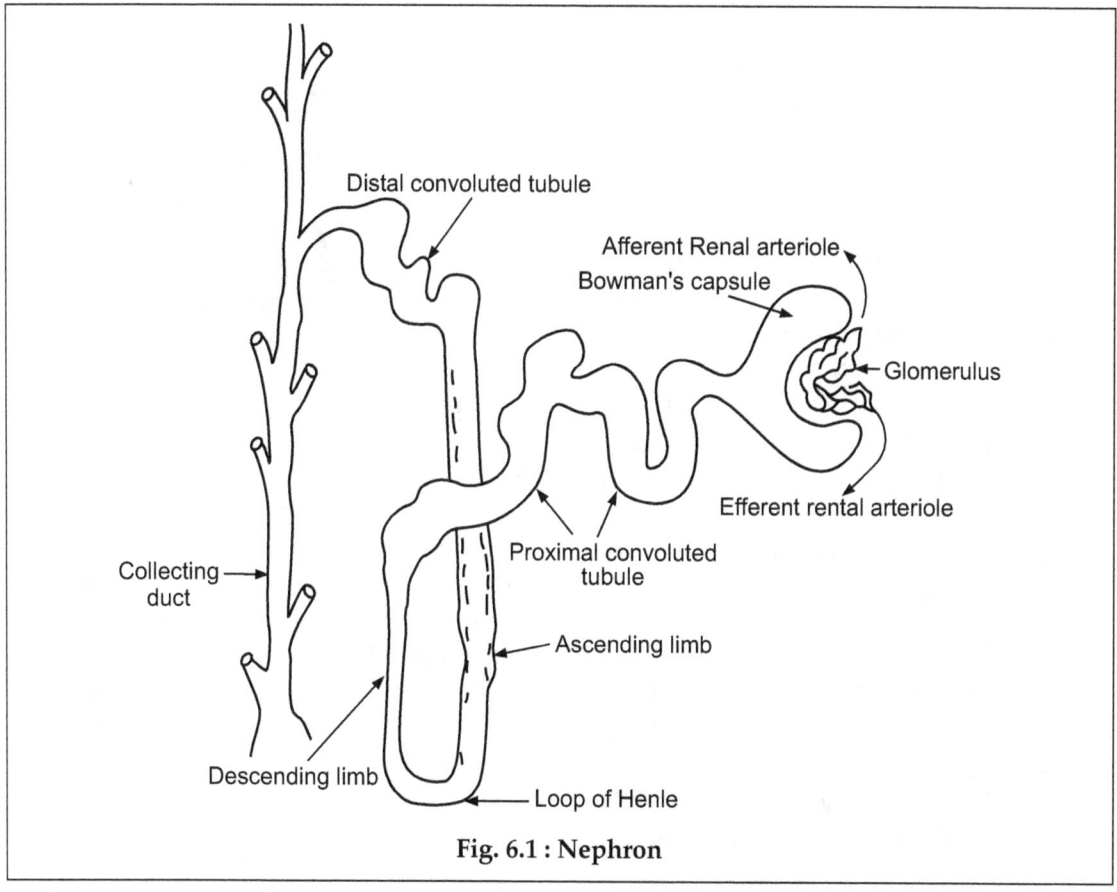

Fig. 6.1 : Nephron

The daily volume of glomerular filtrate in adults is 150 lit. in females and 180 lit. in males, a volume that represents about 65 times the entire blood plasma volume. More than 99% of the glomerular filtrate returns to the bloodstream via tubular reabsorption, however, so only 1-2 lit. are excreted as urine. In the process of urine formation, nephron and collecting ducts perform 3 basic processes.

1. Glomerular filtration (ultra filtration)

2. Tubular reabsorption (selective reabsorption)

3. Tubular secretion

Nephron is a basic functional unit of kidney. Each kidney consists of about one million nephrons, which routinely filter water, electrolytes and non-electrolytes like glucose, urea, uric acid and creatinine. Each nephron has three functional parts.

1. **Bowman's capsule :**

It encloses a microscopic ball of blood vessels, known as glomerulus. The blood enters the glomerulus through afferent arterioles under high capillary pressure. At the exit of glomerulus, the capillaries reunite to form efferent arterioles. After the glomerular filtration, the filtered fraction is collected in the lumen of the capsule. Under normal circumstances, glomerular filtration is independent of arterial blood pressure.

2. The renal tubule :

It is made up of three segments i.e.

1. The proximal convoluted tubule.

2. The loop of Henle, and

3. The distal convoluted tubule.

The renal tubule has the ability, both actively and passively, to reabsorb large amounts of water and other substances (NaCl, glucose, amino acids etc.) that appear in the ultrafiltrate. Blood present in afferent arterioles has a pH of 7.4 while urine has an average pH of 6.00 due to acidification of fluid. This acidification of urine, potassium secretion and ammonia secretion occur in the distal convoluted tubule.

3. The collecting tubule :

Water reabsorption in the distal tubule and collecting ducts is regulated independently by antidiuretic hormone (ADH) which controls the water permeability of this part of the nephron. The collecting

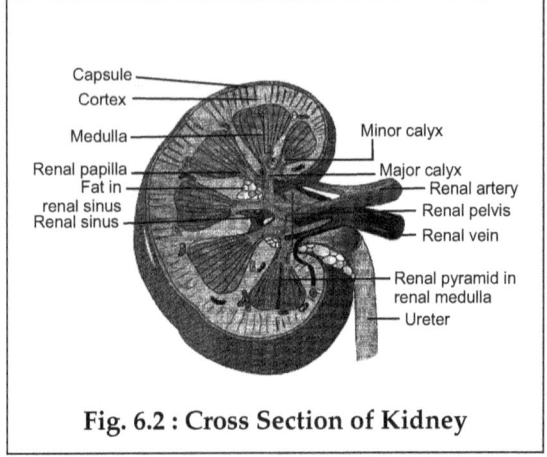

Fig. 6.2 : Cross Section of Kidney

tubule finally joins a large collecting duct via the renal pelvis and ureter. The larger collecting duct releases its contents into urinary bladder where the urine is stored. The total volume of urine formed varies between 1 to 1.5 litres a day.

The term 'diuretics' is derived from the Greek word 'Diouretikos' which means 'to promote urine' in the year 1500.

$$H_2N - \overset{\overset{\displaystyle O}{\|}}{C} - NH_2$$

Urea

D-glucose (Dextrose)

Sucrose

CH₂OH
HO — CH
HO — CH
HC — OH
HC — OH
CH₂OH

Mannitol

Isosorbide

Osmotic agents

The process of diuresis is usually accompanied by mobilization of the edema fluid. In diuresis, increased urine is due to the increased excretion of Na^+, H^+, Cl^-, HPO_4^{--}, Ca^{++}, Mg^{++} and HCO_3^- ions. This may possibly result in hypokalemia, hyperglycemia and hyperuricemia.

6.2 CLASSIFICATION OF DIURETICS

Looking at dose response curve, a diuretic is either called as :

1. **Low-ceiling diuretic :**

In this case, response increases proportionately with an increase in dose upto a threshold value. Thereafter, increase in dose, does not affect the response, or

2. **High-ceiling diuretic :**

Response runs linearly with the dose of the diuretic, even after the threshold value.

We shall study the different diuretic agents under the following heads :
1. Water and osmotic agents
2. Acidifying agents
3. Mercurials
4. Phenoxyacetic acids
5. Xanthines
6. Inhibitors of carbonic anhydrase
7. Benzothiadiazines
8. Sulfamyl benzoic acid derivatives (high-ceiling agents)
9. Potassium sparing diuretics
10. Uricosuric diuretics

6.3 INDIVIDUAL CLASS

1. **Water and Osmotic Agents :**

Diuresis is generally desired to mobilize the edema fluid, resulting in the removal of excess extracellular fluid and electrolytes. Water does not fit in this definition. It is therefore used when it is intended to get increased urine volume without altering the electrolytes or extracellular fluids. Ingested water rapidly dilutes the blood. This water induced fall in blood osmolarity, increases urinary excretion by inhibiting the secretion of antidiuretic hormone (ADH). Water is a diuretic agent which is of no value in the treatment of edema.

Osmotic agents prevent reabsorption of water. They are low molecular weight, non-metabolized, inert substances readily filtered in the glomerulus. They remain poorly reabsorbed in the renal tubule. The diuresis thus produced is proportional to the concentration of non-absorbable osmotic agent.

In the normal course, the solutes get reabsorbed as they pass from one segment to other in the renal tubule. Water also linearly diffuses into tubular cells to maintain the constant tonicity of tubular fluid. This linearity cannot be maintained in presence of osmotic agent. The diffusion of water is reduced. This in turn causes reduction in the net reabsorption of sodium ions, producing a diuretic effect.

Osmotic diuretics : Mannitol is prototype of this class. Urea (1864) is the first osmotic diuretic used.

Commonly used osmotic agents are urea, glucose, sucrose, mannitol and isosorbide. The intestinal wall shares some structural features in common with the renal tubular cells. Naturally, the substances that fail to get reabsorbed in renal tubule, also remain unabsorbed in GIT, if given by oral route. Hence osmotic agents must be administered parenterally to reach the circulation. Exception is urea. The 4 % urea and 10 % invert sugar solution is generally used to cause diuresis. An extensively used agent is mannitol which after intravenous administration causes diuresis within 1 to 3 hours.

Table 6.1

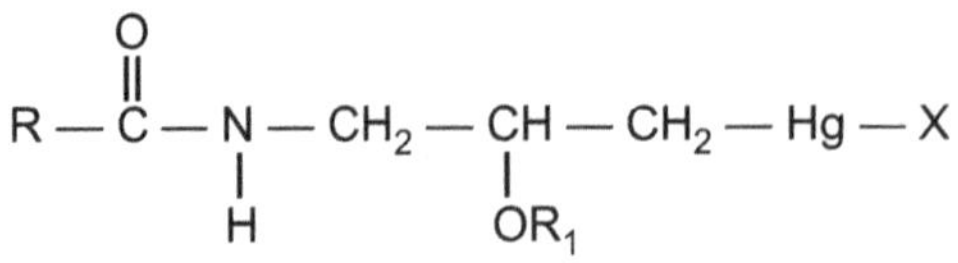

$$R - \overset{\overset{\displaystyle O}{\|}}{C} - \underset{\underset{\displaystyle H}{|}}{N} - CH_2 - \underset{\underset{\displaystyle OR_1}{|}}{CH} - CH_2 - Hg - X$$

Organomercurials

Name	R	R_1	X
1. Mersalyl	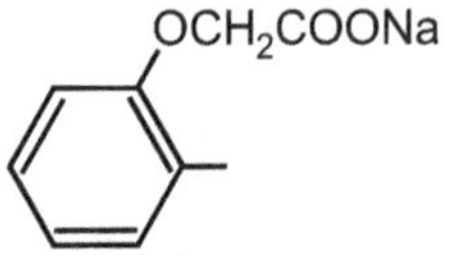 OCH$_2$COONa (benzene ring)	CH_3	Theophylline
2. Mercurophyllin	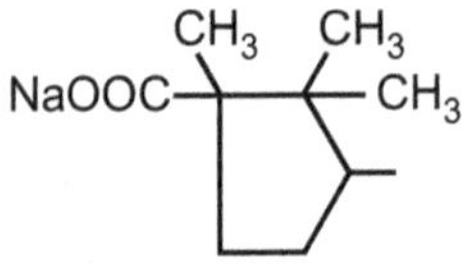 NaOOC— (ring) CH$_3$ CH$_3$ —CH$_3$	CH_3	Theophylline
3. Mercaptomerin	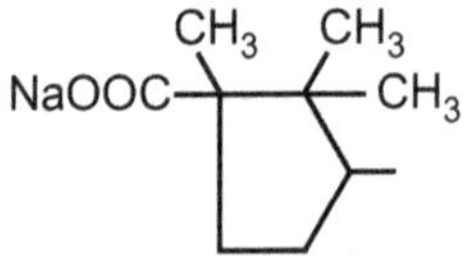 NaOOC— (ring) CH$_3$ CH$_3$ —CH$_3$	CH_3	$- SCH_2COOH$
4. Chlormerodrin	NH_2	CH_3	Cl
5. Merethoxyline	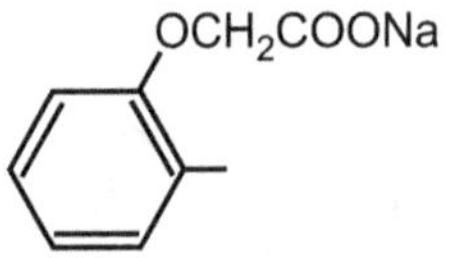 OCH$_2$COONa (benzene ring)	$- CH_2CH_2OCH_3$	OH
6. Meralluride	$NaOOCCH_2CH_2CONH -$	CH_3	OH

2. Acidifying Agents :

Ammonium chloride, ammonium nitrate, calcium chloride and L-lysine monohydrochloride are some examples. These are inorganic salts which produce systemic acidosis and a transient diuresis.

In liver, the ammonium ion is converted into a neutral compound, urea. The excess of chloride ions left is excreted taking with it an equivalent amount of sodium and appropriate amount of water. With this process the renal sodium reserve is exhausted resulting into the renal acidosis. Kidney develops compensatory mechanisms by producing ammonia which is exchanged in terms of sodium ions in the tubule. As a result, Na$^+$ ions are retained and ammonia ions are excreted in the form of ammonium chloride which quantitatively matches the amount ingested. Loss of sodium ions is thus prevented and acidifying agents thus lose their diuretic activity within first 1 - 2 days of treatment. If used alone, they are of no clinical value. They may be used in conjunction with the organomercurials because acidifying agents potentiate their action.

3. Organomercurials :

Calomel (mercurial chloride) was used by Paracelsus in 15th century. Mersalyl is the prototype of this class.

They are potent, relatively non-toxic agents. Though the first clinical use of mercurials (mercury chloride) dates back to sixteenth century, they had to wait until 1919 to get their potential recognised. Thereafter they dominated the diuretic field for more than 30 years. They are usually given by deep intramuscular injection and are still regarded as effective agents against severe edematous states. Most of them are mono or dicarboxylic acid or their amide derivative possessing an alkoxymercuripropyl chain. The clinically useful organomercurials are enlisted in the table 6.1.

SAR studies revealed that any marked deviation in the general structure of organo-mercurials drastically reduce the activity. The nature of R is most related with activity while that of R_1 is least effective. Theophylline attachment to the basic skeleton improves the absorption. Besides this, theophylline itself has weak diuretic activity. It also lowers tissue irritation usually associated with mercurials.

Mercurials impair the activity of enzymes containing sulfhydryl (–SH) groups. This inhibition occurs in both, the proximal renal tubule and loop of the Henle. The most affected enzyme system is sodium - potassium activated ATPase system which governs reabsorption process. Due to this, a moderate increase in potassium loss also occurs. Dimercaprol or other vicinal dithiols have

greater affinity for mercury ion. Hence, if administered, they restore the activity of renal enzyme system and diuresis ceases.

Mercurials mainly interfere with the enzyme systems responsible for reabsorption of chloride ions. Chloride ions alongwith less sodium ions are retained in the renal tubule and also the water. This results in diuresis. It is proposed that mercurials do not directly exhibit the activity. They undergo ionization to release divalent mercury ion in the tubule which is the actual diuretic agent. They exhibit a synergistic activity with acidifying salt.

They are mainly used in mobilization of edema due to cardiac failure. They are also effective in ascites due to cirrhosis of the liver and portal obstruction. Side-effects include nausea, vomiting, tissue irritation and allergic manifestations. Their clinical popularity has sharply declined due to, their toxic effects and availability of newer orally active drugs. e.g., furosemide. Oral administration of mercurials is unsatisfactory owing to irritation of gastro-intestinal tract.

4. Phenoxyacetic Acids :

Mechanism of action of mercurial diuretics indicated the importance of enzymes containing sulfhydryl groups in renal transport mechanisms. Search naturally then began for effective sulfhydryl group blockers. Ethacrynic acid was outcome of this search. First used in 1963, the structure contains a highly reactive ethylene group which reacts with sulfhydryl group to form adduct. While the aryloxyacetic acid part favours the renal localization of the drug.

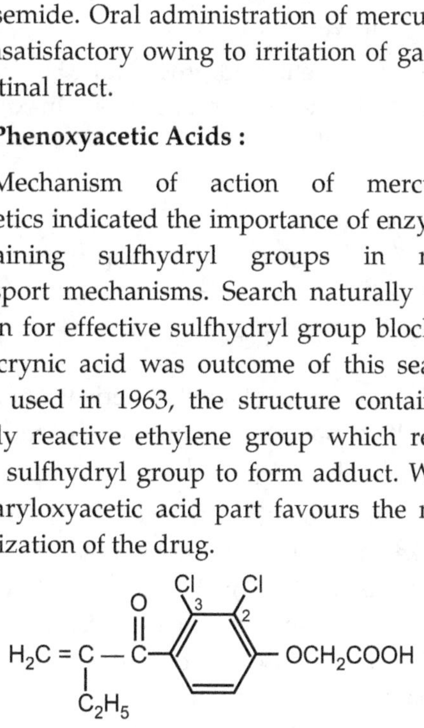

Ethacrynic acid

Ethacrynic acid is an extremely powerful diuretic. On pharmacological basis (i.e. similar site of action), it is grouped together with furosemide and bumetanide into 'high-ceiling' or 'loop diuretic' category. They are most effective agents available. They also possess some carbonic anhydrase inhibiting activity except ethacrynic acid. Diuresis is brought about by inhibition of active Cl⁻ reabsorption in the thick ascending limb of the loop of Henle.

SAR studies in ethacrynic acid series revealed the following points :

1. Halogen (more preferably chlorine) or methyl group may be substituted at position ortho to the unsaturated ketone.

2. It confers the proper lipophilic - hydrophilic balance for maximum activity.

3. Disubstitution at 2, 3 positions may increase the activity.

4. Oxyacetic acid group must be para to the ketone group for maximum activity.

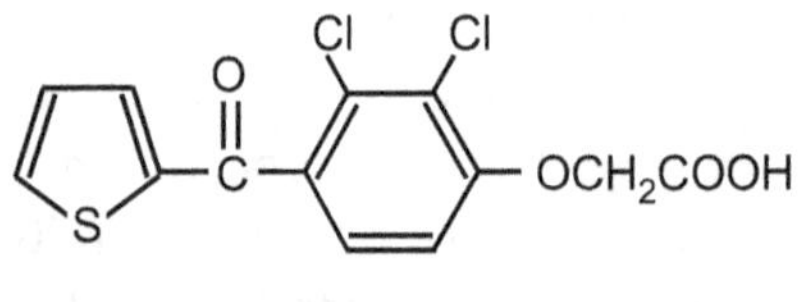

Ticrynafen

Ticrynafen is yet another derivative of this class. It is not a loop diuretic. Severe liver toxicity has been reported with its use.

Nausea, vomiting, dizziness, hypotension, hypokalemia and hypochloremia are side-effects associated with loop - diuretics. Ototoxicity also sometimes occurs which seems to be dose related. Reversible and permanant deafness has been reported to occur with ethacrynic acid in patients with uremia.

Loop diuretics are usually effective in treatment of edemas of cardiac, hepatic, renal or pulmonary origin. They are contraindicated in pregnancy. Ethacrynic acid is a potent saluretic agent and is especially effective in the treatment of refractory edema where it may be used alongwith a potassium sparing diuretic.

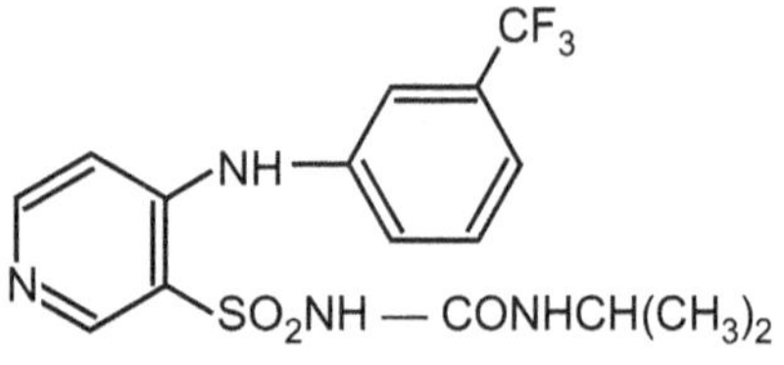

Torsemide

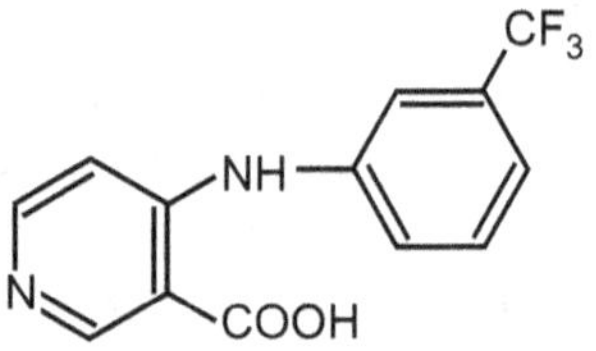

Triflocin

5. Xanthines :

The xanthines are rarely employed as primary diuretics. Theophylline, theobromine and caffeine are all methylated xanthines that occur in nature. They are usually administered as water soluble compounds. e.g. theophylline ethylenediamine (aminophylline). Similarly, xanturil a mannich base of theophylline also possesses good activity.

The 2, 6 - dihydroxypurine is xanthine and theophylline, theobromine and caffeine are N-methylated xanthines. Theophylline is the most potent xanthine diuretic. It is used in conjunction with diuretics to reduce their tissue irritating effects and to improve their absorption. Its derivative, aminophylline is effective as a diuretic only when it is given by the intravenous route.

Mechanism of action of xanthine diuretics still remains unclear. Due to their cardiac actions, there is an increase in the renal blood flow and glomerular filtration rate. Xanthine derivatives also are expected to inhibit reabsorption of Na^+ and Cl^- ions in the proximal tubules without disturbing urinary pH or activity of carbonic anhydrase.

6. **Inhibitors of Carbonic Anhydrase Enzymes :**

The enzyme carbonic anhydrase displays its activity at many sites including renal cortex, gastric mucosa, pancreas, eye, erythrocytes and central nervous system. It is present in dense population particularly in erythrocytes and the renal cortex and plays an important role in the tubular reabsorption of bicarbonate and Na^+ ions.

It catalyses hydration of carbon dioxide to carbonic acid and also its dissociation, back to water and carbon dioxide. In next independant reaction, carbonic acid ionizes to hydrogen ion and a bicarbonate ion.

These reactions occur in the cells of renal tubule. Through the sodium-hydrogen exchange programme, the Na^+ ions in the glomerular filtrate are reabsorbed in the tubules, primarily in the proximal tubule. The HCO_3^- is also reabsorbed from the glomerular filtrate. Under the influence of carbonic anhydrase inhibitors, sodium-hydrogen exchange can not be operated. Sodium and bicarbonate ions are retained in the glomerular filtrate and can not be reabsorbed. This coupled with increased rate of excretion of potassium ions, and osmotic equivalent of water results in diuresis. The use of carbonic anhydrase inhibitors is usually accompanied by systemic acidosis and alkaline urine. This is due to increased renal excretion of K^+, Na^+ and HCO_3^- ions (alkaline urine) and impairment of H^+ secretion (systemic acidosis).

$$H_2O + CO_2 \rightleftharpoons H_2CO_3 \rightleftharpoons H^+ + HCO_3^-$$
Carbonic anhydrase

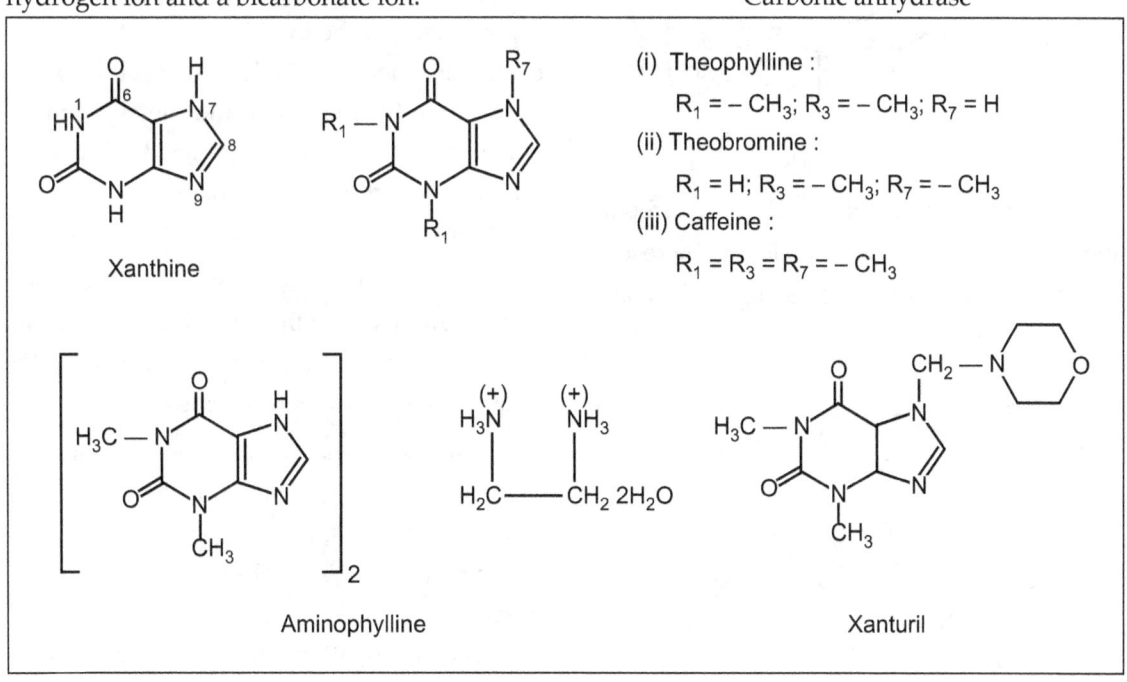

(i) Theophylline :
     $R_1 = -CH_3$; $R_3 = -CH_3$; $R_7 = H$

(ii) Theobromine :
     $R_1 = H$; $R_3 = -CH_3$; $R_7 = -CH_3$

(iii) Caffeine :
     $R_1 = R_3 = R_7 = -CH_3$

Xanthine

Aminophylline

Xanturil

Killin and Mann discovered the carbonic anhydrase inhibitory property of sulphanilamide. Acetazolamide is prototype of this class of drugs.

An unsubstituted sulphonamide (- SO_2NH_2) group seems to be essential for inhibition of carbonic anhydrase enzyme. A large number of aromatic and heterocyclic sulphonamides exhibit this activity. Acetazolamide is the prototype of this class.

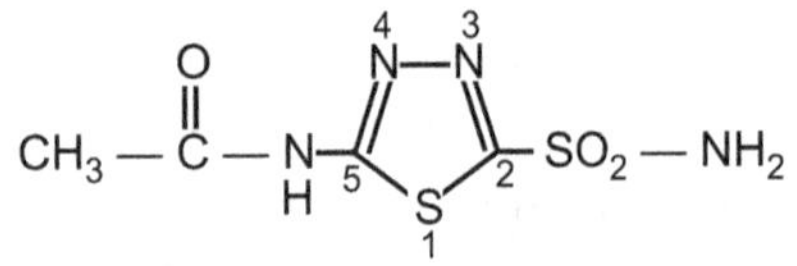

Acetazolamide

Brinzolamide : It is carbonic anhydrase inhibitor used to lower intraocular pressure with open angle glaucoma or ocular hypertension.

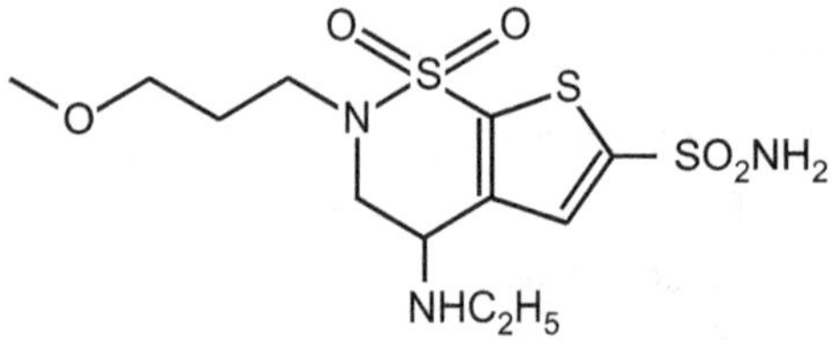

Dorzolamide (1995) : It is carbonic anhydrase inhibitor used to lower increased intraocular pressure in open angle glaucoma and ocular hypertension.

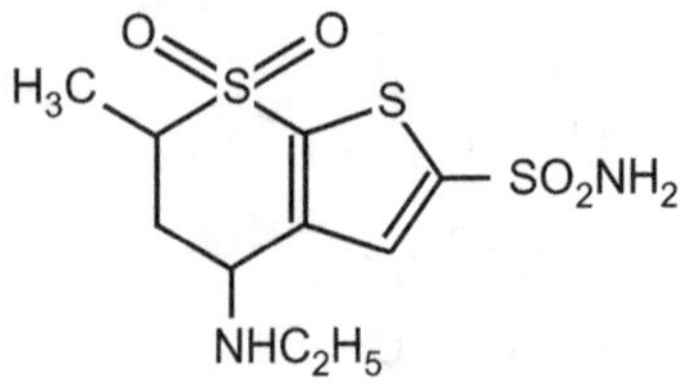

In addition to proximal tubule, these agents also affect both distal tubule and collecting duct.

SAR studies reveal the importance of free amide nitrogen because the mono- and di-substitutions at SO_2NH_2 abolish the activity. Ionizing ability of the drug seems to be proportional to its activity. The free - SO_2NH_2 group is necessary to bind with Zn^{++} ion in the enzyme. The sulfhydryl function of the enzyme engages another drug molecule through the mercury atom. This drug-enzyme complex is of reversible type.

Carbonic anhydrase inhibitors are less preferred diuretics because :

1. They are accompanied by systemic acidosis and alkalinization of the urine. Many drugs are weak acids or weak bases. The metabolic turnover and body life time of such drugs is affected due to systemic acidosis and alkaline urine e.g. amphetamine and urinary tract antiseptic (e g. methenamine).

2. Since the drug-enzyme complex is of reversible type, the inhibitory activity of drug ceases as soon as depletion of bicarbonate store in the tubules occur and they remain no longer effective as diuretic agents. This self limiting action of these agents is a major drawback.

3. An introduction of more effective, orally administered thiazide diuretics further suppressed their use. Hence, they are not used frequently as therapeutic agents.

Their side-effects include drowsiness, confusion and loss of appetite. They are contra-indicated in pregnancy. They are recommended in the treatment of premenstrual edema, glaucoma and to reduce the frequency of attacks in petit mal and grand mal epilepsy. Their place in anticonvulsant therapy is due to their ability to develop systemic acidosis which reduces the frequency of seizures. They also cause a partial depression of aqueous humor formation in the eye which is dependent on their carbonic anhydrase inhibition ability.

7. Benzothiadiazines :

They are also known as thiazide diuretics. They are derivatives of 1, 2, 4 - benzothiadiazine -1, 1 dioxide. They all carry a 3 - sulfamyl - 4 - halogenated benzene ring and all exhibit identical properties, mode of action, site of action and same range of clinical application. They mainly differ in their duration of action, where drug having high lipophilicity displays long duration of action. They appeared on the clinical screen through the efforts to find out better inhibitors of carbonic anhydrase enzymes. The heterocyclic benzothiadiazines are potent, orally active diuretic agents.

Chlorthiazide, the first thiazide diuretic agent was introduced in 1958. Soon after, hydrochlorthiazide was introduced. SAR studies of thiazide diuretics revealed following points :

1. In general, all hydrothiazides are more active than thiazide derivatives.

2. The benzene ring should bear a free sulfamyl group at position 7. In substituted sulfamyl derivatives, the substitution should easily get cleared off in-vivo, to release drug containing free sulfamyl group.

3. Halogen or halogen like group at position 6 increases the potency.

4. Saturation of the 3, 4 double bond potentiates the activity.

5. Lipophilic substitution in position 3 of the heterocyclic ring enlarges the duration of action.

These agents cause diuresis mainly by inhibiting active Cl^- reabsorption in the distal portion of the ascending limb or the initial part of the distal tubule. Their site of action resembles closely with that of mercurials. This is independent of any effect on carbonic anhydrase. They also increase excretion of potassium. Due to their direct action on the renal vasculature, glomerular filtration rate may also be reduced. At therapeutic doses, they exhibit mercurial like activity by impairing Cl^- transport mechanisms. At higher doses, their activity is partly due to carbonic anhydrase inhibition and partly by depressant action on distal tubular reabsorption, and thus may be said to combine the actions of mercurials and carbonic anhydrase inhibitors. In long term treatment, there may be a gradual reduction in the diuretic response, due to depressant action on glomerular filtration rate. This may be due to a slow emergence of the body's compensatory mechanisms (like increased aldosterone secretion). In patients having diabetes insipidus, diuretic action is not observed. In fact thiazide diuretics may exhibit antidiuretic activity in such patients.

The adverse effects of thiazide diuretics are usually rare. Gastrointestinal disturbances, alongwith certain allergic reactions may occur. They should be used with caution in patients suffering from diabetes insipidus and renal or hepatic fault. Hypokalaemia usually occurs with thiazide therapy which may be corrected by giving supplemental administration of potassium or using potassium sparing diuretic alongwith thiazide. But this resulted in development of non-specific small intestinal ulcers in some patients. Hyperglycemia and glycosuria may occur which precipitate the onset of diabetes mellitus.

These agents have restricted advantages during pregnancy.

The thiazides are diuretics of choice in the treatment of edema associated with pre-menstrual tension, hormone therapy and edema of cardiac, liver or renal origin. They also possess mild anti-hypertensive activity and may be used in the treatment of hypertension with or without edema.

Metolazone : It is a thiazoide diuretic used to treat congestive heart failure and high blood pressure.

Metolazone

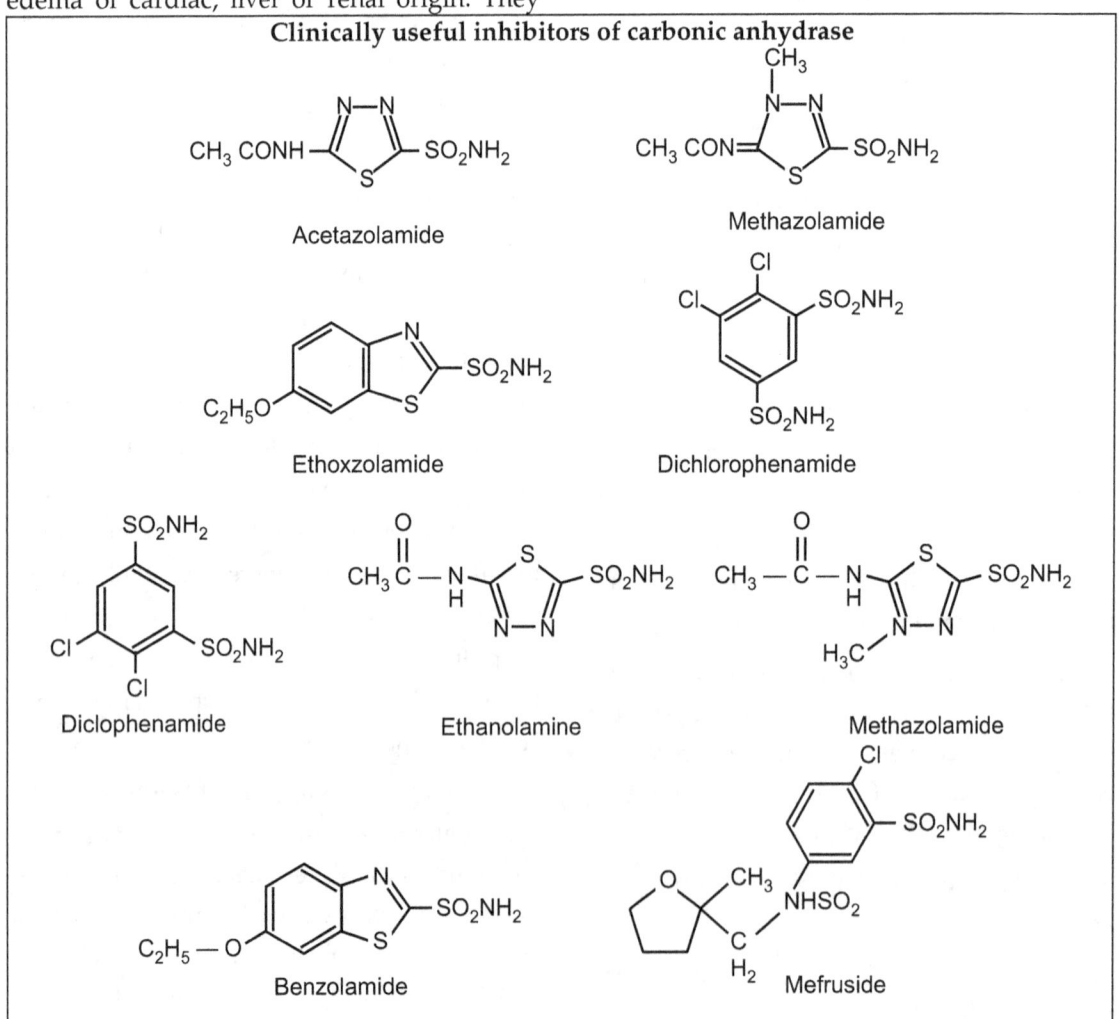

Clinically useful inhibitors of carbonic anhydrase

Acetazolamide

Methazolamide

Ethoxzolamide

Dichlorophenamide

Diclophenamide

Ethanolamine

Methazolamide

Benzolamide

Mefruside

Table 6.2 : Clinically useful benzothiadiazine diuretic agents

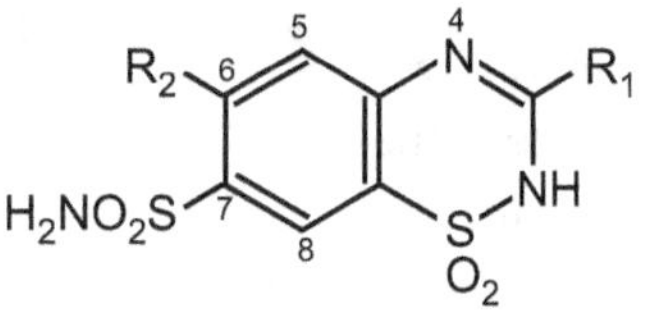

(A) Thiazides :

Name	R_1	R_2
1. Chlorothiazide	H	Cl
2. Flumethiazide	H	CF_3
3. Benzthiazide	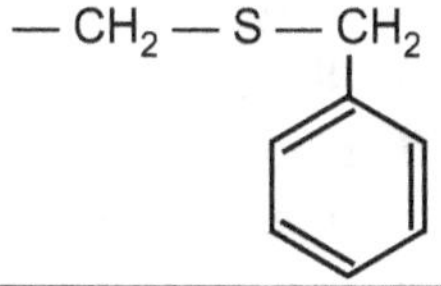 $-CH_2-S-CH_2-$ (benzyl)	Cl

(B) Hydrothiazides :

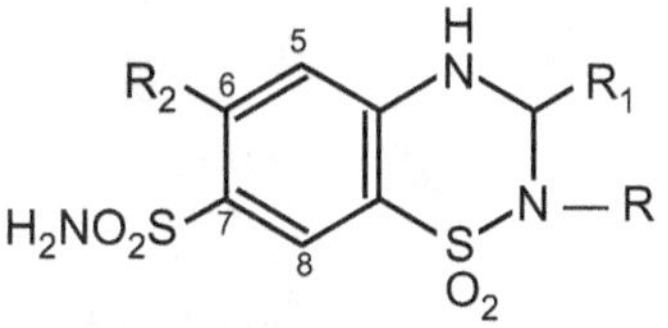

Name	R_1	R_2	R
1. Hydrochlorthiazide	H	Cl	H
2. Hydroflumethiazide	H	CF_3	H
3. Hydrobenzthiazide	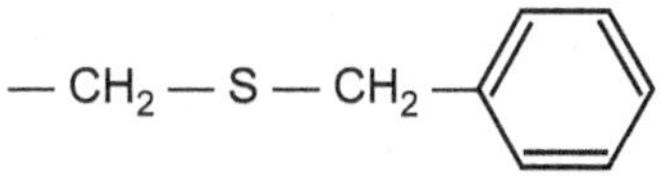 $-CH_2-S-CH_2-$ (phenyl)	Cl	H
4. Cyclothiazide	 (norbornene)	Cl	H
5. Bendroflumethiazide	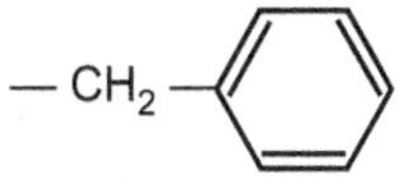 $-CH_2-$ (phenyl)	CF_3	H
6. Polythiazide	$-CH_2-S-CH_2-CF_3$	Cl	CH_3
7. Methyclothiazide	$-CH_2Cl$	Cl	CH_3
8. Trichlormethiazide	$-CHCl_2$	Cl	H

Non-thiazide Analogs of Thiazide Diuretics :

They are also known as quinazolinone derivatives. They closely resemble the benzothiadiazines in their mode of action, therapeutic applications and spectra of side-effects.

They differ chemically from the thiazides by the nature of the heterocyclic ring where the ring sulfone (-SO$_2$ group) is replaced by the carbonyl group. They propogate, comparatively longer duration of action than thiazide diuretics, as indicated in the bracket.

The members of this series belong to chemically distinct categories like, quinazolinone, benzhydrazide, phthalimidine, oxoisoindole etc.

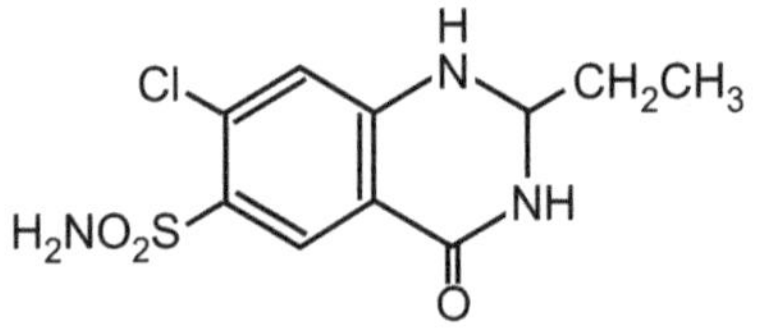

Quinethazone (18 to 24 hours)
(Quinazolinones)

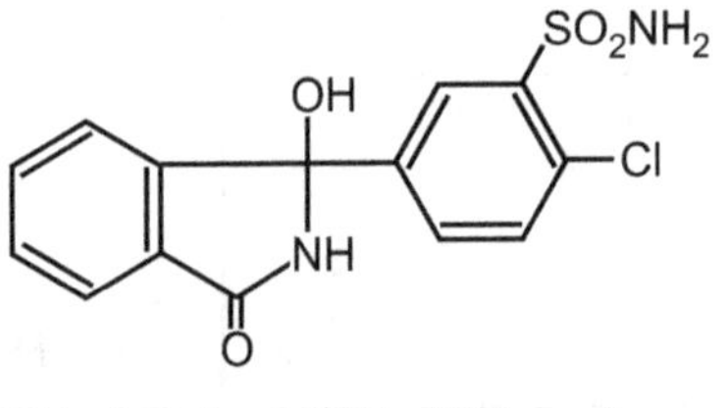

Chlorthalidone (48 to 72 hours)
(Pthalimidine)

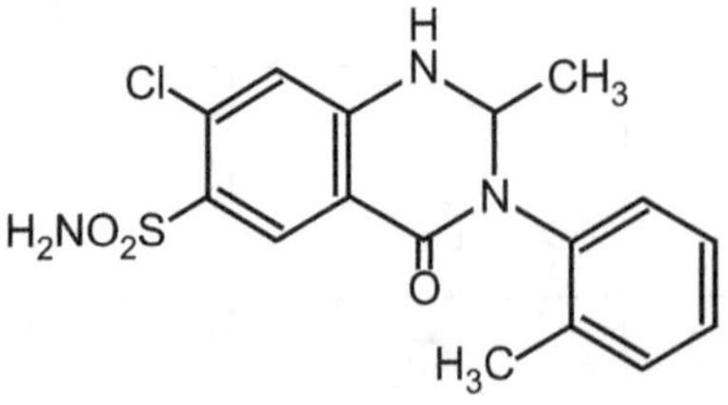

Metolazone (12 to 24 hours)
(Quinazolinones)

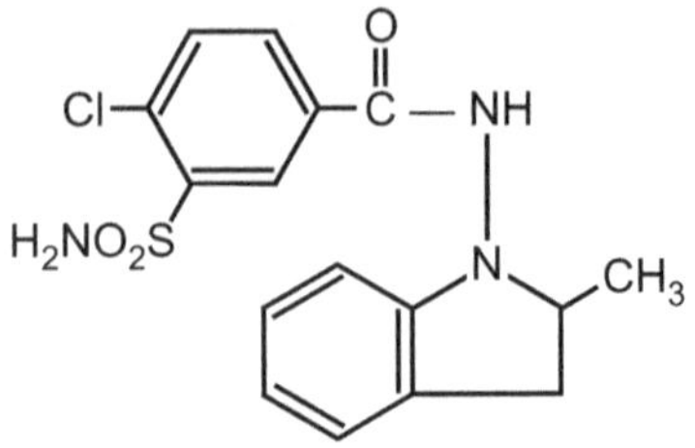

Indapamide
(Benzhydrazides)

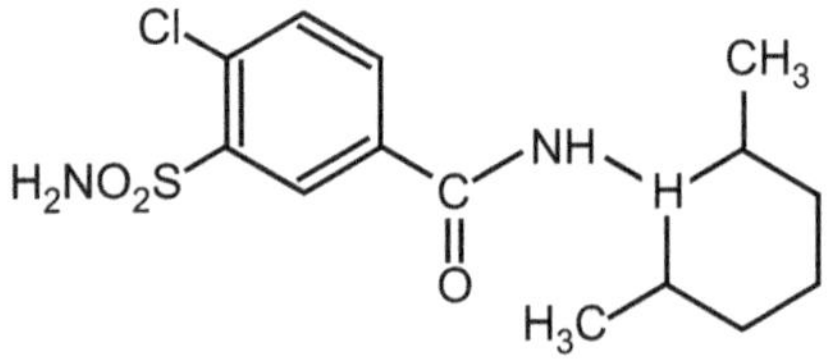

Clopamide
(Benzhydrazides)

8. Sulfomyl Benzoic Acid Derivatives :

Loop or high ceiling diuretics (after 1960) : Furesemide (1964) is prototype of this class.

These analogs share many properties, mode of action, therapeutic applications and side-effects in common with ethacrynic acid, a phenoxyacetic acid derivative. Ethacrynic acid, furosemide and bumetanide are more often grouped together and are called as loop diuretics or high ceiling diuretics. Furosemide is anthranilic acid derivative.

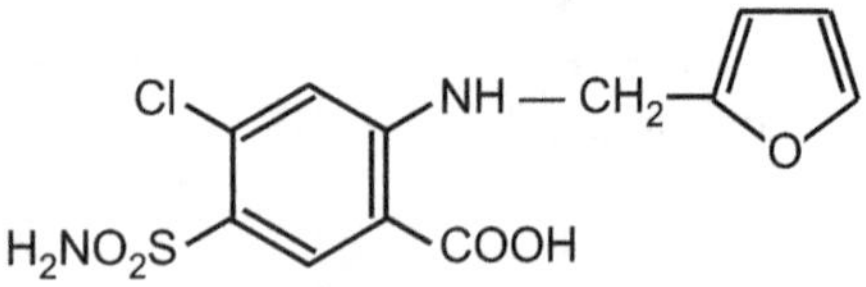

Furosemide

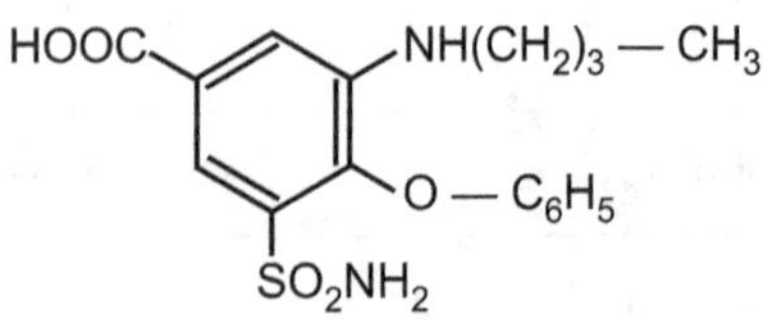

Bumetanide

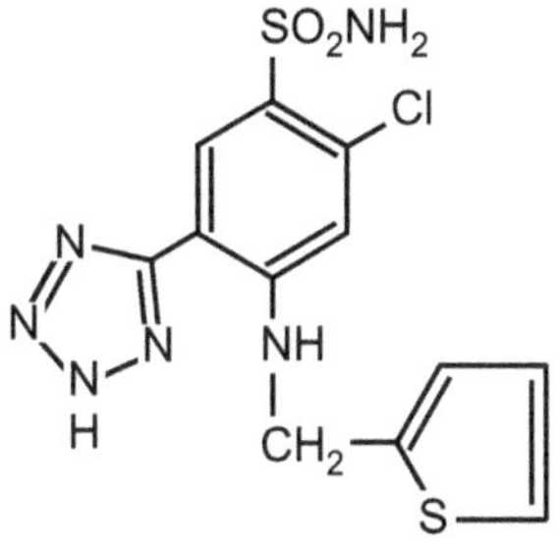

Azosamide
Loop diuretics

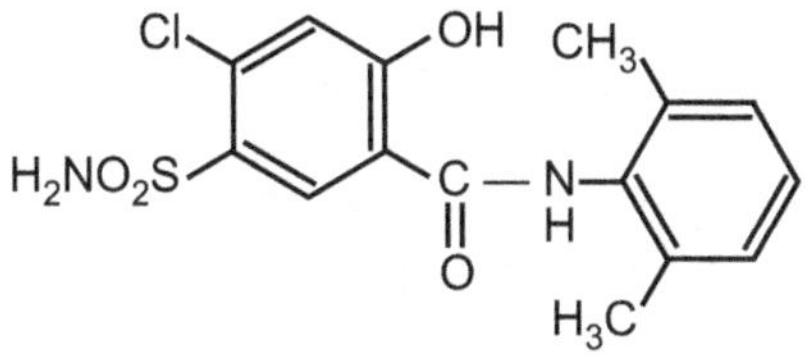

Xipamide (Salicylanilide)

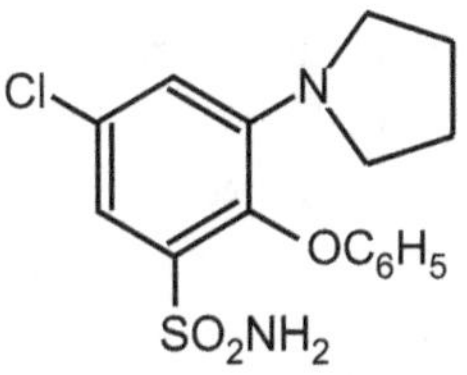

Piretanide

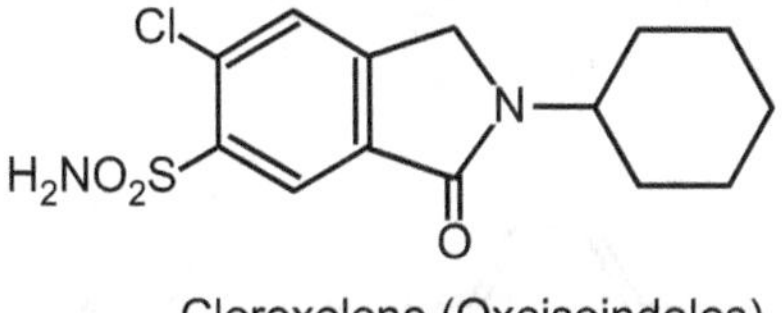

Clorexolone (Oxoisoindoles)

Torsemide : It is a pyridine-sulfonyl urea type loop diuretic used in the management of edema associated with congestive heart failure.

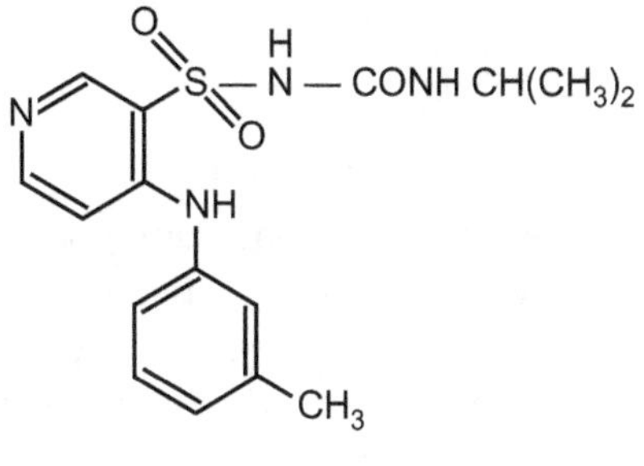

Furosemide and Bumetanide have already been described in phenoxyacetic acid derivatives, alongwith ethacrynic acid. Unlike ethacrynic acid, both agents however induce a loss of bicarbonate ions, probably due to partial inhibition of carbonic anhydrase enzyme.

Xipamide and Clorexolone are the new agents of this class which are under clinical trials.

9. Potassium Sparing Agents :

These agents act at the distal segment of the nephron and decrease the excretion of potassium and hydrogen ions. These agents are preferred in patients with low serum K^+ levels resulting from diuretic therapy with other agents.

Aldosterone plays a physiological role in regulating sodium and water balance by its action on the distal tubule. Renin (released by the juxtaglomerular cells of kidney) and angiotensin govern the secretion of aldosterone in the adrenal cortex. Aldosterone, deoxycorticosterone and hydrocortisone are potent antidiuretic mineralocorticoids. Under the influence of aldosterone, sodium is reabsorbed and is exchanged for potassium. Excretion of potassium is thus promoted. If this process is blocked, sodium and chloride ions alongwith equivalent of water will be retained in the renal tubule, resulting into diuresis. Similarly, potassium ions will not be excreted. Hence, drugs which block this process are known as potassium sparing diuretic agents. They are classified into :

1. Agents that inhibit the production, release or physiological activity of aldosterone. They are called as 'aldosterone antagonists'.

2. Agents that interfere with K^+ transport processes. They are known as 'pteridine derivatives'.

(a) Aldosterone antagonists :

The Na^+ - K^+ exchange is partially under mineralocorticoidal control. Aldosterone is the principal agent amongst them. Aldosterone receptors are located in several tissues, like salivary glands, colon and several segments of the nephron. In nephron, aldosterone receptors are more predominant in the cytoplasm of distal tubule cells and collecting system. Spiranolactone, an aldosterone antagonist is one of a series of steroidal derivatives having a lactone ring in the spiro arrangement at 17th position. It is a synthetic steroid having structural similarity with aldosterone. It competitively inhibits the binding of aldosterone with its receptors. Spiranolactone thus effectively blocks the aldosterone induced Na^+ - K^+ exchange process, which otherwise occurs when aldosterone binds with its receptors in order to release energy necessary for this exchange.

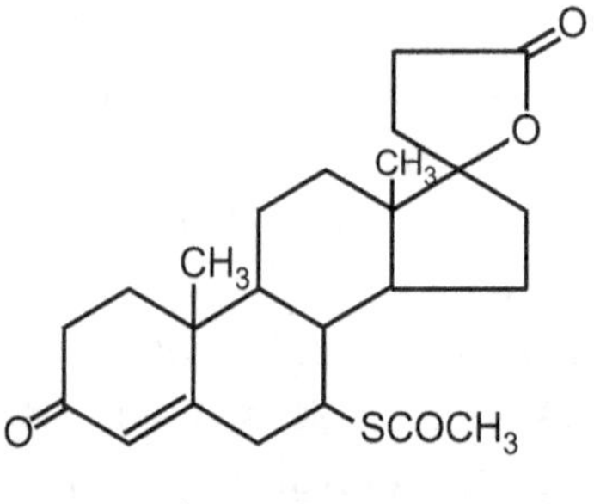

Spironolactone

Spiranolactone increases Na^+ and Cl^- ion excretion alongwith reduction in K^+ ion excretion. It also increases calcium excretion through a direct action on tubular transport. It is effective only when mineralocorticoids are present.

Canrenone and canrenoate are the metabolites of spiranolactone which still retains antialdosterone activity.

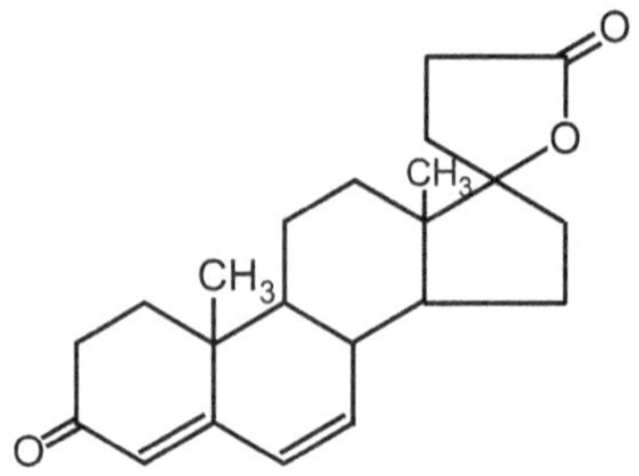

Canrenone

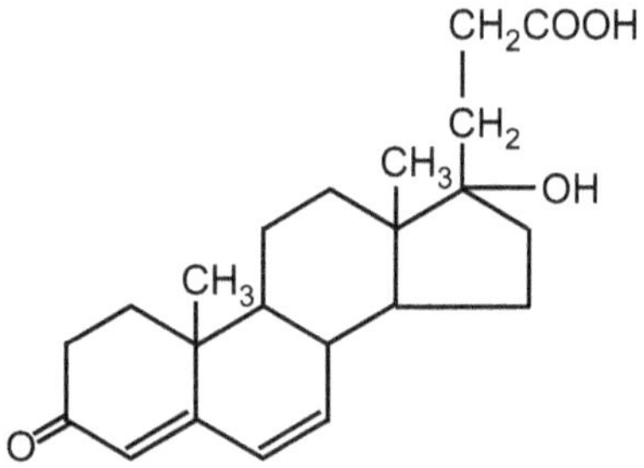

Canrenoate

Since spiranolactone induced antagonism is of reversible nature, spiranolactone is rather disappointing as a diuretic agent. After repeated doses, diuretic activity decreases presumely due to a compensatory change in the proximal tubule.

Amphenone B and metyrapone are the agents which interfere in the biosynthesis of aldosterone but do not qualify the standards for clinical utility.

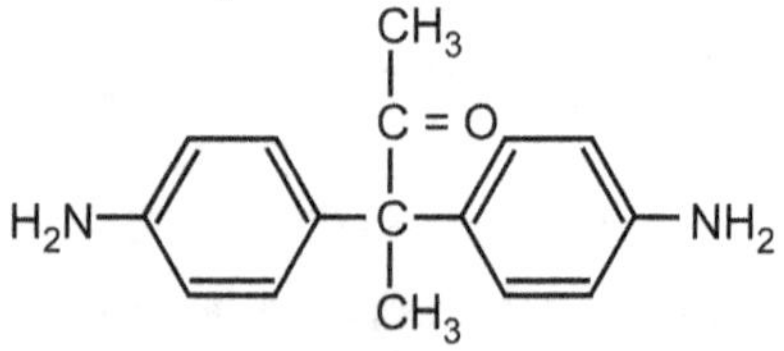

Amphenone B

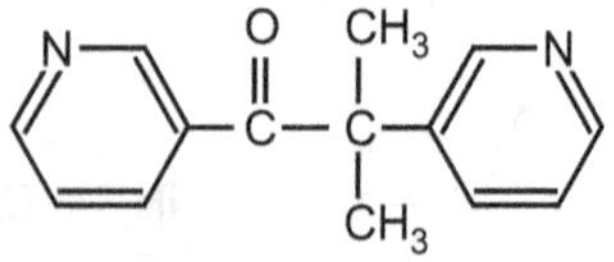

Metyrapone

All these aldosterone antagonists are useful only in those patients (patients suffering from liver cirrhosis or patients under digitalis treatment) for whom hypokalaemia would prove fatal.

(b) Pteridine derivatives and related compounds :

These drugs behave very much similar to spiranolactone. They increase the excretion of sodium and chloride ions, reduce potassium excretion but their mechanism of action is very much different than that of aldosterone antagonist. They cause diuresis even in the absence of mineralocorticoids. Triamterene and amiloride are clinically used agents of this class. They act by interferring with the Na^+ - K^+ exchange processes in the distal renal tubule by a mechanism other than antagonism of aldosterone. The site of action involves a mineralocorticoid-independent portion of the distal tubule. The potassium sparing diuretic agents may also cause slight alkalinization of urine by inhibition of H^+ secretion in the distal tubule.

Triamterene is a synthetic pteridine having structural similarity to folic acid and its related compounds. Amiloride is an aminopyrazine derivative. Both drugs are rarely used alone. They are often used as an adjunct to long term thiazide therapy where they potentiate the diuresis and reduce the loss of potassium. Side-effects include nausea and mental confusion.

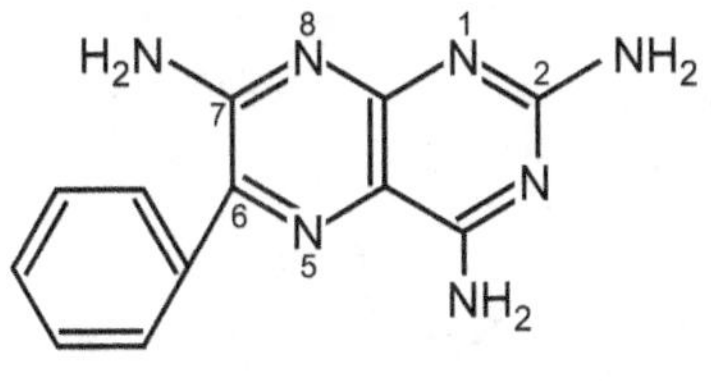

Triamterene

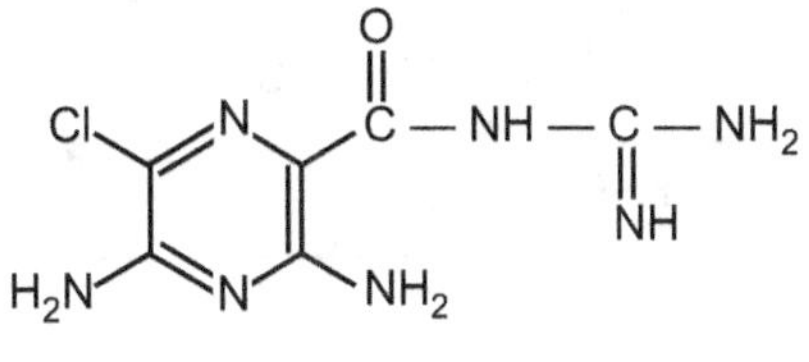

Amiloride

Hyperkalemia is the most serious side-effect associated with all potassium sparing diuretic agents. This emphasises the need of routine check up and monitoring the serum electrolyte balance. Hyperkalemia may generate complications in patients with impaired renal function or who are taking potassium supplements in any form (e.g. potassium penicillin). Spiranolactone showed positive tumorigenic response in animal studies.

10. Uricosuric diuretics :

Uric acid is the principal end product of purine metabolism in man. The increased plasma urate level may be due to increased nucleic acid metabolism in neoplasms (cancers), excessive urate production from an inborn error of metabolism, defective excretion process by the kidney or may be induced by drugs like acetazolamide.

When plasma urate level crosses its solubility limit, it precipitates in the tissues in the form of crystals and may get deposited mainly as monosodium urate in joints, subcutaneous areas and the kidney. These conditions prevail in the attack of gout. Many of the currently used diuretics usually lead to urate retention, which favours and leaves a scope for cardiovascular disease, carbohydrate intolerance or nephropathy. Hence, scientists are interested to develop such diuretics that also possess uricosuric activity. Most uricosuric drugs are acidic in character. They decrease urate clearance in small doses while increase it at higher doses.

Ticrynafen and indacrinone are the examples of diuretic uricosuric agents.

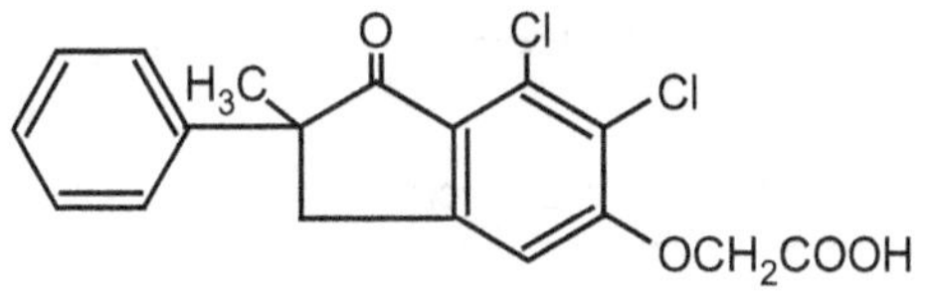

Indacrinone

6.4 ANTI-DIURETIC SUBSTANCES

Body possesses several compensatory mechanisms to get it suited with changing environmental conditions. As per the body's need, these mechanisms are switched ON or OFF. For example, the osmolality and ionic composition of the body's fluids are maintained by modification of blood flow or control of glomerular filtration rate (i.e. renal conservation of water). The only clinical condition where renal conservation of water is needed by anti-diuretics is diabetes insipidus.

This conservation is effected by many drugs e.g., Posterior pituitary gland secretes anti-diuretic hormone which helps to maintain the body's water balance. Similarly, thiazide diuretics and ethacrynic acid exhibit anti-diuretic action in patients with diabetes insipidus. An oral hypoglycemic agent, chlorpropamide is also having anti-diuretic activity and may be used for this purpose in patients with diabetes insipidus.

6.5 SUMMARY

There are many pathological conditions which stress the need of using diuretics. Monitering the dose schedule is necessary to avoid dehydration and electrolyte abnormalities.

The story of diuretics can not be completed without making a reference to mercurials, which full heartedly served the people for nearly a quarter of century. With the introduction of benzothiadiazines, people at once realised drawbacks of organomercurials and started criticising their clinical status.

Many diuretics cause diuresis along with loss of potassium. The hypokalemia thus produced may be harmful to patients suffering from liver cirrhosis or patients under digitalis treatment. In such cases, the therapy solely depends upon spiranolactone, triamterene or amiloride which are 'Potassium sparing diuretics'.

Non-diuretic uricosuric agents

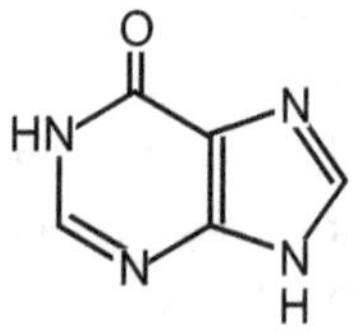

Allopurinol 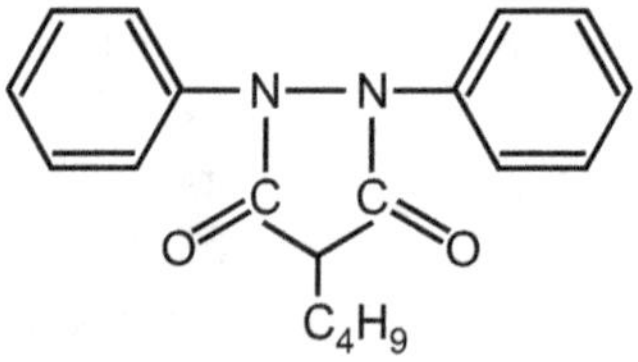   Phenylbutazone 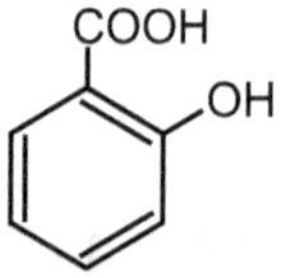   Salicylic acid

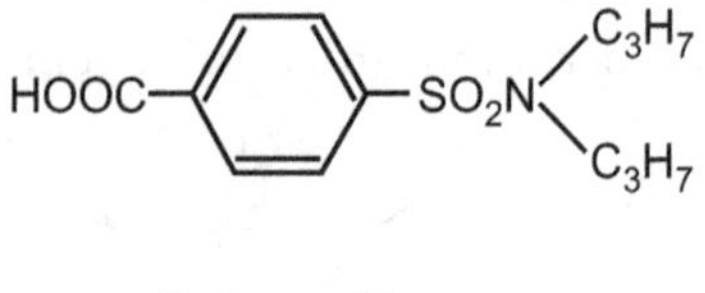

Probenecid 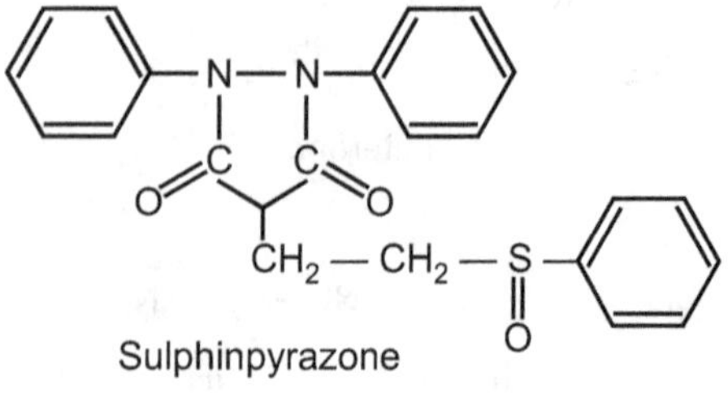   Sulphinpyrazone

Similarly the attack of gout is not unexpected when plasma urate level crosses its solubility limit. This results into deposition of monosodium urate mainly in joints and kidneys. Certain drugs used in this condition are non-diuretic uricosuric agents. Some drugs are designed by blending diuretic activity with uricosuric activity.

Some drugs become naughty and scatter their pharmacological spectra in wavy fashion. They often try to prove their smartness by also influencing the body compartments other than their expected targets. Their ill-mentality can be corrected by modification of their structure. Their SAR successors have to be evaluated to find out further clinical deficiencies.

Synthesis

(i) Furosemide :

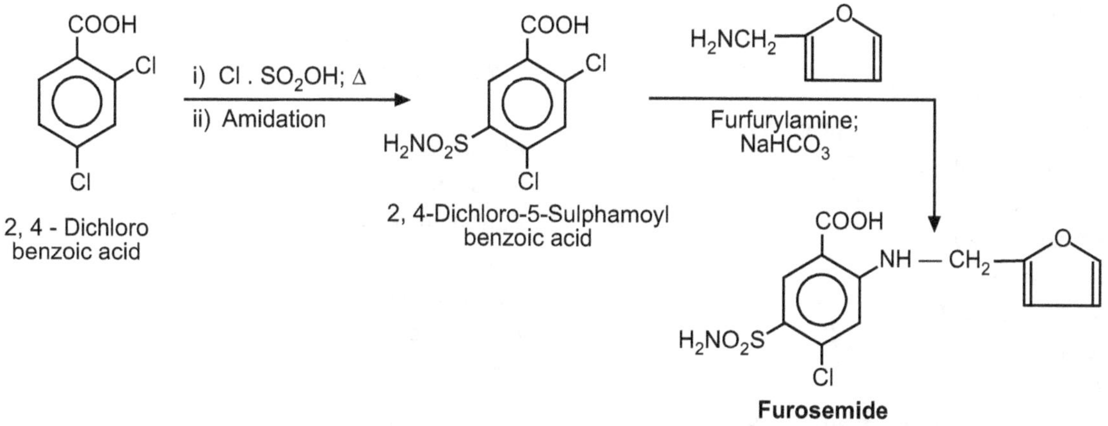

COOH

Cl

Cl

2, 4 - Dichloro
benzoic acid

i) Cl . SO$_2$OH; Δ

ii) Amidation

COOH

Cl

H$_2$NO$_2$S

Cl

2, 4-Dichloro-5-Sulphamoyl
benzoic acid

H$_2$NCH$_2$—

Furfurylamine;
NaHCO$_3$

COOH

NH — CH$_2$—

H$_2$NO$_2$S

Cl

Furosemide

(ii) Chlorthiazide :

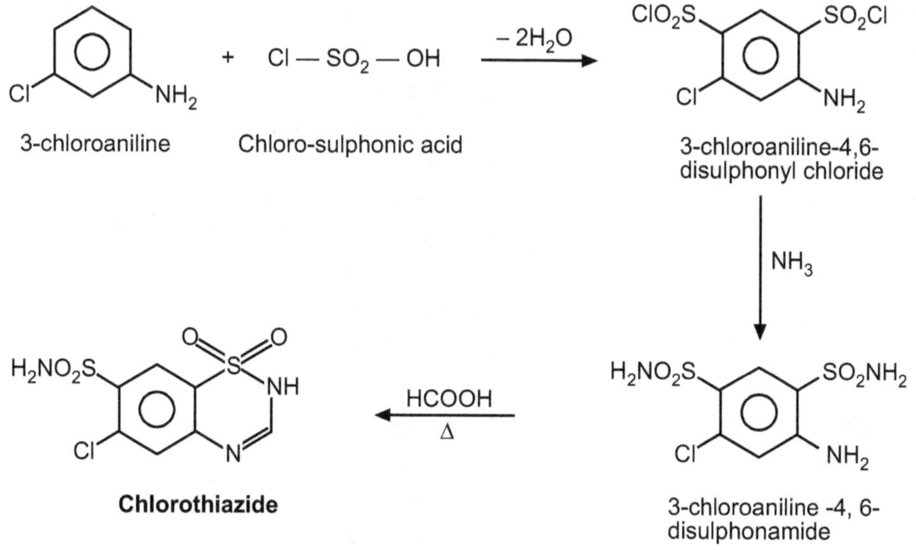

Cl

NH$_2$

3-chloroaniline

+　Cl — SO$_2$ — OH

Chloro-sulphonic acid

$-2H_2O$

ClO$_2$S

SO$_2$Cl

Cl

NH$_2$

3-chloroaniline-4,6-
disulphonyl chloride

NH$_3$

H$_2$NO$_2$S

SO$_2$NH$_2$

Cl

NH$_2$

3-chloroaniline -4, 6-
disulphonamide

HCOOH
Δ

H$_2$NO$_2$S

Cl

O
‖
S
‖
O

NH

N

Chlorothiazide

INDEX

❖ ❖ ❖

www.ingramcontent.com/pod-product-compliance
Lightning Source LLC
Chambersburg PA
CBHW080011040726
47505CB00016B/2215